ROUGHING IT

THE OXFORD MARK TWAIN

Shelley Fisher Fishkin, Editor

The Celebrated Jumping Frog of Calaveras County, and Other Sketches
    Introduction: Roy Blount Jr.
    Afterword: Richard Bucci

The Innocents Abroad
    Introduction: Mordecai Richler
    Afterword: David E. E. Sloane

Roughing It
    Introduction: George Plimpton
    Afterword: Henry B. Wonham

The Gilded Age
    Introduction: Ward Just
    Afterword: Gregg Camfield

Sketches, New and Old
    Introduction: Lee Smith
    Afterword: Sherwood Cummings

The Adventures of Tom Sawyer
    Introduction: E. L. Doctorow
    Afterword: Albert E. Stone

A Tramp Abroad
    Introduction: Russell Banks
    Afterword: James S. Leonard

Roughing It

Mark Twain

FOREWORD

SHELLEY FISHER FISHKIN

INTRODUCTION

GEORGE PLIMPTON

AFTERWORD

HENRY B. WONHAM

New York   Oxford

OXFORD UNIVERSITY PRESS

1996

OXFORD UNIVERSITY PRESS

Oxford   New York

Athens, Auckland, Bangkok, Bogotá, Bombay
Buenos Aires, Calcutta, Cape Town, Dar es Salaam
Delhi, Florence, Hong Kong, Istanbul, Karachi
Kuala Lumpur, Madras, Madrid, Melbourne
Mexico City, Nairobi, Paris, Singapore
Taipei, Tokyo, Toronto
and associated companies in
Berlin, Ibadan

Copyright © 1996 by
Oxford University Press, Inc.
Introduction © 1996 by George Plimpton
Afterword © 1996 by Henry B. Wonham
Illustrators and Illustrations in Mark Twain's
First American Editions © 1996 by Beverly R. David
and Ray Sapirstein
Reading the Illustrations in Roughing It
© 1996 by Beverly R. David and Ray Sapirstein
Text design by Richard Hendel
Composition: David Thorne

Published by
Oxford University Press, Inc.
198 Madison Avenue, New York,
New York 10016

Oxford is a registered trademark of
Oxford University Press

Library of Congress
Cataloging-in-Publication Data

Twain, Mark, 1835–1910.
Roughing it / by Mark Twain; with an introduction
by George Plimpton; and an afterword by Henry B.
Wonham.
p. cm. — (The Oxford Mark Twain)
Includes bibliographical references.
1. Twain, Mark, 1835–1910—Journeys—West (U.S.)
2. West (U.S.)—Description and travel. 3. Authors,
American—19th century—Journeys—West (U.S.)
I. Title. II. Series: Twain, Mark, 1835–1910.
Works. 1996.
PS1318.A1 1996b
813'.403—dc20
96-12323
CIP
ISBN 0-19-510133-2 (trade ed.)
ISBN 0-19-511401-9 (lib. ed.)
ISBN 0-19-509088-8 (trade ed. set)
ISBN 0-19-511345-4 (lib. ed. set)

9 8 7 6 5 4 3 2 1

Printed in the United States of America
on acid-free paper

FRONTISPIECE
Samuel L. Clemens posed for this portrait by
photographer E. H. Paige in Buffalo in 1870, the year
he began to write *Roughing It*. (The Mark Twain
House, Hartford, Connecticut)

CONTENTS

EDITOR'S NOTE

The Oxford Mark Twain consists of twenty-nine volumes of facsimiles of the first American editions of Mark Twain's works, with an editor's foreword, new introductions, afterwords, notes on the texts, and essays on the illustrations in volumes with artwork. The facsimiles have been reproduced from the originals unaltered, except that blank pages in the front and back of the books have been omitted, and any seriously damaged or missing pages have been replaced by pages from other first editions (as indicated in the notes on the texts).

In the foreword, introduction, afterword, and essays on the illustrations, the titles of Mark Twain's works have been capitalized according to modern conventions, as have the names of characters (except where otherwise indicated). In the case of discrepancies between the title of a short story, essay, or sketch as it appears in the original table of contents and as it appears on its own title page, the title page has been followed. The parenthetical numbers in the introduction, afterwords, and illustration essays are page references to the facsimiles.

FOREWORD

Shelley Fisher Fishkin

Samuel Clemens entered the world and left it with Halley's Comet, little dreaming that generations hence Halley's Comet would be less famous than Mark Twain. He has been called the American Cervantes, our Homer, our Tolstoy, our Shakespeare, our Rabelais. Ernest Hemingway maintained that "all modern American literature comes from one book by Mark Twain called *Huckleberry Finn*." President Franklin Delano Roosevelt got the phrase "New Deal" from *A Connecticut Yankee in King Arthur's Court*. *The Gilded Age* gave an entire era its name. "The future historian of America," wrote George Bernard Shaw to Samuel Clemens, "will find your works as indispensable to him as a French historian finds the political tracts of Voltaire."[1]

There is a Mark Twain Bank in St. Louis, a Mark Twain Diner in Jackson Heights, New York, a Mark Twain Smoke Shop in Lakeland, Florida. There are Mark Twain Elementary Schools in Albuquerque, Dayton, Seattle, and Sioux Falls. Mark Twain's image peers at us from advertisements for Bass Ale (his drink of choice was Scotch), for a gas company in Tennessee, a hotel in the nation's capital, a cemetery in California.

Ubiquitous though his name and image may be, Mark Twain is in no danger of becoming a petrified icon. On the contrary: Mark Twain lives. *Huckleberry Finn* is "the most taught novel, most taught long work, and most taught piece of American literature" in American schools from junior high to the graduate level.[2] Hundreds of Twain impersonators appear in theaters, trade shows, and shopping centers in every region of the country.[3] Scholars publish hundreds of articles as well as books about Twain every year, and he is the subject of daily exchanges on the Internet. A journalist somewhere in the world finds a reason to quote Twain just about every day. Television series such as *Bonanza, Star Trek: The Next Generation,* and *Cheers* broadcast episodes that feature Mark Twain as a character. Hollywood screenwriters regularly produce movies inspired by his works, and writers of mysteries and science fiction continue to weave him into their plots.[4]

A century after the American Revolution sent shock waves throughout Europe, it took Mark Twain to explain to Europeans and to his countrymen alike what that revolution had wrought. He probed the significance of this new land and its new citizens, and identified what it was in the Old World that America abolished and rejected. The founding fathers had thought through the political dimensions of making a new society; Mark Twain took on the challenge of interpreting the social and cultural life of the United States for those outside its borders as well as for those who were living the changes he discerned.

Americans may have constructed a new society in the eighteenth century, but they articulated what they had done in voices that were largely inter-changeable with those of Englishmen until well into the nineteenth century. Mark Twain became the voice of the new land, the leading translator of what and who the "American" was — and, to a large extent, is. Frances Trollope's *Domestic Manners of the Americans,* a best-seller in England, Hector St. John de Crèvecoeur's *Letters from an American Farmer,* and Tocqueville's *Democracy in America* all tried to explain America to Europeans. But Twain did more than that: he allowed European readers to *experience* this strange "new world." And he gave his countrymen the tools to do two things they had not quite had the confidence to do before. He helped them stand before the cultural icons of the Old World unembarrassed, unashamed of America's lack of palaces and shrines, proud of its brash practicality and bold inventiveness, unafraid to reject European models of "civilization" as tainted or corrupt. And he also helped them recognize their own insularity, boorishness, arrogance, or ignorance, and laugh at it — the first step toward transcending it and becoming more "civilized," in the best European sense of the word.

Twain often strikes us as more a creature of our time than of his. He appreciated the importance and the complexity of mass tourism and public relations, fields that would come into their own in the twentieth century but were only fledgling enterprises in the nineteenth. He explored the liberating potential of humor and the dynamics of friendship, parenting, and marriage. He narrowed the gap between "popular" and "high" culture, and he meditated on the enigmas of personal and national identity. Indeed, it would be difficult to find an issue on the horizon today that Twain did not touch on somewhere in his work. Heredity versus environment? Animal rights? The boundaries of gender? The place of black voices in the cultural heritage of the United States? Twain was there.

With startling prescience and characteristic grace and wit, he zeroed in on many of the key challenges — political, social, and technological — that would face his country and the world for the next hundred years: the challenge of race relations in a society founded on both chattel slavery and ideals of equality, and the intractable problem of racism in American life; the potential of new technologies to transform our lives in ways that can be both exhilarating and terrifying — as well as unpredictable; the problem of imperialism and the difficulties entailed in getting rid of it. But he never lost sight of the most basic challenge of all: each man or woman's struggle for integrity in the face of the seductions of power, status, and material things.

Mark Twain's unerring sense of the right word and not its second cousin taught people to pay attention when he spoke, in person or in print. He said things that were smart and things that were wise, and he said them incomparably well. He defined the rhythms of our prose and the contours of our moral map. He saw our best and our worst, our extravagant promise and our stunning failures, our comic foibles and our tragic flaws. Throughout the world he is viewed as the most distinctively American of American authors — and as one of the most universal. He is assigned in classrooms in Naples, Riyadh, Belfast, and Beijing, and has been a major influence on twentieth-century writers from Argentina to Nigeria to Japan. The Oxford Mark Twain celebrates the versatility and vitality of this remarkable writer.

The Oxford Mark Twain reproduces the first American editions of Mark Twain's books published during his lifetime.[5] By encountering Twain's works in their original format — typography, layout, order of contents, and illustrations — readers today can come a few steps closer to the literary artifacts that entranced and excited readers when the books first appeared. Twain approved of and to a greater or lesser degree supervised the publication of all of this material.[6] The Mark Twain House in Hartford, Connecticut, generously loaned us its originals.[7] When more than one copy of a first American edition was available, Robert H. Hirst, general editor of the Mark Twain Project, in cooperation with Marianne Curling, curator of the Mark Twain House (and Jeffrey Kaimowitz, head of Rare Books for the Watkinson Library of Trinity College, Hartford, where the Mark Twain House collection is kept), guided our decision about which one to use.[8] As a set, the volumes also contain more than eighty essays commissioned especially for The Oxford Mark Twain, in which distinguished contributors reassess Twain's achievement as a writer and his place in the cultural conversation that he did so much to shape.

Each volume of The Oxford Mark Twain is introduced by a leading American, Canadian, or British writer who responds to Twain — often in a very personal way — as a fellow writer. Novelists, journalists, humorists, columnists, fabulists, poets, playwrights — these writers tell us what Twain taught them and what in his work continues to speak to them. Reading Twain's books, both famous and obscure, they reflect on the genesis of his art and the characteristics of his style, the themes he illuminated, and the aesthetic strategies he pioneered. Individually and collectively their contributions testify to the place Mark Twain holds in the hearts of readers of all kinds and temperaments.

Scholars whose work has shaped our view of Twain in the academy today have written afterwords to each volume, with suggestions for further reading. Their essays give us a sense of what was going on in Twain's life when he wrote the book at hand, and of how that book fits into his career. They explore how each book reflects and refracts contemporary events, and they show Twain responding to literary and social currents of the day, variously accepting, amplifying, modifying, and challenging prevailing paradigms. Sometimes they argue that works previously dismissed as quirky or eccentric departures actually address themes at the heart of Twain's work from the start. And as they bring new perspectives to Twain's composition strategies in familiar texts, several scholars see experiments in form where others saw only formlessness, method where prior critics saw only madness. In addition to elucidating the work's historical and cultural context, the afterwords provide an overview of responses to each book from its first appearance to the present.

Most of Mark Twain's books involved more than Mark Twain's words: unique illustrations. The parodic visual send-ups of "high culture" that Twain himself drew for *A Tramp Abroad*, the sketch of financial manipulator Jay Gould as a greedy and sadistic "Slave Driver" in *A Connecticut Yankee in King Arthur's Court*, and the memorable drawings of Eve in *Eve's Diary* all helped Twain's books to be sold, read, discussed, and preserved. In their essays for each volume that contains artwork, Beverly R. David and Ray Sapirstein highlight the significance of the sketches, engravings, and photographs in the first American editions of Mark Twain's works, and tell us what is known about the public response to them.

The Oxford Mark Twain invites us to read some relatively neglected works by Twain in the company of some of the most engaging literary figures of our time. Roy Blount Jr., for example, riffs in a deliciously Twain-like manner on "An Item Which the Editor Himself Could Not Understand," which may well rank as one of the least-known pieces Twain ever published. Bobbie Ann Mason celebrates the "mad energy" of Twain's most obscure comic novel, *The American Claimant*, in which the humor "hurtles beyond tall tale into simon-pure absurdity."[9] Garry Wills finds that *Christian Science* "gets us very close to the heart of American culture." Lee Smith reads "Political Economy" as a sharp and funny essay on language. Walter Mosley sees "The Stolen White Elephant," a story "reduced to a series of ridiculous telegrams related by an untrustworthy narrator caught up in an adventure that is as impossible as it is ludicrous," as a stunningly compact and economical satire of a world we still recognize as our own. Anne Bernays returns to "The Private History of a Campaign That Failed" and finds "an antiwar manifesto that is also confession, dramatic monologue, a plea for understanding and absolution, and a romp that gradually turns into atrocity even as we watch." After revisiting Captain Stormfield's heaven, Frederik Pohl finds that there "is no imaginable place more pleasant to spend eternity." Indeed, Pohl writes, "one would almost be willing to die to enter it."

While less familiar works receive fresh attention in The Oxford Mark Twain, new light is cast on the best-known works as well. Judith Martin ("Miss Manners") points out that it is by reading a court etiquette book that Twain's pauper learns how to behave as a proper prince. As important as etiquette may be in the palace, Martin notes, it is even more important in the slums.

> That etiquette is a sorer point with the ruffians in the street than with the proud dignitaries of the prince's court may surprise some readers. As in our own streets, etiquette is always a more volatile subject among those who cannot count on being treated with respect than among those who have the power to command deference.

And taking a fresh look at *Adventures of Huckleberry Finn*, Toni Morrison writes,

> much of the novel's genius lies in its quiescence, the silences that pervade it and give it a porous quality that is by turns brooding and soothing. It lies in . . . the subdued images in which the repetition of a simple word, such as "lonesome," tolls like an evening bell; the moments when nothing is said, when scenes and incidents swell the heart unbearably precisely because unarticulated, and force an act of imagination almost against the will.

Engaging Mark Twain as one writer to another, several contributors to The Oxford Mark Twain offer new insights into the processes by which his books came to be. Russell Banks, for example, reads *A Tramp Abroad* as "an important revision of Twain's incomplete first draft of *Huckleberry Finn*, a second draft, if you will, which in turn made possible the third and final draft." Erica Jong suggests that *1601*, a freewheeling parody of Elizabethan manners and mores, written during the same summer Twain began *Huckleberry Finn*, served as "a warm-up for his creative process" and "primed the pump for other sorts of freedom of expression." And Justin Kaplan suggests that "one of the transcendent figures standing behind and shaping" *Joan of Arc* was Ulysses S. Grant, whose memoirs Twain had recently published, and who, like Joan, had risen unpredictably "from humble and obscure origins" to become a "military genius" endowed with "the gift of command, a natural eloquence, and an equally natural reserve."

As a number of contributors note, Twain was a man ahead of his times. *The Gilded Age* was the first "Washington novel," Ward Just tells us, because "Twain was the first to see the possibilities that had eluded so many others." Commenting on *The Tragedy of Pudd'nhead Wilson*, Sherley Anne Williams observes that "Twain's argument about the power of environment in shaping character runs directly counter to prevailing sentiment where the negro was concerned." Twain's fictional technology, wildly fanciful by the standards of his day, predicts developments we take for granted in ours. DNA cloning, fax machines, and photocopiers are all prefigured, Bobbie Ann Mason tells us, in *The American Claimant*. Cynthia Ozick points out that the "telelectrophonoscope" we meet in "From the 'London Times' of 1904" is suspiciously like what we know as "television." And Malcolm Bradbury suggests that in the "phrenophones" of "Mental Telegraphy" "the Internet was born."

Twain turns out to have been remarkably prescient about political affairs as well. Kurt Vonnegut sees in *A Connecticut Yankee* a chilling foreshadowing (or perhaps a projection from the Civil War) of "all the high-tech atrocities which followed, and which follow still." Cynthia Ozick suggests that "The Man That Corrupted Hadleyburg," along with some of the other pieces collected under that title — many of them written when Twain lived in a Vienna ruled by Karl Lueger, a demagogue Adolf Hitler would later idolize — shoot up moral flares that shed an eerie light on the insidious corruption, prejudice, and hatred that reached bitter fruition under the Third Reich. And Twain's portrait in this book of "the dissolving Austria-Hungary of the 1890s," in Ozick's view, presages not only the Sarajevo that would erupt in 1914 but also "the disintegrated components of the former Yugoslavia" and "the *fin-de-siècle* Sarajevo of our own moment."

Despite their admiration for Twain's ambitious reach and scope, contributors to The Oxford Mark Twain also recognize his limitations. Mordecai Richler, for example, thinks that "the early pages of *Innocents Abroad* suffer from being a tad broad, proffering more burlesque than inspired satire," perhaps because Twain was "trying too hard for knee-slappers." Charles Johnson notes that the Young Man in Twain's philosophical dialogue about free will and determinism (*What Is Man?*) "caves in far too soon," failing to challenge what through late-twentieth-century eyes looks like "pseudoscience" and suspect essentialism in the Old Man's arguments.

Some contributors revisit their first encounters with Twain's works, recalling what surprised or intrigued them. When David Bradley came across "Fenimore Cooper's Literary Offences" in his college library, he "did not at first realize that Twain was being his usual ironic self with all this business about the 'nineteen rules governing literary art in the domain of romantic fiction,' but by the time I figured out there was no such list outside Twain's own head, I had decided that the rules made *sense*. . . . It seemed to me they were a pretty good blueprint for writing — Negro writing included." Sherley Anne Williams remembers that part of what attracted her to *Pudd'nhead Wilson* when she first read it thirty years ago was "that Twain, writing at the end of the nineteenth century, could imagine negroes as characters, albeit white ones, who actually thought for and of themselves, whose actions were the product of their thinking rather than the spontaneous ephemera of physical instincts that stereotype assigned to blacks." Frederik Pohl recalls his first reading of *Huckleberry Finn* as "a watershed event" in his life, the first book he read as a child in which "bad people" ceased to exercise a monopoly on doing "bad things." In *Huckleberry Finn* "some seriously bad things — things like the possession and mistreatment of black slaves, like stealing and lying, even like killing other people in duels — were quite often done by people who not only thought of themselves as exemplarily moral but, by any other standards I knew how to apply, actually *were* admirable citizens." The world that

Tom and Huck lived in, Pohl writes, "was filled with complexities and contradictions," and resembled "the world I appeared to be living in myself."

Other contributors explore their more recent encounters with Twain, explaining why they have revised their initial responses to his work. For Toni Morrison, parts of *Huckleberry Finn* that she "once took to be deliberate evasions, stumbles even, or a writer's impatience with his or her material," now strike her "as otherwise: as entrances, crevices, gaps, seductive invitations flashing the possibility of meaning. Unarticulated eddies that encourage diving into the novel's undertow — the real place where writer captures reader." One such "eddy" is the imprisonment of Jim on the Phelps farm. Instead of dismissing this portion of the book as authorial bungling, as she once did, Morrison now reads it as Twain's commentary on the 1880s, a period that "saw the collapse of civil rights for blacks," a time when "the nation, as well as Tom Sawyer, was deferring Jim's freedom in agonizing play." Morrison believes that Americans in the 1880s were attempting "to bury the combustible issues Twain raised in his novel," and that those who try to kick Huck Finn out of school in the 1990s are doing the same: "The cyclical attempts to remove the novel from classrooms extend Jim's captivity on into each generation of readers."

Although imitation-Hemingway and imitation-Faulkner writing contests draw hundreds of entries annually, no one has ever tried to mount a faux-Twain competition. Why? Perhaps because Mark Twain's voice is too much a part of who we are and how we speak even today. Roy Blount Jr. suggests that it is impossible, "at least for an American writer, to parody Mark Twain. It would be like doing an impression of your father or mother: he or she is already there in your voice."

Twain's style is examined and celebrated in The Oxford Mark Twain by fellow writers who themselves have struggled with the nuances of words, the structure of sentences, the subtleties of point of view, and the trickiness of opening lines. Bobbie Ann Mason observes, for example, that "Twain loved the sound of words and he knew how to string them by sound, like different shades of one color: 'The earl's barbaric eye,' 'the Usurping Earl,' 'a double-dyed humbug.'" Twain "relied on the punch of plain words" to show writers how to move beyond the "wordy romantic rubbish" so prevalent in nine-teenth-century fiction, Mason says; he "was one of the first writers in America to deflower literary language." Lee Smith believes that "American writers have benefited as much from the way Mark Twain opened up the possibilities of first-person narration as we have from his use of vernacular language." (She feels that "the ghost of Mark Twain was hovering someplace in the back-ground" when she decided to write her novel *Oral History* from the stand-point of multiple first-person narrators.) Frederick Busch maintains that "A Dog's Tale" "boasts one of the great opening sentences" of all time: "My fa-ther was a St. Bernard, my mother was a collie, but I am a Presbyterian." And Ursula Le Guin marvels at the ingenuity of the following sentence that she en-counters in *Extracts from Adam's Diary.*

> . . . This made her sorry for the creatures which live in there, which she calls fish, for she continues to fasten names on to things that don't need them and don't come when they are called by them, which is a matter of no consequence to her, as she is such a numskull anyway; so she got a lot of them out and brought them in last night and put them in my bed to keep warm, but I have noticed them now and then all day, and I don't see that they are any happier there than they were before, only quieter.[10]

Le Guin responds,

> Now, that is a pure Mark-Twain-tour-de-force sentence, covering an im-mense amount of territory in an effortless, aimless ramble that seems to be heading nowhere in particular and ends up with breathtaking accuracy at the gold mine. Any sensible child would find that funny, perhaps not fol-lowing all its divagations but delighted by the swing of it, by the word "numskull," by the idea of putting fish in the bed; and as that child grew older and reread it, its reward would only grow; and if that grown-up child had to write an essay on the piece and therefore earnestly studied and pored over this sentence, she would end up in unmitigated admiration of its vocabulary, syntax, pacing, sense, and rhythm, above all the beautiful

timing of the last two words; and she would, and she does, still find it funny.

The fish surface again in a passage that Gore Vidal calls to our attention, from *Following the Equator*: "'The Whites always mean well when they take human fish out of the ocean and try to make them dry and warm and happy and comfortable in a chicken coop,' which is how, through civilization, they did away with many of the original inhabitants. Lack of empathy is a principal theme in Twain's meditations on race and empire."

Indeed, empathy — and its lack — is a principal theme in virtually all of Twain's work, as contributors frequently note. Nat Hentoff quotes the following thoughts from Huck in *Tom Sawyer Abroad*:

> I see a bird setting on a dead limb of a high tree, singing with its head tilted back and its mouth open, and before I thought I fired, and his song stopped and he fell straight down from the limb, all limp like a rag, and I run and picked him up and he was dead, and his body was warm in my hand, and his head rolled about this way and that, like his neck was broke, and there was a little white skin over his eyes, and one little drop of blood on the side of his head; and laws! I could n't see nothing more for the tears; and I hain't never murdered no creature since that war n't doing me no harm, and I ain't going to.[11]

"The Humane Society," Hentoff writes, "has yet to say anything as powerful — and lasting."

Readers of The Oxford Mark Twain will have the pleasure of revisiting Twain's Mississippi landmarks alongside Willie Morris, whose own lower Mississippi Valley boyhood gives him a special sense of connection to Twain. Morris knows firsthand the mosquitoes described in *Life on the Mississippi* — so colossal that "two of them could whip a dog" and "four of them could hold a man down"; in Morris's own hometown they were so large during the flood season that "local wags said they wore wristwatches." Morris's Yazoo City and Twain's Hannibal shared a "rough-hewn democracy . . . complicated by all the visible textures of caste and class, . . . harmless boyhood fun and mischief right along with . . . rank hypocrisies, churchgoing sanctimonies, racial hatred, entrenched and unrepentant greed."

For the West of Mark Twain's *Roughing It*, readers will have George Plimpton as their guide. "What a group these newspapermen were!" Plimpton writes about Twain and his friends Dan De Quille and Joe Goodman in Virginia City, Nevada. "Their roisterous carryings-on bring to mind the kind of frat-house enthusiasm one associates with college humor magazines like the *Harvard Lampoon*." Malcolm Bradbury examines Twain as "a living example of what made the American so different from the European." And Hal Holbrook, who has interpreted Mark Twain on stage for some forty years, describes how Twain "played" during the civil rights movement, during the Vietnam War, during the Gulf War, and in Prague on the eve of the demise of Communism.

Why do we continue to read Mark Twain? What draws us to him? His wit? His compassion? His humor? His bravura? His humility? His understanding of who and what we are in those parts of our being that we rarely open to view? Our sense that he knows we can do better than we do? Our sense that he knows we can't? E. L. Doctorow tells us that children are attracted to *Tom Sawyer* because in this book "the young reader confirms his own hope that no matter how troubled his relations with his elders may be, beneath all their disapproval is their underlying love for him, constant and steadfast." Readers in general, Arthur Miller writes, value Twain's "insights into America's always uncertain moral life and its shifting but everlasting hypocrisies"; we appreciate the fact that he "is not using his alienation from the public illusions of his hour in order to reject the country implicitly as though he could live without it, but manifestly in order to correct it." Perhaps we keep reading Mark Twain because, in Miller's words, he "wrote much more like a father than a son. He doesn't seem to be sitting in class taunting the teacher but standing at the head of it challenging his students to acknowledge their own humanity, that is, their immemorial attraction to the untrue."

Mark Twain entered the public eye at a time when many of his countrymen considered "American culture" an oxymoron; he died four years before a world conflagration that would lead many to question whether the contradiction in terms was not "European civilization" instead. In between he worked in journalism, printing, steamboating, mining, lecturing, publishing, and editing, in virtually every region of the country. He tried his hand at humorous sketches, social satire, historical novels, children's books, poetry, drama, science fiction, mysteries, romance, philosophy, travelogue, memoir, polemic, and several genres no one had ever seen before or has ever seen since. He invented a self-pasting scrapbook, a history game, a vest strap, and a gizmo for keeping bed sheets tucked in; he invested in machines and processes designed to revolutionize typesetting and engraving, and in a food supplement called "Plasmon." Along the way he cheerfully impersonated himself and prior versions of himself for doting publics on five continents while playing out a charming rags-to-riches story followed by a devastating riches-to-rags story followed by yet another great American comeback. He had a long-running real-life engagement in a sumptuous comedy of manners, and then in a real-life tragedy not of his own design: during the last fourteen years of his life almost everyone he ever loved was taken from him by disease and death.

Mark Twain has indelibly shaped our views of who and what the United States is as a nation and of who and what we might become. He understood the nostalgia for a "simpler" past that increased as that past receded — and he saw through the nostalgia to a past that was just as complex as the present. He recognized better than we did ourselves our potential for greatness and our potential for disaster. His fictions brilliantly illuminated the world in which he lived, changing it — and us — in the process. He knew that our feet often danced to tunes that had somehow remained beyond our hearing; with perfect pitch he played them back to us.

My mother read *Tom Sawyer* to me as a bedtime story when I was eleven. I thought Huck and Tom could be a lot of fun, but I dismissed Becky Thatcher as a bore. When I was twelve I invested a nickel at a local garage sale in a book that contained short pieces by Mark Twain. That was where I met Twain's Eve. Now, *that's* more like it, I decided, pleased to meet a female character I could identify *with* instead of against. Eve had spunk. Even if she got a lot wrong, you had to give her credit for trying. "The Man That Corrupted

Hadleyburg" left me giddy with satisfaction: none of my adolescent reveries of getting even with my enemies were half as neat as the plot of the man who got back at that town. "How I Edited an Agricultural Paper" set me off in uncontrollable giggles.

People sometimes told me that I looked like Huck Finn. "It's the freckles," they'd explain—not explaining anything at all. I didn't read *Huckleberry Finn* until junior year in high school in my English class. It was the fall of 1965. I was living in a small town in Connecticut. I expected a sequel to *Tom Sawyer*. So when the teacher handed out the books and announced our assignment, my jaw dropped: "Write a paper on how Mark Twain used irony to attack racism in *Huckleberry Finn*."

The year before, the bodies of three young men who had gone to Mississippi to help blacks register to vote—James Chaney, Andrew Goodman, and Michael Schwerner—had been found in a shallow grave; a group of white segregationists (the county sheriff among them) had been arrested in connection with the murders. America's inner cities were simmering with pent-up rage that began to explode in the summer of 1965, when riots in Watts left thirty-four people dead. None of this made any sense to me. I was confused, angry, certain that there was something missing from the news stories I read each day: the why. Then I met Pap Finn. And the Phelpses.

Pap Finn, Huck tells us, "had been drunk over in town" and "was just all mud." He erupts into a drunken tirade about "a free nigger . . . from Ohio—a mulatter, most as white as a white man," with "the whitest shirt on you ever see, too, and the shiniest hat; and there ain't a man in town that's got as fine clothes as what he had."

> . . . they said he was a p'fessor in a college, and could talk all kinds of languages, and knowed everything. And that ain't the wust. They said he could *vote*, when he was at home. Well, that let me out. Thinks I, what is the country a-coming to? It was 'lection day, and I was just about to go and vote, myself, if I warn't too drunk to get there; but when they told me there was a State in this country where they'd let that nigger vote, I drawed out. I says I'll never vote agin. Them's the very words I said. . . . And to see the

cool way of that nigger — why, he wouldn't a give me the road if I hadn't shoved him out o' the way.[12]

Later on in the novel, when the runaway slave Jim gives up his freedom to nurse a wounded Tom Sawyer, a white doctor testifies to the stunning altruism of his actions. The Phelpses and their neighbors, all fine, upstanding, well-meaning, churchgoing folk,

> agreed that Jim had acted very well, and was deserving to have some notice took of it, and reward. So every one of them promised, right out and hearty, that they wouldn't curse him no more.
>
> Then they come out and locked him up. I hoped they was going to say he could have one or two of the chains took off, because they was rotten heavy, or could have meat and greens with his bread and water, but they didn't think of it.[13]

Why did the behavior of these people tell me more about why Watts burned than anything I had read in the daily paper? And why did a drunk Pap Finn railing against a black college professor from Ohio whose vote was as good as his own tell me more about white anxiety over black political power than anything I had seen on the evening news?

Mark Twain knew that there was nothing, absolutely *nothing*, a black man could do — including selflessly sacrificing his freedom, the only thing of value he had — that would make white society see beyond the color of his skin. And Mark Twain knew that depicting racists with chilling accuracy would expose the viciousness of their world view like nothing else could. It was an insight echoed some eighty years after Mark Twain penned Pap Finn's rantings about the black professor, when Malcolm X famously asked, "Do you know what white racists call black Ph.D.'s?" and answered, " '*Nigger!* '"[14]

Mark Twain taught me things I needed to know. He taught me to understand the raw racism that lay behind what I saw on the evening news. He taught me that the most well-meaning people can be hurtful and myopic. He taught me to recognize the supreme irony of a country founded in freedom that continued to deny freedom to so many of its citizens. Every time I hear of another effort to kick Huck Finn out of school somewhere, I recall everything that Mark Twain taught *this* high school junior, and I find myself jumping into the fray.[15] I remember the black high school student who called CNN during the phone-in portion of a 1985 debate between Dr. John Wallace, a black educator spearheading efforts to ban the book, and myself. She accused Dr. Wallace of insulting her and all black high school students by suggesting they weren't smart enough to understand Mark Twain's irony. And I recall the black cameraman on the *CBS Morning News* who came up to me after he finished shooting another debate between Dr. Wallace and myself. He said he had never read the book by Mark Twain that we had been arguing about — but now he really wanted to. One thing that puzzled him, though, was why a white woman was defending it and a black man was attacking it, because as far as he could see from what we'd been saying, the book made whites look pretty bad.

As I came to understand *Huckleberry Finn* and *Pudd'nhead Wilson* as commentaries on the era now known as the nadir of American race relations, those books pointed me toward the world recorded in nineteenth-century black newspapers and periodicals and in fiction by Mark Twain's black contemporaries. My investigation of the role black voices and traditions played in shaping Mark Twain's art helped make me aware of their role in shaping all of American culture.[16] My research underlined for me the importance of changing the stories we tell about who we are to reflect the realities of what we've been.[17]

Ever since our encounter in high school English, Mark Twain has shown me the potential of American literature and American history to illuminate each other. Rarely have I found a contradiction or complexity we grapple with as a nation that Mark Twain had not puzzled over as well. He insisted on taking America seriously. And he insisted on *not* taking America seriously: "I think that there is but a single specialty with us, only one thing that can be called by the wide name 'American,'" he once wrote. "That is the national devotion to ice-water."[18]

Mark Twain threw back at us our dreams and our denial of those dreams, our greed, our goodness, our ambition, and our laziness, all rattling around together in that vast echo chamber of our talk — that sharp, spunky American talk that Mark Twain figured out how to write down without robbing it of its energy and immediacy. Talk shaped by voices that the official arbiters of "culture" deemed of no importance — voices of children, voices of slaves, voices of servants, voices of ordinary people. Mark Twain listened. And he made us listen. To the stories he told us, and to the truths they conveyed. He still has a lot to say that we need to hear.

Mark Twain lives — in our libraries, classrooms, homes, theaters, movie houses, streets, and most of all in our speech. His optimism energizes us, his despair sobers us, and his willingness to keep wrestling with the hilarious and horrendous complexities of it all keeps us coming back for more. As the twenty-first century approaches, may he continue to goad us, chasten us, delight us, berate us, and cause us to erupt in unrestrained laughter in unexpected places.

NOTES

1. Ernest Hemingway, *Green Hills of Africa* (New York: Charles Scribner's Sons, 1935), 22. George Bernard Shaw to Samuel L. Clemens, July 3, 1907, quoted in Albert Bigelow Paine, *Mark Twain: A Biography* (New York: Harper and Brothers, 1912), 3:1398.

2. Allen Carey-Webb, "Racism and *Huckleberry Finn*: Censorship, Dialogue and Change," *English Journal* 82, no. 7 (November 1993):22.

3. See Louis J. Budd, "Impersonators," in J. R. LeMaster and James D. Wilson, eds., *The Mark Twain Encyclopedia* (New York: Garland Publishing Company, 1993), 389–91.

4. See Shelley Fisher Fishkin, "Ripples and Reverberations," part 3 of *Lighting Out for the Territory: Reflections on Mark Twain and American Culture* (New York: Oxford University Press, 1996).

5. There are two exceptions. Twain published chapters from his autobiography in the *North American Review* in 1906 and 1907, but this material was not published in book form in Twain's lifetime; our volume reproduces the material as it appeared in the *North American Review*. The other exception is our final volume, *Mark Twain's Speeches*, which appeared two months after Twain's death in 1910.

An unauthorized handful of copies of *1601* was privately printed by an Alexander Gunn of Cleveland at the instigation of Twain's friend John Hay in 1880. The first American edition authorized by Mark Twain, however, was printed at the United States Military Academy at West Point in 1882; that is the edition reproduced here.

It should further be noted that four volumes — *The Stolen White Elephant and Other Detective Stories*, *Following the Equator and Anti-imperialist Essays*, *The Diaries of Adam and Eve*, and *1601, and Is Shakespeare Dead?* — bind together material originally published separately. In each case the first American edition of the material is the version that has been reproduced, always in its entirety. Because Twain constantly recycled and repackaged previously published works in his collections of short pieces, a certain amount of duplication is unavoidable. We have selected volumes with an eye toward keeping this duplication to a minimum.

Even the twenty-nine-volume Oxford Mark Twain has had to leave much out. No edition of Twain can ever claim to be "complete," for the man was too prolix, and the file drawers of both ephemera and as yet unpublished texts are deep.

6. With the possible exception of *Mark Twain's Speeches*. Some scholars suspect Twain knew about this book and may have helped shape it, although no hard evidence to that effect has yet surfaced. Twain's involvement in the production process varied greatly from book to book. For a fuller sense of authorial intention, scholars will continue to rely on the superb definitive editions of Twain's works produced by the Mark Twain Project at the University of California at Berkeley as they become available. Dense with annotation documenting textual emendation and related issues, these editions add immeasurably to our understanding of Mark Twain and the genesis of his works.

7. Except for a few titles that were not in its collection. The American Antiquarian Society in Worcester, Massachusetts, provided the first edition of *King Leopold's Soliloquy*; the Elmer Holmes Bobst Library of New York University furnished the 1906–7 volumes of the *North American Review* in which *Chapters from My Autobiography* first appeared; the Harry Ransom Humanities Research Center at the University of Texas at Austin made their copy of the West Point edition of *1601* available; and the Mark Twain Project provided the first edition of *Extract from Captain Stormfield's Visit to Heaven*.

8. The specific copy photographed for Oxford's facsimile edition is indicated in a note on the text at the end of each volume.

9. All quotations from contemporary writers in this essay are taken from their introductions to the volumes of The Oxford Mark Twain, and the quotations from Mark Twain's works are taken from the texts reproduced in The Oxford Mark Twain.

10. *The Diaries of Adam and Eve*, The Oxford Mark Twain [hereafter OMT] (New York: Oxford University Press, 1996), p. 33.

11. *Tom Sawyer Abroad*, OMT, p. 74.

12. *Adventures of Huckleberry Finn*, OMT, p. 49–50.

13. Ibid., p. 358.

14. Malcolm X, *The Autobiography of Malcolm X*, with the assistance of Alex Haley (New York: Grove Press, 1965), p. 284.

15. I do not mean to minimize the challenge of teaching this difficult novel, a challenge for which all teachers may not feel themselves prepared. Elsewhere I have developed some concrete strategies for approaching the book in the classroom, including teaching it in the context of the history of American race relations and alongside books by black writers. See Shelley Fisher Fishkin, "Teaching *Huckleberry Finn*," in James S. Leonard, ed., *Making Mark Twain Work in the Classroom* (Durham: Duke University Press, forthcoming). See also Shelley Fisher Fishkin, *Was Huck Black? Mark Twain and African-American Voices* (New York: Oxford University Press, 1993), pp. 106–8, and a curriculum kit in preparation at the Mark Twain House in Hartford, containing teaching suggestions from myself, David Bradley, Jocelyn Chadwick-Joshua, James Miller, and David E. E. Sloane.

16. See Fishkin, *Was Huck Black?* See also Fishkin, "Interrogating 'Whiteness,' Complicating 'Blackness': Remapping American Culture," in Henry Wonham, ed., *Criticism and the Color Line: Desegregating American Literary Studies* (New Brunswick: Rutgers UP, 1996, pp. 251–90 and in shortened form in *American Quarterly* 47, no. 3 (September 1995):428–66.

17. I explore the roots of my interest in Mark Twain and race at greater length in an essay entitled "Changing the Story," in Jeffrey Rubin-Dorsky and Shelley Fisher Fishkin, eds., *People of the Book: Thirty Scholars Reflect on Their Jewish Identity* (Madison: U of Wisconsin Press, 1996), pp. 47–63.

18. "What Paul Bourget Thinks of Us," *How to Tell a Story and Other Essays*, OMT, p. 197.

INTRODUCTION
George Plimpton

I reread *Roughing It* sitting in seat 24F on an American Airlines plane from New York to Los Angeles not long ago — our flight plan four hours out, crossing the Sierra Nevada, not far from where Mark Twain spent the years I was reading about in the book on my lap.

Not long after we had taken off, a man just across the aisle from me took exception to pulling his shade down so the passengers could watch the motion picture in the tourist cabin in relative darkness. He complained to the flight attendant that he had never been in an airplane before and wanted to look down and see the fields and towns go by below — "like being a bird," I heard him say. She was sympathetic, and so was I, but the others were particularly anxious to watch the film, which starred, as I recall, Harrison Ford. As the credits came on the screen, they protested the light streaming across the cabin from the single open window like a laser beam, so adamant about it (one nearby woman called out, "*Nobody* looks out the window anymore") that the flight attendant took the majority view. "Look," she said. "We're above the clouds — 30,000 feet up — and there's nothing to see. Won't you. . . ?"

The man had his back up by this time. He announced that he'd never seen the tops of clouds, not having been in a plane before, and that he fully intended to have his fill of them.

Actually, everything quieted down after that. The man looked gloomily out at the clouds, and after a while, perhaps because he had sneaked a peek at what Harrison Ford was doing on the screen, he pulled the shade down and settled in to watch the film.

I began wondering how Mark Twain would have reported this mild alter-cation. Surely he would have stretched the scene. We would have had some creative journalism. The man would not have backed down. The woman who had announced that nobody looks out airplane windows would have hit him over the head with a handbag. A struggle in the aisle, surely enough malarkey going on to force the pilot to land in Duluth, or some such place. What would have been delivered was what Mark Twain himself called "a fancy sketch."

Mark Twain was often criticized, especially in his later works, for mean-dering, drifting into lengthy asides such as this. In the travel books (*The Innocents Abroad*, *Roughing It*, *A Tramp Abroad*), describing what Twain referred to as his "variegated vagabondizing," his anecdotes, portraits, mus-ings, tall stories enliven the text and seem absolutely essential — his "excur-sions and digressions of all kinds are the very woof of it," as William Dean Howells, the editor of the *Atlantic Monthly* and his great friend, once archly stated it. "Woof" indeed!

As I read along in my little cone of light from the overhead reading lamp (glancing up occasionally to see how Harrison Ford was getting along), I noticed about Twain's asides that the truth is almost invariably stretched to the breaking point in order to give the incident or character a comic twist, and yet the reader never moans, "Oh, come off it!" It is part of Twain's genius that he keeps us on the delicate edge of credulity — a condition which humorists, especially those who perform on the stage, strive to imitate. Every time a hu-morist confides to his audience that what is about to be told is a "true story," one can be fairly sure that it will be nothing of the sort. Even Twain falls back on this on occasion. "That anecdote is *true*," he insists after telling a story in *Roughing It* about a grizzled miner, long in the fields, who pays one hundred and fifty dollars' worth of gold dust in a pouch to kiss a two-year-old child.

Twain at his comic best utilizes the popular conceit of piling on successive stories, increasingly hyperbolic, leading from the original subject. In the first few pages of *Roughing It*, he describes his ill-suited pistol. "One of our 'con-ductors' practiced awhile on a cow with it, and as long as she stood still and behaved herself she was safe; but as soon as she went to moving about, and he got shooting at other things, she came to grief." No sooner has Twain done with this than he obliges us with a description of yet another pistol, a fellow traveler's "pepper box," whose faults are even more formidable. This is a procedure that vaudevillians and comics refer to as providing a "capper" — that is to say, tacking an *extension*, even more hilarious, onto the original.

I was unable to suppress my laughter reading those early chapters — startling those seated around me, since my outbursts of mirth invariably occurred when something dire was happening to Harrison Ford on the screen. Even the man across the aisle who had protested the lowering of his window shade gave me a sharp look or two. Twain should not be read sitting alone in public places! In *The Mysterious Stranger*, Twain wrote that laughter was really the only effective weapon owned by the human race. He didn't add that such a weapon can backfire as well. . . .

2

Some matters of fact about *Roughing It*. In 1870 Mark Twain's publisher, Elisha Bliss, urged him to follow up the phenomenal success of his first travel book, *The Innocents Abroad* (which sold some one hundred thousand copies in its first three years) with an account of his experiences in the West. Twain, living in Buffalo, New York, with his new bride, was eager enough to do this, starting the book in 1870, but he discovered to his dismay that the writing did not come easily. The events he was trying to remember had taken place in the Washoe country of Nevada almost a decade before. In desperation he wrote his brother Orion, who had been with him, that he was going to "do up Nevada & Cal." but remembered "next to *nothing* about the matter." He asked for a memorandum book he knew Orion had kept on the trip, and promised the first thousand dollars out of his royalties in return. Alas, his brother's notes were skimpy and not especially helpful. Twain had his columns from the *Virginia City Territorial Enterprise* and various other local papers to fall back on, but a malaise about the whole project had settled in and the work progressed at a snail's pace.

Then Joseph Thompson Goodman, an old friend from Washoe and indeed the *Enterprise* editor who had given Twain his first writing job back in

1862, turned up in Elmira, where the author had moved. He took a look at what had been written, the early chapters, and praised them so highly that Twain not only got back to work but persuaded Goodman to stay with him for a month and help him in the evenings — doubtless over cigars and Scotch (Twain liked his warm) — to recall more vividly the boisterous days the two of them had spent on the frontier.

In April 1871, Twain sent Bliss chapter 8 of *Roughing It*, along with an assessment that it was "by all odds . . . the finest piece of writing I ever did." It is the chapter which includes the remarkable portrait of the pony express rider overtaking the stagecoach in which Twain and his brother are riding. The stagecoach driver exclaims, "HERE HE COMES!"

> Every neck is stretched further, and every eye strained wider. Away across the endless dead level of the prairie a black speck appears against the sky, and it is plain that it moves. Well, I should think so! In a second or two it becomes a horse and rider, rising and falling, rising and falling — sweeping toward us nearer and nearer — growing more and more distinct, more and more sharply defined — nearer and still nearer, and the flutter of the hoofs comes faintly to the ear — another instant a whoop and a hurrah from our upper deck, a wave of the rider's hand, but no reply, and man and horse burst past our excited faces, and go winging away like a belated fragment of a storm!
>
> So sudden is it all, and so like a flash of unreal fancy, that but for the flake of white foam left quivering and perishing on a mail-sack after the vision had flashed by and disappeared, we might have doubted whether we had seen any actual horse and man at all, maybe.

Twain's work on *Roughing It* speeded up. It seemed to take on the pace of his pony express rider. He reported to Elisha Bliss that he was churning out as many as sixty pages a day — a "bully book," he called it, "a starchy book" that he thought would sell.

3

Mark Twain was just twenty-one when he left Keokuk, Iowa, on the journey that was eventually to give him his material for *Roughing It*. Originally his plan had been to head for the upper reaches of the Amazon, where it was a simple matter to make a fortune in coca plants, he had read, just a question of bending down and picking the stuff off the ground. But when he arrived in New Orleans, he discovered that there weren't any ships leaving for South America and "probably wouldn't be any during that century." It was then that he turned to piloting on the river, the subject of his other great book on domestic travel, *Life on the Mississippi*. He might well have continued his career as a pilot if not for the intervention of the Civil War, which closed down the river traffic.

In 1861 Twain joined the Confederate army in Missouri. It seems a somewhat more quixotic than a serious involvement, the group he joined being a ragtail collection of old friends who called themselves the Marion Rangers. They elected their own officers, and Twain was voted a second lieutenancy. This little group was nearly captured by Union forces. Claiming later that he had been exhausted by continual retreating, Twain left the service after two weeks.

Then, with his brother Orion, ten years older, who had been appointed a territorial secretary, Twain left for the West, arriving in the territory of Nevada (also known as the Land of the Washoe after the local Indian tribes) in the middle of August 1861. He had eight hundred dollars in capital with him, quite a substantial sum in those days since his room and board only set him back ten dollars a week. He was drawn there in part by the lure of what was referred to as going "to see the elephant" — the elephant being the symbol for gold prospecting. In fact, there was much else besides gold. Twain wrote home to his mother, "The country is fabulously rich in gold, silver, copper, lead, coal, iron, quicksilver, marble, granite, chalk, plaster of Paris (gypsum), thieves, murderers, desperadoes, ladies, children, lawyers, Christians, Indians, Chinamen, Spaniards, gamblers, sharpers, coyotes (pronounced Ki-yo-ties), poets, preachers, and jackass rabbits."

As his mention of murderers suggests, life was cheap on the frontier, and he reported as much in another letter to his mother: "I have just heard five pistol shots down the street — as such things are in my line I will go and see about it." He added in a postscript, "The pistol did its work well — one man — a Jackson County Missourian, shot two of my friends (police officers) through the heart — both died within three minutes. Murderer's name is John Campbell."

Effie Mona Mack in her superb book *Mark Twain in Nevada* (for which I am indebted for much background material on life in the territory) gives an example of the indifference to violence in those frontier days: that a man shot between the eyes in a billiard saloon in Virginia City in 1863 lay under one of the billiard tables from four in the morning until noon. The coroner was apparently overworked. The billiard games went on as if nothing had happened — players often making their shots astride the body.

The wealth of the mines, especially the gold fields, was to be denied Twain. But his dismal experiences in them turned out to be, as William Dean Howells later put it, "gold under his hand." Almost in desperation he turned to writing. Composing his first letters by the light of a miner's candle in a cabin in the Sierra Nevada, he signed them "Josh" and sent them off to the editor of the *Territorial Enterprise* in Virginia City, one of the most influential papers west of the Mississippi.

The Josh letters are not extant, but the one that probably landed him his job on the *Enterprise* was titled "Professor Personal Pronoun." It was a spoof on the excessive oratory of Judge George Turner, the chief justice of the territory of Nevada. It was said that the judge's lectures and speeches could not be published in their entirety because the printer invariably ran out of capital I's. The opening line of Twain's burlesque was "I WAS SIRED BY THE GREAT AMERICAN EAGLE AND FOALED BY A CONTINENTAL DAM!"

The judge must have been quite a character, certainly worthy of a parodist's pen. A man who signed his name on hotel registers as "CHIEF JUSTICE OF THE UNITED STATES, U.S.A.," he was in fact an official who fit a description common to those times on the frontier: "An honest judge is a son of a gun who will stay bought." Stories about him (often apocryphal) abound. On one occasion he demanded a ten-thousand-dollar bribe to find on behalf of a litigant, which had to be paid before the court convened the next morning. The briber made the rounds of the saloons and gaming halls in Virginia City that evening and was able to collect the sum in gold coins. Back in Carson City, late at night but with sack in hand, he knocked on the judge's door. The judge's wife answered and allowed that the judge was asleep but that she would undertake to receive the money herself. She spread her nightgown before her like a bowl. The sack of gold was emptied into it, so heavy that it tore the nightgown completely off her body and left her standing in the doorway, naked as a jaybird, the gold in hundreds of twenty-dollar pieces lying at her feet.

The editor who accepted the Josh letters was the aforementioned Joseph Goodman, often referred to as the discoverer of "Mark Twain." A debonair bon vivant, he was known as the "Boss Poet of the Comstock" — inevitably called upon to write commemorative verses on the occasion of national holidays, funerals, and civic events.

The paper he ran was founded in 1858 in the small mining community of Genoa, Nevada. A weekly, it was run off on an ancient "Washington" handpress. The second-story room in the store which contained the press was also used as the town jail — the prisoners chained to the machine until press time, when they were unlocked and guarded by an armed deputy until the press run was done. In 1860 the *Territorial Enterprise* moved with the Gold Rush to Virginia City in the western part of the territory of Nevada, on the eastern slopes of the Sierra Nevada. The first issue appeared on November 12, 1860. The following year Goodman, who had started off as a typesetter, became a partner.

In late August 1862, at the urging of Goodman, Twain gave up his search for "the elephant" and came to the *Enterprise*. One of the reasons Goodman called for him was that his star writer, Dan De Quille, was leaving for his home in Iowa; the hope was that the man who wrote the Josh letters could replace him. In fact, De Quille only stayed away nine months. In 1863, with huge veins of silver ore discovered on the Lode, the Comstock boom under way, De Quille, being the paper's expert on geological matters, was lured back to Virginia City. He and Mark Twain became fast friends.

With the exception of the nine months' hiatus back home De Quille worked for the *Territorial Enterprise* for thirty years, writing local news, scientific mining articles, and fanciful tales, often hoaxes, which he called his "quaints." He was a fine writer in his own stead, and much of his work echoes Mark Twain at his best. It suggests that these young writers fed off each other's wit, style, and hyperbolic approach. Here is De Quille on the ferocious wind gusts, known as Washoe zephyrs, that bedeviled the area.

> The air is filled with dust, rags, tin cans, empty packing cases, old cooking stoves, all manner of second-hand furniture, crowbars, log-chains, lamp posts, and similar rubbish. Hats! More hats are lost during the prevalence of a single zephyr than in any city of the Union on any election held in the last twenty years. These hats all go down the side of the mountain and land in a deep gulch known as Six-mile Cañon. . . .
>
> After a very severe zephyr, it is said, drifts of hats, fully fifteen feet in depth, are to be seen in the bed of the cañon just named. All these hats are found and appropriated by the Piute Indians, who always go down in to the cañon the next morning after a rousing fruitful gale to gather in the hat crop. When the innocent and guileless children of the desert come back to town, they are all loaded down to the guards with hats. Each head is decorated with at least a dozen hats of all kinds and colors — braves, squaws, and papooses are walking pyramids of hats.

What a group these newspapermen were — De Quille, Goodman, and Twain! Accounts of their roisterous carryings-on bring to mind the kind of frat-house enthusiasm one associates with college humor magazines like the *Harvard Lampoon*. Pranks, spoofs, parodies. In Mark Twain's case, it was a characteristic that stayed with him throughout his life. William Dean Howells spoke of him as "a youth to the end of his days, the heart of a boy with the head of a sage; the heart of a good boy, or a bad boy, but always a willful boy."

Mark Twain's wife often despaired of her husband's continuing adolescent exuberance. "Youth" was her nickname for him among friends. "Oh, Youth!" one imagines her exclaiming. "Cut it out!"

Not that there wasn't solid reporting in those early days on the *Enterprise*. Twain was assigned to cover the territorial legislature in Carson City. It was to one of a series of these articles—a piece written on January 30, 1863, and published on February 3—that the name "was first signed Mark Twain." In those times it was the fashion to use pseudonyms, many of them quite odd and quirky. Dan De Quille (a pseudonym itself—his real name was William Wright) also wrote under the names "Ebenezer Queerkut" and "Picaroon Pax." One of Twain's first noms de plume was "Thomas Jefferson Snodgrass," which he signed for some travel articles in the form of letters he wrote for the *Keokuk Saturday Post* back in 1856. "Mark Twain" was a nom de plume, he claimed later, first used by a captain, recently deceased, a "river news" columnist for the *New Orleans Picayune*. "As he could no longer need that signature," Twain confided, "I laid violent hands upon it without asking permission of the proprietor's remains."

It is not an overstatement to emphasize that the year 1863 was notable not only for the mining of great riches in the Washoe (the Comstock Lode) but also for Mark Twain's emergence as a writer. His work was reprinted along the West Coast, and in Eastern journals. A celebrity in Nevada, he was close to being one throughout the country. "Everybody knows me," he wrote his mother, "and I fare like a prince wherever I go, be it on this side of the mountains or the other. And I am proud to say I am the most conceited ass in the Territory."

The popularity of his columns stemmed in considerable part from his lampooning of various personages in the Washoe. His spoofs were often taken seriously—stories so absurd as to suggest that a lot of gullible souls populated those parts. On one occasion Twain fooled his readers so badly that he felt compelled to publish a retraction the next day.

I take it all back.
— Mark Twain

In fact, in 1864 a peppery exchange with the editor of a rival paper in Virginia City, the *Daily Union*, precipitated a situation which almost led to a duel. The rivalry between the local papers was intense. The year before, a series of vicious *ad hominem* editorials had resulted in a duel between Joe Goodman of the *Enterprise* and Tom Fitch of the *Union*. Mark Twain had been one of the spectators. From ten paces Joe Goodman fired the first shot, a bullet into Fitch's leg (he had promised to shoot low) which knocked his rival to the ground. Fitch was unable to return fire and was left with a slight limp for life. Apparently, their differences thus resolved, the two remained close friends. In Mark Twain's case, he had referred to his opposite number as a "liar, a poltroon, and a puppy." There were challenges and acceptances: an affair of honor seemed close at hand. However, following the Fitch-Goodman affair, the territorial legislature had passed a law that anyone involved in the process of a duel had committed a felony, punishable by two years in the penitentiary. Since the preliminaries to a duel had already occurred, a felony thus committed, word was sent to Twain that he had better get out of the territory at once. He took the stage for San Francisco — an episode, oddly, that he does not mention in *Roughing It*. He simply states (in the first sentence of chapter 55), "I began to get tired of staying in one place so long."

After leaving the *Enterprise*, Twain got a job as a reporter on the *San Francisco Morning Call*. He spent some time in the California foothill mining towns — one of them in Calaveras County, which gave him the material for his first story, originally titled "Jim Smiley and His Jumping Frog." It was a yarn he enjoyed telling friends, and he was persuaded by Artemus Ward to put it to paper. Ward intended to publish the story in an anthology, but it arrived in New York too late to be included. Eventually published in the *Saturday Press*, the story caught the public's fancy and was reprinted in a number of newspaper supplements. James Russell Lowell described it as the "finest piece of humorus fiction yet produced in America." Twain himself was somewhat rueful about the story's popularity, complaining in his autobiography, "I was aware that it was only the frog that was celebrated. It wasn't I. I was still an obscurity."

Two years after leaving Virginia City, Twain came back to give a lecture on the Sandwich Islands (Hawaii), which he had visited in the interim. He had been very successful on the lecture circuit with talks in San Francisco and Sacramento, as well as in smaller towns with names like You Bet and Red Dog. The advance announcement in the *Enterprise* proclaimed, among other encomiums,

> Our state can justly claim Mark Twain as its own peculiar production. It was while a resident here and associated with the *Enterprise* that he assumed the name Mark Twain and developed that rich and inexhaustible vein which has made the title famous. True, he has warmed his fancy in tropical climes and expanded his thought by ocean pilgrimages and heated his eloquence in volcanic fires; but all of them rest upon the solid foundation which was originally laid in our native alkali and sagebrush.

His old friend Joseph Goodman of the *Enterprise* had a suggestion about how to open the lecture from the stage of the opera house.

> "Sam, you don't need anybody to introduce you. There's a piano on the stage in the theatre. . . . when the curtain rises, you be seated at the piano, playing and singing that song of yours, 'Had an Old Horse Whose Name Was Jerusalem,' and don't seem to notice that the curtain is up at first; then be surprised when you finally find that it is up, and begin talking without any further preliminaries."

The plan worked well — it started Twain off "with great hilarity and applause." He received a fine write-up for the speech from his friends on the *Enterprise*: "Combining the most valuable statistical and general information with passages of drollest humor, all delivered in the peculiar and inimitable style of the author, it constitutes an entertainment of rare excellence and intelligence."

His friends were not through with him. In the spirit of past pranks they staged a fake hold-up up on the Divide as Twain was coming back to Virginia City from Gold Hill, where he had given another lecture. It was a bitterly cold night, the air full of drifting snow. He would have enjoyed being in on the planning of the prank, but hardly, it turned out, being the victim. A writer from the rival *Virginia City Union* had noted in 1862, "Merciless himself in perpetrating jokes on others, he winces like a cur with a flea in his ear when others retort."

It was surprising that Twain didn't realize his friends were involved. Barely able to suppress their laughter, they communicated with each other in the darkness using the names of Southern generals Beauregard and Stonewall Jackson, and a Northerner, Philip Sheridan. Twain was relieved of twenty-five dollars and his watch. He eventually got both back though not received with very much grace. "Since then," he writes in the final pages of *Roughing It*, "I play no practical jokes on people and generally lose my temper when one is played upon me."

I think it can be assumed, though, that here he is playing with the truth — what Huck Finn called a "stretcher."

4

We were about an hour from Los Angeles. Toward the end of *Roughing It* I came across a holograph (it appears on page 509), a barely decipherable letter purportedly written by Horace Greeley to a retired Michigan preacher named Simon Erickson. Erickson is described as "muttering to himself and nodding his head acquiescingly or shaking it in mild protest." He has written Greeley on behalf of a young boy, an amateur gardener obsessed with the notion of growing turnips on a vine. He wants advice. What comes back from Greeley looks as if written on a stagecoach in the midst of a headlong bucking ride. Erickson spends an agonizing week trying to make out what Greeley has written. Three of his attempts at decoding the letter are given in *Roughing It*. One of them reads:

Poultices do sometimes choke swine; tulips reduce posterity; causes leather to resist. Our notions empower wisdom, her let's afford while we can. Butter but any cakes, fill any undertaker, we'll wean him from his filly. We feel hot.
Yrxwly,
Hevace Eveeloj

Finally, in despair, Erickson writes Greeley ("I fear I do not entirely comprehend your kind note") and asks for clarification. Back it comes, and sure enough, the words emerge from the holograph as if by magic. But it is too late. Typical of so many of Twain's minor characters who fade away under emotional duress, the young gardener is no more. "Poor lad, they laid him to rest with a turnip in each hand."

Rather idly, and perhaps with the stimulus of a Scotch and water (with ice), I took a crack at decoding Greeley's original scrawl, assuming that Twain (or Greeley, for that matter) wouldn't mind. Here is what I wrote sitting in seat 24F:

> Potatoes for solidiers. Gershwin smoothes nerves. Gramps receive green bushels. Eurotrash assigned to Steelers. Frequently the person disclosed his early efforts well. He received red deer. I hastened etc. etc. quarrelsome nearly a mile. Will hasten for dinner with Jell-O for your Nell.
>
> Yours,
>
> Horace Greeley

What is going on here, it seems to me, is a kind of surreal family dinner, perhaps at a military base, music on the phonograph etc. etc. when something goes wrong in the kitchen, driving an angry Horace Greeley out into the streets looking for Jell-O. Apparently some unpleasant European relatives have turned up who have been sent off to the Pittsburgh Steelers training camp. All this is even more farfetched than Simon Erickson's attempts, and it is of very little help to the turnip-crazed youngster, and furthermore, the text, especially the reference to the Pittsburgh Steelers, is not particularly topical. But it's the best I could do. Interested readers, especially those with an interest in cryptology and a bit of time on their hands, such as on a transcontinental flight, may do far better.

5

Somewhere in J. D. Salinger's *Catcher in the Rye*, Holden Caulfield remarks that his idea of a good book is one which makes him want to call up the author and talk to him about it. What a privilege it would have been to talk to Mark Twain, or even better to have met him in person, or especially to hear him lecture. William Dean Howells wrote that he was the "most consummate public performer I ever saw. . . . he knew all the stops of that simple instrument — man." Or even to walk down a street with him. He wore a sealskin coat or later the familiar white serge suit, and an Oxford gown he put on at every possible occasion. Howells wrote that he teased up his hair to make himself look taller than he actually was (five feet eight inches) and that the "splendid shock of red hair . . . tilted from side to side in his undulating walk."

Best to guide him to a café table. There perhaps he'd reminisce about his adventures in *Roughing It*—his troubles with his horse, the Genuine Mexican Plug, the encounter with the "sociable heifer," the night the tarantulas got loose, Bemis's buffalo hunt, Jim Blaine and his grandfather's ram . . . any one of the treasures that await the reader in what follows.

ROUGHING IT

CAMPING IN THE SNOW.

THE MINER'S DREAM.

ROUGHING

IT

BY

MARK TWAIN.
(SAMUEL L. CLEMENS.)

FULLY ILLUSTRATED BY EMINENT ARTISTS.

(ISSUED BY SUBSCRIPTION ONLY, AND NOT FOR SALE IN BOOK STORES.)
(RESIDENTS OF ANY STATE DESIRING A COPY SHOULD ADDRESS THE PUBLISHERS AS BELOW.)

HARTFORD, CONN.:
AMERICAN PUBLISHING COMPANY.
F. G. GILMAN & CO., CHICAGO, ILL.; W. E. BLISS, TOLEDO, OHIO.;
NETTLETON & CO., CINCINNATI, OHIO.; D. ASHMEAD, PHILADELPHIA, PENN.
J. W. GOODSPEED, NEW ORLEANS, LA.;
A. ROMAN & COMPANY, SAN FRANCISCO, CAL.
1872.

TO

CALVIN H. HIGBIE,

Of California,

An Honest Man, a Genial Comrade, and a Steadfast Friend,

THIS BOOK IS INSCRIBED

By the Author,

In Memory of the Curious Time

When We Two

WERE MILLIONAIRES FOR TEN DAYS.

PREFATORY.

THIS book is merely a personal narrative, and not a pretentious history or a philosophical dissertation. It is a record of several years of variegated vagabondizing, and its object is rather to help the resting reader while away an idle hour than afflict him with metaphysics, or goad him with science. Still, there is information in the volume; information concerning an interesting episode in the history of the Far West, about which no books have been written by persons who were on the ground in person, and saw the happenings of the time with their own eyes. I allude to the rise, growth and culmination of the silver-mining fever in Nevada—a curious episode, in some respects; the only one, of its peculiar kind, that has occurred in the land; and the only one, indeed, that is likely to occur in it.

Yes, take it all around, there is quite a good deal of information in the book. I regret this very much; but really it could not be helped: information appears to stew out of me naturally, like the precious ottar of roses out of the otter. Sometimes it has seemed to me that I would give worlds if I could retain my facts; but it cannot be. The more I calk up the sources, and the tighter I get, the more I leak wisdom. Therefore, I can only claim indulgence at the hands of the reader, not justification.

THE AUTHOR.

List of Illustrations

BY FAY & COX, 105 NASSAU ST., N.Y.

CONTENTS.

CHAPTER XLIX.

CHAPTER L.

CHAPTER LI.

CHAPTER LII.

CHAPTER LIII.

CHAPTER LIV.

CHAPTER LV.

CHAPTER LVI.

CHAPTER LVII.

CHAPTER LVIII.

CHAPTER LIX.

CHAPTER LX.

CHAPTER LXI.

CHAPTER LXII.

CHAPTER LXIII.

CHAPTER LXIV.

CHAPTER LXV.

CHAPTER LXVI.

CHAPTER LXVII.

CHAPTER LXVIII.

CHAPTER LXIX.

2†

CHAPTER I.

MY brother had just been appointed Secretary of Nevada Territory — an office of such majesty that it concentrated in itself the duties and dignities of Treasurer, Comptroller, Secretary of State, and Acting Governor in the Governor's absence. A salary of eighteen hundred dollars a year and the title of "Mr. Secretary," gave to the great position an air of wild and imposing grandeur. I was young and ignorant, and I envied my brother. I coveted his distinction and his financial splendor, but particularly and especially the long, strange journey he was going to make, and the curious new world he was going to explore. He was going to travel! I never had been away from home, and that word "travel" had a seductive charm for me. Pretty soon he would be hundreds and hundreds of miles away on the great plains and deserts, and among the mountains of the Far West, and would see buffaloes and Indians, and prairie dogs, and antelopes, and have all kinds of adventures, and may be get hanged or scalped, and have ever such a fine time, and write home and tell us all about it, and be a hero. And he would see the gold mines and the silver mines, and maybe go about of an afternoon when his work was done, and pick up two or three pailfuls of shining slugs, and nuggets of gold and silver on the hillside. And by and by he would become very rich, and return home by sea, and be able to talk as calmly about San Francisco and the ocean, and "the isthmus" as if it was nothing of any consequence to have seen those marvels face to face. What I suffered in contemplating his happiness, pen cannot describe. And so, when he offered me, in cold blood, the sublime position of private secretary under him, it appeared to me that the heavens and the earth passed away, and the firmament was rolled together as a scroll! I had nothing more to desire. My contentment was complete. At the end of an hour or

ENVIOUS CONTEMPLATIONS.

two I was ready for the journey. Not much packing up was necessary, because we were going in the overland stage from the Missouri frontier to Nevada, and passengers were only allowed a small quantity of baggage apiece. There was no Pacific railroad in those fine times of ten or twelve years ago— not a single rail of it.

I only proposed to stay in Nevada three months—I had no thought of staying longer than that. I meant to see all I could that was new and strange, and then hurry home to business. I little thought that I would not see the end of that three-month pleasure excursion for six or seven uncommonly long years!

I dreamed all night about Indians, deserts, and silver bars, and in due time, next day, we took shipping at the St. Louis wharf on board a steamboat bound up the Missouri River.

We were six days going from St. Louis to "St. Jo."—a trip that was so dull, and sleepy, and eventless that it has left no more impression on my memory than if its duration had been six minutes instead of that many days. No record is left in my mind, now, concerning it, but a confused jumble of savage-looking snags, which we deliberately walked over with one wheel or the other; and of reefs which we butted and butted, and then retired from and climbed over in some softer place; and of sand-bars which we roosted on occasionally, and rested, and then got out our crutches and sparred over. In fact, the boat might almost as well have gone to St. Jo. by land, for she was walking most of the time, anyhow—climbing over reefs and clambering over snags patiently and laboriously

INNOCENT DREAMS.

all day long. The captain said she was a "bully" boat, and all she wanted was more "shear" and a bigger wheel. I thought she wanted a pair of stilts, but I had the deep sagacity not to say so.

CHAPTER II.

THE first thing we did on that glad evening that landed us at St. Joseph was to hunt up the stage-office, and pay a hundred and fifty dollars apiece for tickets per overland coach to Carson City, Nevada.

The next morning, bright and early, we took a hasty breakfast, and hurried to the starting-place. Then an inconvenience presented itself which we had not properly appreciated before, namely, that one cannot make a heavy traveling trunk stand for twenty-five pounds of baggage—because it weighs a good deal more. But that was all we could take—twenty-five pounds each. So we had to snatch our trunks open, and make a selection in a good deal of a hurry. We put our lawful twenty-five pounds apiece all in one valise, and shipped the trunks back to St. Louis again. It was a sad parting, for now we had no swallow-tail coats and white kid gloves to wear at Pawnee receptions in the Rocky Mountains, and no stove-pipe hats nor patent-leather boots, nor anything else necessary to make life calm and peaceful. We were reduced to a war-footing. Each of us put on a rough, heavy suit of clothing, woolen army shirt and "stogy" boots included; and into the valise we crowded a few white shirts, some under-clothing and such things. My brother, the Secretary, took along about four pounds of United States statutes and six pounds of Unabridged Dictionary; for we did not know—poor innocents—that such things could be bought in San Francisco on one day and received in Carson City the next. I was armed to the teeth with a pitiful little Smith & Wesson's seven-shooter, which carried a ball like a homœopathic pill, and it took the whole seven to make a dose for an adult. But I thought it was grand. It ap-peared to me to be a dangerous weapon. It only had one fault—you could not hit anything with it. One of our "conductors" practiced awhile on a cow with it, and as long as she stood still and behaved herself she was safe; but as soon as she went to mov-ing about, and he got to shooting at other things, she came to grief. The Secretary had a small-sized Colt's revolver strapped around him for protection against the Indians, and to guard against accidents he carried it uncapped. Mr. George Bemis was dismally

LIGHT TRAVELING ORDER.

formidable. George Bemis was our fellow-traveler. We had never seen him before. He wore in his belt an old original "Allen" revolver, such as irreverent people called a "pepper-box." Simply drawing the trigger back, cocked and fired the pistol. As the trigger came back, the hammer would begin to rise and the barrel to turn over, and presently down would drop the hammer, and away would speed the ball. To aim along the turning barrel and hit the thing aimed at was a feat which was probably never done with an "Allen" in the world. But George's was a reliable weapon,

THE "ALLEN."

nevertheless, because, as one of the stage-drivers afterward said, "If she didn't get what she went after, she would fetch something else." And so she did. She went after a deuce of

spades nailed against a tree, once, and fetched a mule standing
about thirty yards to the left of it.   Bemis did not want the
mule ; but the owner came out with a double-barreled shot-
gun and persuaded him to buy it, anyhow.   It was a cheerful

INDUCEMENTS TO PURCHASE.

weapon—the "Allen."   Sometimes all its six barrels would
go off at once, and then there was no safe place in all the
region round about, but behind it.

We took two or three blankets for protection against frosty
weather in the mountains.   In the matter of luxuries we were
modest—we took none along but some pipes and five pounds
of smoking tobacco.   We had two large canteens to carry
water in, between stations on the Plains, and we also took with
us a little shot-bag of silver coin for daily expenses in the way
of breakfasts and dinners.

By eight o'clock everything was ready, and we were on the other side of the river. We jumped into the stage, the driver cracked his whip, and we bowled away and left "the States" behind us. It was a superb summer morning, and all the landscape was brilliant with sunshine. There was a freshness and breeziness, too, and an exhilarating sense of emancipation from all sorts of cares and responsibilities, that almost made us feel that the years we had spent in the close, hot city, toiling and slaving, had been wasted and thrown away. We were spinning along through Kansas, and in the course of an hour and a half we were fairly abroad on the great Plains. Just here the land was rolling—a grand sweep of regular elevations and depressions as far as the eye could reach—like the stately heave and swell of the ocean's bosom after a storm. And everywhere were cornfields, accenting with squares of deeper green, this limitless expanse of grassy land. But presently this sea upon dry ground was to lose its "rolling" character and stretch away for seven hundred miles as level as a floor!

Our coach was a great swinging and swaying stage, of the most sumptuous description —an imposing cradle on wheels. It was drawn by six handsome horses, and by the side of the driver sat the "conductor," the legitimate captain of the craft; for it was his business to take charge and care of the mails, baggage, express matter, and passengers. We three were the only passengers, this trip. We sat on the back seat,

THE FACETIOUS DRIVER.

inside. About all the rest of the coach was full of mail bags—for we had three days' delayed mails with us. Almost touching our knees, a perpendicular wall of mail matter rose up to the roof. There was a great pile of it strapped on top of the stage, and both the fore and hind boots were full. We had twenty-seven hundred pounds of it aboard, the driver

PLEASING NEWS.

said—"a little for Brigham, and Carson, and 'Frisco, but the heft of it for the Injuns, which is powerful troublesome 'thout they get plenty of truck to read." But as he just then got up a fearful convulsion of his countenance which was suggestive of a wink being swallowed by an earthquake, we guessed that his remark was intended to be facetious, and to mean that we would unload the most of our mail matter somewhere on the Plains and leave it to the Indians, or whosoever wanted it.

We changed horses every ten miles, all day long, and fairly flew over the hard, level road. We jumped out and stretched our legs every time the coach stopped, and so the night found us still vivacious and unfatigued.

After supper a woman got in, who lived about fifty miles

further on, and we three had to take turns at sitting outside
with the driver and conductor. Apparently she was not a,
talkative woman. She would sit there in the gathering twilight and fasten her steadfast eyes on a mosquito rooting into
her arm, and slowly she would raise her other hand till she
had got his range, and then she would launch a slap at him
that would have jolted a cow; and after that she would sit and
contemplate the corpse with tranquil satisfaction—for she
never missed her mosquito; she was a dead shot at short range.
She never removed a carcase, but left them there for bait. I
sat by this grim Sphynx and watched her kill thirty or forty
mosquitoes—watched her, and waited for her to say something,
but she never did. So I finally opened the conversation myself. I said:

"The mosquitoes are pretty bad, about here, madam."

"You bet!"

"What did I understand you to say, madam?"

"You BET!"

Then she cheered up, and faced around and said:

"Danged if I didn't begin to think you fellers was deef
and dumb. I did, b' gosh.
Here I've sot, and sot, and
sot, a-bust'n muskeeters and
wonderin' what was ailin'
ye. Fust I thot you was
deef and dumb, then I thot
you was sick or crazy, or
suthin', and then by and by
I begin to reckon you was
a passel of sickly fools that
couldn't think of nothing
to say. Wher'd ye come
from?"

THE SPHYNX.

The Sphynx was a
Sphynx no more! The fountains of her great deep were
broken up, and she rained the nine parts of speech forty days
and forty nights, metaphorically speaking, and buried us under

a desolating deluge of trivial gossip that left not a crag or pinnacle of rejoinder projecting above the tossing waste of dislocated grammar and decomposed pronunciation!

How we suffered, suffered, suffered! She went on, hour after hour, till I was sorry I ever opened the mosquito question and gave her a start. She never did stop again until she got to her journey's end toward daylight; and then she stirred us up as she was leaving the stage (for we were nodding, by that time), and said:

"Now you git out at Cottonwood, you fellers, and lay over a couple o' days, and I'll be along some time to-night, and if I can do ye any good by edgin' in a word now and then, I'm right thar. Folks 'll tell you 't I've always ben kind o' offish and partic'lar for a gal that's raised in the woods, and I *am*, with the rag-tag and bob-tail, and a gal *has* to be, if she wants to *be* anything, but when people comes along which is my equals, I reckon I'm a pretty sociable heifer after all."

We resolved not to " lay by at Cottonwood."

CHAPTER III.

ABOUT an hour and a half before daylight we were bowling along smoothly over the road—so smoothly that our cradle only rocked in a gentle, lulling way, that was gradually soothing us to sleep, and dulling our consciousness—when something gave away under us! We were dimly aware of it, but indifferent to it. The coach stopped. We heard the driver and conductor talking together outside, and rummaging for a lantern, and swearing because they could not find it—but we had no interest in whatever had happened, and it only added to our comfort to think of those people out there at work in the murky night, and we snug in our nest with the curtains drawn. But presently, by the sounds, there seemed to be an examination going on, and then the driver's voice said:

"By George, the thoroughbrace is broke!"

This startled me broad awake—as an undefined sense of calamity is always apt to do. I said to myself: "Now, a thoroughbrace is probably part of a horse; and doubtless a vital part, too, from the dismay in the driver's voice. Leg, maybe—and yet how could he break his leg waltzing along such a road as this? No, it can't be his leg. That is impossible, unless he was reaching for the driver. Now, what can be the thoroughbrace of a horse, I wonder? Well, whatever comes, I shall not air my ignorance in this crowd, anyway."

Just then the conductor's face appeared at a lifted curtain,

and his lantern glared in on us and our wall of mail matter.
He said :

"Gents, you'll have to turn out a spell.   Thoroughbrace is
broke."

We climbed out into a chill drizzle, and felt ever so homeless and dreary.   When I found that the thing they called a
"thoroughbrace" was the massive combination of belts and
springs which the coach rocks itself in, I said to the driver :

"I never saw a thoroughbrace used up like that, before,
that I can remember.   How did it happen ?"

"Why, it happened by trying to make one coach carry
three days' mail—that's how it happened," said he.   "And
right here is the very direction which is wrote on all the
newspaper-bags which was to be put out for the Injuns for to
keep 'em quiet.   It's most uncommon lucky, becuz it's so
nation dark I should 'a' gone by unbeknowns if that air
thoroughbrace hadn't broke."

I knew that he was in labor with another of those winks
of his, though I could not see his face, because he was bent
down at work ; and wishing him a safe delivery, I turned to
and helped the rest get out the mail-sacks.   It made a great
pyramid by the roadside when it was all out.   When they had
mended the thoroughbrace we filled the two boots again, but
put no mail on top, and only half as much inside as there was
before.   The conductor bent all the seat-backs down, and then
filled the coach just half full of mail-bags from end to end.
We objected loudly to this, for it left us no seats.   But the
conductor was wiser than we, and said a bed was better than
seats, and moreover, this plan would protect his thoroughbraces.
We never wanted any seats after that.   The lazy bed was infinitely preferable.   I had many an exciting day, subsequently,
lying on it reading the statutes and the dictionary, and wondering how the characters would turn out.

The conductor said he would send back a guard from the
next station to take charge of the abandoned mail-bags, and
we drove on.

It was now just dawn ; and as we stretched our cramped

legs full length on the mail sacks, and gazed out through the windows across the wide wastes of greensward clad in cool, powdery mist, to where there was an expectant look in the eastern horizon, our perfect enjoyment took the form of a tranquil and contented ecstasy. The stage whirled along at a spanking gait, the breeze flapping curtains and suspended coats in a most exhilarating way; the cradle swayed and swung luxuriously, the pattering of the horses' hoofs, the cracking of the driver's whip, and his "Hi-yi! g'lang!" were music; the spinning ground and the waltzing trees appeared to give us a mute hurrah as we went by, and then slack up and look after us with interest, or envy, or something; and as we lay and smoked the pipe of peace and compared all this luxury with the years of tiresome city life that had gone before it, we felt that there was only one complete and satisfying happiness in the world, and we had found it.

After breakfast, at some station whose name I have forgotten, we three climbed up on the seat behind the driver, and let the conductor have our bed for a nap. And by and by, when the sun made me drowsy, I lay down on my face on top of the coach, grasping the slender iron railing, and slept for an hour or more. That will give one an appreciable idea of those matchless roads. Instinct will make a sleeping man grip a fast hold of the railing when the stage jolts, but when it only swings and sways, no grip is necessary. Overland drivers and conductors used to sit in their places and sleep thirty or forty minutes at a time, on good roads, while spinning along at the rate of eight or ten miles an hour. I saw them do it, often. There was no danger about it; a sleeping man *will* seize the irons in time when the coach jolts. These men were hard worked, and it was not possible for them to stay awake all the time.

By and by we passed through Marysville, and over the Big Blue and Little Sandy; thence about a mile, and entered Nebraska. About a mile further on, we came to the Big Sandy—one hundred and eighty miles from St. Joseph.

As the sun was going down, we saw the first specimen of

an animal known familiarly over two thousand miles of mountain and desert—from Kansas clear to the Pacific Ocean—as the "jackass rabbit." He is well named. He is just like any other rabbit, except that he is from one third to twice as large, has longer legs in proportion to his size, and has the most preposterous ears that ever were mounted on any creature *but* a jackass. When he is sitting quiet, thinking about his sins, or is absent-minded or unapprehensive of danger, his majestic

MEDITATION.

ears project above him conspicuously; but the breaking of a twig will scare him nearly to death, and then he tilts his ears back gently and starts for home. All you can see, then, for the next minute, is his long gray form stretched out straight and "streaking it" through the low sage-brush, head erect, eyes right, and ears just canted a little to the rear, but showing you where the animal is, all the time, the same as if he carried a jib. Now and then he makes a marvelous spring with his long legs, high over the stunted sage-brush, and scores a leap that would make a horse envious. Presently he comes down to a long, graceful "lope," and shortly he mysteriously disappears. He has crouched behind a sage-bush, and will sit there and listen and tremble until you get within six feet of him, when he will get under way again. But one must shoot at this creature once, if he wishes to see him throw his heart into his heels, and do the best he knows how. He is frightened clear through, now, and he lays his long ears down on his back, straightens himself out like a yard-stick every spring he makes, and scatters miles behind him with an easy indifference that is enchanting.

Our party made this specimen "hump himself," as the

conductor said. The secretary started him with a shot from the Colt; I commenced spitting at him with my weapon; and all in the same instant the old "Allen's" whole broadside let go with a rattling crash, and it is not putting it too strong to say that the rabbit was frantic! He dropped his ears, set up his tail, and left for San Francisco at a speed which

ON BUSINESS.

can only be described as a flash and a vanish! Long after he was out of sight we could hear him whiz.

I do not remember where we first came across "sage-brush," but as I have been speaking of it I may as well describe it. This is easily done, for if the reader can imagine a gnarled

AUTHOR AS GULLIVER.

and venerable live oak-tree reduced to a little shrub two feet high, with its rough bark, its foliage, its twisted boughs, all complete, he can picture the "sage-brush" exactly. Often, on lazy afternoons in the mountains, I have lain on the ground with my face under a sage-bush, and entertained myself with fancying that the gnats among its foliage were liliputian birds, and that the ants marching and countermarching about its base were liliputian flocks and herds, and myself some vast loafer from Brobdignag waiting to catch a little citizen and eat him.

It is an imposing monarch of the forest in exquisite minia-

3†

ture, is the "sage-brush." Its foliage is a grayish green, and
gives that tint to desert and mountain. It smells like our domestic sage, and "sage-tea" made from it tastes like the sage-
tea which all boys are so well acquainted with. The sage-
brush is a singularly hardy plant, and grows right in the midst
of deep sand, and among barren rocks, where nothing else in
the vegetable world would try to grow, except "bunch-
grass." * The sage-bushes grow from three to six or seven
feet apart, all over the mountains and deserts of the Far West,
clear to the borders of California. There is not a tree of any
kind in the deserts, for hundreds of miles—there is no vegetation at all in a regular desert, except the sage-brush and its
cousin the "greasewood," which is so much like the sage-
brush that the difference amounts to little. Camp-fires and
hot suppers in the deserts would be impossible but for the
friendly sage-brush. Its trunk is as large as a boy's wrist (and
from that up to a man's arm), and its crooked branches are
half as large as its trunk—all good, sound, hard wood, very
like oak.

When a party camps, the first thing to be done is to cut
sage-brush; and in a few minutes there is an opulent pile of
it ready for use. A hole a foot wide, two feet deep, and two
feet long, is dug, and sage-brush chopped up and burned in it
till it is full to the brim with glowing coals. Then the cooking
begins, and there is no smoke, and consequently no swearing.
Such a fire will keep all night, with very little replenishing;
and it makes a very sociable camp-fire, and one around which
the most impossible reminiscences sound plausible, instructive,
and profoundly entertaining.

Sage-brush is very fair fuel, but as a vegetable it is a distinguished failure. Nothing can abide the taste of it but the

---

* "Bunch-grass" grows on the bleak mountain-sides of Nevada and
neighboring territories, and offers excellent feed for stock, even in the dead
of winter, wherever the snow is blown aside and exposes it; notwithstanding its unpromising home, bunch-grass is a better and more nutritious diet
for cattle and horses than almost any other hay or grass that is known—so
stock-men say.

jackass and his illegitimate child the mule. But their testimony to its nutritiousness is worth nothing, for they will eat pine knots, or anthracite coal, or brass filings, or lead pipe, or old bottles, or anything that comes handy, and then go off looking as grateful as if they had had oysters for dinner. Mules and donkeys and camels have appetites that anything will relieve temporarily, but nothing satisfy. In Syria, once, at the head-waters of the Jordan, a camel took charge of my overcoat while the tents were being pitched, and examined it with a critical eye, all over, with as much interest as if he had an idea of getting one made like it; and then, after he was

A tough statement.

done figuring on it as an article of apparel, he began to contemplate it as an article of diet. He put his foot on it, and lifted one of the sleeves out with his teeth, and chewed and chewed at it, gradually taking it in, and all the while opening and closing his eyes in a kind of religious ecstasy, as if he had never tasted anything as good as an overcoat before, in his life. Then he smacked his lips once or twice, and reached after the other sleeve. Next he tried the velvet collar, and smiled a smile of such contentment that it was plain to see that he regarded that as the daintiest thing about an overcoat. The tails went next, along with some percussion caps and cough candy, and some fig-paste from Constantinople. And then my newspaper correspondence dropped out, and he took a chance in that—manuscript letters written for the home papers. But he was treading on dangerous ground, now. He began to come across solid wisdom in those documents that was rather weighty on his stomach; and occasionally he would take a joke that would shake him up till it loosened his teeth; it was getting to be perilous times with him, but he held his grip with good courage and hopefully, till at last he began to stumble on statements that not even a camel could swallow with impunity. He began to gag and gasp, and his eyes to stand out, and his forelegs to spread, and in about a quarter of a minute he fell over as stiff as a carpenter's work-bench, and died a death of indescribable agony. I went and pulled the manuscript out of his mouth, and found that the sensitive creature had choked to death on one of the mildest and gentlest statements of fact that I ever laid before a trusting public.

I was about to say, when diverted from my subject, that occasionally one finds sage-bushes five or six feet high, and with a spread of branch and foliage in proportion, but two or two and a half feet is the usual height.

CHAPTER IV.

AS the sun went down and the evening chill came on, we made preparation for bed. We stirred up the hard leather letter-sacks, and the knotty canvas bags of printed matter (knotty and uneven because of projecting ends and corners of magazines, boxes and books). We stirred them up and redisposed them in such a way as to make our bed as level as possible. And we *did* improve it, too, though after all our work it had an upheaved and billowy look about it, like a little piece of a stormy sea. Next we hunted up our boots from odd nooks among the mail-bags where they had settled, and put them on. Then we got down our coats, vests, pantaloons and heavy woolen shirts, from the arm-loops where they had been swinging all day, and clothed ourselves in them—for, there being no ladies either at the stations or in the coach, and the weather being hot, we had looked to our comfort by stripping to our underclothing, at nine o'clock in the morning. All things being now ready, we stowed the uneasy Dictionary where it would lie as quiet as possible, and placed the water-canteens and pistols where we could find them in the dark. Then we smoked a final pipe, and swapped a final yarn; after which, we put the pipes, tobacco and bag of coin in snug holes and caves among the mail-bags, and then fastened down the coach curtains all around, and made the place as " dark as the inside of a cow," as the conductor phrased it in his picturesque way. It was certainly as dark as any place could be— nothing was even dimly visible in it. And finally, we rolled ourselves up like silk-worms, each person in his own blanket, and sank peacefully to sleep.

Whenever the stage stopped to change horses, we would wake up, and try to recollect where we were—and succeed— and in a minute or two the stage would be off again, and we likewise. We began to get into country, now, threaded here and there with little streams. These had high, steep banks on each side, and every time we flew down one bank and scrambled up the other, our party inside got mixed somewhat. First we would all be down in a pile at the forward

THIRD TRIP OF THE UNABRIDGED.

end of the stage, nearly in a sitting posture, and in a second we would shoot to the other end, and stand on our heads. And we would sprawl and kick, too, and ward off ends and corners of mail-bags that came lumbering over us and about us; and as the dust rose from the tumult, we would all sneeze in chorus, and the majority of us would grumble, and probably say some hasty thing, like: "Take your elbow out of my ribs!—can't you quit crowding?"

Every time we avalanched from one end of the stage to the other, the Unabridged Dictionary would come too; and every

time it came it damaged somebody. One trip it "barked"
the Secretary's elbow; the next trip it hurt me in the stomach,
and the third it tilted Bemis's nose up till he could look down
his nostrils—he said. The pistols and coin soon settled to the
bottom, but the pipes, pipe-stems, tobacco and canteens clattered
and floundered after the Dictionary every time it made an assault on us, and aided and abetted the book by spilling tobacco
in our eyes, and water down our backs.

Still, all things considered, it was a very comfortable night.
It wore gradually away, and when at last a cold gray light was
visible through the puckers and chinks in the curtains, we
yawned and stretched with satisfaction, shed our cocoons, and
felt that we had slept as much as was necessary. By and by,
as the sun rose up and warmed the world, we pulled off our
clothes and got ready for breakfast. We were just pleasantly
in time, for five minutes afterward the driver sent the weird
music of his bugle winding over the grassy solitudes, and
presently we detected a low hut or two in the distance. Then
the rattling of the coach, the clatter of our six horses' hoofs,
and the driver's crisp commands, awoke to a louder and stronger
emphasis, and we went sweeping down on the station at our
smartest speed. It was fascinating—that old overland stage-
coaching.

We jumped out in undress uniform. The driver tossed his
gathered reins out on the ground, gaped and stretched complacently, drew off his heavy buckskin gloves with great deliberation and insufferable dignity—taking not the slightest notice
of a dozen solicitous inquiries after his health, and humbly facetious and flattering accostings, and obsequious tenders of service,
from five or six hairy and half-civilized station-keepers and
hostlers who were nimbly unhitching our steeds and bringing
the fresh team out of the stables—for in the eyes of the stage-
driver of that day, station-keepers and hostlers were a sort of
good enough low creatures, useful in their place, and helping
to make up a world, but not the kind of beings which a person
of distinction could afford to concern himself with; while, on
the contrary, in the eyes of the station-keeper and the hostler,

the stage-driver was a hero—a great and shining dignitary, the world's favorite son, the envy of the people, the observed of the nations. When they spoke to him they received his insolent silence meekly, and as being the natural and proper conduct of so great a man; when he opened his lips they all hung on his words with admiration (he never honored a particular individual with a remark, but addressed it with a broad generality to the horses, the stables, the surrounding country *and* the human underlings); when he discharged a facetious insulting personality at a hostler, that hostler was happy for the day; when he uttered his one jest—old as the hills, coarse, profane, witless, and inflicted on the same audience, in the same language, every time his coach drove up there—the varlets roared, and slapped their thighs, and swore it was the best thing they'd ever heard in all their lives. And how they would fly around when he wanted a basin of water, a gourd of the same, or a light for his pipe!—but they would instantly insult a passenger if he so far forgot himself as to crave a favor at their hands. They could do that sort of insolence as well as the driver they copied it from—for, let it be borne in mind, the overland driver had but little less contempt for his passengers than he had for his hostlers.

The hostlers and station-keepers treated the really powerful *conductor* of the coach merely with the best of what was their idea of civility, but the *driver* was the only being they bowed down to and worshipped. How admiringly they would gaze up at him in his high seat as he gloved himself with lingering deliberation, while some happy hostler held the bunch of reins aloft, and waited patiently for him to take it! And how they would bombard him with glorifying ejaculations as he cracked his long whip and went careering away.

The station buildings were long, low huts, made of sundried, mud-colored bricks, laid up without mortar (*adobes*, the Spaniards call these bricks, and Americans shorten it to *'dobies*). The roofs, which had no slant to them worth speaking of, were thatched and then sodded or covered with a thick layer of earth, and from this sprung a pretty rank growth of weeds and grass. It was the first time we had ever seen a man's front yard on top of his house. The buildings consisted of barns, stable-room for twelve or fifteen horses, and a hut for an eating-room for passengers. This latter had bunks in it for the station-keeper and a hostler or two. You could rest your elbow on its eaves, and you had to bend in order to get in at the door. In place of a window there was a square hole about large enough for a man to crawl through, but this had no glass in it. There was no flooring, but the ground was packed hard. There was no stove, but the fire-place served all needful purposes. There were no shelves, no cupboards, no closets. In a corner stood an open sack of flour, and nestling against its base were a couple of black and venerable tin coffee-pots, a tin tea-pot, a little bag of salt, and a side of bacon.

By the door of the station-keeper's den, outside, was a tin wash-basin, on the ground. Near it was a pail of water and a piece of yellow bar soap, and from the eaves hung a hoary blue woolen shirt, significantly—but this latter was the station-keeper's private towel, and only two persons in all the party might venture to use it—the stage-driver and the con-

A POWERFUL GLASS.

ductor. The latter would not, from a sense of decency; the former would not, because he did not choose to encourage the advances of a station-keeper. We had towels—in the valise; they might as well have been in Sodom and Gomorrah. We (and the conductor) used our handkerchiefs, and the driver his pantaloons and sleeves. By the door, inside, was fastened a small old-fashioned looking-glass frame, with two little fragments of the original mirror lodged down in one corner of it. This arrangement afforded a pleasant double-barreled portrait of you when you looked into it, with one half of your head set up a couple of inches above the other half. From the glass frame hung the half of a comb by a string—but if I had to describe that patriarch or die, I believe I would order some

AN HEIRLOOM.

sample coffins. It had come down from Esau and Samson, and had been accumulating hair ever since—along with certain impurities. In one corner of the room stood three or four rifles and muskets, together with horns and pouches of

OUR LANDLORD.

ammunition. The station-men wore pantaloons of coarse, country-woven stuff, and into the seat and the inside of the legs were sewed ample additions of buckskin, to do duty in place of leggings, when the man rode horseback—so the pants were half dull blue and half yellow, and unspeakably picturesque. The pants were stuffed into the tops of high boots, the heels whereof were armed with great Spanish spurs, whose little iron clogs and chains jingled with every step. The man wore a huge beard and mustachios, an old slouch hat, a blue woolen shirt, no suspenders, no vest, no coat—in a leathern sheath in his belt, a great long "navy" re-

volver (slung on right side, hammer to the front), and projecting from his boot a horn-handled bowie-knife. The furniture of the hut was neither gorgeous nor much in the way. The rocking-chairs and sofas were not present, and never had been,

but they were represented by two three-legged stools, a pine-
board bench four feet long, and two empty candle-boxes.
The table was a greasy board on stilts, and the table-cloth and
napkins had not come—and they were not looking for them,
either. A battered tin platter, a knife and fork, and a tin pint
cup, were at each man's place, and the driver had a queensware saucer that had seen better days. Of course this duke
sat at the head of the table. There was one isolated piece of
table furniture that bore about it a touching air of grandeur
in misfortune. This was the caster. It was German silver,
and crippled and rusty, but it was so preposterously out of
place there that it was suggestive of a tattered exiled king
among barbarians, and the majesty of its native position compelled respect even in its degradation. There was only one
cruet left, and that was a stopperless, fly-specked, broken-

necked thing, with two
inches of vinegar in it, and
a dozen preserved flies with
their heels up and looking
sorry they had invested
there.

DIGNIFIED EXILE.

The station-keeper up-
ended a disk of last week's
bread, of the shape and size
of an old-time cheese, and
carved some slabs from it
which were as good as Ni-
cholson pavement, and ten-
derer.

He sliced off a piece of bacon for each man, but only the
experienced old hands made out to eat it, for it was condemned
army bacon which the United States would not feed to its
soldiers in the forts, and the stage company had bought it
cheap for the sustenance of their passengers and employes.
We may have found this condemned army bacon further out
on the plains than the section I am locating it in, but we *found*
it—there is no gainsaying that.

Then he poured for us a beverage which he called " *Slum-*

gullion," and it is hard to think he was not inspired when he named it. It really pretended to be tea, but there was too much dish-rag, and sand, and old bacon-rind in it to deceive

DRINKING SLUMGULLION.

the intelligent traveler. He had no sugar and no milk—not even a spoon to stir the ingredients with.

We could not eat the bread or the meat, nor drink the "slumgullion." And when I looked at that melancholy vinegar-cruet, I thought of the anecdote (a very, very old one, even at that day) of the traveler who sat down to a table which had nothing on it but a mackerel and a pot of mustard. He asked the landlord if this was all. The landlord said:

"*All!* Why, thunder and lightning, I should think there was mackerel enough there for six."

"But I don't like mackerel."

"Oh—then help yourself to the mustard."

In other days I had considered it a good, a very good, anecdote, but there was a dismal plausibility about it, here, that took all the humor out of it.

Our breakfast was before us, but our teeth were idle.
I tasted and smelt, and said I would take coffee, I believed.
The station-boss stopped dead still, and glared at me speechless. At last, when he came to, he turned away and said, as one
who communes with himself upon a matter too vast to grasp:

"*Coffee!* Well, if that
don't go clean ahead of me,
I'm d——d!"

We could not eat, and
there was no conversation
among the hostlers and
herdsmen—we all sat at the
same board. At least there
was no conversation further
than a single hurried request,
now and then, from one em-
ploye to another. It was
always in the same form,
and always gruffly friendly.
Its western freshness and
novelty startled me, at first,
and interested me; but it
presently grew monotonous,
and lost its charm. It was:
"Pass the bread, you son

A JOKE WITHOUT CREAM.

of a skunk!" No, I forget—skunk was not the word; it seems
to me it was still stronger than that; I know it was, in fact,
but it is gone from my memory, apparently. However, it is
no matter—probably it was too strong for print, anyway. It
is the landmark in my memory which tells me where I first
encountered the vigorous new vernacular of the occidental
plains and mountains.

We gave up the breakfast, and paid our dollar apiece and
went back to our mail-bag bed in the coach, and found comfort in our pipes. Right here we suffered the first diminution
of our princely state. We left our six fine horses and took six
mules in their place. But they were wild Mexican fellows, and

a man had to stand at the head of each of them and hold him fast while the driver gloved and got himself ready. And when at last he grasped the reins and gave the word, the men sprung suddenly away from the mules' heads and the coach shot from the station as if it had issued from a cannon. How the frantic animals did scamper! It was a fierce and furious gallop—and the gait never altered for a moment till we reeled off ten or twelve miles and swept up to the next collection of little station-huts and stables.

So we flew along all day. At 2 P.M. the belt of timber that fringes the North Platte and marks its windings through the vast level floor of the Plains came in sight. At 4 P.M. we crossed a branch of the river, and at 5 P.M. we crossed the Platte itself, and landed at Fort Kearney, *fifty-six hours out from St. Joe*—THREE HUNDRED MILES!

Now that was stage-coaching on the great overland, ten or twelve years ago, when perhaps not more than ten men in America, all told, expected to live to see a railroad follow that route to the Pacific. But the railroad is there, now, and it pictures a thousand odd comparisons and contrasts in my mind to read the following sketch, in the New York *Times*, of a recent trip over almost the very ground I have been describing. I can scarcely comprehend the new state of things:

"ACROSS THE CONTINENT.

"At 4.20 P.M., Sunday, we rolled out of the station at Omaha, and started westward on our long jaunt. A couple of hours out, dinner was announced—an "event" to those of us who had yet to experience what it is to eat in one of Pullman's hotels on wheels; so, stepping into the car next forward of our sleeping palace, we found ourselves in the dining-car. It was a revelation to us, that first dinner on Sunday. And though we continued to dine for four days, and had as many breakfasts and suppers, our whole party never ceased to admire the perfection of the arrangements, and the marvelous results achieved. Upon tables covered with snowy linen, and garnished with services of solid silver, Ethiop waiters, flitting about in spotless white, placed as by magic a repast at which Delmonico himself could have had no occasion to blush; and, indeed, in some respects it would be hard for that distinguished *chef* to match our *menu*; for, in addition to all that ordinarily makes up a first-chop dinner, had we not our antelope steak (the gormand who has not experienced this—bah! what does he know of the feast of fat things?) our delicious mountain-brook trout, and choice fruits and berries, and (sauce piquant and unpurchasable!) our sweet-scented, appetite-compelling air of the prairies? You may depend upon it, we all did justice to the good things, and as we washed them down with bumpers of sparkling Krug, whilst we

PULLMAN CAR DINING-SALOON.

sped along at the rate of thirty miles an hour, agreed it was the *fastest* living we had ever experienced. (We beat that, however, two days afterward when we made *twenty-seven miles in twenty-seven minutes*, while our Champagne glasses filled to the brim spilled not a drop!) After dinner we repaired to our drawing-room car, and, as it was Sabbath eve, intoned some of the grand old hymns—"Praise God from whom," etc.; "Shining Shore," "Coronation," etc.—the voices of the men singers and of the women singers blending sweetly in the evening air, while our train, with its great, glaring Polyphemus eye, lighting up long vistas of prairie, rushed into the night and the Wild. Then to bed in luxurious couches, where we slept the sleep of the just and only awoke the next morning (Monday) at eight o'clock, to find ourselves at the crossing of the North Platte, three hundred miles from Omaha—*fifteen hours and forty minutes out.*"

CHAPTER V.

ANOTHER night of alternate tranquillity and turmoil. But morning came, by and by. It was another glad awakening to fresh breezes, vast expanses of level greensward, bright sunlight, an impressive solitude utterly without visible human beings or human habitations, and an atmosphere of such amazing magnifying properties that trees that seemed close at hand were more than three miles away. We resumed undress uniform, climbed a-top of the flying coach, dangled our legs over the side, shouted occasionally at our frantic mules, merely to see them lay their ears back and scamper faster, tied our hats on to keep our hair from blowing away, and leveled an outlook over the world-wide carpet about us for things new and strange to gaze at. Even at this day it thrills me through and through to think of the life, the gladness and the wild sense of freedom that used to make the blood dance in my veins on those fine overland mornings!

Along about an hour after breakfast we saw the first prairie-dog villages, the first antelope, and the first wolf. If I remember rightly, this latter was the regular *cayote* (pronounced ky-*o*-te) of the farther deserts. And if it *was*, he was not a pretty creature or respectable either, for I got well acquainted with his race afterward, and can speak with confidence. The cayote is a long, slim, sick and sorry-looking skeleton, with a gray wolf-skin stretched over it, a tolerably bushy tail that forever sags down with a despairing expression of forsakenness and misery, a furtive and evil eye, and a long,

OUR MORNING RIDE.

sharp face, with slightly lifted lip and exposed teeth. He has a general slinking expression all over. The cayote is a living, breathing allegory of Want. He is *always* hungry. He is always poor, out of luck and friendless. The meanest creatures despise him, and even the fleas would desert him for a velocipede. He is so spiritless and cowardly that even while his exposed teeth are pretending a threat, the rest of his face is apologizing for it. And he is *so* homely!—so scrawny, and ribby, and coarse-haired, and pitiful. When he sees you he lifts his lip and lets a flash of his teeth out, and then turns a little out of the course he was pursuing, depresses his head a bit, and strikes a long, soft-footed trot through the sage-brush, glancing over his shoulder at you, from time to time, till he is about out of easy pistol range, and then he stops and takes a deliberate survey of you; he will trot fifty yards and stop again—another fifty and stop again; and finally the gray of his gliding body blends with the gray of the sage-brush, and he disappears. All this is when you make no demonstration against him; but if you do, he develops a livelier interest in his journey, and instantly electrifies his heels and puts such a deal of real estate between himself and your weapon, that by the time you have raised the hammer you see that you need a minie rifle, and by the

4†

time you have got him in line you need a rifled cannon, and by the time you have "drawn a bead" on him you see well enough that nothing but an unusually long-winded streak of lightning could reach him where he is now. But if you start a swift-footed dog after him, you will enjoy it ever so much— especially if it is a dog that has a good opinion of himself, and has been brought up to think he knows something about speed.

PRAIRIE DOGS.

The cayote will go swinging gently off on that deceitful trot of his, and every little while he will smile a fraudful smile over his shoulder that will fill that dog entirely full of encouragement and worldly ambition, and make him lay his head still lower to the ground, and stretch his neck further to the front, and pant more fiercely, and stick his tail out straighter behind, and move his furious legs with a yet wilder frenzy, and leave a broader and broader, and higher and denser cloud of desert sand smoking behind, and marking his long wake across the level plain! And all this time the dog is only a short twenty feet behind the cayote, and to save the soul of him he cannot understand why it is that he cannot get perceptibly closer; and he begins to get aggravated, and it makes him madder and madder to see how gently the cayote glides along and never pants or sweats or ceases to smile; and he grows still more and more incensed to see how shamefully he has been taken in by an entire stranger, and what an ignoble swindle that long, calm, soft-footed trot is; and next he notices that he is getting fagged, and that the cayote actually has to slacken speed a little to keep from running away from him—and *then* that town-dog is mad in earnest, and he begins to strain and weep and swear, and paw the sand higher than ever, and reach for the cayote with concentrated and desperate energy. This "spurt" finds him six feet behind the gliding enemy, and two miles from his friends. And then, in the instant that a wild new hope is lighting up his face, the cayote turns and smiles blandly upon him once more, and with a something about it which seems to say: "Well, I shall have to tear myself away from you, bub—business is business, and it will not do for me

A CAYOTE.

to be fooling along this way all day"—and forthwith there is a rushing sound, and the sudden splitting of a long crack through the atmosphere, and behold that dog is solitary and alone in the midst of a vast solitude!

It makes his head swim. He stops, and looks all around; climbs the nearest sand-mound, and gazes into the distance; shakes his head reflectively, and then, without a word, he turns and jogs along back to his train, and takes up a humble position under the hindmost wagon, and feels unspeakably mean, and looks ashamed, and hangs his tail at half-mast for a week. And for as much as a year after that, whenever there is a great hue and cry after a cayote, that dog will merely glance in that direction without emotion, and apparently observe to himself, "I believe I do not wish any of the pie."

The cayote lives chiefly in the most desolate and forbidding deserts, along with the lizard, the jackass-rabbit and the raven, and gets an uncertain and precarious living, and earns it. He seems to subsist almost wholly on the carcases of oxen, mules and horses that have dropped out of emigrant trains and died, and upon windfalls of carrion, and occasional legacies of

offal bequeathed to him by white men who have been opulent enough to have something better to butcher than condemned army bacon.

SHOWING RESPECT TO RELATIVES.

He will eat anything in the world that his first cousins, the desert-frequenting tribes of Indians will, and they will eat anything they can bite. It is a curious fact that these latter are the only creatures known to history who will eat nitro-glycerine and ask for more if they survive.

The cayote of the deserts beyond the Rocky Mountains has a peculiarly hard time of it, owing to the fact that his relations, the Indians, are just as apt to be the first to detect a seductive scent on the desert breeze, and follow the fragrance to the late ox it emanated from, as he is himself; and when this occurs he has to content himself with sitting off at a little distance watching those people strip off and dig out everything edible, and walk off with it. Then he and the waiting ravens explore the skeleton and polish the bones. It is considered that the cayote, and the obscene bird, and the Indian of the desert, testify their blood kinship with each other in that they live together in the waste places of the earth on terms of perfect confidence and friendship, while hating all other creatures and yearning to assist at their funerals. He does not mind going a hundred miles to breakfast, and a hundred and fifty to dinner, because he is sure to have three or four days between meals, and he can just as well be traveling and looking at the scenery as lying around doing nothing and adding to the burdens of his parents.

We soon learned to recognize the sharp, vicious bark of the cayote as it came across the murky plain at night to disturb our dreams among the mail-sacks; and remembering his forlorn aspect and his hard fortune, made shift to wish him the blessed novelty of a long day's good luck and a limitless larder the morrow.

CHAPTER VI.

OUR new conductor (just shipped) had been without sleep for twenty hours. Such a thing was very frequent. From St. Joseph, Missouri, to Sacramento, California, by stage-coach, was nearly nineteen hundred miles, and the trip was often made in fifteen days (the cars do it in four and a half, now), but the time specified in the mail contracts, and required by the schedule, was eighteen or nineteen days, if I remember rightly. This was to make fair allowance for winter storms and snows, and other unavoidable causes of detention. The stage company had everything under strict discipline and good system. Over each two hundred and fifty miles of road they placed an agent or superintendent, and invested him with great authority. His beat or jurisdiction of two hundred and fifty miles was called a " division." He purchased horses, mules harness, and food for men and beasts, and distributed these things among his stage stations, from time to time, according to his judgment of what each station needed. He erected station buildings and dug wells. He attended to the paying of the station-keepers, hostlers, drivers and blacksmiths, and discharged them whenever he chose. He was a very, very great man in his " division"—a kind of Grand Mogul, a Sultan of the Indies, in whose presence common men were modest of speech and manner, and in the glare of whose greatness even the dazzling stage-driver dwindled to a penny dip. There were about eight of these kings, all told, on the overland route.

Next in rank and importance to the division-agent came the

"conductor." His beat was the same length as the agent's—two hundred and fifty miles. He sat with the driver, and (when necessary) rode that fearful distance, night and day, without other rest or sleep than what he could get perched thus on top of the flying vehicle. Think of it! He had absolute charge of the mails, express matter, passengers and stage, coach, until he delivered them to the next conductor, and got his receipt for them. Consequently he had to be a man of intelligence, decision and considerable executive ability. He was usually a quiet, pleasant man, who attended closely to his duties, and was a good deal of a gentleman. It was not absolutely necessary that the division-agent should be a gentleman, and occasionally he wasn't. But he was always a general in administrative ability, and a bulldog in courage and determination — otherwise the chieftainship over the lawless underlings of the over-

THE CONDUCTOR.

land service would never in any instance have been to him anything but an equivalent for a month of insolence and distress and a bullet and a coffin at the end of it. There were about sixteen or eighteen conductors on the overland, for there was a daily stage each way, and a conductor on every stage.

Next in *real* and official rank and importance, *after* the conductor, came my delight, the driver—next in real but not in *apparent* importance—for we have seen that in the eyes of the common herd the driver was to the conductor as an admiral is to the captain of the flag-ship. The driver's beat was pretty long, and his sleeping-time at the stations pretty short, sometimes; and so, but for the grandeur of his position his would have been a sorry life, as well as a hard and a wearing one. We took a new driver every day or every night (for they drove backward and forward over the same piece of road all the time), and therefore we never got as well acquainted with them as we did with the conductors; and besides, they would have been above being familiar with such rubbish as passengers, anyhow, as a general thing. Still, we were always eager to get a sight of each and every new driver as soon as the watch changed, for each and every day we were either anxious to get rid of an unpleasant one, or loath to part with a driver we had learned to like and had come to be sociable and friendly with. And so the first question we asked the conductor whenever we got to where we were to exchange drivers, was always, "Which is him?" The grammar was faulty, maybe, but we could not know, then, that it would go into a book some day. As long as everything went smoothly, the overland driver was well enough situated, but if a fellow driver got sick suddenly it made trouble, for the coach *must* go on, and so the potentate who was about to climb down and take a luxurious rest after his long night's siege in the midst of wind and rain and darkness, had to stay where he was and do the sick man's work. Once, in the Rocky Mountains, when I found a driver sound asleep on the box, and the mules going at the usual break-neck pace, the conductor said never mind him, there was no danger, and he was doing double duty—had driven seventy-five miles on one coach, and was now going back over it on this without rest or sleep. A hundred and fifty miles of holding back of six vindictive mules and keeping them from climbing the trees! It sounds incredible, but I remember the statement well enough.

The station-keepers, hostlers, etc., were low, rough characters, as already described; and from western Nebraska to Nevada a considerable sprinkling of them might be fairly set down as outlaws—fugitives from justice, criminals whose best security was a section of country which was without law and without even the pretense of it. When the "division-agent" issued an order to one of these parties he did it with the full understanding that he might have to enforce it with a navy six-shooter, and so he always went "fixed" to make things go along smoothly. Now and then a division-agent was really obliged to shoot a hostler through the head to teach him some

THE SUPERINTENDENT AS A TEACHER.

simple matter that he could have taught him with a club if his circumstances and surroundings had been different. But they were snappy, able men, those division-agents, and when they tried to teach a subordinate anything, that subordinate generally "got it through his head."

A great portion of this vast machinery—these hundreds of men and coaches, and thousands of mules and horses—was in the hands of Mr. Ben Holliday. All the western half of the business was in his hands. This reminds me of an incident of Palestine travel which is pertinent here, and so I will transfer it just in the language in which I find it set down in my Holy Land note-book:

No doubt everybody has heard of Ben Holliday—a man of prodigious energy, who used to send mails and passengers flying across the continent in his overland stage-coaches like a very whirlwind—two thousand long miles in fifteen days and a half, by the watch! But this fragment of history is not about Ben Holliday, but about a young New York boy by the name of Jack, who traveled with our small party of pilgrims in the Holy Land (and who had traveled to California in Mr. Holliday's overland coaches three years before, and had by no means forgotten it or lost his gushing admiration of Mr. H.) Aged nineteen. Jack was a good boy—a good-hearted and always well-meaning boy, who had been reared in the city of New York, and although he was bright and knew a great many useful things, his Scriptural education had been a good deal neglected—to such a degree, indeed, that all Holy Land history was fresh and new to him, and all Bible

JACK AND THE ELDERLY PILGRIM.

names mysteries that had never disturbed his virgin ear. Also in our party was an elderly pilgrim who was the reverse of Jack, in that he was learned in the Scriptures and an enthusiast concerning them. He was our encyclopedia, and we were never tired of listening to his speeches, nor he of making them. He never passed a celebrated locality, from Bashan to Bethlehem, without illuminating it with an oration. One day, when camped near the ruins of Jericho, he burst forth with something like this:

"Jack, do you see that range of mountains over yonder that bounds the Jordan valley? The mountains of Moab, Jack! Think of it, my boy—the

actual mountains of Moab—renowned in Scripture history! We are
actually standing face to face with those illustrious crags and peaks—and
for all we know" [dropping his voice impressively], "*our eyes may be
resting at this very moment upon the spot* WHERE LIES THE MYSTERIOUS
GRAVE OF MOSES! Think of it, Jack!"

"Moses *who?*" (falling inflection).

"Moses *who!* Jack, you ought to be ashamed of yourself—you ought to
be ashamed of such criminal ignorance. Why, Moses, the great guide, soldier, poet, lawgiver of ancient Israel! Jack, from this spot where we stand,
to Egypt, stretches a fearful desert three hundred miles in extent—and
across that desert that wonderful man brought the children of Israel!—
guiding them with unfailing sagacity for forty years over the sandy desolation and among the obstructing rocks and hills, and landed them at last, safe
and sound, with insight of this very spot; and where we now stand they
entered the Promised Land with anthems of rejoicing! It was a wonderful,
wonderful thing to do, Jack! Think of it!"

"*Forty years? Only three hundred miles?* Humph! Ben Holliday
would have fetched them through in thirty-six hours!"

The boy meant no harm. He did not know that he had said anything
that was wrong or irreverent. And so no one scolded him or felt offended
with him—and nobody *could* but some ungenerous spirit incapable of
excusing the heedless blunders of a boy.

At noon on the fifth day out, we arrived at the "Crossing
of the South Platte," *alias* "Julesburg," *alias* "Overland
City," four hundred and seventy miles from St. Joseph—the
strangest, quaintest, funniest frontier town that our untraveled
eyes had ever stared at and been astonished with.

CHAPTER VII.

IT did seem strange enough to see a town again after what appeared to us such a long acquaintance with deep, still, almost lifeless and houseless solitude! We tumbled out into the busy street feeling like meteoric people crumbled off the corner of some other world, and wakened up suddenly in this. For an hour we took as much interest in Overland City as if we had never seen a town before. The reason we had an hour to spare was because we had to change our stage (for a less sumptuous affair, called a "mud-wagon") and transfer our freight of mails.

Presently we got under way again. We came to the shallow, yellow, muddy South Platte, with its low banks and its scattering flat sand-bars and pigmy islands—a melancholy stream straggling through the centre of the enormous flat plain, and only saved from being impossible to find with the naked eye by its sentinel rank of scattering trees standing on either bank. The Platte was "up," they said—which made me wish I could see it when it was down, if it could look any sicker and sorrier. They said it was a dangerous stream to cross, now, because its quicksands were liable to swallow up horses, coach and passengers if an attempt was made to ford it. But the mails had to go, and we made the attempt. Once or twice in midstream the wheels sunk into the yielding sands so threateningly that we half believed we had dreaded and avoided the sea all our lives to be shipwrecked in a "mud-wagon" in the middle of a desert at last. But we dragged through and sped away toward the setting sun.

Next morning, just before dawn, when about five hundred and fifty miles from St. Joseph, our mud-wagon broke down. We were to be delayed five or six hours, and therefore we took horses, by invitation, and joined a party who were just starting on a buffalo hunt. It was noble sport galloping over the plain in the dewy freshness of the morning, but our part of the hunt ended in disaster and disgrace, for a wounded buffalo bull chased the passenger Bemis nearly two miles, and then he forsook his horse and took to a lone tree. He was very sullen about the matter for some twenty-four hours, but at last he began to soften little by little, and finally he said:

"Well, it was not funny, and there was no sense in those gawks making themselves so facetious over it. I tell you I was angry in earnest for awhile. I should have shot that long gangly lubber they called Hank, if I could have done it without crippling six or seven other people—but of course I couldn't, the old 'Allen's' so confounded comprehensive. I wish those loafers had been up in the tree; they wouldn't have wanted to laugh so. If I had had a horse

CROSSING THE PLATTE.

worth a cent—but no, the minute he saw that buffalo bull
wheel on him and give a bellow, he raised straight up in the
air and stood on his heels. The saddle began to slip, and I
took him round the neck and laid close to him, and began
to pray. Then he came down and stood up on the other
end awhile, and the bull actually stopped pawing sand and
bellowing to contemplate the inhuman spectacle. Then the

AN INHUMAN SPECTACLE.

bull made a pass at him and uttered a bellow that sounded
perfectly frightful, it was so close to me, and that seemed
to literally prostrate my horse's reason, and make a raving
distracted maniac of him, and I wish I may die if he didn't
stand on his head for a quarter of a minute and shed tears.
He was absolutely out of his mind—he was, as sure as truth
itself, and he really didn't know what he was doing. Then
the bull came charging at us, and my horse dropped down
on all fours and took a fresh start—and then for the next

ten minutes he would actually throw one hand-spring after another so fast that the bull began to get unsettled, too, and didn't know where to start in—and so he stood there sneezing, and shovelling dust over his back, and bellowing every now and then, and thinking he had got a fifteen-hundred dollar circus horse for breakfast, certain.   Well, I was first out on his neck—the horse's, not the bull's—and then underneath, and next on his rump, and sometimes head up, and sometimes heels—but I tell you it seemed solemn and awful to be ripping and tearing and carrying on so in the presence of death, as you might say.   Pretty soon the bull made a snatch for us and brought away some of my horse's tail (I suppose, but do not know, being pretty busy at the time), but *something* made him hungry for solitude and suggested to him to get up and hunt for it.   And then you ought to have seen that spider-legged old skeleton go! and you ought to have seen the bull

A NEW DEPARTURE.

eat out after him, too—head down, tongue out, tail up, bellowing like everything, and actually mowing down the weeds, and tearing up the earth, and boosting up the sand like a whirlwind! By George, it was a hot race!   I and the saddle were back on the rump, and I had the bridle in my teeth and hold-

ing on to the pommel with both hands. First we left the
dogs behind; then we passed a jackass rabbit; then we overtook a cayote, and were gaining on an antelope when the
rotten girth let go and threw me about thirty yards off to the
left, and as the saddle went down over the horse's rump he
gave it a lift with his heels that sent it more than four hundred yards up in the air, I wish I may die in a minute if he
didn't. I fell at the foot of the only solitary tree there was
in nine counties adjacent (as any creature could see with the
naked eye), and the next second I had hold of the bark with
four sets of nails and my teeth, and the next second after that
I was astraddle of the main limb and blaspheming my luck in
a way that made my breath smell of brimstone. I *had* the
bull, now, if he did not think of *one* thing. But that one
thing I dreaded. I dreaded it very seriously. There was a
possibility that the bull might not think of it, but there were
greater chances that he would. I made up my mind what I
would do in case he did. It was a little over forty feet to
the ground from where I sat. I cautiously unwound the
lariat from the pommel of my saddle—"

"Your *saddle?* Did you take your saddle up in the tree
with you?"

"Take it up in the tree with me? Why, how you talk.
Of course I didn't. No man could do that. It *fell* in the
tree when it came down."

"Oh—exactly."

"Certainly. I unwound the lariat, and fastened one end
of it to the limb. It was the very best green raw-hide, and
capable of sustaining tons. I made a slip-noose in the other
end, and then hung it down to see the length. It reached
down twenty-two feet—half way to the ground. I then
loaded every barrel of the Allen with a double charge. I felt
satisfied. I said to myself, if he never thinks of that one
thing that I dread, all right—but if he does, all right anyhow—I am fixed for him. But don't you know that the very
thing a man dreads is the thing that always happens? Indeed
it is so. I watched the bull, now, with anxiety—anxiety

which no one can conceive of who has not been in such a situation and felt that at any moment death might come. Presently a thought came into the bull's eye. I knew it! said I—if my nerve fails now, I am lost. Sure enough, it was just as I had dreaded, he started in to climb the tree—"

"What, the bull?"

"Of course— who else?"

"But a bull can't climb a tree."

"He can't, can't he? Since you know so much about it, did you ever see a bull try?"

"No! I never dreamt of such a thing."

"Well, then, what is the use of your talking that way, then? Because you never saw a thing done, is that any reason why it can't be done?"

"Well, all right—go on. What did you do?"

"The bull

SUSPENDED OPERATIONS.

started up, and got along well for about ten feet, then slipped and slid back. I breathed easier. He tried it again—got

5†

up a little higher—slipped again. But he came at it once
more, and this time he was careful. He got gradually
higher and higher, and my spirits went down more and
more. Up he came—an inch at a time—with his eyes
hot, and his tongue hanging out. Higher and higher—
hitched his foot over the stump of a limb, and looked up, as
much as to say, 'You are my meat, friend.' Up again—
higher and higher, and getting more excited the closer he got.
He was within ten feet of me! I took a long breath,—and
then said I, 'It is now or never.' I had the coil of the
lariat all ready; I paid it out slowly, till it hung right over
his head; all of a sudden I let go of the slack, and the slip-
noose fell fairly round his neck! Quicker than lightning I
out with the Allen and let him have it in the face. It was an
awful roar, and must have scared the bull out of his senses.
When the smoke cleared away, there he was, dangling in the
air, twenty foot from the ground, and going out of one convulsion into another faster than you could count! I didn't
stop to count, anyhow—I shinned down the tree and shot for
home."

"Bemis, is all that true, just as you have stated it?"

"I wish I may rot in my tracks and die the death of a dog
if it isn't."

"Well, we can't refuse to believe it, and we don't. But
if there 'were some proofs—"

"Proofs! Did I bring back my lariat?"

"No."

"Did I bring back my horse?"

"No."

"Did you ever see the bull again?"

"No."

"Well, then, what more do you want? I never saw anybody as particular as you are about a little thing like that."

I made up my mind that if this man was not a liar he only
missed it by the skin of his teeth. This episode reminds me
of an incident of my brief sojourn in Siam, years afterward.
The European citizens of a town in the neighborhood of Bang-

kok had a prodigy among them by the name of Eckert, an
Englishman—a person famous for the number, ingenuity and
imposing magnitude of his lies.   They were always repeating
his most celebrated falsehoods, and always trying to "draw
him out" before strangers; but they seldom succeeded.   Twice
he was invited to the house where I was visiting, but nothing
could seduce him into a specimen lie.   One day a planter
named Bascom, an influential man, and a proud and sometimes
irascible one, invited me to ride over with him and call on
Eckert.   As we jogged along, said he:

"Now, do you know where the fault lies?   It lies in putting
Eckert on his guard.   The minute the boys go to pumping at
Eckert he knows perfectly well what they are after, and of
course he shuts up his shell.   Anybody might know he would.
But when we get there, we must play him finer than that.
Let him shape the conversation to suit himself—let him drop
it or change it whenever he wants to.   Let him see that nobody is trying to draw him out.   Just let him have his own
way.   He will soon forget himself and begin to grind out lies
like a mill.   Don't get impatient—just keep quiet, and let me
play him.   I will make him lie.   It does seem to me that the
boys must be blind to overlook such an obvious and simple
trick as that."

Eckert received us heartily—a pleasant-spoken, gentle-
mannered creature.   We sat in the veranda an hour, sipping
English ale, and talking about the king, and the sacred white
elephant, the Sleeping Idol, and all manner of things; and I
noticed that my comrade never led the conversation himself
or shaped it, but simply followed Eckert's lead, and betrayed
no solicitude and no anxiety about anything.   The effect was
shortly perceptible.   Eckert began to grow communicative;
he grew more and more at his ease, and more and more talkative and sociable.   Another hour passed in the same way, and
then all of a sudden Eckert said:

"Oh, by the way!   I came near forgetting.   I have got a
thing here to astonish you.   Such a thing as neither you nor
any other man ever heard of—I've got a cat that will eat cocoa-

nut! Common green cocoanut—and not only eat the meat, but drink the milk. It is so—I'll swear to it."

A quick glance from Bascom—a glance that I understood—then:

"Why, bless my soul, I never heard of such a thing. Man, it is impossible."

"I knew you would say it. I'll fetch the cat."

He went in the house. Bascom said:

"There—what did I tell you? Now, that is the way to handle Eckert. You see, I have petted him along patiently, and put his suspicions to sleep. I am glad we came. You tell the boys about it when you go back. Cat eat a cocoanut —oh, my! Now, that is just his way, exactly—he will tell the absurdest lie, and trust to luck to get out of it again. Cat eat a cocoanut—the innocent fool!"

A WONDERFUL LIE.

Eckert approached with his cat, sure enough. Bascom smiled. Said he:

"I'll hold the cat—you bring a cocoanut."

Eckert split one open, and chopped up some pieces. Bascom smuggled a wink to me, and proffered a slice of the fruit to puss. She snatched it, swallowed it ravenously, and asked for more !

We rode our two miles in silence, and wide apart. At least I was silent, though Bascom cuffed his horse and cursed him a good deal, notwithstanding the horse was behaving well enough. When I branched off homeward, Bascom said:

"Keep the horse till morning. And—you need not speak of this —— foolishness to the boys."

CHAPTER VIII.

IN a little while all interest was taken up in stretching our necks and watching for the "pony-rider"—the fleet messenger who sped across the continent from St. Joe to Sacramento, carrying letters nineteen hundred miles in eight days! Think of that for perishable horse and human flesh and blood to do! The pony-rider was usually a little bit of a man, brimful of spirit and endurance. No matter what time of the day or night his watch came on, and no matter whether it was winter or summer, raining, snowing, hailing, or sleeting, or whether his "beat" was a level straight road or a crazy trail over mountain crags and precipices, or whether it led through peaceful regions or regions that swarmed with hostile Indians, he must be always ready to leap into the saddle and be off like the wind! There was no idling-time for a pony-rider on duty. He rode fifty miles without stopping, by daylight, moonlight, starlight, or through the blackness of darkness—just as it happened. He rode a splendid horse that was born for a racer and fed and lodged like a gentleman; kept him at his utmost speed for ten miles, and then, as he came crashing up to the station where stood two men holding fast a fresh, impatient steed, the transfer of rider and mail-bag was made in the twinkling of an eye, and away flew the eager pair and were out of sight before the spectator could get hardly the ghost of a look. Both rider and horse went "flying light." The rider's dress was thin, and fitted close; he wore a "roundabout," and a skull-cap, and tucked his pantaloons into his

boot-tops like a race-rider. He carried no arms—he carried nothing that was not absolutely necessary, for even the postage on his literary freight was worth *five dollars a letter.* He got but little frivo-
lous correspondence to carry — his bag had business letters in it, mostly. His horse was stripped of all unnecessary weight, too. He wore a little wafer of a racing-sad-dle, and no visible blanket. He wore light shoes, or none at all. The little flat mail-pockets strap-

"HERE HE COMES."

ped under the rider's thighs would each hold about the bulk of a child's primer. They held many and many an important business chapter and newspaper letter, but these were written on paper as airy and thin as gold-leaf, nearly, and thus bulk and weight were economized. The stage-coach traveled about a hundred to a hundred and twenty-five miles a day (twenty-four hours), the pony-rider about two hundred and fifty. There were about eighty pony-riders in the saddle all the time, night and day, stretching in a long, scattering procession from Missouri to California, forty flying eastward, and forty toward the west, and among them making four hundred gallant horses earn a stirring livelihood and see a deal of scenery every single day in the year.

We had had a consuming desire, from the beginning, to see a pony-rider, but somehow or other all that passed us and all that met us managed to streak by in the night, and so we heard only a whiz and a hail, and the swift phantom of the desert was gone before we could get our heads out of the windows. But now we were expecting one along every moment, and would see him in broad daylight. Presently the driver exclaims:

"HERE HE COMES!"

Every neck is stretched further, and every eye strained

wider. Away across the endless dead level of the prairie a black speck appears against the sky, and it is plain that it moves. Well, I should think so! In a second or two it becomes a horse

CHANGING HORSES.

and rider, rising and falling, rising and falling— sweeping toward us nearer and nearer—growing more and more distinct, more and more sharply defined— nearer and still nearer, and the flutter of the hoofs comes faintly to the ear—another instant a whoop and a hurrah from our upper deck, a wave of the rider's hand, but no reply, and man and horse burst past our excited faces, and go winging away like a belated fragment of a storm!

So sudden is it all, and so like a flash of unreal fancy, that but for the flake of white foam left quivering and perishing on a mail-sack after the vision had flashed by and disappeared, we might have doubted whether we had seen any actual horse and man at all, maybe.

We rattled through Scott's Bluffs Pass, by and by. It was along here somewhere that we first came across genuine and unmistakable alkali water in the road, and we cordially hailed it as a first-class curiosity, and a thing to be mentioned with eclat in letters to the ignorant at home. This water gave the road a soapy appearance, and in many places the ground looked as if it had been whitewashed. I think the strange alkali water excited us as much as any wonder we had come upon yet, and I know we felt very complacent and conceited, and better satisfied with life after we had added it to our list of things which *we* had seen and some other people had not. In a small way we were the same sort of simpletons as those who climb unnecessarily the perilous peaks of Mont Blanc and the Matterhorn, and derive no pleasure from it except the reflection that it isn't a common experience. But once in a while one of those parties trips and comes darting down the long mountain-crags in a sitting posture, making the crusted snow smoke behind him, flitting from bench to bench, and from terrace to terrace, jarring the earth where he strikes, and still glancing and flitting on again, sticking an iceberg into himself every now and then, and tearing his clothes, snatching at things to save himself, taking hold of trees and fetching them along with him, roots and all, starting little rocks now and then, then big boulders, then acres of ice and snow and patches of forest, gathering and still gathering as he goes, adding and still adding to his massed and sweeping grandeur as he nears a three thousand-foot precipice, till at last he waves his hat magnificently and rides into eternity on the back of a raging and tossing avalanche!

RIDING THE AVALANCHE.

This is all very fine, but let us not be carried away by excitement, but ask calmly, how does this person feel about it in his cooler moments next day, with six or seven thousand feet of snow and stuff on top of him?

We crossed the sand hills near the scene of the Indian mail robbery and massacre of 1856, wherein the driver and conductor perished, and also all the passengers but one, it was supposed; but this must have been a mistake, for at different times afterward on the Pacific coast I was personally acquainted with a hundred and thirty-three or four people who were wounded during that massacre, and barely escaped with their lives.   There was no doubt of the truth of it—I had it from their own lips.   One of these parties told me that he kept coming across arrow-heads in his system for nearly seven years after the massacre ; and another of them told me that he was stuck so literally full of arrows that after the Indians were gone and he could raise up and examine himself, he could not restrain his tears, for his clothes were completely ruined.

The most trustworthy tradition avers, however, that only one man, a person named Babbitt, survived the massacre, and he was desperately wounded.   He dragged himself on his hands and knee (for one leg was broken) to a station several miles away.   He did it during portions of two nights, lying concealed one day and part of another, and for more than forty hours suffering unimaginable anguish from hunger, thirst and bodily pain.   The Indians robbed the coach of everything it contained, including quite an amount of treasure.

CHAPTER IX.

WE passed Fort Laramie in the night, and on the seventh morning out we found ourselves in the Black Hills, with Laramie Peak at our elbow (apparently) looming vast and solitary—a deep, dark, rich indigo blue in hue, so portentously did the old colossus frown under his beetling brows of storm-cloud. He was thirty or forty miles away, in reality, but he only seemed removed a little beyond the low ridge at our right. We breakfasted at Horse-Shoe Station, six hundred and seventy-six miles out from St. Joseph. We had now reached a hostile Indian country, and during the afternoon we passed Laparelle Station, and enjoyed great discomfort all the time we were in the neighborhood, being aware that many of the trees we dashed by at arm's length concealed a lurking Indian or two. During the preceding night an ambushed savage had sent a bullet through the pony-rider's jacket, but he had ridden on, just the same, because pony-riders were not allowed to stop and inquire into such things except when killed. As long as they had life enough left in them they had to stick to the horse and ride, even if the Indians had been waiting for them a week, and were entirely out of patience. About two hours and a half before we arrived at Laparelle Station, the keeper in charge of it had fired four times at an Indian, but he said with an injured air that the Indian had "skipped around so's to spile everything —and ammunition's blamed skurse, too." The most natural

inference conveyed by his manner of speaking was, that in
"skipping around," the Indian had taken an unfair advantage.

INDIAN COUNTRY.

The coach we were
in had a neat hole
through its front—
a reminiscence of
its last trip through
this region. The
bullet that made
it wounded the
driver slightly, but
he did not mind it
much. He said the
place to keep a man
"huffy" was down
on the Southern
Overland, among
the Apaches, be-
fore the company
moved the stage-
line up on the northern route. He said the Apaches used to
annoy him all the time down there, and that he came as near
as anything to starving to death in the midst of abundance,
because they kept him so leaky with bullet holes that he
"couldn't hold his vittles." This person's statement were
not generally believed.

We shut the blinds down very tightly that first night in
the hostile Indian country, and lay on our arms. We slept
on them some, but most of the time we only lay on them.
We did not talk much, but kept quiet and listened. It was
an inky-black night, and occasionally rainy. We were among
woods and rocks, hills and gorges—so shut in, in fact, that
when we peeped through a chink in a curtain, we could discern nothing. The driver and conductor on top were still,
too, or only spoke at long intervals, in low tones, as is the
way of men in the midst of invisible dangers. We listened
to rain-drops pattering on the roof; and the grinding of the

wheels through the muddy gravel; and the low wailing of the wind; and all the time we had that absurd sense upon us, inseparable from travel at night in a close-curtained vehicle, the sense of remaining perfectly still in one place, notwithstanding the jolting and swaying of the vehicle, the trampling of the horses, and the grinding of the wheels. We listened a long time, with intent faculties and bated breath; every time one of us would relax, and draw a long sigh of relief and start to say something, a comrade would be sure to utter a sudden "Hark!" and instantly the experimenter was rigid and listening again. So the tiresome minutes and decades of minutes dragged away, until at last our tense forms filmed over with a dulled consciousness, and we slept, if one might call such a condition by so strong a name—for it was a sleep set with a hair-trigger. It was a sleep seething and teeming with a weird and distressful confusion of shreds and fag-ends of dreams—a sleep that was a chaos. Presently, dreams and sleep and the sullen hush of the night were startled by a ringing report, and cloven by *such* a long, wild, agonizing shriek! Then we heard—ten steps from the stage—

"Help! help! help!" [It was our driver's voice.]

"Kill him! Kill him like a dog!"

"I'm being murdered! Will no man lend me a pistol?"

"Look out! head him off! head him off!"

[Two pistol shots; a confusion of voices and the trampling of many feet, as if a crowd were closing and surging together around some object; several heavy, dull blows, as with a club; a voice that said appealingly, "Don't, gentlemen, please don't —I'm a dead man!" Then a fainter groan, and another blow, and away sped the stage into the darkness, and left the grisly mystery behind us.]

What a startle it was! Eight seconds would amply cover the time it occupied—maybe even five would do it. We only had time to plunge at a curtain and unbuckle and unbutton part of it in an awkward and hindering flurry, when our whip cracked sharply overhead, and we went rumbling and thundering away, down a mountain "grade."

We fed on that mystery the rest of the night—what was left of it, for it was waning fast. It had to remain a present mystery, for all we could get from the conductor in answer to our hails was something that sounded, through the clatter of the wheels, like "Tell you in the morning!"

So we lit our pipes and opened the corner of a curtain for a chimney, and lay there in the dark, listening to each other's story of how he first felt and how many thousand Indians he first thought had hurled themselves upon us, and what his remembrance of the subsequent sounds was, and the order of their occurrence. And we theorized, too, but there was never a theory that would account for our driver's voice being out there, nor yet account for his Indian murderers talking such good English, if they *were* Indians.

So we chatted and smoked the rest of the night comfortably away, our boding anxiety being somehow marvelously dissipated by the real presence of something to be anxious *about*.

We never did get much satisfaction about that dark occurrence. All that we could make out of the odds and ends of the information we gathered in the morning, was that the disturbance occurred at a station; that we changed drivers there, and that the driver that got off there had been talking roughly about some of the outlaws that infested the region ("for there wasn't a man around there but had a price on his head and didn't dare show himself in the settlements," the conductor said); he had talked roughly about these characters, and ought to have "drove up there with his pistol cocked and ready on the seat alongside of him, and begun business himself, because any softy would know they would be laying for him."

That was all we could gather, and we could see that neither the conductor nor the new driver were much concerned about the matter. They plainly had little respect for a man who would deliver offensive opinions of people and then be so simple as to come into their presence unprepared to "back his judgment," as they pleasantly phrased the killing of any fellow-being who did not like said opinions. And likewise they plainly had a contempt for the man's poor discretion in venturing to rouse the wrath of such utterly reckless wild beasts as those outlaws —and the conductor added:

"I tell you it's as much as Slade himself wants to do!"

This remark created an entire revolution in my curiosity. I cared nothing now about the Indians, and even lost interest in the murdered driver. There was such magic in that name, SLADE! Day or night, now, I stood always ready to drop any subject in hand, to listen to something new about Slade and his ghastly exploits. Even before we got to Overland City, we had begun to hear about Slade and his "division" (for he was a "division-agent") on the Overland; and from the hour we had left Overland City we had heard drivers and conductors talk about only three things—"Californy," the Nevada silver mines, and this desperado Slade. And a deal the most of the talk was about Slade. We had gradually come to have a realizing sense of the fact that Slade was a man whose heart and hands and soul were steeped in the blood of offenders against his dignity; a man who awfully avenged all injuries, affronts, insults or slights, of whatever kind—on the spot if he could, years afterward if lack of earlier opportunity compelled it; a man whose hate tortured him day and night till vengeance appeased it—and not an ordinary vengeance either, but his enemy's absolute death—nothing less; a man whose face would light up with a terrible joy when he surprised a foe and had him at a disadvantage. A high and efficient servant of the Overland, an outlaw among outlaws and yet their relentless scourge, Slade was at once the most bloody, the most dangerous and the most valuable citizen that inhabited the savage fastnesses of the mountains.

CHAPTER X.

REALLY and truly, two thirds of the talk of drivers and conductors had been about this man Slade, ever since the day before we reached Julesburg. In order that the eastern reader may have a clear conception of what a Rocky Mountain desperado is, in his highest state of development, I will reduce all this mass of overland gossip to one straightforward narrative, and present it in the following shape :

Slade was born in Illinois, of good parentage. At about twenty-six years of age he killed a man in a quarrel and fled the country. At St. Joseph, Missouri, he joined one of the early California-bound emigrant trains, and was given the post of train-master. One day on the plains he had an angry dispute with one of his wagon-drivers, and both drew their revolvers. But the driver was the quicker artist, and had his weapon cocked first. So Slade said it was a pity to waste life on so small a matter, and proposed that the pistols be thrown on the ground and the quarrel settled by a fist-fight. The unsuspecting driver agreed, and threw down his pistol—whereupon Slade laughed at his simplicity, and shot him dead !

He made his escape, and lived a wild life for awhile, dividing his time between fighting Indians and avoiding an Illinois sheriff, who had been sent to arrest him for his first murder. It is said that in one Indian battle he killed three savages with his own hand, and afterward cut their ears off and sent them, with his compliments, to the chief of the tribe.

Slade soon gained a name for fearless resolution, and this

was sufficient merit to procure for him the important post of overland division-agent at Julesburg, in place of Mr. Jules, removed. For some time previously, the company's horses had been frequent-ly stolen, and the coaches delayed, by gangs of outlaws, who were wont to laugh at the idea of any man's having the temerity to re-sent such outrages. Slade resented them promptly. The out-laws soon found that the new agent was a man who did not fear anything that breathed the breath of life. He made short work of all offenders. The re-sult was that delays ceased, the compa-ny's property was let alone, and no matter what happened or

A PROPOSED FIST-FIGHT.

who suffered, Slade's coaches went through, every time! True, in order to bring about this wholesome change, Slade had to kill several men—some say three, others say four, and others six—but the world was the richer for their loss. The first prominent difficulty he had was with the ex-agent Jules, who bore the reputation of being a reckless and desperate man himself. Jules hated Slade for supplanting him, and a good fair occasion for a fight was all he was waiting for. By and by Slade dared to employ a man whom Jules had once discharged. Next, Slade seized a team of stage-horses which he accused Jules of having driven off and hidden somewhere for his own use. War was declared, and for a day or two the two men walked warily about the streets, seeking each other, Jules armed with a double-barreled shot gun, and Slade with his history-creating revolver. Finally, as Slade stepped into a store, Jules poured the contents of his gun into him from be-

hind the door. Slade was pluck, and Jules got several bad pistol wounds in return. Then both men fell, and were carried to their respective lodgings, both swearing that better aim should do deadlier work next time. Both were bedridden a long time, but Jules got on his feet first, and gathering his possessions together, packed them on a couple of mules, and fled to the Rocky Mountains to gather strength in safety against the day of reckoning.

FROM BEHIND THE DOOR.

For many months he was not seen or heard of, and was gradually dropped out of the remembrance of all save Slade himself. But Slade was not the man to forget him. On the contrary, common report said that Slade kept a reward standing for his capture, dead or alive!

After awhile, seeing that Slade's energetic administration had restored peace and order to one of the worst divisions of the road, the overland stage company transferred him to the Rocky Ridge division in the Rocky Mountains, to see if he could perform a like miracle there. It was the very paradise of outlaws and desperadoes. There was absolutely no semblance of law there. Violence was the rule. Force was the only recognized authority. The commonest misunderstandings were settled on the spot with the revolver or the knife. Murders were done in open day, and with sparkling frequency, and nobody thought of inquiring into them. It was considered that the parties who did the killing had their private reasons for it; for other people to meddle would have been looked upon as indelicate. After a murder, all that Rocky Mountain etiquette required of a spectator was, that he should help the gentleman bury his game—otherwise his churlishness would surely be remembered against him the first time he killed a man himself and needed a neighborly turn in interring him.

Slade took up his residence sweetly and peacefully in the midst of this hive of horse-thieves and assassins, and the very first time one of them aired his insolent swaggerings in his presence he shot him dead! He began a raid on the outlaws, and in a singularly short space of time he had completely stopped their depredations on the stage stock, recovered a large number of stolen horses, killed several of the worst desperadoes of the district, and gained such a dread ascendancy over the rest that they respected him, admired him, feared him, obeyed him! He wrought the same marvelous change in the ways of the community that had marked his administration at Overland City. He captured two men who had stolen overland stock, and with his own hands he hanged them. He was supreme judge in his district, and he was jury and executioner likewise—and not only in the case of offences against his employers, but against passing emigrants as well. On one occasion some emigrants had their stock lost or stolen, and told Slade, who chanced to visit their camp. With a single companion he rode to a ranch, the owners of which he suspected, and opening the door, commenced firing, killing three, and wounding the fourth.

From a bloodthirstily interesting little Montana book * I take this paragraph :

While on the road, Slade held absolute sway. He would ride down to a station, get into a quarrel, turn the house out of windows, and maltreat the occupants most cruelly. The unfortunates had no means of redress, and

SLADE AS EXECUTIONER.

were compelled to recuperate as best they could. On one of these occasions, it is said he killed the father of the fine little half-breed boy Jemmy, whom he adopted, and who lived with his widow after his execution. Stories of Slade's hanging men, and of innumerable assaults, shootings, stabbings and beatings, in which he was a principal actor, form part of the legends of the stage line. As for minor quarrels and shootings, it is absolutely certain that a minute history of Slade's life would be one long record of such practices.

* "The Vigilantes of Montana," by Prof. Thos. J. Dimsdale.

Slade was a matchless marksman with a navy revolver. The legends say that one morning at Rocky Ridge, when he was feeling comfortable, he saw a man approaching who had offended him some days before—observe the fine memory he had for matters like that—and, "Gentlemen," said Slade, drawing, "it is a good twenty-yard shot—I'll clip the third button on his coat!" Which he did. The bystanders all admired it. And they all attended the funeral, too.

On one occasion a man who kept a little whisky-shelf at the station did something which angered Slade—and went and made his will. A day or two afterward Slade came in

AN UNPLEASANT VIEW.

and called for some brandy. The man reached under the counter (ostensibly to get a bottle—possibly to get something else), but Slade smiled upon him that peculiarly bland and satisfied smile of his which the neighbors had long ago learned to recognize as a death-warrant in disguise, and told him to "none of that!—pass out the high-priced article." So the poor bar-keeper had to turn his back and get the high-priced brandy from the shelf; and when he faced around again he was looking into the muzzle of Slade's pistol. "And the next instant," added my informant, impressively, "he was one of the deadest men that ever lived."

The stage-drivers and conductors told us that sometimes Slade would leave a hated enemy wholly unmolested, unnoticed and unmentioned, for weeks together—had done it once or twice at any rate. And some said they believed he did it in order to lull the victims into unwatchfulness, so that he could get the advantage of them, and others said they believed he saved up an enemy that way, just as a schoolboy saves up a cake, and made the pleasure go as far as it would by gloating over the anticipation. One of these cases was that of a Frenchman who had offended Slade. To the surprise of everybody Slade did not kill him on the spot, but let him alone for a considerable time. Finally, however, he went to the Frenchman's house very late one night, knocked, and when his enemy opened the door, shot him dead—pushed the corpse inside the door with his foot, set the house on fire and burned up the dead man, his widow and three children! I heard this story from several different people, and they evidently believed what they were saying. It may be true, and it may not. "Give a dog a bad name," etc.

Slade was captured, once, by a party of men who intended to lynch him. They disarmed him, and shut him up in a strong log-house, and placed a guard over him. He prevailed on his captors to send for his wife, so that he might have a last interview with her. She was a brave, loving, spirited woman. She jumped on a horse and rode for life and death. When she arrived they let her in without searching her, and before the door could be closed she whipped out a couple of revolvers, and she and her lord marched forth defying the party. And then, under a brisk fire, they mounted double and galloped away unharmed!

In the fulness of time Slade's myrmidons captured his

ancient enemy Jules, whom they found in a well-chosen hiding-place in the remote fastnesses of the mountains, gaining a precarious livelihood with his rifle. They brought him to Rocky Ridge, bound hand and foot, and deposited him in the middle of the cattle-yard with his back against a post. It is said that the pleasure that lit Slade's face when he heard of it was something fearful to contemplate. He examined his enemy to see that he was securely tied, and then went to bed, content to wait till morning before enjoying the luxury of killing him. Jules spent the night in the cattle-yard, and it is a region where warm nights are never known. In the morning Slade practised on him with his revolver, nipping the flesh here and there, and occasionally clipping off a finger, while Jules begged him to kill him outright and put him out of his misery. Finally Slade reloaded, and walking up close to his victim, made some characteristic remarks and then dispatched him. The body lay there half a day, nobody venturing to touch it without orders, and then Slade detailed a party and assisted at the burial himself. But he first cut off the dead man's ears and put them in his vest pocket, where he carried them for some time with great satisfaction. That is the story as I have frequently heard it told and seen it in print in California newspapers. It is doubtless correct in all essential particulars.

In due time we rattled up to a stage-station, and sat down to breakfast with a half-savage, half-civilized company of armed and bearded mountaineers, ranchmen and station employees. The most gentlemanly-appearing, quiet and affable officer we had yet found along the road in the Overland Company's service was the person who sat at the head of the table, at my elbow. Never youth stared and shivered as I did when I heard them call him SLADE!

Here was romance, and I sitting face to face with it!— looking upon it—touching it—hobnobbing with it, as it were! Here, right by my side, was the actual ogre who, in fights and brawls and various ways, *had taken the lives of twenty-six human beings,* or all men lied about him! I suppose I was the proudest stripling that ever traveled to see strange lands and wonderful people.

He was so friendly and so gentle-spoken that I warmed to him in spite of his awful history. It was hardly possible to realize that this pleasant person was the pitiless scourge of the outlaws, the raw-head-and-bloody-bones the nursing mothers of the mountains terrified their children with. And to this day I can remember nothing remarkable about Slade except that his face was rather broad across the cheek bones, and that the cheek bones were low and the lips peculiarly thin and straight. But that was enough to leave something of an effect upon me, for since then I seldom see a face possessing those characteristics without fancying that the owner of it is a dangerous man.

The coffee ran out. At least it was reduced to one tin-cupful, and Slade was about to take it when he saw that my cup was empty. He politely offered to fill it, but although I wanted it, I politely declined. I was afraid he had not killed anybody that morning, and might be needing diversion.

UNAPPRECIATED POLITENESS.

But still with firm politeness he insisted on filling my cup, and said I had traveled all night and better deserved it than he—and while he talked he placidly poured the fluid, to the last drop. I thanked him and drank it, but it gave me no comfort, for I

could not feel sure that he would not be sorry, presently, that
he had given it away, and proceed to kill me to distract his
thoughts from the loss.   But nothing of the kind occurred.
We left him with only twenty-six dead people to account
for, and I felt a tranquil satisfaction in the thought that in
so judiciously taking care of No. 1 at that breakfast-table
I had pleasantly escaped being No. 27.   Slade came out to
the coach and saw us off, first ordering certain reärrangements
of the mail-bags for our comfort, and then we took leave of
him, satisfied that we should hear of him again, some day, and
wondering in what connection.

CHAPTER XI.

A ND sure enough, two or three years afterward, we did
hear of him again. News came to the Pacific coast
that the Vigilance Committee in Montana (whither Slade had
removed from Rocky Ridge) had hanged him. I find an
account of the affair in the thrilling little book I quoted a
paragraph from in the last chapter—"The Vigilantes of Montana; being a Reliable Account of the Capture, Trial and
Execution of Henry Plummer's Notorious Road Agent Band:
By Prof. Thos. J. Dimsdale, Virginia City, M. T." Mr.
Dimsdale's chapter is well worth reading, as a specimen of
how the people of the frontier deal with criminals when the
courts of law prove inefficient. Mr. Dimsdale makes two remarks about Slade, both of which are accurately descriptive,
and one of which is exceedingly picturesque: "Those who
saw him in his natural state only, would pronounce him to be
a kind husband, a most hospitable host and a courteous gentleman; on the contrary, those who met him when maddened
with liquor and surrounded by a gang of armed roughs, would
pronounce him a fiend incarnate." And this: "From Fort
Kearney, west, he was feared *a great deal more than the Almighty.*" For compactness, simplicity and vigor of expression, I will "back" that sentence against anything in literature.
Mr. Dimsdale's narrative is as follows. In all places where
italics occur, they are mine:

After the execution of the five men on the 14th of January, the Vigilantes considered that their work was nearly ended. They had freed the

country of highwaymen and murderers to a great extent, and they determined that in the absence of the regular civil authority they would establish a People's Court where all offenders should be tried by judge and jury. This was the nearest approach to social order that the circumstances permitted, and, though strict legal authority was wanting, yet the people were firmly determined to maintain its efficiency, and to enforce its decrees. It may here be mentioned that the overt act which was the last round on the fatal ladder leading to the scaffold on which Slade perished, *was the tearing in pieces and stamping upon a writ of this court, followed by his arrest of the Judge, Alex. Davis, by authority of a presented Derringer, and with his own hands.*

J. A. Slade was himself, we have been informed, a Vigilante; he openly boasted of it, and said he knew all that they knew. He was never accused, or even suspected, of either murder or robbery, committed in this Territory (the latter crime was never laid to his charge, in any place); but that he had killed several men in other localities was notorious, and his bad reputation in this respect was a most powerful argument in determining his fate, when he was finally arrested for the offence above mentioned. On returning from Milk River he became more and more addicted to drinking, until at last it was a common feat for him and his friends to "take the town." He and a couple of his dependents might often be seen on one horse, galloping through the streets, shouting and yelling, firing revolvers, etc. On many occasions he would ride his horse into stores, break up bars, toss the scales out of doors and use most insulting language to parties present. Just previous to the day of his arrest, he had given a fearful beating to one of his followers; but such was his influence over them that the man wept bitterly at the gallows, and begged for his life with all his power. *It had become quite common, when Slade was on a spree, for the shop-keepers and citizens to close the stores and put out all the lights;* being fearful of some outrage at his hands. For his wanton destruction of goods and furniture, he was always ready to pay, when sober, if he had money; but there were not a few who regarded payment as small satisfaction for the outrage, and these men were his personal enemies.

From time to time Slade received warnings from men that he well knew would not deceive him, of the certain end of his conduct. There was not a moment, for weeks previous to his arrest, in which the public did not expect to hear of some bloody outrage. The dread of his very name, and the presence of the armed band of hangers-on who followed him alone prevented a resistance which must certainly have ended in the instant murder or mutilation of the opposing party.

Slade was frequently arrested by order of the court whose organization we have described, and had treated it with respect by paying one or two fines and promising to pay the rest when he had money; but in the transaction that occurred at this crisis, he forgot even this caution, and goaded by passion and the hatred of restraint, he sprang into the embrace of death.

Slade had been drunk and "cutting up" all night. He and his companions had made the town a perfect hell. In the morning, J. M. Fox, the sheriff, met him, arrested him, took him into court and commenced reading a warrant that he had for his arrest, by way of arraignment. He became uncontrollably furious, and *seizing the writ, he tore it up, threw it on the ground*

SLADE IN COURT.

and stamped upon it. The clicking of the locks of his companions' revolvers was instantly heard, and a crisis was expected. The sheriff did not attempt his retention; but being at least as prudent as he was valiant, he succumbed, leaving Slade the *master of the situation and the conqueror and ruler of the courts, law and law-makers.* This was a declaration of war, and was so accepted. The Vigilance Committee now felt that the question of social order and the preponderance of the law-abiding citizens had then and there to be decided. They knew the character of Slade, and they were well aware that they must submit to his rule without murmur, or else that he must be dealt with in such fashion as would prevent his being able to wreak his vengeance on the committee, who could never have hoped to live in the Territory secure from outrage or death, and who could never leave it without encountering his friends, whom his victory would have emboldened and stimulated to a pitch that would have rendered them reckless of consequences. The day previous he had ridden into Dorris's store, and on being requested to leave, he drew his revolver and threatened to kill the gentleman who spoke to him. Another saloon he had led his horse into, and buying a bottle of wine, he tried to make the animal drink it. This was not considered an uncommon performance, as he had often entered saloons and commenced firing at the lamps, causing a wild stampede.

A leading member of the committee met Slade, and informed him in the quiet, earnest manner of one who feels the importance of what he is saying: "Slade, get your horse at once, and go home, or there will be ——— to pay." Slade started and took a long look, with his dark and piercing eyes, at the gentleman. "What do you mean?" said he. "You have no right to ask me what I mean," was the quiet reply, "get your horse at once, and remember what I tell you." After a short pause he promised to do so, and actually got into the saddle; but, being still intoxicated, he began calling aloud to one after another of his friends, and at last seemed to have forgotten the warning he had received and became again uproarious, shouting the name of a well-known courtezan in company with those of two men whom he considered heads of the committee, as a sort of challenge; perhaps, however, as a simple act of bravado. It seems probable that the intimation of personal danger he had received had not been forgotten entirely; though fatally for him, he took a foolish way of showing his remembrance of it. He sought out Alexander Davis, the Judge of the Court, and drawing a cocked Derringer, he presented it at his head, and told him that he should hold him as a hostage for his own safety. As the judge stood perfectly quiet, and offered no resistance to his captor, no further outrage followed on this score. Previous to this, on account of the critical state of affairs, the committee had met, and at last resolved to arrest him. His execution had not been agreed upon, and, at that time, would have been negatived, most assuredly. A messenger rode down to Nevada to inform the leading men of what was on hand, as it was desirable to show that there was a feeling of unanimity on the subject, all along the gulch.

The miners turned out almost *en masse*, leaving their work and forming in solid column. about six hundred strong, armed to the teeth, they marched up to Virginia. The leader of the body well knew the temper of his men on the subject. He spurred on ahead of them, and hastily calling a meeting of the executive, he told them plainly that the miners meant "business," and that, if they came up, they would not stand in the street to be shot down by Slade's friends; but that they would take him and hang him. The meeting was small, as the Virginia men were loath to act at all. This momentous announcement of the feeling of the Lower Town was made to a cluster of men, who were deliberating behind a wagon, at the rear of a store on Main street.

The committee were most unwilling to proceed to extremities. All the duty they had ever performed seemed as nothing to the task before them; but they had to decide, and that quickly. It was finally agreed that if the whole body of the miners were of the opinion that he should be hanged, that the committee left it in their hands to deal with him. Off, at hot speed, rode the leader of the Nevada men to join his command.

Slade had found out what was intended, and the news sobered him instantly. He went into P. S. Pfouts' store, where Davis was, and apologized for his conduct, saying that he would take it all back.

The head of the column now wheeled into Wallace street and marched up at quick time. Halting in front of the store, the executive officer of the committee stepped forward and arrested Slade, who was at once informed of his doom, and inquiry was made as to whether he had any business to settle. Several parties spoke to him on the subject; but to all such inquiries he turned a deaf ear, being entirely absorbed in the terrifying reflections on his own awful position. He never ceased his entreaties for life, and to see his dear wife. The unfortunate lady referred to, between whom and Slade there existed a warm affection, was at this time living at their ranch on the Madison. She was possessed of considerable personal attractions; tall, well-formed, of graceful carriage, pleasing manners, and was, withal, an accomplished horsewoman.

A messenger from Slade rode at full speed to inform her of her husband's arrest. In an instant she was in the saddle, and with all the energy that love and despair could lend to an ardent temperament and a strong physique, she urged her fleet charger over the twelve miles of rough and rocky ground that intervened between her and the object of her passionate devotion.

Meanwhile a party of volunteers had made the necessary preparations for the execution, in the valley traversed by the branch. Beneath the site of Pfouts and Russell's stone building there was a corral, the gate-posts of which were strong and high. Across the top was laid a beam, to which the rope was fastened, and a dry-goods box served for the platform. To this place Slade was marched, surrounded by a guard, composing the best armed and most numerous force that has ever appeared in Montana Territory.

The doomed man had so exhausted himself by tears, prayers and lamentations, that he had scarcely strength left to stand under the fatal beam. He repeatedly exclaimed, "My God! my God! must I die? Oh, my dear wife!"

On the return of the fatigue party, they encountered some friends of Slade, staunch and reliable citizens and members of the committee, but who were personally attached to the condemned. On hearing of his sentence, one of them, a stout-hearted man, pulled out his handkerchief and walked away, weeping like a child. Slade still begged to see his wife, most piteously, and it seemed hard to deny his request; but the bloody consequences that were sure to follow the inevitable attempt at a rescue, that her presence and entreaties would have certainly incited, forbade the granting of his request. Several gentlemen were sent for to see him, in his last moments, one of whom (Judge Davis) made a short address to the people; but in such low tones as to be inaudible, save to a few in his immediate vicinity. One of his friends, after exhausting his powers of entreaty, threw off his coat and declared that the prisoner could not be hanged until he himself was killed. A hundred guns were instantly leveled at him; whereupon he

A WIFE'S LAMENTATION.

turned and fled; but, being brought back, he was compelled to resume his coat, and to give a promise of future peaceable demeanor.

Scarcely a leading man in Virginia could be found, though numbers of the citizens joined the ranks of the guard when the arrest was made. All lamented the stern necessity which dictated the execution.

Everything being ready, the command was given, "Men, do your duty," and the box being instantly slipped from beneath his feet, he died almost instantaneously.

The body was cut down and carried to the Virginia Hotel, where, in a darkened room, it was scarcely laid out, when the unfortunate and bereaved companion of the deceased arrived, at headlong speed, to find that all was over, and that she was a widow. Her grief and heart-piercing cries were terrible evidences of the depth of her attachment for her lost husband, and a considerable period elapsed before she could regain the command of her excited feelings.

There is something about the desperado-nature that is wholly unaccountable—at least it looks unaccountable. It is this. The true desperado is gifted with splendid courage, and yet he will take the most infamous advantage of his enemy; armed and free, he will stand up before a host and fight until he is shot all to pieces, and yet when he is under the gallows and helpless he will cry and plead like a child. Words are cheap, and it is easy to call Slade a coward (all executed men who do not " die game " are promptly called cowards by unreflecting people), and when we read of Slade that he " had so exhausted himself by tears, prayers and lamentations, that he had scarcely strength left to stand under the fatal beam," the disgraceful word suggests itself in a moment—yet in frequently defying and inviting the vengeance of banded Rocky Mountain cut-throats by shooting down their comrades and leaders, and never offering to hide or fly, Slade showed that he was a man of peerless bravery. No coward would dare that. Many a notorious coward, many a chicken-livered poltroon, coarse, brutal, degraded, has made his dying speech without a quaver in his voice and been swung into eternity with what looked liked the calmest fortitude, and so we are justified in believing, from the low intellect of such a creature, that it was not *moral* courage that enabled him to do it. Then, if moral courage is not the requisite quality, what could it have been that this stout-hearted Slade lacked?—this bloody, desperate, kindly-mannered, urbane gentleman, who never hesitated to warn his most ruffianly enemies that he would kill them whenever or wherever he came across them next! I think it is a conundrum worth investigating.

CHAPTER XII.

JUST beyond the breakfast-station we overtook a Mormon emigrant train of thirty-three wagons; and tramping wearily along and driving their herd of loose cows, were dozens of coarse-clad and sad-looking men, women and children, who had walked as they were walking now, day after day for eight lingering weeks, and in that time had compassed the distance our stage had come in *eight days and three hours*—seven hundred and ninety-eight miles! They were dusty and uncombed, hatless, bonnetless and ragged, and they did look so tired!

After breakfast, we bathed in Horse Creek, a (previously) limpid, sparkling stream—an appreciated luxury, for it was very seldom that our furious coach halted long enough for an indulgence of that kind. We changed horses ten or twelve times in every twenty-four hours—changed mules, rather—six mules—and did it nearly every time in *four minutes.* It was lively work. As our coach rattled up to each station six harnessed mules stepped gayly from the stable; and in the twinkling of an eye, almost, the old team was out, and the new one in and we off and away again.

During the afternoon we passed Sweetwater Creek, Independence Rock, Devil's Gate and the Devil's Gap. The latter were wild specimens of rugged scenery, and full of interest—*we were in the heart of the Rocky Mountains, now.* And we also passed by "Alkali" or "Soda Lake," and we woke up to the fact that our journey had stretched a long way across the

7†

world when the driver said that the Mormons often came there from Great Salt Lake City to haul away saleratus. He said that a few days gone by they had shoveled up enough pure saleratus from the ground (it was a *dry* lake) to load two wagons, and that when they got these two wagon-loads of a drug that cost them nothing, to Salt Lake, they could sell it for twenty-five cents a pound.

In the night we sailed by a most notable curiosity, and one we had been hearing a good deal about for a day or two, and were suffering to see. This was what might be called a natural ice-house. It was August, now, and sweltering weather in the daytime, yet at one of the stations the men could scrape the soil on the hill-side under the lee of a range of boulders, and at a depth of six inches cut out pure blocks of ice—hard, compactly frozen, and clear as crystal!

Toward dawn we got under way again, and presently as we sat with raised curtains enjoying our early-morning smoke and contemplating the first splendor of the rising sun as it swept down the long array of mountain peaks, flushing and gilding crag after crag and summit after summit, as if the invisible Creator reviewed his gray veterans and they saluted with a smile, we hove in sight of South Pass City. The hotel-keeper, the postmaster, the blacksmith, the mayor, the constable, the city marshal and the principal citizen and property holder, all came out and greeted us cheerily, and we gave him good day. He gave us a little Indian news, and a little Rocky Mountain news, and we gave him some Plains information in return. He then retired to his lonely grandeur and we climbed on up among the bristling peaks and the ragged clouds. South Pass City consisted of four log cabins, one of which was unfinished, and the gentleman with all those offices and titles was the chiefest of the ten citizens of the place. Think of hotel-keeper, postmaster, blacksmith, mayor, constable, city marshal and principal citizen all condensed into one person and crammed into one skin. Bemis said he was "a perfect Allen's revolver of dignities." And he said that if he were to die as postmaster, or as blacksmith, or as postmaster and blacksmith both, the people might stand it; but if he were to die all over, it would be a frightful loss to the community.

Two miles beyond South Pass City we saw for the first time that mysterious marvel which all Western untraveled boys have heard of and fully believe in, but are sure to be astounded at when they see it with their own eyes, nevertheless — banks of snow in dead summer time. We were now far up toward the sky, and knew all the time that we must presently encounter

THE CONCENTRATED INHABITANT.

lofty summits clad in the " eternal snow " which was so common-place a matter of mention in books, and yet when I did see it glittering in the sun on stately domes in the distance and knew the month was August and that my coat was hanging up because it was too warm to wear it, I was full as much amazed as if I never had heard of snow in August before. Truly, " seeing is believing "—and many a man lives a long life through, *thinking* he believes certain universally received and well established things, and yet never suspects that if he were confronted by those things once, he would discover that he did not *really* believe them before, but only thought he believed them.

In a little while quite a number of peaks swung into view with long claws of glittering snow clasping them; and with here and there, in the shade, down the mountain side, a little solitary patch of snow looking no larger than a lady's pocket-handkerchief, but being in reality as large as a " public square."

And now, at last, we were fairly in the renowned South

Pass, and whirling gayly along high above the common world. We were perched upon the extreme summit of the great range of the Rocky Mountains, toward which we had been climbing, patiently climbing, ceaselessly climbing, for days and nights together—and about us was gathered a convention of Nature's kings that stood ten, twelve, and even thirteen thousand feet high—grand old fellows who would have to stoop to see Mount Washington, in the twilight. We were in such an airy elevation above the creeping populations of the earth, that now and then when the obstructing crags stood out of the way it seemed that we could look around and abroad and contemplate the whole great globe, with its dissolving views of mountains, seas and continents stretching away through the mystery of the summer haze.

As a general thing the Pass was more suggestive of a valley than a suspension bridge in the clouds—but it strongly suggested the latter at one spot. At that place the upper third of one or two majestic purple domes projected above our level on either hand and gave us a sense of a hidden great deep of mountains and plains and valleys down about their bases which we fancied we might see if we could step to the edge and look over. These Sultans of the fastnesses were turbaned with tumbled volumes of cloud, which shredded away from time to time and drifted off fringed and torn, trailing their continents of shadow after them; and catching presently on an intercepting peak, wrapped it about and brooded there —then shredded away again and left the purple peak, as they had left the purple domes, downy and white with new-laid snow. In passing, these monstrous rags of cloud hung low and swept along right over the spectator's head, swinging their tatters so nearly in his face that his impulse was to shrink when they came closest. In the one place I speak of, one could look below him upon a world of diminishing crags and canyons leading down, down, and away to a vague plain with a thread in it which was a road, and bunches of feathers in it which were trees,—a pretty picture sleeping in the sunlight— but with a darkness stealing over it and glooming its features

THE SOUTH PASS.

deeper and deeper under the frown of a coming storm; and then, while no film or shadow marred the noon brightness of his high perch, he could watch the tempest break forth down there and see the lightnings leap from crag to crag and the sheeted rain drive along the canyon-sides, and hear the thunders peal and crash and roar. We had this spectacle; a familiar one to many, but to us a novelty.

We bowled along cheerily, and presently, at the very summit (though it had been all summit to us, and all equally level, for half an hour or more), we came to a spring which spent its water through two outlets and sent it in opposite directions. The conductor said that one of those streams which we were looking at, was just starting on a journey westward to the Gulf of

THE PARTED STREAM.

California and the Pacific Ocean, through hundreds and even thousands of miles of desert solitudes. He said that the other was just leaving its home among the snow-peaks on a similar journey eastward—and we knew that long after we should have forgotten the simple rivulet it would still be plodding its patient way down the mountain sides, and canyon-beds, and between the banks of the Yellowstone; and by and by would join the broad Missouri and flow through unknown plains and deserts and unvisited wildernesses; and add a long and troubled pilgrimage among snags and wrecks and sand-bars; and enter the Mississippi, touch the wharves of St. Louis and still drift on, traversing shoals and rocky channels, then endless chains of bottomless and ample bends, walled with unbroken forests, then mysterious byways and secret pas- ages among woody islands, then the chained bends again, bor- dered with wide levels of shining sugar-cane in place of the sombre forests; then by New Orleans and still other chains of bends—and finally, after two long months of daily and nightly harassment, excitement, enjoyment, adventure, and awful peril of parched throats, pumps and evaporation, pass the Gulf and enter into its rest upon the bosom of the tropic sea, never to look upon its snow-peaks again or regret them.

I freighted a leaf with a mental message for the friends at home, and dropped it in the stream. But I put no stamp on it and it was held for postage somewhere.

On the summit we overtook an emigrant train of many wagons, many tired men and women, and many a disgusted sheep and cow. In the wofully dusty horseman in charge of the expedition I recognized John ——. Of all persons in the world to meet on top of the Rocky Mountains thousands of miles from home, he was the last one I should have looked for. We were school-boys together and warm friends for years. But a boyish prank of mine had disrup- tured this friendship and it had never been renewed. The act of which I speak was this. I had been ac- customed to visit occasion- ally an editor whose room was in the third story of a building and overlooked the street. One day this editor gave me a watermelon which I made preparations

IT SPOILED THE MELON.

to devour on the spot, but chancing to look out of the

window, I saw John standing directly under it and an irresistible desire came upon me to drop the melon on his head, which I immediately did. I was the loser, for it spoiled the melon, and John never forgave me and we dropped all intercourse and parted, but now met again under these circumstances.

We recognized each other simultaneously, and hands were grasped as warmly as if no coldness had ever existed between us, and no allusion was made to any. All animosities were buried and the simple fact of meeting a familiar face in that isolated spot so far from home, was sufficient to make us forget all things but pleasant ones, and we parted again with sincere " good-byes " and " God bless you " from both.

We had been climbing up the long shoulders of the Rocky Mountains for many tedious hours—we started *down* them, now. And we went spinning away at a round rate too.

We left the snowy Wind River Mountains and Uinta Mountains behind, and sped away, always through splendid scenery but occasionally through long ranks of white skeletons of mules and oxen — monuments of the huge emigration of other days—and here and there were up-ended boards or small piles of stones which the driver said marked the resting-place of more precious

GIVEN OVER TO THE CAYOTE AND THE RAVEN.

remains. It was the loneliest land for a grave! A land given over to the cayote and the raven—which is but another name for desolation and utter solitude. On damp, murky nights, these scattered skeletons gave forth a soft, hideous glow, like very faint spots of moonlight starring the vague desert. It was because of the phosphorus in the bones.   But no scientific explanation could keep a body from shivering when he drifted by one of those ghostly lights and knew that a skull held it.

At midnight it began to rain, and I never saw anything like it—indeed, I did not even see this, for it was too dark. We fastened down the curtains and even caulked them with clothing, but the rain streamed in in twenty places, notwithstanding.   There was no escape.   If one moved his feet out of a stream, he brought his body under one; and if he moved his body he caught one somewhere else.   If he struggled out of the drenched blankets and sat up, he was bound to get one down the back of his neck.   Meantime the stage was wandering about a plain with gaping gullies in it, for the driver could not see an inch before his face nor keep the road, and the storm pelted so pitilessly that there was no keeping the horses still.   With the first abatement the conductor turned out with lanterns to look for the road, and the first dash he made was into a chasm about fourteen feet deep, his lantern following

"DON'T COME HERE."

like a meteor.   As soon as he touched bottom he sang out frantically :

"Don't come here!"

To which the driver, who was looking over the precipice where he had disappeared, replied, with an injured air: "Think I'm a dam fool?"

The conductor was more than an hour finding the road —a matter which showed us how far we had wandered and what chances we had been taking.   He traced our wheel-tracks to the imminent verge of danger, in two places.   I have always been glad that we were not killed that night.   I do not know any particular reason, but I have always been glad.

In the morning, the tenth day out, we crossed Green

River, a fine, large, limpid stream—stuck in it, with the water just up to the top of our mail-bed, and waited till extra teams were put on to haul us up the steep bank. But it was nice cool water, and besides it could not find any fresh place on us to wet.

At the Green River station we had breakfast—hot biscuits, fresh antelope steaks, and coffee—the only decent meal we tasted between the United States and Great Salt Lake City, and the only one we were ever really thankful for. Think of the monotonous execrableness of the thirty that went before it, to leave this one simple breakfast looming up in my memory like a shot-tower after all these years have gone by!

At five P.M. we reached Fort Bridger, one hundred and seventeen miles from the South Pass, and one

"THINK I'M A FOOL?"

thousand and twenty-five miles from St. Joseph. Fifty-two miles further on, near the head of Echo Canyon, we met sixty United States soldiers from Camp Floyd. The day before, they had fired upon three hundred or four hundred Indians, whom they supposed gathered together for no good purpose. In the fight that had ensued, four Indians were captured, and the main body chased four miles, but nobody killed. This looked like business. We had a notion to get out and join the sixty soldiers, but upon reflecting that there were four hundred of the Indians, we concluded to go on and join the Indians.

Echo Canyon is twenty miles long. It was like a long, smooth, narrow street, with a gradual descending grade, and shut in by enormous perpendicular walls of coarse conglomerate, four hundred feet high in many places, and turreted like mediæval castles. This was the most faultless piece of road in the mountains, and the driver said he would "let his team out." He did, and if the Pacific express trains whiz through there now any faster than we did then in the stage-coach, I envy the passengers the exhilaration of it. We fairly seemed to pick up our wheels and fly—and the mail matter was lifted up free from everything and held in solution! I am not given to exaggeration, and when I say a thing I mean it.

However, time presses. At four in the afternoon we

arrived on the summit of Big Mountain, fifteen miles from Salt Lake City, when all the world was glorified with the setting sun, and the most stupendous panorama of mountain peaks yet encountered burst on our sight. We looked out upon this sublime spectacle from under the arch of a brilliant rainbow! Even the overland stage-driver stopped his horses and gazed!

Half an hour or an hour later, we changed horses, and took supper with a Mormon "Destroying Angel." "Destroying Angels," as I understand it, are Latter-Day Saints who are set apart by the Church to conduct permanent disappearances of obnoxious citizens. I had heard a deal about these Mormon Destroying Angels and the dark and bloody deeds they had done, and when I entered this one's house I had my shudder all ready. But alas for all our romances, he was nothing but a loud, profane, offensive, old blackguard! He was murderous enough, possibly, to fill the bill of a Destroyer, but would you have *any* kind of an Angel devoid of dignity? Could you abide an Angel in an unclean shirt and no suspenders? Could you respect an Angel with a horse-laugh and a swagger like a buccaneer?

THE "DESTROYING ANGEL."

There were other blackguards present—comrades of this one. And there was one person that looked like a gentleman —Heber C. Kimball's son, tall and well made, and thirty years old, perhaps. A lot of slatternly women flitted hither and thither in a hurry, with coffee-pots, plates of bread, and other appurtenances to supper, and these were said to be the wives of the Angel—or some of them, at least. And of course they were; for if they had been hired "help" they would not have let an angel from above storm and swear at them as he did, let alone one from the place this one hailed from.

This was our first experience of the western "peculiar institution," and it was not very prepossessing. We did not tarry long to observe it, but hurried on to the home of the Latter-Day Saints, the stronghold of the prophets, the capital of the only absolute monarch in America—Great Salt Lake City. As the night closed in we took sanctuary in the Salt Lake House and unpacked our baggage.

CHAPTER XIII.

WE had a fine supper, of the freshest meats and fowls and vegetables—a great variety and as great abundance. We walked about the streets some, afterward, and glanced in at shops and stores; and there was fascination in surreptitiously staring at every creature we took to be a Mormon. This was fairy-land to us, to all intents and purposes—a land of enchantment, and goblins, and awful mystery. We felt a curiosity to ask every child how many mothers it had, and if it could tell them apart; and we experienced a thrill every time a dwelling-house door opened and shut as we passed, disclosing a glimpse of human heads and backs and shoulders—for we so longed to have a good satisfying look at a Mormon family in all its comprehensive ampleness, disposed in the customary concentric rings of its home circle.

By and by the Acting Governor of the Territory introduced us to other "Gentiles," and we spent a sociable hour with them. "Gentiles" are people who are not Mormons. Our fellow-passenger, Bemis, took care of himself, during this part of the evening, and did not make an overpowering success of it, either, for he came into our room in the hotel about eleven o'clock, full of cheerfulness, and talking loosely, disjointedly and indiscriminately, and every now and then tugging out a ragged word by the roots that had more hiccups than syllables in it. This, together with his hanging his coat on the floor on one side of a chair, and his vest on the floor on the other side, and piling his pants on the floor just in front of the same chair, and then contemplating the general result with superstitious awe, and finally pronouncing it "too many for *him*" and going to bed with his boots on, led us to fear that something he had eaten had not agreed with him.

But we knew afterward that it was something he had been drinking. It was the exclusively M o r m o n refresher, "valley tan." Valley tan (or, at least, one form of v a l l e y tan) is a kind of whisky, or first cousin to it; is of Mormon invention and manufactured only in Utah. Tradition says it is made of (imported) fire and brimstone. If

EFFECTS OF "VALLEY TAN."

I remember rightly no public drinking saloons were allowed in the kingdom by Brigham Young, and no private drinking permitted among the faithful, except they confined themselves to "valley tan."

Next day we strolled about everywhere through the broad, straight, level streets, and enjoyed the pleasant strangeness of a city of fifteen thousand inhabitants with no loafers perceptible in it; and no visible drunkards or noisy people; a limpid stream rippling and dancing through every street in place of a filthy gutter; block after block of trim dwellings, built of "frame" and sunburned brick—a great thriving orchard and garden behind every one of them, apparently—branches from the street stream winding and sparkling among the garden beds and fruit trees—and a grand general air of neatness, repair, thrift and comfort, around and about and over the whole.

And everywhere were workshops, factories, and all manner of industries; and intent faces and busy hands were to be seen wherever one looked; and in one's ears was the ceaseless clink of hammers, the buzz of trade and the contented hum of drums and fly-wheels.

The armorial crest of my own State consisted of two dissolute bears holding up the head of a dead and gone cask between them and making the pertinent remark, " United, We Stand——(hic!)—— Divided, We Fall." It was always too figurative for the author of this book. But the Mormon crest was easy. And it was simple, unostentatious, and fitted like a glove. It was a representation of a Golden Beehive, with the bees all at work!

ONE CREST.

The city lies in the edge of a level plain as broad as the State of Connecticut, and crouches close down to the ground under a curving wall of mighty mountains whose heads are hidden in the clouds, and whose shoulders bear relics of the snows of winter all the summer long. Seen from one of these dizzy heights, twelve or fifteen miles off, Great Salt Lake City is toned down and diminished till it is suggestive of a child's toy-village reposing under the majestic protection of the Chinese wall.

THE OTHER.

On some of those mountains, to the southwest, it had been

raining every day for two weeks, but not a drop had fallen in the city. And on hot days in late spring and early autumn the citizens could quit fanning and growling and go out and cool off by looking at the luxury of a glorious snow-storm going on in the mountains. They could enjoy it at a distance, at those seasons, every day, though no snow would fall in their streets, or anywhere near them.

Salt Lake City was healthy—an extremely healthy city. They declared there was only one physician in the place and

THE VAGRANT.

he was arrested every week regularly and held to answer under the vagrant act for having "no visible means of support." [They always give you a good substantial article of truth in

Salt Lake, and good measure and good weight, too. Very often, if you wished to weigh one of their airiest little commonplace statements you would want the hay scales.]

We desired to visit the famous inland sea, the American "Dead Sea," the great Salt Lake—seventeen miles, horseback, from the city—for we had dreamed about it, and thought about it, and talked about it, and yearned to see it, all the first part of our trip; but now when it was only arm's length away it had suddenly lost nearly every bit of its interest. And so we put it off, in a sort of general way, till next day—and that was the last we ever thought of it. We dined with some hospitable Gentiles; and visited the foundation of the prodigious temple; and talked long with that shrewd Connecticut Yankee, Heber C. Kimball (since deceased), a saint of high degree

and a mighty man of commerce. We saw the "Tithing-House," and the "Lion House," and I do not know or remember how many more church and government buildings of various kinds and curious names. We flitted hither and thither and enjoyed every hour, and picked up a great deal of useful information and entertaining nonsense, and went to bed at night satisfied.

The second day, we made the acquaintance of Mr. Street (since deceased) and put on white shirts and went and paid a state visit to the king. He seemed a quiet, kindly, easy-mannered, dignified, self-possessed old gentleman of fifty-five or sixty, and had a gentle craft in his eye that probably belonged there. He was very simply dressed and was just taking off a straw hat as we entered. He talked about Utah, and the Indians, and Nevada, and general American matters and questions, with our secretary and certain government officials who came with us. But he never paid any attention to me, notwithstanding I made several attempts to "draw him out" on federal politics and his high handed attitude toward Congress. I thought some of the things I said were rather fine. But he merely looked around at me, at distant intervals, something as I

BRIGHAM YOUNG.

have seen a benignant old cat look around to see which kitten was meddling with her tail. By and by I subsided into an indignant silence, and so sat until the end, hot and flushed, and execrating him in my heart for an ignorant savage. But he was calm. His conversation with those gentlemen flowed on as sweetly and peacefully and musically as any summer brook. When the audience was ended and we were retiring from the presence, he put his hand on my head, beamed down on me in an admiring way and said to my brother:

"Ah—your child, I presume? Boy, or girl?"

8†

CHAPTER XIV.

MR. STREET was very busy with his telegraphic matters —and considering that he had eight or nine hundred miles of rugged, snowy, uninhabited mountains, and waterless, treeless, melancholy deserts to traverse with his wire, it was natural and needful that he should be as busy as possible. He could not go comfortably along and cut his poles by the road-side, either, but they had to be hauled by ox teams across those exhausting deserts—and it was two days' journey from water to water, in one or two of them. Mr. Street's contract was a vast work, every way one looked at it; and yet to comprehend what the vague words "eight hundred miles of rugged mountains and dismal deserts" mean, one must go over the ground in person—pen and ink descriptions cannot convey the dreary reality to the reader. And after all, Mr. S.'s mightiest difficulty turned out to be one which he had never taken into the account at all. Unto Mormons he had sub-let the hardest and heaviest half of his great undertaking, and all of a sudden they concluded that they were going to make little or nothing, and so they tranquilly threw their poles overboard in mountain or desert, just as it happened when they took the notion, and drove home and went about their customary business! They were under written contract to Mr. Street, but they did not care anything for that. They said they would "admire" to see a "Gentile" force a Mormon to fulfil a losing contract in Utah! And they made themselves very merry over the matter. Street said—for it was he that told us these things:

"I was in dismay. I was under heavy bonds to complete my contract in a given time, and this disaster looked very much like ruin. It was an astounding thing; it was such a wholly unlooked-for difficulty, that I was entirely nonplussed. I am a business man—have always been a business man—do not know anything *but* business—and so you can imagine how like being struck by lightning it was to find myself in a country where *written contracts were worthless!*—that main security, that sheet-anchor, that absolute necessity, of business. My confidence left me. There was no use in making new contracts—that was plain. I talked with first one prominent citizen and then another. They all sympathized with me, first rate, but they did not know how to help me. But at last a Gentile said, 'Go to Brigham Young!—these small fry cannot do you any good.' I did not think much of the idea, for if the *law* could not help me, what could an individual do who had not even anything to do with either making the laws or executing them? He might be a very good patriarch of a church and preacher in its tabernacle, but something sterner than religion and moral suasion was needed to handle a hundred refractory, half-civilized sub-contractors. But what was a man to do? I thought if Mr. Young could not do anything else, he might probably be able to give me some advice and a valuable hint or two, and so I went straight to him and laid the whole case before him. He said very little, but he showed strong interest all the way through. He examined all the papers in detail, and whenever there seemed anything like a hitch, either in the papers or my statement, he would go back and take up the thread and follow it patiently out to an intelligent and satisfactory result. Then he made a list of the contractors' names. Finally he said:

"'Mr. Street, this is all perfectly plain. These contracts are strictly and legally drawn, and are duly signed and certified. These men manifestly entered into them with their eyes open. I see no fault or flaw anywhere.'

"Then Mr. Young turned to a man waiting at the other

end of the room and said: 'Take this list of names to So-and-so, and tell him to have these men here at such-and-such an hour.'

"They were there, to the minute.   So was I.   Mr. Young

THE CONTRACTORS BEFORE THE KING.

asked them a number of questions, and their answers made my statement good.   Then he said to them:

" 'You signed these contracts and assumed these obligations of your own free will and accord?'

" 'Yes.'

" 'Then carry them out to the letter, if it makes paupers of you!   Go!'

"And they *did* go, too!   They are strung across the deserts now, working like bees.   And I never hear a word out of them.   There is a batch of governors, and judges, and other officials here, shipped from Washington, and they maintain the semblance of a republican form of government—but the petrified truth is that Utah is an absolute monarchy and Brigham Young is king!"

Mr. Street was a fine man, and I believe his story. I knew him well during several years afterward in San Francisco.

Our stay in Salt Lake City amounted to only two days, and therefore we had no time to make the customary inquisition into the workings of polygamy and get up the usual

I WAS TOUCHED.

statistics and deductions preparatory to calling the attention of the nation at large once more to the matter. I had the will to do it. With the gushing self-sufficiency of youth I was feverish to plunge in headlong and achieve a great reform here—until I saw the Mormon women. Then I was touched. My heart was wiser than my head. It warmed toward these poor, ungainly and pathetically "homely" creatures, and as I turned to hide the generous moisture in my eyes, I said, "No—the man that marries one of them has done an act of Christian charity which entitles him to the kindly applause of mankind, not their harsh censure—and the man that marries sixty of them has done a deed of open-handed generosity so sublime that the nations should stand uncovered in his presence and worship in silence." *

* For a brief sketch of Mormon history, and the noted Mountain Meadow massacre, see Appendices A and B.

CHAPTER XV.

IT is a luscious country for thrilling evening stories about assassinations of intractable Gentiles. I cannot easily conceive of anything more cosy than the night in Salt Lake which we spent in a Gentile den, smoking pipes and listening to tales of how Burton galloped in among the pleading and defenceless "Morisites" and shot them down, men and women, like so many dogs. And how Bill Hickman, a Destroying Angel, shot Drown and Arnold dead for bringing suit against him for a debt. And how Porter Rockwell did this and that dreadful thing. And how heedless people often come to Utah and make remarks about Brigham, or polygamy, or some other sacred matter, and the very next morning at daylight such parties are sure to be found lying up some back alley, contentedly waiting for the hearse.

And the next most interesting thing is to sit and listen to these Gentiles talk about polygamy; and how some portly old frog of an elder, or a bishop, marries a girl—likes her, marries her sister—likes her, marries another sister—likes her, takes another—likes her, marries her mother—likes her, marries her father, grandfather, great grandfather, and then comes back hungry and asks for more. And how the pert young thing of eleven will chance to be the favorite wife and her own venerable grandmother have to rank away down toward D 4 in their mutual husband's esteem, and have to sleep in the kitchen, as like as not. And how this dreadful sort of thing, this hiving together in one foul nest of mother and daughters, and the making a young daughter superior to her own mother in rank and authority, are things which Mormon women submit to because their religion teaches them that

FAVORITE WIFE AND D 4.

the more wives a man has on earth, and the more children he rears, the higher the place they will all have in the world to come—and the warmer, maybe, though they do not seem to say anything about that.

According to these Gentile friends of ours, Brigham Young's harem contains twenty or thirty wives. They said that some of them had grown old and gone out of active service, but were comfortably housed and cared for in the henery —or the Lion House, as it is strangely named. Along with each wife were her children—fifty altogether. The house was perfectly quiet and orderly, when the children were still. They all took their meals in one room, and a happy and home-like sight it was pronounced to be. None of our party got an opportunity to take dinner with Mr. Young, but a Gentile by the name of Johnson professed to have enjoyed a sociable breakfast in the Lion House. He gave a preposterous account of the "calling of the roll," and other preliminaries, and the carnage that ensued when the buckwheat cakes came in. But he embellished rather too much. He said that Mr. Young told him several smart sayings of certain of his "two-year-olds," observing with some pride that for many years he had been the heaviest contributor in that line to one of the Eastern magazines ; and then he wanted to show Mr. Johnson one of the pets that had said the last good thing, but he could not

NEEDED MARKING.

find the child. He searched the faces of the children in detail, but could not decide which one it was. Finally he gave it up with a sigh and said:

"I thought I would know the little cub again but I don't." Mr. Johnson said further, that Mr. Young observed that life was a sad, sad thing—" because the joy of every new marriage a man contracted was so apt to be blighted by the inopportune funeral of a less recent bride." And Mr. Johnson said that while he and Mr. Young were pleasantly conversing in private, one of the Mrs. Youngs came in and demanded a breast-pin, remarking that she had found out that he had been giving a breast-pin to No. 6, and *she*, for one, did not propose to let this partiality go on without making a satisfactory amount of trouble about it. Mr. Young reminded her that there was a stranger present. Mrs. Young said that if the state of things inside the house was not agreeable to the stranger, he could find room outside. Mr. Young promised the breast-pin, and she went away. But in a minute or two another Mrs. Young came in and demanded a breast-pin. Mr. Young began a remonstrance, but Mrs. Young cut him short. She said No. 6 had got one, and No. 11 was promised one, and it was " no use for him to try to impose on her—she hoped she knew her rights." He gave his promise, and she went. And presently three Mrs. Youngs entered in a body and opened on their husband a tempest of tears, abuse, and entreaty. They had heard all about No. 6, No. 11, and No. 14. Three more breast-pins were promised. They were hardly gone when nine more Mrs. Youngs filed into the presence, and a new tempest burst forth and raged round about the prophet and his guest. Nine breast-pins were promised, and the weird sisters filed out again. And in came eleven more, weeping and wailing and gnashing their teeth. Eleven promised breast-pins purchased peace once more.

" That is a specimen," said Mr. Young. " You see how it is. You see what a life I lead. A man *can't* be wise all the time. In a heedless moment I gave my darling No. 6—excuse my calling her thus, as her other name has escaped me for the moment—a breast-pin. It was only worth twenty-five dollars —that is, *apparently* that was its whole cost—but its ultimate cost was inevitably bound to be a good deal more. You yourself have seen it climb up to six hundred and fifty dollars— and alas, even that is not the end! For I have wives all over this Territory of Utah. I have dozens of wives whose *numbers*, even, I do not know without looking in the family Bible. They are scattered far and wide among the mountains and valleys of my realm. And mark you, every solitary one of them will hear of this wretched breast pin, and every last one of them will have one or die. No. 6's breast pin will cost me twenty-five hundred dollars before I see the end of it. And these creatures will compare these pins together, and if one is a shade finer than the rest, they will all be thrown on my hands, and I will have to order a new lot to keep peace in the family. Sir, you probably did not know it, but all the time you were present with my children your every movement was watched by vigilant servitors of mine. If you had offered to give a child a dime, or a stick of candy, or any trifle of the kind, you would have been snatched out of the house instantly, provided it could be done before your gift left your hand. Otherwise it would be absolutely necessary for you to make an exactly similar gift to all my children—and knowing by experience the importance of the thing, I would have stood by and seen to it myself that you did it, and did it thoroughly. Once a gentleman gave one of my children a tin whistle—a veritable invention of Satan, sir, and one which I have an unspeakable horror of, and so would you if you had eighty or ninety children in your house. But the deed was done—the man escaped. I knew what the result was going to be, and I thirsted for vengeance. I ordered out a flock of Destroying Angels, and they hunted the man far into the fastnesses of the Nevada mountains. But they never caught him. I am not cruel, sir—I am not vindictive except when sorely outraged—but if I had caught him, sir, so help me Joseph Smith, I would have locked him into the nursery till the brats whistled him to death. By the slaughtered body of St. Parley Pratt (whom God assoil !) there was never anything on this earth like it ! *I* knew who gave the whistle to the child, but I could not make those jealous mothers believe me. They believed *I* did it, and the result was just what any man of reflection could have foreseen : I had to order a hundred and ten whistles—I think we had a hundred and ten children in the house then, but some of them are off at college now—I had to order a hundred and ten of those shrieking things, and I wish I may never speak another word if we didn't have to talk on our fingers entirely, from that time forth until the children got tired of the whistles. And if ever another man gives a whistle to a child of mine and I get my hands on him, I will hang him higher than Haman! That is the word with the bark on it! Shade of Nephi! *You* don't know anything about married life. I am rich, and everybody knows it. I am benevolent, and everybody takes advantage of it. I have a strong fatherly instinct and all the foundlings are foisted on me. Every time a woman wants to do well by her darling, she puzzles her brain to cipher out some scheme for getting

"A REMARKABLE RESEMBLANCE."

it into my hands. Why, sir, a woman came here once with a child of a curious lifeless sort of complexion (and so had the woman), and swore that the child was mine and she my wife—

that I had married her at such-and-such a time in such-and-such a place, but she had forgotten her number, and of course I could not remember her name. Well, sir, she called my attention to the fact that the child looked like me, and really it did seem to resemble me—a common thing in the Territory—and, to cut the story short, I put it in my nursery, and she left. And by the ghost of Orson Hyde, when they came to wash the paint off that child it was an Injun! Bless my soul, you don't know anything about married life. It is a perfect dog's life, sir—a perfect dog's life. You can't economize. It isn't possible. I have tried keeping one set of bridal attire for all occasions. But it is of no use. First you'll marry a combination of calico and consumption that's as thin as a rail, and next you'll get a creature that's nothing more than the dropsy in disguise, and then you've got to eke out that bridal dress with an old balloon. That is the way it goes. And think of the wash-bill—(excuse these tears)—nine hundred and eighty-four pieces a week! No, sir, there is no such a thing as economy in a family like mine. Why, just the one item of cradles—think of it! And vermifuge! Soothing syrup! Teething rings! And 'papa's watches' for the babies to play with! And things to scratch the furniture with! And lucifer matches for them to eat, and pieces of glass to cut themselves with! The item of glass alone would support *your* family, I venture to say, sir. Let me scrimp and squeeze all I can, I still can't get ahead as fast as I feel I ought to, with my opportunities. Bless you, sir, at a time when I had seventy-two wives in this house, I groaned under the pressure of keeping thousands of dollars tied up in seventy-two bedsteads when the money ought to have been out at interest; and I just sold out the whole stock, sir, at a sacrifice, and built a bedstead seven feet long and ninety-six feet wide. But it was a failure, sir. I could *not* sleep. It appeared to me that the whole seventy-two women snored at once. The roar was deafening. And then the danger of it! That was what I was looking at. They would all draw in their breath at once, and you could actually see the walls of the house suck in—and then they would all exhale their breath at once, and you could see the walls swell out, and strain, and hear the rafters crack, and the shingles grind together. My friend, take an old man's advice, and *don't* encumber yourself with a large family—mind, I tell you, don't do it. In a small family, and in a small family only, you will find that comfort and that peace of mind which are the best at last of the blessings this world is able to afford us, and for the lack of which no accumulation of wealth, and no acquisition of fame, power, and greatness can ever compensate us. Take my word for it, ten or eleven wives is all you need—never go over it."

THE FAMILY BEDSTEAD.

Some instinct or other made me set this Johnson down as being unreliable. And yet he was a very entertaining person, and I doubt if some of the information he gave us could have been acquired from any other source. He was a pleasant contrast to those reticent Mormons.

CHAPTER XVI.

ALL men have heard of the Mormon Bible, but few except the "elect" have seen it, or, at least, taken the trouble to read it. I brought away a copy from Salt Lake. The book is a curiosity to me, it is such a pretentious affair, and yet so "slow," so sleepy; such an insipid mess of inspiration. It is chloroform in print. If Joseph Smith composed this book, the act was a miracle—keeping awake while he did it was, at any rate. If he, according to tradition, merely translated it from certain ancient and mysteriously-engraved plates of copper, which he declares he found under a stone, in an out-of-the-way locality, the work of translating was equally a miracle, for the same reason.

The book seems to be merely a prosy detail of imaginary history, with the Old Testament for a model; followed by a tedious plagiarism of the New Testament. The author labored to give his words and phrases the quaint, old-fashioned sound and structure of our King James's translation of the Scriptures; and the result is a mongrel—half modern glibness, and half ancient simplicity and gravity. The latter is awkward and constrained; the former natural, but grotesque by the contrast. Whenever he found his speech growing too modern—which was about every sentence or two—he ladled in a few such Scriptural phrases as " exceeding sore," " and it came to pass," etc., and made things satisfactory again. " And it came to pass" was his pet.   If he had left that out, his Bible would have been only a pamphlet.

The title-page reads as follows:

THE BOOK OF MORMON: AN ACCOUNT WRITTEN BY THE HAND OF MOR-
MON, UPON PLATES TAKEN FROM THE PLATES OF NEPHI.

Wherefore it is an abridgment of the record of the people of Nephi, and also of the Lamanites; written to the Lamanites, who are a remnant of the House of Israel; and also to Jew and Gentile; written by way of commandment, and also by the spirit of prophecy and of revelation. Written and sealed up, and hid up unto the Lord, that they might not be destroyed; to come forth by the gift and power of God unto the interpretation thereof; sealed by the hand of Moroni, and hid up unto the Lord, to come forth in due time by the way of Gentile; the interpretation thereof by the gift of God. An abridgment taken from the Book of Ether also; which is a record of the people of Jared; who were scattered at the time the Lord confounded the language of the people when they were building a tower to get to Heaven.

"Hid up" is good.   And so is "wherefore"—though why "wherefore"?   Any other word would have answered as well —though in truth it would not have sounded so Scriptural.

Next comes

THE TESTIMONY OF THREE WITNESSES.

Be it known unto all nations, kindreds, tongues, and people unto whom this work shall come, that we, through the grace of God the Father, and our Lord Jesus Christ, have seen the plates which contain this record, which is a record of the people of Nephi, and also of the Lamanites, their brethren, and also of the people of Jared, who came from the tower of which hath been spoken; and we also know that they have been translated by the gift and power of God, for His voice hath declared it unto us; wherefore we know of a surety that the work is true. And we also testify that we have seen the engravings which are upon the plates; and they have been shown unto us by the power of God, and not of man. And we declare with words of soberness, that an angel of God came down from heaven, and he brought and laid before our eyes, that we beheld and saw the plates, and the engravings thereon; and we know that it is by the grace of God the Father, and our Lord Jesus Christ, that we beheld and bear record that these things are true; and it is marvellous in our eyes; nevertheless the voice of the Lord commanded us that we should bear record of it; wherefore, to be obedient unto the commandments of God, we bear testimony of these things. And we know that if we are faithful in Christ, we shall rid our garments of the blood of all men, and be found spotless before the judgment-seat of Christ, and shall dwell with Him eternally in the heavens. And the honor be to the Father, and to the Son, and to the Holy Ghost, which is one God. Amen.

OLIVER COWDERY,
DAVID WHITMER,
MARTIN HARRIS.

Some people have to have a world of evidence before they can come anywhere in the neighborhood of believing anything; but for me, when a man tells me that he has " seen the engravings which are upon the plates," and not only that, but an angel was there at the time, and saw him see them, and probably took his receipt for it, I am very far on the road to conviction, no matter whether I ever heard of that man before or not, and even if I do not know the name of the angel, or his nationality either.

Next is this:

AND ALSO THE TESTIMONY OF EIGHT WITNESSES.

Be it known unto all nations, kindreds, tongues, and people unto whom this work shall come, that Joseph Smith, Jr., the translator of this work, has shown unto us the plates of which hath been spoken, which have the appearance of gold; and as many of the leaves as the said Smith has translated, we did handle with our hands; and we also saw the engravings thereon, all of which has the appearance of ancient work, and of curious workmanship. And this we bear record with words of soberness, that the said Smith has shown unto us, for we have seen and hefted, and know of a surety that the said Smith has got the plates of which we have spoken. And we give our names unto the world, to witness unto the world that which we have seen; and we lie not, God bearing witness of it.

CHRISTIAN WHITMER,	HIRAM PAGE,
JACOB WHITMER,	JOSEPH SMITH, SR.,
PETER WHITMER, JR.,	HYRUM SMITH,
JOHN WHITMER,	SAMUEL H. SMITH.

And when I am far on the road to conviction, and eight men, be they grammatical or otherwise, come forward and tell me that they have seen the plates too; and not only seen

9†

those plates but "hefted" them, I *am* convinced. I could not feel more satisfied and at rest if the entire Whitmer family had testified.

The Mormon Bible consists of fifteen "books"—being the books of Jacob, Enos, Jarom, Omni, Mosiah, Zeniff, Alma, Helaman, Ether, Moroni, two "books" of Mormon, and three of Nephi.

In the first book of Nephi is a plagiarism of the Old Testament, which gives an account of the exodus from Jerusalem of the "children of Lehi"; and it goes on to tell of their wanderings in the wilderness; during eight years, and their supernatural protection by one of their number, a party by the name of Nephi. They finally reached the land of "Bountiful," and camped by the sea. After they had remained there "for the space of many days"—which is more Scriptural than definite—Nephi was commanded from on high to build a ship wherein to "carry the people across the waters." He travestied Noah's ark—but he obeyed orders in the matter of the plan. He finished the ship *in a single day*, while his brethren stood by and made fun of it—and of him, too—"saying, our brother is a fool, for he thinketh that he can build a ship." They did not wait for the timbers to dry, but the whole tribe or nation sailed the next day. Then a bit of genuine nature cropped out, and is revealed by outspoken Nephi with Scriptural frankness—they all got on a spree! They, "and also their wives, began to make themselves merry, insomuch that they began to dance, and to sing, and to speak with much rudeness; yea, they were lifted up unto exceeding rudeness."

Nephi tried to stop these scandalous proceedings; but they tied him neck and heels, and went on with their lark. But observe how Nephi the prophet circumvented them by the aid of the invisible powers:

And it came to pass that after they had bound me, insomuch that I could not move, the compass, which had been prepared of the Lord, did cease to work; wherefore, they knew not whither they should steer the ship, inso-much that there arose a great storm, yea, a great and terrible tempest, and we were driven back upon the waters for the space of three days; and they began to be frightened exceedingly, lest they should be drowned in the sea; nevertheless they did not loose me. And on the fourth day, which we had been driven back, the tempest began to be exceeding sore.

And it came to pass that we were about to be swallowed up in the depths of the sea.

Then they untied him.

And it came to pass after they had loosed me, behold, I took the compass, and it did work whither I desired it. And it came to pass that I prayed unto the Lord; and after I had prayed, the winds did cease, and the storm did cease, and there was a great calm.

THE MIRACULOUS COMPASS.

Equipped with their compass, these ancients appear to have had the advantage of Noah.

Their voyage was toward a "promised land"—the only name they give it. They reached it in safety.

Polygamy is a recent feature in the Mormon religion, and was added by Brigham Young after Joseph Smith's death. Before that, it was regarded as an "abomination." This verse from the Mormon Bible occurs in Chapter II. of the book of Jacob:

> For behold, thus saith the Lord, this people begin to wax in iniquity; they understand not the Scriptures; for they seek to excuse themselves in committing whoredoms, because of the things which were written concerning David, and Solomon his son. Behold, David and Solomon truly had many wives and concubines, which thing was abominable before me, saith the Lord; wherefore, thus saith the Lord, I have led this people forth out of the land of Jerusalem, by the power of mine arm, that I might raise up unto me a righteous branch from the fruit of the loins of Joseph. Wherefore, I the Lord God, will not suffer that this people shall do like unto them of old.

However, the project failed—or at least the modern Mormon end of it—for Brigham "suffers" it. This verse is from the same chapter:

> Behold, the Lamanites your brethren, whom ye hate, because of their filthiness and the cursings which hath come upon their skins, are more righteous than you; for they have not forgotten the commandment of the Lord, which was given unto our fathers, that they should have, save it were one wife; and concubines they should have none.

The following verse (from Chapter IX. of the Book of Nephi) appears to contain information not familiar to everybody:

> And now it came to pass that when Jesus had ascended into heaven, the multitude did disperse, and every man did take his wife and his children, and did return to his own home.
>
> And it came to pass that on the morrow, when the multitude was gathered together, behold, Nephi and his brother whom he had raised from the dead, whose name was Timothy, and also his son, whose name was Jonas, and also Mathoni, and Mathonihah, his brother, and Kumen, and Kumenonhi, and Jeremiah, and Shemnon, and Jonas, and Zedekiah, and Isaiah; now these were the names of the disciples whom Jesus had chosen.

In order that the reader may observe how much more grandeur and picturesqueness (as seen by these Mormon twelve) accompanied one of the tenderest episodes in the life of our Saviour than other eyes seem to have been aware of, I quote the following from the same " book "—Nephi :

And it came to pass that Jesus spake unto them, and bade them arise. And they arose from the earth, and He said unto them, Blessed are ye because of your faith. And now behold, My joy is full. And when He had said these words, He wept, and the multitude bear record of it, and He took their little children, one by one, and blessed them, and prayed unto the Father for them. And when He had done this He wept again, and He spake unto the multitude, and saith unto them, Behold your little ones. And as they looked to behold, they cast their eyes toward heaven, and they saw the heavens open, and they saw angels descending out of heaven as it were, in the midst of fire ; and they came down and encircled those little ones about, and they were encircled about with fire ; and the angels did minister unto them, and the multitude did see and hear and bear record ; and they know that their record is true, for they all of them did see and hear, every man for himself ; and they were in number about two thousand and five hundred souls ; and they did consist of men, women, and children.

And what else would they be likely to consist of?

The Book of Ether is an incomprehensible medley of " history," much of it relating to battles and sieges among peoples whom the reader has possibly never heard of ; and who inhabited a country which is not set down in the geography. There was a King with the remarkable name of Coriantumr, and he warred with Shared, and Lib, and Shiz, and others, in the "plains of Heshlon" ; and the " valley of Gilgal" ; and the "wilderness of Akish" ; and the "land of Moran" ; and the " plains of Agosh" ; and " Ogath," and " Ramah," and the " land of Corihor," and the "hill Comnor," by "the waters of Ripliancum," etc., etc., etc. " And it came to pass," after a deal of fighting, that Coriantumr, upon making calculation of his losses, found that " there had been slain two millions of mighty men, and also their wives and their children "—say 5,000,000 or 6,000,000 in all—" and he began to sorrow in his heart." Unquestionably it was time. So he wrote to Shiz, asking a cessation of hostilities, and offering to give up his kingdom to save his people. Shiz declined, except upon condition that Coriantumr would come and let him cut his head off first—a thing which Coriantumr would not do. Then there was more fighting for a season ; then *four years* were devoted to gathering the forces for a final struggle—after which ensued a battle, which, I take it, is the most remarkable set forth in history,—except, perhaps, that of the Kilkenny cats, which it resembles in some respects. This is the account of the gathering and the battle :

7. And it came to pass that they did gather together all the people, upon all the face of the land, who had not been slain, save it was Ether. And it came to pass that Ether did behold all the doings of the people ; and he beheld that the people who were for Coriantumr, were gathered together to the army of Coriantumr; and the people who were for Shiz, were gathered together to the army of Shiz ; wherefore they were for the space of four years gathering together the people, that they might get all who were upon the face of the land, and that they might receive all the strength which it was possible that they could receive. And it came to pass that when they were all gathered together, every one to the army which he would, with their wives and their children; both men, women, and children being armed with weapons of war, having shields, and breast-plates, and head-plates, and being clothed after the manner of war, they did march forth one against another, to battle ; and they fought all that day, and conquered not. And it came to pass that when it was night they were weary, and retired to their camps ; and after they had retired to their camps, they took up a howling and a lamentation for the loss of the slain of their people ; and so great were their cries, their howlings and lamentations, that it did rend the air exceedingly. And it came to pass that on the morrow they did go again to battle, and great and terrible was that day ; nevertheless they conquered not, and when the night came again, they did rend the air with their cries, and their howlings, and their mournings, for the loss of the slain of their people.

8. And it came to pass that Coriantumr wrote again an epistle unto Shiz, desiring that he would not come again to battle, but that he would take the kingdom, and spare the lives of the people. But behold, the Spirit of the Lord had ceased striving with them, and Satan had full power over the hearts of the people, for they were given up unto the hardness of their hearts, and the blindness of their minds that they might be destroyed; wherefore they went again to battle. And it came to pass that they fought all that day, and when the night came they slept upon their swords ; and on the morrow they fought even until the night came ; and when the night came they were drunken with anger, even as a man who is drunken with

wine; and they slept again upon their swords; and on the morrow they fought again; and when the night came they had all fallen by the sword save it were fifty and two of the people of Coriantumr, and sixty and nine of the people of Shiz. And it came to pass that they slept upon their swords that night, and on the morrow they fought again, and they contended in their mights with their swords, and with their shields, all that day; and when the night came there were thirty and two of the people of Shiz, and twenty and seven of the people of Coriantumr.

9. And it came to pass that they ate and slept, and prepared for death on the morrow. And they were large and mighty men, as to the strength of men. And it came to pass that they fought for the space of three hours, and they fainted with the loss of blood. And it came to pass that when the men of Coriantumr had received sufficient strength, that they could walk, they were about to flee for their lives, but behold, Shiz arose, and also his men, and he swore in his wrath that he would slay Coriantumr, or he would perish by the sword: wherefore he did pursue them, and on the morrow he did overtake them; and they fought again with the sword. And it came to pass that when they had all fallen by the sword, save it were Coriantumr and Shiz, behold Shiz had fainted with loss of blood. And it came to pass that when Coriantumr had leaned upon his sword, that he rested a little, he smote off the head of Shiz. And it came to pass that after he had smote off the head of Shiz, that Shiz raised upon his hands and fell; and after that he had struggled for breath, he died. And it came to pass that Coriantumr fell to the earth, and became as if he had no life. And the Lord spake unto Ether, and said unto him, go forth. And he went forth, and beheld that the words of the Lord had all been fulfilled; and he finished his record; and the hundredth part I have not written.

It seems a pity he did not finish, for after all his dreary former chapters of commonplace, he stopped just as he was in danger of becoming interesting.

The Mormon Bible is rather stupid and tiresome to read, but there is nothing vicious in its teachings. Its code of morals is unobjectionable—it is " smouched " * from the New Testament and no credit given.

*Milton.

CHAPTER XVII.

AT the end of our two days' sojourn, we left Great Salt Lake City hearty and well fed and happy—physically superb but not so very much wiser, as regards the "Mormon question," than we were when we arrived, perhaps. We had a deal more "information" than we had before, of course, but we did not know what portion of it was reliable and what was not—for it all came from acquaintances of a day—strangers, strictly speaking. We were told, for instance, that the dreadful "Mountain Meadows Massacre" was the work of the Indians entirely, and that the Gentiles had meanly tried to fasten it upon the Mormons; we were told, likewise, that the Indians were to blame, partly, and partly the Mormons; and we were told, likewise, and just as positively, that the Mormons were almost if not wholly and completely responsible for that most treacherous and pitiless butchery. We got the story in all these different shapes, but it was not till several years afterward that Mrs. Waite's book, "The Mormon Prophet," came out with Judge Cradlebaugh's trial of the accused parties in it and revealed the truth that the latter version was the correct one and that the Mormons *were* the assassins. All our "information" had three sides to it, and so I gave up the idea that I could settle the "Mormon question" in two days. Still I have seen newspaper correspondents do it in one.

I left Great Salt Lake a good deal confused as to what state of things existed there—and sometimes even questioning in my own mind whether a state of things existed there at all

or not. But presently I remembered with a lightening sense
of relief that we had learned two or three trivial things there
which we could be certain of; and so the two days were not
wholly lost. For instance, we had learned that we were at last
in a pioneer land, in absolute and tangible reality. The high

THREE SIDES TO A QUESTION.

prices charged for trifles were eloquent of high freights and
bewildering distances of freightage. In the east, in those days,
the smallest moneyed denomination was a penny and it represented the smallest purchasable quantity of any commodity.
West of Cincinnati the smallest coin in use was the silver five-
cent piece and no smaller quantity of an article could be
bought than "five cents' worth." In Overland City the lowest coin appeared to be the ten-cent piece; but in Salt Lake
there did not seem to be any money in circulation smaller
than a quarter, or any smaller quantity purchasable of any
commodity than twenty-five cents' worth. We had always
been used to half dimes and "five cents' worth" as the minimum of financial negotiations; but in Salt Lake if one wanted
a cigar, it was a quarter; if he wanted a chalk pipe, it was a

quarter; if he wanted a peach, or a candle, or a newspaper, or a shave, or a little Gentile whiskey to rub on his corns to arrest indigestion and keep him from having the toothache, twenty-five cents was the price, every time. When we looked at the shot-bag of silver, now and then, we seemed to be

N. York.   St. Louis.   Overland City.   Salt Lake City.

1 Cent.   5 Cents.   10 Cents.   25 Cents.

RESULT OF HIGH FREIGHTS.

wasting our substance in riotous living, but if we referred to the expense account we could see that we had not been doing anything of the kind. But people easily get reconciled to big money and big prices, and fond and vain of both—it is a descent to little coins and cheap prices that is hardest to bear and slowest to take hold upon one's toleration. After a month's acquaintance with the twenty-five cent minimum, the average human being is ready to blush every time he thinks of his despicable five-cent days. How sunburnt with blushes I used to get in gaudy Nevada, every time I thought of my first financial experience in Salt Lake. It was on this wise (which is a favorite expression of great authors, and a very neat one, too, but I never hear anybody *say* on this wise when they are talking). A young half-breed with a complexion like a yellow-jacket asked me if I would have my boots blacked. It was at the Salt Lake House the morning after we arrived. I said yes, and he blacked them. Then I handed him a silver five-cent piece, with the benevolent air of a person who is conferring wealth and blessedness upon poverty and suffering. The yellow-jacket took it with what I judged to be suppressed emotion, and laid it reverently down in the middle of his broad hand. Then he began to contemplate it, much as a philosopher contemplates a gnat's ear in the ample field of his microscope.   Several mountaineers, teamsters, stage-drivers, etc., drew near and dropped into the tableau and fell to surveying the money with that attractive indifference to formality which is noticeable in the hardy pioneer.   Presently the yellow-jacket handed the half dime back to me and told me I ought to keep my money in my pocket-book instead of in my soul, and then I wouldn't get it cramped and shriveled up so!

What a roar of vulgar laughter there was! I destroyed the mongrel reptile on the spot, but I smiled and smiled all the time I was detaching his scalp, for the remark he made *was* good for an "Injun."

Yes, we had learned in Salt Lake to be charged great

A SHRIVELED QUARTER.

prices without letting the inward shudder appear on the surface—for even already we had overheard and noted the tenor of conversations among drivers, conductors, and hostlers, and finally among citizens of Salt Lake, until we were well aware that these superior beings despised "emigrants."   We permitted no tell-tale shudders and winces in our countenances, for we wanted to seem pioneers, or Mormons, half-breeds, teamsters, stage-drivers, Mountain Meadow assassins—anything in the world that the plains and Utah respected and admired— but we were wretchedly ashamed of being "emigrants," and sorry enough that we had white shirts and could not swear in the presence of ladies without looking the other way.

And many a time in Nevada, afterwards, we had occasion

to remember with humiliation that we were "emigrants," and consequently a low and inferior sort of creatures. Perhaps the reader has visited Utah, Nevada, or California, even in these latter days, and while communing with himself upon the sorrowful banishment of those countries from what he considers " the world," has had his wings clipped by finding that *he* is the one to be pitied, and that there are entire populations around him ready and willing to do it for him—yea, who

AN OBJECT OF PITY.

are complacently doing it for him already, wherever he steps his foot. Poor thing, they are making fun of his hat; and the cut of his New York coat; and his conscientiousness about his grammar; and his feeble profanity; and his consumingly ludicrous ignorance of ores, shafts, tunnels, and other things which he never saw before, and never felt enough interest in to read about. And all the time that he is thinking what a sad fate it is to be exiled to that far country, that lonely land, the citizens around him are looking down on him with a blighting compassion because he is an "emigrant" instead of that proudest and blessedest creature that exists on all the earth, a " FORTY-NINER."

The accustomed coach life began again, now, and by midnight it almost seemed as if we never had been out of our snuggery among the mail sacks at all. We had made one alteration, however. We had provided enough bread, boiled ham and hard boiled eggs to last double the six hundred miles of staging we had still to do.

And it was comfort in those succeeding days to sit up and contemplate the majestic panorama of mountains and valleys spread out below us and eat ham and hard boiled

eggs while our spiritual natures revelled alternately in rainbows, thunderstorms, and peerless sunsets.   Nothing helps
scenery like ham and eggs.   Ham and eggs, and after these a
pipe—an old, rank, delicious pipe—ham and eggs and scenery,
a "down grade," a flying coach, a fragrant pipe and a contented heart—these make happiness.   It is what all the ages
have struggled for.

CHAPTER XVIII.

A T eight in the morning we reached the remnant and ruin of what had been the important military station of "Camp Floyd," some forty-five or fifty miles from Salt Lake City. At four P.M. we had doubled our distance and were ninety or a hundred miles from Salt Lake. And now we entered upon one of that species of deserts whose concentrated hideousness shames the diffused and diluted horrors of Sahara —an "*alkali*" desert. For sixty-eight miles there was but one break in it. I do not remember that this was really a break; indeed it seems to me that it was nothing but a watering depot *in the midst* of the stretch of sixty-eight miles. If my memory serves me, there was no well or spring at this place, but the water was hauled there by mule and ox teams from the further side of the desert. There was a stage station there. It was forty-five miles from the beginning of the desert, and twenty-three from the end of it.

We plowed and dragged and groped along, the whole live-long night, and at the end of this uncomfortable twelve hours we finished the forty-five-mile part of the desert and got to the stage station where the imported water was. The sun was just rising. It was easy enough to cross a desert in the night while we were asleep; and it was pleasant to reflect, in the morning, that we in actual person *had* encountered an absolute desert and could always speak knowingly of deserts in presence of the ignorant thenceforward. And it was pleasant also to reflect that this was not an obscure, back country desert, but a very celebrated one, the metropolis itself, as you may say. All this was very well and very comfortable and satisfactory—but now we were to cross a desert in *daylight.* This was fine—novel—romantic—dramatically adventurous— *this*, indeed, was worth living for, worth traveling for! We would write home all about it.

This enthusiasm, this stern thirst for adventure, wilted under the sultry August sun and did not last above one hour. One poor little hour—and then we were ashamed that we had "gushed" so. The poetry was all in the anticipation— there is none in the reality. Imagine a vast, waveless ocean stricken dead and turned to ashes; imagine this solemn waste tufted with ash-dusted sage-bushes; imagine the lifeless silence and solitude that belong to such a place; imagine a coach, creeping like a bug through the midst of this shoreless level, and sending up tumbled volumes of dust as if it were a bug that went by steam; imagine this aching monotony of toiling and plowing kept up hour after hour, and the shore still as far away as ever, apparently; imagine team, driver, coach and passengers so deeply coated with ashes that they are all one colorless color; imagine ash-drifts roosting above moustaches and eyebrows like snow accumulations on boughs and bushes. This is the reality of it.

The sun beats down with dead, blistering, relentless malignity; the perspiration is welling from every pore in man and beast, but scarcely a sign of it finds its way to the surface —it is absorbed before it gets there; there is not the faintest breath of air stirring; there is not a merciful shred of cloud in all the brilliant firmament; there is not a living creature visible in any direction whither one searches the blank level that stretches its monotonous miles on every hand; there is not a sound—not a sigh—not a whisper—not a buzz, or a whir of wings, or distant pipe of bird—not even a sob from the lost souls that doubtless people that dead air. And so the occasional sneezing of the resting mules, and the champing of the bits, grate harshly on the grim stillness, not dissipating the spell but accenting it and making one feel more lonesome and forsaken than before.

The mules, under violent swearing, coaxing and whip-cracking, would make at stated intervals a "spurt," and drag the coach a hundred or may be two hundred yards, stirring up a billowy cloud of dust that rolled back, enveloping the vehicle to the wheel-tops or higher, and making it seem afloat in a fog. Then a rest followed, with the usual sneezing and bit-champing. Then another "spurt" of a hundred yards and another rest at the end of it. All day long we kept this up, without water for the mules and without ever changing the team. At least we kept it up ten hours, which, I take it, is a day, and a pretty honest one, in an alkali desert. It was from four in the morning till two in the afternoon. And it was so hot! and so close! and our water canteens went dry in the middle of the day and we got so thirsty! It was so stupid and tiresome and dull! and the tedious hours did lag and drag and limp along with such a cruel deliberation! It was so trying to give one's watch a good long undisturbed spell and then take it out and find that it had been fooling away the time and not trying to get ahead any! The alkali dust cut through our lips, it persecuted our eyes, it ate through the delicate membranes and made our noses bleed and *kept* them bleeding—and truly and seriously the romance all faded far away and disappeared, and left the desert trip nothing but a harsh reality—a thirsty, sweltering, longing, hateful reality!

Two miles and a quarter an hour for ten hours—that was what we accomplished. It was hard to bring the comprehension away down to such a snail-pace as that, when we had been used to making eight and ten miles an hour. When we reached the station on the farther verge of the desert, we were glad, for the first time, that the dictionary was along, because we never could have found language to tell how glad we were, in any sort of dictionary but an unabridged one with pictures in it. But there could not have been found in a whole library cf dictionaries language sufficient to tell how tired those mules were after their twenty-three mile pull. To try to give the reader an idea of how *thirsty* they were, would be to "gild refined gold or paint the lily."

Somehow, now that it is there, the quotation does not seem to fit—but no matter, let it stay, anyhow. I think it is a graceful and attractive thing, and therefore have tried time and time again to work it in where it *would* fit, but could not succeed. These efforts have kept my mind distracted and ill at ease, and made my narrative seem broken and disjointed, in places. Under these circumstances it seems to me best to leave it in, as above, since this will afford at least a temporary respite from the wear and tear of trying to "lead up" to this really apt and beautiful quotation.

10†

CHAPTER XIX.

ON the morning of the sixteenth day out from St. Joseph we arrived at the entrance of Rocky Canyon, two hundred and fifty miles from Salt Lake. It was along in this wild country somewhere, and far from any habitation of white men, except the stage stations, that we came across the wretchedest type of mankind I have ever seen, up to this writing. I refer to the Goshoot Indians. From what we could see and all we could learn, they are very considerably inferior to even the despised Digger Indians of California; inferior to all races of savages on our continent; inferior to even the Terra del Fuegans; inferior to the Hottentots, and actually inferior in some respects to the Kytches of Africa. Indeed, I have been obliged to look the bulky volumes of Wood's "Uncivilized Races of Men" clear through in order to find a savage tribe degraded enough to take rank with the Goshoots. I find but one people fairly open to that shameful verdict. It is the Bosjesmans (Bushmen) of South Africa. Such of the Goshoots as we saw, along the road and hanging about the stations, were small, lean, "scrawny" creatures; in complexion a dull black like the ordinary American negro; their faces and hands bearing dirt which they had been hoarding and accumulating for months, years, and even generations, according to the age of the proprietor; a silent, sneaking, treacherous looking race; taking note of everything, covertly, like all the other "Noble Red Men" that we (do not) read about, and betraying no sign in their countenances; indolent, everlastingly patient and tireless, like all other Indians; prideless beggars—for if the beggar in-

stinct were left out of an Indian he would not "go," any more
than a clock without a pendulum; hungry, always hungry,
and yet never refusing anything that a hog would eat, though
often eating what a hog would decline; hunters, but having
no higher
ambition
than to kill
and eat jack-
ass rabbits,

GOSHOOT INDIANS HANGING AROUND STATIONS.

crickets and grasshoppers, and embezzle carrion from the buz-
zards and cayotes; savages who, when asked if they have the
common Indian belief in a Great Spirit show a something
which almost amounts to emotion, thinking whiskey is referred
to; a thin, scattering race of almost naked black children, these
Goshoots are, who produce nothing at all, and have no villages,
and no gatherings together into strictly defined tribal communities—a people whose only shelter is a rag cast on a bush
to keep off a portion of the snow, and yet who inhabit one of
the most rocky, wintry, repulsive wastes that our country or
any other can exhibit.

The Bushmen and our Goshoots are manifestly descended
from the self-same gorilla, or kangaroo, or Norway rat, whichever animal-Adam the Darwinians trace them to.

One would as soon·expect the rabbits to fight as the

Goshoots, and yet they used to live off the offal and refuse of the stations a few months and then come some dark night when no mischief was expected, and burn down the buildings and kill the men from ambush as they rushed out.   And once, in the night, they attacked the stage-coach when a District Judge, of Nevada Territory, was the only passenger, and with their first volley of arrows (and a bullet or two) they riddled the stage curtains, wounded a horse or two and mortally wounded the driver.   The latter was full of pluck, and so was his passenger.   At the driver's call Judge Mott swung himself out, clambered to the box and seized the reins of the team, and away they plunged, through the racing mob of skeletons and under a hurtling storm of missiles.   The stricken driver had sunk down on the boot as soon as he was wounded, but had held on to the reins and said he would manage to keep hold of them until relieved.

THE DRIVE FOR LIFE.

And after they were taken from his relaxing grasp, he lay with his head between Judge Mott's feet, and tranquilly gave directions about the road; he said he believed he could live till the miscreants were outrun and left behind, and that if he managed that, the main difficulty would be at an end, and then if the Judge drove so and so (giving directions about bad places in the road, and general course) he would reach the next station without trouble.   The Judge distanced the enemy and at last rattled up to the station and knew that the night's perils were done; but there was no comrade-in-arms for him to rejoice with, for the soldierly driver was dead.

Let us forget that we have been saying harsh things about the Overland drivers, now. The disgust which the Goshoots gave me, a disciple of Cooper and a worshipper of the Red Man—even of the scholarly savages in the "Last of the Mohicans" who are fittingly associated with backwoodsmen who divide each sentence into two equal parts: one part critically grammatical, refined and choice of language, and the other part just such an attempt to talk like a hunter or a mountaineer, as a Broadway clerk might make after eating an edition of Emerson Bennett's works and studying frontier life at the Bowery Theatre a couple of weeks—I say that the nausea which the Goshoots gave me, an Indian worshipper, set me to examining authorities, to see if perchance I had been over-estimating the Red Man while viewing him through the mellow moonshine of romance. The revelations that came were disenchanting. It was curious to see how quickly the paint and tinsel fell away from him and left him treacherous, filthy and repulsive—and how quickly the evidences accumulated that wherever one finds an Indian tribe he has only found Goshoots more or less modified by circumstances and surroundings—but Goshoots, after all. They deserve pity, poor creatures; and they can have mine—at this distance. Nearer by, they never get anybody's.

There is an impression abroad that the Baltimore and Washington Railroad Company and many of its employés are Goshoots; but it is an error. There is only a plausible resemblance, which, while it is apt enough to mislead the ignorant, cannot deceive parties who have contemplated both tribes. But seriously, it was not only poor wit, but very wrong to start the report referred to above; for however innocent the motive may have been, the necessary effect was to injure the reputation of a class who have a hard enough time of it in the pitiless deserts of the Rocky Mountains, Heaven knows! If we cannot find it in our hearts to give those poor naked creatures our Christian sympathy and compassion, in God's name let us at least not throw mud at them.

CHAPTER XX.

ON the seventeenth day we passed the highest mountain peaks we had yet seen, and although the day was very warm the night that followed upon its heels was wintry cold and blankets were next to useless.

On the eighteenth day we encountered the eastward-bound telegraph-constructors at Reese River station and sent a message to his Excellency Gov. Nye at Carson City (distant one hundred and fifty-six miles).

On the nineteenth day we crossed the Great American Desert—forty memorable miles of bottomless sand, into which the coach wheels sunk from six inches to a foot. We worked our passage most of the way across. That is to say, we got out and walked. It was a dreary pull and a long and thirsty one, for we had no water. From one extremity of this desert to the other, the road was white with the bones of oxen and horses. It would hardly be an exaggeration to say that we could have walked the forty miles and set our feet on a bone at every step! The desert was one prodigious graveyard. And the log-chains, wagon tyres, and rotting wrecks of vehicles were almost as thick as the bones. I think we saw log-chains enough rusting there in the desert, to reach across any State in the Union. Do not these relics suggest something of an idea of the fearful suffering and privation the early emigrants to California endured?

At the border of the Desert lies Carson Lake, or The "Sink" of the Carson, a shallow, melancholy sheet of water some eighty or a hundred miles in circumference. Carson River empties into it and is lost—sinks mysteriously into the earth and never appears in the light of the sun again—for the lake has no outlet whatever.

There are several rivers in Nevada, and they all have this mysterious fate. They end in various lakes or "sinks," and that is the last of them. Carson Lake, Humboldt Lake, Walker Lake, Mono Lake, are all great sheets of water without any visible outlet. Water is always flowing into them; none is ever seen to flow out of them, and yet they remain always level full, neither receding nor overflowing. What they do with their surplus is only known to the Creator.

GREELEY'S RIDE.

On the western verge of the Desert we halted a moment at Ragtown. It consisted of one log-house and is not set down on the map.

This reminds me of a circumstance. Just after we left Julesburg, on the Platte, I was sitting with the driver, and he said:

"I can tell you a most laughable thing indeed, if you would like to listen to it. Horace Greeley went over this road once. When he was leaving Carson City he told the driver, Hank Monk, that he had an engagement to lecture at Placerville and was very anxious to go through quick. Hank Monk cracked his whip and started off at an awful pace. The coach bounced up and down in such a terrific way that it jolted the buttons all off of Horace's coat, and finally shot his head clean through the roof of the stage, and then he yelled at Hank Monk and begged him to go easier—said he warn't in as much of a hurry as he was awhile ago. But Hank Monk said, 'Keep your seat, Horace, and I'll get you there on time'— and you bet you he did, too, what was left of him!"

A day or two after that we picked up a Denver man at the cross roads, and he told us a good deal about the country and the Gregory Diggings. He seemed a very entertaining person and a man well posted in the affairs of Colorado. By and by he remarked:

"I can tell you a most laughable thing indeed, if you would like to listen to it. Horace Greeley went over this road once. When he was leaving Carson City he told the driver, Hank Monk, that he had an engagement to lecture at Placerville and was very anxious to go through quick. Hank Monk cracked his whip and started off at an awful pace. The coach bounced up and down in such a terrific way that it jolted the buttons all off of Horace's coat, and finally shot his head clean through the roof of the stage, and then he yelled at Hank Monk and begged him to go easier—said he warn't in as much of a hurry as he was awhile ago. But Hank Monk said, 'Keep your seat, Horace, and I'll get you there on time!'— and you bet you he did, too, what was left of him!"

At Fort Bridger, some days after this, we took on board a cavalry sergeant, a very proper and soldierly person indeed. From no other man during the whole journey, did we gather such a store of concise and well-arranged military information. It was surprising to find in the desolate wilds of our country a man so thoroughly acquainted with everything useful to know in his line of life, and yet of such inferior rank and unpretentious bearing. For as much as three hours we listened to him with unabated interest. Finally he got upon the subject of trans-continental travel, and presently said:

"I can tell you a very laughable thing indeed, if you would like to listen to it. Horace Greeley went over this road once. When he was leaving Carson City he told the driver, Hank Monk, that he had an engagement to lecture at Placerville and was very anxious to go through quick. Hank Monk cracked his whip and started off at an awful pace. The coach bounced up and down in such a terrific way that it jolted the buttons all off of Horace's coat, and finally shot his head clean through the roof of the stage, and then he yelled at Hank Monk and begged him to go easier—said he warn't in as much of a hurry as he was awhile ago. But Hank Monk said, 'Keep your seat, Horace, and I'll get you there on time!'—and you bet you he did, too, what was left of him!"

When we were eight hours out from Salt Lake City a Mormon preacher got in with us at a way station—a gentle, soft-spoken, kindly man, and one whom any stranger would warm to at first sight. I can never forget the pathos that was in his voice as he told, in simple language, the story of his people's wanderings and unpitied sufferings. No pulpit eloquence was ever so moving and so beautiful as this outcast's picture of the first Mormon pilgrimage across the plains, struggling sorrowfully onward to the land of its banishment and marking its desolate way with graves and watering it with tears. His words so wrought upon us that it was a relief to us all when the conversation drifted into a more cheerful channel and the natural features of the curious country we were in came under treatment. One matter after another was pleasantly discussed, and at length the stranger said:

"I can tell you a most laughable thing indeed, if you would like to listen to it. Horace Greeley went over this road once. When he was leaving Carson City he told the driver, Hank Monk, that he had an engagement to lecture in Placerville, and was very anxious to go through quick. Hank Monk cracked his whip and started off at an awful pace. The coach bounced up and down in such a terrific way that it jolted the buttons all off of Horace's coat, and finally shot his head clean through the roof of the stage, and then he yelled at Hank Monk and begged him to go easier—said he warn't in as much of a hurry as he was awhile ago. But Hank Monk said, 'Keep your seat, Horace, and I'll get you there on time!'— and you bet you he did, too, what was left of him!"

Ten miles out of Ragtown we found a poor wanderer who had lain down to die. He had walked as long as he could, but his limbs had failed him at last. Hunger and fatigue had conquered him. It would have been inhuman to leave him there. We paid his fare to Carson and lifted him into the coach. It was some little time before he showed any very decided signs of life; but by dint of chafing him and pouring brandy between his lips we finally brought him to a languid consciousness. Then we fed him a little, and by and by he seemed to comprehend the situation and a grateful light softened his eye. We made his mail-sack bed as comfortable as possible, and constructed a pillow for him with our coats. He seemed very thankful. Then he looked up in our faces, and said in a feeble voice that had a tremble of honest emotion in it:

"Gentlemen, I know not who you are, but you have saved my life; and although I can never be able to repay you for it, I

BOTTLING AN ANECDOTE.

feel that I can at least make one hour of your long journey lighter. I take it you are strangers to this great thoroughfare, but I am entirely familiar with it. In this connection I can tell you a most laughable thing indeed, if you would like to listen to it. Horace Greeley—"

I said, impressively:

"Suffering stranger, proceed at your peril. You see in me the melancholy wreck of a once stalwart and magnificent manhood. What has brought me to this? That thing which you are about to tell. Gradually but surely, that tiresome old anecdote has sapped my strength, undermined my constitution, withered my life. Pity my helplessness. Spare me only just this once, and tell me about young George Washington and his little hatchet for a change."

We were saved. But not so the invalid. In trying to retain the anecdote in his system he strained himself and died in our arms.

I am aware, now, that I ought not to have asked of the sturdiest citizen of all that region, what I asked of that mere shadow of a man; for, after seven years' residence on the Pacific coast, I know that no passenger or driver on the Overland ever corked that anecdote in, when a stranger was by, and survived. Within a period of six years I crossed and recrossed the Sierras between Nevada and California thirteen times by stage and listened to that deathless incident four hundred and eighty-one or eighty-two times. I have the list somewhere. Drivers always told it, conductors told it, landlords told it, chance passengers told it, the very Chinamen and vagrant Indians recounted it. I have had the same driver tell it to me two or three times in the same afternoon. It has come to me in all the multitude of tongues that Babel bequeathed to earth, and flavored with whiskey, brandy, beer, cologne, sozodont, tobacco, garlic, onions, grasshoppers—everything that has a fragrance to it through all the long list of things that are gorged or guzzled by the sons of men. I never have smelt any anecdote as often as I have smelt that one; never have smelt any anecdote that smelt so variegated as that one. And you never could learn to know it by its smell, because every time you thought you had learned the smell of it, it would turn up with a different smell. Bayard Taylor has written about this hoary anecdote, Richardson has published it; so have Jones, Smith, Johnson, Ross Browne, and every other correspondence-inditing being that ever set his foot upon the great overland road anywhere between Julesburg and San Francisco; and I have heard that it is in the Talmud. I have seen it in print in nine different foreign languages; I have been told that it is employed in the inquisition in Rome; and I now learn with regret that it is going to be set to music. I do not think that such things are right.

Stage-coaching on the Overland is no more, and stage drivers are a race defunct. I wonder if they bequeathed that bald-headed anecdote to their successors, the railroad brake-men and conductors, and if these latter still persecute the helpless passenger with it until he concludes, as did many a tourist of other days, that the real grandeurs of the Pacific coast are not Yo Semite and the Big Trees, but Hank Monk and his adventure with Horace Greeley.*

---

* And what makes that worn anecdote the more aggravating, is, that the adventure it celebrates *never occurred.* If it were a good anecdote, that seeming demerit would be its chiefest virtue, for creative power belongs to greatness; but what ought to be done to a man who would wantonly contrive so flat a one as this? If *I* were to suggest what ought to be done to him, I should be called extravagant—but what does the thirteenth chapter of Daniel say? Aha!

CHAPTER XXI.

WE were approaching the end of our long journey. It was the morning of the twentieth day. At noon we would reach Carson City, the capital of Nevada Territory. We were not glad, but sorry. It had been a fine pleasure trip; we had fed fat on wonders every day; we were now well accustomed to stage life, and very fond of it; so the idea of coming to a stand-still and settling down to a humdrum existence in a village was not agreeable, but on the contrary depressing.

Visibly our new home was a desert, walled in by barren, snow-clad mountains. There was not a tree in sight. There was no vegetation but the endless sage-brush and greasewood. All nature was gray with it. We were plowing through great deeps of powdery alkali dust that rose in thick clouds and floated across the plain like smoke from a burning house. We were coated with it like millers; so were the coach, the mules, the mail-bags, the driver—we and the sage-brush and the other scenery were all one monotonous color. Long trains of freight wagons in the distance enveloped in ascending masses of dust suggested pictures of prairies on fire. These teams and their masters were the only life we saw. Otherwise we moved in the midst of solitude, silence and desolation. Every twenty steps we passed the skeleton of some dead beast of burthen, with its dust-coated skin stretched tightly over its empty ribs. Frequently a solemn raven sat upon the skull or the hips and contemplated the passing coach with meditative serenity.

By and by Carson City was pointed out to us. It nestled in the edge of a great plain and was a sufficient number of

CONTEMPLATION.

miles away to look like an assemblage of mere white spots in the shadow of a grim range of mountains overlooking it, whose summits seemed lifted clear out of companionship and consciousness of earthly things.

We arrived, disembarked, and the stage went on. It was a "wooden" town; its population two thousand souls. The main street consisted of four or five blocks of little white frame stores which were too high to sit down on, but not too high for various other purposes; in fact, hardly high enough. They were packed close together, side by side, as if room were scarce in that mighty plain. The sidewalk was of boards that were more or less loose and inclined to rattle when walked upon. In the middle of the town, opposite the stores, was the "plaza" which is native to all towns beyond the Rocky Mountains—a large, unfenced, level vacancy, with a liberty pole in it, and very useful as a place for public auctions, horse trades, and mass meetings, and likewise for teamsters to camp in. Two other sides of the plaza were faced by stores, offices and stables. The rest of Carson City was pretty scattering.

We were introduced to several citizens, at the stage-office and on the way up to the Governor's from the hotel—among others, to a Mr. Harris, who was on horseback; he began to say something, but interrupted himself with the remark:

"I'll have to get you to excuse me a minute; yonder is the witness that swore I helped to rob the California coach—a piece of impertinent intermeddling, sir, for I am not even acquainted with the man."

Then he rode over and began to rebuke the stranger with a six-shooter, and the stranger began to explain with another.

When the pistols were emptied, the stranger resumed his work (mending a whip-lash), and Mr. Harris rode by with a polite nod, homeward bound, with a bullet through one of his lungs, and several in his hips; and from them issued little rivulets of blood that coursed down the horse's sides and made the animal look quite picturesque. I never saw Harris shoot a man after that but it recalled to mind that first day in Carson.

This was all we saw that day, for it was two o'clock, now, and according to custom the daily "Washoe Zephyr" set in; a soaring dust-drift about the size of the United States set up edgewise came with it, and the capital of Nevada Territory

THE WASHOE ZEPHYR.

disappeared from view. Still, there were sights to be seen which were not wholly uninteresting to new comers; for the vast dust cloud was thickly freckled with things strange to the upper air—things living and dead, that flitted hither and thither, going and coming, appearing and disappearing among the rolling billows of dust—hats, chickens and parasols sailing in the remote heavens; blankets, tin signs, sage-brush and shingles a shade lower; door-mats and buffalo robes lower still; shovels and coal scuttles on the next grade; glass doors, cats and little children on the next; disrupted lumber yards, light buggies and wheelbarrows on the next; and down only thirty or forty feet above ground was a scurrying storm of emigrating roofs and vacant lots.

It was something to see that much. I could have seen more, if I could have kept the dust out of my eyes.

But seriously a Washoe wind is by no means a trifling matter. It blows flimsy houses down, lifts shingle roofs occasionally, rolls up tin ones like sheet music, now and then blows a stage coach over and spills the passengers; and tradition says the reason there are so many bald people there, is, that the wind blows the hair off their heads while they are looking skyward after their hats. Carson streets seldom look inactive on Summer afternoons, because there are so many citizens skipping around their escaping hats, like chambermaids trying to head off a spider.

The "Washoe Zephyr" (Washoe is a pet nickname for Nevada) is a peculiarly Scriptural wind, in that no man knoweth "whence it cometh." That is to say, where it *originates*. It comes right over the mountains from the West, but when one crosses the ridge he does not find any of it on the other side! It probably is manufactured on the mountain-top for the occasion, and starts from there. It is a pretty regular wind, in the summer time. Its office hours are from two in the afternoon till two the next morning; and anybody venturing abroad during those twelve hours needs to allow for the wind or he will bring up a mile or two. to leeward of the point he is aiming at. And yet the first complaint a Washoe visitor to San Francisco makes, is that the sea winds blow so, there! There is a good deal of human nature in that.

We found the state palace of the Governor of Nevada Territory to consist of a white frame one-story house with two small rooms in it and a stanchion supported shed in front—for grandeur—it compelled the respect of the citizen and inspired the Indians with awe. The newly arrived Chief and Associate Justices of the Territory, and other machinery of the government, were domiciled with less splendor. They were boarding around privately, and had their offices in their bedrooms.

The Secretary and I took quarters in the "ranch" of a worthy French lady by the name of Bridget O'Flannigan, a camp follower of his Excellency the Governor. She had known him in his prosperity as commander-in-chief of the Metropolitan Police of New York, and she would not desert

THE GOVERNOR'S HOUSE.

him in his adversity as Governor of Nevada. Our room was on the lower floor, facing the plaza, and when we had got our bed, a small table, two chairs, the government fire-proof safe, and the Unabridged Dictionary into it, there was still room enough left for a visitor—may be two, but not without straining the walls. But the walls could stand it—at least the partitions could, for they consisted simply of one thickness of white "cotton domestic" stretched from corner to corner of the room. This was the rule in Carson—any other kind of partition was the rare exception. And if you stood in a dark

11†

room and your neighbors in the next had lights, the shadows on your canvas told queer secrets sometimes! Very often

DARK DISCLOSURES.

these partitions were made of old flour sacks basted together; and then the difference between the common herd and the aristocracy was, that the common herd had unornamented sacks, while the walls of the aristocrat were overpowering with rudimental fresco— i. e., red and blue mill brands on the flour sacks. Occasionally, also, the better classes embellished their canvas by pasting pictures from *Harper's Weekly* on them. In many cases, too, the wealthy and the cultured rose to spittoons and other evidences of a sumptuous and luxurious taste.* We had a carpet and a genuine queen's-ware washbowl. Consequently we were hated without reserve by the other tenants of the O'Flannigan "ranch." When we added a painted oil-cloth window curtain, we simply took our lives into our own hands. To prevent bloodshed I removed up stairs and took up quarters with the untitled plebeians in one of the fourteen white pine cot-bedsteads that stood in two long ranks in the one sole room of which the second story consisted.

It was a jolly company, the fourteen. They were principally voluntary camp-followers of the Governor, who had joined his retinue by their own election at New York and

---

* Washoe people take a joke so hard that I must explain that the above description was only the rule; there were many honorable exceptions in Carson—plastered ceilings and houses that had considerable furniture in them.—M. T.

San Francisco and came along, feeling that in the scuffle for
little territorial crumbs and offices they could not make their
condition more precarious than it was, and might reasonably
expect to make it better.   They were popularly known as the
"Irish Brigade," though there were only four or five Irish-
men among all the Governor's retainers.   His good-natured

THE IRISH BRIGADE.

Excellency was much annoyed at the gossip his henchmen
created—especially when there arose a rumor that they were
paid assassins of his, brought along to quietly reduce the
democratic vote when desirable !

Mrs. O'Flannigan was boarding and lodging them at ten
dollars a week apiece, and they were cheerfully giving their
notes for it.   They were perfectly satisfied, but Bridget presently found that notes that could not be discounted were but
a feeble constitution for a Carson boarding-house.   So she
began to harry the Governor to find employment for the
"Brigade."   Her importunities and theirs together drove him
to a gentle desperation at last, and he finally summoned the
Brigade to the presence.   Then, said he:

"Gentlemen, I have planned a lucrative and useful service for you—a service which will provide you with recreation amid noble landscapes, and afford you never ceasing opportunities for enriching your minds by observation and study. I want you to survey a railroad from Carson City westward to a certain point! When the legislature meets I will have the necessary bill passed and the remuneration arranged."

"What, a railroad over the Sierra Nevada Mountains?"

"Well, then, survey it eastward to a certain point!"

He converted them into surveyors, chain-bearers and so on, and turned them loose in the desert. It was "recreation" with a vengeance! Recreation on foot, lugging chains through sand and sage-brush, under a sultry sun and among cattle bones, cayotes and tarantulas. "Romantic adventure" could go no further. They surveyed very slowly, very deliberately, very carefully. They returned every night during the first week, dusty, footsore, tired, and hungry, but very jolly. They brought in great store of prodigious hairy spiders—tarantulas—and imprisoned them in covered tumblers up stairs in the "ranch."

RECREATION.

After the first week, they had to camp on the field, for they were getting well eastward. They made a good many inquiries as to the location of that indefinite "certain point," but got no information. At last, to a peculiarly urgent inquiry of "How far eastward?" Governor Nye telegraphed back:

"To the Atlantic Ocean, blast you!—and then bridge it and go on!"

This brought back the dusty toilers, who sent in a report and ceased from their labors. The Governor was always comfortable about it; he said Mrs. O'Flannigan would hold him for the Brigade's board anyhow, and he intended to get what entertainment he could out of the boys; he said, with his old-time pleasant twinkle, that he meant to survey them into Utah and then telegraph Brigham to hang them for trespass!

The surveyors brought back more tarantulas with them, and so we had quite a menagerie arranged along the shelves of the room. Some of these spiders could straddle over a common saucer with their hairy, muscular legs, and when their feelings were hurt, or their dignity offended, they were the wickedest-looking desperadoes the animal world can fur-

THE TARANTULA.

nish. If their glass pris-on-houses were touched ever so lightly they were up and spoiling for a fight in a minute. Starchy?—proud? Indeed, they would take up a straw and pick their teeth like a member of Congress. There was as usual a furious "zephyr" blowing the first night of the brigade's return, and about midnight the roof of an adjoining stable blew off, and a corner of it came crashing through the side of our ranch. There was a simultaneous awakening, and a tumultuous muster of the brigade in the dark, and a general tumbling and sprawling over each other in the narrow aisle between the bed-rows. In the midst of the turmoil, Bob H—— sprung up out of a sound sleep, and knocked down a shelf with his head. Instantly he shouted:

"Turn out, boys—the tarantulas is loose!"

No warning ever sounded so dreadful. Nobody tried, any longer, to leave the room, lest he might step on a tarantula. Every man groped for a trunk or a bed, and jumped on it. Then followed the strangest silence—a silence of grisly suspense it was, too—waiting, expectancy, fear. It was as dark as pitch, and one had to imagine the spectacle of those fourteen scant-clad men roosting gingerly on trunks and beds, for not a thing could be seen. Then came occasional little interruptions of the silence, and one could recognize a man and tell his locality by his voice, or locate any other sound a sufferer made by his gropings or changes of position. The occasional voices were not given to much speaking—you simply heard a gentle ejaculation of "Ow!" followed by a solid thump, and you knew the gentleman had felt a hairy blanket or something touch his bare skin and had skipped from a bed to the floor. Another silence. Presently you would hear a gasping voice say:

"Su-su-something's crawling up the back of my neck!"

Every now and then you could hear a little subdued scramble and a sorrowful "O Lord!" and then you knew that somebody was getting away from something he took for a tarantula, and not losing any time about it, either. Directly a voice in the corner rang out wild and clear:

"I've got him! I've got him!" [Pause, and probable change of circumstances.] "No, he's got me! Oh, ain't they *never* going to fetch a lantern!"

The lantern came at that moment, in the hands of Mrs. O'Flannigan, whose anxiety to know the amount of damage

LIGHT THROWN ON THE SUBJECT.

done by the assaulting roof had not prevented her waiting a judicious interval, after getting out of bed and lighting up, to see if the wind was done, now, up stairs, or had a larger contract.

The landscape presented when the lantern flashed into the room was picturesque, and might have been funny to some people, but was not to us. Although we were perched so strangely upon boxes, trunks and beds, and so strangely attired, too, we were too earnestly distressed and too genuinely miserable to see any fun about it, and there was not the semblance of a smile anywhere visible. I know I am not capable of suffering more than I did during those few minutes of suspense in the dark, surrounded by those creeping, bloody-minded tarantulas. I had skipped from bed to bed and from box to box in a cold agony, and every time I touched anything that was furzy I fancied I felt the fangs. I had rather go to war than live that episode over again. Nobody was hurt. The man who thought a tarantula had "got him" was mistaken—only a crack in a box had caught his finger. Not one of those escaped tarantulas was ever seen again. There were ten or twelve of them. We took candles and hunted the place high and low for them, but with no success. Did we go back to bed then? We did nothing of the kind. Money could not have persuaded us to do it. We sat up the rest of the night playing cribbage and keeping a sharp lookout for the enemy.

CHAPTER XXII.

IT was the end of August, and the skies were cloudless and the weather superb. In two or three weeks I had grown wonderfully fascinated with the curious new country, and concluded to put off my return to "the States" awhile. I had grown well accustomed to wearing a damaged slouch hat, blue woolen shirt, and pants crammed into boot-tops, and gloried in the absence of coat, vest and braces. I felt rowdyish and "bully," (as the historian Josephus phrases it, in his fine chapter upon the destruction of the Temple). It seemed to me that nothing could be so fine and so romantic. I had become an officer of the government, but that was for mere sublimity. The office was an unique sinecure. I had nothing to do and no salary. I was private Secretary to his majesty the Secretary and there was not yet writing enough for two of us. So Johnny K—— and I devoted our time to amusement. He was the young son of an Ohio nabob and was out there for recreation. He got it. We had heard a world of talk about the marvellous beauty of Lake Tahoe, and finally curiosity drove us thither to see it. Three or four members of the Brigade had been there and located some timber lands on its shores and stored up a quantity of provisions in their camp. We strapped a couple of blankets on our shoulders and took an axe apiece and started—for we intended to take up a wood ranch or so ourselves and become wealthy. We were on foot. The reader will find it advantageous to go horseback. We were told that the distance was eleven miles.

We tramped a long time on level ground, and then toiled laboriously up a mountain about a thousand miles high and looked over. No lake there. We descended on the other side, crossed the valley and toiled up another mountain three or four thousand miles high, apparently, and looked over again. No lake yet. We sat down tired and perspiring, and hired a couple of Chinamen to curse those people who had beguiled us. Thus refreshed, we presently resumed the march with renewed vigor and determination. We plodded on, two or three hours longer, and at last the Lake burst upon us—a noble sheet of blue water lifted six thousand three hundred feet above the level of the sea, and walled in by a rim of snow-clad mountain peaks that towered aloft full three thousand feet higher still! It was a vast oval, and one would have to use up eighty or a hundred good miles in traveling around it. As it lay there with the shadows of the mountains brilliantly photographed upon its still surface I thought it must surely be the fairest picture the whole earth affords.

We found the small skiff belonging to the Brigade boys, and without loss of time set out across a deep bend of the lake toward the land-marks that signified the lo-cality of the camp. I got Johnny to row — not be-cause I mind exertion my-self, but because it makes me sick to ride backwards when I am at work. But

I STEERED.

I steered. A three-mile pull brought us to the camp just as the night fell, and we stepped ashore very tired and wolfishly hun-gry. In a "cache" among the rocks we found the provisions and the cooking utensils, and then, all fatigued as I was, I sat down on a boulder and superintended while Johnny gathered wood and cooked supper. Many a man who had gone through what I had, would have wanted to rest.

It was a delicious supper—hot bread, fried bacon, and black coffee. It was a delicious solitude we were in, too. Three miles away was a saw-mill and some workmen, but there were not fifteen other human beings throughout the wide circumference of the lake. As the darkness closed down and the stars came out and spangled the great mirror with jewels, we smoked meditatively in the solemn hush and forgot our troubles and our pains. In due time we spread our blankets in the warm sand between two large boulders and soon fell asleep, careless of the procession of ants that passed in through rents in our clothing and explored our persons. Nothing could disturb the sleep that fettered us, for it had been fairly earned, and if our consciences had any sins on them they had to adjourn court for that night, any way. The wind rose just as we were losing consciousness, and we were lulled to sleep by the beating of the surf upon the shore.

It is always very cold on that lake shore in the night, but we had plenty of blankets and were warm enough. We never

THE INVALID.

moved a muscle all night, but waked at early dawn in the original positions, and got up at once, thoroughly refreshed, free from soreness, and brim full of friskiness. There is no end of wholesome medicine in such an experience. That morning we could have whipped ten such people as we were the day before—sick ones at any rate. But the world is slow, and people will go to "water cures" and "movement cures" and to foreign lands for health. Three months of camp life on Lake Tahoe would restore an Egyptian mummy to his pristine vigor, and give him an appetite like an alligator. I do not mean the oldest and driest mummies, of course, but the fresher ones. The air up there in the clouds is very pure and fine, bracing and delicious. And why shouldn't it be?—it is the same the angels breathe. I think that hardly any amount of fatigue can be gathered together that a man cannot sleep off in one night on the sand by its side. Not under a roof, but under the sky; it seldom or never rains there in the summer time. I know a man who went there to die. But he made a failure of it. He was a skeleton when he came, and could barely stand. He had no appetite, and did nothing but read tracts and reflect on the future. Three months later he was sleeping out of doors regularly, eating all he could hold, three times a day, and chasing game over mountains three thousand feet high for recreation. And he was a skeleton no longer, but weighed part of a ton. This is no fancy sketch, but the truth. His disease was consumption. I confidently commend his experience to other skeletons.

I superintended again, and as soon as we had eaten break-fast we got in the boat and skirted along the lake shore about three miles and disembarked. We liked the appearance of the place, and so we claimed some three hundred acres of it and stuck our "notices" on a tree. It was yellow pine timber land—a dense forest of trees a hundred feet high and from one to five feet through at the butt. It was necessary to fence our property or we could not hold it. That is to say, it was necessary to cut down trees here and there and make them fall in such a way as to form a sort of enclosure (with pretty wide gaps

THE RESTORED.

in it). We cut down three trees apiece, and found it such heart-breaking work that we decided to "rest our case" on those; if they held the property, well and good; if they didn't, let the property spill out through the gaps and go; it was no use to work ourselves to death merely to save a few

acres of land. Next day we came back to build a house—
for a house was also necessary, in order to hold the property.
We decided to build a substantial log-house and excite the
envy of the Brigade boys; but by the time we had cut and
trimmed the first log it seemed unnecessary to be so elaborate,
and so we concluded to build it of saplings. However, two
saplings, duly cut and trimmed, compelled recognition of the
fact that a still modester architecture would satisfy the law,
and so we concluded to build a "brush" house. We devoted
the next day to this work, but we did so much "sitting
around" and discussing, that by the middle of the afternoon
we had achieved only a half-way sort of affair which one of us

OUR HOUSE.

had to watch while the other
cut brush, lest if both turned
our backs we might not be
able to find it again, it had
such a strong family resemblance to the surrounding
vegetation. But we were
satisfied with it.

We were land owners
now, duly seized and pos-
sessed, and within the protection of the law. Therefore we decided to take up
our residence on our own
domain and enjoy that large sense of
independence which only such an experience can bring. Late the next afternoon, after a good long rest, we sailed
away from the Brigade camp with all
the provisions and cooking utensils we could carry off—borrow
is the more accurate word—and just as the night was falling
we beached the boat at our own landing.

CHAPTER XXIII.

IF there is any life that is happier than the life we led on our timber ranch for the next two or three weeks, it must be a sort of life which I have not read of in books or experienced in person. We did not see a human being but ourselves during the time, or hear any sounds but those that were made by the wind and the waves, the sighing of the pines, and now and then the far-off thunder of an avalanche. The forest about us was dense and cool, the sky above us was cloudless and brilliant with sunshine, the broad lake before us was glassy and clear, or rippled and breezy, or black and storm-tossed, according to Nature's mood; and its circling border of mountain domes, clothed with forests, scarred with land-slides, cloven by cañons and valleys, and helmeted with glittering snow, fitly framed and finished the noble picture. The view was always fascinating, bewitching, entrancing. The eye was never tired of gazing, night or day, in calm or storm; it suffered but one grief, and that was that it could not look always, but must close sometimes in sleep.

We slept in the sand close to the water's edge, between two protecting boulders, which took care of the stormy night-winds for us. We never took any paregoric to make us sleep. At the first break of dawn we were always up and running foot-races to tone down excess of physical vigor and exuberance of spirits. That is, Johnny was—but I held his hat. While smoking the pipe of peace after breakfast we watched the sentinel peaks put on the glory of the sun, and followed the conquering light as it swept down among the shadows, and set the captive crags and forests free.   We watched the tinted pictures grow and brighten upon the water till every little detail of forest, precipice and pinnacle was wrought in and finished, and the miracle of the enchanter complete.   Then to " business."

That is, drifting around in the boat.   We were on the north shore.   There, the rocks on the bottom are sometimes

AT BUSINESS.

gray, sometimes white. This gives the marvelous transparency of the water a fuller advantage than it has elsewhere on the lake. We usually pushed out a hundred yards or so from shore, and then lay down on the thwarts, in the sun, and let the boat drift by the hour whither it would.   We seldom talked.   It interrupted the Sabbath stillness, and marred the dreams the luxurious rest and indolence brought.   The shore all along was indented with deep, curved bays and coves, bordered by narrow sand-beaches; and where the sand ended, the steep mountain-sides rose right up aloft into space—rose up like a vast wall a little out of the perpendicular, and thickly wooded with tall pines.

So singularly clear was the water, that where it was only twenty or thirty feet deep the bottom was so perfectly distinct that the boat seemed floating in the air!   Yes, where it was even *eighty* feet deep.   Every little pebble was distinct, every speckled trout, every hand's-breadth of sand.   Often, as we lay on our faces, a granite boulder, as large as a village church, would start out of the bottom apparently, and seem climbing up rapidly to the surface, till presently it threatened to touch our faces, and we could not resist the impulse to seize an oar and avert the danger.   But the boat would float on, and the boulder descend again, and then we could see that when we had been exactly above it, it must still have been twenty or thirty feet below the surface. Down through the transparency of these great depths, the water was not *merely* transparent, but dazzlingly, brilliantly so. All objects seen through it had a bright, strong vividness, not only of outline, but of every minute detail, which they would not have had when seen simply through the same depth of atmosphere. So empty and airy did all spaces seem below us, and so strong was the sense of floating high aloft in mid-nothingness, that we called these boat-excursions "balloon-voyages."

We fished a good deal, but we did not average one fish a week. We could see trout by the thousand winging about in the emptiness under us, or sleeping in shoals on the bottom, but they would not bite—they could see the line too plainly, perhaps. We frequently selected the trout we wanted, and rested the bait patiently and persistently on the end of his nose at a depth of eighty feet, but he would only shake it off with an annoyed manner, and shift his position.

We bathed occasionally, but the water was rather chilly, for all it looked so sunny. Sometimes we rowed out to the "blue water," a mile or two from shore. It was as dead blue as indigo there, because of the immense depth. By official measurement the lake in its centre is one thousand five hundred and twenty-five feet deep!

Sometimes, on lazy afternoons, we lolled on the sand in camp, and smoked pipes and read some old well-worn novels. At night, by the camp-fire, we played euchre and seven-up to strengthen the mind—and played them with cards so greasy and defaced that only a whole summer's acquaintance with them could enable the student to tell the ace of clubs from the jack of diamonds.

We never slept in our "house." It never recurred to us, for one thing; and besides, it was built to hold the ground, and that was enough. We did not wish to strain it.

By and by our provisions began to run short, and we went back to the old camp and laid in a new supply. We were gone all day, and reached home again about night-fall, pretty tired and hungry. While Johnny was carrying the main bulk of the provisions up to our "house" for future use, I took the loaf of bread, some slices of bacon, and the coffee-pot, ashore, set them down by a tree, lit a fire, and went back to the boat to get the frying-pan. While I was at this, I heard a shout from Johnny, and looking up I saw that my fire was galloping all over the premises!

Johnny was on the other side of it. He had to run through the flames to get to the lake shore, and then we stood helpless and watched the devastation.

The ground was deeply carpeted with dry pine-needles, and the fire touched them off as if they were gunpowder. It was wonderful to see with what fierce speed the tall sheet of flame traveled! My coffee-pot was gone, and everything with it. In a minute and a half the fire seized upon a dense growth of dry manzanita chapparal six or eight feet high, and then the roaring and popping and crackling was something terrific. We were driven to the boat by the intense heat, and there we remained, spell-bound.

Within half an hour all before us was a tossing, blinding tempest of flame! It went surging up adjacent ridges—surmounted them and disappeared in the cañons beyond—burst into view upon higher and farther ridges, presently—shed a grander illumination abroad, and dove again—flamed out again, directly, higher and still higher up the mountain-side—threw out skirmishing parties of fire here and there, and sent them trailing their crimson spirals away among remote ramparts and ribs and gorges, till as far as the eye could reach the lofty mountain-fronts were webbed as it were with a tangled network of red lava streams. Away across the water the crags and domes were lit with a ruddy glare, and the firmament above was a reflected hell!

Every feature of the spectacle was repeated in the glowing mirror of the lake! Both pictures were sublime, both were beautiful; but that in the lake had a bewildering richness about it that enchanted the eye and held it with the stronger fascination.

We sat absorbed and motionless through four long hours.

FIRE AT LAKE TAHOE.

We never thought of supper, and never felt fatigue. But at eleven o'clock the conflagration had traveled beyond our range of vision, and then darkness stole down upon the landscape again.

Hunger asserted itself now, but there was nothing to eat. The provisions were all cooked, no doubt, but we did not go to see. We were homeless wanderers again, without any property. Our fence was gone, our house burned down; no insurance. Our pine forest was well scorched, the dead trees all burned up, and our broad acres of manzanita swept away. Our blankets were on our usual sand-bed, however, and so we lay down and went to sleep. The next morning we started back to the old camp, but while out a long way from shore, so great a storm came up that we dared not try to land. So I baled out the seas we shipped, and Johnny pulled heavily through the billows till we had reached a point three or four miles beyond the camp. The storm was increasing, and it became evident that it was better to take the hazard of beaching the boat than go down in a hundred fathoms of water; so we ran in, with tall white-caps following, and I sat down in the stern-sheets and pointed her head-on to the shore. The instant the bow struck, a wave came over the stern that washed crew and cargo ashore, and saved a deal of trouble. We shivered in the lee of a boulder all the rest of the day, and froze all the night through. In the morning the tempest had gone down, and we paddled down to the camp without any unnecessary delay. We were so starved that we ate up the rest of the Brigade's provisions, and then set out to Carson to tell them about it and ask their forgiveness. It was accorded, upon payment of damages.

We made many trips to the lake after that, and had many a hair-breadth escape and blood-curdling adventure which will never be recorded in any history.

CHAPTER XXIV.

I RESOLVED to have a horse to ride. I had never seen such wild, free, magnificent horsemanship outside of a circus as these picturesquely-clad Mexicans, Californians and Mexicanized Americans displayed in Carson streets every day. How they rode! Leaning just gently forward out of the perpendicular, easy and nonchalant, with broad slouch-hat brim blown square up in front, and long *riata* swinging above the head, they swept through the town like the wind! The next minute they were only a sailing puff of dust on the far desert. If they trotted, they sat up gallantly and gracefully, and seemed part of the horse; did not go jiggering up and down after the silly Miss-Nancy fashion of the riding-schools. I had quickly learned to tell a horse from a cow, and was full of anxiety to learn more. I was resolved to buy a horse.

While the thought was rankling in my mind, the auctioneer came skurrying through the plaza on a black beast that had as many humps and corners on him as a dromedary, and was necessarily uncomely; but he was "going, going, at twenty-two!—horse, saddle and bridle at twenty-two dollars, gentlemen!" and I could hardly resist.

A man whom I did not know (he turned out to be the auctioneer's brother) noticed the wistful look in my eye, and observed that that was a very remarkable horse to be going at such a price; and added that the saddle alone was worth the money. It was a Spanish saddle, with ponderous *tapidaros,* and furnished with the ungainly sole-leather covering with

the unspellable name. I said I had half a notion to bid.
Then this keen-eyed person appeared to me to be " taking my
measure " ; but I dismissed the suspicion when he spoke, for his
manner was full of guileless candor and truthfulness.   Said he :
"I know that horse—know him well.   You are a stranger,
I take it, and so you might think he was an American horse,

"YOU MIGHT THINK HIM AN AMERICAN HORSE."

maybe, but I assure you he is not.   He is nothing of the kind ;
but—excuse my speaking in a low voice, other people being
near—he is, without the shadow of a doubt, a Genuine Mexican Plug ! "
I did not know what a Genuine Mexican Plug was, but
there was something about this man's way of saying it, that
made me swear inwardly that I would own a Genuine Mexican Plug, or die.
"Has he any other—er—advantages?" I inquired, sup-
pressing what eagerness I could.

He hooked his forefinger in the pocket of my army-shirt, led me to one side, and breathed in my ear impressively these words:

"He can out-buck anything in America!"

"Going, going, going—at *twent–ty*-four dollars and a half, gen—"

"Twenty-seven!" I shouted, in a frenzy.

"And sold!" said the auctioneer, and passed over the Genuine Mexican Plug to me.

I could scarcely contain my exultation. I paid the money, and put the animal in a neighboring livery-stable to dine and rest himself.

In the afternoon I brought the creature into the plaza, and certain citizens held him by the head, and others by the tail, while I mounted him. As soon as they let go, he placed all his feet in a bunch together, lowered his back, and then suddenly arched it upward, and shot me straight into the air a matter of three or four feet! I came as straight down again, lit in the saddle, went instantly up again, came down almost on the high pommel, shot up again, and came down on the horse's neck—all in the space of three or four seconds. Then he rose and stood almost straight up on his hind feet, and I, clasping his lean neck desperately, slid back into the saddle, and held on. He came down, and immediately hoisted his heels into the air, delivering a vicious kick at the sky, and stood on his forefeet.

UNEXPECTED ELEVATION.

And then down he came once more, and began the original exercise of shooting me straight up again. The third time I went up I heard a stranger say:

"Oh, *don't* he buck, though!"

While I was up, somebody struck the horse a sounding thwack with a leathern strap, and when I arrived again the Genuine Mexican Plug was not there. A Californian youth chased him up and caught him, and asked if he might have a ride. I granted him that luxury. He mounted the Genuine, got lifted into the air once, but sent his spurs home as he descended, and the horse darted away like a telegram. He soared over three fences like a bird, and disappeared down the road toward the Washoe Valley.

UNIVERSALLY UNSETTLED.

I sat down on a stone, with a sigh, and by a natural impulse one of my hands sought my forehead, and the other the base of my stomach. I believe I never appreciated, till then, the poverty of the human machinery—for I still needed a hand or two to place elsewhere. Pen cannot describe how I was jolted up. Imagination cannot conceive how disjointed I was—how internally, externally and universally I was unsettled, mixed up and ruptured. There was a sympathetic crowd around me, though.

One elderly-looking comforter said:

"Stranger, you've been taken in. Everybody in this camp knows that horse. Any child, any Injun, could have told you that he'd buck; he is the very worst devil to buck on the continent of America. You hear *me*. I'm Curry. *Old* Curry. Old *Abe* Curry. And moreover, he is a simon-pure, out-and-out, genuine d—d Mexican plug, and an uncommon

mean one at that, too.   Why, you turnip, if you had laid low
and kept dark, there's chances to buy an *American* horse for
mighty little more than you paid for that bloody old foreign
relic."

I gave no sign; but I made up my mind that if the
auctioneer's brother's funeral took place while I was in the
Territory I would postpone all other recreations and attend it.

After a gallop of sixteen miles the Californian youth and
the Genuine Mexican Plug came tearing into town again,
shedding foam-flakes like the spume-spray that drives before a
typhoon, and, with one final skip over a wheelbarrow and a
Chinaman, cast anchor in front of the "ranch."

Such panting and blowing!   Such spreading and contract-
ing of the red equine nostrils, and glaring of the wild equine
eye!   But was the imperial beast subjugated?   Indeed he
was not.
His lord-
ship the
Speaker of
the House
thought he
was, and
mounted
him to go
down to the
Capitol; but
the first
dash the
creature

RIDING THE PLUG.

made was over a pile of telegraph poles half as high as a
church; and his time to the Capitol—one mile and three
quarters—remains unbeaten to this day.   But then he took an
advantage—he left out the mile, and only did the three quarters.   That is to say, he made a straight cut across lots, prefer-
ring fences and ditches to a crooked road; and when the
Speaker got to the Capitol he said he had been in the air so
much he felt as if he had made the trip on a comet.

In the evening the Speaker came home afoot for exercise, and got the Genuine towed back behind a quartz wagon. The next day I loaned the animal to the Clerk of the House to go down to the Dana silver mine, six miles, and *he* walked back for exercise, and got the horse towed. Everybody I loaned him to always walked back; they never could get enough exercise any other way. Still, I continued to loan him to anybody who was willing to borrow him, my idea being to get him crippled, and throw him on the borrower's hands, or killed, and make the borrower pay for him. But somehow nothing ever happened to him. He took chances that no other horse ever took and survived, but he always came out safe.

WANTED EXERCISE.

It was his daily habit to try experiments that had always before been considered impossible, but he always got through. Sometimes he miscalculated a little, and did not get his rider through intact, but *he* always got through himself. Of course I had tried to sell him; but that was a stretch of simplicity which met with little sympathy. The auctioneer stormed up and down the streets on him for four days, dispersing the populace, interrupting business, and destroying children, and never got a bid—at least never any but the eighteen-dollar one he hired a notoriously substanceless bummer to make. The people only smiled pleasantly, and restrained their desire to buy, if they had any. Then the auctioneer brought in his bill, and I withdrew the horse from the market. We tried to trade him off at private vendue next, offering him at a sacrifice for second-hand tombstones, old iron, temperance tracts—any kind of property. But holders were stiff, and we retired from the market again. I never tried to ride the horse any more. Walking was good enough exercise for a man like me, that had nothing the matter with him except ruptures, internal injuries, and such things. Finally I tried to *give* him away. But it was a failure. Parties said earthquakes were handy enough on the Pacific coast—they did not wish to own one. As a last resort I offered him to the Governor for the use of the "Brigade." His face lit up eagerly at first, but toned down again, and he said the thing would be too palpable.

Just then the livery stable man brought in his bill for six weeks' keeping—stall-room for the horse, fifteen dollars; hay for the horse, two hundred and fifty! The Genuine Mexican Plug had eaten a ton of the article, and the man said he would have eaten a hundred if he had let him.

I will remark here, in all seriousness, that the regular price of hay during that year and a part of the next was really two hundred and fifty dollars a ton. During a part of the previous year it had sold at five hundred a ton, in gold, and during the winter before that there was such scarcity of the article that in several instances small quantities had brought eight hundred dollars a ton in coin! The consequence might be guessed without my telling it: peopled turned their stock loose to starve, and before the spring arrived Carson and Eagle valleys were almost literally carpeted with their carcases! Any old settler there will verify these statements.

I managed to pay the livery bill, and that same day I gave the Genuine Mexican Plug to a passing Arkansas emigrant whom fortune delivered into my hand. If this ever meets his eye, he will doubtless remember the donation.

Now whoever has had the luck to ride a real Mexican plug will recognize the animal depicted in this chapter, and hardly consider him exaggerated—but the uninitiated will feel justified in regarding his portrait as a fancy sketch, perhaps.

CHAPTER XXV.

ORIGINALLY, Nevada was a part of Utah and was called Carson county; and a pretty large county it was, too. Certain of its valleys produced no end of hay, and this attracted small colonies of Mormon stock-raisers and farmers to them. A few orthodox Americans straggled in from California, but no love was lost between the two classes of colonists. There was little or no friendly intercourse; each party staid to itself. The Mormons were largely in the majority, and had the additional advantage of being peculiarly under the protection of the Mormon government of the Territory. Therefore they could afford to be distant, and even peremptory toward their neighbors. One of the traditions of Carson Valley illustrates the condition of things that prevailed at the time I speak of. The hired girl of one of the American families was Irish, and a Catholic; yet it was noted with surprise that she was the only person outside of the Mormon ring who could get favors from the Mormons. She asked kindnesses of them often, and always got them. It was a mystery to everybody. But one day as she was passing out at the door, a large bowie knife dropped from under her apron, and when her mistress asked for an explanation she observed that she was going out to " borry a wash-tub from the Mormons!"

In 1858 silver lodes were discovered in " Carson County," and then the aspect of things changed. Californians began to flock in, and the American element was soon in the majority.

Allegiance to Brigham Young and Utah was renounced, and a temporary territorial government for "Washoe" was instituted by the citizens. Governor Roop was the first and only chief magistrate of it. In due course of time Congress passed a bill to organize "Nevada Territory," and President Lincoln sent out Governor Nye to supplant Roop.

At this time the population of the Territory was about twelve or fifteen thousand, and rapidly increasing. Silver mines were being vigorously developed and silver mills erected. Business of all kinds was active and prosperous and growing more so day by day.

BORROWING MADE EASY.

The people were glad to have a legitimately constituted government, but did not particularly enjoy having strangers from distant States put in authority over them—a sentiment that was natural enough. They thought the officials should have been chosen from among themselves —from among prominent citizens who had earned a right to such promotion, and who would be in sympathy with the populace and likewise thoroughly acquainted with the needs of the Territory. They were right in viewing the matter thus, without doubt. The new officers were "emigrants," and that was no title to anybody's affection or admiration either.

The new government was received with considerable coolness. It was not only a foreign intruder, but a poor one. It was not even worth plucking—except by the smallest of small fry office-seekers and such. Everybody knew that Congress had appropriated only twenty thousand dollars a year in greenbacks for its support—about money enough to run a quartz mill a month. And everybody knew, also, that the first year's money was still in Washington, and that the getting hold of it would be a tedious and difficult process. Carson City was too wary and too wise to open up a credit account with the imported bantling with anything like indecent haste.

There is something solemnly funny about the struggles of a new-born Territorial government to get a start in this world. Ours had a trying time of it. The Organic Act and the "instructions" from the State Department commanded that a legislature should be elected at such-and-such a time, and its sittings inaugurated at such-and-such a date. It was easy to get legislators, even at three dollars a day, although board was four dollars and fifty cents, for distinction has its charm in Nevada as well as elsewhere, and there were plenty of patriotic souls out of employment; but to get a legislative hall for them to meet in was another matter altogether. Carson blandly declined to give a room rent-free, or let one to the government on credit.

But when Curry heard of the difficulty, he came forward, solitary and alone, and shouldered the Ship of State over the bar and got her afloat again. I refer to "Curry—*Old* Curry —Old *Abe* Curry." But for him the legislature would have been obliged to sit in the desert. He offered his large stone building just outside the capital limits, rent-free, and it was gladly accepted. Then he built a horse-railroad from town to the capitol, and carried the legislators gratis. He also furnished pine benches and chairs for the legislature, and

FREE RIDES.

covered the floors with clean saw-dust by way of carpet and spittoon combined. But for Curry the government would have died in its tender infancy. A canvas partition to separate the Senate from the House of Representatives was put up by the Secretary, at a cost of three dollars and forty cents, but the United States declined to pay for it. Upon being reminded that the "instructions" permitted the payment of a liberal rent for a legislative hall, and that that money was saved to the country by Mr. Curry's generosity, the United States said that did not alter the matter, and the three dollars and forty cents would be subtracted from the Secretary's eighteen hundred dollar salary—and it *was!*

The matter of printing was from the beginning an interesting feature of the new government's difficulties. The Secretary was sworn to obey his volume of written "instructions," and these commanded him to do two certain things without fail, viz.:

1. Get the House and Senate journals printed; and,

2. For this work, pay one dollar and fifty cents per "thousand" for composition, and one dollar and fifty cents per "token" for press-work, in greenbacks.

It was easy to swear to do these two things, but it was entirely impossible to do more than one of them. When greenbacks had gone down to forty cents on the dollar, the prices regularly charged everybody by printing establishments were one dollar and fifty cents per "thousand" and one dollar and fifty cents per "token," in *gold*. The "instructions" commanded that the Secretary regard a paper dollar issued by the government as equal to any other dollar issued by the government. Hence the printing of the journals was discontinued. Then the United States sternly rebuked the Secretary for disregarding the "instructions," and warned him to correct his ways. Wherefore he got some printing done, forwarded the bill to Washington with full exhibits of the high prices of things in the Territory, and called attention to a printed market report wherein it would be observed that even hay was two hundred and fifty dollars a ton. The United States responded by subtracting the printing-bill from the Secretary's suffering salary—and moreover remarked with dense gravity that he would find nothing in his "instructions" requiring him to purchase hay !

Nothing in this world is palled in such impenetrable obscurity as a U. S. Treasury Comptroller's understanding. The very fires of the hereafter could get up nothing more than a fitful glimmer in it. In the days I speak of he never could be made to comprehend why it was that twenty thousand dollars would not go as far in Nevada, where all commodities ranged at an enormous figure, as it would in the other Territories, where exceeding cheapness was the rule. He was an officer who looked out for the little expenses all the time. The Secretary of the Territory kept his office in his bedroom, as I before remarked; and he charged the United States no rent, although his "instructions" provided for that item and he could have justly taken advantage of it (a thing which I would have done with more than lightning promptness if I had been Secretary myself). But the United States never applauded this devotion. Indeed, I think my country was ashamed to have so improvident a person in its employ.

Those "instructions" (we used to read a chapter from them every morning, as intellectual gymnastics, and a couple of chapters in Sunday school every Sabbath, for they treated of all subjects under the sun and had much valuable religious matter in them along with the other statistics) those "instructions" commanded that pen-knives, envelopes, pens and writing-paper be furnished the members of the legislature. So the Secretary made the purchase and the distribution. The knives cost three dollars apiece. There was one too many, and the Secretary gave it to the Clerk of the House of Representatives. The United States said the Clerk of the House was not a "member" of the legislature, and took that three dollars out of the Secretary's salary, as usual.

White men charged three or four dollars a "load" for sawing up stove-wood. The Secretary was sagacious enough to know that the United States would never pay any such price as that; so he got an Indian to saw up a load of office wood at one dollar and a half. He made out the usual voucher, but signed no name to it—simply appended a note explaining that an Indian had done the work, and had done it in a very capable and satisfactory way, but could not sign the voucher owing to lack of ability in the necessary direction. The Secretary had to pay that dollar and a half. He thought the United States would admire both his economy and his honesty in getting the work done at half price and not putting a pretended Indian's signature to the voucher, but the United States did not see it in that light. The United States was too much accustomed to employing dollar-and-a-half

SATISFACTORY VOUCHER.

thieves in all manner of official capacities to regard his explanation of the voucher as having any foundation in fact.

But the next time the Indian sawed wood for us I taught him to make a cross at the bottom of the voucher—it looked like a cross that had been drunk a year—and then I "witnessed" it and it went through all right. The United States never said a word. I was sorry I had not made the voucher for a thousand loads of wood instead of one. The govern-

NEEDS PRAYING FOR.

ment of my country snubs honest simplicity but fondles artistic villainy, and I think I might have developed into a very capable pickpocket if I had remained in the public service a year or two.

That was a fine collection of sovereigns, that first Nevada legislature. They levied taxes to the amount of thirty or forty thousand dollars and ordered expenditures to the extent of about a million.   Yet they had their little periodical explosions of economy like all other bodies of the kind.   A member proposed to save three dollars a day to the nation by dispensing with the Chaplain.   And yet that short-sighted man needed the Chaplain more than any other member, perhaps, for he generally sat with his feet on his desk, eating raw turnips, during the morning prayer.

The legislature sat sixty days, and passed private toll-road franchises all the time.   When they adjourned it was estimated that every citizen owned about three franchises, and it was believed that unless Congress gave the Territory another degree of longitude there would not be room enough to accommodate the toll-roads.   The ends of them were hanging over the boundary line everywhere like a fringe.

MAP OF TOLL-ROADS.

The fact is, the freighting business had grown to such important proportions that there was nearly as much excitement over suddenly acquired toll-road fortunes as over the wonderful silver mines.

CHAPTER XXVI.

BY and by I was smitten with the silver fever. "Prospecting parties" were leaving for the mountains every day, and discovering and taking possession of rich silver-bearing lodes and ledges of quartz. Plainly this was the road to fortune. The great "Gould and Curry" mine was held at three or four hundred dollars a foot when we arrived; but in two months it had sprung up to eight hundred. The "Ophir" had been worth only a mere trifle, a year gone by, and now it was selling at nearly *four thousand dollars a foot!* Not a mine could be named that had not experienced an astonishing advance in value within a short time. Everybody was talking about these marvels. Go where you would, you heard nothing else, from morning till far into the night. Tom So-and-So had sold out of the "Amanda Smith" for $40,000—hadn't a cent when he "took up" the ledge six months ago. John Jones had sold half his interest in the "Bald Eagle and Mary Ann" for $65,000, gold coin, and gone to the States for his family. The widow Brewster had "struck it rich" in the "Golden Fleece" and sold ten feet for $18,000—hadn't money enough to buy a crape bonnet when Sing-Sing Tommy killed her husband at Baldy Johnson's wake last spring. The "Last Chance" had found a "clay casing" and knew they were "right on the ledge"—consequence, "feet" that went begging yesterday were worth a brick house apiece to-day, and seedy owners who could not get trusted for a drink at any bar in the country yesterday were roaring drunk on champagne to-day

13†

and had hosts of warm personal friends in a town where they had forgotten how to bow or shake hands from long-continued want of practice. Johnny Morgan, a common loafer, had gone to sleep in the gutter and waked up worth a hundred thousand dollars, in consequence of the decision in the "Lady Franklin and Rough and Ready" lawsuit. And so on—day in and day

UNLOADING SILVER BRICKS.

out the talk pelted our ears and the excitement waxed hotter and hotter around us.

I would have been more or less than human if I had not gone mad like the rest. Cart-loads of solid silver bricks, as large as pigs of lead, were arriving from the mills every day, and such sights as that gave substance to the wild talk about me. I succumbed and grew as frenzied as the craziest.

Every few days news would come of the discovery of a bran-new mining region; immediately the papers would teem with accounts of its richness, and away the surplus population would scamper to take possession. By the time I was fairly inoculated with the disease, "Esmeralda" had just had a run and "Humboldt" was beginning to shriek for attention. "Humboldt! Humboldt!" was the new cry, and straightway Humboldt, the newest of the new, the richest of the rich, the most marvellous of the marvellous discoveries in silver-land, was occupying two columns of the public prints to "Esmeralda's" one. I was just on the point of starting to Esmeralda, but turned with the tide and got ready for Humboldt. That the reader may see what moved me, and what would as surely have moved him had he been there, I insert here one of the newspaper letters of the day. It and several other letters from the same calm hand were the main means of converting me. I shall not garble the extract, but put it in just as it appeared in the *Daily Territorial Enterprise:*

But what about our mines? I shall be candid with you. I shall express an honest opinion, based upon a thorough examination. Humboldt county is the richest mineral region upon God's footstool. Each mountain range is gorged with the precious ores. Humboldt is the true Golconda.

The other day an assay of mere *croppings* yielded exceeding *four thousand dollars to the ton.* A week or two ago an assay of just such surface developments made returns of *seven thousand* dollars to the ton. Our mountains are full of rambling prospectors. Each day and almost every hour reveals new and more startling evidences of the profuse and intensified wealth of our favored county. The metal is not silver alone. There are distinct ledges of auriferous ore. A late discovery plainly evinces cinnabar. The coarser metals are in gross abundance. Lately evidences of bituminous coal have been detected. My theory has ever been that coal is a ligneous formation. I told Col. Whitman, in times past, that the neighborhood of Dayton (Nevada) betrayed no present or previous manifestations of a ligneous foundation, and that hence I had no confidence in his lauded coal mines. I repeated the same doctrine to the exultant coal discoverers of Humboldt. I talked with my friend Captain Burch on the subject. My pyrhanism vanished upon his statement that in the very region referred to he had seen petrified trees of the length of two hundred feet. Then is the fact established that huge forests once cast their grim shadows over this remote section. I am firm in the coal faith. Have no fears of the mineral resources of Humboldt county. They are immense—incalculable.

Let me state one or two things which will help the reader to better comprehend certain items in the above. At this time, our near neighbor, Gold Hill, was the most successful silver mining locality in Nevada. It was from there that more than half the daily shipments of silver bricks came. "Very rich" (and scarce) Gold Hill ore yielded from $100 to $400 to the ton; but the usual yield was only $20 to $40 per ton— that is to say, each hundred pounds of ore yielded from one dollar to two dollars. But the reader will perceive by the above extract, that in Humboldt from one fourth to nearly half the mass was silver! That is to say, every one hundred dred pounds of the ore had from *two hundred* dollars up to about *three hundred and fifty* in it. Some days later this same correspondent wrote:

I have spoken of the vast and almost fabulous wealth of this region—it is incredible. The intestines of our mountains are gorged with precious ore to plethora. I have said that nature has so shaped our mountains as to furnish most excellent facilities for the working of our mines. I have also told you that the country about here is pregnant with the finest mill sites in the world. But what is the mining history of Humboldt? The Sheba mine is in the hands of energetic San Francisco capitalists. It would seem that the ore is combined with metals that render it difficult of reduction with our im-

VIEW IN HUMBOLDT MOUNTAINS.

perfect mountain machinery. The proprietors have combined the capital and labor hinted at in my exordium. They are toiling and probing. Their tunnel has reached the length of one hundred feet. From primal assays alone, coupled with the development of the mine and public confidence in the continuance of effort, the stock had reared itself to eight hundred dollars market value. I do not know that one ton of the ore has been converted into current metal. I do know that there are many lodes in this section that surpass the Sheba in primal assay value. Listen a moment to the calculations of the Sheba operators. They purpose transporting the ore concentrated to Europe. The conveyance from Star City (its locality) to Virginia City will cost seventy dollars per ton; from Virginia to San Francisco, forty dollars per ton; from thence to Liverpool, its destination, ten dollars per ton. Their idea is that its conglomerate metals will reimburse them their cost of original extraction, the price of transportation, and the expense of reduction, and that then a ton of the raw ore will net them twelve hundred dollars. The estimate may be extravagant. Cut it in twain, and the product is enormous, far transcending any previous developments of our racy Territory.

A very common calculation is that many of our mines will yield five hundred dollars to the ton. Such fecundity throws the Gould & Curry, the Ophir and the Mexican, of your neighborhood, in the darkest shadow. I have given you the estimate of the value of a single developed mine. Its richness is indexed by its market valuation. The people of Humboldt county are *feet* crazy. As I write, our towns are near deserted. They look as languid as a consumptive girl. What has become of our sinewy and athletic fellow-citizens? They are coursing through ravines and over mountain tops. Their tracks are visible in every direction. Occasionally a horseman will dash among us. His steed betrays hard usage. He alights before his adobe dwelling, hastily exchanges courtesies with his townsmen, hurries to an assay office and from thence to the District Recorder's. In the morning, having renewed his provisional supplies, he is off again on his wild and unbeaten route. Why, the fellow numbers already his feet by the thousands. He is the horse-leech. He has the craving stomach of the shark or anaconda. He would conquer metallic worlds.

This was enough. The instant we had finished reading the above article, four of us decided to go to Humboldt. We commenced getting ready at once. And we also commenced upbraiding ourselves for not deciding sooner—for we were in terror lest all the rich mines would be found and secured before we got there, and we might have to put up with ledges that would not yield more than two or three hundred dollars a ton, maybe. An hour before, I would have felt opulent if I had owned ten feet in a Gold Hill mine whose ore produced twenty-five dollars to the ton; now I was already annoyed at the prospect of having to put up with mines the poorest of which would be a marvel in Gold Hill.

CHAPTER XXVII.

HURRY, was the word! We wasted no time. Our party consisted of four persons—a blacksmith sixty years of age, two young lawyers, and myself. We bought a wagon and two miserable old horses. We put eighteen hundred pounds of provisions and mining tools in the wagon and drove out of Carson on a chilly December afternoon. The horses were so weak and old that we soon found that it would be better if one or two of us got out and walked. It was an improvement. Next, we found that it would be better if a third man got out. That was an improvement also. It was at this time that I volunteered to drive, although I had never driven a harnessed horse before and many a man in such a position would have felt fairly excused from such a responsibility. But in a little while it was found that it would be a fine thing if the driver got out and walked also. It was at this time that I resigned the position of driver, and never resumed it again. Within the hour, we found that it would not only be better, but was absolutely necessary, that we four, taking turns, two at a time, should put our hands against the end of the wagon and push it through the sand, leaving the feeble horses little to do but keep out of the way and hold up the tongue. Perhaps it is well for one to know his fate at first, and get reconciled to it. We had learned ours in one afternoon. It was plain that we had to walk through the sand and shove that wagon and those horses two hundred miles. So we accepted the situation, and from that time forth we never rode. More than that, we stood regular and nearly constant watches pushing up behind.

We made seven miles, and camped in the desert. Young Clagett (now member of Congress from Montana) unharnessed and fed and watered the horses; Oliphant and I cut sage-brush, built the fire and brought water to cook with; and old Mr. Ballou the blacksmith did the cooking. This division of labor, and this appointment, was adhered to throughout the journey. We had no tent, and so we slept under our blankets in the open plain. We were so tired that we slept soundly.

We were fifteen days making the trip—two hundred miles; thirteen, rather, for we lay by a couple of days, in one

GOING TO HUMBOLDT.

place, to let the horses rest. We could really have accomplished the journey in ten days if we had towed the horses behind the wagon, but we did not think of that until it was too late, and so went on shoving the horses and the wagon too when we might have saved half the labor. Parties who met us, occasionally, advised us to put the horses *in* the wagon, but Mr. Ballou, through whose iron-clad earnestness no sarcasm could pierce, said that that would not do, because the provisions were exposed and would suffer, the horses being "bituminous from long deprivation." The reader will excuse me from translating. What Mr. Ballou customarily meant, when he used a long word, was a secret between himself and his Maker. He was one of the best and kindest hearted men that ever graced a humble sphere of life. He was gentleness

and simplicity itself—and unselfishness, too.   Although he was
more than twice as old as the eldest of us, he never gave himself any airs, privileges, or exemptions on that account.   He did
a *young* man's share of the work ; and did his share of conversing and entertaining from the general stand-point of *any* age—
not from the arrogant, overawing summit-height of sixty years.
His one striking peculiarity was his Partingtonian fashion of
loving and using big words *for their own sakes*, and independent of any bearing they might have upon the thought he
was purposing to convey.   He always let his ponderous syllables fall with an easy unconsciousness that left them wholly
without offensiveness.   In truth his air was so natural and so
simple that one was always catching himself accepting his
stately sentences as meaning something, when they really
meant nothing in the world.   If a word was long and grand
and resonant, that was sufficient to win the old man's love,
and he would drop that word into the most out-of-the-way
place in a sentence or a subject, and be as pleased with it as
if it were perfectly luminous with meaning.

We four always spread our common stock of blankets
together on the frozen ground, and slept side by side ; and
finding that our foolish, long-legged hound pup had a deal of
animal heat in him, Oliphant got to admitting him to the bed,
between himself and Mr. Ballou, hugging the dog's warm
back to his breast and finding great comfort in it.   But in the
night the pup would get stretchy and brace his feet against the
old man's back and shove, grunting complacently the while ;
and now and then, being warm and snug, grateful and happy,
he would paw the old man's back simply in excess of comfort ;
and at yet other times he would dream of the chase and in
his sleep tug at the old man's back hair and bark in his ear.
The old gentleman complained mildly about these familiarities,
at last, and when he got through with his statement he said
that such a dog as that was not a proper animal to admit to bed
with tired men, because he was " so meretricious in his movements and so organic in his emotions."   We turned the dog out.

It was a hard, wearing, toilsome journey, but it had its

bright side; for after each day was done and our wolfish
hunger appeased with a hot supper of fried bacon, bread, mo-

BALLOU'S BEDFELLOW.

lasses and black coffee, the pipe-smoking, song-singing and
yarn-spinning around the evening camp-fire in the still solitudes of the desert was a happy, care-free sort of recreation
that seemed the very summit and culmination of earthly
luxury. It is a kind of life that has a potent charm for all
men, whether city or country-bred. We are descended from
desert-lounging Arabs, and countless ages of growth toward
perfect civilization have failed to root out of us the nomadic
instinct. We all confess to a gratified thrill at the thought of
" camping out."

Once we made twenty-five miles in a day, and once we
made forty miles (through the Great American Desert), and
ten miles beyond—fifty in all—in twenty-three hours, without
halting to eat, drink or rest. To stretch out and go to sleep,
even on stony and frozen ground, after pushing a wagon and
two horses fifty miles, is a delight so supreme that for the
moment it almost seems cheap at the price.

We camped two days in the neighborhood of the "Sink
of the Humboldt." We tried to use the strong alkaline water
of the Sink, but it would not answer. It was like drinking
lye, and not weak lye, either. It left a taste in the mouth,

bitter and every way execrable, and a burning in the stomach
that was very uncomfortable.   We put molasses in it, but that
helped it very little; we added a pickle, yet the alkali was the
prominent taste, and so it was unfit for drinking.   The coffee

PLEASURES OF CAMPING OUT.

we made of this water was
the meanest compound man
has yet invented.   It was
really viler to the taste than
the unameliorated water itself.   Mr. Ballou, being the
architect and builder of the
beverage felt constrained to endorse and uphold it, and so
drank half a cup, by little sips, making shift to praise it faintly
the while, but finally threw out the remainder, and said frankly
it was "too technical for *him*."

But presently we found a spring of fresh water, convenient, and then, with nothing to mar our enjoyment, and no
stragglers to interrupt it, we entered into our rest.

CHAPTER XXVIII.

AFTER leaving the Sink, we traveled along the Humboldt river a little way. People accustomed to the monster mile-wide Mississippi, grow accustomed to associating the term "river" with a high degree of watery grandeur. Consequently, such people feel rather disappointed when they stand on the shores of the Humboldt or the Carson and find that a "river" in Nevada is a sickly rivulet which is just the counterpart of the Erie canal in all respects save that the canal is twice as long and four times as deep. One of the pleasantest and most invigorating exercises one can contrive is to run and jump across the Humboldt river till he is overheated, and then drink it dry.

On the fifteenth day we completed our march of two hundred miles and entered Unionville, Humboldt county, in the midst of a driving snow-storm. Unionville consisted of eleven cabins and a liberty-pole. Six of the cabins were strung along one side of a deep canyon, and the other five faced them. The rest of the landscape was made up of bleak mountain walls that rose so high into the sky from both sides of the canyon that the village was left, as it were, far down in the bottom of a crevice. It was always daylight on the mountain tops a long time before the darkness lifted and revealed Unionville.

We built a small, rude cabin in the side of the crevice and roofed it with canvas, leaving a corner open to serve as a chimney, through which the cattle used to tumble occasionally, at night, and mash our furniture and interrupt our sleep. It was very cold weather and fuel was scarce. Indians brought brush and bushes several miles on their backs; and when we could catch a laden Indian it was well—and when we could not (which was the rule, not the exception), we shivered and bore it.

I confess, without shame, that I expected to find masses of silver lying all about the ground. I expected to see it glittering in the sun on the mountain summits. I said nothing about this, for some instinct told me that I might possibly have an exaggerated idea about it, and so if I betrayed my thought I might bring derision upon myself. Yet I was as perfectly satisfied in my own mind as I could be of anything, that I was going to gather up, in a day or two, or at furthest a week or two, silver enough to make me satisfactorily wealthy—and so my fancy was already busy with plans for spending this money. The first opportunity that offered, I sauntered carelessly away from the cabin, keeping an eye on the other boys, and stopping and contemplating the sky when they seemed to be observing me; but as soon as the coast was manifestly clear, I fled away as guiltily as a thief might have done and never halted till I was far beyond sight and call. Then I began my search with a feverish excitement that was brimful of expectation—almost of certainty. I crawled about the ground, seizing and examining bits of stone, blowing the dust from them or rubbing them on my clothes, and then peering at them with anxious hope. Presently I found a bright fragment and my heart bounded! I hid behind a boulder and polished it and scrutinized it with a nervous eagerness and a delight that was more pronounced than absolute certainty itself could have afforded. The more I examined the fragment the more I was convinced that I had found the door to fortune. I marked the spot and carried away my specimen. Up and down the rugged mountain side I searched, with always increasing interest and always augmenting gratitude that I had come to Humboldt and come in time. Of all the experiences of my life, this secret search among the hidden treasures of silver-land was the nearest to unmarred ecstasy. It was a delirious revel. By and by, in the bed of a shallow rivulet, I found a deposit of shining yellow scales, and my breath almost forsook me! A gold mine, and in my simplicity I had been content with vulgar silver! I was so excited that I half believed my overwrought imagination was deceiving me. Then a fear came upon me that people might be observing me and would guess my secret.

THE SECRET SEARCH.

Moved by this thought, I made a circuit of the place, and ascended a knoll to reconnoiter. Solitude. No creature was near. Then I returned to my mine, fortifying myself against possible disappointment, but my fears were groundless—the shining scales were still there. I set about scooping them out, and for an hour I toiled down the windings of the stream and robbed its bed. But at last the descending sun warned me to give up the quest, and I turned homeward laden with wealth. As I walked along I could not help smiling at the thought of my being so excited over my fragment of silver when a nobler metal was almost under my nose. In this little time the former had so fallen in my estimation that once or twice I was on the point of throwing it away.

The boys were as hungry as usual, but I could eat nothing. Neither could I talk. I was full of dreams and far away.

Their conversation interrupted the flow of my fancy somewhat, and annoyed me a little, too. I despised the sordid and commonplace things they talked about. But as they proceeded, it began to amuse me. It grew to be rare fun to hear them planning their poor little economies and sighing over possible privations and distresses when a gold mine, all our own, lay within sight of the cabin and I could point it out at any moment. Smothered hilarity began to oppress me, presently. It was hard to resist the impulse to burst out with exultation and reveal everything; but I did resist. I said within myself that I would filter the great news through my lips calmly and be serene as a summer morning while I watched its effect in their faces. I said:

"Where have you all been?"

"Prospecting."

"What did you find?"

"Nothing."

"Nothing? What do you think of the country?"

"Can't tell, yet," said Mr. Ballou, who was an old gold miner, and had likewise had considerable experience among the silver mines.

"Well, haven't you formed any sort of opinion?"

"Yes, a sort of a one. It's fair enough here, may be, but overrated. Seven thousand dollar ledges are scarce, though. That Sheba may be rich enough, but we don't own it; and besides, the rock is so full of base metals that all the science in the world can't work it. We'll not starve, here, but we'll not get rich, I'm afraid."

"So you think the prospect is pretty poor?"

"No name for it!"

"Well, we'd better go back, hadn't we?"

"Oh, not yet—of course not. We'll try it a riffle, first."

"Suppose, now—this is merely a supposition, you know—suppose you could find a ledge that would yield, say, a hundred and fifty dollars a ton—would that satisfy you?"

"Try us once!" from the whole party.

"Or suppose—merely a supposition, of course—suppose

you were to find a ledge that would yield two thousand dollars a ton—would *that* satisfy you?"

"Here—what do you mean? What are you coming at? Is there some mystery behind all this?"

"Never mind. I am not saying anything. You know perfectly well there are no rich mines here—of course you do. Because you have been around and examined for yourselves. Anybody would know that, that had been around. But just for the sake of argument, suppose—in a kind of general way—suppose some person were to tell you that two-thousand-dollar ledges were simply contemptible—contemptible, understand—and that right yonder in sight of this very cabin there were piles of pure gold and pure silver—oceans of it—enough to make you all rich in twenty-four hours! Come!"

"CAST YOUR EYE ON THAT!"

"I should say he was as crazy as a loon!" said old Ballou, but wild with excitement, nevertheless.

"Gentlemen," said I, "I don't say anything—*I* haven't

been around, you know, and of course don't know anything—
but all I ask of you is to cast your eye on *that*, for instance,
and tell me what you think of it!" and I tossed my treasure
before them.

There was an eager scramble for it, and a closing of heads
together over it under the candle-light. Then old Ballou
said:

"Think of it? I think it is nothing but a lot of granite
rubbish and nasty glittering mica that isn't worth ten cents
an acre!"

So vanished my dream. So melted my wealth away. So
toppled my airy castle to the earth and left me stricken and
forlorn.

Moralizing, I observed, then, that "all that glitters is not
gold."

Mr. Ballou said I could go further than that, and lay it
up among my treasures of knowledge, that *nothing* that glitters is gold. So I learned then, once for all, that gold in its
native state is but dull, unornamental stuff, and that only low-
born metals excite the admiration of the ignorant with an
ostentatious glitter. However, like the rest of the world, I
still go on underrating men of gold and glorifying men of
mica. Commonplace human nature cannot rise above that.

CHAPTER XXIX.

TRUE knowledge of the nature of silver mining came fast enough. We went out "prospecting" with Mr. Ballou. We climbed the mountain sides, and clambered among sagebrush, rocks and snow till we were ready to drop with exhaustion, but found no silver—nor yet any gold. Day after day we did this. Now and then we came upon holes burrowed a few feet into the declivities and apparently abandoned; and now and then we found one or two listless men still burrowing. But there was no appearance of silver. These holes were the beginnings of tunnels, and the purpose was to drive them hundreds of feet into the mountain, and some day tap the hidden ledge where the silver was. Some day! It seemed far enough away, and very hopeless and dreary. Day after day we toiled, and climbed and searched, and we younger partners grew sicker and still sicker of the promiseless toil. At last we halted under a beetling rampart of rock which projected from the earth high upon the mountain. Mr. Ballou broke off some fragments with a hammer, and examined them long and attentively with a small eye-glass; threw them away and broke off more; said this rock was quartz, and quartz was the sort of rock that contained silver. *Contained* it! I had thought that at least it would be caked on the outside of it like a kind of veneering. He still broke off pieces and critically examined them, now and then wetting the piece with his tongue and applying the glass. At last he exclaimed:

14†

"We've got it!"

We were full of anxiety in a moment. The rock was clean and white, where it was broken, and across it ran a ragged thread of blue. He said that that little thread had

"WE'VE GOT IT!"

silver in it, mixed with base metals, such as lead and antimony, a n d o t h e r rubbish, and that there was a speck or two of gold visible. A f t e r a great deal of effort we managed to discern some little fine yellow s p e c k s, a n d judged t h a t a couple of tons of them massed together might make a gold dollar, possibly. We were not jubilant, but Mr. Ballou said there were worse ledges in the world

than that. He saved what he called the "richest" piece of the rock, in order to determine its value by the process called the "fire-assay." Then we named the mine "Monarch of the Mountains" (modesty of nomenclature is not a prominent feature in the mines), and Mr. Ballou wrote out and stuck up the following "notice," preserving a copy to be entered upon the books in the mining recorder's office in the town.

" NOTICE."

" We the undersigned claim three claims, of three hundred feet each [and one for discovery), on this silver-bearing quartz lead or lode, extending north and south from this notice, with all its dips, spurs, and angles, variations and sinuosities, together with fifty feet of ground on either side for working the same."

We put our names to it and tried to feel that our fortunes were made. But when we talked the matter all over with Mr. Ballou, we felt depressed and dubious. He said that this surface quartz was not all there was of our mine; but that the wall or ledge of rock called the " Monarch of the Mountains," extended down hundreds and hundreds of feet into the earth—he illustrated by saying it was like a curb-stone, and maintained a nearly uniform thickness—say twenty feet—away down into the bowels of the earth, and was perfectly distinct from the casing rock on each side of it; and that it kept to itself, and maintained its distinctive character always, no matter how deep it extended into the earth or how far it stretched itself through and across the hills and valleys. He said it might be a mile deep and ten miles long, for all we knew; and that wherever we bored into it above ground or below, we would find gold and silver in it, but no gold or silver in the meaner rock it was cased between. And he said that down in the great depths of the ledge was its richness, and the deeper it went the richer it grew. Therefore, instead of working here on the surface, we must either bore down into the rock with a shaft till we came to where it was rich—say a hundred feet or so—or else we must go down into the valley and bore a long tunnel into the mountain side and tap the ledge far under the earth. To do either was plainly the labor of months; for we could blast and bore only a few feet a day—some five or six. But this was not all. He said that after we got the ore out it must be hauled in wagons to a distant silver-mill, ground up, and the silver extracted by a tedious and costly process. Our fortune seemed a century away!

But we went to work. We decided to sink a shaft. So, for a week we climbed the mountain, laden with picks, drills,

gads, crowbars, shovels, cans of blasting powder and coils of
fuse and strove with might and main.   At first the rock was
broken and loose and we dug it up with picks and threw it out
with shovels, and the hole progressed very well.   But the rock
became more compact, presently, and gads and crowbars came
into play.   But shortly nothing could make an impression but
blasting powder.   That was the weariest work!   One of us
held the iron drill in its place and another would strike with
an eight-pound sledge—it was like driving nails on a large
scale.   In the course of an hour or two the drill would reach

INCIPIENT MILLIONAIRES.

a depth of two or three feet, making a hole a couple of
inches in diameter.   We would put in a charge of powder, in-

sert half a yard of fuse, pour in sand and gravel and ram it down, then light the fuse and run.   When the explosion came and the rocks and smoke shot into the air, we would go back and find about a bushel of that hard, rebellious quartz jolted out.   Nothing more.   One week of this satisfied me.   I resigned.   Clagget and Oliphant followed.   Our shaft was only twelve feet deep.   We decided that a tunnel was the thing we wanted.

So we went down the mountain side and worked a week; at the end of which time we had blasted a tunnel about deep enough to hide a hogshead in, and judged that about nine hundred feet more of it would reach the ledge.   I resigned again, and the other boys only held out one day longer.   We decided that a tunnel was not what we wanted.   We wanted a ledge that was already "developed."   There were none in the camp.

We dropped the "Monarch" for the time being.

Meantime the camp was filling up with people, and there was a constantly growing excitement about our Humboldt mines.   We fell victims to the epidemic and strained every nerve to acquire more "feet."   We prospected and took up new claims, put "notices" on them and gave them grandiloquent names.   We traded some of our "feet" for "feet" in other people's claims.   In a little while we owned largely in the "Gray Eagle," the "Columbiana," the "Branch Mint," the "Maria Jane," the "Universe," the "Root-Hog-or-Die," the "Samson and Delilah," the "Treasure Trove," the "Golconda," the "Sultana," the "Boomerang," the "Great Republic," the "Grand Mogul," and fifty other "mines" that had never been molested by a shovel or scratched with a pick.   We had not less than thirty thousand "feet" apiece in the "richest mines on earth" as the frenzied cant phrased it—and were in debt to the butcher.   We were stark mad with excitement—drunk with happiness—smothered under mountains of prospective wealth—arrogantly compassionate toward the plodding millions who knew not our marvellous canyon—but our credit was not good at the grocer's.

It was the strangest phase of life one can imagine. It was a beggars' revel. There was nothing doing in the district— no mining—no milling—no productive effort—no income— and not enough money in the entire camp to buy a corner lot in an eastern village, hardly; and yet a stranger would have supposed he was walking among bloated millionaires. Prospecting parties swarmed out of town with the first flush of dawn, and swarmed in again at nightfall laden with spoil— rocks. Nothing but rocks. Every man's pockets were full of them; the floor of his cabin was littered with them; they were disposed in labeled rows on his shelves.

CHAPTER XXX.

I MET men at every turn who owned from one thousand to thirty thousand "feet" in undeveloped silver mines, every single foot of which they believed would shortly be worth from fifty to a thousand dollars—and as often as any other way they were men who had not twenty-five dollars in the world. Every man you met had his new mine to boast of, and his "specimens" ready; and if the opportunity offered, he would infallibly back you into a corner and offer as a favor to *you*, not to *him*, to part with just a few feet in the "Golden Age," or the "Sarah Jane," or some other unknown stack of croppings, for money enough to get a "square meal" with, as the phrase went. And you were never to reveal that he had made you the offer at such a ruinous price, for it was only out of friendship for you that he was willing to make the sacrifice. Then he would fish a piece of rock out of his pocket, and after looking mysteriously around as if he feared he might be waylaid and robbed if caught with such wealth in his possession, he would dab the rock against his tongue, clap an eyeglass to it, and exclaim:

"Look at that! Right there in that red dirt! See it? See the specks of gold? And the streak of silver? That's from the 'Uncle Abe.' There's a hundred thousand tons like that in sight! Right in sight, mind you! And when we get down on it and the ledge comes in solid, it will be the richest thing in the world! Look at the assay! I don't want you to believe *me*—look at the assay!"

Then he would get out a greasy sheet of paper which showed that the portion of rock assayed had given evidence of containing silver and gold in the proportion of so many hundreds or thousands of dollars to the ton. I little knew, then, that the custom was to hunt out the *richest* piece of rock and get it assayed! Very often, that piece, the size of a filbert, was the only fragment in a ton that had a particle of metal in it— and yet the assay made it pretend to represent the average value of the ton of rubbish it came from!

" DO YOU SEE IT ? "

On such a system of assaying as that, the Humboldt world had gone crazy. On the authority of such assays its newspaper correspondents were frothing about rock worth four and seven thousand dollars a ton!

And does the reader remember, a few pages back, the calculations, of a quoted correspondent, whereby the ore is to be mined and shipped all the way to England, the metals extracted, and the gold and silver contents received back by the miners as clear profit, the copper, antimony and other things in the ore being sufficient to pay all the expenses incurred? Everybody's head was full of such "calculations" as those— such raving insanity, rather. Few people took *work* into their calculations—or outlay of money either; except the work and expenditures of other people.

We never touched our tunnel or our shaft again. Why? Because we judged that we had learned the *real* secret of success in silver mining—which was, *not* to mine the silver ourselves by the sweat of our brows and the labor of our hands, but to *sell* the ledges to the dull slaves of toil and let them do the mining!

Before leaving Carson, the Secretary and I had purchased "feet" from various Esmeralda stragglers. We had expected immediate returns of bullion, but were only afflicted with regular and constant "assessments" instead—demands for money wherewith to develop the said mines. These assessments had grown so oppressive that it seemed necessary to look into the matter personally. Therefore I projected a pilgrimage to Carson and thence to Esmeralda. I bought a horse and started, in company with Mr. Ballou and a gentleman named Ollendorff, a Prussian—not the party who has inflicted so much suffering on the world with his wretched foreign grammars, with their interminable repetitions of questions which never have occurred and are never likely to occur in any conversation among human beings. We rode through a snow-storm for two or three days, and arrived at "Honey Lake Smith's," a sort of isolated inn on the Carson river. It was a two-story log house situated on a small knoll in the midst of the vast basin or desert through which the sickly Carson winds its melancholy way. Close to the house were the Overland stage stables, built of sun-dried bricks. There was not another building within several leagues of the place. Towards sunset about twenty hay-wagons arrived and camped around the house and all the teamsters came in to supper—a very, very rough set. There were one or two Overland stage drivers there, also, and half a dozen vagabonds and stragglers; consequently the house was well crowded.

We walked out, after supper, and visited a small Indian camp in the vicinity. The Indians were in a great hurry about something, and were packing up and getting away as fast as they could.   In their broken English they said, "By'm-by, heap water!" and by the help of signs made us under-stand that in their opinion a flood was coming.   The weather was perfectly clear, and this was not the rainy season.   There was about a foot of water in the insignificant river—or maybe two feet; the stream was not wider than a back alley in a village, and its banks were scarcely higher than a man's head. So, where was the flood to come from? We canvassed the subject a-while and then concluded it was a ruse, and that the Indians

FAREWELL SWEET RIVER.

had some better reason for leaving in a hurry than fears of a flood in such an exceedingly dry time.

At seven in the evening we went to bed in the second story—with our clothes on, as usual, and all three in the same bed, for every available space on the floors, chairs, etc., was in request, and even then there was barely room for the housing of the inn's guests.   An hour later we were awakened by a great turmoil, and springing out of bed we picked our way nimbly among the ranks of snoring teamsters on the floor and got to the front windows of the long room.   A glance revealed a strange spectacle, under the moonlight. The crooked Carson was full to the brim, and its waters were raging and foaming in the wildest way—sweeping around the sharp bends at a furious speed, and bearing on their surface a chaos of logs, brush and all sorts of rubbish.   A depression, where its bed had once been, in other times, was already filling, and in one or two places the water was beginning to wash over the main bank.   Men were flying hither and thither, bringing

cattle and wagons close up to the house, for the spot of high
ground on which it stood extended only some thirty feet in
front and about a hundred in the rear. Close to the old river
bed just spoken of, stood a little log stable, and in this our

THE RESCUE.

horses were lodged.
While we looked, the
waters increased so fast
in this place that in a
few minutes a torrent
was roaring by the little
stable and its margin
encroaching steadily on
the logs. We suddenly
realized that this flood
was not a mere holiday spectacle, but meant damage—and not
only to the small log stable but to the Overland buildings
close to the main river, for the waves had now come ashore
and were creeping about the foundations and invading the

great hay-corral adjoining.   We ran down and joined the
crowd of excited men and frightened animals.   We waded
knee-deep into the log stable, unfastened the horses and
waded out almost *waist*-deep, so fast the waters increased.
Then the crowd rushed in a body to the hay-corral and began
to tumble down the huge stacks of baled hay and roll the
bales up on the high ground by the house.   Meantime it was
discovered that Owens, an overland driver, was missing, and a
man ran to the large stable, and wading in, boot-top deep,
discovered him asleep in his bed, awoke him, and waded out
again.   But Owens was drowsy and resumed his nap; but
only for a minute or two, for presently he turned in his bed,
his hand dropped over the side and came in contact with the
cold water !   It was up level with the mattrass !   He waded
out, breast-deep, almost, and the next moment the sun-burned
bricks melted down like sugar and the big building crumbled
to a ruin and was washed away in a twinkling.

At eleven o'clock only the roof of the little log stable was
out of water, and our inn was on an island in mid-ocean.   As
far as the eye could reach, in the moonlight, there was no
desert visible, but only a level waste of shining water.   The
Indians were true prophets, but how did they get their information ?   I am not able to answer the question.

We remained cooped up eight days and nights with that
curious crew.   Swearing, drinking and card playing were the
order of the day, and occasionally a fight was thrown in for
variety.   Dirt and vermin—but let us forget those features;
their profusion is simply inconceivable—it is better that they
remain so.

There were two men—however, this chapter is long enough.

CHAPTER XXXI.

THERE were two men in the company who caused me particular discomfort. One was a little Swede, about twenty-five years old, who knew only one song, and he was forever singing it. By day we were all crowded into one small, stifling barroom, and so there was no escaping this person's music. Through all the profanity, whisky-guzzling, "old sledge" and quarreling, his monotonous song meandered with never a variation in its tiresome sameness, and it seemed to me, at last, that I would be content to die, in order to be rid of the torture. The other man was a stalwart ruffian called "Arkansas," who carried two revolvers in his belt and a bowie knife projecting from his boot, and who was always drunk and always suffering for a fight. But he was so feared, that nobody would accommodate him. He would try all manner of little wary ruses to entrap somebody into an offensive remark, and his face would light up now and then when he fancied he was fairly on the scent of a fight, but invariably his victim would elude his toils and then he would show a disappointment that was almost pathetic. The landlord, Johnson, was a meek, well-meaning fellow, and Arkansas fastened on him early, as a promising subject, and gave him no rest day or night, for awhile. On the fourth morning, Arkansas got drunk and sat himself down to wait for an opportunity. Presently Johnson came in, just comfortably sociable with whisky, and said:

"I reckon the Pennsylvania 'lection—"

Arkansas raised his finger impressively and Johnson stopped. Arkansas rose unsteadily and confronted him. Said he:

"Wha-what do you know a-about Pennsylvania? **Answer** me that. Wha-what do you know 'bout Pennsylvania?"

"I was only goin' to say—"

"You was only goin' to *say*. *You* was! You was only goin' to say—*what* was you goin' to say? That's it! That's what *I* want to know. *I* want to know wha-what you (*'ic*) what you know about Pennsylvania, since you're makin' yourself so d—d free. Answer me that!"

"MR. ARKANSAS."

"Mr. Arkansas, if you'd only let me—"

"Who's a henderin' you? Don't you insinuate nothing agin me!—don't you do it. Don't you come in here bullyin' around, and cussin' and goin' on like a lunatic—don't you do it. 'Coz *I* won't *stand* it. If fight's what you want, out with it! I'm your man! Out with it!"

Said Johnson, backing into a corner, Arkansas following, menacingly:

"Why, *I* never said nothing, Mr. Arkansas. You don't give a man no chance. I was only goin' to say that Pennsylvania was goin' to have an election next week—that was all—that was everything I was goin' to say—I wish I may never stir if it wasn't."

"Well then why d'n't you say it? What did you come swellin' around that way for, and tryin' to raise trouble?"

"Why *I* didn't come swellin' around, Mr. Arkansas—I just—"

"I'm a liar am I! Ger-reat Cæsar's ghost—"

"Oh, please, Mr. Arkansas, I never meant such a thing as that, I wish I may die if I did. All the boys will tell you that I've always spoke well of you, and respected you more'n any man in the house. Ask Smith. Ain't it so, Smith? Didn't I say, no longer ago than last night, that for a man that was a gentleman *all* the time and every way you took him, give me Arkansas? I'll leave it to any gentleman here if them warn't the very words I used. Come, now, Mr. Arkansas, le's take a drink—le's shake hands and take a drink. Come up—everybody! It's my treat. Come up, Bill, Tom, Bob, Scotty—come up. I want you all to take a drink with me and Arkansas—*old* Arkansas, I call him—bully old Arkansas. Gimme your hand agin. Look at him, boys—just take a *look* at him. Thar stands the whitest man in America!—and the man that denies it has got to fight *me*, that's all. Gimme that old flipper agin!"

They embraced, with drunken affection on the landlord's part and unresponsive toleration on the part of Arkansas, who, bribed by a drink, was disappointed of his prey once more. But the foolish landlord was so happy to have escaped butchery, that he went on talking when he ought to have marched himself out of danger. The consequence was that Arkansas shortly began to glower upon him dangerously, and presently said:

"Lan'lord, will you p-please make that remark over agin if you please?"

"I was a-sayin' to Scotty that my father was up'ards of eighty year old when he died."

"Was that *all* that you said?"

"Yes, that was all."

"Didn't say nothing but that?"

"No—nothing."

Then an uncomfortable silence.

Arkansas played with his glass a moment, lolling on his elbows on the counter. Then he meditatively scratched his left shin with his right boot, while the awkward silence continued. But presently he loafed away toward the stove, looking dissatisfied; roughly shouldered two or three men out of a comfortable position; occupied it himself, gave a sleeping dog a kick that sent him howling under a bench, then spread his long legs and his blanket-coat tails apart and proceeded to warm his back. In a little while he fell to grumbling to himself, and soon he slouched back to the bar and said:

"Lan'lord, what's your idea for rakin' up old personalities and blowin' about your father? Ain't this company agreeable to you? Ain't it? If this company ain't agreeable to you, p'r'aps we'd better leave. Is that your idea? Is that what you're coming at?"

"Why bless your soul, Arkansas, I warn't thinking of such a thing. My father and my mother—"

"Lan'lord, *don't* crowd a man! Don't do it. If nothing'll do you but a disturbance, out with it like a man ('*ic*)—but *don't* rake up old bygones and fling 'em in the teeth of a passel of people that wants to be peaceable if they could git a chance. What's the matter with you this mornin', anyway? I never see a man carry on so."

"Arkansas, I reely didn't mean no harm, and I won't go on with it if it's onpleasant to you. I reckon my licker's got into my head, and what with the flood, and havin' so many to feed and look out for—"

"So *that's* what's a-ranklin' in your heart, is it? You want us to leave do you? There's too many on us. You want us to pack up and swim. Is that it? Come!"

"Please be reasonable, Arkansas. Now *you* know that I ain't the man to—"

"Are you a threatenin' me? Are you? By George, the man don't live that can skeer me! Don't you try to come that game, my chicken—'cuz I can stand a good deal, but I won't stand that. Come out from behind that bar till I clean you! You want to drive us out, do you, you sneakin' underhanded hound! Come out from behind that bar! *I'll* learn you to bully and badger and browbeat a gentleman that's forever trying to befriend you and keep you out of trouble!"

"Please, Arkansas, please don't shoot! If there's got to be bloodshed—"

"Do you hear that, gentlemen? Do you hear him talk about bloodshed? So it's blood you want, is it, you ravin' desperado! You'd made up your mind to murder somebody this mornin'—I knowed it perfectly well. I'm the man, am I? It's me you're goin' to murder, is it? But you can't do it 'thout I get one chance first, you thievin' black-hearted, white-livered son of a nigger! Draw your weepon!"

AN ARMED ALLY.

With that, Arkansas began to shoot, and the landlord to clamber over benches, men and every sort of obstacle in a frantic desire to escape. In the midst of the wild hubbub the landlord crashed through a glass door, and as Arkansas charged after him the landlord's wife suddenly appeared in the door-

†15

way and confronted the desperado with a pair of scissors! Her fury was magnificent. With head erect and flashing eye she stood a moment and then advanced, with her weapon raised. The astonished ruffian hesitated, and then fell back a step. She followed. She backed him step by step into the middle of the bar-room, and then, while the wondering crowd closed up and gazed, she gave him such another tongue-lashing as never a cowed and shamefaced braggart got before, perhaps! As she finished and retired victorious, a roar of applause shook the house, and every man ordered " drinks for the crowd " in one and the same breath.

The lesson was entirely sufficient. The reign of terror was over, and the Arkansas domination broken for good. During the rest of the season of island captivity, there was one man who sat apart in a state of permanent humiliation, never mixing in any quarrel or uttering a boast, and never resenting the insults the once cringing crew now constantly leveled at him, and that man was " Arkansas."

By the fifth or sixth morning the waters had subsided from the land, but the stream in the old river bed was still high and swift and there was no possibility of crossing it. On the eighth it was still too high for an entirely safe passage, but life in the inn had become next to insupportable by reason of the dirt, drunkenness, fighting, etc., and so we made an effort to get away. In the midst of a heavy snow-storm we embarked in a canoe, taking our saddles aboard and towing our horses after us by their halters. The Prussian, Ollendorff, was in the bow, with a paddle, Ballou paddled in the middle, and I sat in the stern holding the halters. When the horses lost their footing and began to swim, Ollendorff got frightened, for there was great danger that the horses would make our aim uncertain, and it was plain that if we failed to land at a certain spot the current would throw us off and almost surely cast us into the main Carson, which was a boiling torrent, now. Such a catastrophe would be death, in all probability, for we would be swept to sea in the " Sink " or overturned and drowned. We warned Ollendorff to keep his wits about him and handle himself carefully, but it was useless; the moment the bow touched the bank, he made a spring and the canoe whirled upside down in

CROSSING THE FLOOD.

ten-foot water. Ollendorff seized some brush and dragged himself ashore, but Ballou and I had to swim for it, encumbered with our overcoats. But we held on to the canoe, and although we were washed down nearly to the Carson, we managed to push the boat ashore and make a safe landing. We were cold and water-soaked, but safe. The horses made a landing, too, but our saddles were gone, of course. We tied the animals in the sage-brush and there they had to stay for twenty-four hours. We baled out the canoe and ferried over some food and blankets for them, but we slept one more night in the inn before making another venture on our journey.

The next morning it was still snowing furiously when we

got away with our new stock of saddles and accoutrements. We mounted and started. The snow lay so deep on the ground that there was no sign of a road perceptible, and the snow-fall was so thick that we could not see more than a hundred yards ahead, else we could have guided our course by the mountain ranges. The case looked dubious, but Ollendorff said his instinct was as sensitive as any compass, and that he could "strike a bee-line" for Carson city and never diverge from it. He said that if he were to straggle a single point out of the true line his instinct would assail him like an outraged conscience. Consequently we dropped into his wake happy and content. For half an hour we poked along warily enough, but at the end of that time we came upon a fresh trail, and Ollendorff shouted proudly:

"I knew I was as dead certain as a compass, boys! Here we are, right in somebody's tracks that will hunt the way for us without any trouble. Let's hurry up and join company with the party."

So we put the horses into as much of a trot as the deep snow would allow, and before long it was evident that we were gaining on our predecessors, for the tracks grew more distinct. We hurried along, and at the end of an hour the tracks looked still newer and fresher—but what surprised us was, that the *number* of travelers in advance of us seemed to steadily increase. We wondered how so large a party came to be traveling at such a time and in such a solitude. Somebody suggested that it must be a company of soldiers from the fort, and so we accepted that solution and jogged along a little faster still, for they could not be far off now. But the tracks still multiplied, and we began to think the platoon of soldiers was miraculously expanding into a regiment—Ballou said they had already increased to five hundred! Presently he stopped his horse and said:

"Boys, these are our own tracks, and we've actually been circussing round and round in a circle for more than two hours, out here in this blind desert! By George this is perfectly hydraulic!"

Then the old man waxed wroth and abusive. He called Ollendorff all manner of hard names—said he never saw such a lurid fool as he was, and ended with the peculiarly venomous opinion that he "did not know as much as a logarythm!"

We certainly had been following our own tracks. Ollen-

ADVANCE IN A CIRCLE.

dorff and his "mental compass" were in disgrace from that moment. After all our hard travel, here we were on the bank of the stream again, with the inn beyond dimly outlined through the driving snow-fall. While we were considering what to do, the young Swede landed from the canoe and took his pedestrian way Carson-wards, singing his same tiresome song about his "sister and his brother" and "the child in the grave with its mother," and in a short minute faded and disappeared in the white oblivion. He was never heard of again. He no doubt got bewildered and lost, and Fatigue delivered him over to Sleep and Sleep betrayed him to Death. Possibly he followed our treacherous tracks till he became exhausted and dropped.

THE SONGSTER.

Presently the Overland stage forded the now fast receding stream and started toward Carson on its first trip since the flood came. We hesitated no longer, now, but took up our march in its wake, and trotted merrily along, for we had good confidence in the driver's bump of locality. But our horses were no match for the fresh stage team. We were soon left out of sight; but it was no matter, for we had the deep ruts the wheels made for a guide. By this time it was three in the afternoon, and consequently it was not very long before night came—and not with a lingering twilight, but with a sudden shutting down like a cellar door, as is its habit in that country. The snow-fall was still as thick as ever, and of course we could not see fifteen steps before us; but all about us the white glare of the snow-bed enabled us to discern the smooth sugar-loaf mounds made by the covered sage-bushes, and just in front of us the two faint grooves which we knew were the steadily filling and slowly disappearing wheel-tracks.

Now those sage-bushes were all about the same height— three or four feet; they stood just about seven feet apart, all over the vast desert; each of them was a mere snow-mound, now; in *any* direction that you proceeded (the same as in a well laid out orchard) you would find yourself moving down a distinctly defined avenue, with a row of these snow-mounds an either side of it—an avenue the customary width of a road, nice and level in its breadth, and rising at the sides in the most natural way, by reason of the mounds. But we had not thought of this. Then imagine the chilly thrill that shot through us when it finally occurred to us, far in the night,

that since the last faint trace of the wheel-tracks had long ago
been buried from sight, we might now be wandering down a
mere sage-brush avenue, miles away from the road and diverging further and further away from it all the time.   Having a
cake of ice slipped down one's back is placid comfort compared
to it.   There was a sudden leap and stir of blood that had
been asleep for an hour, and as sudden a rousing of all the
drowsing activities in our minds and bodies.   We were alive
and awake at once—and shaking and quaking with consternation, too.   There was an instant halting and dismounting, a
bending low and an anxious scanning of the road-bed.   Useless, of course ; for if a faint depression could not be discerned
from an altitude of four or five feet above it, it certainly could
not with one's nose nearly against it.

CHAPTER XXXII.

WE seemed to be in a road, but that was no proof. We tested this by walking off in various directions—the regular snow-mounds and the regular avenues between them convinced each man that *he* had found the true road, and that the others had found only false ones. Plainly the situation was desperate. We were cold and stiff and the horses were tired. We decided to build a sage-brush fire and camp out till morning. This was wise, because if we were wandering from the right road and the snow-storm continued another day our case would be the next thing to hopeless if we kept on.

All agreed that a camp fire was what would come nearest to saving us, now, and so we set about building it. We could find no matches, and so we tried to make shift with the pistols. Not a man in the party had ever tried to do such a thing before, but not a man in the party doubted that it *could* be done, and without any trouble—because every man in the party had read about it in books many a time and had naturally come to believe it, with trusting simplicity, just as he had long ago accepted and believed *that other* common book-fraud about Indians and lost hunters making a fire by rubbing two dry sticks together.

We huddled together on our knees in the deep snow, and the horses put their noses together and bowed their patient heads over us; and while the feathery flakes eddied down and turned us into a group of white statuary, we proceeded with the momentous experiment. We broke twigs

from a sage bush and piled them on a little cleared place
in the shelter of our bodies. In the course of ten or fifteen
minutes all was ready, and then, while conversation ceased
and our pulses beat low with anxious suspense, Ollendorff
applied his revolver, pulled the trigger and blew the pile
clear out of the county! It was the flattest failure that ever
was.

This was distressing, but it paled before a greater horror—

A FLAT FAILURE.

the horses were gone! I had been appointed to hold the
bridles, but in my absorbing anxiety over the pistol experiment I had unconsciously dropped them and the released
animals had walked off in the storm. It was useless to try to
follow them, for their footfalls could make no sound, and one
could pass within two yards of the creatures and never see
them. We gave them up without an effort at recovering
them, and cursed the lying books that said horses would stay

by their masters for protection and companionship in a distressful time like ours.

We were miserable enough, before; we felt still more forlorn, now. Patiently, but with blighted hope, we broke more sticks and piled them, and once more the Prussian shot them into annihilation. Plainly, to light a fire with a pistol was an art requiring practice and experience, and the middle of a desert at midnight in a snow-storm was not a good place or time for the acquiring of the accomplishment. We gave it up and tried the other. Each man took a couple of sticks and fell to chafing them together. At the end of half an hour we were thoroughly chilled, and so were the sticks. We bitterly execrated the Indians, the hunters and the books that had betrayed us with the silly device, and wondered dismally what was next to be done. At this critical moment Mr. Ballou fished out four matches from the rubbish of an overlooked pocket. To have found four gold bars would have seemed poor and cheap good luck compared to this. One

THE LAST MATCH.

cannot think how good a match looks under such circumstances—or how lovable and precious, and sacredly beautiful to the eye. This time we gathered sticks with high hopes; and when Mr. Ballou prepared to light the first match, there was an amount of interest centred upon him that pages of writing could not describe. The match burned hopefully a moment, and then went out. It could not have carried more regret with it if it had been a human life. The next match simply flashed and died. The wind puffed the third one out just as it was on the imminent verge of success. We gathered together closer than ever, and developed a solicitude that was rapt and painful, as Mr. Ballou scratched our last hope on his leg. It lit, burned blue and sickly, and then budded into a robust flame. Shading it with his hands, the old gentleman bent gradually down and every heart went with him—everybody, too, for that matter—and blood and breath stood still. The flame touched the sticks at last, took gradual hold upon them—hesitated—took a stronger hold—hesitated again—held its breath five heart-breaking seconds, then gave a sort of human gasp and went out.

Nobody said a word for several minutes. It was a solemn sort of silence; even the wind put on a stealthy, sinister quiet, and made no more noise than the falling flakes of snow. Finally a sad-voiced conversation began, and it was soon apparent that in each of our hearts lay the conviction that this was our last night with the living. I had so hoped that I was the only one who felt so. When the others calmly acknowledged their conviction, it sounded like the summons itself. Ollendorff said:

" Brothers, let us die together. And let us go without one hard feeling towards each other. Let us forget and forgive bygones. I know that you have felt hard towards me for turning over the canoe, and for knowing too much and leading you round and round in the snow—but I meant well; forgive me. I acknowledge freely that I have had hard feelings against Mr. Ballou for abusing me and calling me a logarythm, which is a thing I do not know what, but no doubt a thing considered disgraceful and unbecoming in America, and it has scarcely been out of my mind and has hurt me a great deal—but let it go; I forgive Mr. Ballou with all my heart, and— "

Poor Ollendorff broke down and the tears came. He was not alone, for I was crying too, and so was Mr. Ballou. Ollendorff got his voice again and forgave me for things I had done and said. Then he got out his bottle of whisky and said that whether he lived or died he would never touch another drop. He said he had given up all hope of life, and although ill-prepared, was ready to submit humbly to his fate; that he wished he could be spared a little longer, not for any selfish reason, but to make a thorough reform in his character, and by devoting himself to helping the poor, nursing the sick, and pleading with the people to guard themselves against the evils of intemperance, make his life a beneficent example to the young, and lay it down at last with the precious reflection that it had not been lived in vain. He ended by saying that his reform should begin at this moment, even here in the presence of death, since no longer time was to be vouchsafed wherein to prosecute it to men's help and benefit—and with that he threw away the bottle of whisky.

Mr. Ballou made remarks of similar purport, and began the reform he could not live to continue, by throwing away the ancient pack of cards that had solaced our captivity during the flood and made it bearable. He said he never gambled, but still was satisfied that the meddling with cards in any way was

DISCARDED VICES.

immoral and injurious, and no man could be wholly pure and blemishless without eschewing them. "And therefore," continued he, "in doing this act I already feel more in sympathy with that spiritual saturnalia necessary to entire and obsolete reform." These rolling syllables touched him as no intelligible eloquence could have done, and the old man sobbed with a mournfulness not unmingled with satisfaction.

My own remarks were of the same tenor as those of my comrades, and I know that the feelings that prompted them were heartfelt and sincere. We were all sincere, and all deeply moved and earnest, for we were in the presence of death and without hope. I threw away my pipe, and in doing it felt that at last I was free of a hated vice and one that had ridden me like a tyrant all my days. While I yet talked, the thought of the good I might have done in the world and the still greater good I might *now* do, with these new incentives and higher and better aims to guide me if I could only be spared a few years longer, overcame me and the tears came again. We put our arms about each other's necks and awaited the warning drowsiness that precedes death by freezing.

It came stealing over us presently, and then we bade each other a last farewell. A delicious dreaminess wrought its web about my yielding senses, while the snow-flakes wove a winding sheet about my conquered body. Oblivion came. The battle of life was done.

CHAPTER XXXIII.

I DO not know how long I was in a state of forgetfulness, but it seemed an age. A vague consciousness grew upon me by degrees, and then came a gathering anguish of pain in my limbs and through all my body. I shuddered. The thought flitted through my brain, "this is death—this is the hereafter."

Then came a white upheaval at my side, and a voice said, with bitterness:

"Will some gentleman be so good as to kick me behind?"

It was Ballou—at least it was a towzled snow image in a sitting posture, with Ballou's voice.

I rose up, and there in the gray dawn, not fifteen steps from us, were the frame buildings of a stage station, and under a shed stood our still saddled and bridled horses!

An arched snow-drift broke up, now, and Ollendorff emerged from it, and the three of us sat and stared at the houses without speaking a word. We really had nothing to say. We were like the profane man who could not "do the subject justice," the whole situation was so painfully ridiculous and humiliating that words were tame and we did not know where to commence anyhow.

The joy in our hearts at our deliverance was poisoned; well-nigh dissipated, indeed. We presently began to grow pettish by degrees, and sullen; and then, angry at each other, angry at ourselves, angry at everything in general, we moodily dusted the snow from our clothing and in unsociable single file plowed our way to the horses, unsaddled them, and sought shelter in the station.

I have scarcely exaggerated a detail of this curious and

absurd adventure. It occurred almost exactly as I have stated it. We actually went into camp in a snow-drift in a desert, at midnight in a storm, forlorn and hopeless, within fifteen steps of a comfortable inn.

For two hours we sat apart in the station and ruminated in disgust. The mystery was gone, now, and it was plain enough why the horses had deserted us. Without a doubt they were under that shed a quarter of a minute after they had left us, and they must have overheard and enjoyed all our confessions and lamentations.

After breakfast we felt better, and the zest of life soon came back. The world looked bright again, and existence was as dear to us as ever. Presently an uneasiness came over me—grew upon me—assailed me without ceasing. Alas, my regeneration was not complete—I wanted to smoke! I resisted with all my strength, but the flesh was weak. I wandered away alone and wrestled with myself an hour. I recalled my promises of reform and preached to myself persuasively, upbraidingly, exhaustively. But it was all vain, I shortly found myself sneaking among the snow-drifts hunting for my pipe. I discovered it after a considerable search, and crept away to hide myself and enjoy it. I remained behind the barn a good while, asking myself how I would feel if my braver, stronger, truer comrades should catch me in my degradation. At last I lit the pipe, and no human being can feel meaner and baser than I did then. I was ashamed of being in my own pitiful company. Still dreading discovery, I felt that perhaps the further side of the barn would be somewhat safer, and so I turned the corner. As I turned the one corner, smoking, Ollendorff turned the other with his bottle to his lips, and between us sat unconscious Ballou deep in a game of "solitaire" with the old greasy cards!

Absurdity could go no farther. We shook hands and agreed to say no more about "reform" and "examples to the rising generation."

The station we were at was at the verge of the Twenty-six-Mile Desert. If we had approached it half an hour earlier the night before, we must have heard men shouting there and firing pistols; for they were expecting some sheep drovers

IT WAS THUS WE MET.

and their flocks and knew that they would infallibly get lost and wander out of reach of help unless guided by sounds. While we remained at the station, three of the drovers arrived, nearly exhausted with their wanderings, but two others of their party were never heard of afterward.

We reached Carson in due time, and took a rest. This rest, together with preparations for the journey to Esmeralda, kept us there a week, and the delay gave us the opportunity to be present at the trial of the great land-slide case of Hyde *vs.* Morgan—an episode which is famous in Nevada to this day. After a word or two of necessary explanation, I will set down the history of this singular affair just as it transpired.

CHAPTER XXXIV

THE mountains are very high and steep about Carson, Eagle and Washoe Valleys—very high and very steep, and so when the snow gets to melting off fast in the Spring and the warm surface-earth begins to moisten and soften, the disastrous land-slides commence. The reader cannot know what a land-slide is, unless he has lived in that country and seen the whole side of a mountain taken off some fine morning and deposited down in the valley, leaving a vast, treeless, unsightly scar upon the mountain's front to keep the circumstance fresh in his memory all the years that he may go on living within seventy miles of that place.

General Buncombe was shipped out to Nevada in the invoice of Territorial officers, to be United States Attorney. He considered himself a lawyer of parts, and he very much wanted an opportunity to manifest it—partly for the pure gratification of it and partly because his salary was Territorially meagre (which is a strong expression). Now the older citizens of a new territory look down upon the rest of the world with a calm, benevolent compassion, as long as it keeps out of the way—when it gets in the way they snub it. Sometimes this latter takes the shape of a practical joke.

One morning Dick Hyde rode furiously up to General Buncombe's door in Carson city and rushed into his presence without stopping to tie his horse. He seemed much excited. He told the General that he wanted him to conduct a suit for him and would pay him five hundred dollars if he achieved a victory. And then, with violent gestures and a world of profanity, he poured out his griefs. He said it was pretty

16†

well known that for some years he had been farming (or ranching as the more customary term is) in Washoe District, and making a successful thing of it, and furthermore it was known that his ranch was situated just in the edge of the valley, and that Tom Morgan owned a ranch immediately above it on the mountain side. And now the trouble was, that one of those hated and dreaded land-slides had come and slid

Morgan's ranch, fences, cabins, cattle, barns and everything down on top of *his* ranch and exactly covered up every single vestige of his property, to a depth of about thirty-eight feet. Morgan was in possession and refused to vacate the premises—said he was occupying his own cabin and not interfering with anybody else's—and said the cabin was standing on the same dirt and same ranch it had always stood on, and he would like to see anybody make him vacate.

TAKING POSSESSION.

"And when I reminded him," said Hyde, weeping, "that it was on top of my ranch and that he was trespassing, he had the infernal meanness to ask me why didn't I *stay* on my ranch and hold possession when I see him a-coming! Why didn't I *stay* on it, the blathering lunatic—by George, when I heard that racket and looked up that hill it was just like the whole world was a-ripping and a-tearing down that mountain side—splinters, and cord-wood, thunder and lightning, hail and snow, odds and ends of hay stacks, and awful clouds of dust!—trees going end over end in the air, rocks as big as a house jumping 'bout a thousand feet high and busting into ten million pieces, cattle turned inside out and a-coming head on with their tails hanging out between their teeth!—and in the midst of all that wrack and destruction sot that cussed Morgan on his gate-post, a-wondering why I didn't *stay and hold possession!* Laws bless me, I just took one glimpse, General, and lit out'n the county in three jumps exactly.

"But what grinds me is that that Morgan hangs on there and won't move off'n that ranch—says it's his'n and he's going to keep it—likes it better'n he did when it was higher up the hill. Mad! Well, I've been so mad for two days I couldn't find my way to town—been wandering around in the brush in a starving condition—got anything here to drink, General? But I'm here *now*, and I'm a-going to law. You hear *me!*"

Never in all the world, perhaps, were a man's feelings so outraged as were the General's. He said he had never heard of such high-handed conduct in all his life as this Morgan's. And he said there was no use in going to law—Morgan had no shadow of right to remain where he was—nobody in the wide world would uphold him in it, and no lawyer would take his case and no judge listen to it. Hyde said that right there was where he was mistaken—everybody in town sustained Morgan; Hal Brayton, a very smart lawyer, had taken his case; the courts being in vacation, it was to be tried before a referee, and ex-Governor Roop had already been appointed to that office and would open his court in a large public hall near the hotel at two that afternoon.

The General was amazed. He said he had suspected before that the people of that Territory were fools, and now he knew it. But he said rest easy, rest easy and collect the witnesses, for the victory was just as certain as if the conflict were already over. Hyde wiped away his tears and left.

At two in the afternoon referee Roop's Court opened, and Roop appeared throned among his sheriffs, the witnesses, and spectators, and wearing upon his face a solemnity so awe-inspiring that some of his fellow-conspirators had misgivings that maybe he had not comprehended, after all, that this was merely a joke. An unearthly stillness prevailed, for at the slightest noise the judge uttered sternly the command :

"Order in the Court!"

And the sheriffs promptly echoed it. Presently the General elbowed his way through the crowd of spectators, with his arms full of law-books, and on his ears fell an order from the judge which was the first respectful recognition of his high official dignity that had ever saluted them, and it trickled pleasantly through his whole system :

"Way for the United States Attorney!"

The witnesses were called—legislators, high government

A GREAT EFFORT.

officers, ranchmen, miners, Indians, Chinamen, negroes. Three fourths of them were called by the defendant Morgan, but no matter, their testimony invariably went in favor of the plaintiff Hyde. Each new witness only added new testimony to the absurdity of a man's claiming to own another man's property because his farm had slid down on top of it. Then the Morgan lawyers made their speeches, and seemed to make singularly weak ones—they did really nothing to help the Morgan cause. And now the General, with exultation in his face, got up and made an impassioned effort; he pounded the table, he banged the law-books, he shouted, and roared, and howled, he quoted from everything and everybody, poetry, sarcasm, statistics, history, pathos, bathos, blasphemy, and wound up with a grand war-whoop for free speech, freedom of the press, free schools, the Glorious Bird of America and the principles of eternal justice! [Applause.]

When the General sat down, he did it with the conviction that if there was anything in good strong testimony, a great speech and believing and admiring countenances all around, Mr. Morgan's case was killed. Ex-Governor Roop leant his head upon his hand for some minutes, thinking, and the still audience waited for his decision. Then he got up and stood erect, with bended head, and thought again. Then he walked the floor with long, deliberate strides, his chin in his hand, and still the audience waited. At last he returned to his throne, seated himself, and began, impressively:

"Gentlemen, I feel the great responsibility that rests upon me this day. This is no ordinary case. On the contrary it is plain that it is the most solemn and awful that ever man was called upon to decide. Gentlemen, I have listened attentively to the evidence, and have perceived that the weight of it, the overwhelming weight of it, is in favor of the plaintiff Hyde. I have listened also to the remarks of counsel, with high interest—and especially will I commend the masterly and irrefutable logic of the distinguished gentleman who represents the plaintiff. But gentlemen, let us beware how we allow mere human testimony, human ingenuity in argument and human ideas of equity, to influence us at a moment so solemn as this. Gentlemen, it ill becomes us, worms as we are, to meddle with the decrees of Heaven. It is plain to me that

Heaven, in its inscrutable wisdom, has seen fit to move this defendant's ranch for a purpose. We are but creatures, and we must submit. If Heaven has chosen to favor the defendant Morgan in this marked and wonderful manner; and if Heaven, dissatisfied with the position of the Morgan ranch upon the mountain side, has chosen to remove it to a position more eligible and more advantageous for its owner, it ill becomes us, insects as we are, to question the legality of the act or inquire into the reasons that prompted it. No—Heaven created the ranches and it is Heaven's prerogative to rearrange them, to experiment with them, to shift them around at its pleasure.

REARRANGING AND SHIFTING.

It is for us to submit, without repining. I warn you that this thing which has happened is a thing with which the sacrilegious hands and brains and tongues of men must not meddle. Gentlemen, it is the verdict of this court that the plaintiff,

Richard Hyde, has been deprived of his ranch by the visitation of God! And from this decision there is no appeal."

Buncombe seized his cargo of law-books and plunged out
of the court-room frantic with indignation. He pronounced
Roop to be a miraculous fool, an inspired idiot. In all good
faith he returned at night and remonstrated with Roop upon
his extravagant decision, and implored him to walk the floor
and think for half an hour, and see if he could not figure out
some sort of modification of the verdict. Roop yielded at last
and got up to walk. He walked two hours and a half, and at
last his face lit up happily and he told Buncombe it had occurred to him that the ranch underneath the new Morgan ranch
still belonged to Hyde, that his title to the ground was just
as good as it had ever been, and therefore he was of opinion
that Hyde had a right to dig it out from under there and—

The General never waited to hear the end of it. He was
always an impatient and irascible man, that way. At the end
of two months the fact that he had been played upon with a
joke had managed to bore itself, like another Hoosac Tunnel,
through the solid adamant of his understanding.

CHAPTER XXXV.

WHEN we finally left for Esmeralda, horseback, we had an addition to the company in the person of Capt. John Nye, the Governor's brother. He had a good memory, and a tongue hung in the middle. This is a combination which gives immortality to conversation. Capt. John never suffered the talk to flag or falter once during the hundred and twenty miles of the journey. In addition to his conversational powers, he had one or two other endowments of a marked character. One was a singular "handiness" about doing anything and everything, from laying out a railroad or organizing a political party, down to sewing on buttons, shoeing a horse, or setting a broken leg, or a hen. Another was a spirit of accommodation that prompted him to take the needs, difficulties and perplexities of anybody and everybody upon his own shoulders at any and all times, and dispose of them with admirable facility and alacrity—hence he always managed to find vacant beds in crowded inns, and plenty to eat in the emptiest larders. And finally, wherever he met a man, woman or child, in camp, inn or desert, he either knew such parties personally or had been acquainted with a relative of the same. Such another traveling comrade was never seen before. I cannot forbear giving a specimen of the way in which he overcame difficulties. On the second day out, we arrived, very tired and hungry, at a poor little inn in the desert, and were told that the house was full, no provisions on hand, and neither hay nor barley to spare for the horses—we must move on. The rest of us wanted to hurry on while it was yet light, but Capt. John insisted on stopping awhile. We dismounted and entered. There was no welcome for us on any face. Capt. John began his blandishments, and within twenty minutes he had accomplished the following things, viz.: found old acquaintances in three teamsters; discovered that he used to go to school with the landlord's mother; recognized his wife as a lady whose life he had saved once in California, by stopping her runaway horse; mended a child's broken toy and won the favor of its mother, a guest of the inn; helped the hostler bleed a horse, and prescribed for another horse that had the "heaves"; treated the entire party three times at the landlord's bar; produced a later paper than anybody had seen for a week and sat himself down to read the news to a deeply interested audience. The result, summed up, was as follows: The hostler found plenty of feed for our horses; we had a trout supper, an exceedingly sociable time after it, good beds to sleep in, and a surprising breakfast in the morning—and when we left, we left lamented by all! Capt.

WE LEFT LAMENTED.

John had some bad traits, but he had some uncommonly valuable ones to offset them with.

Esmeralda was in many respects another Humboldt, but in a little more forward state. The claims we had been paying assessments on were entirely worthless, and we threw them away. The principal one cropped out of the top of a knoll that was fourteen feet high, and the inspired Board of

Directors were running a tunnel under that knoll to strike the ledge. The tunnel would have to be seventy feet long, and would then strike the ledge at the same depth that a *shaft* twelve feet deep would have reached! The Board were living on the "assessments." [N. B.—This hint comes too late for the enlightenment of New York silver miners; they have already learned all about this neat trick by experience.] The Board had no desire to strike the ledge, knowing that it was as barren of silver as a curbstone. This reminiscence calls to mind Jim Townsend's tunnel. He had paid assessments on a mine called the "Daley" till he was well-nigh penniless. Finally an assessment was levied to run a tunnel two hundred and fifty feet on the Daley, and Townsend went up on the hill to look into matters. He found the Daley cropping out of the apex

PICTURE OF TOWNSEND'S TUNNEL.

of an exceedingly sharp-pointed peak, and a couple of men up there "facing" the proposed tunnel. Townsend made a calculation. Then he said to the men:

"So you have taken a contract to run a tunnel into this hill two hundred and fifty feet to strike this ledge?"

"Yes, sir."

"Well, do you know that you have got one of the most expensive and arduous undertakings before you that was ever conceived by man?"

"Why no—how is that?"

"Because this hill is only twenty-five feet through from side to side; and so you have got to build two hundred and twenty-five feet of your tunnel on trestle-work!"

The ways of silver mining Boards are exceedingly dark and sinuous.

We took up various claims, and *commenced* shafts and tunnels on them, but never finished any of them. We had to do a certain amount of work on each to "hold" it, else other parties could seize our property after the expiration of ten days. We were always hunting up new claims and doing a little work on them and then waiting for a buyer—who never came. We never found any ore that would yield more than fifty dollars a ton; and as the mills charged fifty dollars a ton for *working* ore and extracting the silver, our pocket-money melted steadily away and none returned to take its place. We lived in a little cabin and cooked for ourselves; and altogether it was a hard life, though a hopeful one—for we never ceased to expect fortune and a customer to burst upon us some day.

At last, when flour reached a dollar a pound, and money could not be borrowed on the best security at less than *eight per cent a month* (I being without the security, too), I abandoned mining and went to milling. That is to say, I went to work as a common laborer in a quartz mill, at ten dollars a week and board.

CHAPTER XXXVI.

I HAD already learned how hard and long and dismal a task it is to burrow down into the bowels of the earth and get out the coveted ore; and now I learned that the burrowing was only half the work; and that to get the silver out of the ore was the dreary and laborious other half of it. We had to turn out at six in the morning and keep at it till dark. This mill was a six-stamp affair, driven by steam. Six tall, upright rods of iron, as large as a man's ankle, and heavily shod with a mass of iron and steel at their lower ends, were framed together like a gate, and these rose and fell, one after the other, in a ponderous dance, in an iron box called a "battery." Each of these rods or stamps weighed six hundred pounds. One of us stood by the battery all day long, breaking up masses of silver-bearing rock with a sledge and shoveling it into the battery. The ceaseless dance of the stamps pulverized the rock to powder, and a stream of water that trickled into the battery turned it to a creamy paste. The minutest particles were driven through a fine wire screen which fitted close around the battery, and were washed into great tubs warmed by super-heated steam—amalgamating pans, they are called. The mass of pulp in the pans was kept constantly stirred up by revolving "mullers." A quantity of quicksilver was kept always in the battery, and this seized some of the liberated gold and silver particles and held on to them; quicksilver was shaken in a fine shower into the pans, also, about every half hour, through a buckskin sack. Quantities of coarse salt and sulphate of copper were added, from time to time to assist the amalgamation by destroying base metals which coated the gold and silver and would not let it unite with the quicksilver. All these tiresome things we had to

QUARTZ MILL IN NEVADA.

attend to constantly. Streams of dirty water flowed always from the pans and were carried off in broad wooden troughs to the ravine. One would not suppose that atoms of gold and silver would float on top of six inches of water, but they did; and in order to catch them, coarse blankets were laid in the troughs, and little obstructing "riffles" charged with quicksilver were placed here and there across the troughs also. These riffles had to be cleaned and the blankets washed out every evening, to get their precious accumulations—and after all this eternity of trouble one third of the silver and gold in a ton of rock would find its way to the end of the troughs in the ravine at last and have to be worked over again some day. There is nothing so aggravating as silver milling. There never was any idle time in that mill. There was always something to do. It is a pity that Adam could not have gone

straight out of Eden into a quartz mill, in order to understand
the full force of his doom to "earn his bread by the sweat of
his brow." Every now and then, during the day, we had to
scoop some pulp out of the pans, and tediously "wash" it in a
horn spoon—wash it little by little over the edge till at last
nothing was left but some little dull globules of quicksilver in
the bottom. If they were soft and yielding, the pan needed
some salt or some sulphate of copper or some other chemical
rubbish to assist digestion; if they were crisp to the touch and
would retain a dint, they were freighted with all the silver and
gold they could seize and hold, and consequently the pans
needed a fresh charge of quicksilver. When there was nothing else to do, one could always "screen tailings." That is to
say, he could shovel up the dried sand that had washed down
to the ravine through the troughs and dash it against an upright wire screen to free it from pebbles and prepare it for

ANOTHER PROCESS OF AMALGAMATION.

working over. The process of amalgamation differed in the
various mills, and this included changes in style of pans and
other machinery, and a great diversity of opinion existed as to
the best in use, but none of the methods employed, involved

the principle of milling ore without "screening the tailings." Of all recreations in the world, screening tailings on a hot day, with a long-handled shovel, is the most undesirable.

At the end of the week the machinery was stopped and we "cleaned up." That is to say, we got the pulp out of the pans and batteries, and washed the mud patiently away till nothing was left but the long accumulating mass of quicksilver, with its imprisoned treasures. This we made into heavy, compact snow-balls, and piled them up in a bright, luxurious heap for inspection. Making these snow-balls cost me a fine gold ring—that and ignorance together; for the quicksilver invaded the ring with the same facility with which water saturates a sponge—separated its particles and the ring crumbled to pieces.

We put our pile of quicksilver balls into an iron retort that had a pipe leading from it to a pail of water, and then applied a roasting heat. The quicksilver turned to vapor, escaped through the pipe into the pail, and the water turned it into good wholesome quicksilver again. Quicksilver is very costly, and they never waste it. On opening the retort, there was our week's work—a lump of pure white, frosty looking silver, twice as large as a man's head. Perhaps a fifth of the mass was gold, but the color of it did not show—would not have shown if two thirds of it had been gold. We melted it up and made a solid brick of it by pouring it into an iron brick-mould.

By such a tedious and laborious process were silver bricks obtained. This mill was but one of many others in operation at the time. The first one in Nevada was built at Egan Canyon and was a small insignificant affair and compared most unfavorably with some of the immense establishments afterwards located at Virginia City and elsewhere.

From our bricks a little corner was chipped off for the "fire-assay"—a method used to determine the proportions of gold, silver and base metals in the mass. This is an interesting process. The chip is hammered out as thin as paper and weighed on scales so fine and sensitive that if you weigh a two-inch scrap of paper on them and then write your name on the paper with a coarse, soft pencil and weigh it again, the

FIRST QUARTZ MILL IN NEVADA.

scales will take marked notice of the addition. Then a little lead (also weighed) is rolled up with the flake of silver and the two are melted at a great heat in a small vessel called a cupel, made by compressing bone ashes into a cup-shape in a steel mold. The base metals oxydize and are absorbed with the lead into the pores of the cupel. A button or globule of perfectly pure gold and silver is left behind, and by weighing it and noting the loss, the assayer knows the proportion of base metal the brick contains. He has to separate the gold from the silver now. The button is hammered out flat and thin, put in the furnace and kept some time at a red heat; after cooling it off it is rolled up like a quill and heated in a glass vessel containing nitric acid; the acid dissolves the silver and leaves the gold pure and ready to be weighed on its own merits.

Then salt water is poured into the vessel containing the dissolved silver and the silver returns to palpable form again and sinks to the bottom. Nothing now remains but to weigh it; then the proportions of the several metals contained in the brick are known, and the assayer stamps the value of the brick upon its surface.

The sagacious reader will know now, without being told, that the speculative miner, in getting a "fire-assay" made of a piece of rock from his mine (to help him sell the same), was not in the habit of picking out the least valuable fragment of rock on his dump-pile, but quite the contrary. I have seen men hunt over a pile of nearly worthless quartz for an hour, and at last find a little piece as large as a filbert, which was rich in gold and silver—and this was reserved for a fire-assay! Of course the fire-assay would demonstrate that a ton of such rock would yield hundreds of dollars—and on such assays many an utterly worthless mine was sold.

A SLICE OF RICH ORE.

Assaying was a good business, and so some men engaged in it, occasionally, who were not strictly scientific and capable. One assayer got such rich results out of all specimens brought to him that in time he acquired almost a monopoly of the business. But like all men who achieve success, he became an object of envy and suspicion. The other assayers entered into a conspiracy against him, and let some prominent citizens into the secret in order to show that they meant fairly. Then they broke a little fragment off a carpenter's grindstone and got a stranger to take it to the popular scientist and get it assayed.

17†

In the course of an hour the result came—whereby it appeared that a ton of that rock would yield $1,284.40 in silver and $366.36 in gold!

Due publication of the whole matter was made in the paper, and the popular assayer left town "between two days."

I will remark, in passing, that I only remained in the milling business one week. I told my employer I could not stay longer without an advance in my wages; that I liked quartz milling, indeed was infatuated with it; that I had never before grown so tenderly attached to an occupation in so short a time; that nothing, it seemed to me, gave such scope to intellectual activity as feeding a battery and screening tailings, and nothing so stimulated the moral attributes as retorting bullion and washing blankets—still, I felt constrained to ask an increase of salary.

He said he was paying me ten dollars a week, and thought it a good round sum. How much did I want?

I said about four hundred thousand dollars a month, and board, was about all I could reasonably ask, considering the hard times.

I was ordered off the premises! And yet, when I look back to those days and call to mind the exceeding hardness of the labor I performed in that mill, I only regret that I did not ask him seven hundred thousand.

Shortly after this I began to grow crazy, along with the rest of the population, about the mysterious and wonderful "cement mine," and to make preparations to take advantage of any opportunity that might offer to go and help hunt for it.

CHAPTER XXXVII.

IT was somewhere in the neighborhood of Mono Lake that the marvellous Whiteman cement mine was supposed to lie. Every now and then it would be reported that Mr. W. had passed stealthily through Esmeralda at dead of night, in disguise, and then we would have a wild excitement—because he must be steering for his secret mine, and now was the time to follow him. In less than three hours after daylight all the horses and mules and donkeys in the vicinity would be bought, hired or stolen, and half the community would be off for the mountains, following in the wake of Whiteman. But W. would drift about through the mountain gorges for days together, in a purposeless sort of way, until the provisions of the miners ran out, and they would have to go back home. I have known it reported at eleven at night, in a large mining camp, that Whiteman had just passed through, and in two hours the streets, so quiet before, would be swarming with men and animals. Every individual would be trying to be very secret, but yet venturing to whisper to just one neighbor that W. had passed through. And long before daylight—this in the dead of Winter—the stampede would be complete, the camp deserted, and the whole population gone chasing after W.

The tradition was that in the early immigration, more than twenty years ago, three young Germans, brothers, who had survived an Indian massacre on the Plains, wandered on foot through the deserts, avoiding all trails and roads, and simply holding a westerly direction and hoping to find California before they starved, or died of fatigue. And in a gorge in the mountains they sat down to rest one day, when one of them noticed a curious vein of cement running along the ground, shot full of lumps of dull yellow metal. They saw that it was gold, and that here was a fortune to be acquired in a single day. The vein was about as wide as a curbstone, and fully two thirds of it was pure gold. Every pound of the wonderful cement was

THE SAVED BROTHER.

worth well-nigh $200. Each of the brothers loaded himself with about twenty-five pounds of it, and then they covered up all traces of the vein, made a rude drawing of the locality and the principal landmarks in the vicinity, and started westward again. But troubles thickened about them. In their wanderings one brother fell and broke his leg, and the others were obliged to go on and leave him to die in the wilderness. Another, worn out and starving, gave up by and by, and laid down to die, but after two or three weeks of incredible hardships, the third reached the settlements of California exhausted, sick, and his mind deranged by his sufferings. He had thrown away all his cement but a few fragments, but these were sufficient to set everybody wild with excitement. However, he had had enough of the cement country, and nothing could induce him to lead a party thither. He was entirely content to work on a farm for wages. But he gave Whiteman his map, and described the cement region as well as he could, and thus transferred the curse to that gentleman—for when I had my one accidental glimpse of Mr. W. in Esmeralda he had been hunting for the lost mine, in hunger and thirst, poverty and sickness, for twelve or thirteen years. Some people believed he had found it, but most people believed he had not. I saw a piece of cement as large as my fist which was said to have been given to Whiteman by the young German, and it was of a seductive nature. Lumps of virgin gold were as thick in it as raisins in a slice of fruit cake. The privilege of working such a mine one week would be sufficient for a man of reasonable desires.

A new partner of ours, a Mr. Higbie, knew Whiteman well by sight, and a friend of ours, a Mr. Van Dorn, was well acquainted with him, and not only that, but had Whiteman's promise that he should have a private hint in time to enable him to join the next cement expedition. Van Dorn had promised to extend the hint to us. One evening Higbie came in greatly excited, and said he felt certain he had recognized Whiteman, up town, disguised and in a pretended state of intoxication. In a little while Van Dorn arrived and confirmed the news; and so we gathered in our cabin and with heads close together arranged our plans in impressive whispers.

We were to leave town quietly, after midnight, in two or three small parties, so as not to attract attention, and meet at dawn on the " divide " overlooking Mono Lake, eight or nine miles distant. We were to make no noise after starting, and not speak above a whisper under any circumstances. It was believed that for once Whiteman's presence was unknown in the town and his expedition unsuspected. Our conclave broke up at nine o'clock, and we set about our preparations diligently and with profound secrecy. At eleven o'clock we saddled our horses, hitched them with their long *riatas* (or lassos), and then brought out a side of bacon, a sack of beans, a small sack of coffee, some sugar, a hundred pounds of flour in sacks, some tin cups and a coffee pot, frying pan and some few other necessary articles. All these things were " packed " on the back of a led horse—and whoever has not been taught, by a Spanish adept, to pack an animal, let him never hope to do the thing by natural smartness. That is impossible. Higbie had had some experience, but was not perfect. He put on the pack saddle (a thing like a saw-buck), piled the property on it and then wound a rope all over and about it and under it, "every which way," taking a hitch in it every now and then, and occasionally surging back on it till the horse's sides sunk in and he gasped for breath—but every time the lashings grew tight in one place they loosened in another. We never did get the load tight all over, but we got it so that it would do, after a fashion, and then we started, in single file, close order, and without a word. It was a dark night. We kept the middle of the road, and proceeded in a slow walk past the rows of cabins, and whenever a miner came to his door I trembled for fear the light would shine on us and excite curiosity. But nothing happened. We began the long winding ascent of the canyon, toward the "divide," and presently the cabins began to grow infrequent, and the intervals between them wider and wider, and then I began to breathe tolerably freely and feel less like a thief and a murderer. I was in the rear, leading the pack horse. As the ascent grew steeper he grew proportionately less satisfied with his cargo, and began to pull back on his *riata* occasionally and delay progress. My comrades were passing out of sight in the gloom. I was getting anxious. I coaxed and bullied the pack horse till I presently got him into a trot, and then the tin cups and pans strung about his person frightened him and he ran. His *riata* was wound around the pummel of my saddle, and so, as he went by he dragged me from my horse and the two animals traveled briskly on without me. But I was not alone—the loosened cargo tumbled overboard from the pack horse and fell close to me. It was abreast of almost the last cabin. A miner came out and said:

"Hello!"

I was thirty steps from him, and knew he could not see me, it was so very dark in the shadow of the mountain. So I lay still. Another head appeared in the light of the cabin door, and presently the two men walked toward me. They stopped within ten steps of me, and one said:

"'St! Listen."

ON A SECRET EXPEDITION.

I could not have been in a more distressed state if I had been escaping justice with a price on my head. Then the miners appeared to sit down on a boulder, though I could not see them distinctly enough to be very sure what they did. One said:

"I heard a noise, as plain as I ever heard anything. It seemed to be about there—"

A stone whizzed by my head. I flattened myself out in the dust like a postage stamp, and thought to myself if he mended his aim ever so little he would probably hear another noise. In my heart, now, I execrated secret expeditions. I promised myself that this should be my last, though the Sierras were ribbed with cement veins. Then one of the men said:

"I'll tell you what! Welch knew what he was talking about

when he said he saw Whiteman to-day. I heard horses—that was the noise. I am going down to Welch's, right away."

They left and I was glad. I did not care whither they went, so they went. I was willing they should visit Welch, and the sooner the better.

As soon as they closed their cabin door my comrades emerged from the gloom; they had caught the horses and were waiting for a clear coast again. We remounted the cargo on the pack horse and got under way, and as day broke we reached the "divide" and joined Van Dorn. Then we journeyed down into the valley of the Lake, and feeling secure, we halted to cook breakfast, for we were tired and sleepy and hungry. Three hours later the rest of the population filed over the "divide" in a long procession, and drifted off out of sight around the borders of the Lake!

Whether or not my accident had produced this result we never knew, but at least one thing was certain—the secret was out and Whiteman would not enter upon a search for the cement mine this time. We were filled with chagrin.

We held a council and decided to make the best of our misfortune and enjoy a week's holiday on the borders of the curious Lake. Mono, it is sometimes called, and sometimes the "Dead Sea of California." It is one of the strangest freaks of Nature to be found in any land, but it is hardly ever mentioned in print and very seldom visited, because it lies away off the usual routes of travel and besides is so difficult to get at that only men content to endure the roughest life will consent to take upon themselves the discomforts of such a trip. On the morning of our second day, we traveled around to a remote and particularly wild spot on the borders of the Lake, where a stream of fresh, ice-cold water entered it from the mountain side, and then we went regularly into camp. We hired a large boat and two shot-guns from a lonely ranchman who lived some ten miles further on, and made ready for comfort and recreation. We soon got thoroughly acquainted with the Lake and all its peculiarities.

LAKE MONO.

CHAPTER XXXVIII.

MONO LAKE lies in a lifeless, treeless, hideous desert, eight thousand feet above the level of the sea, and is guarded by mountains two thousand feet higher, whose summits are always clothed in clouds. This solemn, silent, sailless sea—this lonely tenant of the loneliest spot on earth—is little graced with the picturesque. It is an unpretending expanse of grayish water, about a hundred miles in circumference, with two islands in its centre, mere upheavals of rent and scorched and blistered lava, snowed over with gray banks and drifts of pumice-stone and ashes, the winding sheet of the dead volcano, whose vast crater the lake has seized upon and occupied.

The lake is two hundred feet deep, and its sluggish waters are so strong with alkali that if you only dip the most hopelessly soiled garment into them once or twice, and wring it out, it will be found as clean as if it had been through the ablest of washerwomen's hands. While we camped there our laundry work was easy. We tied the week's washing astern of our boat, and sailed a quarter of a mile, and the job was complete, all to the wringing out. If we threw the water on our heads and gave them a rub or so, the white lather would pile up three inches high. This water is not good for bruised places and abrasions of the skin. We had a valuable dog. He had raw places on him. He had more raw places on him than sound ones. He was the rawest dog I almost ever saw. He jumped overboard one day to get away from the flies. But it was bad

judgment.   In his condition, it would have been just as comfortable to jump into the fire.   The alkali water nipped him

RATHER SOAPY.

in all the raw places
simultaneously, and
he struck out for the
shore with consider-
able interest.   He
yelped and barked
and howled as he
went—and by the
time he got to the
shore there was no
bark to him—for he
had barked the bark
all out of his inside,
and the alkali water
had cleaned the bark
all off his outside,

and he probably wished he had never embarked in any such
enterprise.   He ran round and round in a circle, and pawed

A BARK UNDER FULL SAIL.

the earth and clawed the air, and threw double somersaults,
sometimes backward and sometimes forward, in the most

extraordinary manner. He was not a demonstrative dog, as a general thing, but rather of a grave and serious turn of mind, and I never saw him take so much interest in anything before. He finally struck out over the mountains, at a gait which we estimated at about two hundred and fifty miles an hour, and he is going yet. This was about nine years ago. We look for what is left of him along here every day.

A white man cannot drink the water of Mono Lake, for it is nearly pure lye. It is said that the Indians in the vicinity drink it sometimes, though. It is not improbable, for they are among the purest liars I ever saw. [There will be no additional charge for this joke, except to parties requiring an explanation of it. This joke has received high commendation from some of the ablest minds of the age.]

There are no fish in Mono Lake—no frogs, no snakes, no polliwigs—nothing, in fact, that goes to make life desirable. Millions of wild ducks and sea-gulls swim about the surface, but no living thing exists *under* the surface, except a white feathery sort of worm, one half an inch long, which looks like a bit of white thread frayed out at the sides. If you dip up a gallon of water, you will get about fifteen thousand of these. They give to the water a sort of grayish-white appearance. Then there is a fly, which looks something like our house fly. These settle on the beach to eat the worms that wash ashore —and any time, you can see there a belt of flies an inch deep and six feet wide, and this belt extends clear around the lake —a belt of flies one hundred miles long. If you throw a stone among them, they swarm up so thick that they look dense, like a cloud. You can hold them under water as long as you please —they do not mind it—they are only proud of it. When you let them go, they pop up to the surface as dry as a patent office report, and walk off as unconcernedly as if they had been educated especially with a view to affording instructive entertainment to man in that particular way. Providence leaves nothing to go by chance. All things have their uses and their part and proper place in Nature's economy: the ducks eat the flies—the flies eat the worms—the Indians eat all three—the

wild cats eat the Indians—the white folks eat the wild cats—
and thus all things are lovely.

Mono Lake is a hundred miles in a straight line from the
ocean—and between it and the ocean are one or two ranges
of mountains—yet thousands of sea-gulls go there every season
to lay their eggs and rear their young. One would as soon
expect to find sea-gulls in Kansas. And in this connection let
us observe another instance of Nature's wisdom. The islands
in the lake being merely huge masses of lava, coated over with
ashes and pumice-stone, and utterly innocent of vegetation or
anything that would burn; and sea-gulls' eggs being entirely
useless to anybody unless they be cooked, Nature has provided
an unfailing spring of boiling water on the largest island, and
you can put your eggs in there, and in four minutes you can
boil them as hard as any statement I have made during the past
fifteen years. Within ten feet of the boiling spring is a spring
of pure cold water, sweet and wholesome. So, in that island

A MODEL BOARDING-HOUSE.

you get your board and washing free of charge—and if nature
had gone further and furnished a nice American hotel clerk
who was crusty and disobliging, and didn't know anything
about the time tables, or the railroad routes—or—anything—
and was proud of it—I would not wish for a more desirable
boarding-house.

Half a dozen little mountain brooks flow into Mono
Lake, but *not a stream of any kind flows out of it*. It neither

rises nor falls, apparently, and what it does with its surplus water is a dark and bloody mystery.

There are only two seasons in the region round about Mono Lake—and these are, the breaking up of one Winter and the beginning of the next. More than once (in Esmeralda) I have seen a perfectly blistering morning open up with the thermometer at ninety degrees at eight o'clock, and seen the snow fall fourteen inches deep and that same identical thermometer go down to forty-four degrees under shelter, before nine o'clock at night. Under favorable circumstances it snows at least once in every single month in the year, in the little town of Mono. So uncertain is the climate in Summer that a lady who goes out visiting cannot hope to be prepared for all emergencies unless she takes her fan under one arm and her snow shoes under the other. When they have a Fourth of July procession it generally snows on them, and they do say that as a general thing when a man calls for a brandy toddy there, the bar keeper chops it off with a hatchet and wraps it up in a paper, like maple sugar. And it is further reported that the old soakers haven't any teeth—wore them out eating gin cocktails and brandy punches. I do not endorse that statement—I simply give it for what it is worth—and it is worth—well, I should say, millions, to any man who can believe it without straining himself. But I do endorse the snow on the Fourth of July—because I know that to be true.

CHAPTER XXXIX.

ABOUT seven o'clock one blistering hot morning—for it was now dead summer time—Higbie and I took the boat and started on a voyage of discovery to the two islands. We had often longed to do this, but had been deterred by the fear of storms; for they were frequent, and severe enough to capsize an ordinary row-boat like ours without great difficulty —and once capsized, death would ensue in spite of the bravest swimming, for that venomous water would eat a man's eyes out like fire, and burn him out inside, too, if he shipped a sea. It was called twelve miles, straight out to the islands—a long pull and a warm one—but the morning was so quiet and sunny, and the lake so smooth and glassy and dead, that we could not resist the temptation. So we filled two large tin canteens with water (since we were not acquainted with the locality of the spring said to exist on the large island), and started. Higbie's brawny muscles gave the boat good speed, but by the time we reached our destination we judged that we had pulled nearer fifteen miles than twelve.

We landed on the big island and went ashore. We tried the water in the canteens, now, and found that the sun had spoiled it; it was so brackish that we could not drink it; so we poured it out and began a search for the spring—for thirst augments fast as soon as it is apparent that one has no means at hand of quenching it. The island was a long, moderately high hill of ashes—nothing but gray ashes and pumice-stone, in which we sunk to our knees at every step—and all around the top was a forbidding wall of scorched and blasted rocks. When we reached the top and got within the wall, we found simply a shallow, far-reaching basin, carpeted with ashes, and here and there a patch of fine sand. In places, picturesque jets of steam shot up out of crevices, giving evidence that although this ancient crater had gone out of active business, there was still some fire left in its furnaces. Close to one of these jets of steam stood the only tree on the island—a small pine of most graceful shape and most faultless symmetry; its color was a brilliant green, for the steam drifted unceasingly through its branches and kept them always moist. It contrasted strangely enough, did this vigorous and beautiful outcast, with its dead and dismal surroundings. It was like a cheerful spirit in a mourn-

LIFE AMID DEATH.

ing household.

We hunted for the spring everywhere, traversing the full length of the island (two or three miles), and crossing it twice— climbing ash-hills patiently, and then sliding down the other side in a sitting posture, plowing up smothering volumes of gray dust. But we found nothing but solitude, ashes and a heart-breaking silence. Finally we noticed that the wind had risen, and we forgot our thirst in a solicitude of greater importance; for, the lake being quiet, we had not taken pains about securing the boat. We hurried back to a point overlooking our landing place, and then—but mere words cannot describe our dismay—the boat was gone! The chances were that there was not another boat on the entire lake. The situation was not comfortable—in truth, to speak plainly, it was frightful. We were prisoners on a desolate island, in aggravating proximity to friends who were for the present helpless to aid us; and what was still more uncomfortable was the reflection that we had neither food nor water. But presently we sighted the boat. It was drifting along, leisurely, about fifty yards from shore, tossing in a foamy sea. It drifted, and continued to drift, but at the same safe distance from land, and we walked along abreast it and waited for fortune to favor us. At the end of an hour it approached a jutting cape, and Higbie ran ahead and posted himself on the utmost verge and prepared for the assault. If we failed there, there was no hope for us. It was driving gradually shoreward all the time, now; but whether it was driving fast enough to make the connection or not was the momentous question. When it got within thirty steps of Higbie I was so excited that I fancied I could hear my own heart beat. When, a little later, it dragged slowly along and seemed about to go by, only one little yard out of reach, it seemed as if my heart stood still; and when it was exactly abreast him and began to widen away, and he still standing like a watching statue, I knew my heart did stop. But when he gave a great spring, the next instant, and lit fairly in the stern, I discharged a war-whoop that woke the solitudes!

But it dulled my enthusiasm, presently, when he told me he had not been caring whether the boat came within jumping distance or not, so that it passed within eight or ten yards of him, for he had made up his mind to shut his eyes and mouth and swim that trifling distance. Imbecile that I was, I had not thought of that. It was only a long swim that could be fatal.

The sea was running high and the storm increasing. It was growing late, too—three or four in the afternoon. Whether to venture toward the mainland or not, was a question of some moment. But we were so distressed by thirst that we decided to try it, and so Higbie fell to work and I took the steering-oar. When we had pulled a mile, laboriously, we were evidently in serious peril, for the storm had greatly

A JUMP FOR LIFE.

augmented; the billows ran very high and were capped with foaming crests, the heavens were hung with black, and the wind blew with great fury. We would have gone back, now, but we did not dare to turn the boat around, because as soon as she got in the trough of the sea she would upset, of course. Our only hope lay in keeping her head-on to the seas. It was hard work to do this, she plunged so, and so beat and belabored the billows with her rising and falling bows. Now and then one of Higbie's oars would trip on the top of a wave, and the other one would snatch the boat half around in spite of my cumbersome steering apparatus. We were drenched by the sprays constantly, and the boat occasionally shipped water. By and by, powerful as my comrade was, his great exertions began to tell on him, and he was anxious that I should change places with him till he could rest a little. But I told him this was impossible; for if the steering oar were dropped a

18†

moment while we changed, the boat would slue around into the trough of the sea, capsize, and in less than five minutes we would have a hundred gallons of soap-suds in us and be eaten up so quickly that we could not even be present at our own inquest.

But things cannot last always. Just as the darkness shut down we came booming into port, head on. Higbie dropped his oars to hurrah—I dropped mine to help—the sea gave the boat a twist, and over she went!

The agony that alkali water inflicts on bruises, chafes and blistered hands, is unspeakable, and nothing but greasing all over will modify it—but we ate, drank and slept well, that night, notwithstanding.

In speaking of the peculiarities of Mono Lake, I ought to have mentioned that at intervals all around its shores stand picturesque turret-looking masses and clusters of a whitish, coarse-grained rock that resembles inferior mortar dried hard; and if one breaks off fragments of this rock he will find perfectly shaped and thoroughly petrified gulls' eggs deeply imbedded in the mass. How did they get there? I simply state the fact—for it is a fact—and leave the geological reader to crack the nut at his leisure and solve the problem after his own fashion.

At the end of a week we adjourned to the Sierras on a fishing excursion, and spent several days in camp under snowy Castle Peak, and fished successfully for trout in a bright, miniature lake whose surface was between ten and eleven thousand feet above the level of the sea; cooling ourselves during the hot August noons by sitting on snow banks ten feet deep, under whose sheltering edges *fine grass and dainty flowers flourished luxuriously;* and at night entertaining ourselves by almost freezing to death. Then we returned to Mono Lake, and finding that the cement excitement was over for the present, packed up and went back to Esmeralda. Mr. Ballou reconnoitred awhile, and not liking the prospect, set out alone for Humboldt.

About this time occurred a little incident which has always

had a sort of interest to me, from the fact that it came so near "instigating" my funeral. At a time when an Indian attack had been expected, the citizens hid their gunpowder where it would be safe and yet convenient to hand when wanted. A neighbor of ours hid six cans of rifle powder in the bake-oven of an old discarded cooking stove which stood on the open ground near a frame out-house or shed, and from and after that day never thought of it again. We hired a half-tamed Indian to do some washing for us, and he took up quarters under the shed with his tub. The ancient stove reposed within six feet of him, and before his face. Finally it occurred to him that hot water would be better than cold, and he went out and fired up under that forgotten powder magazine and set on a kettle of water. Then he returned to his tub. I

"STOVE HEAP GONE."

entered the shed presently and threw down some more clothes, and was about to speak to him when the stove blew up with a prodigious crash, and disappeared, leaving not a splinter behind. Fragments of it fell in the streets full two hundred yards away. Nearly a third of the shed roof over our heads

was destroyed, and one of the stove lids, after cutting a small
stanchion half in two in front of the Indian, whizzed between
us and drove partly through the weather-boarding beyond. I
was as white as a sheet and as weak as a kitten and speechless.
But the Indian betrayed no trepidation, no distress, not even
discomfort. He simply stopped washing, leaned forward and
surveyed the clean, blank ground a moment, and then remarked:

"Mph! Dam stove heap gone!"—and resumed his scrub-
bing as placidly as if it were an entirely customary thing for a
stove to do. I will explain, that "heap" is "Injun-English"
for "very much." The reader will perceive the exhaustive
expressiveness of it in the present instance.

CHAPTER XL.

I NOW come to a curious episode—the most curious, I think, that had yet accented my slothful, valueless, heedless career. Out of a hillside toward the upper end of the town, projected a wall of reddish looking quartz-croppings, the exposed comb of a silver-bearing ledge that extended deep down into the earth, of course. It was owned by a company entitled the "Wide West." There was a shaft sixty or seventy feet deep on the under side of the croppings, and everybody was acquainted with the rock that came from it—and tolerably rich rock it was, too, but nothing extraordinary. I will remark here, that although to the inexperienced stranger all the quartz of a particular "district" looks about alike, an old resident of the camp can take a glance at a mixed pile of rock, separate the fragments and tell you which mine each came from, as easily as a confectioner can separate and classify the various kinds and qualities of candy in a mixed heap of the article.

All at once the town was thrown into a state of extraordinary excitement. In mining parlance the Wide West had "struck it rich!" Everybody went to see the new developments, and for some days there was such a crowd of people about the Wide West shaft that a stranger would have supposed there was a mass meeting in session there. No other topic was discussed but the rich strike, and nobody thought or dreamed about anything else. Every man brought away a specimen, ground it up in a hand mortar, washed it out in his horn spoon, and glared speechless upon the marvelous result. It was not hard rock, but black, decomposed stuff which could be crumbled in the hand like a baked potato, and when spread out on a paper exhibited a thick sprinkling of gold and particles of "native" silver. Higbie brought a handful to the cabin, and when he had washed it out his amazement was beyond description. Wide West stock soared skywards. It was said that repeated offers had been made for it at a thousand dollars a foot, and promptly refused. We have all had the "blues"—the mere sky-blues—but mine were indigo, now —because I did not own in the Wide West. The world seemed hollow to me, and existence a grief. I lost my appetite, and ceased to take an interest in anything. Still I had to stay, and listen to other people's rejoicings, because I had no money to get out of the camp with.

The Wide West company put a stop to the carrying away of "specimens," and well they might, for every handful of the ore was worth a sum of some consequence. To show the exceeding value of the ore, I will remark that a sixteen-hundred-pounds parcel of it was sold, just as it lay, at the mouth of the shaft, at *one dollar a pound ;* and the man who bought it "packed" it on mules a hundred and fifty or two hundred miles, over the mountains, to San Francisco, satisfied that it would yield at a rate that would richly compensate him for his trouble. The Wide West people also commanded their foreman to refuse any but their own operatives permission to enter the mine at any time or for any purpose. I kept up my "blue" meditations and Higbie kept up a deal of thinking, too, but of a different sort. He puzzled over the "rock," examined it with a glass, inspected it in different lights and from different points of view, and after each experiment delivered himself, in soliloquy, of one and the same unvarying opinion in the same unvarying formula:

"It is *not* Wide West rock !"

He said once or twice that he meant to have a look into the Wide West shaft if he got shot for it. I was wretched, and did not care whether he got a look into it or not. He failed that day, and tried again at night; failed again; got up at dawn and tried, and failed again. Then he lay in ambush in the sage brush hour after hour, waiting for the two or three hands to adjourn to the shade of a boulder for dinner; made a start once, but was premature—one of the men came back for something; tried it again, but when almost at the mouth of the shaft, another of the men rose up from behind the boulder as if to reconnoitre, and he dropped on the ground and lay quiet; presently he crawled on his hands and knees to the mouth of the shaft, gave a quick glance around, then seized the rope and slid down the shaft. He disappeared in the gloom of a "side drift" just as a head appeared in the mouth of the shaft and somebody shouted "Hello!"—which he did not answer. He was not disturbed any more. An hour later he entered the cabin, hot, red, and ready to burst with smothered excitement, and exclaimed in a stage whisper:

"I knew it! We are rich! It's A BLIND LEAD!"

I thought the very earth reeled under me. Doubt—conviction—doubt again—exultation—hope, amazement, belief, unbelief—every emo-

INTERVIEWING THE "WIDE WEST."

tion imaginable swept in wild procession through my heart and brain, and I could not speak a word. After a moment or two of this mental fury, I shook myself to rights, and said:

"Say it again!"

"It's a blind lead!"

"Cal., let's—let's burn the house—or kill somebody! Let's get out where there's room to hurrah! But what is the use? It is a hundred times too good to be true."

"It's a blind lead, for a million!—hanging wall—foot wall —clay casings—everything complete!" He swung his hat and gave three cheers, and I cast doubt to the winds and chimed in with a will. For I was worth a million dollars, and did not care "whether school kept or not!"

But perhaps I ought to explain. A "blind lead" is a lead or ledge that does not "crop out" above the surface. A miner does not know where to look 'for such leads, but they are often stumbled upon by accident in the course of driving a tunnel or sinking a shaft. Higbie knew the Wide West rock perfectly well, and the more he had examined the new developments the more he was satisfied that the ore could not have come from the Wide West vein.

WORTH A MILLION.

And so had it occurred to him alone, of all the camp, that there was a blind lead down in the shaft, and that even the Wide West people themselves did not suspect it. He was right. When he went down the shaft, he found that the blind lead held its independent way through the Wide West vein, cutting it diagonally, and that it was enclosed in its own well-defined casing-rocks and clay. Hence it was public prop-

erty. Both leads being perfectly well defined, it was easy for
any miner to see which one belonged to the Wide West and
which did not.

We thought it well to have a strong friend; and therefore
we brought the foreman of the Wide West to our cabin that
night and revealed the great surprise to him. Higbie said:

"We are going to take possession of this blind lead, record
it and establish ownership, and then forbid the Wide West
company to take out any more of the rock. You cannot help
your company in this matter—nobody can help them. I will
go into the shaft with you and prove to your entire satisfaction.
that it *is* a blind lead. Now we propose to take you in with
us, and claim the blind lead in our three names. What do
you say?"

What could a man say who had an opportunity to simply
stretch forth his hand and take possession of a fortune without
risk of any kind and without wronging any one or attaching
the least taint of dishonor to his name? He could only say,
"Agreed."

The notice was put up that night, and duly spread upon
the recorder's books before ten o'clock. We claimed two hundred feet each—six hundred feet in all—the smallest and com-
pactest organization in the district, and the easiest to manage.

No one can be so thoughtless as to suppose that we slept, that
night. Higbie and I went to bed at midnight, but it was only
to lie broad awake and think, dream, scheme. The floorless,
tumble-down cabin was a palace, the ragged gray blankets silk,
the furniture rosewood and mahogany. Each new splendor
that burst out of my visions of the future whirled me bodily
over in bed or jerked me to a sitting posture just as if an elec-
tric battery had been applied to me. We shot fragments of
conversation back and forth at each other. Once Higbie said:

"When are you going home—to the States?"

"To-morrow!"—with an evolution or two, ending with a
sitting position. "Well—no—but next month, at furthest."

"We'll go in the same steamer."

"Agreed."

A pause.

"Steamer of the 10th?"

"Yes.   No, the 1st."

"All right."

Another pause.

"Where are you going to live?" said Higbie.

"San Francisco."

"That's me!"

Pause.

"Too high—too much climbing"—from Higbie.

"What is?"

"I was thinking of Russian Hill—building a house up there."

"Too much climbing?   Shan't you keep a carriage?"

"Of course.   I forgot that."

Pause.

"Cal., what kind of a house are you going to build?"

MILLIONAIRES LAYING PLANS.

"I was thinking about that.   Three-story and an attic."

"But what *kind?*"

"Well, I don't hardly know.   Brick, I suppose."

"Brick—bosh."

"Why? What is your idea?"

"Brown stone front—French plate glass—billiard-room off the dining-room—statuary and paintings—shrubbery and two-acre grass plat—greenhouse—iron dog on the front stoop—gray horses—landau, and a coachman with a bug on his hat!"

"By George!"

A long pause.

"Cal., when are you going to Europe?"

"Well—I hadn't thought of that. When are you?"

"In the Spring."

"Going to be gone all summer?"

"All summer! I shall remain there three years."

"No—but are you in earnest?"

"Indeed I am."

"I will go along too."

"Why of course you will."

"What part of Europe shall you go to?"

"All parts. France, England, Germany—Spain, Italy, Switzerland, Syria, Greece, Palestine, Arabia, Persia, Egypt—all over—everywhere."

"I'm agreed."

"All right."

"Won't it be a swell trip!"

"We'll spend forty or fifty thousand dollars trying to make it one, anyway."

Another long pause.

"Higbie, we owe the butcher six dollars, and he has been threatening to stop our—"

"Hang the butcher!"

"Amen."

And so it went on. By three o'clock we found it was no use, and so we got up and played cribbage and smoked pipes till sunrise. It was my week to cook. I always hated cooking—now, I abhorred it.

The news was all over town. The former excitement was great—this one was greater still. I walked the streets serene and happy. Higbie said the foreman had been offered two hundred thousand dollars for his third of the mine. I said I would like to see myself selling for any such price. My ideas were lofty. My figure was a million. Still, I honestly believe that if I had been offered it, it would have had no other effect than to make me hold off for more.

I found abundant enjoyment in being rich. A man offered me a three-hundred-dollar horse, and wanted to take my simple, unendorsed note for it. That brought the most realizing sense I had yet had that I was actually rich, beyond shadow of doubt. It was followed by numerous other evidences of a similar nature—among which I may mention the fact of the butcher leaving us a double supply of meat and saying nothing about money.

By the laws of the district, the "locators" or claimants of a ledge were obliged to do a fair and reasonable amount of work on their new property within ten days after the date of the location, or the property was forfeited, and anybody could go and seize it that chose. So we determined to go to work the next day. About the middle of the afternoon, as I was coming out of the post office, I met a Mr. Gardiner, who told me that Capt. John Nye was lying dangerously ill at his place (the "Nine-Mile Ranch"), and that he and his wife were not able to give him nearly as much care and attention as his case demanded. I said if he would wait for me a moment, I would go down and help in the sick room. I ran to the cabin to tell Higbie. He was not there, but I left a note on the table for him, and a few minutes later I left town in Gardiner's wagon.

CHAPTER XLI.

CAPTAIN NYE was very ill indeed, with spasmodic rheumatism. But the old gentleman was himself— which is to say, he was kind-hearted and agreeable when comfortable, but a singularly violent wild-cat when things did not go well. He would be smiling along pleasantly enough, when a sudden spasm of his disease would take him and he would go out of his smile into a perfect fury. He would groan and wail and howl with the anguish, and fill up the odd chinks with the most elaborate profanity that strong convictions and a fine fancy could contrive. With fair opportunity he could swear very well and handle his adjectives with considerable judgment; but when the spasm was on him it was painful to listen to him, he was so awkward. However, I had seen him nurse a sick man himself and put up patiently with the inconveniences of the situation, and consequently I was willing that he should have full license now that his own turn had come. He could not disturb me, with all his raving and ranting, for my mind had work on hand, and it labored on diligently, night and day, whether my hands were idle or employed. I was altering and amending the plans for my house, and thinking over the propriety of having the billiard-room in the attic, instead of on the same floor with the dining-room; also, I was trying to decide between green and blue for the upholstery of the drawing-room, for, although my preference was blue I feared it was a color that would be too easily damaged by dust and sunlight; likewise while I was content to put the coach-

man in a modest livery, I was uncertain about a footman—I
needed one, and was even resolved to have one, but wished he
could properly appear and perform his functions out of livery,
for I somewhat dreaded so much show ; and yet, inasmuch as
my late grandfather had had a coachman and such things, but
no liveries, I felt rather drawn to beat him ;—or beat his ghost,
at any rate ; I was also systematizing the European trip, and
managed to get it all laid out, as to route and length of time
to be devoted to it—everything, with one exception—namely,
whether to cross the desert from Cairo to Jerusalem per camel,
or go by sea to Beirut, and thence down through the country
per caravan.   Meantime I was writing to the friends at home
every day, instructing them concerning all my plans and intentions, and directing them to look up a handsome homestead
for my mother and agree upon a price for it against my coming, and also directing them to sell my share of the Tennessee
land and tender the proceeds to the widows' and orphans'
fund of the typographical union of which I had long been a
member in good standing.   [This Tennessee land had been in
the possession of the family many years, and promised to confer high fortune upon us some day ; it still promises it, but in
a less violent way.]

When I had been nursing the Captain nine days he was
somewhat better, but very feeble.   During the afternoon we
lifted him into a chair and gave him an alcoholic vapor bath,
and then set about putting him on the bed again.   We had
to be exceedingly careful, for the least jar produced pain.
Gardiner had his shoulders and I his legs; in an unfortunate
moment I stumbled and the patient fell heavily on the bed in
an agony of torture.   I never heard a man swear so in my life.
He raved like a maniac, and tried to snatch a revolver from
the table—but I got it.   He ordered me out of the house, and
swore a world of oaths that he would kill me wherever he
caught me when he got on his feet again.   It was simply a
passing fury, and meant nothing.   I knew he would forget it in
an hour, and maybe be sorry for it, too ; but it angered me a
little, at the moment.   So much so, indeed, that I determined

to go back to Esmeralda. I thought he was able to get along alone, now, since he was on the war path. I took supper, and as soon as the moon rose, began my nine-mile journey, on foot.

DANGEROUSLY SICK.

Even millionaires needed no horses, in those days, for a mere nine-mile jaunt without baggage.

As I "raised the hill" overlooking the town, it lacked fifteen minutes of twelve. I glanced at the hill over beyond the canyon, and in the bright moonlight saw what appeared to be about half the population of the village massed on and around the Wide West croppings. My heart gave an exulting bound, and I said to myself, "They have made a new strike to-night—and struck it richer than ever, no doubt." I started over there, but gave it up. I said the "strike" would keep, and I had climbed hills enough for one night. I went on down through the town, and as I was passing a little German bakery, a woman ran out and begged me to come in and help her. She said her husband had a fit. I went in, and judged she was right—he appeared to have a hundred of them, compressed into one. Two Germans were there, trying to hold him, and not making much of a success of it. I ran up the street half a block or so and routed out a sleeping doctor, brought him down half dressed, and we four wrestled with the maniac, and doctored, drenched and bled him, for more than an hour, and the poor German woman did the crying. He grew quiet, now, and the doctor and I withdrew and left him to his friends.

It was a little after one o'clock. As I entered the cabin door, tired but jolly, the dingy light of a tallow candle revealed Higbie, sitting by the pine table gazing stupidly at my note, which he held in his fingers, and looking pale, old, and hag-

WORTH NOTHING.

gard. I halted, and looked at him. He looked at me, stolidly. I said:

"Higbie, what—what is it?"

"We're ruined—we didn't do the work — THE BLIND LEAD'S RELOCATED!"

It was enough. I sat down sick, grieved—broken-hearted, indeed. A minute before, I was rich and brimful of vanity; I was a pauper now, and very meek. We sat still an hour, busy with thought, busy with vain and useless self-upbraidings, busy with "Why *didn't* I do this, and why *didn't* I do that," but neither spoke a word. Then we dropped into mutual explanations, and the mystery was cleared away. It came out that Higbie had depended on me, as I had on him, and as both of us had on the foreman. The folly of it! It was the first time that ever staid and steadfast Higbie had left an important matter to chance or failed to be true to his full share of a responsibility.

But he had never seen my note till this moment, and this moment was the first time he had been in the cabin since the day he had seen me last. He, also, had left a note for me, on that same fatal afternoon—had ridden up on horseback, and looked through the window, and being in a hurry and not seeing me, had tossed the note into the cabin through a broken pane. Here it was, on the floor, where it had remained undisturbed for nine days:

"Don't fail to do the work before the ten days expire. W. has passed through and given me notice. I am to join him at Mono Lake, and we shall go on from there to-night. He says he will find it this time, sure. CAL."

"W." meant Whiteman, of course. That thrice accursed "cement!"

That was the way of it. An old miner, like Higbie, could no more withstand the fascination of a mysterious mining excitement like this "cement" foolishness, than he could refrain from eating when he was famishing. Higbie had been dreaming about the marvelous cement for months; and now, against his better judgment, he had gone off and "taken the chances" on my keeping secure a mine worth a million undiscovered cement veins. They had not been followed this time. His riding out of town in broad daylight was such a commonplace thing to do that it had not attracted any attention. He said they prosecuted their search in the fastnesses of the mountains during nine days, without success; they could not find the cement. Then a ghastly fear came over him that something might have happened to prevent the doing of the necessary work to hold the blind lead (though indeed he thought such a thing hardly possible), and forthwith he started home with all speed. He would have reached Esmeralda in time, but his horse broke down and he had to walk a great part of the distance. And so it happened that as he came into Esmeralda by one road, I entered it by another. His was the superior energy, however, for he went straight to the Wide West, instead of turning aside as I had done—and he arrived there about five or ten minutes too late! The "notice"

19†

was already up, the "relocation" of our mine completed beyond recall, and the crowd rapidly dispersing. He learned
some facts before he left the ground. The foreman had not
been seen about the streets since the night we had located the
mine—a telegram had called him to California on a matter of
life and death, it was said. At any rate he had done no work
and the watchful eyes of the community were taking note of
the fact. At midnight of this woful tenth day, the ledge
would be "relocatable," and by eleven o'clock the hill was
black with men prepared to do the relocating. That was the
crowd I had seen when I fancied a new "strike" had been

ENFORCING A COMPROMISE.

made—idiot that I was.
[We three had the same
right to relocate the lead
that other people had,
provided we were quick
enough.] As midnight
was announced, fourteen
men, duly armed and ready
to back their proceedings,
put up their "notice" and proclaimed their ownership of the
blind lead, under the new name of the "Johnson." But A.
D. Allen our partner (the foreman) put in a sudden appearance
about that time, with a cocked revolver in his hand, and said
his name must be added to the list, or he would "thin out the
Johnson company some." He was a manly, splendid, de-

termined fellow, and known to be as good as his word, and therefore a compromise was effected. They put in his name for a hundred feet, reserving to themselves the customary two hundred feet each. Such was the history of the night's events, as Higbie gathered from a friend on the way home.

Higbie and I cleared out on a new mining excitement the next morning, glad to get away from the scene of our sufferings, and after a month or two of hardship and disappointment, returned to Esmeralda once more. Then we learned that the Wide West and the Johnson companies had consolidated; that the stock, thus united, comprised five thousand feet, or shares; that the foreman, apprehending tiresome litigation, and considering such a huge concern unwieldy, had sold his hundred feet for ninety thousand dollars in gold and gone home to the States to enjoy it. If the stock was worth such a gallant figure, with five thousand shares in the corporation, it makes me dizzy to think what it would have been worth with only our original six hundred in it. It was the difference between six hundred men owning a house and five thousand owning it. We would have been millionaires if we had only worked with pick and spade one little day on our property and so secured our ownership!

It reads like a wild fancy sketch, but the evidence of many witnesses, and likewise that of the official records of Esmeralda District, is easily obtainable in proof that it is a true history. I can always have it to say that I was absolutely and unquestionably worth a million dollars, once, for ten days.

A year ago my esteemed and in every way estimable old millionaire partner, Higbie, wrote me from an obscure little mining camp in California that after nine or ten years of buffetings and hard striving, he was at last in a position where he could command twenty-five hundred dollars, and said he meant to go into the fruit business in a modest way. How such a thought would have insulted him the night we lay in our cabin planning European trips and brown stone houses on Russian Hill!

CHAPTER XLII.

WHAT to do next?

It was a momentous question. I had gone out into the world to shift for myself, at the age of thirteen (for my father had endorsed for friends; and although he left us a sumptuous legacy of pride in his fine Virginian stock and its national distinction, I presently found that I could not live on that alone without occasional bread to wash it down with). I had gained a livelihood in various vocations, but had not dazzled anybody with my successes; still the list was before me, and the amplest liberty in the matter of choosing, provided I wanted to work—which I did not, after being so wealthy. I had once been a grocery clerk, for one day, but had consumed so much sugar in that time that I was relieved from further duty by the proprietor; said he wanted me outside, so that he could have my custom. I had studied law an entire week, and then given it up because it was so prosy and tiresome. I had engaged briefly in the study of blacksmithing, but wasted so much time trying to fix the bellows so that it would blow itself, that the master turned me adrift in disgrace, and told me I would come to no good. I had been a bookseller's clerk for awhile, but the customers bothered me so much I could not read with any comfort, and so the proprietor gave me a furlough and forgot to put a limit to it. I had clerked in a drug store part of a summer, but my prescriptions were unlucky, and we appeared to sell more stomach pumps than soda water. So I had to go. I had made of myself a tolerable printer, under the impression that I would be another Franklin some day, but somehow had missed the connection thus far. There was no berth open in the Esmeralda *Union*, and besides I had always been such a slow compositor that I looked with envy upon the achievements of apprentices of two years' standing; and when I took a "take," foremen were in the habit of suggesting that it would be wanted "some time during the year." I was a good average St. Louis and New Orleans pilot and by

ONE OF MY FAILURES.

no means ashamed of my abilities in that line; wages were two hundred and fifty dollars a month and no board to pay, and I did long to stand behind a wheel again and never roam any more—but I had been making such an ass of myself lately in grandiloquent letters home about my blind lead and my European excursion that I did what many and many a poor disappointed miner had done before; said "It is all over with me now, and I will never go back home to be pitied—and snubbed." I had been a private secretary, a silver miner and a silver mill operative, and amounted to less than nothing in each, and now—

What to do next?

I yielded to Higbie's appeals and consented to try the mining once more. We climbed far up on the mountain side and went to work on a little rubbishy claim of ours that had a shaft on it eight feet deep. Higbie descended into it and worked bravely with his pick till he had loosened up a deal of rock and dirt and then I went down with a long-handled shovel (the most awkward invention yet contrived by man) to throw it out. You must brace the shovel forward with the side of your knee till it is full, and then, with a skilful toss, throw it backward over your left shoulder. I made the toss and landed the mess just on the edge of the shaft and it all came back on my head and down the back of my neck. I

TARGET SHOOTING.

never said a word, but climbed out and walked home. I inwardly resolved that I would starve before I would make a target of myself and shoot rubbish at it with a long-handled shovel. I sat down, in the cabin, and gave myself up to solid misery—so to speak. Now in pleasanter days I had amused myself with writing letters to the chief paper of the Territory, the Virginia *Daily Territorial Enterprise*, and had always been surprised when they appeared in print. My good opinion of the editors had steadily declined; for it seemed to me that they might have found something better to fill up with than my literature. I had found a letter in the post office as I came home from the hill side, and finally I opened it. Eureka! [I never did know what Eureka meant, but it seems to be as proper a word to heave in as any when no other that sounds pretty offers.] It was a deliberate offer to me of Twenty-Five Dollars a week to come up to Virginia and be city editor of the *Enterprise*.

I would have challenged the publisher in the "blind lead" days—I wanted to fall down and worship him, now. Twenty-Five Dollars a week—it looked like bloated luxury—a fortune —a sinful and lavish waste of money. But my transports cooled when I thought of my inexperience and consequent unfitness for the position—and straightway, on top of this, my long array of failures rose up before me. Yet if I refused this place I must presently become dependent upon somebody for my bread, a thing necessarily distasteful to a man who had never experienced such a humiliation since he was thirteen years old. Not much to be proud of, since it is so common —but then it was all I had to *be* proud of. So I was scared into being a city editor. I would have declined, otherwise. Necessity is the mother of "taking chances." I do not doubt that if, at that time, I had been offered a salary to translate the Talmud from the original Hebrew, I would have accepted —albeit with diffidence and some misgivings—and thrown as much variety into it as I could for the money.

I went up to Virginia and entered upon my new vocation. I was a rusty looking city editor, I am free to confess—coatless, slouch hat, blue woolen shirt, pantaloons stuffed into boot-tops, whiskered half down to the waist, and the universal navy revolver slung to my belt. But I secured a more Christian costume and discarded the revolver. I had never had occasion to kill anybody, nor ever felt a desire to do so, but had worn the thing in deference to popular sentiment, and in order that I might not, by its absence, be offensively conspicuous, and a subject of remark. But the other editors, and all the printers, carried revolvers. I asked

AS CITY EDITOR.

the chief editor and proprietor (Mr. Goodman, I will call him, since it describes him as well as any name could do) for some instructions with regard to my duties, and he told me to go all over town and ask all sorts of people all sorts of questions, make notes of the information gained, and write them out for publication. And he added :

"Never say 'We learn' so-and-so, or 'It is reported, or 'It is rumored,' or 'We understand' so-and-so, but go to head-quarters and get the absolute facts, and then speak out and say 'It *is* so-and-so.' Otherwise, people will not put confidence in your news. Unassailable certainty is the thing that gives a newspaper the firmest and most valuable reputation."

It was the whole thing in a nut-shell; and to this day when I find a reporter commencing his article with "We understand," I gather a suspicion that he has not taken as much pains to inform himself as he ought to have done. I moralize well, but I did not always practise well when I was a city editor; I let fancy get the upper hand of fact too often when there was a dearth of news. I can never forget my first day's experience as a reporter. I wandered about town questioning everybody, boring everybody, and finding out that nobody knew anything. At the end of five hours my note-book was still barren. I spoke to Mr. Goodman. He said :

"Dan used to make a good thing out of the hay wagons in a dry time when there were no fires or inquests. Are there no hay wagons in from the Truckee? If there are, you might

THE ENTIRE MARKET.

speak of the re-newed activity and all that sort of thing, in the hay business, you know. It isn't sensational or ex-citing, but it fills up and looks business like."

I canvassed the city again and found one wretched old hay truck dragging in from the country. But I made affluent use of it. I multiplied it by sixteen, brought it into town from sixteen different directions, made sixteen separate items out of it, and got up such another sweat about hay as Virginia City had never seen in the world before.

This was encouraging. Two nonpareil columns had to be filled, and I was getting along. Presently, when things began to look dismal again, a desperado killed a man in a saloon and joy returned once more. I never was so glad over any mere trifle before in my life. I said to the murderer:

"Sir, you are a stranger to me, but you have done me a kindness this day which I can never forget. If whole years of gratitude can be to you any slight compensation, they shall be yours. I was in trouble and you have relieved me nobly and at a time when all seemed dark and drear. Count me your friend from this time forth, for I am not a man to forget a favor."

A FRIEND INDEED.

If I did not really say that to him I at least felt a sort of itching desire to do it. I wrote up the murder with a hungry attention to details, and when it was finished experienced but one regret—namely, that they had not hanged my bene-factor on the spot, so that I could work him up too.

Next I discovered some emigrant wagons going into camp on the plaza and found that they had lately come through the hostile Indian country and had fared rather roughly. I made the best of the item that the circumstances permitted, and felt that if I were not confined within rigid limits by the presence of the reporters of the other papers I could add particulars that would make the article much more interesting. However, I found one wagon that was going on to California, and made some judicious inquiries of the proprietor. When I learned, through his short and surly answers to my cross-questioning, that he was certainly going on and would not be in the city next day to make trouble, I got ahead of the other papers, for I took down his list of names and added his party to the killed and wounded. Having more scope here, I put this wagon through an Indian fight that to this day has no parallel in history.

My two columns were filled. When I read them over in the morning I felt that I had found my legitimate occupation at last. I reasoned within myself that news, and stirring news, too, was what a paper needed, and I felt that I was peculiarly endowed with the ability to furnish it. Mr. Goodman said that I was as good a reporter as Dan. I desired no higher commendation. With encouragement like that, I felt that I could take my pen and murder all the immigrants on the plains if need be and the interests of the paper demanded it.

CHAPTER XLIII.

HOWEVER, as I grew better acquainted with the business and learned the run of the sources of information I ceased to require the aid of fancy to any large extent, and became able to fill my columns without diverging noticeably from the domain of fact.

I struck up friendships with the reporters of the other journals, and we swapped "regulars" with each other and thus economized work. "Regulars" are permanent sources of news, like courts, bullion returns, "clean-ups" at the quartz mills, and inquests. Inasmuch as everybody went armed, we had an inquest about every day, and so this department was naturally set down among the "regulars." We had lively papers in those days. My great competitor among the reporters was Boggs of the *Union*. He was an excellent reporter. Once in three or four months he would get a little intoxicated, but as a general thing he was a wary and cautious drinker although always ready to tamper a little with the enemy. He had the advantage of me in one thing; he could get the monthly public school report and I could not, because the principal hated the *Enterprise*. One snowy night when the report was due, I started out sadly wondering how I was going to get it. Presently, a few steps up the almost deserted street I stumbled on Boggs and asked him where he was going.

"After the school report."

"I'll go along with you."

"No, *sir*. I'll excuse you."

"Just as you say."

A saloon-keeper's boy passed by with a steaming pitcher

of hot punch, and Boggs snuffed the fragrance gratefully. He gazed fondly after the boy and saw him start up the *Enterprise* stairs. I said :

"I wish you could help me get that school business, but since you can't, I must run up to the *Union* office and see if I can get them to let me have a proof of it after they have set it up, though I don't begin to suppose they will. Good night."

"Hold on a minute. I don't mind getting the report and sitting around with the boys a little, while you copy it, if you're willing to drop down to the principal's with me."

"Now you talk like a rational being. Come along."

We plowed a couple of blocks through the snow, got the report and returned to our office. It was a short document and soon copied. Meantime Boggs helped himself to the punch. I gave the manuscript back to him and we started out to get an inquest, for we heard pistol shots near by. We got the particulars with little loss of time, for it was only an inferior sort of bar-room murder, and of little interest to the public, and then we separated. Away at three o'clock in the morning, when we had gone to press and were having a relaxing concert as usual—for some of the printers were good singers and others good performers on the guitar and on that atrocity the accordeon—the proprietor of the *Union* strode in and desired to know if anybody had heard anything of Boggs or the school report. We stated the case, and all turned out to help hunt for the delinquent. We found him standing on a table in a saloon, with an old tin lantern in one hand and the school report in the other, haranguing a gang of intoxicated Cornish miners on the iniquity of squandering the public moneys on education "when hundreds and hundreds of honest hard-working men are literally starving for whiskey." [Riotous applause.] He had been assisting in a regal spree with those parties for hours. We dragged him away and put him to bed.

Of course there was no school report in the *Union*, and Boggs held me accountable, though I was innocent of any intention or desire to compass its absence from that paper and was as sorry as any one that the misfortune had occurred.

But we were perfectly friendly. The day that the school
report was next due, the proprietor of the "Genessee" mine

AN EDUCATIONAL REPORT.

furnished us a buggy and asked us to go down and write something about the property—a very common request and one
always gladly acceded to when people furnished buggies, for
we were as fond of pleasure excursions as other people. In due
time we arrived at the "mine"—nothing but a hole in the
ground ninety feet deep, and no way of getting down into it
but by holding on to a rope and being lowered with a windlass.
The workmen had just gone off somewhere to dinner. I was
not strong enough to lower Boggs's bulk; so I took an un-
lighted candle in my teeth, made a loop for my foot in the
end of the rope, implored Boggs not to go to sleep or let the
windlass get the start of him, and then swung out over the
shaft. I reached the bottom muddy and bruised about the
elbows, but safe. I lit the candle, made an examination of
the rock, selected some specimens and shouted to Boggs to

hoist away. No answer. Presently a head appeared in the circle of daylight away aloft, and a voice came down:

NO PARTICULAR HURRY.

"Are you all set?"

"All set—hoist away."

"Are you comfortable?"

"Perfectly."

"Could you wait a little?"

"Oh c e r t a i n l y—no particular hurry."

"Well—good by."

"Why? Where are you going?"

"After the school report!"

And he did. I staid down there an hour, and surprised t h e workmen when they hauled up and found a man on the rope instead of a bucket of rock. I walked home, too—five miles—up hill. We had no school report next morning; but the *Union* had.

Six months after my entry into journalism the grand "flush times" of Silverland began, and they continued with unabated splendor for three years. All difficulty about filling up the "local department" ceased, and the only trouble now was how to make the lengthened columns hold the world of incidents and happenings that came to our literary net every day. Virginia had grown to be the "livest" town, for its age and population, that America had ever produced. The sidewalks swarmed with people—to such an extent, indeed, that it was generally no easy matter to stem the human tide. The streets themselves were just as crowded with quartz wagons, freight teams and other vehicles. The procession was endless. So great was the pack, that buggies frequently had to wait half an hour for an opportunity to cross the principal street. Joy sat on every countenance, and there was a glad, almost fierce, intensity in every eye, that told of the money-getting schemes that were seething in every brain and the high hope that held sway in every heart. Money was as plenty as dust; every individual considered himself wealthy, and a melancholy countenance was nowhere to be seen. There were military companies, fire companies, brass bands, banks, hotels, theatres, "hurdy-gurdy houses," wide-open gambling palaces, political pow-wows, civic processions, street fights, murders, inquests, riots, a whiskey mill every fifteen steps, a Board of Aldermen, a Mayor, a City Surveyor, a City Engineer, a Chief of the Fire Department, with First, Second and Third Assistants, a Chief of Police, City Marshal and a large police force, two Boards of Mining Brokers, a dozen breweries and half a dozen jails and station-houses in full operation, and some talk of building a church. The "flush times" were in magnificent flower! Large fire-proof brick buildings were going up in the principal streets, and the wooden suburbs were spreading out in all directions. Town lots soared up to prices that were amazing.

The great "Comstock lode" stretched its opulent length straight through the town from north to south, and every mine on it was in diligent process of development. One of these mines alone employed six hundred and seventy-five men, and in the matter of elections the adage was, "as the 'Gould and Curry' goes, so goes the city." Laboring men's wages were four and six dollars a day, and they worked in three "shifts" or gangs, and the blasting and picking and shoveling went on without ceasing, night and day.

The "city" of Virginia roosted royally midway up the steep side of Mount Davidson, seven thousand two hundred

BIRD'S EYE VIEW OF VIRGINIA AND MOUNT DAVIDSON.

feet above the level of the sea, and in the clear Nevada atmosphere was visible from a distance of fifty miles! It claimed a population of fifteen thousand to eighteen thousand, and all day long half of this little army swarmed the streets like bees and the other half swarmed among the drifts and tunnels of the "Comstock," hundreds of feet down in the earth directly under those same streets. Often we felt our chairs jar, and heard the faint boom of a blast down in the bowels of the earth under the office.

The mountain side was so steep that the entire town had a slant to it like a roof. Each street was a terrace, and from each to the next street below the descent was forty or fifty feet. The fronts of the houses were level with the street they faced, but their rear first floors were propped on lofty stilts; a man could stand at a rear first floor window of a C street house and look down the chimneys of the row of houses below him facing D street. It was a laborious climb, in that thin atmosphere, to ascend from D to A street, and you were panting and out of breath when you got there; but you could turn around and go down again like a house a-fire—so to speak. The atmosphere was so rarified, on account of the great altitude, that one's blood lay near the surface always, and the scratch of a pin was a disaster worth worrying about, for the chances were that a grievous erysipelas would ensue. But to offset this, the thin atmosphere seemed to carry healing to gunshot wounds, and therefore, to simply shoot your adversary through both lungs was a thing not likely to afford you any permanent satisfaction, for he would be nearly certain to be around looking for you within the month, and not with an opera glass, either.

From Virginia's airy situation one could look over a vast, far-reaching panorama of mountain ranges and deserts; and whether the day was bright or overcast, whether the sun was rising or setting, or flaming in the zenith, or whether night and the moon held sway, the spectacle was always impressive and beautiful. Over your head Mount Davidson lifted its gray dome, and before and below you a rugged canyon clove the battlemented hills, making a sombre gateway through which a soft-tinted desert was glimpsed, with the silver thread of a river winding through it, bordered with trees which many miles of distance diminished to a delicate fringe; and still further away the snowy mountains rose up and stretched their long barrier to the filmy horizon—far enough beyond a lake that burned in the desert like a fallen sun, though that, itself, lay fifty miles removed. Look from your window where you would, there was fascination in the picture. At rare intervals—but very rare—there were clouds in our skies, and then the setting sun would gild and flush and glorify this mighty expanse of scenery with a bewildering pomp of color that held the eye like a spell and moved the spirit like music.

20†

CHAPTER XLIV.

MY salary was increased to forty dollars a week. But I seldom drew it. I had plenty of other resources, and what were two broad twenty-dollar gold pieces to a man who had his pockets full of such and a cumbersome abundance of bright half dollars besides? [Paper money has never come into use on the Pacific coast.] Reporting was lucrative, and every man in the town was lavish with his money and his "feet." The city and all the great mountain side were riddled with mining shafts. There were more mines than miners. True, not ten of these mines were yielding rock worth hauling to a mill, but everybody said, "Wait till the shaft gets down where the ledge comes in solid, and then you will see!" So nobody was discouraged. These were nearly all "wild cat" mines, and wholly worthless, but nobody believed it then. The "Ophir," the "Gould & Curry," the "Mexican," and other great mines on the Comstock lead in Virginia and Gold Hill were turning out huge piles of rich rock every day, and every man believed that his little wild cat claim was as good as any on the "main lead" and would infallibly be worth a thousand dollars a foot when he "got down where it came in solid." Poor fellow, he was blessedly blind to the fact that he never would see that day. So the thousand wild cat shafts burrowed deeper and deeper into the earth day by day, and all men were beside themselves with hope and happiness. How they labored, prophesied, exulted! Surely nothing like it was ever seen before since the world began. Every one of these wild cat mines—not mines, but holes in the ground over imaginary mines—was incorporated and had handsomely engraved "stock" and the stock was salable, too. It was bought and sold with a feverish avidity in the boards every day. You could go up on the mountain side, scratch around and find a ledge (there was no lack of them), put up a "notice" with a grandiloquent name in it, start a shaft, get your stock printed, and with nothing whatever to prove that your mine was worth a straw, you could put your stock on the market and sell out for hundreds and even thousands of dollars. To make money, and make it fast, was as easy as it was to eat your dinner. Every man owned "feet" in fifty different wild cat mines and considered his fortune made. Think of a city with not one

A NEW MINE.

solitary poor man in it! One would suppose that when month after month went by and still not a wild cat mine [by wild cat I mean, in general terms, *any* claim not located on the mother vein, *i. e.*, the "Comstock") yielded a ton of rock worth crushing, the people would begin to wonder if they were not putting too much faith in their prospective riches; but there was not a thought of such a thing. They burrowed away, bought and sold, and were happy.

New claims were taken up daily, and it was the friendly custom to run straight to the newspaper offices, give the re-

porter forty or fifty "feet," and get them to go and examine
the mine and publish a notice of it. They did not care a fig
what you said about the property so you said something.
Consequently we generally said a word or two to the effect
that the "indications" were good, or that the ledge was "six
feet wide," or that the rock "resembled the Comstock" (and
so it did—but as a general thing the resemblance was not
startling enough to knock you down). If the rock was moderately promising, we followed the custom of the country, used
strong adjectives and frothed at the mouth as if a very marvel
in silver discoveries had transpired. If the mine was a "developed" one, and had no pay ore to show (and of course it
hadn't), we praised the tunnel; said it was one of the most
infatuating tunnels in the land; driveled and driveled about
the tunnel till we ran entirely out of ecstasies—but never said
a word about the rock. We would squander half a column of
adulation on a shaft, or a new wire rope, or a dressed pine
windlass, or a fascinating force pump, and close with a burst of
admiration of the "gentlemanly and efficient Superintendent"
of the mine—but never utter a whisper about the rock. And
those people were always pleased, always satisfied. Occasionally we patched up and varnished our reputation for discrimi-
nation and stern, undeviating accuracy, by giving some old
abandoned claim a blast that ought to have made its dry bones
rattle—and then somebody would seize it and sell it on the
fleeting notoriety thus conferred upon it.

There was *nothing* in the shape of a mining claim that was
not salable. We received presents of "feet" every day. If
we needed a hundred dollars or so, we sold some; if not, we
hoarded it away, satisfied that it would ultimately be worth
a thousand dollars a foot. I had a trunk about half full of
"stock." When a claim made a stir in the market and went
up to a high figure, I searched through my pile to see if I had
any of its stock—and generally found it.

The prices rose and fell constantly; but still a fall disturbed
us little, because a thousand dollars a foot was our figure, and
so we were content to let it fluctuate as much as it pleased till it

reached it. My pile of stock was not all given to me by people who wished their claims "noticed." At least half of it was given me by persons who had no thought of such a thing, and looked for nothing more than a simple verbal "thank you;" and you were not even obliged by law to furnish that. If you are coming up the street with a couple of baskets of apples in your hands, and you meet a friend, you naturally invite him to take a few. That describes the condition of things in Virginia in the "flush times." Every man had his pockets full of stock, and it was the actual *custom* of the country to part with small quantities of it to friends without the asking. Very often it was a good idea to close the transaction instantly, when a man offered a stock present to a friend, for the offer was only good and binding at that moment, and if the price went to a high figure shortly afterward the procrastination was a thing to be regretted. Mr. Stewart (Senator, now, from Nevada) one day told me he

"TRY A FEW?"

would give me twenty feet of "Justis" stock if I would walk over to his office. It was worth five or ten dollars a foot. I asked him to make the offer good for next day, as I was just going to dinner. He said he would not be in town; so I risked it and took my dinner instead of the stock: Within the week the price went up to seventy dollars and afterward to a hundred and fifty, but nothing could make that man yield. I suppose he sold that stock of mine and placed the guilty proceeds in his own pocket. [My revenge will be found in the accompanying portrait.] I met three friends one afternoon, who said they had been buying "Overman" stock at

auction at eight dollars a foot.   One said if I would come up
to his office he would give me fifteen feet; another said he
would add fifteen; the third said he would do the same.   But

I was going after an inquest
and could not stop.   A few
weeks afterward they sold all
their " Overman " at six hundred dollars a foot and generously came around to tell
me about it—and also to urge
me to accept of the next forty-
five feet of it that people tried
to force on me.   These are
actual facts, and I could make
the list a long one and still
confine myself strictly to the
truth.   Many a time friends

PORTRAIT OF MR. STEWART.

gave us as much as twenty-five feet of stock that was selling
at twenty-five dollars a foot, and they thought no more of it
than they would of offering a guest a cigar.   These were
" flush times " indeed !   I thought they were going to last
always, but somehow I never was much of a prophet.

To show what a wild spirit possessed the mining brain of
the community, I will remark that " claims " were actually
" located " in excavations for cellars, where the pick had exposed what seemed to be quartz veins—and not cellars in the
suburbs, either, but in the very heart of the city; and forthwith stock would be issued and thrown on the market.   It was
small matter who the cellar belonged to—the " ledge " belonged
to the finder, and unless the United States government interfered (inasmuch as the government holds the primary right to
mines of the noble metals in Nevada—or at least did then),
it was considered to be his privilege to work it.   Imagine a
stranger staking out a mining claim among the costly shrubbery in your front yard and calmly proceeding to lay waste
the ground with pick and shovel and blasting powder !   It has
been often done in California.   In the middle of one of the

principal business streets of Virginia, a man "located" a mining claim and began a shaft on it. He gave me a hundred feet of the stock and I sold it for a fine suit of clothes because I was afraid somebody would fall down the shaft and sue for damages. I owned in another claim that was located in the middle of another street; and to show how absurd people can be, that "East India" stock (as it was called) sold briskly although there was an ancient tunnel running directly under the claim and any man could go into it and see that it did not cut a quartz ledge or anything that remotely resembled one.

One plan of acquiring sudden wealth was to "salt" a wild cat claim and sell out while the excitement was up. The process was simple. The schemer located a worthless ledge, sunk a shaft on it, bought a wagon load of rich "Comstock" ore, dumped a portion of it into the shaft and piled the rest by its side, above ground. Then he showed the property to a simpleton and sold it to

SELLING A MINE.

him at a high figure. Of course the wagon load of rich ore was all that the victim ever got out of his purchase. A most remarkable case of "salting" was that of the "North Ophir." It was claimed that this vein was a remote "extension " of the original " Ophir," a valuable mine on the " Comstock." For a few days everybody was talking about the rich developments in the North Ophir. It was said that it yielded perfectly pure silver in small, solid lumps. I went to the place with the owners, and found a shaft six or eight feet deep, in the bottom of which was a badly shattered vein of dull, yellowish, unpromising rock. One would as soon expect to find silver in a grindstone. We got out a pan of the rubbish and washed it in a puddle, and sure enough, among the sediment we found half a dozen black, bullet-looking pellets of unimpeachable "native" silver. Nobody had ever heard of such a thing before; science could not account for such a queer novelty. The stock rose to sixty-five dollars a foot, and at this figure the world-renowned tragedian, McKean Buchanan, bought a commanding interest and prepared to quit the stage once more—he was always doing that. And then it transpired that the mine had been "salted"—and not in any hackneyed way, either, but in a singularly bold, barefaced and peculiarly original and outrageous fashion. On one of the lumps of "native" silver was discovered the minted legend, "TED STATES OF," and then it was plainly apparent that the mine had been "salted" with melted half-dollars! The lumps thus obtained had been blackened till they resembled native silver, and were then mixed with the shattered rock in the bottom of the shaft. It is literally true. Of course the price of the stock at once fell to nothing, and the tragedian was ruined. But for this calamity we might have lost McKean Buchanan from the stage.

CHAPTER XLV.

THE "flush times" held bravely on. Something over two years before, Mr. Goodman and another journeyman printer, had borrowed forty dollars and set out from San Francisco to try their fortunes in the new city of Virginia. They found the *Territorial Enterprise*, a poverty-stricken weekly journal, gasping for breath and likely to die. They bought it, type, fixtures, good-will and all, for a thousand dollars, on long time. The editorial sanctum, news-room, press-room, publication office, bed-chamber, parlor, and kitchen were all compressed into one apartment and it was a small one, too. The editors and printers slept on the floor, a China-man did their cooking, and the "imposing-stone" was the general dinner table. But now things were changed. The paper was a great daily, printed by steam; there were five editors and twenty-three compositors; the subscription price was sixteen dollars a year; the advertising rates were exorbitant, and the columns crowded. The paper was clearing from six to ten thousand dollars a month, and the "Enterprise Building" was finished and ready for occupation—a stately fire-proof brick. Every day from five all the way up to eleven columns of "live" advertisements were left out or crowded into spasmodic and irregular "supplements."

The "Gould & Curry" company were erecting a monster hundred-stamp mill at a cost that ultimately fell little short of a million dollars. Gould & Curry stock paid heavy dividends —a rare thing, and an experience confined to the dozen or fifteen claims located on the "main lead," the "Comstock." The Superintendent of the Gould & Curry lived, rent free, in a fine house built and furnished by the company. He drove a fine pair of horses which were a present from the company, and his salary was twelve thousand dollars a year. The superintendent of another of the great mines traveled in grand state, had a salary of twenty-eight thousand dollars a year, and in a law suit in after days claimed that he was to have had one per cent. on the gross yield of the bullion likewise.

Money was wonderfully plenty. The trouble was, not how to get it,—but how to spend it, how to lavish it, get rid of it, squander it. And so it was a happy thing that just at this juncture the news came over the wires that a great United States Sanitary Commission had been formed and money was wanted for the relief of the wounded sailors and soldiers of the Union languishing in the Eastern hospitals. Right on the heels of it came word that San Francisco had responded superbly before the telegram was half a day old. Virginia rose as one man! A Sanitary Committee was hurriedly organized, and its chairman mounted a vacant cart in C street and tried to make the clamorous multitude understand that the rest of the committee were flying hither and thither and working with all their might and main, and that if the town would only wait an hour, an office would be ready, books opened, and the Commission prepared to receive contributions. His voice was drowned and his information lost in a ceaseless roar of cheers, and demands that the money be received *now*—they swore they would not wait. The chairman pleaded and argued, but, deaf to all entreaty, men plowed their way through the throng and rained checks of gold coin into the cart and skurried away for more. Hands clutching money, were thrust aloft out of the jam by men who hoped this eloquent appeal would cleave a road their strugglings could not open. The very Chinamen and Indians caught the excitement and dashed their half dollars into the cart without knowing or caring what it was all about. Women plunged into the crowd, trimly attired, fought their way to the cart with their coin, and emerged again, by and by, with their apparel in a state of hopeless dilapidation.   It was the wildest mob Virginia had ever seen and the most determined and ungovernable ; and when at last it abated its fury and dispersed,

COULDN'T WAIT.

it had not a penny in its pocket.   To use its own phraseology, it came there " flush " and went away " busted."

After that, the Commission got itself into systematic working order, and for weeks the contributions flowed into its treasury in a generous stream.   Individuals and all sorts of organizations levied upon themselves a regular weekly tax for the sanitary fund, graduated according to their means, and there was not another grand universal outburst till the famous "Sanitary Flour Sack" came our way. Its history is peculiar and interesting. A former schoolmate of mine, by the name of Reuel Gridley, was living at the little city of Austin, in the Reese river country, at this time, and was the Democratic candidate for mayor. He and the Republican candidate made an agreement that the defeated man should be publicly presented with a fifty-pound sack of flour by the successful one, and should carry it home on his shoulder. Gridley was defeated. The new mayor gave him the sack of flour, and he shouldered it and carried it a mile or two, from Lower Austin to his home in Upper Austin, attended by a band of music and the whole population. Arrived there, he said he did not need the flour, and asked what the people thought he had better do with it. A voice said:

"Sell it to the highest bidder, for the benefit of the Sanitary fund."

The suggestion was greeted with a round of applause, and Gridley mounted a dry-goods box and assumed the role of auctioneer. The bids went higher and higher, as the sympathies of the pioneers awoke and expanded, till at last the sack was knocked down to a mill man at two hundred and fifty dollars, and his check taken. He was asked where he would have the flour delivered, and he said:

"Nowhere—sell it again."

Now the cheers went up royally, and the multitude were fairly in the spirit of the thing. So Gridley stood there and shouted and perspired till the sun went down; and when the crowd dispersed he had sold the sack to three hundred different people, and had taken in eight thousand dollars in gold. And still the flour sack was in his possession.

The news came to Virginia, and a telegram went back:

"Fetch along your flour sack!"

Thirty-six hours afterward Gridley arrived, and an afternoon mass meeting was held in the Opera House, and the auction began. But the sack had come sooner than it was

THE GREAT FLOUR SACK PROCESSION.

expected; the people were not thoroughly aroused, and the sale dragged. At nightfall only five thousand dollars had been secured, and there was a crestfallen feeling in the community. However, there was no disposition to let the matter rest here and acknowledge vanquishment at the hands of the village of Austin. Till late in the night the principal citizens were at work arranging the morrow's campaign, and when they went to bed they had no fears for the result. At eleven the next morning a procession of open carriages, attended by clamorous bands of music and adorned with a moving display of flags, filed along C street and was soon in danger of blockade by a huzzaing multitude of citizens. In the first carriage sat Gridley, with the flour sack in prominent view, the latter splendid with bright paint and gilt lettering; also in the same carriage sat the mayor and the recorder. The other carriages contained the Common Council, the editors and reporters, and other people of imposing consequence. The crowd pressed to the corner of C and Taylor streets, expecting the sale to begin there, but they were disappointed, and also unspeakably surprised; for the cavalcade moved on as if Virginia had ceased to be of importance, and took its way over the "divide," toward the small town of Gold Hill. Telegrams had gone ahead to Gold Hill, Silver City and Dayton, and those communities were at fever heat and rife for the conflict. It was a very hot day, and wonderfully dusty. At the end of a short half hour we descended into Gold Hill with drums beating and colors flying, and enveloped in imposing clouds of dust. The whole population—men, women and children, Chinamen and Indians, were massed in the main street, all the flags in town were at the mast head, and the blare of the bands was drowned in cheers. Gridley stood up and asked who would make the first bid for the National Sanitary Flour Sack. Gen. W. said:

"The Yellow Jacket silver mining company offers a thousand dollars, coin!"

A tempest of applause followed. A telegram carried the news to Virginia, and fifteen minutes afterward that city's

population was massed in the streets devouring the tidings—
for it was part of the programme that the bulletin boards
should do a good work that day. Every few minutes a new
dispatch was bulletined from Gold Hill, and still the excitement grew. Telegrams began to return to us from Virginia
beseeching Gridley to bring back the flour sack; but such
was not the plan of the campaign. At the end of an hour
Gold Hill's small population had paid a figure for the flour
sack that awoke all the enthusiasm of Virginia when the grand
total was displayed upon the bulletin boards. Then the
Gridley cavalcade moved on, a giant refreshed with new lager
beer and plenty of it—for the people brought it to the
carriages without waiting to measure it—and within three
hours more the expedition had carried Silver City and Dayton
by storm and was on its way back covered with glory. Every
move had been telegraphed and bulletined, and as the procession entered Virginia and filed down C street at half past
eight in the evening the town was abroad in the thorough-
fares, torches were glaring, flags flying, bands playing, cheer
on cheer cleaving the air, and the city ready to surrender at
discretion. The auction began, every bid was greeted with
bursts of applause, and at the end of two hours and a half a
population of fifteen thousand souls had paid in coin for a
fifty-pound sack of flour a sum equal to forty thousand dollars
in greenbacks! It was at a rate in the neighborhood of three
dollars for each man, woman and child of the population.
The grand total would have been twice as large, but the
streets were very narrow, and hundreds who wanted to bid
could not get within a block of the stand, and could not make
themselves heard. These grew tired of waiting and many of
them went home long before the auction was over. This was
the greatest day Virginia ever saw, perhaps.

Gridley sold the sack in Carson city and several California
towns; also in San Francisco. Then he took it east and sold
it in one or two Atlantic cities, I think. I am not sure of
that, but I know that he finally carried it to St. Louis, where a
monster Sanitary Fair was being held, and after selling it

there for a large sum and helping on the enthusiasm by displaying the portly silver bricks which Nevada's donation had produced, he had the flour baked up into small cakes and retailed them at high prices.

It was estimated that when the flour sack's mission was ended it had been sold for a grand total of a hundred and fifty thousand dollars in greenbacks! This is probably the only instance on record where common family flour brought three thousand dollars a pound in the public market.

It is due to Mr. Gridley's memory to mention that the expenses of his sanitary flour sack expedition of fifteen thousand miles, going and returning, were paid in large part, if not entirely, out of his own pocket. The time he gave to it was not less than three months. Mr. Gridley was a soldier in the Mexican war and a pioneer Californian. He died at Stockton, California, in December, 1870, greatly regretted.

CHAPTER XLVI.

THERE were nabobs in those days—in the "flush times," I mean. Every rich strike in the mines created one or two. I call to mind several of these. They were careless, easy-going fellows, as a general thing, and the community at large was as much benefited by their riches as they were themselves—possibly more, in some cases.

Two cousins, teamsters, did some hauling for a man and had to take a small segregated portion of a silver mine in lieu of $300 cash. They gave an outsider a third to open the mine, and they went on teaming. But not long. Ten months afterward the mine was out of debt and paying each·owner $8,000 to $10,000 a month—say $100,000 a year.

One of the earliest nabobs that Nevada was delivered of wore $6,000 worth of diamonds in his bosom, and swore he was unhappy because he could not spend his money as fast as he made it.

Another Nevada nabob boasted an income that often reached $16,000 a month ; and he used to love to tell how he had worked in the very mine that yielded it, for five dollars a day, when he first came to the country.

The silver and sage-brush State has knowledge of another of these pets of fortune—lifted from actual poverty to affluence almost in a single night—who was able to offer $100,000 for a position of high official distinction, shortly afterward, and did offer it—but failed to get it, his politics not being as sound as his bank account.

Then there was John Smith. He was a good, honest, kind-hearted soul, born and reared in the lower ranks of life, and miraculously ignorant. He drove a team, and owned a small ranch—a ranch that paid him a comfortable living, for although it yielded but little hay, what little it did yield was worth from $250 to $300 in gold per ton in the market. Presently Smith traded a few acres of the ranch for a small undeveloped silver mine in Gold Hill. He opened the mine and built a little unpretending ten-stamp mill. Eighteen months afterward he retired from the hay business, for his mining income had reached a most comfortable figure. Some people said it was $30,000 a month, and others said it was $60,000. Smith was very rich at any rate.

And then he went to Europe and traveled. And when he came back he was never tired of telling about the fine hogs he had seen in England, and the gorgeous sheep he had seen in Spain, and the fine cattle he had noticed in the vicinity of Rome. He was full of the wonders of the old world, and advised every-body to travel. He said a man never imagined what surprising things there were in the world till he had traveled.

A NABOB.

One day, on board ship, the passengers made up a pool of $500, which was to be the property of the man who should come nearest to guessing the run of the ves-sel for the next twenty-four hours. Next day, toward noon, the figures were all in the purser's hands in sealed en-velopes. Smith was serene and happy, for he had been bribing the engineer. But another party won the prize! Smith said:

"Here, that won't do! He guessed two miles wider of the mark than I did."

The purser said, "Mr. Smith, you missed it further than any man on board. We traveled two hundred and eight miles yesterday."

"Well, sir," said Smith, "that's just where I've got you, for I guessed two hundred and nine. If you'll look at my figgers again you'll find a 2 and two 0's, which stands for 200, don't it?—and after 'em you'll find a 9 (2009), which stands for two hundred and nine. I reckon I'll take that money, if you please."

The Gould & Curry claim comprised twelve hundred feet, and it all belonged originally to the two men whose names it bears. Mr. Curry owned two thirds of it—and he said that he sold it out for twenty-five hundred dollars in cash, and an old plug horse that ate up his market value in hay and barley in seventeen days by the watch. And he said that Gould sold out for a pair of second-hand government blankets and a bottle of whisky that killed nine men in three hours, and that an unoffending stranger that smelt the cork was disabled for life. Four years afterward the mine thus disposed of was worth in the San Francisco market seven millions six hundred thousand dollars in gold coin.

In the early days a poverty-stricken Mexican who lived in a canyon directly back of Virginia City, had a stream of water as large as a man's wrist trickling from the hill-side on his premises. The Ophir Company segregated a hundred feet of their mine and traded it to him for the stream of water. The hundred feet proved to be the richest part of the entire mine; four years after the swap, its market value (including its mill) was $1,500,000.

An individual who owned twenty feet in the Ophir mine before its great riches were revealed to men, traded it for a horse, and a very sorry looking brute he was, too. A year or so afterward, when Ophir stock went up to $3,000 a foot, this man, who had not a cent, used to say he was the most startling example of magnificence and misery the world had ever seen —because he was able to ride a sixty-thousand-dollar horse— yet could not scrape up cash enough to buy a saddle, and was obliged to borrow one or ride bareback. He said if fortune were to give him another sixty-thousand-dollar horse it would ruin him.

A youth of nineteen, who was a telegraph operator in Virginia on a salary of a hundred dollars a month, and who, when he could not make out German names in the list of San Francisco steamer arrivals, used to ingeniously select and supply substitutes for them out of an old Berlin city directory, made himself rich by watching the mining

MAGNIFICENCE AND MISERY.

telegrams that passed through his hands and buying and selling stocks accordingly, through a friend in San Francisco. Once when a private dispatch was sent from Virginia announcing a rich strike in a prominent mine and advising that the matter be kept secret till a large amount of the stock could be secured, he bought forty "feet" of the stock at twenty dollars a foot, and afterward sold half of it at eight hundred dollars a foot and the rest at double that figure. Within three months he was worth $150,000, and had resigned his telegraphic position.

Another telegraph operator who had been discharged by the company for divulging the secrets of the office, agreed

with a moneyed man in San Francisco to furnish him the
result of a great Virginia mining lawsuit within an hour after
its private reception by the parties to it in San Francisco.
For this he was to have a large percentage of the profits on
purchases and sales made on it by his fellow-conspirator. So
he went, disguised as a teamster, to a little wayside telegraph
office in the mountains, got acquainted with the operator, and
sat in the office day after day, smoking his pipe, complaining
that his team was fagged out and unable to travel—and meantime listening to the dispatches as they passed clicking through
the machine from Virginia. Finally the private dispatch announcing the result of the lawsuit sped over the wires, and as
soon as he heard it he telegraphed his friend in San Francisco:

"Am tired waiting. Shall sell the team and go home."

It was the signal agreed upon. The word "waiting" left
out, would have signified that the suit had gone the other way.
The mock teamster's friend picked up a deal of the mining
stock, at low figures, before the news became public, and a
fortune was the result.

For a long time after one of the great Virginia mines had
been incorporated, about fifty feet of the original location were
still in the hands of a man who had never signed the incorpo-
ration papers. The stock became very valuable, and every
effort was made to find this man, but he had disappeared.
Once it was heard that he was in New York, and one or two
speculators went east but failed to find him. Once the news
came that he was in the Bermudas, and straightway a specu-
lator or two hurried east and sailed for Bermuda—but he was
not there. Finally he was heard of in Mexico, and a friend
of his, a bar-keeper on a salary, scraped together a little money
and sought him out, bought his "feet" for a hundred dollars,
returned and sold the property for $75,000.

But why go on? The traditions of Silverland are filled
with instances like these, and I would never get through enu-
merating them were I to attempt do it. I only desired to give
the reader an idea of a peculiarity of the "flush times" which
I could not present so strikingly in any other way, and which

some mention of was necessary to a realizing comprehension
of the time and the country.

I was personally acquainted with the majority of the
nabobs I have referred to, and so, for old acquaintance sake,
I have shifted their occupations and experiences around in
such a way as to keep the Pacific public from recognizing
these once notorious men. No longer notorious, for the
majority of them have drifted back into poverty and obscurity
again.

In Nevada there used to be current the story of an adventure of two of her nabobs, which may or may not have
occurred. I give it for what it is worth:

Col. Jim had seen somewhat of the world, and knew more
or less of its ways; but Col. Jack was from the back settlements of the States, had led a life of arduous toil, and had
never seen a city. These two, blessed with sudden wealth,
projected a visit to New York,—Col. Jack to see the sights,
and Col. Jim to guard his unsophistication from misfortune.
They reached San Francisco in the night, and sailed in the
morning. Arrived in New York, Col. Jack said:

"I've heard tell of carriages all my life, and now I mean to
have a ride in one; I don't care what it costs. Come along."

They stepped out on the sidewalk, and Col. Jim called a
stylish barouche. But Col. Jack said:

"*No*, sir! None of your cheap-John turn-outs for me.
I'm here to have a good time, and money ain't any object. I
mean to have the nobbiest rig that's going. Now here comes
the very trick. Stop that yaller one with the pictures on it—
don't you fret—I'll stand all the expenses myself."

So Col. Jim stopped an empty omnibus, and they got in.
Said Col. Jack:

"Ain't it gay, though? Oh, no, I reckon not! Cush-
ions, and windows, and pictures, till you can't rest. What
would the boys say if they could see us cutting a swell like
this in New York? By George, I wish they *could* see us."

Then he put his head out of the window, and shouted to
the driver:

"Say, Johnny, this suits *me!*—suits yours truly, you bet, you! I want this shebang all day. I'm *on* it, old man! Let 'em out! Make 'em go! We'll make it all right with *you*, sonny!"

The driver passed his hand through the strap-hole, and tapped for his fare—it was before the gongs came into common use. Col. Jack took the hand, and shook it cordially. He said:

"You twig me, old pard! All right between gents. Smell of *that*, and see how you like it!"

And he put a twenty-dollar gold piece in the driver's hand. After a moment the driver said he could not make change.

"Bother the change! Ride it out. Put it in your pocket."

Then to Col. Jim, with a sounding slap on his thigh:

"*Ain't* it style, though? Hanged if I don't hire this thing every day for a week."

The omnibus stopped, and a young lady got in. Col. Jack stared a moment, then nudged Col. Jim with his elbow:

"Don't say a word," he whispered. "Let her

A FRIENDLY DRIVER.

ride, if she wants to. Gracious, there's room enough."

The young lady got out her porte-monnaie, and handed her fare to Col. Jack.

"What's this for?" said he.

"Give it to the driver, please."

"Take back your money, madam. We can't allow it.

You're welcome to ride here as long as you please, but this she-bang's chartered, and we can't let you pay a cent."

The girl shrunk into a corner, bewildered. An old lady with a basket climbed in, and proffered her fare.

"Excuse me," said Col. Jack. "You're perfectly welcome here, madam, but we can't allow you to pay. Set right down there, mum, and don't you be the least uneasy. Make yourself just as free as if you was in your own turn-out."

Within two minutes, three gentlemen, two fat women, and a couple of children, entered.

"Come right along, friends," said Col. Jack; "don't mind *us*. This is a free blow-out." Then he whispered to Col. Jim, "New York ain't no sociable place, I don't reckon—it ain't no *name* for it!"

He resisted every effort to pass fares to the driver, and

ASTONISHES THE NATIVES.

made everybody cordially welcome. The situation dawned on the people, and they pocketed their money, and delivered themselves up to covert enjoyment of the episode. Half a dozen more passengers entered.

"Oh, there's *plenty* of room," said Col. Jack. "Walk right in, and make yourselves at home. A blow-out ain't worth anything *as* a blow-out, unless a body has company." Then in a whisper to Col. Jim: "But *ain't* these New Yorkers friendly? And ain't they cool about it, too? Icebergs ain't anywhere. I reckon they'd tackle a hearse, if it was going their way."

More passengers got in; more yet, and still more. Both seats were filled, and a file of men were standing up, holding on to the cleats overhead. Parties with baskets and bundles were climbing up on the roof. Half-suppressed laughter rippled up from all sides.

"Well, for clean, cool, out-and-out cheek, if this don't bang anything that ever I saw, I'm an Injun!" whispered Col. Jack.

A Chinaman crowded his way in.

"I weaken!" said Col. Jack. "Hold on, driver! Keep your seats, ladies and gents. Just make yourselves free— everything's paid for. Driver, rustle these folks around as long as they're a mind to go—friends of ours, you know. Take them everywheres—and if you want more money, come

COL. JACK "WEAKENS."

to the St. Nicholas, and we'll make it all right. Pleasant journey to you, ladies and gents—go it just as long as you please—it shan't cost you a cent!"

The two comrades got out, and Col. Jack said:

"Jimmy, it's the sociablest place *I* ever saw. The China-man waltzed in as comfortable as anybody. If we'd staid awhile, I reckon we'd had some niggers. B' George, we'll have to barricade our doors to-night, or some of these ducks will be trying to sleep with us."

CHAPTER XLVII.

SOMEBODY has said that in order to know a community, one must observe the style of its funerals and know what manner of men they bury with most ceremony. I cannot say which class we buried with most eclat in our "flush times," the distinguished public benefactor or the distinguished rough—possibly the two chief grades or grand divisions of society honored their illustrious dead about equally; and hence, no doubt the philosopher I have quoted from would have needed to see two representative funerals in Virginia before forming his estimate of the people.

There was a grand time over Buck Fanshaw when he died. He was a representative citizen. He had "killed his man"— not in his own quarrel, it is true, but in defence of a stranger unfairly beset by numbers. He had kept a sumptuous saloon. He had been the proprietor of a dashing helpmeet whom he could have discarded without the formality of a divorce. He had held a high position in the fire department and been a very Warwick in politics. When he died there was great lamentation throughout the town, but especially in the vast bottom-stratum of society.

On the inquest it was shown that Buck Fanshaw, in the delirium of a wasting typhoid fever, had taken arsenic, shot himself through the body, cut his throat, and jumped out of a four-story window and broken his neck—and after due deliberation, the jury, sad and tearful, but with intelligence unblinded by its sorrow, brought in a verdict of death "by the visitation of God." What could the world do without juries?

Prodigious preparations were made for the funeral. All the vehicles in town were hired, all the saloons put in mourning, all the municipal and fire-company flags hung at half-mast, and all the firemen ordered to muster in uniform and bring their machines duly draped in black.   Now—let us remark in parenthesis—as all the peoples of the earth had representative adventurers in the Silverland, and as each adventurer had brought the slang of his nation or his locality with him, the combination made the slang of Nevada the richest and the most infinitely varied and copious that had ever existed any-where in the world, perhaps, except in the mines of California in the "early days."   Slang was the language of Nevada.   It was hard to preach a sermon without it, and be understood. Such phrases as "You bet!" "Oh, no, I reckon not!" "No Irish need apply," and a hundred others, became so common as to fall from the lips of a speaker unconsciously—and very often when they did not touch the subject under discussion and consequently failed to mean anything.

After Buck Fanshaw's inquest, a meeting of the short-haired brotherhood was held, for nothing can be done on the Pacific coast without a public meeting and an expression of sentiment.   Regretful resolutions were passed and various committees appointed ; among others, a committee of one was deputed to call on the minister, a fragile, gentle ,spirituel new fledgling from an Eastern theological seminary, and as yet un-acquainted with the ways of the mines.   The committeeman, "Scotty" Briggs, made his visit; and in after days it was worth something to hear the minister tell about it.   Scotty was a stalwart rough, whose customary suit, when on weighty official business, like committee work, was a fire helmet, flam-ing red flannel shirt, patent leather belt with spanner and revolver attached, coat hung over arm, and pants stuffed into boot tops.   He formed something of a contrast to the pale theological student.   It is fair to say of Scotty, however, in passing, that he had a warm heart, and a strong love for his friends, and never entered into a quarrel when he could rea-sonably keep out of it.   Indeed, it was commonly said that whenever one of Scotty's fights was investigated, it always turned out that it had originally been no affair of his, but that out of native goodheartedness he had dropped in of his own accord to help the man who was getting the worst of it. He and Buck Fanshaw were bosom friends, for years, and had often taken adventurous "pot-luck" together. On one occasion, they had thrown off their coats and taken the weaker side in a fight among strangers, and after gaining a hard-earned victory, turned and found that the men they were helping had deserted early, and not only that, but had stolen their coats and made off with them! But to return to Scotty's visit to the minister. He was on a sorrowful mission, now, and his face was the picture of woe. Being admitted to the presence he sat down before the clergyman, placed his fire-hat on an unfinished manuscript sermon under the minister's nose, took from it a red silk handkerchief, wiped his brow and heaved a sigh of dismal impressiveness, explanatory of his business.

COMMITTEEMAN AND MINISTER.

He choked, and even shed tears; but with an effort he mastered his voice and said in lugubrious tones:

"Are you the duck that runs the gospel-mill next door?"

"Am I the—pardon me, I believe I do not understand?"

With another sigh and a half-sob, Scotty rejoined:

"Why you see we are in a bit of trouble, and the boys thought maybe you would give us a lift, if we'd tackle you— that is, if I've got the rights of it and you are the head clerk of the doxology-works next door."

"I am the shepherd in charge of the flock whose fold is next door."

"The which?"

"The spiritual adviser of the little company of believers whose sanctuary adjoins these premises."

Scotty scratched his head, reflected a moment, and then said:

"You ruther hold over me, pard. I reckon I can't call that hand. Ante and pass the buck."

"How? I beg pardon. What did I understand you to say?"

"Well, you've ruther got the bulge on me. Or maybe we've both got the bulge, somehow. You don't smoke me and I don't smoke you. You see, one of the boys has passed in his checks and we want to give him a good send-off, and so the thing I'm on now is to roust out somebody to jerk a little chin-music for us and waltz him through handsome."

"My friend, I seem to grow more and more bewildered. Your observations are wholly incomprehensible to me. Cannot you simplify them in some way? At first I thought perhaps I understood you, but I grope now. Would it not expedite matters if you restricted yourself to categorical statements of fact unencumbered with obstructing accumulations of metaphor and allegory?"

Another pause, and more reflection. Then, said Scotty:

"I'll have to pass, I judge."

"How?"

"You've raised me out, pard."

"I still fail to catch your meaning."

"Why, that last lead of yourn is too many for me—that's the idea. I can't neither trump nor follow suit."

The clergyman sank back in his chair perplexed. Scotty leaned his head on his hand and gave himself up to thought. Presently his face came up, sorrowful but confident.

"I've got it now, so's you can savvy," he said. "What we want is a gospel-sharp. See?"

"A what?"

"Gospel-sharp. Parson."

"Oh! Why did you not say so before? I am a clergy-man—a parson."

"Now you talk! You see my blind and straddle it like a man. Put it there!"—extending a brawny paw, which closed over the minister's small hand and gave it a shake indicative of fraternal sympathy and fervent gratification.

"Now we're all right, pard. Let's start fresh. Don't you mind my snuffling a little—becuz we're in a power of trouble. You see, one of the boys has gone up the flume—"

"Gone where?"

"Up the flume—throwed up the sponge, you understand."

"Thrown up the sponge?"

"Yes—kicked the bucket—"

"Ah—has departed to that mysterious country from whose bourne no traveler returns."

"Return! I reckon not. Why pard, he's *dead!*"

"Yes, I understand."

"Oh, you do? Well I thought maybe you might be get-ting tangled some more. Yes, you see he's dead again—"

"*Again?* Why, has he ever been dead before?"

"Dead before? No! Do you reckon a man has got as many lives as a cat? But you bet you he's awful dead now, poor old boy, and I wish I'd never seen this day. I don't want no better friend than Buck Fanshaw. I knowed him by the back; and when I know a man and like him, I freeze to him—you hear *me.* Take him all round, pard, there never was a bullier man in the mines. No man ever knowed Buck Fanshaw to go back on a friend. But it's all up, you know, it's all up. It ain't no use. They've scooped him."

"Scooped him?"

"Yes—death has. Well, well, well, we've got to give him up. Yes indeed. It's a kind of a hard world, after all, *ain't it?* But pard, he was a rustler! You ought to seen him get started once. He was a bully boy with a glass eye! Just spit in his face and give him room according to his strength, and it was just beautiful to see him peel and go in. He was the worst son of a thief that ever drawed breath. Pard, he was *on* it! He was on it bigger than an Injun!"

"On it? On what?"

"On the shoot. On the shoulder. On the fight, you understand. *He* didn't give a continental for *any*body. *Beg* your pardon, friend, for coming so near saying a cuss-word—but you see I'm on an awful strain, in this palaver, on account of having to cramp down and draw everything so mild. But we've got to give him up. There ain't any getting around that, I don't reckon. Now if we can get you to help plant him—"

"Preach the funeral discourse? Assist at the obsequies?"

"Obs'quies is good. Yes. That's it—that's our little game. We are going to get the thing up regardless, you know. He was always nifty himself, and so you bet you his funeral ain't going to be no slouch—solid silver door-plate on his coffin, six plumes on the hearse, and a nigger on the box in a biled shirt and a plug hat—how's that for high? And we'll take care of *you*, pard. We'll fix you all right. There'll be a kerridge for you; and whatever you want, you just 'scape out and we'll 'tend to it. We've got a shebang fixed up for you to stand behind, in No. 1's house, and don't you be afraid. Just go in and toot your horn, if you don't sell a clam. Put Buck through as bully as you can, pard, for anybody that knowed him will tell you that he was one of the whitest men that was ever in the mines. You can't draw it too strong. He never could stand it to see things going wrong. He's done more to make this town quiet and peaceable than any man in it. I've seen him lick four Greasers in eleven minutes, myself. If a thing wanted regulating, *he* warn't a man to go browsing around after somebody to do it, but he would prance in and regulate it himself. He warn't a Catholic. Scasely. He was down on 'em. His word was, 'No Irish need apply!' But it didn't make no difference about that when it came down to what a man's rights was—and so, when some roughs jumped the Catholic bone-yard and started in to stake out town-lots in it he *went* for 'em! And he *cleaned* 'em, too! I was there, pard, and I seen it myself."

"That was very well indeed—at least the impulse was—whether the act was strictly defensible or not. Had deceased

SCOTTY REGULATING MATTERS.

any religious convictions? That is to say, did he feel a dependence upon, or acknowledge allegiance to a higher power?'

More reflection.

"I reckon you've stumped me again, pard. Could you say it over once more, and say it slow?"

"Well, to simplify it somewhat, was he, or rather had he ever been connected with any organization sequestered from secular concerns and devoted to self-sacrifice in the interests of morality?"

"All down but nine—set 'em up on the other alley, pard."

"What did I understand you to say?"

"Why, you're most too many for me, you know. When you get in with your left I hunt grass every time. Every time you draw, you fill; but I don't seem to have any luck. Lets have a new deal."

"How? Begin again?"

"That's it."

"Very well. Was he a good man, and—"

"There—I see that; don't put up another chip till I look at my hand. A good man, says you? Pard, it ain't no name for it. He was the best man that ever—pard, you would have doted on that man. He could lam any galoot of his inches in America. It was him that put down the riot last election before it got a start; and everybody said he was the only man that could have done it. He waltzed in with a spanner in one hand and a trumpet in the other, and sent fourteen men home on a shutter in less than three minutes. He had that riot all broke up and prevented nice before anybody ever got a chance to strike a blow. He was always for peace, and he would *have* peace—he could not stand disturbances. Pard, he was a great loss to this town. It would please the boys if you could chip in something like that and do him justice. Here once when the Micks got to throwing stones through the Methodis' Sunday school windows, Buck Fanshaw, all of his own notion, shut up his saloon and took a couple of six-shooters and mounted guard over the Sunday school. Says he, 'No Irish need apply!' And they didn't. He was the bulliest man in the mountains, pard! He could run faster, jump higher, hit harder, and hold more tangle-foot whisky without spilling it than any man in seventeen counties. Put that in, pard—it'll please the boys more than anything you could say. And you can say, pard, that he never shook his mother."

"Never shook his mother?"

"That's it—any of the boys will tell you so."

"Well, but why *should* he shake her?"

"That's what *I* say—but some people does."

"Not people of any repute?"

"Well, some that averages pretty so-so."

"In my opinion the man that would offer personal violence to his own mother, ought to—"

"Cheese it, pard; you've banked your ball clean outside the string. What I was a drivin' at, was, that he never *throwed off* on his mother—don't you see? No indeedy. He give her a house to live in, and town lots, and plenty of money; and he looked after her and took care of her all the time; and when she was down with the small-pox I'm d—d if he didn't set up nights and nuss her himself! *Beg* your pardon for say-ing it, but it hopped out too quick for yours tru-ly. You've treated me like a gen-tleman, pard, and I ain't the man to hurt your feel-ings inten-tional. I think you're white.

DIDN'T SHOOK HIS MOTHER.

I think you're a square man, pard. I like you, and I'll lick any man that don't. I'll lick him till he can't tell himself from a last year's corpse! Put it *there!* " [Another fraternal hand-shake—and exit.]

The obsequies were all that " the boys " could desire. Such a marvel of funeral pomp had never been seen in Virginia. The plumed hearse, the dirge-breathing brass bands, the closed marts of business, the flags drooping at half mast, the long, plodding procession of uniformed secret societies, military battalions and fire companies, draped engines, carriages of officials, and citi-zens in vehicles and on foot, attracted multitudes of spectators to the sidewalks, roofs and windows; and for years afterward, the degree of grandeur attained by any civic display in Virginia was determined by comparison with Buck Fanshaw's funeral.

Scotty Briggs, as a pall-bearer and a mourner, occupied a prominent place at the funeral, and when the sermon was

22†

finished and the last sentence of the prayer for the dead man's soul ascended, he responded, in a low voice, but with feeling:

"AMEN. No Irish need apply."

As the bulk of the response was without apparent relevancy, it was probably nothing more than a humble tribute to the memory of the friend that was gone; for, as Scotty had once said, it was "his word."

Scotty Briggs, in after days, achieved the distinction of becoming the only convert to religion that was ever gathered from the Virginia roughs; and it transpired that the man who had it in him to espouse the quarrel of the weak out of inborn nobility of spirit was no mean timber whereof to construct a Christian. The making him one did not warp his generosity or diminish his courage; on the contrary it gave intelligent

direction to the one and a broader field to the other. If his Sunday-school class progressed faster than the other classes, was it matter for wonder? I think not. He talked to

SCOTTY AS A SUNDAY-SCHOOL TEACHER.

his pioneer small-fry in a language they understood! It was my large privilege, a month before he died, to hear him tell the beautiful story of Joseph and his brethren to his class "without looking at the book." I leave it to the reader to fancy what it was like, as it fell, riddled with slang, from the lips of that grave, earnest teacher, and was listened to by his little learners with a consuming interest that showed that they were as unconscious as he was that any violence was being done to the sacred proprieties!

CHAPTER XLVIII.

THE first twenty-six graves in the Virginia cemetery were occupied by *murdered* men. So everybody said, so everybody believed, and so they will always say and believe. The reason why there was so much slaughtering done, was, that in a new mining district the rough element predominates, and a person is not respected until he has "killed his man." That was the very expression used.

If an unknown individual arrived, they did not inquire if he was capable, honest, industrious, but—had he killed his man? If he had not, he gravitated to his natural and proper position, that of a man of small consequence; if he had, the cordiality of his reception was graduated according to the number of his dead. It was tedious work struggling up to a position of influence with bloodless hands; but when a man came with the blood of half a dozen men on his soul, his worth was recognized at once and his acquaintance sought.

In Nevada, for a time, the lawyer, the editor, the banker, the chief desperado, the chief gambler, and the saloon keeper, occupied the same level in society, and it was the highest. The cheapest and easiest way to become an influential man and be looked up to by the community at large, was to stand behind a bar, wear a cluster-diamond pin, and sell whisky. I am not sure but that the saloon-keeper held a shade higher rank than any other member of society. His opinion had weight. It was his privilege to say how the elections should

go. No great movement could succeed without the countenance and direction of the saloon-keepers. It was a high favor
when the chief saloon-keeper consented to serve in the legislature or the board of aldermen. Youthful ambition hardly

THE MAN WHO HAD KILLED A DOZEN.

aspired so much to the honors of the law, or the army and
navy as to the dignity of proprietorship in a saloon.

To be a saloon-keeper and kill a man was to be illustrious.
Hence the reader will not be surprised to learn that more
than one man was killed in Nevada under hardly the pretext
of provocation, so impatient was the slayer to achieve reputation and throw off the galling sense of being held in indifferent

repute by his associates. I knew two youths who tried to "kill their men" for no other reason—and got killed themselves for their pains. "There goes the man that killed Bill Adams" was higher praise and a sweeter sound in the ears of this sort of people than any other speech that admiring lips could utter.

The men who murdered Virginia's original twenty-six cemetery-occupants were never punished. Why? Because Alfred the Great, when he invented trial by jury, and knew that he had admirably framed it to secure justice in his age of the world, was not aware that in the nineteenth century the condition of things would be so entirely changed that unless he rose from the grave and altered the jury plan to meet the emergency, it would prove the most ingenious and infallible agency for *defeating* justice that human wisdom could contrive. For how could he imagine that we simpletons would go on using his jury plan after circumstances had stripped it of its usefulness, any more than he could imagine that we would go on using his candle-clock after we had invented chronometers? In his day news could not travel fast, and hence he could easily find a jury of honest, intelligent men who had not heard of the case they were called to try—but in our day of telegraphs and newspapers his plan compels us to swear in juries composed of fools and rascals, because the system rigidly excludes honest men and men of brains.

I remember one of those sorrowful farces, in Virginia, which we call a jury trial. A noted desperado killed Mr. B., a good citizen, in the most wanton and cold-blooded way. Of course the papers were full of it, and all men capable of reading, read about it. And of course all men not deaf and dumb and idiotic, talked about it. A jury-list was made out, and Mr. B. L., a prominent banker and a valued citizen, was questioned precisely as he would have been questioned in any court in America:

"Have you heard of this homicide?"

"Yes."

"Have you held conversations upon the subject?"

"Yes."

"Have you formed or expressed opinions about it?"

"Yes."

"Have you read the newspaper accounts of it?"

"Yes."

"We do not want you."

A minister, intelligent, esteemed, and greatly respected; a merchant of high character and known probity; a mining superintendent of intelligence and unblemished reputation; a quartz mill owner of excellent standing, were all questioned in the same way, and all set aside. Each said the public talk and the newspaper reports had not so biased his mind but that sworn testimony would overthrow his previously formed opinions and enable him to render a verdict without prejudice and in accordance with the facts. But of course such men could not be trusted with the case. Ignoramuses alone could mete out unsullied justice.

When the peremptory challenges were all exhausted, a jury of twelve men was impaneled—a jury who swore they had neither heard, read, talked about nor expressed an opinion concerning a murder which the very cattle in the corrals, the Indians in the sage-brush and the stones in the streets were

THE UNPREJUDICED JURY.

cognizant of! It was a jury composed of two desperadoes, two low beer-house politicians, three bar-keepers, two ranchmen who could not read, and three dull, stupid, human donkeys!

It actually came out afterward, that one of these latter thought that incest and arson were the same thing.

The verdict rendered by this jury was, Not Guilty. What else could one expect?

The jury system puts a ban upon intelligence and honesty, and a premium upon ignorance, stupidity and perjury. It is a shame that we must continue to use a worthless system because it *was* good a thousand years ago. In this age, when a gentleman of high social standing, intelligence and probity, swears that testimony given under solemn oath will outweigh, with him, street talk and newspaper reports based upon mere hearsay, he is worth a hundred jurymen who will swear to their own ignorance and stupidity, and justice would be far safer in his hands than in theirs. Why could not the jury law be so altered as to give men of brains and honesty an *equal chance* with fools and miscreants? Is it right to show the present favoritism to one class of men and inflict a disability on another, in a land whose boast is that all its citizens are free and equal? I am a candidate for the legislature. I desire to tamper with the jury law. I wish to so alter it as to put a premium on intelligence and character, and close the jury box against idiots, blacklegs, and people who do not read newspapers. But no doubt I shall be defeated—every effort I make to save the country "misses fire."

My idea, when I began this chapter, was to say something about desperadoism in the "flush times" of Nevada. To attempt a portrayal of that era and that land, and leave out the blood and carnage, would be like portraying Mormondom and leaving out polygamy. The desperado stalked the streets with a swagger graded according to the number of his homicides, and a nod of recognition from him was sufficient to make a humble admirer happy for the rest of the day. The deference that was paid to a desperado of wide reputation, and who "kept his private graveyard," as the phrase went, was marked, and cheerfully accorded. When he moved along the sidewalk in his excessively long-tailed frock-coat, shiny stump-toed boots, and with dainty little slouch hat tipped over left eye, the small-fry roughs made room for his majesty; when he entered the restaurant, the waiters deserted bankers and merchants to overwhelm him with obsequious

A DESPERADO GIVING REFERENCE.

service; when he shouldered his way to a bar, the shouldered parties wheeled indignantly, recognized him, and—apologized. They got a look in return that froze their marrow, and by that time a curled and breast-pinned bar keeper was beaming over the counter, proud of the established acquaintanceship that permitted such a familiar form of speech as:

"How 're ye, Billy, old fel? Glad to see you. What'll you take—the old thing?"

The "old thing" meant his customary drink, of course.

The best known names in the Territory of Nevada were those belonging to these long-tailed heroes of the revolver. Orators, Governors, capitalists and leaders of the legislature enjoyed a degree of fame, but it seemed local and meagre when contrasted with the fame of such men as Sam Brown, Jack Williams, Billy Mulligan, Farmer Pease, Sugarfoot Mike, Pock-Marked Jake, El Dorado Johnny, Jack McNabb, Joe McGee, Jack Harris, Six-fingered Pete, etc., etc. There was a long list of them. They were brave, reckless men, and traveled with their lives in their hands. To give them their due, they did their killing principally among themselves, and seldom molested peaceable citizens, for they considered it small credit to add to their trophies so cheap a bauble as the death of a man who was "not on the shoot," as they phrased it. They killed each other on slight provocation, and hoped and expected to be killed themselves—for they held it almost shame to die otherwise than "with their boots on," as they expressed it.

I remember an instance of a desperado's contempt for such small game as a private citizen's life. I was taking a late supper in a restaurant one night, with two reporters and a little printer named—Brown, for instance—any name will do. Presently a stranger with a long-tailed coat on came in, and not noticing Brown's hat, which was lying in a chair, sat down on it. Little Brown sprang up and became abusive in a moment. The stranger smiled, smoothed out the hat, and offered it to Brown with profuse apologies couched in caustic sarcasm, and begged Brown not to destroy him. Brown threw off his coat and challenged the man to fight—abused him, threatened him, impeached his courage, and urged and even implored him to fight; and in the meantime the smiling stranger placed himself under our protection in mock distress. But presently he assumed a serious tone, and said:

"Very well, gentlemen, if we must fight, we must, I suppose. But don't rush into danger and then say I gave you no warning. I am more than a match for all of you when I get started. I will give you proofs, and then if my friend here still insists, I will try to accommodate him."

The table we were sitting at was about five feet long, and unusually cumbersome and heavy. He asked us to put our hands on the dishes and hold them in their places a moment —one of them was a large oval dish with a portly roast on it. Then he sat down, tilted up one end of the table, set two of the legs on his knees, took the end of the table between his teeth, took his hands away, and pulled down with his teeth till the table came up to a level position, dishes and all! He said he could lift a keg of nails with his teeth. He picked up a common glass tumbler and bit a semi-circle out of it. Then he opened his bosom and showed us a net-work of knife and bullet scars; showed us more on his arms and face, and said he believed he had bullets enough in his body to make a

SATISFYING A FOE.

pig of lead. He was armed to the teeth. He closed with the remark that he was Mr. —— of Cariboo—a celebrated name whereat we shook in our shoes. I would publish the name, but for the suspicion that he might come and carve me. He finally inquired if Brown still thirsted for blood. Brown turned the thing over in his mind a moment, and then—asked him to supper.

With the permission of the reader, I will group together, in the next chapter, some samples of life in our small mountain village in the old days of desperadoism. I was there at the time. The reader will observe peculiarities in our *official* society; and he will observe also, an instance of how, in new countries, murders breed murders.

CHAPTER XLIX.

A N extract or two from the newspapers of the day will furnish a photograph that can need no embellishment:

FATAL SHOOTING AFFRAY.—An affray occurred, last evening, in a billiard saloon on C street, between *Deputy Marshal Jack Williams* and Wm. Brown, which resulted in the immediate death of the latter. There had been some difficulty between the parties for several months.

An inquest was immediately held, and the following testimony adduced:

Officer GEO. BIRDSALL, sworn, says:—I was told Wm. Brown was drunk and was looking for Jack Williams; so soon as I heard that I started for the parties to prevent a collision; went into the billiard saloon; saw Billy Brown running around, saying if anybody had anything against him to show cause; he was talking in a boisterous manner, and officer Perry took him to the other end of the room to talk to him; Brown came back to me; remarked to me that he thought he was as good as anybody, and knew how to take care of himself; he passed by me and went to the bar; don't know whether he drank or not; Williams was at the end of the billiard-table, next to the stairway; Brown, after going to the bar, came back and said he was as good as any man in the world; he had then walked out to the end of the first billiard-table from the bar; I moved closer to them, supposing there would be a fight; as Brown drew his pistol I caught hold of it; he had fired one shot at Williams; don't know the effect of it; caught hold of him with one hand, and took hold of the pistol and turned it up; think he fired once after I caught hold of the pistol; I wrenched the pistol from him; walked to the end of the billiard-table and told a party that I had Brown's pistol, and to stop shooting; I think four shots were fired in all; after walking out, Mr. Foster remarked that Brown was shot dead.

Oh, there was no excitement about it—he merely "remarked" the small circumstance!

Four months later the following item appeared in the same paper (the *Enterprise*). In this item the name of one of the city officers above referred to (*Deputy Marshal Jack Williams*) occurs again:

ROBBERY AND DESPERATE AFFRAY.—On Tuesday night, a German named Charles Hurtzal, engineer in a mill at Silver City, came to this place, and visited the hurdy-gurdy house on B street. The music, dancing and Teutonic maidens awakened memories of Faderland until our German friend was carried away with rapture. He evidently had money, and was spending it freely. Late in the evening Jack Williams and Andy Blessington invited him down stairs to take a cup of coffee. Williams proposed a game of cards and went up stairs to procure a deck, but not finding any returned. On the stairway he met the German, and drawing his pistol knocked him down and rifled his pockets of some seventy dollars. Hurtzal dared give no alarm, as he was told, with a pistol at his head, if he made any noise or exposed them, they would blow his brains out. So effectually was he frightened that he made no complaint, until his friends forced him. Yesterday a warrant was issued, but the culprits had disappeared.

This efficient city officer, Jack Williams, had the common reputation of being a burglar, a highwayman and a desperado. It was said that he had several times drawn his revolver and levied money contributions on citizens at dead of night in the public streets of Virginia.

Five months after the above item appeared, Williams was assassinated while sitting at a card table one night; a gun was thrust through the crack of the door and Williams dropped from his chair riddled with balls. It was said, at the time, that Williams had been for some time aware that a party of his own sort (desperadoes) had sworn away his life; and it was generally believed among the people that Williams's friends and enemies would make the assassination memorable—and useful, too—by a wholesale destruction of each other.*

---

* However, one prophecy was verified, at any rate. It was asserted by the desperadoes that one of their brethren (Joe McGee, *a special policeman*) was known to be the conspirator chosen by lot to assassinate Williams; and they also asserted that doom had been pronounced against McGee, and that he would be assassinated in exactly the same manner that had been adopted for the destruction of Williams—a prophecy which came true a year later. After twelve months of distress (for McGee saw a fancied assassin in every man that approached him), he made the last of many efforts to get out of the country unwatched. He went to Carson and sat down in a saloon to wait for the stage—it would leave at four in the morning. But as the night

It did not so happen, but still, times were not dull during the next twenty-four hours, for within that time a woman was killed by a pistol shot, a man was brained with a slung shot, and a man named Reeder was also disposed of permanently. Some matters in the *Enterprise* account of the killing of Reeder are worth noting—especially the accommodating complaisance of a Virginia justice of the peace. The italics in the following narrative are mine:

MORE CUTTING AND SHOOTING.—The devil seems to have again broken loose in our town. Pistols and guns explode and knives gleam in our streets as in early times. When there has been a long season of quiet, people are slow to wet their hands in blood; but once blood is spilled, cutting and shooting come easy. Night before last Jack Williams was assassinated, and yesterday forenoon we had more bloody work, growing out of the killing of Williams, and on the same street in which he met his death. It appears that Tom Reeder, a friend of Williams, and George Gumbert were talking, at the meat market of the latter, about the killing of Williams the previous night, when Reeder said it was a most cowardly act to shoot a man in such a way, giving him "no show." Gumbert said that Williams had "as good a show as he gave Billy Brown," meaning the man killed by Williams last March. Reeder said it was a d—d lie, that Williams had no show at all. At this, Gumbert drew a knife and stabbed Reeder, cutting him in two places in the back. One stroke of the knife cut into the sleeve of Reeder's coat and passed downward in a slanting direction through his clothing, and entered his body at the small of the back; another blow struck more squarely, and made a much more dangerous wound. Gumbert gave himself up to the officers of justice, and was shortly after discharged by Justice Atwill, *on his own recognizance,* to appear for trial at six o'clock in the evening. In the meantime Reeder had been taken into the office of Dr. Owens, where his wounds were properly dressed. *One of his wounds was considered quite dangerous, and it was thought by many that it would prove*

waned and the crowd thinned, he grew uneasy, and told the bar-keeper that assassins were on his track. The bar-keeper told him to stay in the middle of the room, then, and not go near the door, or the window by the stove. But a fatal fascination seduced him to the neighborhood of the stove every now and then, and repeatedly the bar-keeper brought him back to the middle of the room and warned him to remain there. But he could not. At three in the morning he again returned to the stove and sat down by a stranger. Before the bar-keeper could get to him with another warning whisper, some one outside fired through the window and riddled McGee's breast with slugs, killing him almost instantly. By the same discharge the stranger at McGee's side also received attentions which proved fatal in the course of two or three days.

fatal. But being considerably under the influence of liquor, Reeder did not feel his wounds as he otherwise would, and he got up and went into the street. He went to the meat market and renewed his quarrel with Gumbert, threatening his life. Friends tried to interfere to put a stop to the quarrel and get the parties away from each other. In the Fashion Saloon Reeder made threats against the life of Gumbert, saying he would kill him, and it is said that *he requested the officers not to arrest Gumbert, as he intended to kill him.* After these threats Gumbert went off and procured a double-barreled shot gun, loaded with buck-shot or revolver balls, and went after Reeder. Two or three persons were assisting him along the street, trying to get him home, and had him just in front of the store of Klopstock & Harris, when Gumbert came across toward him from the opposite side of the street with his gun. He came up within about ten or fifteen feet of Reeder, and called out to those with him to "look out! get out of the way!" and they had only time to heed the warning, when he fired. Reeder was at the time attempting to screen himself behind a large cask, which stood against the awning post of Klopstock & Harris's store, but some of the balls took effect in the lower part of his breast, and he reeled around forward and fell in front of the cask. Gumbert then raised his gun and fired the second barrel, which missed Reeder and entered the ground. At the time that this occurred, there were a great many persons on the street in the vicinity, and a number of them called out to Gumbert, when they saw him raise his gun, to "hold on," and "don't shoot!" The cutting took place about ten o'clock and the shooting about twelve. After the shooting the street was instantly crowded with the inhabitants of that part of the town, some appearing much excited and laughing—declaring that it looked like the "good old times of '60." Marshal Perry and officer Birdsall were near when the shooting occurred, and Gumbert was immediately arrested and his gun taken from him, when he was marched off to jail. Many persons who were attracted to the spot where this bloody work had just taken place, looked bewildered and seemed to be asking themselves what was to happen next, appearing in doubt as to whether the killing mania had reached its climax, or whether we were to turn in and have a grand killing spell, shooting whoever might have given us offence. It was whispered around that it was not all over yet—five or six more were to be killed before night. Reeder was taken to the Virginia City Hotel, and doctors called in to examine his wounds. They found that two or three balls had entered his right side; one of them appeared to have passed through the substance of the lungs, while another passed into the liver. Two balls were also found to have struck one of his legs. As some of the balls struck the cask, the wounds in Reeder's leg were probably from these, glancing downwards, though they might have been caused by the second shot fired. After being shot, Reeder said when he got on his feet—smiling as he spoke—"It will take better shooting than that to kill me." The doctors consider it almost impossible for him to recover, but as he has an excellent constitution he may survive, notwithstanding the number and dangerous character of the wounds he has received. The town appears to be perfectly quiet at present, as though the late stormy times had cleared our moral atmosphere ; but who can tell in what quarter clouds are lowering or plots ripening ?

Reeder—or at least what was left of him—survived his wounds two days ! Nothing was ever done with Gumbert.

Trial by jury is the palladium of our liberties. I do not know what a palladium is, having never seen a palladium, but it is a good thing no doubt at any rate. Not less than a hundred men have been murdered in Nevada—perhaps I would be within bounds if I said three hundred—and as far as I can learn, only two persons have suffered the death penalty there. However, four or five who had no money and no political influence have been punished by imprisonment—one languished in prison as much as eight months, I think. However, I do not desire to be extravagant—it may have been less.

CHAPTER L.

THESE murder and jury statistics remind me of a certain very extraordinary trial and execution of twenty years ago; it is a scrap of history familiar to all old Californians, and worthy to be known by other peoples of the earth that love simple, straightforward justice unencumbered with nonsense. I would apologize for this digression but for the fact that the information I am about to offer is apology enough in itself. And since I digress constantly anyhow, perhaps it is as well to eschew apologies altogether and thus prevent their growing irksome.

Capt. Ned Blakely—that name will answer as well as any other fictitious one (for he was still with the living at last accounts, and may not desire to be famous)—sailed ships out of the harbor of San Francisco for many years. He was a stalwart, warm-hearted, eagle-eyed veteran, who had been a sailor nearly fifty years—a sailor from early boyhood. He was a rough, honest creature, full of pluck, and just as full of hardheaded simplicity, too. He hated trifling conventionalities— "business" was the word, with him. He had all a sailor's vindictiveness against the quips and quirks of the law, and steadfastly believed that the first and last aim and object of the law and lawyers was to defeat justice.

He sailed for the Chincha Islands in command of a guano ship. He had a fine crew, but his negro mate was his pet— on him he had for years lavished his admiration and esteem. It was Capt. Ned's first voyage to the Chinchas, but his fame had gone before him—the fame of being a man who would fight at the dropping of a handkerchief, when imposed upon, and would stand no nonsense. It was a fame well earned. Arrived in the islands, he found that the staple of conversation was the exploits of one Bill Noakes, a bully, the mate of a trading ship. This man had created a small reign of terror there. At nine o'clock at night, Capt. Ned, all alone, was pacing his deck in the starlight. A form ascended the side, and approached him. Capt. Ned said:

"Who goes there?"

"I'm Bill Noakes, the best man in the islands."

"What do you want aboard this ship?"

IMPARTING INFORMATION.

"I've heard of Capt. Ned Blakely, and one of us is a better man than 'tother—I'll know which, before I go ashore."

"You've come to the right shop—I'm your man. I'll learn you to come aboard this ship without an *invite*."

He seized Noakes, backed him against the mainmast, pounded his face to a pulp, and then threw him overboard.

Noakes was not convinced. He returned the next night, got the pulp renewed, and went overboard head first, as before. He was satisfied.

A week after this, while Noakes was carousing with a sailor crowd on shore, at noonday, Capt. Ned's colored mate came along, and Noakes tried to pick a quarrel with him. The negro evaded the trap, and tried to get away. Noakes followed him up; the negro began to run; Noakes fired on him with a revolver and killed him. Half a dozen sea-captains witnessed the whole affair. Noakes retreated to the small after-cabin of his ship, with two other bullies, and gave out that death would be the portion of any man that intruded there. There was no attempt made to follow the villains; there was no disposition to do it, and indeed very little thought of such an enterprise. There were no courts and no officers; there was no government; the islands belonged to Peru, and Peru was far away; she had no official representative on the ground; and neither had any other nation.

However, Capt. Ned was not perplexing his head about such things. They concerned him not. He was boiling with rage and furious for justice. At nine o'clock at night he loaded a double-barreled gun with slugs, fished out a pair of handcuffs, got a ship's lantern, summoned his quartermaster, and went ashore. He said:

"Do you see that ship there at the dock?"

"Ay-ay, sir."

"It's the Venus."

"Ay-ay, sir."

"You—you know *me*."

"Ay-ay, sir."

"Very well, then. Take the lantern. Carry it just under your chin. I'll walk behind you and rest this gun-barrel on your shoulder, p'inting forward—so. Keep your lantern well up, so's I can see things ahead of you good. I'm going to march in on Noakes—and take him—and jug the other chaps. If you flinch—well, you know *me*."

"Ay-ay, sir."

In this order they filed aboard softly, arrived at Noakes's den, the quartermaster pushed the door open, and the lantern revealed the three desperadoes sitting on the floor.   Capt. Ned said:

"I'm Ned Blakely.   I've got you under fire.   Don't **you**

A WALKING BATTERY.

move without orders—any of you.   You two kneel down in the corner; faces to the wall—now.   Bill Noakes, put these hand-cuffs on; now come up close.   Quartermaster, fasten 'em.   All right.   Don't stir, sir.   Quartermaster, put the key in the out-side of the door.   Now, men, I'm going to lock you two in; and if you try to burst through this door—well, you've heard of *me*.   Bill Noakes, fall in ahead, and march.   All set. Quartermaster, lock the door."

Noakes spent the night on board Blakely's ship, a prisoner under strict guard.   Early in the morning Capt. Ned called in all the sea-captains in the harbor and invited them, with nauti-cal ceremony, to be present on board his ship at nine o'clock to witness the hanging of Noakes at the yard-arm!

"What! The man has not been tried."

"Of course he hasn't. But didn't he kill the nigger?"

"Certainly he did; but you are not thinking of hanging him without a trial?"

"*Trial!* What do I want to try him for, if he killed the nigger?"

"Oh, Capt. Ned, this will *never* do. Think how it will sound."

"Sound be hanged! *Didn't he kill the nigger?*"

"Certainly, certainly, Capt. Ned,—nobody denies that,—but—"

"Then I'm going to *hang* him, that's all. Everybody I've talked to talks just the same way you do. Everybody says he killed the nigger, everybody knows he killed the nigger, and yet every lubber of you wants him *tried* for it. I don't understand such bloody foolishness as that. *Tried!* Mind you, I don't object to trying him, if it's got to be done to give satisfaction; and I'll be there, and chip in and help, too; but put it off till afternoon—put it off till afternoon, for I'll have my hands middling full till after the burying—"

"Why, what do you mean? Are you going to hang him *any how*—and try him afterward?"

"Didn't I *say* I was going to hang him? I never saw such people as you. What's the difference? You ask a favor, and then you ain't satisfied when you get it. Before or after's all one—*you* know how the trial will go. He killed the nigger. Say—I must be going. If your mate would like to come to the hanging, fetch him along. I like him."

There was a stir in the camp. The captains came in a body and pleaded with Capt. Ned not to do this rash thing. They promised that they would create a court composed of captains of the best character; they would empanel a jury; they would conduct everything in a way becoming the serious nature of the business in hand, and give the case an impartial hearing and the accused a fair trial. And they said it would be murder, and punishable by the American courts if he persisted and hung the accused on his ship. They pleaded hard. Capt. Ned said:

"Gentlemen, I'm not stubborn and I'm not unreasonable. I'm always willing to do just as near right as I can. How long will it take?"

"Probably only a little while."

"And can I take him up the shore and hang him as soon as you are done?"

"If he is proven guilty he shall be hanged without unnecessary delay."

"*If* he's proven guilty. Great Neptune, *ain't* he guilty? This beats my time. Why you all *know* he's guilty."

But at last they satisfied him that they were projecting nothing underhanded. Then he said:

"Well, all right. You go on and try him and I'll go down and overhaul his conscience and prepare him to go—like enough he needs it, and I don't want to send him off without a show for hereafter."

This was another obstacle. They finally convinced him that it was necessary to have the accused in court. Then they said they would send a guard to bring him.

"No, sir, I prefer to fetch him myself—he don't get out of *my* hands. Besides, I've got to go to the ship to get a rope, anyway."

The court assembled with due ceremony, empaneled a jury, and presently Capt. Ned entered, leading the prisoner with one hand and carrying a Bible and a rope in the other. He seated himself by the side of his captive and told the court to "up anchor and make sail." Then he turned a searching eye on the jury, and detected Noakes's friends, the two bullies. He strode over and said to them confidentially:

"You're here to interfere, you see. Now you vote right, do you hear?—or else there'll be a double-barreled inquest here when this trial's off, and your remainders will go home in a couple of baskets."

The caution was not without fruit. The jury was a unit —the verdict, "Guilty."

Capt. Ned sprung to his feet and said:

"Come along—you're my meat *now*, my lad, anyway.

Gentlemen you've done yourselves proud. I invite you all to come and see that I do it all straight. Follow me to the canyon, a mile above here."

The court informed him that a sheriff had been appointed to do the hanging, and—

Capt. Ned's patience was at an end. His wrath was boundless. The subject of a sheriff was judiciously dropped.

When the crowd arrived at the canyon, Capt. Ned climbed a tree and arranged the halter, then came down and noosed his man. He opened his Bible, and laid aside his hat. Selecting a chapter at random, he read it through, in a deep bass voice and with sincere solemnity. Then he said:

OVERHAULING HIS MANIFEST.

"Lad, you are about to go aloft and give an account of yourself; and the lighter a man's manifest is, as far as sin's concerned, the better for him. Make a clean breast, man, and carry a log with you that'll bear inspection. You killed the nigger?"

No reply. A long pause.

The captain read another chapter, pausing, from time to time, to impress the effect. Then he talked an earnest, persuasive sermon to him, and ended by repeating the question:

"Did you kill the nigger?"

No reply—other than a malignant scowl. The captain now read the first and second chapters of Genesis, with deep feeling—paused a moment, closed the book reverently, and said with a perceptible savor of satisfaction :

"There. Four chapters. There's few that would have took the pains with you that I have."

Then he swung up the condemned, and made the rope fast; stood by and timed him half an hour with his watch, and then delivered the body to the court. A little after, as he stood contemplating the motionless figure, a doubt came into his face; evidently he felt a twinge of conscience—a misgiving— and he said with a sigh :

"Well, p'raps I ought to burnt him, maybe. But I was trying to do for the best."

When the history of this affair reached California (it was in the "early days") it made a deal of talk, but did not diminish the captain's popularity in any degree. It increased it, indeed. California had a population then that "inflicted" justice after a fashion that was simplicity and primitiveness itself, and could therefore admire appreciatively when the same fashion was followed elsewhere.

CHAPTER LI.

VICE flourished luxuriantly during the hey-day of our "flush times." The saloons were overburdened with custom; so were the police courts, the gambling dens, the brothels and the jails—unfailing signs of high prosperity in a mining region—in any region for that matter. Is it not so? A crowded police court docket is the surest of all signs that trade is brisk and money plenty. Still, there is one other sign; it comes last, but when it does come it establishes beyond cavil that the "flush times" are at the flood. This is the birth of the "literary" paper. The *Weekly Occidental*, "devoted to literature," made its appearance in Virginia. All the literary people were engaged to write for it. Mr. F. was to edit it. He was a felicitous skirmisher with a pen, and a man who could say happy things in a crisp, neat way. Once, while editor of the *Union*, he had disposed of a labored, incoherent, two-column attack made upon him by a cotemporary, with a single line, which, at first glance, seemed to contain a solemn and tremendous compliment—viz.: "THE LOGIC OF OUR ADVERSARY RESEMBLES THE PEACE OF GOD,"—and left it to the reader's memory and after-thought to invest the remark with another and "more different" meaning by supplying for himself and at his own leisure the rest of the Scripture—"*in that it passeth understanding.*" He once said of a little, half-starved, wayside community that had no subsistence except what they could get by preying upon chance passengers who stopped over with them a day when traveling by the overland stage, that in their Church service they had altered the Lord's Prayer to read: "Give us this day our daily stranger!"

We expected great things of the *Occidental*. Of course it could not get along without an original novel, and so we made arrangements to hurl into the work the full strength of the company. Mrs. F. was an able romancist of the ineffable school—I know no other name to apply to a school whose heroes are all dainty and all perfect. She wrote the opening chapter, and introduced a lovely blonde simpleton who talked nothing but pearls and poetry and who was virtuous to the verge of eccentricity. She also introduced a young French Duke of aggravated refinement, in love with the blonde. Mr. F. followed next week, with a brilliant lawyer who set about getting the Duke's estates into trouble, and a sparkling young lady of high society who fell to fascinating the Duke and impairing the appetite of the blonde. Mr. D., a dark and bloody editor of one of the dailies, followed Mr. F., the third

THE HEROES AND HEROINES OF THE STORY.

week, introducing a mysterious Roscicrucian who transmuted metals, held consultations with the devil in a cave at dead of night, and cast the horoscope of the several heroes and heroines in such a way as to provide plenty of trouble for their future careers and breed a solemn and awful public interest in the novel. He also introduced a cloaked and masked melodramatic miscreant, put him on a salary and set him on the midnight tract of the Duke with a poisoned dagger. He also created an Irish coachman with a rich brogue and placed him in the service of the society-young-lady with an ulterior mission to carry billet-doux to the Duke.

About this time there arrived in Virginia a dissolute stranger with a literary turn of mind—rather seedy he was, but very quiet and unassuming; almost diffident, indeed. He was so gentle, and his manners were so pleasing and kindly, whether he was sober or intoxicated, that he made friends of all who came in contact with him. He applied for literary work, offered conclusive evidence that he wielded an easy and practiced pen, and so Mr. F. engaged him at once to help write the novel. His chapter was to follow Mr. D.'s, and mine was to come next. Now what does this fellow do but go off and get drunk and then proceed to his quarters and set to work with his imagination in a state of chaos, and that chaos in a condition of extravagant activity. The result may be guessed. He scanned the chapters of his predecessors, found plenty of heroes and heroines already created, and was satisfied with them; he decided to introduce no more; with all the confidence that whisky inspires and all the easy complacency it gives to its servant, he then launched himself lovingly into his work: he married the coachman to the society-young-lady for the sake of the scandal; married the Duke to the blonde's stepmother, for the sake of the sensation; stopped the desperado's salary; created a mis-

DISSOLUTE AUTHOR.

understanding between the devil and the Roscicrucian; threw the Duke's property into the wicked lawyer's hands; made the lawyer's upbraiding conscience drive him to drink, thence to *delirium tremens,* thence to suicide; broke the coachman's neck; let his widow succumb to contumely, neglect, poverty and consumption; caused the blonde to drown herself, leaving her clothes on the bank with the customary note pinned to them forgiving the Duke and hoping he would be happy; revealed to the Duke, by means of the usual strawberry mark on left arm, that he had married his own long-lost mother and destroyed his long-lost sister; instituted the proper and necessary suicide of the Duke and the Duchess in order to compass poetical justice; opened the earth and let the Roscicrucian through, accompanied with the accustomed smoke and thunder and smell of brimstone, and finished with the promise that in the next chapter, after holding a general inquest, he would take up the surviving character of the novel and tell what became of the devil!

It read with singular smoothness, and with a "dead" earnestness that was funny enough to suffocate a body. But there was war when it came in. The other novelists were furious. The mild stranger, not yet more than half sober, stood there, under a scathing fire of vituperation, meek and bewildered, looking from one to another of his assailants, and wondering what he could have done to invoke such a storm. When a lull came at last, he said his say gently and appealingly—said he did not rightly remember what he had written, but was sure he had tried to do the best he could, and knew his object had been to make the novel not only pleasant and plausible but instructive and—

The bombardment began again. The novelists assailed his ill-chosen adjectives and demolished them with a storm of denunciation and ridicule. And so the siege went on. Every time the stranger tried to appease the enemy he only made matters worse. Finally he offered to rewrite the chapter. This arrested hostilities. The indignation gradually quieted down, peace reigned again and the sufferer retired in safety and got him to his own citadel.

But on the way thither the evil angel tempted him and he got drunk again. And again his imagination went mad. He led the heroes and heroines a wilder dance than ever; and yet all through it ran that same convincing air of honesty and earnestness that had marked his first work. He got the characters into the most extraordinary situations, put them through the most surprising performances, and made them talk the strangest talk! But the chapter cannot be described. It was symmetrically crazy; it was artistically absurd; and it had explanatory footnotes that were fully as curious as the text. I remember one of the " situations," and will offer it as an example of the whole. He altered the character of the brilliant lawyer, and made him a great-hearted, splendid fellow; gave him fame and riches, and set his age at thirty-three years. Then he made the blonde discover, through the help of the Roscicrucian and the melodramatic miscreant, that while the Duke loved her money ardently and wanted it, he secretly felt a sort of leaning toward the society-young-lady. Stung to the quick, she tore her affections from him and bestowed them with tenfold power upon the lawyer, who responded with consuming zeal. But the parents would none of it. What they wanted in the family was a Duke; and a Duke they were determined to have; though they confessed that next to the Duke the lawyer had their preference. Necessarily the blonde now went into a decline. The parents were alarmed. They pleaded with her to marry the Duke, but she steadfastly refused, and pined on. Then they laid a plan. They told her to wait a year and a day, and if at the end of that time she still felt that she could not marry the Duke, she might marry the lawyer with their full consent. The result was as they had foreseen: gladness came again, and the flush of returning health. Then the parents took the next step in their scheme. They had the family physician recommend a long sea voyage and much land travel for the thorough restoration of the blonde's strength; and they invited the Duke to be of the party. They judged that the Duke's constant presence and the lawyer's protracted absence would do the rest—for they did not invite the lawyer.

So they set sail in a steamer for America—and the third

day out, when their sea-sickness called truce and permitted them to take their first meal at the public table, behold there sat the lawyer! The Duke and party made the best of an

UNLOOKED-FOR APPEARANCE OF THE LAWYER.

awkward situation; the voyage progressed, and the vessel neared America. But, by and by, two hundred miles off New Bedford, the ship took fire; she burned to the water's edge; of all her crew and passengers, only thirty were saved. They floated about the sea half an afternoon and all night long. Among them were our friends. The lawyer, by superhuman exertions, had saved the blonde and her parents, swimming back and forth two hundred yards and bringing one each time—(the girl first). The Duke had saved himself. In the morning two whale ships arrived on the scene and sent their boats. The weather was stormy and the embarkation was attended with much confusion and excitement. The lawyer did his duty like a man; helped his exhausted and insensible blonde, her parents and some others into a boat (the Duke helped himself in); then a child fell overboard at the other end of the raft and the lawyer rushed thither and helped half a dozen people fish it out, under the stimulus of its mother's screams. Then he ran back —a few seconds too late—the blonde's boat was under way. So

he had to take the other boat, and go to the other ship.   The
storm increased and drove the vessels out of sight of each other

THE STORM INCREASED.

—drove them whither it would.   When it calmed, at the end
of three days, the blonde's ship was seven hundred miles north
of Boston and the other about seven hundred south of that
port.   The blonde's captain was bound on a whaling cruise
in the North Atlantic and could not go back such a distance
or make a port without orders; such being nautical law.   The
lawyer's captain was to cruise in the North Pacific, and *he*
could not go back or make a port without orders.   All the lawyer's money and baggage were in the blonde's boat and went
to the blonde's ship—so his captain made him work his passage
as a common sailor.   When both ships had been cruising nearly
a year, the one was off the coast of Greenland and the other in

Behring's Strait. The blonde had long ago been well-nigh persuaded that her lawyer had been washed overboard and lost just before the whale ships reached the raft, and now, under the pleadings of her parents and the Duke she was at last beginning to nerve herself for the doom of the covenant,

JONAH OUTDONE.

and prepare for the hated marriage. But she would not yield a day before the date set. The weeks dragged on, the time narrowed, orders were given to deck the ship for the wedding—a wedding at sea among icebergs and walruses. Five days more and all would be over. So the blonde reflected, with a sigh and a tear. Oh where was her true love —and why, why did he not come and save her? At that moment he was lifting his harpoon to strike a whale in Behring's Strait, five thousand miles away, by the way of the Arctic Ocean, or twenty thousand by the way of the Horn—that was the reason. He struck, but not with perfect aim—his foot slipped and he fell in the whale's mouth and went down his throat. He was insensible five days. Then he came to himself and heard voices; daylight was streaming through a hole cut in the whale's roof. He climbed out and astonished the sailors who were hoisting blubber up a ship's side. He recognized the vessel, flew aboard, surprised the wedding party at the altar and exclaimed:

"Stop the proceedings—I'm here! Come to my arms, my own!"

There were foot-notes to this extravagant piece of literature wherein the author endeavored to show that the whole thing was within the possibilities; he said he got the incident of the whale traveling from Behring's Strait to the coast of Greenland, five thousand miles in five days, through the Arctic Ocean, from Charles Reade's "Love Me Little Love Me Long," and considered that that established the fact that the thing could be done; and he instanced Jonah's adventure as proof that a man could live in a whale's belly, and added that if a preacher could stand it three days a lawyer could surely stand it five!

There was a fiercer storm than ever in the editorial sanctum now, and the stranger was peremptorily discharged, and his manuscript flung at his head. But he had already delayed things so much that there was not time for some one else to rewrite the chapter, and so the paper came out without any novel in it. It was but a feeble, struggling, stupid journal, and the absence of the novel probably shook public confidence; at any rate, before the first side of the next issue went to press, the *Weekly Occidental* died as peacefully as an infant.

An effort was made to resurrect it, with the proposed advantage of a telling new title, and Mr. F. said that *The Phenix* would be just the name for it, because it would give the idea of a resurrection from its dead ashes in a new and undreamed of condition of splendor; but some low-priced smarty on one of the dailies suggested that we call it the *Lazarus;* and inasmuch as the people were not profound in Scriptural matters but thought the resurrected Lazarus and the dilapidated mendicant that begged in the rich man's gateway were one and the same person, the name became the laughing stock of the town, and killed the paper for good and all.

I was sorry enough, for I was very proud of being connected with a literary paper—prouder than I have ever been of anything since, perhaps. I had written some rhymes for it—poetry I considered it—and it was a great grief to me that the production was on the "first side" of the issue that was not completed, and hence did not see the light. But time brings its revenges—I can put it in here; it will answer in place of a tear dropped to the memory of the lost *Occidental*. The idea (not the chief idea, but the vehicle that bears it) was probably suggested by the old song called "The Raging Canal," but I cannot remember now. I do remember, though, that at that time I thought my doggerel was one of the ablest poems of the age:

THE AGED PILOT MAN.

On the Erie Canal, it was,
  All on a summer's day,
I sailed forth with my parents
  Far away to Albany.

From out the clouds at noon that day
  There came a dreadful storm,
That piled the billows high about,
  And filled us with alarm.

A man came rushing from a house,
  Saying, " Snub up * your boat I pray,
Snub up your boat, snub up, alas,
  Snub up while yet you may."

Our captain cast one glance astern,
  Then forward glancèd he,
And said, " My wife and little ones
  I never more shall see."

Said Dollinger the pilot man,
  In noble words, but few,—
" Fear not, but lean on Dollinger,
  And he will fetch you through."

---

* The customary canal technicality for " tie up."

24†

The boat drove on, the frightened mules
  Tore through the rain and wind,
And bravely still, in danger's post,
  The whip-boy strode behind.

" Come 'board, come 'board," the captain cried,
  " Nor tempt so wild a storm ; "
But still the raging mules advanced,
  And still the boy strode on.

Then said the captain to us all,
  " Alas, 'tis plain to me,
The greater danger is not there,
  But here upon the sea.

So let us strive, while life remains,
  To save all souls on board,
And then if die at last we must,
  Let . . . . I *cannot* speak the word ! "

DOLLINGER.

Said Dollinger the pilot man,
  Tow'ring above the crew,

"Fear not, but trust in Dollinger,
   And he will fetch you through."

"Low bridge! low bridge!" all heads went down,
   The laboring bark sped on;
A mill we passed, we passed a church,
   Hamlets, and fields of corn;
And all the world came out to see,
   And chased along the shore

"LOW BRIDGE."

Crying, "Alas, alas, the sheeted rain,
   The wind, the tempest's roar!
Alas, the gallant ship and crew,
   Can *nothing* help them more?"

And from our deck sad eyes looked out
   Across the stormy scene:
The tossing wake of billows aft,
   The bending forests green,

The chickens sheltered under carts
  In lee of barn the cows,
The skurrying swine with straw in mouth,
  The wild spray from our bows!

    "She balances!
      She wavers!
Now let her go about!
  If she misses stays and broaches to,
We're all"—[then with a shout,]
    "Huray! huray!
      Avast! belay!
      Take in more sail!
      Lord, what a gale!
Ho, boy, haul taut on the hind mule's tail!"

SHORTENING SAIL.

"Ho! lighten ship! ho! man the pump!
  Ho, hostler, heave the lead!

"A quarter-three!—'tis shoaling fast!
  Three feet large!—t-h-r-e-e feet!—
·Three feet scant!" I cried in fright
  "Oh, is there *no* retreat?"

Said Dollinger, the pilot man,
  As on the vessel flew,
"Fear not, but trust in Dollinger,
  And he will fetch you through."

A panic struck the bravest hearts,
  The boldest cheek turned pale;
For plain to all, this shoaling said
A leak had burst the ditch's bed!
And, straight as bolt from crossbow sped,
Our ship swept on, with shoaling lead,
  Before the fearful gale!

"Sever the tow line! Cripple the mules!"
  Too late! . . . . . There comes a shock!
*   *   *   *   *   *
Another length, and the fated craft
  Would have swum in the saving lock!

Then gathered together the shipwrecked crew
  And took one last embrace,
While sorrowful tears from despairing eyes
  Ran down each hopeless face;
And some did think of their little ones
  Whom they never more might see,
And others of waiting wives at home,
  And mothers that grieved would be.

But of all the children of misery there
  On that poor sinking frame,
But one spake words of hope and faith,
  And I worshipped as they came:
Said Dollinger the pilot man,—
  (O brave heart, strong and true!)—
"Fear not, but trust in Dollinger,
  For he will fetch you through."

Lo! scarce the words have passed his lips
  The dauntless prophet say'th,
When every soul about him seeth
  A wonder crown his faith!

And count ye all, both great and small,
　　As numbered with the dead!
For mariner for forty year,
　　On Erie, boy and man,
I never yet saw such a storm,
　　Or one 't with it began!"

So overboard a keg of nails
　　And anvils three we threw,
Likewise four bales of gunny-sacks,
　　Two hundred pounds of glue,
Two sacks of corn, four ditto wheat,
　　A box of books, a cow,
A violin, Lord Byron's works,
　　A rip-saw and a sow.

LIGHTENING SHIP.

A curve! a curve! the dangers grow!
　"Labbord!—stabbord!—s-t-e-a-d-y!—so!—
Hard-a-port, Dol!—hellum-a-lee!
　Haw the head mule!—the aft one gee!
Luff!—bring her to the wind!"

For straight a farmer brought a plank,—
  (Mysteriously inspired)—
And laying it unto the ship,
  In silent awe retired.

THE MARVELOUS RESCUE.

Then every sufferer stood amazed
  That pilot man before;
A moment stood.   Then wondering turned,
  And speechless walked ashore.

CHAPTER LII.

SINCE I desire, in this chapter, to say an instructive word or two about the silver mines, the reader may take this fair warning and skip, if he chooses. The year 1863 was perhaps the very top blossom and culmination of the "flush times." Virginia swarmed with men and vehicles to that degree that the place looked like a very hive—that is when one's vision could pierce through the thick fog of alkali dust that was generally blowing in summer. I will say, concerning this dust, that if you drove ten miles through it, you and your horses would be coated with it a sixteenth of an inch thick and present an outside appearance that was a uniform pale yellow color, and your buggy would have three inches of dust in it, thrown there by the wheels. The delicate scales used by the assayers were inclosed in glass cases intended to be air-tight, and yet some of this dust was so impalpable and so invisibly fine that it would get in, somehow, and impair the accuracy of those scales.

Speculation ran riot, and yet there was a world of substantial business going on, too. All freights were brought over the mountains from California (150 miles) by pack-train partly, and partly in huge wagons drawn by such long mule teams that each team amounted to a procession, and it did seem, sometimes, that the grand combined procession of animals stretched unbroken from Virginia to California. Its long route was traceable clear across the deserts of the Territory by the writhing serpent of dust it lifted up. By these wagons, freights over that hundred and fifty miles were $200 a ton for small lots (same price for all express matter brought by stage), and $100 a ton for full loads. One Virginia firm received one hundred tons of freight a month, and paid $10,000 a month freightage. In the winter the freights were much higher. All the bullion was shipped in bars by stage to San Francisco (a bar was usually about twice the size of a pig of lead and contained from $1,500 to $3,000 according to the amount of gold mixed with the silver), and the freight on it (when the shipment was large) was one and a quarter per cent. of its intrinsic value. So, the freight on these bars probably averaged something more than $25 each. Small shippers paid two per cent. There were three stages a day, each way, and I have seen the out-going stages carry away a

SILVER BRICKS.

third of a ton of bullion each, and more than once I saw them divide a two-ton lot and take it off. However, these were extraordinary events.* Two tons of silver bullion would be in

---

* Mr. Valentine, Wells Fargo's agent, has handled all the bullion shipped through the Virginia office for many a month. To his memory—which is excellent—we are indebted for the following exhibit of the company's business in the Virginia office since the first of January, 1862: From January 1st to April 1st, about $270,000 worth of bullion passed through that office ; during the next quarter, $570,000; next quarter, $800,000; next quarter, $956,000; next quarter, $1,275,000; and for the quarter ending on the 30th of last June, about $1,600,000. Thus in a year and a half, the Virginia office only shipped $5,330,000 in bullion. During the year 1862 they shipped $2,615,000, so we perceive the average shipments have more than doubled in the last six months. This gives us room to promise for the Virginia office $500,000 a month for the year 1863 (though perhaps, judging by the steady increase in the business, we are under estimating, somewhat). This gives us $6,000,000 for the year. Gold Hill and Silver City together can beat us—we will give them $10,000,000. To Dayton, Empire City, Ophir and Carson City, we will allow an aggregate of $8,000,000, which is not over

the neighborhood of forty bars, and the freight on it over $1,000. Each coach always carried a deal of ordinary express matter beside, and also from fifteen to twenty passengers at from $25 to $30 a head. With six stages going all the time, Wells, Fargo and Co.'s Virginia City business was important and lucrative.

All along under the centre of Virginia and Gold Hill, for a couple of miles, ran the great Comstock silver lode—a vein of ore from fifty to eighty feet thick between its solid walls of rock—a vein as wide as some of New York's streets. I will remind the reader that in Pennsylvania a coal vein only eight feet wide is considered ample.

Virginia was a busy city of streets and houses above ground. Under it was another busy city, down in the bowels of the earth, where a great population of men thronged in and out among an intricate maze of tunnels and drifts, flitting hither and thither under a winking sparkle of lights, and over their heads towered a vast web of interlocking timbers that held the walls of the gutted Comstock apart. These timbers were as large as a man's body, and the framework stretched upward so far that no eye could pierce to its top through the closing gloom. It was like peering up through the clean-picked ribs and bones of some colossal skeleton. Imagine such a framework two miles long, sixty feet wide, and higher than any church spire in America. Imagine this stately lattice-work stretching down Broadway, from the St. Nicholas to Wall street, and a Fourth

---

the mark, perhaps, and may possibly be a little under it. To Esmeralda we give $4,000,000. To Reese River and Humboldt $2,000,000, which is liberal now, but may not be before the year is out. So we prognosticate that the yield of bullion this year will be about $30,000,000. Placing the number of mills in the Territory at one hundred, this gives to each the labor of producing $300,000 in bullion during the twelve months. Allowing them to run three hundred days in the year (which none of them more than do), this makes their work average $1,000 a day. Say the mills average twenty tons of rock a day and this rock worth $50 as a general thing, and you have the actual work of our one hundred mills figured down "to a spot"—$1,000 a day each, and $30,000,000 a year in the aggregate.—*Enterprise.*

[A considerable over estimate.—M. T.]

of July procession, reduced to pigmies, parading on top of it and flaunting their flags, high above the pinnacle of Trinity steeple. One can imagine that, but he cannot well imagine what that forest of timbers cost, from the time they were felled in the pineries beyond Washoe Lake, hauled up and around Mount Davidson at atrocious rates of freightage, then squared, let down into the deep maw of the mine and built up there. Twenty ample fortunes would not timber one of the greatest of those silver mines. The Spanish proverb says it requires a gold mine to " run " a silver one, and it is true. A beggar with a silver mine is a pitiable pauper indeed if he cannot sell.

TIMBER SUPPORTS.

I spoke of the underground Virginia as a city. The Gould and Curry is only one single mine under there, among a great many others; yet the Gould and Curry's streets of dismal drifts and tunnels were five miles in extent, altogether, and its population five hundred miners. Taken as a whole, the underground city had some thirty miles of streets and a population of five or six thousand. In this present day some of those populations are at work from twelve to sixteen hundred feet under Virginia and Gold Hill, and the signal-bells that tell them what the superintendent above ground desires them to do are struck by telegraph as we strike a fire alarm. Sometimes men fall down a shaft, there, a thousand feet deep. In such cases, the usual plan is to hold an inquest.

If you wish to visit one of those mines, you may walk

FROM GALLERY TO GALLERY.

through a tunnel about half a mile long if you prefer it, or you may take the quicker plan of shooting like a dart down a shaft, on a small platform. It is like tumbling down through an empty steeple, feet first. When you reach the bottom, you take a candle and tramp through drifts and tunnels where throngs of men are digging and blasting; you watch them send up tubs full of great lumps of stone—silver ore; you select choice specimens from the mass, as souvenirs; you admire the world of skeleton timbering; you reflect frequently that you are buried under a mountain, a thousand feet below daylight; being in the bottom of the mine you climb from "gallery" to "gallery," up endless ladders that stand straight up and down; when your legs fail you at last, you lie down in a small box-car in a cramped "incline" like a half-up-ended sewer and are dragged up to daylight feeling as if you are crawling through a coffin that has no end to it. Arrived at the top, you find a busy crowd of men receiving the ascending cars and tubs and dumping the ore from an elevation into long rows of bins capable of holding half a dozen tons each; under the bins are rows of wagons loading from chutes and trap-doors in the bins, and down the long street is a procession of these wagons wending toward the silver mills with their rich freight. It is all "done," now, and there you are. You need never go down again, for you have seen it all. If you have forgotten the process of reducing the ore in the mill and making the silver bars, you can go back and find it again in my Esmeralda chapters if so disposed.

Of course these mines cave in, in places, occasionally, and then it is worth one's while to take the risk of descending into them and observing the crushing power exerted by the pressing weight of a settling mountain. I published such an experience in the *Enterprise*, once, and from it I will take an extract:

AN HOUR IN THE CAVED MINES.—We journeyed down into the Ophir mine, yesterday, to see the earthquake. We could not go down the deep incline, because it still has a propensity to cave in places. Therefore we traveled through the long tunnel which enters the hill above the Ophir office, and then by means of a series of long ladders, climbed away down from the first to the fourth gallery. Traversing a drift, we came to the Spanish line, passed five sets of timbers still uninjured, and found the earthquake. Here was as complete a chaos as ever was seen—vast masses of earth and splintered and broken timbers piled confusedly together, with scarcely an aperture left large enough for a cat to creep through. Rubbish was still falling at intervals from above, and one timber which had braced others earlier in the day, was *now* crushed down out of its former position, showing that the caving and settling of the tremendous mass was still going on. We were in that portion of the Ophir known as the "north mines." Returning to the surface, we entered a tunnel leading into the Central, for the purpose of getting into the main Ophir. Descending a long incline in this tunnel, we traversed a drift or so, and then went down a deep shaft from whence we proceeded into the fifth gallery of the Ophir. From a side-drift we crawled through a small hole and got into the midst of the earthquake again—earth and broken timbers mingled together without regard to grace or symmetry. A large portion of the second, third and fourth galleries had caved in and gone to destruction—the two latter at seven o'clock on the previous evening.

At the turn-table, near the northern extremity of the fifth gallery, two big piles of rubbish had forced their way through from the fifth gallery, and from the looks of the timbers, more was about to come. These beams are solid—eighteen inches square; first, a great beam is laid on the floor, then upright ones, five feet high, stand on it, supporting another horizontal beam, and so on, square above square, like the framework of a window. The superincumbent weight was sufficient to mash the ends of those great upright beams fairly into the solid wood of the horizontal ones three inches, compressing and bending the upright beam till it curved like a bow. Before the Spanish caved in, some of their twelve-inch horizontal timbers were compressed in this way until they were only five inches thick! Imagine the power it must take to squeeze a solid log together in that way. Here, also, was a range of timbers, for a distance of twenty feet, tilted six inches out of the perpendicular by the weight resting upon them from the caved galleries above. You could hear things cracking and giving way, and it was not pleasant to know that the world overhead was slowly and silently sinking down upon you. The men down in the mine do not mind it, however.

Returning along the fifth gallery, we struck the safe part of the Ophir incline, and went down it to the sixth; but we found ten inches of water there, and had to come back. In repairing the damage done to the incline, the pump had to be stopped for two hours, and in the meantime the water gained about a foot. However, the pump was at work again, and the floodwater was decreasing. We climbed up to the fifth gallery again and sought a deep shaft, whereby we might descend to another part of the sixth, out of reach of the water, but suffered disappointment, as the men had gone to dinner, and there was no one to man the windlass. So, having seen the earthquake, we climbed out at the Union incline and tunnel, and adjourned, all dripping with candle grease and perspiration, to lunch at the Ophir office.

During the great flush year of 1863, Nevada [claims to have] produced $25,000,000 in bullion—almost, if not quite, a round million to each thousand inhabitants, which is very well, considering that she was without agriculture and manufactures.*   Silver mining was her sole productive industry.

---

* Since the above was in type, I learn from an official source that the above figure is too high, and that the yield for 1863 did not exceed $20,000,000. However, the day for large figures is approaching; the Sutro Tunnel is to plow through the Comstock lode from end to end, at a depth of two thousand feet, and then mining will be easy and comparatively inexpensive; and the momentous matters of drainage, and hoisting and hauling of ore will cease to be burdensome. This vast work will absorb many years, and millions of dollars, in its completion; but it will early yield money, for that desirable epoch will begin as soon as it strikes the first end of the vein. The tunnel will be some eight miles long, and will develop astonishing riches. Cars will carry the ore through the tunnel and dump it in the mills and thus do away with the present costly system of double handling and transportation by mule teams. The water from the tunnel will furnish the motive power for the mills. Mr. Sutro, the originator of this prodigious enterprise, is one of the few men in the world who is gifted with the pluck and perseverance necessary to follow up and hound such an undertaking to its completion. He has converted several obstinate Congresses to a deserved friendliness toward his important work, and has gone up and down and to and fro in Europe until he has enlisted a great moneyed interest in it there.

CHAPTER LIII.

EVERY now and then, in these days, the boys used to tell me I ought to get one Jim Blaine to tell me the stirring story of his grandfather's old ram—but they always added that I must not mention the matter unless Jim was drunk at the time—just comfortably and sociably drunk. They kept this up until my curiosity was on the rack to hear the story. I got to haunting Blaine; but it was of no use, the boys always found fault with his condition; he was often moderately but never satisfactorily drunk. I never watched a man's condition with such absorbing interest, such anxious solicitude; I never so pined to see a man uncompromisingly drunk before. At last, one evening I hurried to his cabin, for I learned that this time his situation was such that even the most fastidious could find no fault with it—he was tranquilly, serenely, symmetrically drunk—not a hiccup to mar his voice, not a cloud upon his brain thick enough to obscure his memory. As I entered, he was sitting upon an empty powder-keg, with a clay pipe in one hand and the other raised to command silence. His face was round, red, and very serious; his throat was bare and his hair tumbled; in general appearance and costume he was a stalwart miner of the period. On the pine table stood a candle, and its dim light revealed "the boys" sitting here and there on bunks, candle-boxes, powder-kegs, etc. They said:

"Sh—! Don't speak—he's going to commence."

THE STORY OF THE OLD RAM.

I found a seat at once, and Blaine said:

"I don't reckon them times will ever come again. There

never was a more bullier old ram than what he was. Grandfather fetched him from Illinois—got him of a man by the name of Yates —Bill Yates— maybe you might have heard of him; his father was a deacon — B a p - tist—and he was a rustler, too; a man had to get up ruther early to get the start of old Thankful Yates; it was him that put the Greens up to jining teams with my grandfather when he

JIM BLAINE.

moved west. Seth Green was prob'ly the pick of the flock · he married a Wilkerson—Sarah Wilkerson—good cretur, she was—one of the likeliest heifers that was ever raised in old Stoddard, everybody said that knowed her. She could heft a bar'l of flour as easy as I can flirt a flapjack. And spin ? Don't mention it! Independent ? Humph! When Sile Hawkins come a browsing around her, she let him know that for all his tin he couldn't trot in harness alongside of *her*. You see, Sile Hawkins was—no, it warn't Sile Hawkins, after all—it was a galoot by the name of Filkins—I disremember his first name; but he *was* a stump—come into pra'r meeting drunk, one night, hooraying for Nixon, becuz he thought it was a primary; and old deacon Ferguson up and scooted him through the window and he lit on old Miss Jefferson's head, poor old filly. She was a good soul—had a glass eye and used to lend it to old Miss Wagner, that hadn't any, to receive company in; it warn't big enough, and when Miss Wagner warn't noticing, it would get twisted around in the socket, and

HURRAH FOR NIXON.

look up, maybe, or out to one side, and every which way, while t' other one was looking as straight ahead as a spy-glass. Grown people didn't mind it, but it most always made the children cry, it was so sort of scary. She tried packing it in raw cotton, but it wouldn't work, somehow—the cotton would get loose and stick out and look so kind of awful that the children couldn't stand it no way. She was always dropping it out, and turning up her old dead-light on the company empty, and making them oncomfortable, becuz *she* never could tell when it hopped out, being blind on that side, you see. So somebody would have to hunch her and say, "Your game eye has fetched loose, Miss Wagner dear "—and then all of them would have to sit and wait till she jammed it in again—wrong side before, as a general thing, and green as a bird's egg, being a bashful cretur and easy sot back before company. But

25†

being wrong side before warn't much difference, anyway, becuz her own eye was sky-blue and the glass one was yaller

MISS WAGNER.

on the front side, so whichever way she turned it it didn't match nohow. Old Miss Wagner was considerable on the borrow, she was. When she had a quilting, or Dorcas S'iety at her house she gen'ally borrowed Miss Higgins's wooden leg to stump around on; it was considerable shorter than her other pin, but much *she* minded that. She said she couldn't abide crutches when she had company, becuz they were so slow; said when she had company and things had to be done, she wanted to get up and hump herself. She was as bald as a jug, and so she used to borrow Miss Jacops's wig—Miss Jacops was the coffin-peddler's wife—a ratty old buzzard, he was, that used to go roosting around where people was sick, waiting for 'em; and there that old rip would sit all day, in the shade, on a coffin that he judged would fit the can'idate; and if it was a slow customer and kind of uncertain, he'd fetch his rations and a blanket along and sleep in the coffin nights. He was anchored out that way, in frosty weather, for about three weeks, once, before old Robbins's place, waiting for him; and after that, for as much as two years, Jacops was not on speaking terms with the old man, on account of his disapp'inting him. He got one of his feet froze, and lost money, too, becuz old Robbins took a favorable turn and got well. The next time Robbins got sick, Jacops tried to make up with him, and varnished up the same old coffin and fetched it along; but old Robbins was too many for him; he had him in, and 'peared to be powerful weak; he bought the coffin for ten dollars and Jacops was to pay it back and twenty-five more

besides if Robbins didn't like the coffin after he'd tried it.
And then Robbins died, and at the funeral he bursted off the

WAITING FOR A CUSTOMER.

lid and riz up in his shroud and told the parson to let up on
the performances, becuz he could *not* stand such a coffin as
that. You see he had been in a trance once before, when he
was young, and he took the chances on another, cal'lating that
if he made the trip it was money in his pocket, and if he
missed fire he couldn't lose a cent. And by George he sued
Jacops for the rhino and got jedgment; and he set up the
coffin in his back parlor and said he 'lowed to take his time,
now. It was always an aggravation to Jacops, the way that
miserable old thing acted. He moved back to Indiany pretty
soon—went to Wellsville—Wellsville was the place the Hog-
adorns was from. Mighty fine family. Old Maryland stock.
Old Squire Hogadorn could carry around more mixed licker,
and cuss better than most any man I ever see. His second
wife was the widder Billings—she that was Becky Martin;
her dam was deacon Dunlap's first wife. Her oldest child,
Maria, married a missionary and died in grace—et up by the

savages. They et *him*, too, poor feller—biled him. It warn't the custom, so they say, but they explained to friends of his'n that went down there to bring away his things, that they'd tried missionaries every other way and never could get any good out of 'em—and so it annoyed all his relations to find out that that man's life was fooled away just out of a dern'd experiment, so to speak. But mind you, there ain't anything ever reely lost; everything that people can't understand and don't see the reason of does good if you only hold on and give it a fair shake; Prov'dence don't fire no blank ca'tridges, boys. That there missionary's substance, unbeknowns to himself, actu'ly converted every last one of them heathens that took a chance at the barbacue. Nothing ever fetched them but that. Don't tell *me* it was an accident that he was biled. There

WAS TO BE THERE.

ain't no such a thing as an accident. When my uncle Lem was leaning up agin a scaffolding once, sick, or drunk, or suthin, an Irishman with a hod full of bricks fell on him out of the third story and broke the old man's back in two places. People said it was an accident. Much accident there was about that. He didn't know what he was there for, but he was there for a good object. If he hadn't been there the Irishman would have been killed. Nobody can ever make me believe anything different from that. Uncle Lem's dog was there. Why didn't the Irishman fall on the dog? Becuz the dog would a seen him a coming and stood from under. That's the reason the dog warn't appinted. A dog can't be depended on to carry out a special providence. Mark my words it was a put-up thing. Accidents don't happen, boys. Uncle Lem's dog—I wish you could a seen that dog. He was a reglar shepherd—or ruther he was part bull and part shepherd—splendid animal; belonged to parson Hagar before Uncle Lem got him. Parson Hagar belonged to the Western Reserve Hagars; prime family; his mother was a Watson; one of his sisters married a Wheeler; they settled in Morgan county, and he got nipped by the machinery in a carpet factory and went through in less than a quarter of a minute; his widder bought the piece of carpet that had his remains wove in, and people come a hundred mile to 'tend the funeral. There was fourteen yards in the piece. She wouldn't let them roll him up, but planted him just so —full length. The church was middling small where they preached the funeral, and they had to let one end of the coffin stick out of the window. They didn't bury him —they planted one end, and let him stand up, same as a monument. And they nailed a sign on it and put—put on—put on it— sacred to—the m-e-m-o-r-y—of fourteen y-a-r-d-s—of three-ply—car - - - pet—containing all that was—m-o-r-t-a-l—of—of— W-i-l-l-i-a-m—W-h-e-- "

THE MONUMENT.

Jim Blaine had been growing gradually drowsy and drowsier—his head nodded, once, twice, three times—dropped peacefully upon his breast, and he fell tranquilly asleep. The tears were running down the boys' cheeks—they were suffocating with suppressed laughter—and had been from the start, though I had never noticed it. I perceived that I was "sold." I learned then that Jim Blaine's peculiarity was that whenever he reached a certain stage of intoxication, no human power could keep him from setting out, with impressive unction, to tell about a wonderful adventure which he had once had with his grandfather's old ram—and the mention of the ram in the first sentence was as far as any man had ever heard him get, concerning it. He always maundered off, interminably, from one thing to another, till his whisky got the best of him and he fell asleep. What the thing was that happened to him and his grandfather's old ram is a dark mystery to this day, for nobody has ever yet found out.

CHAPTER LIV.

OF course there was a large Chinese population in Virginia —it is the case with every town and city on the Pacific coast. They are a harmless race when white men either let them alone or treat them no worse than dogs; in fact they are almost entirely harmless anyhow, for they seldom think of resenting the vilest insults or the cruelest injuries. They are quiet, peaceable, tractable, free from drunkenness, and they are as industrious as the day is long. A disorderly Chinaman is rare, and a lazy one does not exist. So long as a Chinaman has strength to use his hands he needs no support from anybody; white men often complain of want of work, but a Chinaman offers no such complaint; he always manages to find something to do. He is a great convenience to everybody— even to the worst class of white men, for he bears the most of their sins, suffering fines for their petty thefts, imprisonment for their robberies, and death for their murders. Any white man can swear a Chinaman's life away in the courts, but no Chinaman can testify against a white man. Ours is the "land of the free"—nobody denies that—nobody challenges it. [Maybe it is because we won't let other people testify.] As I write, news comes that in broad daylight in San Francisco, some boys have stoned an inoffensive Chinaman to death, and that although a large crowd witnessed the shameful deed, no one interfered.

There are seventy thousand (and possibly one hundred thousand) Chinamen on the Pacific coast. There were about a thousand in Virginia. They were penned into a " Chinese quarter "—a thing which they do not particularly object to, as they are fond of herding together. Their buildings were of wood; usually only one story high, and set thickly together along streets scarcely wide enough for a wagon to pass through. Their quarter was a little removed from the rest of the town. The chief employment of Chinamen in towns is to wash clothing. They always send a bill, like this below, pinned to the clothes. It is mere ceremony, for it does not enlighten the customer much. Their price for washing was $2.50 per dozen—rather cheaper than white people could afford to wash for at that time. A very common sign on the Chinese houses was: " See Yup, Washer and Ironer "; " Hong Wo, Washer "; " Sam Sing & Ah Hop, Washing." The house servants, cooks, etc., in California and Nevada, were chiefly Chinamen. There were few white servants and no Chinawomen so employed. Chinamen make good house servants, being quick, obedient, patient, quick to learn and tirelessly industrious. They do not need to be taught a thing twice, as a general thing. They are imitative. If a Chinaman were to see his master break up a centre table, in a passion, and kindle a fire with it, that Chinaman would be likely to resort to the furniture for fuel forever afterward.

All Chinamen can read, write and cipher with easy facility—pity but all our petted *voters* could. In California they rent little patches of ground and do a deal of gardening. They will raise surprising crops of vegetables on a sand pile. They waste nothing. What is rubbish to a Christian, a Chinaman carefully preserves and makes useful in one way or another. He gathers up all the old oyster and sardine cans that white people throw away, and procures marketable tin and solder from them by melting.

He gathers up old bones and turns them into manure. In California he gets a living out of old mining claims that white men have abandoned as exhausted and worthless—and then the officers come down on him once a month with an exorbitant swindle to which the legislature has given the broad, general name of "foreign" mining tax, but it is usually inflicted on no foreigners but Chinamen. This swindle has in some cases been repeated

IMITATION.

once or twice on the same victim in the course of the same month—but the public treasury was not additionally enriched by it, probably.

Chinamen hold their dead in great reverence—they worship their departed ancestors, in fact. Hence, in China, a man's front yard, back yard, or any other part of his premises, is made his family burying ground, in order that he may visit the graves at any and all times. Therefore that huge empire is one mighty cemetery; it is ridged and wringled from its centre to its circumference with graves—and inasmuch as every foot of ground must be made to do its utmost, in China, lest the swarming population suffer for food, the very graves are cultivated and yield a harvest, custom holding this to be no dishonor to the dead. Since the departed are held in such worshipful reverence, a Chinaman cannot bear that any indignity be offered the places where they sleep. Mr. Burlingame said that herein lay China's bitter opposition to railroads; a road could not be built anywhere in the empire without disturbing the graves of their ancestors or friends.

A Chinaman hardly believes he could enjoy the hereafter except his body lay in his beloved China; also, he desires to receive, himself, after death, that worship with which he has honored his dead that preceded him. Therefore, if he visits a foreign country, he makes arrangements to have his bones returned to China in case he dies; if he hires to go to a foreign country on a labor contract, there is always a stipulation that his body shall be taken back to China if he dies; if the government sells a gang of Coolies to a foreigner for the usual five-year term, it is specified in the contract that their bodies shall be restored to China in case of death. On the Pacific coast the Chinamen all belong to one or another of several great companies or organizations, and these companies keep track of their members, register their names, and ship their bodies home when they die. The See Yup Company is held to be the largest of these. The Ning Yeong Company is next, and numbers eighteen thousand members on the coast. Its headquarters are at San Francisco, where it has a costly temple, several great officers (one of whom keeps regal state in seclusion and cannot be approached by common humanity), and a numerous priesthood. In it I was shown a register of its members, with the dead and the date of their shipment to China duly marked. Every ship that sails from San Francisco carries away a heavy freight of Chinese corpses—or did, at least, until the legislature, with an ingenious refinement of Christian cruelty, forbade the shipments, as a neat underhanded way of deterring Chinese immigration. The bill was offered, whether it passed or not. It is my impression that it passed. There was another bill—it became a law—compelling every incoming Chinaman to be vaccinated on the wharf and pay a duly appointed quack (no decent doctor would defile himself with such legalized robbery) ten dollars for it. As few importers of Chinese would want to go to an expense like that, the lawmakers thought this would be another heavy blow to Chinese immigration.

What the Chinese quarter of Virginia was like—or, indeed, what the Chinese quarter of any Pacific coast town was and is like—may be gathered from this item which I printed in the *Enterprise* while reporting for that paper:

CHINATOWN.—Accompanied by a fellow reporter, we made a trip through our Chinese quarter the other night. The Chinese have built their portion of the city to suit themselves; and as they keep neither carriages nor wagons, their streets are not wide enough, as a general thing, to admit of the passage of vehicles. At ten o'clock at night the Chinaman may be seen in all his glory. In every little cooped-up, dingy cavern of a hut, faint with the odor of burning Josh-lights and with nothing to see the gloom by save the sickly, guttering tallow candle, were two or three yellow, long-tailed vagabonds, coiled up on a sort of short truckle-bed, smoking opium, motionless and with their lustreless eyes turned inward from excess of satisfaction —or rather the recent smoker looks thus, immediately after having passed the pipe to his neighbor—for opium-smoking is a comfortless operation, and requires constant attention. A lamp sits on the bed, the length of the long pipe-stem from the smoker's mouth; he puts a pellet of opium on the end of a wire, sets it on fire, and plasters it into the pipe much as a Christian would fill a hole with putty; then he applies the bowl to the lamp and proceeds to smoke—and the stewing and frying of the drug and the gurgling of the juices in the stem would wellnigh turn the stomach of a statue. John likes it, though; it soothes him, he takes about two dozen whiffs, and then rolls over to dream, Heaven only knows what, for we could not imagine by looking at the soggy creature. Possibly in his visions he travels far away from the gross world and his regular washing, and feasts on succulent rats and birds'-nests in Paradise.

Mr. Ah Sing keeps a general grocery and provision store at No. 13 Wang street. He lavished his hospitality upon our party in the friendliest way. He had various kinds of colored and colorless wines and brandies, with unpronounceable names, imported from China in little crockery jugs, and which he offered to us in dainty little miniature wash-basins of porcelain. He offered us a mess of birds'-nests; also, small, neat sausages, of which we could have swallowed several yards if we had chosen to try, but we suspected that each link contained the corpse of a mouse, and therefore refrained. Mr. Sing had in his store a thousand articles of merchandise, curious to behold, impossible to imagine the uses of, and beyond our ability to describe.

His ducks, however, and his eggs, we could understand; the former were split open and flattened out like codfish, and came from China in that shape, and the latter were plastered over with some kind of paste which kept them fresh and palatable through the long voyage.

We found Mr. Hong Wo, No. 37 Chow-chow street, making up a lottery scheme—in fact we found a dozen others occupied in the same way in various parts of the quarter, for about every third Chinaman runs a lottery, and the balance of the tribe "buck" at it. "Tom," who speaks faultless English, and used to be chief and only cook to the *Territorial Enterprise*, when the establishment kept bachelor's hall two years ago, said that "Sometime Chinaman buy ticket one dollar hap, ketch um two tree hundred, sometime no ketch um anyting; lottery like one man fight um seventy—may-be he whip, may-be he get whip heself, welly good." However, the percentage being sixty-nine against him, the chances are, as a general thing, that "he

CHINESE LOTTERY.

get whip heself." We could not see that these lotteries differed in any respect from our own, save that the figures being Chinese, no ignorant white man might ever hope to succeed in telling "t'other from which;" the manner of drawing is similar to ours.

Mr. See Yup keeps a fancy store on Live Fox street. He sold us fans of white feathers, gorgeously ornamented; perfumery that smelled like Limburger cheese, Chinese pens, and watch-charms made of a stone unscratchable with steel instruments, yet polished and tinted like the inner coat of a sea-shell.* As tokens of his esteem, See Yup presented the party with gaudy plumes made of gold tinsel and trimmed with peacocks' feathers.

We ate chow-chow with chop-sticks in the celestial restaurants; our comrade chided the moon-eyed damsels in front of the houses for their want of feminine reserve; we received protecting Josh-lights from our hosts and "dick-

* A peculiar species of the "jade-stone"—to a Chinaman peculiarly precious.

ered " for a pagan God or two.   Finally, we were impressed with the genius
of a Chinese book-keeper ; he figured up his accounts on a machine like a gridiron with buttons strung on its bars ; the different rows represented units,
tens, hundreds and thousands.   He fingered them with incredible rapidity—
in fact, he pushed them from place to place as fast as a musical professor's
fingers travel over the keys of a piano.

They are a kindly disposed, well-meaning race, and are
respected and well treated by the upper classes, all over the
Pacific coast.   No Californian *gentleman or lady* ever abuses
or oppresses a Chinaman, under any circumstances, an explanation that seems to be much needed in the East.   Only the scum
of the population do it—they and their children ; they, and,
naturally and consistently, the policemen and politicians, likewise, for these are the dust-licking pimps and slaves of the
scum, there as well as elsewhere in America.

CHAPTER LV.

I BEGAN to get tired of staying in one place so long. There was no longer satisfying variety in going down to Carson to report the proceedings of the legislature once a year, and horse-races and pumpkin-shows once in three months; (they had got to raising pumpkins and potatoes in Washoe Valley, and of course one of the first achievements of the legislature was to institute a ten-thousand-dollar Agricultural Fair to show off forty dollars' worth of those pumpkins in— however, the territorial legislature was usually spoken of as the "asylum"). I wanted to see San Francisco. I wanted to go somewhere. I wanted—I did not know *what* I wanted. I had the "spring fever" and wanted a change, principally, no doubt. Besides, a convention had framed a State Constitution; nine men out of every ten wanted an office; I believed that these gentlemen would "treat" the moneyless and the irresponsible among the population into adopting the constitution and thus wellnigh killing the country (it could not well carry such a load as a State government, since it had nothing to tax that could stand a tax, for undeveloped mines could not, and there were not fifty developed ones in the land, there was but little realty to tax, and it did seem as if nobody was ever going to think of the simple salvation of inflicting a money penalty on murder). I believed that a State government would destroy the "flush times," and I wanted to get away. I believed that the mining stocks I had on hand would soon be worth $100,000, and thought if they reached that before the Constitution was adopted, I would sell out and make myself

secure from the crash the change of government was going to
bring. I considered $100,000 sufficient to go home with
decently, though it was but a small amount compared to what
I had been expecting to return with. I felt rather down-
hearted about it, but I tried to comfort myself with the reflection that with such a sum I could not fall into want.
About this time a schoolmate of mine whom I had not seen
since boyhood, came tramping in on foot from Reese River, a
very allegory of Poverty. The son of wealthy parents, here
he was, in a strange land, hungry, bootless, mantled in an
ancient horse-blanket, roofed

with a brimless hat, and so
generally and so extrava-
gantly dilapidated that he
could have "taken the shine
out of the Prodigal Son
himself," as he pleasantly
remarked. He wanted to
borrow forty-six dollars—
twenty-six to take him to
San Francisco, and twenty
for something else ; to buy
some soap with, maybe, for
he needed it. I found I had
but little more than the
amount wanted, in my pocket ; so I stepped in and borrowed forty-six dollars of a
banker (on twenty days' time,
without the formality of a
note), and gave it him, rather
than walk half a block to the

AN OLD FRIEND.

office, where I had some specie laid up. If anybody had told
me that it would take me two years to pay back that forty-six
dollars to the banker (for I did not expect it of the Prodigal,
and was not disappointed), I would have felt injured. And
so would the banker.

I wanted a change. I wanted variety of some kind. It came. Mr. Goodman went away for a week and left me the post of chief editor. It destroyed me. The first day, I wrote my "leader" in the forenoon. The second day, I had no subject and put it off till the afternoon. The third day I put it off till evening, and then copied an elaborate editorial out of the "American Cyclopedia," that steadfast friend of the editor, all over this land. The fourth day I "fooled around" till midnight, and then fell back on the Cyclopedia again. The fifth day I cudgeled my brain till midnight, and then kept the press waiting while I penned some bitter personalities on six different people. The sixth day I labored in anguish till far into the night and brought forth—nothing. The paper went to press without an editorial. The seventh day I resigned. On the eighth, Mr. Goodman returned and found six duels on his hands—my personalities had borne fruit.

Nobody, except he has tried it, knows what it is to be an editor. It is easy to scribble local rubbish, with the facts all before you; it is easy to clip selections from other papers; it is easy to string out a correspondence from any locality; but it is unspeakable hardship to write editorials. *Subjects* are the trouble—the dreary lack of them, I mean. Every day, it is drag, drag, drag—think, and worry and suffer—all the world is a dull blank, and yet the editorial columns *must* be filled. Only give the editor a *subject*, and his work is done—it is no trouble to write it up; but fancy how you would feel if you had to pump your brains dry every day in the week, fifty-two weeks in the year. It makes one low spirited simply to think of it. The matter that each editor of a daily paper in America writes in the course of a year would fill from four to eight bulky volumes like this book! Fancy what a library an editor's work would make, after twenty or thirty years' service. Yet people often marvel that Dickens, Scott, Bulwer, Dumas, etc., have been able to produce so many books. If these authors had wrought as voluminously as newspaper editors do, the result would be something to marvel at, indeed. How editors can continue this tremendous labor, this exhausting consumption of brain fibre (for their work is creative, and not a mere mechanical laying-up of facts, like reporting), day after day and year after year, is incomprehensible. Preachers take two months' holiday in midsummer, for they find that to produce two sermons a week is wearing, in the long run. In truth it must be so, and is so; and therefore, how an editor can take from ten to twenty texts and build upon them from ten to twenty painstaking editorials a week and keep it up all the year round, is farther beyond comprehension than ever. Ever since I survived my week as editor, I have found at least one pleasure in any newspaper that comes to my hand; it is in admiring the long columns of editorial, and wondering to myself how in the mischief he did it !

Mr. Goodman's return relieved me of employment, unless I chose to become a reporter again. I could not do that; I could not serve in the ranks after being General of the army. So I thought I would depart and go abroad into the world somewhere. Just at this juncture, Dan, my associate in the reportorial department, told me, casually, that two citizens had been trying to persuade him to go with them to New York and aid in selling a rich silver mine which they had discovered and secured in a new mining district in our neighborhood. He said they offered to pay his expenses and give him one third of the proceeds of the sale. He had refused to go. It was the very opportunity I wanted. I abused him for keeping so quiet about it, and not mentioning it sooner. He said it had not occurred to him that I would like to go, and so he had recommended them to apply to Marshall, the reporter of the other paper. I asked Dan if it was a good, honest mine, and no swindle. He said the men had shown him nine tons of the rock, which they had got out to take to New York, and he could cheerfully say that he had seen but little rock in Nevada that was richer; and moreover, he said that they had secured a tract of valuable timber and a mill-site, near the mine. My first idea was to kill Dan. But I changed my mind, notwithstanding I was so angry, for I thought maybe the chance was not yet lost. Dan said it was by no means lost; that the men

26†

were absent at the mine again, and would not be in Virginia to leave for the East for some ten days; that they had requested him to do the talking to Marshall, and he had promised that he would either secure Marshall or somebody else for them by the time they got back; he would now say nothing to anybody till they returned, and then fulfil his promise by furnishing me to them.

It was splendid. I went to bed all on fire with excitement; for nobody had yet gone East to sell a Nevada silver mine, and the field was white for the sickle. I felt that such a mine as the one described by Dan would bring a princely sum in New York, and sell without delay or difficulty. I could not sleep, my fancy so rioted through its castles in the air. It was the "blind lead" come again.

Next day I got away, on the coach, with the usual eclat attending departures of old citizens,—for if you have only half a dozen friends out there they will make noise for a hundred rather than let you seem to go away neglected and unregretted —and Dan promised to keep strict watch for the men that had the mine to sell.

The trip was signalized but by one little incident, and that occurred just as we were about to start. A very seedy looking vagabond passenger got out of the stage a moment to wait till the usual ballast of silver bricks was thrown in. He was standing on the pavement, when an awkward express employé, carrying a brick weighing a hundred pounds, stumbled and let it fall on the bummer's foot. He instantly dropped on the ground and began to howl in the most heart-breaking way. A sympathizing crowd gathered around and were going to pull his boot off; but he screamed louder than ever and they desisted; then he fell to gasping, and between the gasps ejaculated "Brandy! for Heaven's sake, brandy!" They poured half a pint down him, and it wonderfully restored and comforted him. Then he begged the people to assist him to the stage, which was done. The express people urged him to have a doctor at their expense, but he declined, and said that if he only had a little brandy to take along with him, to soothe his paroxyms of pain when they came on, he would be grateful and content. He was quickly supplied with two bottles, and we drove off. He was so smiling and happy after that, that I could not refrain from asking him how he could possibly be so comfortable with a crushed foot.

"Well," said he, "I hadn't had a drink for twelve hours, and hadn't a cent to my name. I was most perishing—and so, when that duffer dropped that hundred-pounder on my foot, I see my chance. Got a cork leg, you know!" and he pulled up his pantaloons and proved it.

He was as drunk as a lord all day long, and full of chucklings over his timely ingenuity.

One drunken man necessarily reminds one of an-

FAREWELL AND ACCIDENT.

other. I once heard a gentleman tell about an incident which he witnessed in a Californian bar-room. He entitled it "Ye Modest Man Taketh a Drink." It was nothing but a bit of acting, but it seemed to me a perfect rendering, and worthy of Toodles himself. The modest man, tolerably far gone with beer and other matters, enters a saloon (twenty-five cents is the price for anything and everything, and specie the only money used) and lays down a half dollar; calls for whiskey and drinks it;

the bar-keeper makes change and lays the quarter in a wet place on the counter; the modest man fumbles at it with nerveless fingers, but it slips and the water holds it; he contemplates it, and tries again; same result; observes that people are interested in what he is at, blushes; fumbles at the quarter again—blushes—puts his forefinger carefully, slowly down, to make sure of his aim—pushes the coin toward the bar-keeper, and says with a sigh:

"('ic!) Gimme a cigar!"

Naturally, another gentleman present told about another drunken man. He said he reeled toward home late at night; made a mistake and entered the wrong gate; thought he saw a dog on the stoop; and it was—an iron one. He stopped and considered; wondered if it was a dangerous dog; ventured to say "Be (hic) begone!" No effect. Then he approached warily, and adopted conciliation; pursed up his lips and tried to whistle, but failed; still approached, saying, "Poor dog!—doggy, doggy, doggy!—poor doggy-dog!" Got up on the stoop, still petting with fond names; till master of the advantages; then exclaimed, "Leave, you thief!"—planted a vindictive kick in his ribs, and went head-over-

"GIMME A CIGAR!"

heels overboard, of course. A pause; a sigh or two of pain, and then a remark in a reflective voice:

"Awful solid dog. What could he ben eating? ('ic!) Rocks, p'raps. Such animals is dangerous. 'At's what *I* say —they're dangerous. If a man—('ic!)—if a man wants to feed a dog on rocks, let him *feed* him on rocks; 'at's all right;

but let him keep him at *home*—not have him layin' round promiscuous, where ('ic!) where people's liable to stumble over him when they ain't noticin'!"

It was not without regret that I took a last look at the tiny flag (it was thirty-five feet long and ten feet wide) fluttering like a lady's handkerchief from the topmost peak of Mount Davidson, two thousand feet above Virginia's roofs, and felt that doubtless I was bidding a permanent farewell to a city which had afforded me the most vigorous enjoyment of life I had ever experienced. And this reminds me of an incident which the dullest memory Virginia could boast at the time it happened must vividly recall, at times, till its possessor dies. Late one summer afternoon we had a rain shower. That was astonishing enough, in itself, to set the whole town buzzing, for it only rains (during a week or two weeks) in the winter in Nevada, and even then not enough at a time to make it worth while for any merchant to keep umbrellas for sale. But the rain was not the chief wonder. It only lasted five or ten minutes; while the people were still talking about it all the heavens gathered to themselves a dense blackness as of midnight. All the vast eastern front of Mount Davidson, overlooking the city, put on such a funereal gloom that only the nearness and solidity of the mountain made its outlines even faintly distinguishable from the dead blackness of the heavens they rested against. This unaccustomed sight turned all eyes toward the mountain; and as they looked, a little tongue of rich golden flame was seen waving and quivering in the heart of the midnight, away up on the extreme summit! In a few minutes the streets were packed with people, gazing with hardly an uttered word, at the one brilliant mote in the brooding world of darkness. It flicked like a candle-flame, and looked no larger; but with such a background it was wonderfully bright, small as it was. It was the flag!—though no one suspected it at first, it seemed so like a supernatural visitor of some kind—a mysterious messenger of good tidings, some were fain to believe. It was the nation's emblem transfigured by the departing rays of a sun that was entirely palled from view ; and on no other object did the glory fall, in all the broad panorama of mountain ranges and deserts. Not even upon the staff of the flag—for that, a needle in the distance at any time, was now untouched by the light and undistinguishable in the gloom. For a whole hour the weird visitor winked and burned in its lofty solitude, and still the thousands of uplifted eyes watched it with fascinated interest. How the people were wrought up! The superstition grew apace that this was a mystic courier come with great news from the war —the poetry of the idea excusing and commending it—and on

THE HERALD OF GLAD NEWS.

it spread, from heart to heart, from lip to lip and from street to street, till there was a general impulse to have out the military and welcome the bright waif with a salvo of artillery!

And all that time one sorely tried man, the telegraph operator sworn to official secrecy, had to lock his lips and chain his tongue with a silence that was like to rend them ; for he, and he only, of all the speculating multitude, knew the great

things this sinking sun had seen that day in the east—Vicks-
burg fallen, and the Union arms victorious at Gettysburg!

But for the journalistic monopoly that forbade the slightest
revealment of eastern news till a day after its publication in
the California papers, the glorified flag on Mount Davidson
would have been saluted and re-saluted, that memorable evening, as long as there was a charge of powder to thunder with;
the city would have been illuminated, and every man that had
any respect for himself would have got drunk,—as was the
custom of the country on all occasions of public moment.
Even at this distant day I cannot think of this needlessly
marred supreme opportunity without regret. What a time
we might have had!

CHAPTER LVI.

WE rumbled over the plains and valleys, climbed the Sierras to the clouds, and looked down upon summer-clad California. And I will remark here, in passing, that all scenery in California requires *distance* to give it its highest charm. The mountains are imposing in their sublimity and their majesty of form and altitude, from any point of view—but one must have distance to soften their ruggedness and enrich their tintings; a Californian forest is best at a little distance, for there is a sad poverty of variety in species, the trees being chiefly of one monotonous family—redwood, pine, spruce, fir—and so, at a near view there is a wearisome sameness of attitude in their rigid arms, stretched downward and outward in one continued and reiterated appeal to all men to "Sh ⊢—don't say a word!—you might disturb somebody!" Close at hand, too, there is a reliefless and relentless smell of pitch and turpentine; there is a ceaseless melancholy in their sighing and complaining foliage; one walks over a soundless carpet of beaten yellow bark and dead spines of the foliage till he feels like a wandering spirit bereft of a footfall; he tires of the endless tufts of needles and yearns for substantial, shapely leaves; he looks for moss and grass to loll upon, and finds none, for where there is no bark there is naked clay and dirt, enemies to pensive musing and clean apparel. Often a grassy plain in California, is what it should be, but often, too, it is best contemplated at a distance, because although its grass blades are tall, they stand up vindictively straight and self-sufficient, and are unsociably wide apart, with uncomely spots of barren sand between.

One of the queerest things I know of, is to hear tourists

from "the States" go into ecstasies over the loveliness of "ever-blooming California." And they always do go into that sort of ecstasies. But perhaps they would modify them if they knew how old Californians, with the memory full upon them of the dust-covered and questionable summer greens of Cali-

fornian "verdure," stand astonished, and filled with w o r s h i p-ping admiration, in the presence of the lavish richness, the brilliant green, the i n f i n i t e freshness, the spend-thrift variety of form and species and foli-age that make an Eastern landscape a vision of Paradise it-self. The idea of a man falling into rap-tures over grave and s o m b r e California, when that man has

AN EASTERN LANDSCAPE.

seen New England's meadow-expanses and her maples, oaks and cathedral-windowed elms decked in summer attire, or the opaline splendors of autumn descending upon her forests, comes very near being funny—would be, in fact, but that it is so pathetic. No land with an unvarying climate can be very beautiful. The tropics are not, for all the sentiment that is wasted on them. They seem beautiful at first, but sameness impairs the charm by and by. *Change* is the handmaiden Nature requires to do her miracles with. The land that has four well-defined seasons, cannot lack beauty, or pall with monotony. Each season brings a world of enjoyment and interest in the watching of its unfolding, its gradual, harmo-nious development, its culminating graces—and just as one begins to tire of it, it passes away and a radical change comes, with new witcheries and new glories in its train. And I think that to one in sympathy with nature, each season, in its turn, seems the loveliest.

San Francisco, a truly fascinating city to live in, is

A VARIABLE CLIMATE.

stately and handsome at a fair distance, but close at hand one notes that the architecture is mostly old-fashioned, many streets are made up of decaying, smoke-grimed, wooden houses, and the barren sand-hills toward the outskirts obtrude themselves too prominently. Even the kindly climate is sometimes pleasanter when read about than personally experienced, for a lovely, cloudless sky wears out its welcome by and by, and then when the longed for rain does come it *stays*. Even the playful earthquake is better contemplated at a dis—

However there are varying opinions about that.

The climate of San Francisco is mild and singularly equable. The thermometer stands at about seventy degrees the year round. It hardly changes at all. You sleep under one or two light blankets Summer and Winter, and never use a mosquito bar. Nobody ever wears Summer clothing. You wear black broadcloth—if you have it—in August and January, just the same. It is no colder, and no warmer, in the one month than the other. You do not use overcoats and you do not use fans. It is as pleasant a climate as could well be contrived, take it all around, and is doubtless the most unvarying in the whole world. The wind blows there a good deal in the

Summer months, but then you can go over to Oakland, if you choose—three or four miles away—it does not blow there. It has only snowed twice in San Francisco in nineteen years, and then it only remained on the ground long enough to astonish the children, and set them to wondering what the feathery stuff was.

During eight months of the year, straight along, the skies are bright and cloudless, and never a drop of rain falls. But when the other four months come along, you will need to go and steal an umbrella. Because you will require it. Not just one day, but one hundred and twenty days in hardly varying succession. When you want to go visiting, or attend church, or the theatre, you never look up at the clouds to see whether it is likely to rain or not—you look at the almanac. If it is Winter, it will *rain*—and if it is Summer, it *won't* rain, and you cannot help it. You never need a lightning-rod, because it never thunders and it never lightens. And after you have listened for six or eight weeks, every night, to the dismal monotony of those quiet rains, you will wish in your heart the thunder *would* leap and crash and roar along those drowsy skies once, and make everything alive—you will wish the prisoned lightnings *would* cleave the dull firmament asunder and light it with a blinding glare for *one* little instant. You would give *anything* to hear the old familiar thunder again and see the lightning strike somebody. And along in the Summer, when you have suffered about four months of lustrous, pitiless sunshine, you are ready to go down on your knees and plead for rain—hail—snow—thunder and lightning —anything to break the monotony—you will take an earth-quake, if you cannot do any better. And the chances are that you'll get it, too.

San Francisco is built on sand hills, but they are prolific sand hills. They yield a generous vegetation. All the rare flowers which people in "the States" rear with such patient care in parlor flower-pots and green-houses, flourish luxu-riantly in the open air there all the year round. Calla lilies, all sorts of geraniums, passion flowers, moss roses—I do not know the names of a tenth part of them. I only know that while

New Yorkers are burdened with banks and drifts of snow, Californians are burdened with banks and drifts of flowers, if they only keep their hands off and let them grow. And I have heard that they have also that rarest and most curious of all the flowers, the beautiful *Espiritu Santo*, as the Spaniards call it—or flower of the Holy Spirit—though I thought it grew only in Central America—down on the Isthmus. In its cup is the daintiest little fac-simile of a dove, as pure as snow. The Spaniards have a superstitious reverence for it. The blossom has been conveyed to the States, submerged in ether; and the bulb has been taken thither also, but every attempt to make it bloom after it arrived, has failed.

I have elsewhere spoken of the endless Winter of Mono, California, and but this moment of the eternal Spring of San Francisco. Now if we travel a hundred miles in a straight line, we come to the eternal Summer of Sacramento. One never sees Summer-clothing or mosquitoes in San Francisco— but they can be found in Sacramento. Not always and unvaryingly, but about one hundred and forty-three months out of twelve years, perhaps. Flowers bloom there, always, the reader can easily believe—people suffer and sweat, and swear, morning, noon and night, and wear out their stanchest energies fanning themselves. It gets hot there, but if you go down to Fort Yuma you will find it hotter. Fort Yuma is probably the hottest place on earth. The thermometer stays at one hundred and twenty in the shade there all the time—except when it varies and goes higher. It is a U. S. military post, and its occupants get so used to the terrific heat that they suffer without it. There is a tradition (attributed to John Phenix*) that a very, very wicked soldier died there, once, and of course, went straight to the hottest corner of perdition,—and the next day he *telegraphed back for his blankets*. There is no doubt about the truth of this statement—there can be no doubt about it. I have seen the place where that soldier used to board. In Sacramento it is fiery Summer always, and you can gather roses, and eat strawberries and ice-cream, and wear

* It has been purloined by fifty different scribblers who were too poor to invent a fancy but not ashamed to steal one.—M. T.

white linen clothes, and pant and perspire, at eight or nine
o'clock in the morning, and then take the cars, and at noon
put on your furs and your skates, and go skimming over frozen

SACRAMENTO.   THREE HOURS AWAY.

Donner Lake, seven thousand feet above the valley, among
snow banks fifteen feet deep, and in the shadow of grand
mountain peaks that lift their frosty crags ten thousand feet
above the level of the sea.   There is a transition for you!
Where will you find another like it in the Western hemis-
phere?   And some of us have swept around snow-walled
curves of the Pacific Railroad in that vicinity, six thousand
feet above the sea, and looked down as the birds do, upon the
deathless Summer of the Sacramento Valley, with its fruitful
fields, its feathery foliage, its silver streams, all slumbering in
the mellow haze of its enchanted atmosphere, and all infinitely
softened and spiritualized by distance—a dreamy, exquisite
glimpse of fairyland, made all the more charming and striking
that it was caught through a forbidden gateway of ice and
snow, and savage crags and precipices.

CHAPTER LVII.

IT was in this Sacramento Valley, just referred to, that a deal of the most lucrative of the early gold mining was done, and you may still see, in places, its grassy slopes and levels torn and guttered and disfigured by the avaricious spoilers of fifteen and twenty years ago. You may see such disfigurements far and wide over California—and in some such places, where only meadows and forests are visible—not a living creature, not a house, no stick or stone or remnant of a ruin, and not a sound, not even a whisper to disturb the Sabbath stillness—you will find it hard to believe that there stood at one time a fiercely-flourishing little city, of two thousand or three thousand souls, with its newspaper, fire company, brass band, volunteer militia, bank, hotels, noisy Fourth of July processions and speeches, gambling hells crammed with tobacco smoke, profanity, and rough-bearded men of all nations and colors, with tables heaped with gold dust sufficient for the revenues of a German principality—streets crowded and rife with business—town lots worth four hundred dollars a front foot—labor, laughter, music, dancing, swearing, fighting, shooting, stabbing—a bloody inquest and a man for breakfast every morning—*everything* that delights and adorns existence—all the appointments and appurtenances of a thriving and prosperous and promising young city,—and *now* nothing is left of it all but a lifeless, homeless solitude. The men are gone, the houses have vanished, even the *name* of the place is forgotten. In no other land, in modern times, have towns so absolutely died and disappeared, as in the old mining regions of California.

It was a driving, vigorous, restless population in those days. It was a *curious* population. It was the *only* population of the kind that the world has ever seen gathered together, and it is not likely that the world will ever see its like again. For, observe, it was an assemblage of two hundred thousand *young* men—not simpering, dainty, kid-gloved weaklings, but stalwart, muscular, dauntless young braves, brimful of push and energy, and royally endowed with every attribute that goes to make up a peerless and magnificent manhood—the very pick and choice of the world's glorious ones. No women, no children, no gray and stooping veterans,—none but erect, bright-eyed, quick-moving, strong-handed young giants—the strangest population, the finest population, the most gallant host that ever trooped down the startled solitudes of an unpeopled land. And where are they now? Scattered to the ends of the earth—or prematurely aged and decrepit—or shot or stabbed in street affrays—or dead of disappointed hopes and broken hearts—all gone, or nearly all—victims devoted upon the altar of the golden calf—the noblest holocaust that ever wafted its sacrificial incense heavenward. It is pitiful to think upon.

It was a splendid population—for all the slow, sleepy, sluggish-brained sloths staid at home—you never find that sort of people among pioneers—you cannot build pioneers out of that sort of material. It was that population that gave to California a name for getting up astounding enterprises and rushing them through with a magnificent dash and daring and a recklessness of cost or consequences, which she bears unto this day—and when she projects a new surprise, the grave world smiles as usual, and says "Well, that is California all over."

But they were rough in those times! They fairly reveled in gold, whisky, fights, and fandangoes, and were unspeakably happy. The honest miner raked from a hundred to a thousand dollars out of his claim a day, and what with the gambling dens and the other entertainments, he hadn't a

cent the next morning, if he had any sort of luck. They
cooked their own bacon and beans, sewed on their own
buttons, washed their own shirts—blue woollen ones; and if
a man wanted a fight on his hands without any annoying
delay, all he had to do was to appear in public in a white
shirt or a stove-pipe hat, and he would be accommodated. For
those people hated aristocrats. They had a particular and
malignant animosity toward what they called a "biled shirt."

It was a wild, free, disorderly, grotesque society! *Men*—
only swarming hosts of stalwart *men*—nothing juvenile, nothing feminine, visible anywhere!

In those days miners would flock in crowds to catch a
glimpse of that rare and blessed spectacle, a woman! Old

"FETCH HER OUT."

inhabitants tell how, in a certain camp, the news went abroad
early in the morning that a woman was come! They had
seen a calico dress hanging out of a wagon down at the
camping-ground—sign of emigrants from over the great plains.
Everybody went down there, and a shout went up when an

actual, bona fide dress was discovered fluttering in the wind! The male emigrant was visible. The miners said:

"Fetch her out!"

He said: "It is my wife, gentlemen—she is sick—we have been robbed of money, provisions, everything, by the Indians—we want to rest."

"Fetch her out! We've got to see her!"

"But, gentlemen, the poor thing, she—"

"FETCH HER OUT!"

He "fetched her out," and they swung their hats and sent up three rousing cheers and a tiger; and they crowded around and gazed at her, and touched her dress, and listened to her voice with the look of men who listened to a *memory* rather than a present reality—and then they collected twenty-five hundred dollars in gold and gave it to the man, and swung their hats again and gave three more cheers, and went home satisfied.

Once I dined in San Francisco with the family of a pioneer, and talked with his daughter, a young lady whose first experience in San Francisco was an adventure, though she herself did not remember it, as she was only two or three years old at the time. Her father said that, after landing from the ship, they were walking up the street, a servant lead-

"WELL, IF IT AIN'T A CHILD!"

ing the party with the little girl in her arms. And presently

27†

a huge miner, bearded, belted, spurred, and bristling with deadly weapons—just down from a long campaign in the mountains, evidently—barred the way, stopped the servant, and stood gazing, with a face all alive with gratification and astonishment. Then he said, reverently:

"Well, if it ain't a child!" And then he snatched a little leather sack out of his pocket and said to the servant:

"There's a hundred and fifty dollars in dust, there, and I'll give it to you to let me kiss the child!"

That anecdote is *true*.

But see how things change. Sitting at that dinner-table, listening to that anecdote, if I had offered double the money for the privilege of kissing the same child, I would have been refused. Seventeen added years have far more than doubled the price.

And while upon this subject I will remark that once in Star City, in the Humboldt Mountains, I took my place in a sort of long, post-office single file of miners, to patiently await my chance to peep through a crack in the cabin and get a sight of the splendid new sensation—a genuine, live Woman! And at the end of half of an hour my turn came, and I put my eye to the crack, and there she was, with one arm akimbo, and tossing flap-jacks in a frying-pan with the other. And she was one hundred and sixty-five* years old, and hadn't a tooth in her head.

* Being in calmer mood, now, I voluntarily knock off a hundred from that.—M. T.

CHAPTER LVIII.

FOR a few months I enjoyed what to me was an entirely new phase of existence—a butterfly idleness; nothing to do, nobody to be responsible to, and untroubled with financial uneasiness. I fell in love with the most cordial and sociable city in the Union. After the sage-brush and alkali deserts of Washoe, San Francisco was Paradise to me. I lived at the best hotel, exhibited my clothes in the most conspicuous places, infested the opera, and learned to seem enraptured with music which oftener afflicted my ignorant ear than enchanted it, if I had had the vulgar honesty to confess it. However, I suppose I was not greatly worse than the most of my countrymen in that. I had longed to be a butterfly, and I was one at last. I attended private parties in sumptuous evening dress, simpered and aired my graces like a born beau, and polked and schottisched with a step peculiar to myself—and the kangaroo. In a word, I kept the due state of a man worth a hundred thousand dollars (prospectively,) and likely to reach absolute affluence when that silvermine sale should be ultimately achieved in the East. I spent money with a free hand, and meantime watched the stock sales with an interested eye and looked to see what might happen in Nevada.

Something very important happened. The property holders of Nevada voted against the State Constitution; but the folks who had nothing to lose were in the majority, and carried the measure over their heads. But after all it did not immediately look like a disaster, though unquestionably it was one.

I hesitated, calculated the chances, and then concluded not to sell. Stocks went on rising; speculation went mad; bankers, merchants, lawyers, doctors, mechanics, laborers, even the

THE GRACE OF A KANGAROO.

very washerwomen and servant girls, were putting up their earnings on silver stocks, and every sun that rose in the morning went down on paupers enriched and rich men beggared. What a gambling carnival it was! Gould and Curry soared to six thousand three hundred dollars a foot! And then—all of a sudden, out went the bottom and everything and everybody went to ruin and destruction! The wreck was complete. The bubble scarcely left a microscopic moisture behind it. I was an early beggar and a thorough one. My hoarded stocks were not worth the paper they were printed on. I threw them all away. I, the cheerful idiot that had been squandering money like water, and thought myself beyond the reach of misfortune, had not now as much as fifty dollars when I gathered together my various debts and paid them. I removed from the hotel to a very private boarding house. I took a reporter's berth and went to work. I was not entirely broken in spirit, for I was building confidently on the sale of the silver mine in the east. But I could not hear from Dan. My letters miscarried or were not answered.

One day I did not feel vigorous and remained away from the office. The next day I went down toward noon as usual, and found a note on my desk which had been there twenty-four hours. It was signed "Marshall"—the Virginia reporter—and contained a request that I should call at the hotel and see him and a friend or two that night, as they would sail for the east in the morning. A postscript added that their errand was a big mining speculation! I was hardly ever so sick in my life. I abused myself for leaving Virginia and entrusting to another man a matter I ought to have attended to myself; I abused myself for remaining away from the office on the one day of all the year that I should have been there. And thus berating myself I trotted a mile to the steamer wharf and arrived just in time to be too late. The ship was in the stream and under way.

I comforted myself with the thought that may be the speculation would amount to nothing—poor comfort at best—and then went back to my slavery, resolved to put up with my thirty-five dollars a week and forget all about it.

A month afterward I enjoyed my first earthquake. It was one which was long called the "great" earthquake, and is doubtless so distinguished till this day. It was just after noon, on a bright October day. I was coming down Third street. The only objects in motion anywhere in sight in that thickly built and populous quarter, were a man in a buggy behind me, and a street car wending slowly up the cross street. Otherwise, all

DREAMS DISSIPATED.

was solitude and a Sabbath stillness. As I turned the corner, around a frame house, there was a great rattle and jar, and it occurred to me that here was an item!—no doubt a fight in that house. Before I could turn and seek the door, there came a really terrific shock; the ground seemed to roll under me in waves, interrupted by a violent joggling up and down, and there was a heavy grinding noise as of brick houses rubbing together. I fell up against the frame house and hurt my elbow. I knew what it was, now, and from mere reportorial instinct, nothing else, took out my watch and noted the time of day; at that moment a third and still severer shock came, and as I reeled about on the pavement trying to keep my footing, I saw a sight! The entire front of a tall four-story brick building in Third street sprung outward like a door and fell sprawling across the street, raising a dust like a great volume of smoke! And here came the buggy—overboard went the man, and in

THE "ONE-HORSE SHAY" OUT-DONE.

less time than I can tell it the vehicle was distributed in small fragments along three hundred yards of street. One could have fancied that somebody had fired a charge of chair-rounds and rags down the thoroughfare. The street car had stopped, the horses were rearing and plunging, the passengers were pouring out at both ends, and one fat man had crashed half way through a glass window on one side of the car, got wedged fast and was squirming and screaming like an impaled madman.

Every door, of every house, as far as the eye could reach, was vomiting a stream of human beings; and almost before one could execute a wink and begin another, there was a massed multitude of people stretching in endless procession down every street my position commanded. Never was solemn solitude turned into teeming life quicker.

Of the wonders wrought by "the great earthquake," these were all that came under my eye; but the tricks it did, elsewhere, and far and wide over the town, made toothsome gossip for nine days.

HARD ON THE INNOCENTS.

DRY BONES SHAKEN.

The destruction of property was trifling—the injury to it was wide-spread and somewhat serious.

The "curiosities" of the earthquake were simply endless. Gentlemen and ladies who were sick, or were taking a siesta, or had dissipated till a late hour and were making up lost sleep, thronged into the public streets in all sorts of queer apparel, and some without any at all. One woman who had been washing a naked child, ran down the street holding it by the ankles as if it were a dressed turkey. Prominent citizens who were supposed to keep the Sabbath strictly, rushed out of saloons in their shirt-sleeves, with billiard cues in their hands. Dozens of men with necks swathed in napkins, rushed from barber-shops, lathered to the eyes or with one cheek clean shaved and the other still bearing a hairy stubble. Horses broke from stables, and a frightened dog rushed up a short attic ladder and out on to a roof, and when his scare was over had not the nerve to go down again the same way he had gone up. A

"OH, WHAT SHALL I DO?"

prominent editor flew down stairs, in the principal hotel, with nothing on but one brief undergarment—met a chambermaid, and exclaimed:

"Oh, what *shall* I do! Where shall I go!"

She responded with naive serenity:

"If you have no choice, you might try a clothing-store!"

A certain foreign consul's lady was the acknowledged leader of fashion, and every time she appeared in anything new or extraordinary, the ladies in the vicinity made a raid on their husbands' purses and arrayed themselves similarly. One man who had suffered considerably and growled accordingly, was standing at the window when the shocks came, and the next instant the consul's wife, just out of the bath, fled by with no ot'.er apology for clothing than—a bath-towel! The sufferer rose superior to the terrors of the earthquake, and said to his wife:

"Now *that* is something *like*! Get out your towel my dear!"

The plastering that fell from ceilings in San Francisco that day, would have covered several acres of ground. For some days afterward, groups of eyeing and pointing men stood about many a building, looking at long zig-zag cracks that extended from the eaves to the ground. Four feet of the tops of three chimneys on one house were broken square off and turned around in such a way as to completely stop the draft. A crack a hundred feet long gaped open six inches wide in the middle of one street and then shut together again

"GET OUT YOUR TOWEL, MY DEAR."

with such force, as to ridge up the meeting earth like a slender grave. A lady sitting in her rocking and quaking parlor, saw the wall part at the ceiling, open and shut twice, like a mouth, and then-drop the end of a brick on the floor like a tooth. She was a woman easily disgusted with foolishness, and she arose and went out of there. One lady who was coming down stairs was astonished to see a bronze Hercules lean forward on its pedestal as if to strike her with its club. They both reached the bottom of the flight at the same time,—the woman insensible from the fright. Her child, born some little time afterward, was club-footed. However—on second thought,—if the reader sees any coincidence in this, he must do it at his own risk.

The first shock brought down two or three huge organ-pipes in one of the churches. The minister, with uplifted hands, was just closing the services. He glanced up, hesitated, and said:

"However, we will omit the benediction!"—and the next instant there was a vacancy in the atmosphere where he had stood.

After the first shock, an Oakland minister said:

"WE WILL OMIT THE BENEDICTION.

"Keep your seats! There is no better place to die than this "—

And added, after the third:

"But outside is good enough!" He then skipped out at the back door.

Such another destruction of mantel ornaments and toilet bottles as the earthquake created, San Francisco never saw before. There was hardly a girl or a matron in the city but suffered losses of this kind. Suspended pictures were thrown down, but oftener still, by a curious freak of the earthquake's humor, they were whirled completely around with their faces to the wall! There was great difference of opinion, at first, as to the course or direction the earthquake traveled, but water that splashed out of various tanks and buckets settled that. Thousands of people were made so sea-sick by the rolling and pitching of floors and streets that they were weak and bed-ridden for hours, and some few for even days afterward.—Hardly an individual escaped nausea entirely.

The queer earthquake—episodes that formed the staple of

San Francisco gossip for the next week would fill a much larger book than this, and so I will diverge from the subject.

By and by, in the due course of things, I picked up a copy of the *Enterprise* one day, and fell under this cruel blow :

NEVADA MINES IN NEW YORK.—G. M. Marshall, Sheba Hurs and Amos H. Rose, who left San Francisco last July for New York City, with ores from mines in Pine Wood District, Humboldt County, and on the Reese River range, have disposed of a mine containing six thousand feet and called the Pine Mountains Consolidated, for the sum of $3,000,000. The stamps on the deed, which is now on its way to Humboldt County, from New York, for record, amounted to $3,000, which is said to be the largest amount of stamps ever placed on one document. A working capital of $1,000,000 has been paid into the treasury, and machinery has already been purchased for a large quartz mill, which will be put up as soon as possible. The stock in this company is all full paid and entirely unassessable. The ores of the mines in this district somewhat resemble those of the Sheba mine in Humboldt. Sheba Hurst, the discoverer of the mines, with his friends corralled all the best leads and all the land and timber they desired before making public their whereabouts. Ores from there, assayed in this city, showed them to be exceedingly rich in silver and gold—silver predominating. There is an abundance of wood and water in the District. We are glad to know that New York capital has been enlisted in the development of the mines of this region. Having seen the ores and assays, we are satisfied that the mines of the District are very valuable—anything but wild-cat.

Once more native imbecility had carried the day, and I had lost a million ! It was the "blind lead" over again.

Let us not dwell on this miserable matter. If I were inventing these things, I could be wonderfully humorous over them ; but they are too true to be talked of with hearty levity, even at this distant day.* Suffice it that I so lost heart, and so yielded myself up to repinings and sighings and foolish regrets, that I neglected my duties and became about worthless, as a reporter for a brisk newspaper. And at last one of the proprietors took me aside, with a charity I still remember with considerable respect, and gave me an opportunity to resign my berth and so save myself the disgrace of a dismissal.

*True, and yet not exactly as given in the above figures, possibly. I saw Marshall, months afterward, and although he had plenty of money he did not claim to have captured an entire *million*. In fact I gathered that he had not then received $50,000. Beyond that figure his fortune appeared to consist of uncertain vast expectations rather than prodigious certainties. However, when the above item appeared in print I put full faith in it, and incontinently wilted and went to seed under it.

CHAPTER LIX.

FOR a time I wrote literary screeds for the *Golden Era.*
C. H. Webb had established a very excellent literary
weekly called the *Californian*, but high merit was no guaranty
of success; it languished, and he sold out to three printers, and
Bret Harte became editor at $20 a week, and I was employed
to contribute an article a week at $12. But the journal still
languished, and the printers sold out to Captain Ogden, a rich
man and a pleasant gentleman who chose to amuse himself
with such an expensive luxury without much caring about the
cost of it. When he grew tired of the novelty, he re-sold to
the printers, the paper presently died a peaceful death, and I was
out of work again. I would not mention these things but for
the fact that they so aptly illustrate the ups and downs that
characterize life on the Pacific coast. A man could hardly stumble into such a variety of queer vicissitudes in any other
country.

For two months my sole occupation was avoiding acquaintances; for during that time I did not earn a penny, or buy an
article of any kind, or pay my board. I became a very adept
at "slinking." I slunk from back street to back street, I slunk
away from approaching faces that looked familiar, I slunk to my
meals, ate them humbly and with a mute apology for every
mouthful I robbed my generous landlady of, and at midnight,
after wanderings that were but slinkings away from cheerfulness and light, I slunk to my bed. I felt meaner, and lowlier
and more despicable than the worms. During all this time I

had but one piece of money—a silver ten cent piece—and I held to it and would not spend it on any account, lest the consciousness coming strong upon me that I was *entirely* penniless, might suggest suicide. I had pawned every thing but the clothes I had on; so I clung to my dime desperately, till it was smooth with handling.

However, I am forgetting. I did have one other occupation beside that of "slinking." It was the entertaining of a collector (and being entertained by him,) who had in his hands the Virginia banker's bill for the forty-six dollars which I had loaned my schoolmate, the "Prodigal." This man used to call regularly once a week and dun me, and sometimes oftener. He did it from sheer force of habit, for he knew he could get nothing. He would get out

SLINKING.

his bill, calculate the interest for me, at five per cent a month, and show me clearly that there was no attempt at fraud in it and no mistakes; and then plead, and argue and dun with all his might for any sum—any little trifle—even a dollar—even half a dollar, on account. Then his duty was accomplished and his conscience free. He immediately dropped the subject there always; got out a couple of cigars and divided, put his feet in the window, and then we would have a long, luxurious talk about everything and everybody, and he would furnish me a world of curious dunning adventures out of the ample store in his memory. By and by he would clap his hat on his head, shake hands and say briskly:

"Well, business is business—can't stay with you always!"— and was off in a second.

The idea of pining for a dun! And yet I used to long for

him to come, and would get as uneasy as any mother if the day
went by without his visit, when I was expecting him.   But he
never collected that bill, at last nor any part of it.   I lived to
pay it to the banker myself.

Misery loves company.   Now and then at night, in out-of-the
way, dimly lighted places, I found myself happening on another
child of misfortune.   He looked so seedy and forlorn, so homeless and friendless and forsaken, that I yearned toward him as
a brother.   I wanted to claim kinship with him and go about
and enjoy our wretchedness together.   The drawing toward
each other must have been mutual; at any rate we got to falling together oftener, though still seemingly by accident; and
although we did not speak or evince any recognition, I think
the dull anxiety passed out of both of us when we saw each
other, and then for several hours we would idle along contentedly, wide apart, and glancing furtively in at home lights and
fireside gatherings, out of the night shadows, and very much
enjoying our dumb companionship.

Finally we spoke, and were inseparable after that.   For our
woes were identical, almost.   He had been a reporter too, and
lost his berth, and this was his experience, as nearly as I can
recollect it.   After losing his berth, he had gone down, down,
down, with never a halt: from a boarding house on Russian
Hill to a boarding house in Kearney street; from thence to
Dupont; from thence to a low sailor den; and from thence to lodgings in goods boxes and empty hogsheads near the wharves.
Then, for a while, he had gained a meagre living by sewing up
bursted sacks of grain on the piers; when that failed he had
found food here and there as chance threw it in his way.   He
had ceased to show his face in daylight, now, for a reporter
knows everybody, rich and poor, high and low, and cannot well
avoid familiar faces in the broad light of day.

This mendicant Blucher—I call him that for convenience—
was a splendid creature.   He was full of hope, pluck and philosophy; he was well read and a man of cultivated taste; he
had a bright wit and was a master of satire; his kindliness and
his generous spirit made him royal in my eyes and changed his
curb-stone seat to a throne and his damaged hat to a crown.

He had an adventure, once, which sticks fast in my memory as the most pleasantly grotesque that ever touched my sympathies. He had been without a penny for two months. He had shirked about obscure streets, among friendly dim lights, till the thing had become second nature to him. But at last he was driven abroad in daylight. The cause was sufficient; *he had not tasted food for forty-eight hours*, and he could not endure the misery of his hunger in idle hiding. He came along a back street, glowering at the loaves in bake-shop windows, and feeling that he could trade his life away for a morsel to eat. The sight of the bread doubled his hunger; but it was good to look at it, any how, and imagine what one might do if one only had it. Presently, in the middle of the street he saw a shining spot—looked again—did not, and could not, believe his eyes—turned away, to try them, then looked again. It was a verity—no vain, hunger-inspired delusion—it was a silver dime! He snatched it— gloated over it; doubted it—bit it—found it genuine—choked his heart down, and smothered a halleluiah. Then he looked around—saw that nobody was looking at him—threw the dime down where it was before— walked away a few steps, and approached again, pretending he did not know it was there, so that

A PRIZE.

he could re-enjoy the luxury of finding it. He walked around it, viewing it from different points; then sauntered about with his hands in his pockets, looking up at the signs and now and then glancing at it and feeling the old thrill again. Finally he took it up, and went away, fondling it in his pocket. He idled through unfrequented streets, stopping in doorways and corners to take it out and look at it. By and by he went home to his lodgings—an empty queensware hogshead,—and employed himself till night trying to make up his mind what to buy with it. But it was hard to do. To get the most for it was the idea. He knew that at the Miner's Restaurant he could get a plate of beans and a piece of bread for ten cents; or a fish-ball and some few trifles, but they gave "no bread with one fish-ball" there. At French Pete's he could get a veal cutlet, plain, and some radishes and bread, for ten cents; or a cup of coffee—a pint at least—and a slice of bread; but the slice was not thick enough by the eighth of an inch, and sometimes they were still more criminal than that in the cutting of it. At seven o'clock his hunger was wolfish; and still his mind was not made up. He turned out and went up Merchant street, still ciphering; and chewing a bit of stick, as is the way of starving men. He passed before the lights of Martin's restaurant, the most aristo-

cratic in the city, and stopped. It was a place where he had often dined, in better days, and Martin knew him well. Standing aside, just out of the range of the light, he worshiped the quails and steaks in the show window, and imagined that may be the fairy times were not gone yet and some prince in disguise would come along presently and tell him to go in there and take whatever he wanted. He chewed his stick with a hungry interest as he warmed to his subject. Just at this juncture he was conscious of some one at his side, sure enough;

A LOOK IN AT THE WINDOW.

and then a finger touched his arm. He looked up, over his shoulder, and saw an apparition—a very allegory of Hunger! It was a man six feet high, gaunt, unshaven, hung with rags; with a haggard face and sunken cheeks, and eyes that pleaded piteously. This phantom said:

"Come with me—please."

He locked his arm in Blucher's and walked up the street to where the passengers were few and the light not strong, and then facing about, put out his hands in a beseeching way, and said:

"Friend—stranger—look at me! Life is easy to you—you go about, placid and content, as I did once, in my day—you have been in there, and eaten your sumptuous supper, and picked your teeth, and hummed your tune, and thought your pleasant

DO IT STRANGER.

thoughts, and said to yourself it is a good world—but you've never *suffered*! You don't know what trouble is—you don't know what misery is—nor hunger! Look at me! Stranger have pity on a poor friendless, homeless dog! As God is my judge,
28†

I have not tasted food for eight and forty hours!—look in my eyes and see if I lie! Give me the least trifle in the world to keep me from starving—anything—twenty-five cents! Do it, stranger—do it, *please*. It will be nothing to you, but life to me. Do it, and I will go down on my knees and lick the dust before you! I will kiss your footprints—I will worship the very ground you walk on! Only twenty-five cents! I am famishing—perishing—starving by inches! For God's sake don't desert me!"

Blucher was bewildered—and touched, too—stirred to the depths. He reflected. Thought again. Then an idea struck him, and he said:

"Come with me."

He took the outcast's arm, walked him down to Martin's restaurant, seated him at a marble table, placed the bill of fare before him, and said:

"Order what you want, friend. Charge it to me, Mr. Martin."

"All right, Mr. Blucher," said Martin.

Then Blucher stepped back and leaned against the counter and watched the man stow away cargo after cargo of buckwheat cakes at seventy-five cents a plate; cup after cup of coffee, and porter house steaks worth two dollars apiece; and when six dollars and a half's worth of destruction had been accomplished, and the stranger's hunger appeased, Blucher went down to French Pete's, bought a veal cutlet plain, a slice of bread, and three radishes, with his dime, and set to and feasted like a king!

Take the episode all around, it was as odd as any that can be culled from the myriad curiosities of Californian life, perhaps.

CHAPTER LX.

BY and by, an old friend of mine, a miner, came down from one of the decayed mining camps of Tuolumne, California, and I went back with him. We lived in a small cabin on a verdant hillside, and there were not five other cabins in view over the wide expanse of hill and forest. Yet a flourishing city of two or three thousand population had occupied this grassy dead solitude during the flush times of twelve or fifteen years before, and where our cabin stood had once been the heart of the teeming hive, the centre of the city. When the mines gave out the town fell into decay, and in a few years wholly disappeared—streets, dwellings, shops, everything—and left no sign. The grassy slopes were as green and smooth and desolate of life as if they had never been disturbed. The mere handful of miners still remaining, had seen the town spring up, spread, grow and flourish in its pride; and they had seen it sicken and die, and pass away like a dream. With it their hopes had died, and their zest of life. They had long ago resigned themselves to their exile, and ceased to correspond with their distant friends or turn longing eyes toward their early homes. They had accepted banishment, forgotten the world and been forgotten of the world. They were far from telegraphs and railroads, and they stood, as it were, in a living grave, dead to the events that stirred the globe's great populations, dead to the common interests of men, isolated and outcast from brotherhood with their kind. It was the most singular, and almost the most touching and melancholy exile that fancy can imagine.—One of my associates in this locality, for

two or three months, was a man who had had a university education; but now for eighteen years he had decayed there by
inches, a bearded, rough-clad, clay-stained miner, and at times,

among his sighings and solilo-
quizings, he unconsciously in-
terjected vaguely remembered
Latin and Greek sentences—
dead and musty tongues, meet
vehicles for the thoughts of one
whose dreams were all of the
past, whose life was a failure;
a tired man, burdened with the
present, and indifferent to the
future; a man without ties,
hopes, interests, waiting for
rest and the end.

In that one little corner of
California is found a species of
mining which is seldom or never mentioned in print. It is
called "pocket mining" and I

THE OLD COLLEGIATE.

am not aware that any of it is done outside of that little corner.
The gold is not evenly distributed through the surface dirt, as
in ordinary placer mines, but is collected in little spots, and
they are very wide apart and exceedingly hard to find, but when
you do find one you reap a rich and sudden harvest. There
are not now more than twenty pocket miners in that entire little region. I think I know every one of them personally. I
have known one of them to hunt patiently about the hill-sides
every day for eight months without finding gold enough to
make a snuff-box—his grocery bill running up relentlessly all
the time—and then find a pocket and take out of it two
thousand dollars in two dips of his shovel. I have known him
to take out three thousand dollars in two hours, and go and
pay up every cent of his indebtedness, then enter on a dazzling
spree that finished the last of his treasure before the night was
gone. And the next day he bought his groceries on credit as
usual, and shouldered his pan and shovel and went off to the

hills hunting pockets again happy and content. This is the
most fascinating of all the different kinds of mining, and furnishes
a very handsome percentage of victims to the lunatic asylum.

Pocket hunting is an ingenious process. You take a spadeful of earth from the hill-side and put it in a large tin pan and
dissolve and wash it gradually away till nothing is left but a
teaspoonful of fine sediment. Whatever gold was in that earth
has remained, because, being the heaviest, it has sought the
bottom. Among the sediment you will find half a dozen yellow
particles no larger than pin-heads. You are delighted. You
move off to one side and wash another pan. If you find gold
again, you move to one side further, and wash a third pan. If
you find *no* gold this time, you
are delighted again, because you
know you are on the right scent.
You lay an imaginary plan,
shaped like a fan, with its handle up the hill—for just where
the end of the handle is, you
argue that the rich deposit lies
hidden, whose vagrant grains of
gold have escaped and been
washed down the hill, spreading farther and farther apart
as they wandered. And so you
proceed up the hill, washing
the earth and narrowing your
lines every time the absence of
gold in the pan shows that you
are outside the spread of the fan;

STRIKING A POCKET.

and at last, twenty yards up the hill your lines have converged
to a point—a single foot from that point you cannot find any
gold. Your breath comes short and quick, you are feverish
with excitement; the dinner-bell may ring its clapper off, you
pay no attention; friends may die, weddings transpire, houses
burn down, they are nothing to you; you sweat and dig and
delve with a frantic interest—and all at once you strike it!
Up comes a spadeful of earth and quartz that is all lovely with

soiled lumps and leaves ánd sprays of gold. Sometimes that one spadeful is all—$500. Sometimes the nest contains $10,000, and it takes you three or four days to get it all out. The pocket-miners tell of one nest that yielded $60,000 and two men exhausted it in two weeks, and then sold the ground for $10,-000 to a party who never got $300 out of it afterward.

The hogs are good pocket hunters. All the summer they root around the bushes, and turn up a thousand little piles of dirt, and then the miners long for the rains; for the rains beat upon these little piles and wash them down and expose the gold, possibly right over a pocket. Two pockets were found in this way by the same man in one day. One had $5,000 in it and the other $8,000. That man could appreciate it, for he hadn't had a cent for about a year.

In Tuolumne lived two miners who used to go to the neighboring village in the afternoon and return every night with household supplies. Part of the distance they traversed a trail, and nearly always sat down to rest on a great boulder that lay beside the path. In the course of thirteen years they had worn that boulder tolerably smooth, sitting on it. By and by two vagrant Mexicans came along and occupied the seat. They began to amuse themselves by chipping off flakes from the boulder with a sledge-hammer. They examined one of these flakes and found it rich with gold. That boulder paid them $800 afterward. But the aggravating circumstance was that these " Greasers " knew that there must be more gold where that boulder came from, and so they went panning up the hill and found what was probably the richest pocket that region has yet produced. It took three months to exhaust it, and it yielded $120,000. The two American miners who used to sit on the boulder are poor yet, and they take turn about in getting up early in the morning to curse those Mexicans—and when it comes down to pure ornamental cursing, the native American is gifted above the sons of men.

I have dwelt at some length upon this matter of pocket mining because it is a subject that is seldom referred to in print, and therefore I judged that it would have for the reader that interest which naturally attaches to novelty.

CHAPTER LXI.

ONE of my comrades there—another of those victims of eighteen years of unrequited toil and blighted hopes—was one of the gentlest spirits that ever bore its patient cross in a weary exile: grave and simple Dick Baker, pocket-miner of Dead-House Gulch.—He was forty-six, gray as a rat, earnest, thoughtful, slenderly educated, slouchily dressed and clay-soiled, but his heart was finer metal than any gold his shovel ever brought to light—than any, indeed, that ever was mined or minted.

Whenever he was out of luck and a little down-hearted, he would fall to mourning over the loss of a wonderful cat he used to own (for where women and children are not, men of kindly impulses take up with pets, for they must love something). And he always spoke of the strange sagacity of that cat with the air of a man who believed in his secret heart that there was something human about it—may be even supernatural.

I heard him talking about this animal once. He said:

"Gentlemen, I used to have a cat here, by the name of Tom Quartz, which you'd a took an interest in I reckon—most any body would. I had him here eight year—and he was the re-markablest cat I ever see. He was a large gray one of the Tom specie, an' he had more hard, natchral sense than any man in this camp—'n' a *power* of dignity—he wouldn't let the Gov'ner of Californy be familiar with him. He never ketched a rat in his life—'peared to be above it. He never cared for nothing but mining. He knowed more about mining, that cat did, than any man *I* ever, ever see. You couldn't tell *him* noth'n' 'bout placer diggin's—'n' as for pocket mining, why he was just born for it. He would dig out after me an' Jim

TOM QUARTZ.

when we went over the hills prospect'n', and he would trot along behind us for as much as five mile, if we went so fur. An' he had the best judgment about mining ground—why you never see anything like it. When we went to work, he'd scatter a glance around, 'n' if he didn't think much of the indications, he would give a look as much as to say, 'Well, I'll have to get you to excuse *me*,' 'n' without another word he'd hyste his nose into the air 'n' shove for home. But if the ground suited him, he would lay low 'n' keep dark till the first pan was washed, 'n' then he would sidle up 'n' take a look, an' if there was about six or seven grains of gold *he* was satisfied—he didn't want no better prospect 'n' that—'n' then he would lay down on our coats and snore like a steamboat till we'd struck the pocket, an' then get up 'n' superintend. He was nearly lightnin' on superintending.

"Well, bye an' bye, up comes this yer quartz excitement. Every body was into it—every body was pick'n' 'n' blast'n' instead of shovelin' dirt on the hill side—every body was put'n' down a shaft instead of scrapin' the surface. Noth'n' would do Jim, but *we* must tackle the ledges, too, 'n' so we did. We commenced put'n' down a shaft, 'n' Tom Quartz he begin to wonder what in the Dickens it was all about. *He* hadn't ever seen any mining like that before, 'n' he was all upset, as you may say—he couldn't come to a right understanding of it no way—it was too many for *him*. He was down on it, too, you bet you—he was down on it powerful—'n' always appeared to consider it the cussedest foolishness out. But that cat, you know, was *always* agin new fangled arrangements—somehow he never could abide 'em. *You* know how it is with old habits.

But by an' by Tom Quartz begin to git sort of reconciled a little, though he never *could* altogether understand that eternal sinkin' of a shaft an' never pannin' out any thing. At last he got to comin' down in the shaft, hisself, to try to cipher it out. An' when he'd git the blues. 'n' feel kind o' scruffy, 'n' aggravated 'n' disgusted—knowin' as he did, that the bills was runnin' up all the time an' we warn't makin' a cent—he would curl up on a gunny sack in the corner an' go to sleep. Well, one day when the shaft was down about eight foot, the rock got so hard that we had to put in a blast—the first blast'n' we'd ever done since Tom Quartz was born. An' then we lit the fuse 'n' clumb out 'n' got off 'bout fifty yards—'n' forgot 'n' left Tom Quartz sound asleep on the gunny sack. In 'bout a minute we seen a puff of smoke bust up out of the hole, 'n' then everything let go with an awful crash, 'n' about four

AN ADVANTAGE TAKEN.

million ton of rocks 'n' dirt 'n' smoke 'n' splinters shot up 'bout a mile an' a half into the air, an' by George, right in the dead centre of it was old Tom Quartz a goin' end over end, an' a snortin' an' a sneez'n', an' a clawin' an' a reachin' for things like all possessed. But it warn't no use, you know, it warn't no use. An' that was the last we see of *him* for about two minutes 'n' a half, an' then all of a sudden it begin to rain rocks and rubbage, an' directly he come down ker-whop about ten foot off f'm where we stood Well, I reckon he was p'raps the orneriest lookin' beast you ever see. One ear was sot back on his neck, 'n' his tail was stove up, 'n' his eye-winkers was swinged off, 'n' he was all

AFTER AN EXCURSION.

blacked up with powder an' smoke, an' all sloppy with mud 'n' slush f'm one end to the other. Well sir, it warn't no use to try to apologize—we couldn't say a word. He took a sort of a disgusted look at his-self, 'n' then he looked at us— an' it was just exactly the same as if he had said—'Gents, may be *you* think it's smart to take advantage of a cat that 'ain't had no experience of quartz minin', but *I* think *different*' —an' then he turned on his heel 'n' marched off home without ever saying another word.

"That was jest his style. An' may be you won't believe it, but after that you never see a cat so prejudiced agin quartz mining as what he was. An' by an' bye when he *did* get to goin' down in the shaft agin, you'd 'a been astonished at his sagacity. The minute we'd tetch off a blast 'n' the fuse'd begin to sizzle, he'd give a look as much as to say : 'Well, I'll have to git you to excuse *me*,' an' it was surpris'n' the way he'd shin out of that hole 'n' go f'r a tree. Sagacity? It ain't no name for it. 'Twas *inspiration* !"

I said, " Well, Mr. Baker, his prejudice against quartz-mining *was* remarkable, considering how he came by it. Couldn't you ever cure him of it ?"

" *Cure him !* No! When Tom Quartz was sot once, he was *always* sot—and you might a blowed him up as much as three million times 'n' you'd never a broken him of his cussed prejudice agin quartz mining."

The affection and the pride that lit up Baker's face when he delivered this tribute to the firmness of his humble friend of other days, will always be a vivid memory with me.

At the end of two months we had never " struck " a pocket. We had panned up and down the hillsides till they looked plowed like a field ; we could have put in a crop of grain, then, but there would have been no way to get it to market. We got many good " prospects," but when the gold gave out in the pan and we dug down, hoping and longing, we found only emptiness—the pocket that should have been there was as barren as our own.—At last we shouldered our pans and shovels and struck out over the hills to try new localities. We prospected around Angel's Camp, in Calaveras county, during three weeks, but had no success. Then we wandered on foot among the mountains, sleeping under the trees at night, for the weather was mild, but still we remained as centless as the last rose of summer. That is a poor joke, but it is in pathetic harmony with the circumstances, since we were so poor ourselves. In accordance with the custom of the country, our door had always stood open and our board welcome to tramping miners—they drifted along nearly every day, dumped their paust shovels by the threshold and took " pot luck " with us—and now on our own tramp we never found cold hospitality.

Our wanderings were wide and in many directions ; and now I could give the reader a vivid description of the Big Trees and the marvels of the Yo Semite—but what has this reader done to me that I should persecute him ? I will deliver him into the hands of less conscientious tourists and take his blessing. Let me be charitable, though I fail in all virtues else.

Some of the phrases in the above are mining technicalities, purely, and may be a little obscure to the general reader. In "*placer diggings*" the gold is scattered all through the surface dirt; in "*pocket*" diggings it is concentrated in one little spot; in "*quartz*" the gold is in a solid, continuous vein of rock, enclosed between distinct walls of some other kind of stone—and this is the most laborious and expensive of all the different kinds of mining. "*Prospecting*" is hunting for a "*placer*"; "*indications*" are signs of its presence; "*panning out*" refers to the washing process by which the grains of gold are separated from the dirt; a "*prospect*" is what one finds in the first panful of dirt—and its value determines whether it is a good or a bad prospect, and whether it is worth while to tarry there or seek further.

CHAPTER LXII.

AFTER a three months' absence, I found myself in San Francisco again, without a cent. When my credit was about exhausted, (for I had become too mean and lazy, now, to work on a morning paper, and there were no vacancies on the evening journals,) I was created San Francisco correspondent of the *Enterprise*, and at the end of five months I was out of debt, but my interest in my work was gone; for my correspondence being a daily one, without rest or respite, I got unspeakably tired of it. I wanted another change. The vagabond instinct was strong upon me. Fortune favored and I got a new berth and a delightful one. It was to go down to the Sandwich Islands and write some letters for the Sacramento *Union*, an excellent journal and liberal with employés.

We sailed in the propeller *Ajax*, in the middle of winter. The almanac called it winter, distinctly enough, but the weather was a compromise between spring and summer. Six days out of port, it became summer altogether. We had some thirty passengers; among them a cheerful soul by the name of Williams, and three sea-worn old whaleship captains going down to join their vessels. These latter played euchre in the smoking room day and night, drank astonishing quantities of raw whisky without being in the least affected by it, and were the happiest people I think I ever saw. And then there was " the old Admiral—" a retired whaleman. He was a roaring, terrific combination of wind and lightning and thunder, and earnest, whole-souled profanity. But nevertheless he was tender-hearted as a girl. He was a raving, deafening, devastating typhoon, laying waste the cowering seas but with an unvexed refuge in the centre where all comers were safe and at rest. Nobody could know the "Admiral" without liking him; and in a sudden and dire emergency I think no friend of his would know which to choose—to be cursed by him or prayed for by a less efficient person.

His title of "Admiral" was more strictly "official" than any ever worn by a naval officer before or since, perhaps—for it was the voluntary offering of a whole nation, and came direct from the *people* themselves without any intermediate red tape—the people of the Sandwich Islands. It was a title that

THE THREE CAPTAINS.

came to him freighted with affection, and honor, and appreciation of his unpretending merit. And in testimony of the genuineness of the title it was publicly ordained that an exclusive flag should be devised for him and used solely to welome his coming and wave him God-speed in his going. From that time forth, whenever his ship was signaled in the offing, or he catted his anchor and stood out to sea, that ensign streamed from the royal halliards on the parliament house and the nation lifted their hats to it with spontaneous accord.

Yet he had never fired a gun or fought a battle in his life.

When I knew him on board the *Ajax*, he was seventy-two years old and had plowed the salt water sixty-one of them. For sixteen years he had gone in and out of the harbor of Honolulu in command of a whaleship, and for sixteen more had been captain of a San Francisco and Sandwich Island passenger packet and had never had an accident or lost a vessel. The simple natives knew him for a friend who never failed them, and regarded him as children regard a father. It was a dangerous thing to oppress them when the roaring Admiral was around.

Two years before I knew the Admiral, he had retired from the sea on a competence, and had sworn a colossal nine-jointed oath that he would "never go within *smelling* distance of the salt water again as long as he lived." And he had conscientiously kept it. That is to say, *he* considered he had kept it, and it would have been more than dangerous to suggest to him, even in the gentlest way, that making eleven long sea voyages, as a passenger, during the two years that had transpired since he "retired," was only keeping the general spirit of it and not the strict letter.

The Admiral knew only one narrow line of conduct to pursue in any and all cases where there was a fight, and that was to shoulder his way straight in without an inquiry as to the rights or the merits of it, and take the part of the weaker side.—And this was the reason why he was always sure to be present at the trial of any universally execrated criminal to oppress and intimidate the jury with a vindictive pantomime of what he would do to them if he ever caught them out of the box. And this was why harried cats and outlawed dogs that knew him confidently took sanctuary under his chair in time of trouble. In the beginning he was the most frantic and bloodthirsty Union man that drew breath in the shadow of the Flag; but the instant the Southerners began to go down before the sweep of the Northern armies, he ran up the Confederate colors and from that time till the end was a rampant and inexorable secessionist.

He hated intemperance with a more uncompromising ani-

mosity than any individual I have ever met, of either sex; and
he was never tired of storming against it and beseeching friends
and strangers alike to be wary and drink with moderation.
And yet if any creature had been guileless enough to intimate
that his absorbing nine gallons of "straight" whisky during
our voyage was any fraction short of rigid or inflexible abste-
miousness, in that self-same moment the old man would have
spun him to the uttermost parts of the earth in the whirlwind
of his wrath. Mind, I am not saying his whisky ever affected
his head or his legs, for it did not, in even the slightest degree.
He was a capacious container, but he did not hold enough for
that. He took a level tumblerful of whisky every morning before
he put his clothes on—" to sweeten his bilgewater," he said.—
He took another after he got the most of his clothes on, "to settle his mind and give him his bearings." He then shaved, and
put on a clean shirt; after which he recited the Lord's Prayer
in a fervent, thundering bass that shook the ship to her kelson
and suspended all conversation in the main cabin. Then, at
this stage, being invariably " by the head," or " by the stern,"
or " listed to port or starboard," he took one more to " put him
on an even keel so that he would mind his hellum and not
miss stays and go about, every time he came up in the wind."
—And now, his state-room door swung open and the sun of
his benignant face beamed redly out upon men and women and
children, and he roared his "Shipmets a'hoy!" in a way that
was calculated to wake the dead and precipitate the final resurrection; and forth he strode, a picture to look at and a presence to
enforce attention. Stalwart and portly; not a gray hair; broad-
brimmed slouch hat; semi-sailor toggery of blue navy flannel
—roomy and ample; a stately expanse of shirt-front and a liberal amount of black silk neck-cloth tied with a sailor knot;
large chain and imposing seals impending from his fob; awe-
inspiring feet, and " a hand like the hand of Providence," as
his whaling brethren expressed it; wrist-bands and sleeves
pushed back half way to the elbow, out of respect for the warm
weather, and exposing hairy arms, gaudy with red and blue
anchors, ships, and goddesses of liberty tattooed in India ink.

But these details were only secondary matters—his face was the lodestone that chained the eye. It was a sultry disk, glowing determinedly out through a weather beaten mask of mahogany, and studded with warts, seamed with scars, "blazed" all over with unfailing fresh slips of the razor; and with cheery eyes, under shaggy brows, contemplating the world from over the back of a gnarled crag of a nose that loomed vast and lonely out of the undulating immensity that spread away from its foundations. At his heels frisked the darling of his bachelor estate, his terrier "Fan," a creature no larger than a squirrel. The main part of his daily life was occupied in looking after "Fan," in a motherly way, and doctoring her for a hundred ailments which existed only in his imagination.

THE OLD ADMIRAL.

The Admiral seldom read newspapers; and when he did he never believed anything they said. He read nothing, and believed in nothing, but "The Old Guard," a secession periodical published in New York. He carrried a dozen copies of it with him, always, and referred to them for all required information. If it was not there, he supplied it himself, out of a bountiful fancy, inventing history, names, dates, and every thing else necessary to make his point good in an argument. Consequently he was a formidable antagonist in a dispute. Whenever he swung clear of the record and began to create history, the enemy was helpless and had to surrender. Indeed, the enemy could not keep from betraying some little spark of indignation at his manufactured history—and when it came to indignation, that was the Admiral's very "best hold." He was always ready for a political argument, and if nobody started one he would do it himself. With his third retort his temper would begin to rise, and within five minutes he would be blowing a gale, and within fifteen his smoking-room audience would be utterly stormed away and the old man left solitary and alone, banging the table with his fist, kicking the chairs, and roaring

a hurricane of profanity. It got so, after a while, that whenever the Admiral approached, with politics in his eye, the passengers would drop out with quiet accord, afraid to meet him; and he would camp on a deserted field.

But he found his match at last, and before a full company. At one time or another, everybody had entered the lists against

DESERTED FIELD.

him and been routed, except the quiet passenger Williams. He had never been able to get an expression of opinion out of him on politics. But now, just as the Admiral drew near the door and the company were about to slip out, Williams said:

"Admiral, are you *certain* about that circumstance concerning the clergymen you mentioned the other day?"—referring to a piece of the Admiral's manufactured history.

Every one was amazed at the man's rashness. The idea of deliberately inviting annihilation was a thing incomprehensible. The retreat came to a halt; then everybody sat down again wondering, to await the upshot of it. The Admiral himself was as surprised as any one. He paused in the door, with his red handkerchief half raised to his sweating face, and contemplated the daring reptile in the corner.

29†

" *Certain* of it? Am I *certain* of it? Do you think I've been lying about it? What do you take me for? Anybody that don't know that circumstance, don't know anything; a child ought to know it. Read up your history! Read it up —— —— —— ——, and don't come asking a man if he's *certain* about a bit of A B C stuff that the very southern niggers know all about."

Here the Admiral's fires began to wax hot, the atmosphere thickened, the coming earthquake rumbled, he began to thunder and lighten. Within three minutes his volcano was in full irruption and he was discharging flames and ashes of indignation, belching black volumes of foul history aloft, and vomiting red-hot torrents of profanity from his crater. Meantime Williams sat silent, and apparently deeply and earnestly interested in what the old man was saying. By and by, when the lull came, he said in the most deferential way, and with the gratified air of a man who has had a mystery cleared up which had been puzzling him uncomfortably :

" *Now* I understand it. I always thought I knew that piece of history well enough, but was still afraid to trust it, because there was not that convincing particularity about it that one likes to have in history ; but when you mentioned every name, the other day, and every date, and every little circumstance, in their just order and sequence, I said to myself, *this* sounds something like—*this* is history—*this* is putting it in a shape that gives a man confidence ; and I said to myself afterward, I will just ask the Admiral if he is perfectly certain about the details, and if he is I will come out and thank him for clearing this matter up for me. And that is what I want to do now— for until you set that matter right it was nothing but just a confusion in my mind, without head or tail to it."

Nobody ever saw the Admiral look so mollified before, and so pleased. Nobody had ever received his bogus history as gospel before; its genuineness had always been called in question either by words or looks; but here was a man that not only swallowed it all down, but was grateful for the dose. He was taken a back; he hardly knew what to say; even his profanity failed him. Now, Williams continued, modestly and earnestly :

"But Admiral, in saying that this was the first stone thrown, and that this precipitated the war, you have overlooked a circumstance which you are perfectly familiar with, but which has escaped your memory. Now I grant you that what you have stated is correct in every detail—to wit: that on the 16th of October, 1860, two Massachusetts clergymen, named Waite and Granger, went in disguise to the house of John Moody, in Rockport, at dead of night, and dragged forth two southern women and their two little children, and after tarring and feathering them conveyed them to Boston and burned them alive in the State House square; and I also grant your proposition that this deed is what led to the secession of South Carolina on the 20th of December following. Very well." [Here the company were pleasantly surprised to hear Williams proceed to come back at the Admiral with his own invincible weapon —clean, pure, *manufactured history*, without a word of truth in it.] "Very well, I say. But Admiral, why overlook the Willis and Morgan case in South Carolina? You are too well informed a man not to know all about that circumstance. Your arguments and your conversations have shown you to be intimately conversant with every detail of this national quarrel. You develop matters of history every day that show plainly that you are no smatterer in it, content to nibble about the surface, but a man who has searched the depths and possessed yourself of everything that has a bearing upon the great question. Therefore, let me just recall to your mind that Willis and Morgan case—though I see by your face that the whole thing is already passing through your memory at this moment. On the 12th of August, 1860, *two months* before the Waite and Granger affair, two South Carolina clergymen, named John H. Morgan and Winthrop L. Willis, one a Methodist and the other an Old School Baptist, disguised themselves, and went at midnight to the house of a planter named Thompson— Archibald F. Thompson, Vice President under Thomas Jefferson,—and took thence, at midnight, his widowed aunt, (a Northern woman,) and her adopted child, an orphan named

Mortimer Highie, afflicted with epilepsy and suffering at the time from white swelling on one of his legs, and compelled to walk on crutches in consequence ; and the two ministers, in spite of the pleadings of the victims, dragged them to the bush, tarred and feathered them, and afterward burned them at the stake in the city of Charleston.   You remember perfectly well what a stir it made ; you remember perfectly well that even the Charleston *Courier* stigmatized the act as being unpleasant, of questionable propriety, and scarcely justifiable, and likewise that it would not be matter of surprise if retaliation ensued. And you remember also, that this thing was the *cause* of the Massachusetts outrage.   Who, indeed, were the two Massachusetts ministers ? and who were the two Southern women they burned ?   I do not need to remind *you*, Admiral, with your intimate knowledge of history, that Waite was the nephew of the woman burned in Charleston ; that Granger was her cousin in the second degree, and that the woman they burned in Boston was the wife of John H. Morgan, and the still loved but divorced wife of Winthrop L. Willis.   Now, Admiral, it is only fair that you should acknowledge that the first provocation came from the Southern preachers and that the Northern ones were justified in retaliating.   In your arguments you never yet have shown the least disposition to withhold a just verdict or be in anywise unfair, when authoritative history condemned your position, and therefore I have no hesitation in asking you to take the original blame from the Massachusetts ministers, in this matter, and transfer it to the South Carolina clergymen where it justly belongs."

The Admiral was conquered.   This sweet spoken creature who swallowed his fraudulent history as if it were the bread of life ; basked in his furious blasphemy as if it were generous sunshine ; found only calm, even-handed justice in his rampart partisanship ; and flooded him with invented history so sugar-coated with flattery and deference that there was no rejecting it, was " too many " for him.   He stammered some awkward, profane sentences about the —— —— —— —— Willis and

Morgan business having escaped his memory, but that he "remembered it now," and then, under pretence of giving Fan some medicine for an imaginary cough, drew out of the battle and went away, a vanquished man.   Then cheers and laughter went up, and Williams, the ship's benefactor was a hero.   The news went about the vessel, champagne was ordered, an enthu-

siastic reception instituted in the smoking room, and everybody flocked thither to shake hands with the conqueror. The wheelsman said afterward, that the Admiral stood up behind the pilot house and "ripped and cursed all to himself" till he loosened the smokestack guys and becalmed the mainsail.

WILLIAMS.

The Admiral's power was broken.   After that, if he began an argument, somebody would bring Williams, and the old man would grow weak and begin to quiet down at once.   And as soon as he was done, Williams in his dulcet, insinuating way, would invent some history (referring for proof, to the old man's own excellent memory and to copies of "The Old Guard" known not to be in his possession) that would turn the tables completely and leave the Admiral all abroad and helpless.   By and by he came to so dread Williams and his gilded tongue that he would stop talking when he saw him approach, and finally ceased to mention politics altogether, and from that time forward there was entire peace and serenity in the ship.

CHAPTER LXIII.

ON a certain bright morning the Islands hove in sight, lying low on the lonely sea, and everybody climbed to the upper deck to look. After two thousand miles of watery solitude the vision was a welcome one. As we approached, the imposing promontory of Diamond Head rose up out of the ocean its rugged front softened by the hazy distance, and presently the details of the land began to make themselves manifest: first the line of beach; then the plumed coacoanut trees of the tropics; then cabins of the natives; then the white town of Honolulu, said to contain between twelve and fifteen thousand inhabitants spread over a dead level; with streets from twenty to thirty feet wide, solid and level as a floor, most of them straight as a line and few as crooked as a corkscrew.

The further I traveled through the town the better I liked it. Every step revealed a new contrast—disclosed something I was unaccustomed to. In place of the grand mud-colored brown fronts of San Francisco, I saw dwellings built of straw, adobies, and cream-colored pebble-and-shell-conglomerated coral, cut into oblong blocks and laid in cement; also a great number of neat white cottages, with green window-shutters; in place of front yards like billiard-tables with iron fences around them, I saw these homes surrounded by ample yards, thickly clad with green grass, and shaded by tall trees, through whose dense foliage the sun could scarcely penetrate; in place of the customary geranium, calla lily, etc., languishing in dust and general debility, I saw luxurious banks and thickets of flowers, fresh as a meadow after a rain, and glowing with the richest dyes; in place of the dingy horrors of San Francisco's pleasure grove, the "Willows," I saw huge-bodied, wide-spreading forest trees, with strange names and stranger appearance —trees that cast a shadow like a thunder-cloud, and were able to stand alone without being tied to green poles; in place of gold fish, wiggling around in glass globes, assuming countless shades and

SCENES ON THE ISLANDS.

degrees of distortion through the magnifying and diminishing qualities of their transparent prison houses, I saw cats—Tom-cats, Mary Ann cats, long-tailed cats, bob-tailed cats, blind cats, one-eyed cats, wall-eyed cats, cross-eyed cats, gray cats, black cats, white cats, yellow cats, striped cats, spotted cats, tame cats, wild cats, singed cats, individual cats, groups of cats, platoons of cats, companies of cats, regiments of cats, armies of cats, multitudes of cats, millions of cats, and all of them sleek, fat, lazy and sound asleep.

I looked on a multitude of people, some white, in white coats, vests, pantaloons, even white cloth shoes, made snowy with chalk duly laid on every morning; but the majority of the people were almost as dark as negroes—women with comely features, fine black eyes, rounded forms, inclining to the

FASHIONABLE ATTIRE.

voluptuous, clad in a single bright red or white' garment that fell free and unconfined from shoulder to heel, long black hair falling loose, gypsy hats, encircled with wreaths of natural flowers of a brilliant carmine tint; plenty of dark men in various costumes, and some with nothing on but a battered stove-pipe hat tilted on the nose, and a very scant breech - clout ;—certain smoke-dried children were clothed in nothing but sunshine—a very neat fitting and picturesque apparel indeed.

In place of roughs and rowdies staring and blackguarding on the corners, I saw long-haired, saddle-colored Sandwich Island maidens sitting on the ground in the shade of corner houses, gazing indolently at whatever or whoever happened along; instead of wretched cobble-stone pavements, I walked on a firm foundation of coral, built up from the bottom of the sea by the absurd but persevering insect of that name, with a light layer of lava and cinders overlying the coral, belched up out of fathomless perdition long ago through the seared and blackened crater that stands dead and harmless in the distance now; instead of cramped and crowded street-cars, I met dusky native women sweeping by, free as the wind, on fleet horses and astride, with gaudy riding-sashes, streaming like banners behind them; instead of the combined stenches of Chinadom and Brannan street slaughter-houses, I breathed the balmy fragrance of jessamine, oleander, and the Pride of India ; in place of the hurry and bustle and noisy confusion of San Francisco, I moved in the midst of a Summer calm as tranquil as dawn in the Garden of Eden ; in place of the Golden City's skirting sand hills and the placid bay, I saw on the one side a frame-work of tall, precipitous mountains close at hand, clad in refreshing green, and cleft by deep, cool, chasm-like valleys—and in front the grand sweep of the ocean : a brilliant, transparent green near the shore, bound and bordered by a long white line of foamy spray dashing against the reef, and further out the dead blue water of the deep sea, flecked with "white caps," and in the far horizon a single, lonely sail—a mere accent-mark to emphasize a slumberous calm and a solitude that were without sound or limit.   When the sun sunk down—the one intruder from other realms and persistent in suggestions of them—it was tranced luxury to sit in the perfumed air and forget that there was any world but these enchanted islands.

It was such ecstacy to dream, and dream—till you got a bite.

A scor-
pion bite.
Then the
first duty
was to get
up out of
the grass
and kill
the scor-
pion ; and
the next
to bathe
the bit-
ten place

A BITE.

with alcohol or brandy ; and the next to resolve to keep out of the grass in future.   Then came an adjournment to the bed-chamber and the pastime of writing up the day's journal with one hand and the destruction of mosquitoes with the other—a whole community of them at a slap.   Then, observing an enemy approaching,—a hairy tarantula on stilts—why not set the spittoon on him ?   It is done, and the projecting ends of his paws give a luminous idea of the magnitude of his reach. Then to bed and become a promenade for a centipede with forty-two legs on a side and every foot hot enough to burn a hole through a raw-hide. More soaking with alcohol, and a resolution to examine the bed before entering it, in future. Then wait, and suffer, till all the mosquitoes in the neighbor-

hood have crawled in under the bar, then slip out quickly, shut them in and sleep peacefully on the floor till morning. Meantime it is com-

RECONNOITERING.

forting to curse the tropics in occasional wakeful intervals.

We had an abundance of fruit in Honolulu, of course. Oranges, pine-apples, bananas, strawberries, lemons, limes, mangoes, guavas, melons, and a rare and curious luxury called the chirimoya, which is deliciousness itself. Then there is the tamarind. I thought tamarinds were made to eat, but that was probably not the idea. I ate several, and it seemed to me that they were rather sour that year. They pursed up my

lips, till they resembled the stem-end of a tomato, and I had to take my sustenance through a quill for twenty-four hours. They sharpened my teeth till I could have shaved with them, and gave them a "wire edge" that I was afraid would stay; but a citizen said "no, it will come off when the enamel does"—which was

EATING TAMARINDS.

comforting, at any rate. I found, afterward, that only strangers eat tamarinds—but they only eat them once.

CHAPTER LXIV.

IN my diary of our third day in Honolulu, I find this:

I am probably the most sensitive man in Hawaii to-night—especially about sitting down in the presence of my betters. I have ridden fifteen or twenty miles on horse-back since 5 P.M. and to tell the honest truth, I have a delicacy about sitting down at all.

An excursion to Diamond Head and the King's Coacoanut Grove was planned to-day—time, 4:30 P.M.—the party to consist of half a dozen gentlemen and three ladies. They all started at the appointed hour except myself. I was at the Government prison, (with Captain Fish and another whaleship-skipper, Captain Phillips,) and got so interested in its examination that I did not notice how quickly the time was passing. Somebody remarked that it was twenty minutes past five o'clock, and that woke me up. It was a fortunate circumstance that Captain Phillips was along with his "turn out," as he calls a top-buggy that Captain Cook brought here in 1778, and a horse that was here when Captain Cook came. Captain Phillips takes a just pride in his driving and in the speed of his horse, and to his passion for displaying them I owe it that we were only sixteen minutes coming from the prison to the American Hotel—a distance which has been estimated to be over half a mile. But it took some fearful driving. The Captain's whip came down fast, and the blows started so much dust out of the horse's hide that during the last half of the journey we rode through an impenetrable fog, and ran by a pocket compass in the hands of Captain Fish, a whaler of twenty-six years experience, who sat there through the perilous voyage as self-possessed as if he had been on the euchre-deck of his own

ship, and calmly said, " Port your helm—port," from time to
time, and " Hold her a little free—steady—so-o," and " Luff—
hard down to starboard !" and never once lost his presence
of mind or betrayed the least anxiety by voice or manner.
When we came to anchor at last, and Captain Phillips looked
at his watch and said, " Sixteen minutes—I told you it was in
her! that's over three miles an hour!" I could see he felt
entitled to a compliment, and so I said I had never seen lightning go like that horse.   And I never had.

The landlord of the American said the party had been gone
nearly an hour, but that he could give me my choice of several
horses that could overtake them.   I said, never mind—I preferred a safe horse to a fast one—I would like to have an
excessively gentle horse—a horse with no spirit whatever—a
lame one, if he had such a thing.   Inside of five minutes I
was mounted, and perfectly satisfied with my outfit.   I had no
time to label him " This is a horse," and so if the public took
him for a sheep I cannot help it.   I was satisfied, and that was
the main thing.   I could see that he had as many fine points
as any man's horse, and so I hung my hat on one of
them, behind the saddle, and swabbed the perspiration from
my face and started.   I named him after this island, " Oahu "
(pronounced O-waw-hee).   The first gate he came to he started
in; I had neither whip nor spur, and so I simply argued
the case with him.   He resisted argument, bnt ultimately
yielded to insult and abuse.   He backed out of that gate and
steered for another one on the other side of the street.   I
triumphed by my former process.   Within the next six hundred yards he crossed the street fourteen times and attempted
thirteen gates, and in the meantime the tropical sun was beating down and threatening to cave the top of my head in, and
I was literally dripping with perspiration.   He abandoned the
gate business after that and went along peaceably enough, but
absorbed in meditation.   I noticed this latter circumstance,
and it soon began to fill me with apprehension.   I said to myself, this creature is planning some new outrage, some fresh
deviltry or other—no horse ever thought over a subject so profoundly as this one is doing just for nothing.   The more this

thing preyed upon my mind the more uneasy I became, until
the suspense became almost unbearable and I dismounted to
see if there was anything wild in his eye—for I had heard
that the eye of this noblest of our domestic animals is very
expressive. I cannot describe what a load of anxiety was

LOOKING FOR MISCHIEF.

lifted from my mind when I found that he was only asleep.
I woke him up and started him into a faster walk, and then
the villainy of his nature came out again. He tried to climb
over a stone wall, five or six feet high. I saw that I must
apply force to this horse, and that I might as well begin first
as last. I plucked a stout switch from a tamarind tree, and the
moment he saw it, he surrendered. He broke into a convul-
sive sort of a canter, which had three short steps in it and one
long one, and reminded me alternately of the clattering shake
of the great earthquake, and the sweeping plunging of the Ajax
in a storm.

And now there can be no fitter occasion than the present to
pronounce a left-handed blessing upon the man who invented
the American saddle. There is no seat to speak of about it—

one might as well sit in a shovel—and the stirrups are nothing but an ornamental nuisance. If I were to write down here all the abuse I expended on those stirrups, it would make a large book, even without pictures. Sometimes I got one foot so far through, that the stirrup partook of the nature of an anklet; sometimes both feet were through, and I was handcuffed by the legs; and sometimes my feet got clear out and left the stirrups wildly dangling about my shins. Even when I was in proper position and carefully balanced upon the balls of my feet, there was no comfort in it, on account of my nervous dread that they were going to slip one way or the other in a moment. But the subject is too exasperating to write about.

A mile and a half from town, I came to a grove of tall cocoanut trees, with clean, branchless stems reaching straight up sixty or seventy feet and topped with a spray of green foliage sheltering clusters of cocoa-nuts—not more picturesque than a forest of collossal ragged parasols, with bunches of magnified grapes under them, would

A FAMILY LIKENESS

be. I once heard a grouty northern invalid say that a cocoanut tree might be poetical, possibly it was; but it looked like a feather-duster struck by lightning. I think that describes it better than a picture—and yet, without any question, there is something fascinating about a cocoa-nut tree—and graceful, too.

About a dozen cottages, some frame and the others of native grass, nestled sleepily in the shade here and there. The grass cabins are of a grayish color, are shaped much like our own cottages, only with higher and steeper roofs usually, and are made of some kind of weed strongly bound together in bundles. The roofs are very thick, and so are the walls; the latter have square holes in them for windows. At a little distance these cabins have a furry appearance, as if they might be made of bear skins. They are very cool and pleasant inside. The King's flag was flying from the roof of one of the cottages, and His Majesty was probably within. He owns the whole concern thereabouts, and passes his time there frequently, on sultry days "laying off." The spot is called "The King's Grove."

Near by is an interesting ruin—the meagre remains of an ancient heathen temple—a place where human sacrifices were offered up in those old bygone days when the simple child of nature, yielding momentarily to sin when sorely tempted, acknowledged his error when calm reflection had shown it him, and came forward with noble frankness and offered up his grandmother as an atoning sacrifice—in those old days when the luckless sinner could keep on cleansing his conscience and achieving periodical happiness as long as his relations held out; long, long before the missionaries braved a thousand privations to come and make them permanently miserable by telling them how beautiful and how blissful a place heaven is, and how nearly impossible it is to get there; and showed the poor native how dreary a place perdition is and what unnecessarily liberal facilities there are for going to it; showed him how, in his ignorance he had gone and fooled away all his kinfolks to no purpose; showed him what rapture it is to work all day long for fifty cents to buy food for next day with, as compared with fishing for pastime and lolling in the shade through eternal Summer, and eating of the bounty that nobody labored to provide but Nature. How sad it is to think of the multitudes who have gone to their graves in this beautiful island and never knew there was a hell!

This ancient temple was built of rough blocks of lava, and was simply a roofless inclosure a hundred and thirty feet long and seventy wide—nothing but naked walls, very thick, but not much higher than a man's head. They will last for ages no doubt, if left unmolested. Its three altars and other sacred appurtenances have crumbled and passed away years ago. It is said that in the old times thousands of human beings were slaughtered here, in the presence of naked and howling savages. If these mute stones could speak, what tales they could tell, what pictures they could describe, of fettered victims writhing under the knife ; of massed forms straining forward out of the gloom, with ferocious faces lit up by the sacrificial fires ; of the background of ghostly trees ; of the dark pyramid of Diamond Head standing-sentinel over the uncanny scene, and the peaceful moon looking down upon it through rifts in the cloud-rack !

When Kamehameha (pronounced Ka-may-ha-may-ah) the Great—who was a sort of a Napoleon in military genius and uniform success—invaded this island of Oahu three quarters of a century ago, and exterminated the army sent to oppose him, and took full and final possession of the country, he searched out the dead body of the King of Oahu, and those of the principal chiefs, and impaled their heads on the walls of this temple.

Those were savage times when this old slaughter-house was in its prime. The King and the chiefs ruled the common herd with a rod of iron ; made them gather all the provisions the masters needed ; build all the houses and temples ; stand all the expenses, of whatever kind ; take kicks and cuffs for thanks ; drag out lives well flavored with misery, and then suffer death for trifling offences or yield up their lives on the sacrificial altars to purchase favors from the gods for their hard rulers. The missionaries have clothed them, educated them, broken up the tyrannous authority of their chiefs, and given them freedom and the right to enjoy whatever their hands and brains produce with equal laws for all, and punishment for all alike who transgress them. The contrast is so strong—the benefit conferred upon this people by the missionaries is so prominent, so palpable and so unquestionable, that the frankest compliment I can pay them, and the best, is simply to point to the condition of the Sandwich Islanders of Captain Cook's time, and their condition to-day. Their work speaks for itself.

CHAPTER LXV.

BY and by, after a rugged climb, we halted on the summit of a hill which commanded a far-reaching view. The moon rose and flooded mountain and valley and ocean with a mellow radiance, and out of the shadows of the foliage the distant lights of Honolulu glinted like an encampment of fire-flies. The air was heavy with the fragrance of flowers. The halt was brief.—Gayly laughing and talking, the party galloped on, and I clung to the pommel and cantered after. Presently we came to a place where no grass grew—a wide expanse of deep sand. They said it was an old battle ground. All around everywhere, not three feet apart, the bleached bones of men gleamed white in the moonlight. We picked up a lot of them for mementoes. I got quite a number of arm bones and leg bones—of great chiefs, may be, who had fought savagely in that fearful battle in the old days, when blood flowed like wine where we now stood.—and wore the choicest of them out on Oahu afterward, trying to make him go. All sorts of bones could be found except skulls; but a citizen said, irreverently, that there had been an unusual number of " skull-hunters " there lately—a species of sportsmen I had never heard of before.

Nothing whatever is known about this place—its story is a secret that will never be revealed. The oldest natives make no pretense of being possessed of its history. They say these
30†

bones were here when they were children. They were here when their grandfathers were children—but how they came here, they can only conjecture. Many people believe this spot to be an ancient battle-ground, and it is usual to call it so; and they believe that these skeletons have lain for ages just where their proprietors fell in the great fight. Other people believe that Kamehameha I. fought his first battle here. On this point, I have heard a story, which may have been taken from one of the numerous books which have been written concerning these islands—I do not know where the narrator got it. He said that when Kamehameha (who was at first merely a subordinate chief on the island of Hawaii), landed here, he brought a large army with him, and encamped at Waikiki. The Oahuans marched against him, and so confident were they of success that they readily acceded to a demand of their priests that they should draw a line where these bones now lie, and take an oath that, if forced to retreat at all, they would never retreat beyond this boundary. The priests told them that death and everlasting punishment would overtake any who violated the oath, and the march was resumed. Kamehameha drove them back step by step; the priests fought in the front rank and exhorted them both by voice and inspiriting example to remember their oath—to die, if need be, but never cross the fatal line. The struggle was manfully maintained, but at last the chief priest fell, pierced to the heart with a spear, and the unlucky omen fell like a blight upon the brave souls at his back; with a triumphant shout the invaders pressed forward—the line was crossed—the offended gods deserted the despairing army, and, accepting the doom their perjury had brought upon them, they broke and fled over the plain where Honolulu stands now—up the beautiful Nuuanu Valley—paused a moment, hemmed in by precipitous mountains on either hand and the frightful precipice of the Pari in front, and then were driven over—a sheer plunge of six hundred feet!

The story is pretty enough, but Mr. Jarves' excellent history says the Oahuans were intrenched in Nuuanu Valley; that

Kamehameha ousted them, routed them, pursued them up the valley and drove them over the precipice. He makes no mention of our bone-yard at all in his book.

Impressed by the profound silence and repose that rested over the beautiful landscape, and being, as usual, in the rear, I gave voice to my thoughts. I said:

"What a picture is here slumbering in the solemn glory of the moon! How strong the rugged outlines of the dead volcano stand out against the clear sky! What a snowy fringe marks the bursting of the surf over the long, curved reef! How calmly the dim city sleeps yonder in the plain! How soft the shadows lie upon the stately mountains that border the dream-haunted Mauoa Valley! What a grand pyramid of billowy clouds towers above the storied Pari! How the grim warriors of the past seem flocking in ghostly squadrons to their ancient battlefield again—how the wails of the dying well up from the——"

At this point the horse called Oahu sat down in the sand.

Sat down to listen, I suppose. Never mind what he heard, I stopped apostrophising and convinced him that I was not a man to allow contempt of Court on the part of a horse. I broke the back-bone of a Chief over his rump and set out to join the cavalcade again.

SAT DOWN TO LISTEN.

Very considerably fagged out we arrived in town at 9 o'clock at night, myself in the lead—for when my horse finally came to understand that he was homeward bound and hadn't far to go, he turned his attention strictly to business.

This is a good time to drop in a paragraph of information.

There is no regular livery stable in Honolulu, or, indeed, in any part of the kingdom of Hawaii; therefore unless you are acquainted with wealthy residents (who all have good horses), you must hire animals of the wretchedest description from the Kanakas. (i. e. natives.) Any horse you hire, even though it be from a white man, is not often of much account, because it will be brought in for you from some ranch, and has necessarily been leading a hard life. If the Kanakas who have been caring for him (inveterate riders they are) have not ridden him half to death every day themselves, you can depend upon it they have been doing the same thing by proxy, by clandestinely hiring him out. At least, so I am informed. The result is, that no horse has a chance to eat, drink, rest, recuperate, or look well or feel well, and so strangers go about the Islands mounted as I was to-day.

In hiring a horse from a Kanaka, you must have all your eyes about you, because you can rest satisfied that you are dealing with a shrewd unprincipled rascal. You may leave your door open and your trunk unlocked as long as you please, and he will not meddle with your property; he has no important vices and no inclination to commit robbery on a large scale; but if he can get ahead of you in the horse business, he will take a genuine delight in doing it. This trait is characteristic of horse jockeys, the world over, is it not? He will overcharge you if he can; he will hire you a fine-looking horse at night (anybody's—may be the King's, if the royal steed be in convenient view), and bring you the mate to my Oahu in the morning, and contend that it is the same animal. If you make trouble, he will get out by saying it was not himself who made the bargain with you, but his brother, "who went out in the country this morning." They have always got a "brother" to shift the responsibility upon. A victim said to one of these fellows one day:

"But I know I hired the horse of you, because I noticed that scar on your cheek."

The reply was not bad: "Oh, yes—yes—my brother all same—we twins!"

A friend of mine, J. Smith, hired a horse yesterday, the

MY BROTHER—WE TWINS.

Kanaka warranting him to be in excellent condition. Smith had a saddle and blanket of his own, and he ordered the Kanaka to put these on the horse. The Kanaka protested that he was perfectly willing to trust the gentleman with the saddle that was already on the animal, but Smith refused to use it. The change was made; then Smith noticed that the Kanaka had only changed the saddles, and had left the original blanket on the horse; he said he forgot to change the blankets, and so, to cut the bother short, Smith mounted and rode away. The horse went lame a mile from town, and afterward got to cutting up some extraordinary capers. Smith got down and took off the saddle, but the blanket stuck fast to the horse—glued to a

procession of raw places. The Kanaka's mysterious conduct stood explained.

Another friend of mine bought a pretty good horse from a native, a day or two ago, after a tolerably thorough examination of the animal. He discovered to-day that the horse was as blind as a bat, in one eye. He meant to have examined

EXTRAORDINARY CAPERS.   that eye, and came home

with a general notion that he had done it; but he remembers now that every time he made the attempt his attention was called to something else by his victimizer.

One more instance, and then I will pass to something else. I am informed that when a certain Mr. L., a visiting stranger, was here, he bought a pair of very respectable-looking match horses from a native. They were in a little stable with a partition through the middle of it—one horse in each apartment. Mr. L. examined one of them critically through a window (the Kanaka's "brother" having gone to the country with the key), and then went around the house and examined the other through a window on the other side. He said it was the neatest match he had ever seen, and paid for the horses on the spot. Whereupon the Kanaka departed to join his brother in the country. The fellow had shamefully swindled L. There was only one "match" horse, and he had examined his starboard side through one window and his port side through another! I decline to believe this story, but I give it because it is worth something as a fanciful illustration of a fixed fact—namely, that the Kanaka horse-jockey is fertile in invention and elastic in conscience.

You can buy a pretty good horse for forty or fifty dollars, and a good enough horse for all practical purposes for two dollars and a half. I estimate " Oahu" to be worth somewhere in the neighborhood of thirty-five cents. A good deal better animal than he is was sold here day before yesterday for a dollar and seventy-five cents, and sold again to-day for two dollars and twenty-five cents; Wiiliams bought a handsome and lively little pony yesterday for ten dollars; and about the best common horse on the island (and he is a really good one) sold yesterday, with Mexican saddle and bridle, for seventy dollars—a horse which is well and widely known, and greatly respected for his speed, good disposi-

A LOAD OF HAY.

tion and everlasting bottom. You give your horse a little grain once a day; it comes from San Francisco, and is worth about two cents a pound; and you give him as much hay as he wants; it is cut and brought to the market by natives, and is not very good it is baled into long, round bundles, about the size of a large man; one of them is stuck by the middle on each end of a six foot pole, and the Kanaka shoulders the pole and walks about the streets between the upright bales in search of customers. These hay bales, thus carried, have a general resemblance to a colossal capital H.

The hay-bundles cost twenty-five cents apiece, and one will last a horse about a day. You can get a horse for a song, a week's hay for another song, and you can turn your animal loose among the luxuriant grass in your neighbor's broad front yard without a song at all—you do it at midnight, and stable the beast again before morning. You have been at no expense thus far, but when you come to buy a saddle and bridle they will cost you from twenty to thirty-five dollars. You can hire a horse, saddle and bridle at from seven to ten dollars a week, and the owner will take care of them at his own expense.

It is time to close this day's record—bed time. As I prepare for sleep, a rich voice rises out of the still night, and, far as this ocean rock is toward the ends of the earth, I recognize a familiar home air. But the words seem somewhat out of joint:

"Waikiki lantoni œ Kaa hooly hooly wawhoo."

Translated, that means "When we were marching through Georgia."

CHAPTER LXVI.

PASSING through the market place we saw that feature of Honolulu under its most favorable auspices—that is, in the full glory of Saturday afternoon, which is a festive day with the natives. The native girls by twos and threes and parties of a dozen, and sometimes in whole platoons and companies, went cantering up and down the neighboring streets astride of fleet but homely horses, and with their guady riding habits streaming like banners behind them. Such a troop of free and easy riders, in their natural home, the saddle, makes a gay and graceful spectacle. The riding habit I speak of is simply a long, broad scarf, like a tavern table cloth brilliantly colored, wrapped around the loins once, then apparently passed between the limbs and each end thrown backward over the same, and floating and flapping behind on both sides beyond the horse's tail like a couple of fancy flags; then, slipping the stirrup-irons between her toes, the girl throws her chest for ward, sits up like a Major General and goes sweeping by like the wind.

The girls put on all the finery they can on Saturday afternoon —fine black silk robes; flowing red ones that nearly put your eyes out; others as white as snow; still others that discount the rainbow; and they wear their hair in nets, and trim their jaunty hats with fresh flowers, and encircle their dusky throats with home-made necklaces of the brilliant vermillion-tinted blossom of the *ohia*; and they fill the markets and the adjacent streets with their bright presences, and smell like a rag factory on fire with their offensive cocoanut oil.

Occasionally you see a heathen from the sunny isles away down in the South Seas, with his face and neck tatooed till he looks like the customary mendicant from Washoe who has been blown up in a mine.   Some are tattooed a dead blue color down to the upper lip—masked, as it were—leaving the natural light yellow skin of Micronesia unstained from thence down; some with broad marks drawn down from hair to neck, on both sides of the face. and a strip of the original yellow skin, two inches

SANDWICH ISLAND GIRLS.

wide, down the center—a gridiron with a spoke broken out; and some with the entire face discolored with the popular mortification tint, relieved only by one or two thin, wavy threads of natural yellow running across the face from ear to ear, and eyes twinkling out of this darkness, from under shadowing hat-brims, like stars in the dark of the moon.

Moving among the stirring crowds, you come to the poi merchants, squatting in the shade on their hams, in true native fashion, and surrounded by purchasers.   (The Sandwich Islanders always squat on their hams, and who knows but they may be the old original "ham sandwiches?" The thought is pregnant with interest.) The poi looks like common flour paste, and is kept in large bowls formed of a species of gourd, and capable of holding from one to three or four gallons. Poi is the chief article of food among the natives, and is prepared from the *taro* plant. The taro root looks like a thick, or, if you please, a corpulent sweet potato, in shape, but is of a light purple color when boiled. When boiled it answers as a passable substitute for bread. The buck Kanakas bake it under ground, then mash it up well with a heavy lava pestle, mix water

ORIGINAL HAM SANDWICH.

with it until it becomes a paste, set it aside and let it ferment, and then it is poi—and an unseductive mixture it is, almost tasteless before it ferments and too sour for a luxury afterward. But nothing is more nutritious. When solely used, however, it produces acrid humors, a fact which sufficiently accounts for the humorous character of the Kanakas. I think there must be as much of a knack in handling poi as there is in eating with chopsticks. The forefinger is thrust into the mess and stirred quickly round several times and drawn as quickly out, thickly coated, just as if it were poulticed; the head is thrown back, the finger inserted in the mouth and the delicacy stripped off and swallowed—the eye closing gently, meanwhile, in a languid sort of ecstasy. Many a different finger goes into the same bowl and many a different kind of dirt and shade and quality of flavor is added to the virtues of its contents.

Around a small shanty was collected a crowd of natives buying the *awa* root. It is said that but for the use of this root the destruction of the people in former times by certain imported diseases would have been far greater than it was, and by others it is said that this is merely a fancy. All agree that poi will rejuvenate a man who is used up and his vitality almost annihilated by hard drinking, and that in some kinds of diseases it will restore health after all medicines have failed ; but all are not willing to allow to the *awa* the virtues claimed for it. The natives manufacture an intoxicating drink from it which is fearful in its effects when persistently indulged in. It covers the body with dry, white scales, inflames the eyes, and causes premature decrepitude. Although the man before whose establishment we stopped has to pay a Government license of eight hundred dollars a year for the exclusive right to sell *awa* root, it is said that he makes a small fortune every twelve-month ; while saloon keepers, who pay a thousand dollars a year for the privilege of retailing whiskey, etc., only make a bare living.

We found the fish market crowded ; for the native is very fond of fish, and *eats the article raw and alive !* Let us change the subject.

In old times here Saturday was a grand gala day indeed. All the native population of the town forsook their labors, and those of the surrounding country journeyed to the city. Then the white folks had to stay indoors, for every street was so packed with charging cavaliers and cavalieresses that it was next to impossible to thread one's way through the cavalcades without getting crippled.

At night they feasted and the girls danced the lascivious *hula hula*—a dance that is said to exhibit the very perfection of educated motion of limb and arm, hand, head and body, and the exactest uniformity of movement and accuracy of " time." It was performed by a circle of girls with no raiment on them to speak of, who went through an infinite variety of motions and figures without prompting, and yet so true was their " time," and in such perfect concert did they move that when they were placed in a straight line, hands, arms, bodies, limbs and heads waved, swayed, gesticulated, bowed, stooped, whirled, squirmed, twisted and undulated as if they were part and parcel of a single individual ; and it was difficult to believe they were not moved in a body by some exquisite piece of mechanism.

Of late years, however, Saturday has lost most of its quondam gala features.   This weekly stampede of the natives interfered too much with labor and the interests of the white folks, and by sticking in a law here, and preaching a sermon there, and by various other means, they gradually broke it up.   The demoralizing *hula hula* was forbidden to be performed, save at night, with closed doors, in presence of few spectators, and only by permission duly procured from the authorities and the payment of ten dollars for the same.   There are few girls now-a-days able to dance this ancient national dance in the highest perfection of the art.

The missionaries have christianized and educated all the natives.   They all belong to the Church, and there is not one of them, above the age of eight years, but can read and write with facility in the native tongue.   It is the most universally educated race of people outside of China.   They have any quantity of books, printed in the Kanaka language, and all the natives are fond of reading.   They are inveterate church-goers —nothing can keep them away.   All this ameliorating cultivation has at last built up in the native women a profound respect for chastity—in other people.   Perhaps that is enough to say on that head.   The national sin will die out when the race does, but perhaps not earlier.—But doubtless this purifying is not far off, when we reflect that contact with civilization and the whites has reduced the native population from *four hundred thousand* (Captain Cook's estimate,) to *fifty-five thousand* in something over eighty years !

Society is a queer medley in this notable missionary, whaling and governmental centre.   If you get into conversation with a stranger and experience that natural desire to know what sort of ground you are treading on by finding out what manner of man your stranger is, strike out boldly and address him as " Captain."   Watch him narrowly, and if you see by his countenance that you are on the wrong tack, ask him where he preaches.   It is a safe bet that he is either a missionary or captain of a whaler.   I am now personally acquainted with seventy-two captains and ninety-six missionaries.   The captains and ministers form one-half of the population ; the third fourth is composed of common Kanakas and mercantile foreigners and their families, and the final fourth is made up of high officers of the Hawaiian Government. And there are just about cats enough for three apiece all around.

A solemn stranger met me in the suburbs the other day, and said:

"Good morning, your reverence. Preach in the stone church yonder, no doubt?"

"No, I don't. I'm not a preacher."

"Really, I beg your pardon, Captain. I trust you had a good season. How much oil"—

"Oil? What do you take me for? I'm not a whaler."

"Oh, I beg a thousand pardons, your Excellency. Major General in the household troops, no doubt? Minister of the

"I KISSED HIM FOR HIS MOTHER."

Interior, likely? Secretary of war? First Gentleman of the Bed-chamber? Commissioner of the Royal"—

"Stuff! I'm no official. I'm not connected in any way with the Government."

"Bless my life! Then, who the mischief are you? what the mischief are you? and how the mischief did you get here, and where in thunder did you come from?"

"I'm only a private personage—an unassuming stranger— lately arrived from America."

"No? Not a missionary! Not a whaler! not a member of his Majesty's Government! not even Secretary of the Navy! Ah, Heaven! it is too blissful to be true; alas, I do but dream. And yet that noble, honest countenance—those oblique, ingenuous eyes—that massive head, incapable of—of—anything; your hand; give me your hand, bright waif. Excuse these tears. For sixteen weary years I have yearned for a moment like this, and "--

Here his feelings were too much for him, and he swooned away. I pitied this poor creature from the bottom of my heart. I was deeply moved. I shed a few tears on him and kissed him for his mother. I then took what small change he had and "shoved."

CHAPTER LXVII.

I STILL quote from my journal:

I found the national Legislature to consist of half a dozen white men and some thirty or forty natives. It was a dark assemblage. The nobles and Ministers (about a dozen of them altogether) occupied the extreme left of the hall, with David Kalakaua (the King's Chamberlain) and Prince William at the head. The President of the Assembly, His Royal Highness M. Kekuanaoa,* and the Vice President (the latter a white man,) sat in the pulpit, if I may so term it.

The President is the King's father. He is an erect, strongly built, massive featured, white-haired, tawny old gentleman of eighty years of age or thereabouts. He was simply but well dressed, in a blue cloth coat and white vest, and white pantaloons, without spot, dust or blemish upon them. He bears himself with a calm, stately dignity, and is a man of noble presence. He was a young man and a distinguished warrior under that terrific fighter, Kamehameha I., more than half a century ago. A knowledge of his career suggested some such thought as this: "This man, naked as the day he was born, and war-club and spear in hand, has charged at the head of a horde of savages against other hordes of savages more than a generation and a half ago, and reveled in slaughter and carnage; has worshipped wooden images on his devout knees; has seen hundreds of his race offered up in heathen temples as sacrifices

*Since dead.

to wooden idols, at a time when no missionary's foot had ever pressed this soil, and he had never heard of the white man's God; has believed his enemy could secretly pray him to death; has seen the day, in his childhood, when it was a crime punishable by death for a man to eat with his wife, or for a plebeian to let his shadow fall upon the King—and now look at him; an educated Christian; neatly and handsomely dressed; a high-minded, elegant gentleman; a traveler, in some degree, and one who has been the honored guest of royalty in Europe; a man practiced in holding the reins of an enlightened government, and well versed in the politics of his country and in general, practical information.   Look at him, sitting there presiding over the deliberations of a legislative body, among whom are white men—a grave, dignified, statesmanlike personage, and as seemingly natural and fitted to the place as if he had been born in it and had never been out of it in his life time.   How the experiences of this old man's eventful life shame the cheap inventions of romance!"

Kekuanaoa is not of the blood royal.   He derives his princely rank from his wife, who was a daughter of Kamehameha the Great.   Under other monarchies the male line takes precedence of the female in tracing genealogies, but here the opposite is the case—the female line takes precedence.   Their reason for this is exceedingly sensible, and I recommend it to the aristocracy of Europe: They say it is easy to know who a man's mother was, but, etc., etc.

The christianizing of the natives has hardly even weakened some of their barbarian superstitions, much less destroyed them. I have just referred to one of these.   It is still a popular belief that if your enemy can get hold of any article belonging to you he can get down on his knees over it and *pray you to death*. Therefore many a native gives up and dies merely because he *imagines* that some enemy is putting him through a course of damaging prayer.   This praying an individual to death seems absurd enough at a first glance, but then when we call to mind

31†

some of the pulpit efforts of certain of our own ministers the thing looks plausible.

In former times, among the Islanders, not only a plurality of wives was customary, but a *plurality of husbands* likewise. Some native women of noble rank had as many as six husbands. A woman thus supplied did not reside with all her husbands at once, but lived several months with each in turn. An understood sign hung at her door during these months. When the sign was taken down, it meant " NEXT."

In those days woman was rigidly taught to "know her place." Her place was to do all the work, take all the cuffs, provide all the food, and content herself with what was left after her lord had finished his dinner. She was not only forbidden, by ancient law, and

AN ENEMY'S PRAYER.

under penalty of death, to eat with her husband or enter a canoe, but was debarred, under the same penalty, from eating bananas, pine-apples, oranges and other choice fruits at any time or in any place. She had to confine herself pretty strictly to "poi" and hard work. These poor ignorant heathen seem to have had a sort of groping idea of what came of woman eating fruit in the garden of Eden, and they did not choose to take any more chances. But the missionaries broke up this satisfactory arrangement of things. They liberated woman and made her the equal of man.

The natives had a romantic fashion of burying some of their children alive when the family became larger than necessary. The missionaries interfered in this matter too, and stopped it.

To this day the natives are able to *lie down and die whenever they want to*. whether there is anything the matter with them or not. If a Kanaka takes a notion to die, that is the end of him ; nobody can persuade him to hold on ; all the doctors in the world could not save him.

A luxury which they enjoy more than anything else, is a large funeral. If a person wants to get rid of a troublesome native, it is only necessary to promise him a fine funeral and name the hour and he will be on hand to the minute—at least his remains will.

All the natives are Christians, now, but many of them still desert to the Great Shark God for temporary succor in time of trouble. An irruption of the great volcano of Kilauea, or an earthquake, always brings a deal of latent loyalty to the Great Shark God to the surface. It is common report that the King, educated, cultivated and refined Christian gentleman as he undoubtedly is, still turns to the idols of his fathers for help when disaster threatens. A planter caught a shark, and one of his christianized natives testified his emancipation from the thrall of ancient superstition by assisting to dissect the shark after a fashion forbidden by his abandoned creed. But remorse shortly began to torture him. He grew moody and sought solitude ; brooded over his sin, refused food, and finally said he must die and ought to die, for he had sinned against the Great Shark God and could never know peace any more. He was proof against persuasion and ridicule, and in the course of a day or two took to his bed and died, although he showed no symptom of disease. His young daughter followed his lead and suffered a like fate within the week. Superstition is ingrained in the native blood and bone and it is only natural that it should crop out in time of distress. Wherever one goes in the Islands, he will find small piles of stones by the wayside, covered with leafy offerings, placed there by the natives to appease evil spirits or honor local deities belonging to the mythology of former days.

In the rural districts of any of the Islands, the traveler hourly comes upon parties of dusky maidens bathing in the streams or in the sea without any clothing on and exhibiting no very

intemperate zeal in the matter of hiding their nakedness. When
the missionaries first took up their residence in Honolulu, the
native women would pay their families frequent friendly visits,
day by day, not even clothed with a blush. It was found a
hard matter to convince them that this was rather indelicate.
Finally the missionaries provided them with long, loose calico
robes, and that ended the difficulty—for the women would
troop through the town, stark naked, with their robes folded
under their arms, march to the missionary houses and then

VISITING THE MISSIONARIES.

proceed to dress!—The natives soon manifested a strong pro-
clivity for clothing, but it was shortly apparent that they only
wanted it for grandeur. The missionaries imported a quantity
of hats, bonnets, and other male and female wearing apparel,
instituted a general distribution, and begged the people not to
come to church naked, next Sunday, as usual. And they did
not; but the national spirit of unselfishness led them to divide
up with neighbors who were not at the distribution, and next
Sabbath the poor preachers could hardly keep countenance before their vast congregations. In the midst of the reading of

a hymn a brown, stately dame would sweep up the aisle with
a world of airs, with nothing in the world on but a "stovepipe"
hat and a pair of cheap gloves; another dame would follow,
tricked out in a man's shirt, and nothing else; another one
would enter with a flourish, with simply the sleeves of a bright
calico dress tied around her waist and the rest of the garment
dragging behind like a peacock's tail off duty; a stately "buck"
Kanaka would stalk in with a woman's bonnet on, wrong side
before—only this, and nothing more; after him would stride
his fellow, with the legs of a pair of pantaloons tied around his
neck, the rest of his person untrammeled; in his rear would
come another gentleman simply gotten up in a fiery neck-tie
and a striped vest.   The poor creatures were beaming with

FULL CHURCH DRESS.

complacency and wholly unconscious of any absurdity in their
appearance.   They gazed at each other with happy admiration,
and it was plain to see that the young girls were taking note
of what each other had on, as naturally as if they had always
lived in a land of Bibles and knew what churches were made

for; here was the evidence of a dawning civilization. The spectacle which the congregation presented was so extraordinary and withal so moving, that the missionaries found it difficult to keep to the text and go on with the services; and by and by when the simple children of the sun began a general swapping of garments in open meeting and produced some irresistibly grotesque effects in the course of re-dressing, there was nothing for it but to cut the thing short with the benediction and dismiss the fantastic assemblage.

In our country, children play " keep house;" and in the same high-sounding but miniature way the grown folk here, with the poor little material of slender territory and meagre population, play " empire." There is his royal Majesty the King, with a New York detective's income of thirty or thirty-five thousand dollars a year from the " royal civil list" and the " royal domain." He lives in a two-story frame " palace."

And there is the " royal family "—the customary hive of

PLAYING EMPIRE.

royal brothers, sisters, cousins and other noble drones and vagrants usual to monarchy,—all with a spoon in the national pap-dish, and all bearing such titles as his or her Royal Highness the Prince or Princess So-and-so. Few of them can carry their royal splendors far enough to ride in carriages, however; they sport the economical Kanaka horse or " hoof it "* with the plebeians.

Then there is his Excellency the " royal Chamberlain "—a sinecure, for his majesty dresses himself with his own hands, except when he is ruralizing at Waikiki and then he requires no dressing.

Next we have his Excellency the Commander-in-chief of the

*Missionary phrase.

Household Troops, whose forces consist of about the number of soldiers usually placed under a corporal in other lands.

Next comes the royal Steward and the Grand Equerry in Waiting—high dignitaries with modest salaries and little to do.

Then we have his Excellency the First Gentleman of the Bed-chamber—an office as easy as it is magnificent.

Next we come to his Excellency the Prime Minister, a renegade American from New Hampshire, all jaw, vanity, bombast and ignorance, a lawyer of "shyster" calibre, a fraud by nature, a humble worshiper of the sceptre above him, a reptile never tired of sneering at the land of his birth or glorifying the ten-acre kingdom that has adopted him—salary, $4,000 a year, vast consequence, and no perquisites.

Then we have his Excellency the Imperial Minister of Finance, who handles a million dollars of public money a year, sends in his annual "budget" with great ceremony, talks prodigiously of "finance," suggests imposing schemes for paying off the "national debt" (of $150,000,) and does it all for $4,000 a year and unimaginable glory.

Next we have his Excellency the Minister of War, who holds sway over the royal armies—they consist of two hundred and thirty uniformed Kanakas, mostly Brigadier Generals, and if the country ever gets into trouble with a foreign power we shall probably hear from them. I knew an American whose copper-plate visiting card bore this impressive legend: "Lieutenant-Colonel in the Royal Infantry. To say that he was proud of this distinction is stating it but tamely. The Minister of War has also in his charge some venerable swivels on Punch-Bowl Hill wherewith royal salutes are fired when foreign vessels of war enter the port.

Next comes his Excellency the Minister of the Navy—a nabob who rules the "royal fleet," (a steam-tug and a sixty-ton schooner.)

And next comes his Grace the Lord Bishop of Honolulu, the chief dignitary of the "Established Church"—for when the American Presbyterian missionaries had completed the reduction of the nation to a compact condition of **Christianity,** native royalty stepped in and erected the grand dignity of an "Established (Episcopal) Church" over it, and imported **a** cheap ready-made Bishop from England to take charge.   The chagrin of the missionaries has never been comprehensively expressed, to this day, profanity not being admissible.

Next comes his Excellency the Minister of Public Instruction.

Next, their Excellencies the Governors of Oahu, Hawaii, etc., and after them a string of High Sheriffs and other small fry too numerous for computation.

Then there are their Excellencies the Envoy Extraordinary and Minister Plenipotentiary of his Imperial Majesty the Em-

ROYALTY AND ITS SATELLITES.

peror of the French ; her British Majesty's Minister ; the Minister Resident, of the United States ; and some six or eight representatives of other foreign nations, all with sounding titles, imposing dignity and prodigious but economical state.

Imagine all this grandeur in a play-house " kingdom " whose population falls absolutely short of sixty thousand souls !

The people are so accustomed to nine-jointed titles and colossal magnates that a foreign prince makes very little more stir in Honolulu than a Western Congressman does in New York.

And let it be borne in mind that there is a strictly defined " court costume " of so " stunning " a nature that it would make the clown in a circus look tame and commonplace by comparison ; and each Hawaiian official dignitary has a gorgeous vari-colored, gold-laced uniform peculiar to his office—no two of them are alike, and it is hard to tell which one is the " loudest." The King had a " drawing-room " at stated intervals, like other monarchs, and when these varied uniforms congregate there weak-eyed people have to contemplate the spectacle through smoked glass. Is there not a gratifying contrast between this latter-day exhibition and the one the ancestors of some of these magnates afforded the missionaries the Sunday after the old-time distribution of clothing? Behold what religion and civilization have wrought !

CHAPTER LXVIII.

WHILE I was in Honolulu I witnessed the ceremonious funeral of the King's sister, her Royal Highness the Princess Victoria. According to the royal custom, the remains had lain in state at the palace *thirty days*, watched day and night by a guard of honor. And during all that time a great multitude of natives from the several islands had kept the palace grounds well crowded and had made the place a pandemonium every night with their howlings and wailings, beating of tom-toms and dancing of the (at other times) forbidden "hula-hula" by half-clad maidens to the music of songs of questionable decency chanted in honor of the deceased. The printed programme of the funeral procession interested me at the time; and after what I have just said of Hawaiian grandiloquence in the matter of "playing empire," I am persuaded that a perusal of it may interest the reader:

After reading the long list of dignitaries, etc., and remembering the sparseness of the population, one is almost inclined to wonder where the material for that portion of the procession devoted to "Hawaiian Population Generally" is going to be procured:

Undertaker.

Royal School.　Kawaiahao School.　Roman Catholic School.　Miæmæ School.

Honolulu Fire Department.

Mechanics' Benefit Union.

Attending Physicians.

Knonohikis (Superintendents) of the Crown Lands, Konohikis of the Private Lands of His Majesty· Konohikis of Private Lands of Her late Royal Highness.

Governor of Oahu and Staff.
Hulumanu (Military Company).
Household Troops.
The Prince of Hawaii's Own (Military Company).
The King's household servants.
Servants of Her late Royal Highness.
Protestant Clergy.   The Clergy of the Roman Catholic Church.
His Lordship Louis Maigret, The Right Rev. Bishop of Arathea, Vicar-Apostolic
of the Hawaiian Islands.
The Clergy of the Hawaiian Reformed Catholic Church.
His Lordship the Right Rev. Bishop of Honolulu.

Escort Hawaiian Cavalry.
Large Kahilis.
Small Kahilis.
Pall Bearers.

[HEARSE.]

Escort Hawaiian Cavalry.
Large Kahilis.*
Small Kahilis.
Pall Bearers.

Her Majesty Queen Emma's Carriage.
His Majesty's Staff.
Carriage of Her late Royal Highness.
Carriage of Her Majesty the Queen Dowager.
The King's Chancellor.
Cabinet Ministers.
His Excellency the Minister Resident of the United States.
H. I. M's Commissioner.
H. B. M's Acting Commissioner.
Judges of Supreme Court.
Privy Councillors.
Members of Legislative Assembly.
Consular Corps.
Circuit Judges.
Clerks of Government Departments.
Members of the Bar.
Collector General, Custom-house Officers and Officers of the Customs.
Marshal and Sheriffs of the different Islands.
King's Yeomanry.
Foreign Residents.
Ahahui Kaahumanu.
Hawaiian Population Generally.
Hawaiian Cavalry.
Police Force.

*Ranks of long-handled mops made of gaudy feathers—sacred to royalty·   They
are stuck in the ground around the tomb and left there.

I resume my journal at the point where the procession arrived at the royal mausoleum :

As the procession filed through the gate, the military deployed handsomely to the right and left and formed an avenue through which the long column of mourners passed to the tomb. The coffin was borne through the door of the mausoleum, followed by the King and his chiefs, the great officers of the kingdom, foreign Consuls, Embassadors and distinguished guests (Burlingame and General Van Valkenburgh). Several of the kahilis were then fastened to a frame-work in front of the tomb, there to remain until they decay and fall to pieces, or, forestalling this, until another scion of royalty dies. At this point of the proceedings the multitude set up such a heart-broken wailing as I hope never to hear again. The soldiers fired three volleys of musketry—the wailing being previously silenced to

A MODERN FUNERAL.

permit of the guns being heard. His Highness Prince William, in a showy military uniform (the " true prince," this—scion of the house over-thrown by the present dynasty—he was formerly betrothed to the Princess but was not allowed to marry her), stood guard and paced back and forth within the door. The privileged few who followed the coffin into the mausoleum remained sometime, but the King soon came out and stood in the door and near one side of it. A stranger could have guessed his rank (although he was so simply and unpretentiously dressed) by the profound deference paid him by all persons in his vicinity; by seeing his high officers receive his quiet orders and suggestions with bowed and uncovered heads; and by observing how careful those persons who came out of the mausoleum were to avoid "crowding" him (although there was room enough in the door-way for a wagon to pass, for that matter); how respectfully they edged out sideways, scraping their backs against the wall and always presenting a front view of their persons to his Majesty, and never putting their hats on until they were well out of the royal presence.

He was dressed entirely in black—dress-coat and silk hat—and looked rather democratic in the midst of the showy uniforms about him. On his breast he wore a large gold star, which was half hidden by the lappel of his coat. He remained at the door a half hour, and occasionally gave an order to the men who were erecting the *kahilis* before the tomb. He had the good taste to make one of them substitute black crape for the ordinary hempen rope he was about to tie one of them to the frame-work with. Finally he entered his carriage and drove away, and the populace shortly began to drop into his wake. While he was in view there was but one man who attracted more attention than himself, and that was Harris (the Yankee Prime Minister). This feeble personage had crape enough around his hat to express the grief of an entire nation, and as usual he neglected no opportunity of making himself conspicuous and exciting the admiration of the simple Kanakas. Oh! noble ambition of this modern Richelieu!

It is interesting to contrast the funeral ceremonies of the Princess Victoria with those of her noted ancestor Kamehameha the Conqueror, who died fifty years ago—in 1819, the year before the first missionaries came.

"On the 8th of May, 1819, at the age of sixty-six, he died, as he had lived, in the faith of his country. It was his misfortune not to have come in contact with men who could have rightly influenced his religious aspirations. Judged by his advantages and compared with the most eminent of his countrymen he may be justly styled not only great, but good. To this day his memory warms the heart and elevates the national feelings of Hawaiians. They are proud of their old warrior King; they love his name; his deeds form their historical age; and an enthusiasm everywhere prevails, shared even by foreigners who knew his worth, that constitutes the firmest pillar of the throne of his dynasty.

"In lieu of human victims (the custom of that age), a sacrifice of three hundred dogs attended his obsequies—no mean holocaust when their national value and the estimation in which they were held are considered. The bones of Kamehameha, after being kept for a while, were so carefully concealed that all knowledge of their final resting place is now lost. There was a proverb current among the common people that the bones of a cruel King could not be hid; they made fish-hooks and arrows of them, upon which, in using them, they vented their abhorrence of his memory in bitter execrations."

The account of the circumstances of his death, as written by the native historians, is full of minute detail, but there is scarcely a line of it which does not mention or illustrate some by-gone custom of the country. In this respect it is the most comprehensive document I have yet met with. I will quote it entire:

"When Kamehameha was dangerously sick, and the priests were unable to cure him, they said: 'Be of good courage and build a house for the god' (his own private god or idol), that thou mayest recover.' The chiefs corroborated this advice of the priests, and a place of worship was prepared for Kukailimoku, and consecrated in the evening. They proposed also to the King, with a view to prolong his life, that human victims should be sacrificed to his deity; upon which the greater part of the people absconded through fear of death, and concealed themselves in hiding places till the *tabu** in which destruction impended, was past. It is doubtful whether Kamehameha approved of the plan of the chiefs and priests to sacrifice men, as he was known to say, 'The men are sacred for the King;' meaning that they were for the service of his successor. This information was derived from Liholiho, his son.

"After this, his sickness increased to such a degree that he had not strength to turn himself in his bed. When another season, consecrated for worship at the new temple (*heiau*) arrived, he said to his son, Liholiho, 'Go thou and make supplication to thy god; I am not able to go, and will offer my prayers at home.' When his devotions to his feathered god, Kukailimoku, were concluded, a certain religiously disposed individual, who had a bird god, suggested to the King that through its influence his sickness might be removed. The name of this god was Pua; its body was made of a bird, now eaten by the Hawaiians, and called in their language *alae*. Kamehameha was willing that a trial should be made, and two houses were constructed to facilitate the experiment; but while dwelling in them he became so very weak as not to receive food. After lying there three days, his wives, children and chiefs, perceiving that he was very low, returned him to his own house. In the evening he was carried to the eating house,† where he took a little food in his mouth which he did not swallow; also a cup of water. The chiefs requested him to give them his counsel; but he made no reply, and was carried back to the dwelling house; but when near midnight—ten o'clock, perhaps—he was carried again to the place to eat; but, as before, he merely tasted of what was presented to him. Then Kaikioewa addressed him thus: 'Here we all are, your younger brethren, your son Liholiho and your foreigner; impart to us your dying charge, that Liholiho and Kaahumanu may hear.' Then Kamehameha inquired, 'What do you say?' Kaikioewa repeated, 'Your counsels for us.'

* *Tabu* (pronounced tah-boo,) means prohibition (we have borrowed it,) or sacred. The tabu was sometimes permanent, sometimes temporary; and the person or thing placed under tabu was for the time being sacred to the purpose for which it was set apart. In the above case the victims selected under the tabu would be sacred to the sacrifice.

†It was deemed pollution to eat in the same hut a person slept in—the fact that the patient was dying could not modify the rigid etiquette.

He then said, 'Move on in my good way and—.' He could proceed no further. The foreigner, Mr. Young, embraced and kissed him. Hoapili also embraced him, whispering something in his ear, after which he was taken back to the house. About twelve he was carried once more to the house for eating, into which his head entered, while his body was in the dwelling house immediately adjoining.   It should be remarked that this frequent carrying of a sick chief from one house to another resulted from the *tabu* system, then in force.   There were at that time six houses (huts) connected with an establishment—one was for worship, one for the men to eat in, an eating house for the women, a house to sleep in, a house in which to manufacture kapa (native cloth) and one where, at certain intervals, the women might dwell in seclusion.

"The sick was once more taken to his house, when he expired; this was at two o'clock, a circumstance from which Leleiohoku derived his name.   As he breathed his last, Kalaimoku came to the eating house to order those in it to go out.   There were two aged persons thus directed to depart; one went, the other remained on account of love to the King, by whom he had formerly been kindly sustained. The children also were sent away.   Then Kalaimoku came to the house, and the chiefs had a consultation.   One of them spoke thus : 'This is my thought—we will eat him raw.'* Kaahumanu (one of the dead King's widows) replied, 'Perhaps his body is not at our disposal; that is more properly with his successor. Our part in him—his breath—has departed; his remains will be disposed of by Liholiho.'

"After this conversation the body was taken into the consecrated house for the performance of the proper rites by the priest and the new King.   The name of this ceremony is *uko;* and when the sacred hog was baked the priest offered it to the dead body, and it became a god, the King at the same time repeating the customary prayers.

"Then the priest, addressing himself to the King and chiefs, said : 'I will now make known to you the rules to be observed respecting persons to be sacrificed on the burial of this body.   If you obtain one man before the corpse is removed, one will be sufficient ; but after it leaves this house four will be required.   If delayed until we carry the corpse to the grave there must be ten ; but after it is deposited in the grave there must be fifteen.   To-morrow morning there will be a *tabu*, and, if the sacrifice be delayed until that time, forty men must die.'

"Then the high priest, Hewahewa, inquired of the chiefs, 'Where shall be the residence of King Liholiho ? ' They replied, 'Where, indeed ? You, of all men, ought to know.'   Then the priest observed, 'There are two suitable places; one is Kau, the other is Kohala.' The chiefs preferred the latter, as it was more thickly inhabited.   The priest added, ' These are proper places for the King's residence; but he must not remain in Kona, for it is polluted.' This was agreed to. It was now break of day. As he was being carried to the place of burial the peo-

---

*This sounds suspicious, in view of the fact that all Sandwich Island historians, white and black, protest that cannibalism never existed in the islands.   However, since they only proposed to "eat him raw" we "won't count that". But it would certainly have been cannibalism if they had cooked him.—[M. T.]

ple perceived that their King was dead, and they wailed. When the corpse was removed from the house to the tomb, a distance of one chain, the procession was met by a certain man who was ardently attached to the deceased. He leaped upon the chiefs who were carrying the King's body; he desired to die with him on account of his love. The chiefs drove him away. He persisted in making numerous attempts, which were unavailing. Kalaimoka also had it in his heart to die with him, but was prevented by Hookio.

" The morning following Kamehameha's death, Liholiho and his train departed for Kohala, according to the suggestions of the priest, to avoid the defilement occasioned by the dead. At this time if a chief died the land was polluted, and the heirs sought a residence in another part of the country until the corpse was dissected and the bones tied in a bundle, which being done, the season of defilement terminated. If the deceased were not a chief, the house only was defiled which became pure again on the burial of the body. Such were the laws on this subject.

"On the morning on which Liholiho sailed in his canoe for Kohala, the chiefs and people mourned after their manner on occasion of a chief's death, conducting themselves like madmen and like beasts. Their conduct was such as to forbid description; The priests, also, put into action the sorcery apparatus, that the person who had prayed the King to death might die; for it was not believed that Kamehameha's departure was the effect either of sickness or old age. When the sorcerers set up by their fire-places stick with a strip of kapa flying at the top, the chief Keeaumoku, Kaahumaun's brother, came in a state of intoxication and broke the flag-staff of the sorcerers, from which it was inferred that Kaahumanu and her friends had been instrumental in the King's death. On this account they were subjected to abuse."

You have the contrast, now, and a strange one it is. This great Queen, Kaahumanu, who was "subjected to abuse" during the frightful orgies that followed the King's death, in accordance with ancient custom, afterward became a devout Christian and a steadfast and powerful friend of the missionaries.

Dogs were, and still are, reared and fattened for food, by the natives—hence the reference to their value in one of the above paragraphs.

Forty years ago it was the custom in the Islands to suspend all law for a certain number of days after the death of a royal personage; and then a saturnalia ensued which one may picture to himself after a fashion, but not in the full horror of the reality. The people shaved their heads, knocked out a tooth or two, plucked out an eye sometimes, cut, bruised, mutilated or burned their flesh, got drunk, burned each other's huts, maimed or murdered one another according to the caprice of the moment, and both sexes gave themselves up to brutal and unbridled licentiousness.   And after it all, came a torpor from which

FORMER FUNERAL ORGIES.

the nation slowly emerged bewildered and dazed, as if from a hideous half-remembered nightmare.   They were not the salt of the earth, those " gentle children of the sun."

The natives still keep up an old custom of theirs which cannot be comforting to an invalid.   When they think a sick friend is going to die, a couple of dozen neighbors surround his hut and keep up a deafening wailing night and day till he either dies or gets well.   No doubt this arrangement has helped many a subject to a shroud before his appointed time.

They surround a hut and wail in the same heart-broken way when its occupant returns from a journey.   This is their dismal idea of a welcome.   A very little of it would go a great way with most of us.

32†

CHAPTER LXIX.

BOUND for Hawaii (a hundred and fifty miles distant,) to visit the great volcano and behold the other notable things which distinguish that island above the remainder of the group, we sailed from Honolulu on a certain Saturday afternoon, in the good schooner Boomerang.

The Boomerang was about as long as two street cars, and about as wide as one. She was so small (though she was larger than the majority of the inter-island coasters) that when I stood on her deck I felt but little smaller than the Colossus of Rhodes must have felt when he had a man-of-war under him. I could reach the water when she lay over under a strong breeze. When the Captain and my comrade (a Mr. Billings), myself and four other persons were all assembled on the little after portion of the deck which is sacred to the cabin passengers, it was full—there was not room for any more quality folks. Another section of the deck, twice as large as ours, was full of natives of both sexes, with their customary dogs, mats, blankets, pipes, calabashes of poi, fleas, and other luxuries and baggage of minor importance. As soon as we set sail the natives all lay down on the deck as thick as negroes in a slave-pen, and smoked, conversed, and spit on each other, and were truly sociable.

The little low-ceiled cabin below was rather larger than a hearse, and as dark as a vault. It had two coffins on each side —I mean two bunks. A small table, capable of accommodating three persons at dinner, stood against the forward bulkhead, and over it hung the dingiest whale oil lantern that ever peopled the obscurity of a dungeon with ghostly shapes. The floor room unoccupied was not extensive. One might swing a cat in it, perhaps, but not a long cat. The hold forward of the bulkhead had but little freight in it, and from morning till

A PASSENGER.

night a portly old rooster, with a voice like Baalam's ass, and the same disposition to use it, strutted up and down in that part of the vessel and crowed. He usually took dinner at six o'clock, and then, after an hour devoted to meditation, he mounted a barrel and crowed a good part of the night. He got hoarser and hoarser all the time, but he scorned to allow any personal consideration to interfere with his duty, and kept up his labors in defiance of threatened diphtheria.

Sleeping was out of the question when he was on watch. He was a source of genuine aggravation and annoyance. It was worse than useless to shout at him or apply offensive epithets to him—he only took these things for applause, and strained himself to make more noise. Occasionally, during the day, I threw potatoes at him through an aperture in the bulkhead, but he only dodged and went on crowing.

The first night, as I lay in my coffin, idly watching the dim lamp swinging to the rolling of the ship, and snuffing the nauseous odors of bilge water, I felt something gallop over me. I turned out promptly. However, I turned in again when I found it was only a rat. Presently something galloped over me once more. I knew it was not a rat this time, and I thought it might be a centipede, because the Captain had killed one on deck in the afternoon. I turned out. The first glance at the pillow showed me a repulsive sentinel perched upon each end of it—cockroaches as large as peach leaves—fellows with long, quivering antennæ and fiery, malignant eyes. They were grating their teeth like tobacco worms, and appeared to be dissatisfied about something. I had often heard that these reptiles were in the habit of eating off sleeping sailors' toe nails down to the quick, and I would not get in the bunk any more. I lay down on the floor. But a rat came and bothered me, and shortly afterward a procession of cockroaches arrived and camped in my hair. In a few moments the rooster was crowing with uncommon spirit and a party of fleas were throwing double somersaults about my person in the wildest disorder, and taking a bite every time they struck. I was beginning to feel really annoyed. I got up and put my clothes on and went on deck.

The above is not overdrawn; it is a truthful sketch of interisland schooner life. There is no such thing as keeping a vessel in elegant condition, when she carries molasses and Kanakas.

It was compensation for my sufferings to come unexpectedly upon so beautiful a scene as met my eye—to step suddenly out of the sepulchral gloom of the cabin and stand under the strong light of the moon—in the centre, as it were, of a glittering sea of liquid silver—to see the broad sails straining in the gale, the ship keeled over on her side, the angry foam hissing past her lee bulwarks, and sparkling sheets of spray dashing high over her bows and raining upon her decks; to brace myself and hang fast to the first object that presented itself, with hat jammed down and coat tails whipping in the breeze, and feel that exhilaration that thrills in one's hair and quivers down his back bone when he knows that every inch of canvas is drawing and the vessel cleaving through the waves at her utmost speed. There was no darkness, no dimness, no obscurity there. All was brightness, every object was vividly defined. Every prostrate Kanaka; every coil of rope; every calabash of poi; every puppy; every seam in the flooring; every bolthead; every object, however minute, showed sharp and distinct in its every outline; and the shadow of the broad mainsail lay black as a pall upon the deck, leaving Billings's white upturned face glorified and his body in a total eclipse.

Monday morning we were close to the island of Hawaii. Two of its high mountains were in view—Mauna Loa and Hualaiai. The latter is an imposing peak, but being only ten

MOONLIGHT ON THE WATER.

thousand feet high is seldom mentioned or heard of. Mauna Loa is said to be sixteen thousand feet high. The rays of glittering snow and ice, that clasped its summit like a claw, looked refreshing when viewed from the blistering climate we were in. One could stand on that mountain (wrapped up in blankets and furs to keep warm), and while he nibbled a snow-ball or an icicle to quench his thirst he could look down the long sweep of its sides and see spots where plants are growing that grow only where the bitter cold of Winter prevails; lower down he could see sections devoted to productions that thrive in the temperate zone alone; and at the bottom of the mountain he could see the home of the tufted cocoa-palms and other species of vegetation that grow only in the sultry atmosphere of eternal Summer. He could see all the climes of the world at a single glance of the eye, and that glance would only pass over a distance of four or five miles as the bird flies!

By and by we took boat and went ashore at Kailua, designing to ride horseback through the pleasant orange and coffee region of Kona, and rejoin the vessel at a point some leagues distant. This journey is well worth taking. The trail passes along on high ground—say a thousand feet above sea level—and usually about a mile distant from the ocean, which is always in sight, save that occasionally you find yourself buried in the forest in the midst of a rank tropical vegetation and a dense growth of trees, whose great bows overarch the road and shut out sun and sea and everything, and leave you in a dim, shady tunnel, haunted with invisible singing birds and fragrant with the odor of flowers. It was pleasant to ride occasionally in the warm sun, and feast the eye upon the ever-changing panorama of the forest (beyond and below us), with its many tints, its softened lights and shadows, its billowy undulations sweeping gently down from the mountain to the sea. It was pleasant also, at intervals, to leave the sultry sun and pass into the cool, green depths of this forest and indulge in sentimental reflections under the inspiration of its brooding twilight and its whispering foliage.

We rode through one orange grove that had ten thousand trees in it! They were all laden with fruit.

At one farmhouse we got some large peaches of excellent flavor. This fruit, as a general thing, does not do well in the Sandwich Islands. It takes a sort of almond shape, and is small and bitter. It needs frost, they say, and perhaps it does; if this be so, it will have a good opportunity to go on needing it, as it will not be likely to get it. The trees from which the fine fruit I have spoken of, came, had been planted and replanted *sixteen times*, and to this treatment the proprietor of the orchard attributed his success.

GOING INTO THE MOUNTAINS.

We passed several sugar plantations—new ones and not very extensive. The crops were, in most cases, third rattoons. [NOTE.—The first crop is called "plant cane;" subsequent crops which spring from the original roots, without replanting, are called "rattoons."] Almost everywhere on the island of Hawaii sugar-cane matures in twelve months, both rattoons and plant, and although it ought to be taken off as soon as it tassels, no doubt, it is not absolutely necessary to do it until about four months afterward. In Kona, the average yield of an acre of ground is *two tons* of sugar, they say. This is only a moderate yield for these islands, but would be astounding for Louisiana and most other sugar growing countries. The plantations in Kona being on pretty high ground—up among the light and frequent rains—no irrigation whatever is required.

CHAPTER LXX.

WE stopped some time at one of the plantations, to rest ourselves and refresh the horses. We had a chatty conversation with several gentlemen present; but there was one person, a middle aged man, with an absent look in his face, who simply glanced up, gave us good-day and lapsed again into the meditations which our coming had interrupted. The planters whispered us not to mind him—crazy. They said he was in the Islands for his health; was a preacher; his home, Michigan. They said that if he woke up presently and fell to talking about a correspondence which he had some time held with Mr. Greeley about a trifle of some kind, we must humor him and listen with interest; and we must humor his fancy that this correspondence was the talk of the world.

It was easy to see that he was a gentle creature and that his madness had nothing vicious in it. He looked pale, and a little worn, as if with perplexing thought and anxiety of mind. He sat a long time, looking at the floor, and at intervals muttering to himself and nodding his head acquiescingly or shaking it in mild protest. He was lost in his thought, or in his memories. We continued our talk with the planters, branching from subject to subject. But at last the word " circumstance," casually dropped, in the course of conversation, attracted his attention and brought an eager look into his countenance. He faced about in his chair and said:

"Circumstance? What circumstance? Ah, I know—I

know too well. So you have heard of it too." [With a sigh.] "Well, no matter—all the world has heard of it. All the world. The whole world. It is a large world, too, for a thing to travel so far in—now isn't it? Yes, yes—the Greeley correspondence with Erickson has created the saddest and bitterest controversy on both sides of the ocean—and still they keep it up! It makes us famous, but at what a sorrowful sacrifice! I was so sorry when I heard that it had caused that bloody and distressful war over there in Italy. It was little comfort to me, after so much bloodshed, to know that the victors sided with me, and the vanquished with Greeley.—It is little comfort to know that Horace Greeley is responsible for the battle of Sadowa, and not me. Queen Victoria wrote me that she felt just as I did about it—she said that as much as she was op-

THE DEMENTED.

posed to Greeley and the spirit he showed in the correspondence with me, she would not have had Sadowa happen for hundreds of dollars. I can show you her letter, if you would like to see it. But gentlemen, much as you may think you know about that unhappy correspondence, you cannot know the *straight* of it till you hear it from my lips. It has always been garbled in the journals, and even in history. Yes, even in history—think of it! Let me—*please* let me, give you the matter, exactly as it occurred. I truly will not abuse your confidence."

Then he leaned forward, all interest, all earnestness, and told his story—and told it appealingly, too, and yet in the simplest and most unpretentious way; indeed, in such a way as to suggest to one, all the time, that this was a faithful, honorable witness, giving evidence in the sacred interest of justice, and under oath. He said:

"Mrs. Beazeley—Mrs. Jackson Beazeley, widow, of the village of Campbellton, Kansas,—wrote me about a matter which was near her heart—a matter which many might think trivial, but to her it was a thing of deep concern. I was living in Michigan, then—serving in the ministry. She was, and is, an estimable woman—a woman to whom poverty and hardship have proven incentives to industry, in place of discouragements. Her only treasure was her son William, a youth just verging upon manhood; religious, amiable, and sincerely attached to agriculture. He was the widow's comfort and her pride. And so, moved by her love for him, she wrote me about a matter, as I have said before, which lay near her heart—because it lay near her boy's. She desired me to confer with Mr. Greeley about turnips. Turnips were the dream of her child's young ambition. While other youths were frittering away in frivolous amusements the precious years of budding vigor which God had given them for useful preparation, this boy was patiently enriching his mind with information concerning turnips. The sentiment which he felt toward the turnip was akin to adoration. He could not think of the turnip without emotion; he could not speak of it calmly; he could not contemplate it without exaltation. He could not eat it without shedding tears. All the poetry in his sensitive nature was in sympathy with the gracious vegetable. With the earliest pipe of dawn he sought his patch, and when the curtaining night drove him from it he shut himself up with his books and garnered statistics till sleep overcame him. On rainy days he sat and talked hours together with his mother about turnips. When company came, he made it his loving duty to put aside everything else and converse with them all the day long of his great joy in

DISCUSSING TURNIPS.

the turnip. And yet, was this joy rounded and complete? Was there no secret alloy of unhappiness in it? Alas, there was. There was a canker gnawing at his heart; the noblest inspiration of his soul eluded his endeavor—viz: he could not make of the turnip a climbing vine. Months went by; the bloom forsook his cheek, the fire faded out of his eye; sighings and abstraction usurped the place of smiles and cheerful converse. But a watchful eye noted these things and in time a motherly sympathy unsealed the secret. Hence the letter to me. She pleaded for attention—she said her boy was dying by inches.

"I was a stranger to Mr. Greeley, but what of that? The matter was urgent. I wrote and begged him to solve the difficult problem if possible and save the student's life. My interest grew, until it partook of the anxiety of the mother. I waited in much suspense.— At last the answer came.

"I found that I could not read it readily, the handwriting being unfamiliar and my emotions somewhat wrought up. It seemed to refer in part to the boy's case, but chiefly to other and irrelevant matters—such as paving-stones, electricity, oysters, and something which I took to be 'absolution' or 'agrarianism,' I could not be certain which; still, these appeared to be simply casual mentions, nothing more; friendly in spirit, without doubt, but lacking the connection or coherence necessary to make them useful.—I judged that my understanding was affected by my feelings, and so laid the letter away till morning.

"In the morning I read it again, but with difficulty and uncertainty still, for I had lost some little rest and my mental vision seemed clouded. The note was more connected, now, but did not meet the emergency it was expected to meet. It was too discursive. It appeared to read as follows, though I was not certain of some of the words:

'Polygamy dissembles majesty; extracts redeem polarity; causes hitherto exist. Ovations pursue wisdom, or warts inherit and condemn. Boston, botany, cakes, folony undertakes, but who shall allay? We fear not. Yrxwly,

HEVACE EVEELOJ.'

"But there did not seem to be a word about turnips. There seemed to be no suggestion as to how they might be made to grow like vines. There was not even a reference to the Beazeleys. I slept upon the matter; I ate no supper, neither any breakfast next morning. So I resumed my work with a brain refreshed, and was very hopeful. *Now* the letter took a different aspect—all save the signature, which latter I judged to be only a harmless affectation of Hebrew. The epistle was necessarily from Mr. Greeley, for it bore the printed heading of *The Tribune*, and I had written to no one else there. The letter, I say, had taken a different aspect, but still its language was eccentric and avoided the issue. It now appeared to say:

'Bolivia extemporizes mackerel; borax esteems polygamy; sausages wither in the east. Creation perdu, is done; for woes inherent one can damn. Buttons, buttons, corks, geology underrates but we shall allay. My beer's out. Yrxwly,

HEVACE EVEELOJ.'

New-York Tribune.

"I was evidently overworked. My comprehension was impaired. Therefore I gave two days to recreation, and then returned to my task greatly refreshed. The letter now took this form :

'Poultices do sometimes choke swine ; tulips reduce posterity ; causes leather to resist. Our notions empower wisdom, her let's afford while we can. Butter but any cakes, fill any undertaker, we'll wean him from his filly. We feel hot.

Yrxwly,   HEVACE EVEELOJ.'

"I was still not satisfied. These generalities did not meet the question. They were crisp, and vigorous, and delivered with a confidence that almost compelled conviction; but at such a time as this, with a human life at stake, they seemed inappropriate, worldly, and in bad taste. At any other time I would have been not only glad, but proud, to receive from a man like Mr. Greeley a letter of this kind, and would have studied it earnestly and tried to improve myself all I could; but now, with that poor boy in his far home languishing for relief, I had no heart for learning.

"Three days passed by, and I read the note again. Again its tenor had changed. It now appeared to say:

'Potations do sometimes wake wines; turnips restrain passion; causes necessary to state. Infest the poor widow; her lord's effects will be void. But dirt, bathing, etc., etc., followed unfairly, will worm him from his folly—so swear not.
                    Yrxwly,   HEVACE EVEELOJ.'

"This was more like it. But I was unable to proceed. I was too much worn. The word 'turnips' brought temporary joy and encouragement, but my strength was so much impaired, and the delay might be so perilous for the boy, that I relinquished the idea of pursuing the translation further, and resolved to do what I ought to have done at first. I sat down and wrote Mr. Greeley as follows:

"DEAR SIR: I fear I do not entirely comprehend your kind note. It cannot be possible, Sir, that 'turnips restrain passion'—at least the study or contemplation of turnips cannot—for it is this very employment that has scorched our poor friend's mind and sapped his bodily strength.—But if they do restrain it, will you bear with us a little further and explain how they should be prepared? I observe that you say 'causes necessary to state,' but you have omitted to state them.

"Under a misapprehension, you seem to attribute to me interested motives in this matter—to call it by no harsher term. But I assure you, dear sir, that if I seem to be 'infesting the widow,' it is all seeming, and void of reality. It is from no seeking of mine that I am in this position. She asked me, herself, to write you. I never have infested her—indeed I scarcely know her. I do not infest anybody. I try to go along, in my humble way, doing as near right as I can, never harming anybody, and never throwing out insinuations. As for 'her lord and his effects,' they are of no interest to me. I trust I have effects enough of my own —shall endeavor to get along with them, at any rate, and not go mousing around to get hold of somebody's that are 'void'' But do you not see?—this woman is a widow—she has no 'lord.' He is dead—or pretended to be, when they buried him. Therefore, no amount of 'dirt, bathing,' etc., etc., howsoever 'unfairly followed' will be likely to 'worm him from his folly'—if being dead and a ghost is 'folly.' Your closing remark is as unkind as it was uncalled for; and if report says true you might have applied it to yourself, sir, with more point and less impropriety.　　　　　　　　　　Very Truly Yours,　　SIMON ERICKSON.

"In the course of a few days, Mr. Greeley did what would have saved a world of trouble, and much mental and bodily suffering and misunderstanding, if he had done it sooner.　To-wit, he sent an intelligible rescript or translation of his original note, made in a plain hand by his clerk.　Then the mystery cleared, and I saw that his heart had been right, all the time. I will recite the note in its clarified form :

[Translation.]

'Potatoes do sometimes make vines ; turnips remain passive : cause unnecessary to state.　Inform the poor widow her lad's efforts will be vain.　But diet, bathing, etc. etc., followed uniformly, will wean him from his folly—so fear not.
　　　　　　　　Yours,　　　　　　HORACE GREELEY.'

"But alas, it was too late, gentlemen—too late.　The criminal delay had done its work—young Beazely was no more. His spirit had taken its flight to a land where all anxieties shall be charmed away, all desires gratified, all ambitions realized.　Poor lad, they laid him to his rest with a turnip in each hand."

So ended Erickson, and lapsed again into nodding, mumbling, and abstraction.　The company broke up, and left him so. . . . But they did not say what drove him crazy.　In the momentary confusion, I forgot to ask.

CHAPTER LXXI.

AT four o'clock in the afternoon we were winding down a mountain of dreary and desolate lava to the sea, and closing our pleasant land journey. This lava is the accumulation of ages; one torrent of fire after another has rolled down here in old times, and built up the island structure higher and higher. Underneath, it is honey-combed with caves; it would be of no use to dig wells in such a place; they would not hold water—you would not find any for them to hold, for that matter. Consequently, the planters depend upon cisterns.

The last lava flow occurred here so long ago that there are none now living who witnessed it. In one place it enclosed and burned down a grove of cocoa-nut trees, and the holes in the lava where the trunks stood are still visible; their sides retain the impression of the bark; the trees fell upon the burning river, and becoming partly submerged, left in it the perfect counterpart of every knot and branch and leaf, and even nut, for curiosity seekers of a long distant day to gaze upon and wonder at.

There were doubtless plenty of Kanaka sentinels on guard hereabouts at that time, but they did not leave casts of their figures in the lava as the Roman sentinels at Herculaneum and Pompeii did. It is a pity it is so, because such things are so interesting; but so it is. They probably went away. They went away early, perhaps. However, they had their merits; the Romans exhibited the higher pluck, but the Kanakas showed the sounder judgment.

Shortly we came in sight of that spot whose history is so familiar to every school-boy in the wide world—Kealakekua Bay—the place where Captain Cook, the great circumnavigator, was killed by the natives, nearly a hundred years ago. The setting sun was flaming upon it, a Summer shower was falling, and it was spanned by two magnificent rainbows. Two men who were in advance of us rode through one of these and for a moment their garments shone with a more than regal splendor. Why did not Captain Cook have taste enough to call his great discovery the Rainbow Islands? These charming spectacles are present to you at every turn; they are common in all the islands; they are visible every day, and frequently at night also—not the silvery bow we see once in an age in the States, by moonlight, but barred with all bright and beautiful colors, like the children of the sun and rain. I saw one of them a few nights ago. What the sailors call "rain-dogs"—little patches of rainbow—are often seen drifting about the heavens in these latitudes, like stained cathedral windows.

Kealakekua Bay is a little curve like the last kink of a snail-shell, winding deep into the land, seemingly not more than a mile wide from shore to shore. It is bounded on one side—where the murder was done—by a little flat plain, on which stands a cocoanut grove and some ruined houses; a steep wall of lava, a thousand feet high at the upper end and three or four hundred at the lower, comes down from the mountain and bounds the inner extremity of it. From this wall the place takes its name, *Kealakekua*, which in the native tongue signifies " The Pathway of the Gods." They say, (and still believe, in spite of their liberal education in Christianity), that the great god *Lono*, who used to live upon the hillside, always traveled that causeway when urgent business connected with heavenly affairs called him down to the seashore in a hurry.

As the red sun looked across the placid ocean through the tall, clean stems of the cocoanut trees, like a blooming whiskey bloat through the bars of a city prison, I went and stood in the edge of the water on the flat rock pressed by Captain

33†

Cook's feet when the blow was dealt which took away his life, and tried to picture in my mind the doomed man struggling in the midst of the multitude of exasperated savages—the men

KEALAKEKUA BAY AND COOK'S MONUMENT.

in the ship crowding to the vessel's side and gazing in anxious dismay toward the shore—the—but I discovered that I could not do it.

It was growing dark, the rain began to fall, we could see that the distant Boomerang was helplessly becalmed at sea, and so I adjourned to the cheerless little box of a warehouse and sat down to smoke and think, and wish the ship would make the land—for we had not eaten much for ten hours and were viciously hungry.

Plain unvarnished history takes the romance out of Captain Cook's assassination, and renders a deliberate verdict of justifiable homicide. Wherever he went among the islands, he was cordially received and welcomed by the inhabitants, and his ships lavishly supplied with all manner of food. He returned these kindnesses with insult and ill-treatment. Perceiving that the people took him for the long vanished and lamented god Lono, he encouraged them in the delusion for the sake of the limitless power it gave him ; but during the famous disturbance at this spot, and while he and his comrades were surrounded by fifteen thousand maddened savages, he received a hurt and betrayed his earthly origin with a groan. It was his death-warrant. Instantly a shout went up : " He groans !—he is not a god !" So they closed in upon him and dispatched him.

His flesh was stripped from the bones and burned (except nine pounds of it which were sent on board the ships). The heart was hung up in a native hut, where it was found and eaten by three children, who mistook it for the heart of a dog. One of these children grew to be a very old man, and died in Honolulu a few years ago. Some of Cook's bones were recovered and consigned to the deep by the officers of the ships.

Small blame should attach to the natives for the killing of Cook. They treated him well. In return, he abused them. He and his men inflicted bodily injury upon many of them at different times, and killed at least three of them before they offered any proportionate retaliation.

Near the shore we found " Cook's Monument "—only a cocoa-nut stump, four feet high and about a foot in diameter at the butt. It had lava boulders piled around its base to hold it up and keep it in its place, and it was entirely sheathed over, from top to bottom, with rough, discolored sheets of copper, such as ships' bottoms are coppered with. Each sheet had a rude inscription scratched upon it—with a nail, apparently—and in every case the execution was wretched. Most of these merely recorded the visits of British naval commanders to the spot, but one of them bore this legend :

"Near this spot fell
CAPTAIN JAMES COOK,
The Distinguished Circumnavigator, who Discovered these
Islands A. D. 1778.

After Cook's murder, his second in command, on board the ship, opened fire upon the swarms of natives on the beach, and one of his cannon balls cut this cocoanut tree short off and left this monumental stump standing. It looked sad and lonely enough to us, out there in the rainy twilight. But there is no other monument to Captain Cook. True, up on the mountain side we had passed by a large inclosure like an ample hog-pen, built of lava blocks, which marks the spot where Cook's flesh was stripped from his bones and burned; but this is not properly a monument, since it was erected by the natives themselves, and less to do honor to the circumnavigator than for the sake of convenience in roasting him. A thing like a guide-board was elevated above this pen on a tall pole, and formerly there was an inscription upon it describing the memorable occurrence that had there taken place; but the sun and the wind have long ago so defaced it as to render it illegible.

Toward midnight a fine breeze sprang up and the schooner soon worked herself into the bay and cast anchor. The boat came ashore for us, and in a little while the clouds and the rain were all gone. The moon was beaming tranquilly down on land and sea, and we two were stretched upon the deck sleeping the refreshing sleep and dreaming the happy dreams that are only vouchsafed to the weary and the innocent.

CHAPTER LXXII.

IN the breezy morning we went ashore and visited the ruined temple of the last god Lono. The high chief cook of this temple—the priest who presided over it and roasted the human sacrifices—was uncle to Obookia, and at one time that youth was an apprentice-priest under him. Obookia was a young native of fine mind, who, together with three other native boys, was taken to New England by the captain of a whaleship during the reign of Kamehameha I, and they were the means of attracting the attention of the religious world to their country. This resulted in the sending of missionaries there. And this Obookia was the very same sensitive savage who sat down on the church steps and wept because his people did not have the Bible. That incident has been very elaborately painted in many a charming Sunday School book—aye, and told so plaintively and so tenderly that I have cried over it in Sunday School myself, on general principles, although at a time when I did not know much and could not understand why the people of the Sandwich Islands needed to worry so much about it as long as they did not know there was a Bible at all.

Obookia was converted and educated, and was to have returned to his native land with the first missionaries, had he lived. The other native youths made the voyage, and two of them did good service, but the third, William Kanui, fell from grace afterward, for a time, and when the gold excitement broke out in California he journeyed thither and went to min-

ing, although he was fifty years old. He succeeded pretty
well, but the failure of Page, Bacon & Co. relieved him of six
thousand dollars, and then, to all intents and purposes, he was
a bankrupt in his old age and he resumed service in the pulpit
again. He died in Honolulu in 1864.

Quite a broad tract of land near the temple, extending from
the sea to the mountain top, was sacred to the god Lono in
olden times—so sacred that if a common native set his sacrilegious foot upon it it was judicious for him to make his will,
because his time had come. He might go around it by water,
but he could not cross it. It was well sprinkled with pagan
temples and stocked with awkward, homely idols carved out
of logs of wood. There was a temple devoted to prayers for
rain—and with fine sagacity it was placed at a point so well
up on the mountain side that if you prayed there twenty-four
times a day for rain you would be likely to get it every time.

THE GHOSTLY BUILDERS.

You would seldom get to your Amen before you would have
to hoist your umbrella.

And there was a large temple near at hand which was built
in a single night, in the midst of storm and thunder and rain,
by the ghastly hands of dead men! Tradition says that by the

wierd glare of the lightning a noiseless multitude of phantoms were seen at their strange labor far up the mountain side at dead of night—flitting hither and thither and bearing great lava-blocks clasped in their nerveless fingers—appearing and disappearing as the pallid lustre fell upon their forms and faded away again.   Even to this day, it is said, the natives hold this dread structure in awe and reverence, and will not pass by it in the night.

At noon I observed a bevy of nude native young ladies bathing in the sea, and went and sat down on their clothes to keep them from being stolen.   I begged them to come out, for the sea was rising and I was satisfied that they were running some risk.   But they were not afraid, and presently went on with their sport.   They were finished swimmers and divers, and en-

ON GUARD.

joyed themselves to the last degree.   They swam races, splashed and ducked and tumbled each other about, and filled the air with their laughter.   It is said that the first thing an Islander learns is how to swim; learning to walk being a matter of smaller consequence, comes afterward.   One hears tales of native men and women swimming ashore from vessels many miles at sea—more miles, indeed, than I dare vouch for or even mention.   And they tell of a native diver who went down in thirty or forty-foot waters and brought up an anvil!   I think he swallowed the anvil afterward, if my memory serves me. However I will not urge this point.

I have spoken, several times, of the god Lono—I may as well furnish two or three sentences concerning him.

The idol the natives worshiped for him was a slender, unornamented staff twelve feet long. Tradition says he was a favorite god on the Island of Hawaii—a great king who had been deified for meritorious services—just our own fashion of rewarding heroes, with the difference that we would have made him a Postmaster instead of a god, no doubt. In an angry moment he slew his wife, a goddess named Kaikilani Aiii. Remorse of conscience drove him mad, and tradition presents us the singular spectacle of a god traveling " on the shoulder;" for in his gnawing grief he wandered about from place to place boxing and wrestling with all whom he met. Of course this pastime soon lost its novelty, inasmuch as it must necessarily have been the case that when so powerful a deity sent a frail human opponent "to grass" he never came back any more. Therefore, he instituted games called makahiki, and ordered that they should be held in his honor, and then sailed for foreign lands on a three-cornered raft, stating that he would return some day—and that was the last of Lono. He was never seen any more; his raft got swamped, perhaps. But the people always expected his return, and thus they were easily led to accept Captain Cook as the restored god.

Some of the old natives believed Cook was Lono to the day of their death; but many did not, for they could not understand how he could die if he was a god.

Only a mile or so from Kealakekua Bay is a spot of historic interest—the place where the last battle was fought for idolatry. Of course we visited it, and came away as wise as most people do who go and gaze upon such mementoes of the past when in an unreflective mood.

While the first missionaries were on their way around the Horn, the idolatrous customs which had obtained in the island, as far back as tradition reached were suddenly broken up. Old

Kamehameha I., was dead, and his son, Liholiho, the new King was a free liver, a roystering, dissolute fellow, and hated the restraints of the ancient *tabu*.   His assistant in the Government, Kaahumanu, the Queen dowager, was proud and high-spirited, and hated the *tabu* because it restricted the privileges of her sex and degraded all women very nearly to the level of brutes.   So the case stood.   Liholiho had half a mind to put his foot down, Kaahumahu had a whole mind to badger him into doing it, and whiskey did the rest.   It was probably the rest.   It was probably the first time whiskey ever prominently figured as an aid to civilization.   Liholiho came up to Kailua as drunk as a piper, and attended a great feast ; the determined Queen spurred his drunken courage up to a reckless pitch, and then, while all the multitude stared in blank dismay, he moved deliberately forward and sat down with the women!   They

THE TABU BROKEN.

saw him eat from the same vessel with them, and were appalled ! Terrible moments drifted slowly by, and still the King ate, still he lived, still the lightnings of the insulted gods were withheld! Then conviction came like a revelation—the superstitions of a hundred generations passed from before the people like a cloud, and a shout went up, "the *tabu* is broken! the *tabu* is broken!"

Thus did King Liholiho and his dreadful whiskey preach the first sermon and prepare the way for the new gospel that was speeding southward over the waves of the Atlantic.

The *tabu* broken and destruction failing to follow the awful sacrilege, the people, with that childlike precipitancy which has always characterized them, jumped to the conclusion that their gods were a weak and wretched swindle, just as they formerly jumped to the conclusion that Captain Cook was no god, merely because he groaned, and promptly killed him without stopping to inquire whether a god might not groan as well as a man if it suited his convenience to do it; and satisfied that the idols were powerless to protect themselves they went to work at once and pulled them down—hacked them to pieces—applied the torch—annihilated them!

The pagan priests were furious. And well they might be; they had held the fattest offices in the land, and now they were beggared; they had been great—they had stood above the chiefs—and now they were vagabonds. They raised a revolt; they scared a number of people into joining their standard, and Bekuokalani, an ambitious offshoot of royalty, was easily persuaded to become their leader.

In the first skirmish the idolaters triumphed over the royal army sent against them, and full of confidence they resolved to march upon Kailua. The King sent an envoy to try and conciliate them, and came very near being an envoy short by the operation; the savages not only refused to listen to him, but wanted to kill him. So the King sent his men forth under Major General Kalaimoku and the two hosts met at Kuamoo. The battle was long and fierce—men and women fighting side by side, as was the custom—and when the day was done the rebels were flying in every direction in hopeless panic, and idolatry and the *tabu* were dead in the land!

The royalists marched gayly home to Kailua glorifying the new dispensation. "There is no power in the gods," said they; "they are a vanity and a lie. The army with idols was weak; the army without idols was strong and victorious!"

The nation was without a religion.

The missionary ship arrived in safety shortly afterward, timed by providential exactness to meet the emergency, and the Gospel was planted as in a virgin soil.

CHAPTER LXXIII.

AT noon, we hired a Kanaka to take us down to the ancient ruins at Honaunau in his canoe—price two dollars—reasonable enough, for a sea voyage of eight miles, counting both ways.

The native canoe is an irresponsible looking contrivance. I cannot think of anything to liken it to but a boy's sled runner hollowed out, and that does not quite convey the correct idea. It is about fifteen feet long, high and pointed at both ends, is a foot and a half or two feet deep, and so narrow that if you wedged a fat man into it you might not get him out again. It sits on top of the water like a duck, but it has an outrigger and does not upset easily, if you keep still. This outrigger is formed of two long bent sticks like plow handles, which project from one side, and to their outer ends is bound a curved beam composed of an extremely light wood, which skims along the surface of the water and thus saves you from an upset on that side, while the outrigger's weight is not so easily lifted as to make an upset on the other side a thing to be greatly feared. Still, until one gets used to sitting perched upon this knife-blade, he is apt to reason within himself that it would be more comfortable if there were just an outrigger or so on the other side also.

I had the bow seat, and Billings sat amidships and faced the Kanaka, who occupied the stern of the craft and did the paddling. With the first stroke the trim shell of a thing shot out from the shore like an arrow. There was not much to see. While we were on the shallow water of the reef, it was pastime to look down into the limpid depths at the large bunches of branching coral—the unique shrubbery of the sea. We lost that, though, when we got out into the dead blue water of the deep. But we had the picture of the surf, then, dashing angrily against the crag-bound shore and sending a foaming spray high into the air. There was interest in this beetling border, too, for it was honey-combed with quaint caves and arches

SURF-BATHING—SUCCESS.

and tunnels, and had a rude semblance of the dilapidated architecture of ruined keeps and castles rising out of the restless sea. When this novelty ceased to be a novelty, we turned our eyes shoreward and gazed at the long mountain with its rich green forests stretching up into the curtaining clouds, and at the specks of houses in the rearward distance and the diminished schooner riding sleepily at anchor. And when these grew tiresome we dashed boldly into the midst of a school of huge, beastly porpoises engaged at their eternal game of arching over a wave and disappearing, and then doing it over again and keeping it up—always circling over, in that way, like so many well-submerged wheels. But the porpoises wheeled themselves away, and then we were thrown upon our own resources. It did not take many minutes to discover that the sun was blazing like a bonfire, and that the weather was of a melting temperature. It had a drowsing effect, too.

In one place we came upon a large company of naked natives, of both sexes and all ages, amusing themselves with the national pastime of surf-bathing. Each heathen would paddle three or four hundred yards out to sea, (taking a short board with him), then face the shore and wait for a particularly prodigious billow to come along; at the right moment he would fling his board upon its foamy crest and himself upon the board, and here he would come whizzing by like a bombshell! It did not seem that a lightning express train could shoot along at a more hair-lifting speed. I tried surf-bathing once, subsequently, but made a failure of it. I got the board placed right, and at the right moment, too; but missed the connection myself.—The

board struck the shore in three quarters of a second, without any cargo, and I struck the bottom about the same time, with a couple of barrels of water in me. None but natives ever master the art of surf-bathing thoroughly.

SURF-BATHING—FAILURE.

At the end of an hour, we had made the four miles, and landed on a level point of land, upon which was a wide extent of old ruins, with many a tall cocoanut tree growing among them. Here was the ancient City of Refuge—a vast inclosure, whose stone walls were twenty feet thick at the base, and fifteen feet high; an oblong square, a thousand and forty feet one way and a fraction under seven hundred the other. Within this inclosure, in early times, has been three rude temples; each two hundred and ten feet long by one hundred wide, and thirteen high.

In those days, if a man killed another anywhere on the island the relatives were privileged to take the murderer's life; and then á chase for life and liberty began—the outlawed criminal flying through pathless forests and over mountain and plain, with his hopes fixed upon the protecting walls of the City of Refuge, and the avenger of blood following hotly after him! Sometimes the race was kept up to the very gates of the temple, and the panting pair sped through long files of excited natives, who watched the contest with flashing eye and dilated nostril, encouraging the hunted refugee with sharp, inspiriting ejaculations, and sending up a ringing shout of exultation when the saving gates closed upon him and the cheated pursuer sank

THE CITY OF REFUGE.

exhausted at the threshold. But sometimes the flying criminal fell under the hand of the avenger at the very door, when one more brave stride, one more brief second of time would have brought his feet upon the sacred ground and barred him against all harm. Where did these isolated pagans get this idea of a City of Refuge—this ancient Oriental custom?

This old sanctuary was sacred to all—even to rebels in arms and invading armies. Once within its walls, and confession made to the priest and absolution obtained, the wretch with a price upon his head could go forth without fear and without danger—he was *tabu*, and to harm him was death. The routed rebels in the lost battle for idolatry fled to this place to claim sanctuary, and many were thus saved.

Close to the corner of the great inclosure is a round structure of stone, some six or eight feet high, with a level top about ten or twelve in diameter. This was the place of execution. A high palisade of cocoanut piles shut out the cruel scenes from the vulgar multitude. Here criminals were killed, the flesh stripped from the bones and burned, and the bones secreted in holes in the body of the structure. If the man had been guilty of a high crime, the entire corpse was burned.

The walls of the temple are a study. The same food for speculation that is offered the visitor to the Pyramids of Egypt he will find here—the mystery of how they were constructed by a people unacquainted with science and mechanics. The natives have no invention of their own for hoisting heavy weights, they had no beasts of burden, and they have never even shown any knowledge of the properties of the lever. Yet some of the lava blocks quarried out, brought over rough, broken ground, and built into this wall, six or seven feet from the ground, are of prodigious size and would weigh tons. How did they transport and how raise them?

Both the inner and outer surfaces of the walls present a smooth front and are very creditable specimens of masonry. The blocks are of all manner of shapes and sizes, but yet are fitted together with the neatest exactness. The gradual narrowing of the wall from the base upward is accurately preserved.

No cement was used, but the edifice is firm and compact and is capable of resisting storm and decay for centuries. Who built this temple, and how was it built, and when, are mysteries that may never be unraveled.

Outside of these ancient walls lies a sort of coffin-shaped stone eleven feet four inches long and three feet square at the small end (it would weigh a few thousand pounds), which the high chief who held sway over this district many centuries ago brought thither on his shoulder one day to use as a lounge! This circumstance is established by the most reliable traditions. He used to lie down on it, in his indolent way, and keep an eye on his subjects at work for him and see that there was no "soldiering" done. And no doubt there was not any done to speak of, because he was a man of that sort of build that incites to attention to business on the part of an employee. He was fourteen or fifteen feet high. When he stretched himself at full length on his lounge, his legs hung down over the end, and when he snored he woke the dead. These facts are all attested by irrefragable tradition.

On the other side of the temple is a monstrous seven-ton rock, eleven feet long, seven feet wide and three feet thick. It is raised a foot or a

THE QUEEN'S ROCK.

foot and a half above the ground, and rests upon half a dozen little stony pedestals. The same old fourteen-footer brought it down from the mountain, merely for fun (he had his own

34†

notions about fun), and propped it up as we find it now and as others may find it a century hence, for it would take a score of horses to budge it from its position. They say that fifty or sixty years ago the proud Queen Kaahumanu used to fly to this rock for safety, whenever she had been making trouble with her fierce husband, and hide under it until his wrath was appeased. But these Kanakas will lie, and this statement is one of their ablest efforts—for Kaahumanu was six feet high— she was bulky—she was built like an ox—and she could no more have squeezed herself under that rock than she could have passed between the cylinders of a sugar mill. What could she gain by it, even if she succeeded? To be chased and abused by a savage husband could not be otherwise than humiliating to her high spirit, yet it could never make her feel so flat as an hour's repose under that rock would.

We walked a mile over a raised macadamized road of uniform width; a road paved with flat stones and exhibiting in its every detail a considerable degree of engineering skill. Some say that that wise old pagan, Kamehameha I. planned and built it, but others say it was built so long before his time that the knowledge of who constructed it has passed out of the traditions. In either case, however, as the handiwork of an untaught and degraded race it is a thing of pleasing interest. The stones are worn and smooth, and pushed apart in places, so that the road has the exact appearance of those ancient paved highways leading out of Rome which one sees in pictures.

The object of our tramp was to visit a great natural curiosity at the base of the foothills—a congealed cascade of lava. Some old forgotten volcanic eruption sent its broad river of fire down the mountain side here, and it poured down in a great torrent from an overhanging bluff some fifty feet high to the ground below. The flaming torrent cooled in the winds from the sea, and remains there to-day, all seamed, and frothed and rippled a petrified Niagara. It is very picturesque, and withal so natural that one might almost imagine it still flowed. A smaller stream trickled over the cliff and built up an isolated pyramid about thirty feet high, which has the semblance of a mass of large gnarled and knotted vines and roots and stems intricately twisted and woven together.

We passed in behind the cascade and the pyramid, and found the bluff pierced by several cavernous tunnels, whose crooked courses we followed a long distance.

Two of these winding tunnels stand as proof of Nature's mining abilities. Their floors are level, they are seven feet wide, and their roofs are gently arched. Their height is not uniform, however. We passed through one a hundred feet long, which leads through a spur of the hill and opens out well up in the sheer wall of a precipice whose foot rests in the waves of the sea. It is a commodious tunnel, except that there are occasional places in it where one must stoop to pass under. The roof is lava, of course, and is thickly studded with little lava-pointed icicles an inch long, which hardened as they dripped. They project as closely together as the iron teeth of a corn-sheller, and if one will stand up straight and walk any distance there, he can get his hair combed free of charge.

CHAPTER LXXIV.

WE got back to the schooner in good time, and then sailed down to Kau, where we disembarked and took final leave of the vessel. Next day we bought horses and bent our way over the summer-clad mountain-terraces, toward the great volcano of Kilauea (Ke-low-way-ah). We made nearly a two days' journey of it, but that was on account of laziness. Toward sunset on the second day, we reached an elevation of some four thousand feet above sea level, and as we picked our careful way through billowy wastes of lava long generations ago stricken dead and cold in the climax of its tossing fury, we began to come upon signs of the near presence of the volcano—signs in the nature of ragged fissures that discharged jets of sulphurous vapor into the air, hot from the molten ocean down in the bowels of the mountain.

Shortly the crater came into view. I have seen Vesuvius since, but it was a mere toy, a child's volcano, a soup-kettle, compared to this. Mount Vesuvius is a shapely cone thirty-six hundred feet high; its crater an inverted cone only three hundred feet deep, and not more than a thousand feet in diameter, if as much as that; its fires meagre, modest, and docile.—But here was a vast, perpendicular, walled cellar, nine hundred feet deep in some places, thirteen hundred in others, level-floored, and *ten miles in circumference!* Here was a yawning pit upon whose floor the armies of Russia could camp, and have room to spare.

Perched upon the edge of the crater, at the opposite end

from where we stood, was a small look-out house—say three miles away. It assisted us, by comparison, to comprehend and appreciate the great depth of the basin—it looked like a tiny martin-box clinging at the eaves of a cathedral. After some little time spent in resting and looking and ciphering, we hurried on to the hotel.

By the path it is half a mile from the Volcano House to the lookout-house. After a hearty supper we waited until it was thoroughly dark and then started to the crater. The first glance in that direction revealed a scene of wild beauty. There was a heavy fog over the crater and it was splendidly illuminated by the glare from the fires below. The illumination was two miles wide and a mile high, perhaps; and if you ever, on a dark night and at a distance beheld the light from thirty or forty blocks of distant build-ings all on fire at once, re-flected strongly against over-hanging clouds, you can form a fair idea of what this looked like.

A colossal column of cloud towered to a great height in the air immediately above the crater, and the outer swell of every one of its vast folds was dyed with a rich crimson luster, which was subdued to a pale rose tint in the depressions between. It glowed like a muffled torch and stretched upward to a dizzy height toward the zenith. I thought it just

THE PILLAR OF FIRE.

possible that its like had not been seen since the children of Israel wandered on their long march through the desert so many centuries ago over a path illuminated by the mysterious "pillar of fire." And I was sure that I now had a vivid conception of what the majestic "pillar of fire" was like, which almost amounted to a revelation.

Arrived at the little thatched lookout house, we rested our elbows on the railing in front and looked abroad over the wide crater and down over the sheer precipice at the seething fires beneath us. The view was a startling improvement on my daylight experience. I turned to see the effect on the balance of the company and found the reddest-faced set of men I almost ever saw. In the strong light every countenance glowed like red-hot iron, every shoulder was suffused with crimson and shaded rearward into dingy, shapeless obscurity! The place below looked like the infernal regions and these men like half-cooled devils just come up on a furlough.

I turned my eyes upon the volcano again. The "cellar" was tolerably well lighted up. For a mile and a half in front of us and half a mile on either side, the floor of the abyss was magnificently illuminated; beyond these limits the mists hung down their gauzy curtains and cast a deceptive gloom over all that made the twinkling fires in the remote corners of the crater seem countless leagues removed—made them seem like the camp-fires of a great army far away. Here was room for the imagination to work! You could imagine those lights the width of a continent away—and that hidden under the intervening darkness were hills, and winding rivers, and weary wastes of plain and desert—and even then the tremendous vista stretched on, and on, and on!—to the fires and far beyond! You could not compass it—it was the idea of eternity made tangible—and the longest end of it made visible to the naked eye!

The greater part of the vast floor of the desert under us was as black as ink, and apparently smooth and level; but over a mile square of it was ringed and streaked and striped with a thousand branching streams of liquid and gorgeously brilliant fire! It looked like a colossal railroad map of the State of Massachusetts done in chain lightning on a midnight sky. Imagine it—im-

agine a coal-black sky shivered into a tangled net-work of angry
fire!

Here and there were gleaming holes a hundred feet in diameter, broken in the dark crust, and in them the melted lava—
the color a dazzling white just tinged with yellow—was boiling

THE CRATER.

and surging furiously; and from these holes branched number-
less bright torrents in many directions, like the spokes of a
wheel, and kept a tolerably straight course for a while and then

swept round in huge rainbow curves, or made a long succession of sharp worm-fence angles, which looked precisely like the fiercest jagged lightning. These streams met other streams, and they mingled with and crossed and recrossed each other in every conceivable direction, like skate tracks on a popular skating ground. Sometimes streams twenty or thirty feet wide flowed from the holes to some distance without dividing—and through the opera-glasses we could see that they ran down small, steep hills and were genuine cataracts of fire, white at their source, but soon cooling and turning to the richest red, grained with alternate lines of black and gold. Every now and then masses of the dark crust broke away and floated slowly down these streams like rafts down a river. Occasionally the molten lava flowing under the superincumbent crust broke through—split a dazzling streak, from five hundred to a thousand feet long, like a sudden flash of lightning, and then acre after acre of the cold lava parted into fragments, turned up edgewise like cakes of ice when a great river breaks up, plunged downward and were swallowed in the crimson cauldron. Then the wide expanse of the " thaw " maintained a ruddy glow for a while, but shortly cooled and became black and level again. During a " thaw," every dismembered cake was marked by a glittering white border which was superbly shaded inward by aurora borealis rays, which were a flaming yellow where they joined the white border, and from thence toward their points tapered into glowing crimson, then into a rich, pale carmine, and finally into a faint blush that held its own a moment and then dimmed and turned black. Some of the streams preferred to mingle together in a tangle of fantastic circles, and then they looked something like the confusion of ropes one sees on a ship's deck when she has just taken in sail and dropped anchor —provided one can imagine those ropes on fire.

Through the glasses, the little fountains scattered about looked very beautiful. They boiled, and coughed, and spluttered, and discharged sprays of stringy red fire—of about the consistency of mush, for instance—from ten to fifteen feet into the air, along with a shower of brilliant white sparks—a quaint and unnatural mingling of gouts of blood and snow-flakes !

We had circles and serpents and streaks of lightning all twined and wreathed and tied together, without a break throughout an area more than a mile square (that amount of ground was covered, though it was not strictly "square"), and it was with a feeling of placid exultation that we reflected that many years had elapsed since any visitor had seen such a splendid display—since any visitor had seen anything more than the now snubbed and insignificant "North" and "South" lakes in action. We had been reading old files of Hawaiian newspapers and the "Record Book" at the Volcano House, and were posted.

I could see the North Lake lying out on the black floor away off in the outer edge of our panorama, and knitted to it by a web-work of lava streams. In its individual capacity it looked very little more respectable than a schoolhouse on fire. True, it was about nine hundred feet long and two or three hundred wide, but then, under the present circumstances, it necessarily appeared rather insignificant, and besides it was so distant from us.

I forgot to say that the noise made by the bubbling lava is not great, heard as we heard it from our lofty perch. It makes three distinct sounds—a rushing, a hissing, and a coughing or puffing sound; and if you stand on the brink and close your eyes it is no trick at all to imagine that you are sweeping down a river on a large low-pressure steamer, and that you hear the hissing of the steam about her boilers, the puffing from her escape-pipes and the churning rush of the water abaft her wheels. The smell of sulphur is strong, but not unpleasant to a sinner.

We left the lookout house at ten o'clock in a half cooked condition, because of the heat from Pele's furnaces, and wrapping up in blankets, for the night was cold, we returned to our Hotel.

CHAPTER LXXV.

THE next night was appointed for a visit to the bottom of the crater, for we desired to traverse its floor and see the "North Lake" (of fire) which lay two miles away, toward the further wall. After dark half a dozen of us set out, with lanterns and native guides, and climbed down a crazy, thousand-foot pathway in a crevice fractured in the crater wall, and reached the bottom in safety.

The irruption of the previous evening had spent its force and the floor looked black and cold; but when we ran out upon it we found it hot yet, to the feet, and it was likewise riven with crevices which revealed the underlying fires gleaming vindictively. A neighboring cauldron was threatening to overflow, and this added to the dubiousness of the situation. So the native guides refused to continue the venture, and then every body deserted except a stranger named Marlette. He said he had been in the crater a dozen times in daylight and believed he could find his way through it at night. He thought that a run of three hundred yards would carry us over the hottest part of the floor and leave us our shoe-soles. His pluck gave me back-bone. We took one lantern and instructed the guides to hang the other to the roof of the look-out house to serve as a beacon for us in case we got lost, and then the party started back up the precipice and Marlette and I made our run. We skipped over the hot floor and over the red crevices with brisk dispatch and reached the cold lava safe but with pretty warm feet. Then we took things leisurely and comfortably,

jumping tolerably wide and probably bottomless chasms, and
threading our way through picturesque lava upheavals with
considerable confidence. When we got fairly away from the
cauldrons of boiling fire, we seemed to be in a gloomy desert,
and a suffocatingly dark one, surrounded by dim walls that
seemed to tower to the sky. The only cheerful objects were
the glinting stars high overhead.

By and by Marlette shouted "Stop!" I never stopped
quicker in my life. I asked what the matter was. He said
we were out of the path. He said we must not try to go on
till we found it again, for we were surrounded with beds of
rotten lava through which we could easily break and plunge
down a thousand feet. I thought eight hundred would answer
for me, and was about to say so when Marlette partly proved
his statement by accidentally crushing through and disappear-

BREAKING THROUGH.

ing to his arm-pits. He got out and we hunted for the path with
the lantern. He said there was only one path and that it was
but vaguely defined. We could not find it. The lava surface
was all alike in the lantern light. But he was an ingenious
man. He said it was not the lantern that had informed him
that we were out of the path, but his *feet*. He had noticed a
crisp grinding of fine lava-needles under his feet, and some
instinct reminded him that in the path these were all worn
away. So he put the lantern behind him, and began to search
with his boots instead of his eyes. It was good sagacity. The

first time his foot touched a surface that did not grind under it he announced that the trail was found again; and after that we kept up a sharp listening for the rasping sound and it always warned us in time.

It was a long tramp, but an exciting one. We reached the North Lake between ten and eleven o'clock, and sat down on a huge overhanging lava-shelf, tired but satisfied. The spectacle presented was worth coming double the distance to see. Under us, and stretching away before us, was a heaving sea of molten fire of seemingly limitless extent. The glare from it was so blinding that it was some time before we could bear to look upon it steadily. It was like gazing at the sun at noonday, except that the glare was not quite so white. At unequal distances all around the shores of the lake were nearly white-hot chimneys or hollow drums of lava, four or five feet high, and up through them were bursting gorgeous sprays of lava-gouts and gem spangles, some white, some red and some golden

FIRE FOUNTAINS.

—a ceaseless bombardment, and one that fascinated the eye with its unapproachable splendor. The more distant jets, sparkling up through an intervening gossamer veil of vapor, seemed miles away; and the further the curving ranks of fiery fountains receded, the more fairy-like and beautiful they appeared.

Now and then the surging bosom of the lake under our noses would calm down ominously and seem to be gathering strength for an enterprise; and then all of a sudden a red dome of lava of the bulk of an ordinary dwelling would heave itself aloft like an escaping balloon, then burst asunder, and out of its heart would flit a pale-green film of vapor, and float upward and vanish in the darkness—a released soul soaring homeward from captivity with the damned, no doubt. The crashing plunge of the ruined dome into the lake again would send a world of seething billows lashing against the shores and shaking the foundations of our perch. By and by, a loosened mass of the hanging shelf we sat on tumbled into the lake, jarring the surroundings like an earthquake and delivering a suggestion that may have been intended for a hint, and may not. We did not wait to see.

We got lost again on our way back, and were more than an hour hunting for the path. We were where we could see the beacon lantern at the look-out house at the time, but thought it was a star and paid no attention to it. We reached the hotel at two o'clock in the morning pretty well fagged out.

Kilauea never overflows its vast crater, but bursts a passage for its lava through the mountain side when relief is necessary, and then the destruction is fearful. About 1840 it rent its overburdened stomach and sent a broad river of fire careering down to the sea, which swept away forests, huts, plantations and every thing else that lay in its path. The stream was *five miles broad*, in places, and *two hundred feet deep*, and the distance it traveled was forty miles. It tore up and bore away acre-patches of land on its bosom like rafts—rocks, trees and all intact. At night the red glare was visible a hundred miles at sea; and at a distance of forty miles fine print could be read at midnight. The atmosphere was poisoned with sulphurous vapors and choked with falling ashes, pumice stones and cinders; countless columns of smoke rose up and blended together in a tumbled canopy that hid the heavens and glowed with a

ruddy flush reflected from the fires below ; here and there jets
of lava sprung hundreds of feet into the air and burst into rock-
et-sprays that returned to earth in a crimson rain ; and all the
while the laboring mountain shook with Nature's great palsy,

LAVA STREAM.

and voiced its distress in moanings and the muffled booming
of subterranean thunders.

Fishes were killed for twenty miles along the shore, where

the lava entered the sea. The earthquakes caused some loss
of human life, and a prodigious tidal wave swept inland, carrying every thing before it and drowning a number of natives.
The devastation consummated along the route traversed by the

A TIDAL WAVE.

river of lava was complete and incalculable. Only a **Pompeii**
and a Herculaneum were needed at the foot of Kilauea to **make**
the story of the irruption immortal.

CHAPTER LXXVI.

WE rode horseback all around the island of Hawaii (the crooked road making the distance two hundred miles), and enjoyed the journey very much. We were more than a week making the trip, because our Kanaka horses would not go by a house or a hut without stopping—whip and spur could not alter their minds about it, and so we finally found that it economized time to let them have their way. Upon inquiry the mystery was explained: the natives are such thorough-going gossips that they never pass a house without stopping to swap news, and consequently their horses learn to regard that sort of thing as an essential part of the whole duty of man, and his salvation not to be compassed without it. However, at a former crisis of my life I had once taken an aristocratic young lady out driving, behind a horse that had just retired from a long and honorable career as the moving impulse of a milk wagon, and so this present experience awoke a reminiscent sadness in me in place of the exasperation more natural to the occasion. I remembered how helpless I was that day, and how humiliated; how ashamed I was of having intimated to the girl that I had always owned the horse and was accustomed to grandeur; how hard I tried to appear easy, and even vivacious, under suffering that was consuming my vitals; how placidly and maliciously the girl smiled, and kept on smiling, while my hot blushes baked themselves into a permanent blood-pudding in my face; how the horse ambled from one side of the street to the other and waited complacently before every third house

two minutes and a quarter while I belabored his back and re-
viled him in my heart; how I tried to keep him from turning
corners, and failed; how I moved heaven and earth to get him
out of town, and did not succeed; how he traversed the entire
settlement and delivered imaginary milk at a hundred and
sixty-two different domiciles, and how he finally brought up at
a dairy depot and refused to budge further, thus rounding and

TRIP ON THE MILKY WAY.

completing the revealment of what the plebeian service of his
life had been; how, in eloquent silence, I walked the girl home,
and how, when I took leave of her, her parting remark scorched
my soul and appeared to blister me all over: she said that my
horse was a fine, capable animal, and I must have taken great
comfort in him in my time—but that if I would take along
some milk-tickets next time, and appear to deliver them at the
various halting places, it might expedite his movements a little.
There was a coolness between us after that.

    In one place in the island of Hawaii, we saw a laced and
35†

ruffled cataract of limpid water leaping from a sheer precipice fifteen hundred feet high; but that sort of scenery finds its stanchest ally in the arithmetic rather than in spectacular effect. If one desires to be so stirred by a poem of Nature wrought in the happily commingled graces of picturesque rocks, glimpsed distances, foliage, color, shifting lights and shadows, and falling water, that the tears almost come into his eyes so potent is the charm exerted, he need not go away from America to enjoy such an experience. The Rainbow Fall, in Watkins Glen (N. Y.), on the Erie railway, is an example. It would recede into pitiable insignificance if the callous tourist drew an arithmetic on it; but left to compete for the honors simply on scenic grace and beauty—the grand, the august and the sublime being barred the contest—it could challenge the old world and the new to produce its peer.

In one locality, on our journey, we saw some horses that had been born and reared on top of the mountains, above the range of running water, and consequently they had never drank that fluid in their lives, but had been always accustomed to quenching their thirst by eating dew-laden or shower-wetted leaves. And now it was destructively funny to see them sniff suspiciously at a pail of water, and then put in their noses and try to take a *bite* out of the fluid, as if it were a solid. Finding it liquid, they would snatch away their heads and fall to trembling, snorting and showing other evidences of fright. When they became convinced at last that the water was friendly and harmless, they thrust in their noses up to their eyes, brought out a mouthful of the water, and proceeded to *chew* it complacently. We saw a man coax, kick and spur one of them five or ten minutes before he could make it cross a running stream. It spread its nostrils, distended its eyes and trembled all over, just as horses customarily do in the presence of a serpent—and for aught I know it thought the crawling stream *was* a serpent.

In due course of time our journey came to an end at Kawaehae (usually pronounced To-a-*hi*—and before we find fault with this elaborate orthographical method of arriving at such

A VIEW IN THE IAO VALLEY.

an unostentatious result, let us lop off the *ugh* from our word
"though"). I made this horseback trip on a mule. I paid ten
dollars for him at Kau (Kah-oo), added four to get him shod,
rode him two hundred miles, and then sold him for fifteen dollars. I mark the circumstance with a white stone (in the absence of chalk—for I never saw a white stone that a body could
mark anything with, though out of respect for the ancients I
have tried it often enough); for up to that day and date it was
the first strictly commercial transaction I had ever entered into,
and come out winner. We returned to Honolulu, and from
thence sailed to the island of Maui, and spent several weeks
there very pleasantly. I still remember, with a sense of indolent luxury, a picnicing excursion up a romantic gorge there,
called the Iao Valley. The trail lay along the edge of a brawl-
ing stream in the bottom of the gorge—a shady route, for it
was well roofed with the verdant domes of forest trees. Through
openings in the foliage we glimpsed picturesque scenery that
revealed ceaseless changes and new charms with every step of
our progress. Perpendicular walls from one to three thousand
feet high guarded the way, and were sumptuously plumed with
varied foliage, in places, and in places swathed in waving ferns.
Passing shreds of cloud trailed their shadows across these shining fronts, mottling them with blots; billowy masses of white
vapor hid the turreted summits, and far above the vapor swelled
a background of gleaming green crags and cones that came and
went, through the veiling mists, like islands drifting in a fog;
sometimes the cloudy curtain descended till half the cañon wall
was hidden, then shredded gradually away till only airy glimpses
of the ferny front appeared through it—then swept aloft and
left it glorified in the sun again. Now and then, as our position changed, rocky bastions swung out from the wall, a mimic
ruin of castellated ramparts and crumbling towers clothed with
mosses and hung with garlands of swaying vines, and as we
moved on they swung back again and hid themselves once
more in the foliage. Presently a verdure-clad needle of stone,
a thousand feet high, stepped out from behind a corner, and
mounted guard over the mysteries of the valley. It seemed to

me that if Captain Cook needed a monument, here was one ready made—therefore, why not put up his sign here, and sell out the venerable cocoanut stump?

But the chief pride of Maui is her dead volcano of Haleakala—which means, translated, "the house of the sun." We climbed a thousand feet up the side of this isolated colossus one afternoon; then camped, and next day climbed the remaining nine thousand feet, and anchored on the summit, where we built a fire and froze and roasted by turns, all night. With the first pallor of dawn we got up and saw things that were new to us. Mounted on a commanding pinnacle, we watched Nature work her silent wonders. The sea was spread abroad on every hand, its tumbled surface seeming only wrinkled and dimpled in the distance. A broad valley below appeared like an ample checker-board, its velvety green sugar plantations alternating with dun squares of barrenness and groves of trees diminished to mossy tufts. Beyond the valley were mountains picturesquely grouped together; but bear in mind, we fancied that we were looking *up* at these things—not down. We seemed to sit in the bottom of a symmetrical bowl ten thousand feet deep, with the valley and the skirting sea lifted away into the sky above us! It was curious; and not only curious, but aggravating; for it was having our trouble all for nothing, to climb ten thousand feet toward heaven and then have to look *up* at our scenery. However, we had to be content with it and make the best of it; for, all we could do we could not coax our landscape down out of the clouds. Formerly, when I had read an article in which Poe treated of this singular fraud perpetrated upon the eye by isolated great altitudes, I had looked upon the matter as an invention of his own fancy.

I have spoken of the outside view—but we had an inside one, too. That was the yawning dead crater, into which we now and then tumbled rocks, half as large as a barrel, from our perch, and saw them go careering down the almost perpendicular sides, bounding three hundred feet at a jump; kicking up dust-clouds wherever they struck; diminishing to our view as they sped farther into distance; growing invisible, finally, and only betraying their course by faint little puffs of dust; and coming to a halt at last in the bottom of the abyss, two thousand five

MAGNIFICENT SPORT.

hundred feet down from where they started! It was magnificent sport. We wore ourselves out at it.

The crater of Vesuvius, as I have before remarked, is a modest pit about a thousand feet deep and three thousand in circumference; that of Kilauea is somewhat deeper, and *ten miles* in circumference. But what are either of them compared to the vacant stomach of Haleakala? I will not offer any figures of my own, but give official ones—those of Commander Wilkes, U. S. N., who surveyed it and testifies that it is *twenty-seven miles in circumference!* If it had a level bottom it would make a fine site for a city like London. It must have afforded a spectacle worth contemplating in the old days when its furnaces gave full rein to their anger.

Presently vagrant white clouds came drifting along, high over the sea and the valley; then they came in couples and groups; then in imposing squadrons; gradually joining their forces, they banked themselves solidly together, a thousand feet under us, and *totally shut out land and ocean*—not a vestige of *anything* was left in view but just a little of the rim of the crater, circling away from the pinnacle whereon we sat (for a ghostly procession of wanderers from the filmy hosts without had drifted through a chasm in the crater wall and filed round and round, and gathered and sunk and blended together till the abyss was stored to the brim with a fleecy fog). Thus banked, motion ceased, and silence reigned. Clear to the horizon, league on league, the snowy floor stretched without a break—not level, but in rounded folds, with shallow creases between, and with here and there stately piles of vapory architecture lifting themselves aloft out of the common plain—some near at hand, some in the middle distances, and others relieving the monotony of the remote solitudes. There was little conversation, for the impressive scene overawed speech. I felt like the Last Man, neglected of the judgment, and left pinnacled in mid-heaven, a forgotten relic of a vanished world.

While the hush yet brooded, the messengers of the coming resurrection appeared in the East. A growing warmth suffused the horizon, and soon the sun emerged and looked out over the cloud-waste, flinging bars of ruddy light across it, staining its folds and billow-caps with blushes, purpling the shaded troughs between, and glorifying the massy vapor-palaces and cathedrals with a wasteful splendor of all blendings and combinations of rich coloring.

It was the sublimest spectacle I ever witnessed, and I think the memory of it will remain with me always.

CHAPTER LXXVII.

I STUMBLED upon one curious character in the Island of
Mani. He became a sore annoyance to me in the course
of time. My first glimpse of him was in a sort of public room
in the town of Lahaina. He occupied a chair at the opposite
side of the apartment, and sat eyeing our party with interest
for some minutes, and listening as critically to what we were
saying as if he fancied we were talking to him and expecting
him to reply. I thought it very sociable in a stranger. Presently, in the course of conversation, I made a statement bearing
upon the subject under discussion—and I made it with due
modesty, for there was nothing extraordinary about it, and it
was only put forth in illustration of a point at issue. I had
barely finished when this person spoke out with rapid utterance
and feverish anxiety :

" Oh, that was certainly remarkable, after a fashion, but you
ought to have seen *my* chimney—you ought to have seen *my*
chimney, sir! Smoke! I wish I may hang if—Mr. Jones,
you remember that chimney—you *must* remember that chimney! No, no—I recollect, now, you warn't living on this side
of the island then. But I am telling you nothing but the truth,
and I wish I may never draw another breath if that chimney
didn't smoke so that the smoke actually got *caked* in it and I
had to dig it out with a pickaxe! You may smile, gentlemen,
but the High Sheriff's got a hunk of it which I dug out before
his eyes, and so it's perfectly easy for you to go and examine
for yourselves."

The interruption broke up the conversation, which had already begun to lag, and we presently hired some natives and an out-rigger canoe or two, and went out to overlook a grand surf-bathing contest.

Two weeks after this, while talking in a company, I looked up and detected this same man boring through and through me with his intense eye, and noted again his twitching muscles and his feverish anxiety to speak. The moment I paused, he said :

" *Beg* your pardon, sir, beg your pardon, but it can only be considered remarkable when brought into strong outline by isolation. Sir, contrasted with a circumstance which occurred in my own experience, it instantly becomes commonplace. No, not that—for I will not speak so discourteously of any experience in the career of a stranger and a gentleman—but I am *obliged* to say that you could not, and you *would* not ever again refer to this tree as a *large* one, if you could behold, as I have, the great Yakmatack tree, in the island of Ounaska, sea of Kamtchatka—a tree, sir, not one inch less than four hundred and fifteen feet in solid diameter !—and I wish I may die in a minute if it isn't so ! Oh, you needn't look so questioning, gentlemen ; here's old Cap Saltmarsh can say whether I know what I'm talking about or not. I showed him the tree."

Captain Saltmarsh.—" Come, now, cat your anchor, lad— you're heaving too taut. You *promised* to show me that stunner, and I walked more than eleven mile with you through the cussedest jungle *I* ever see, a hunting for it ; but the tree you showed me finally warn't as big around as a beer cask, and *you* know that your own self, Markiss."

" Hear the man talk ! Of *course* the tree was reduced that way, but didn't I *explain* it ? Answer me, didn't I ? Didn't I say I wished you could have seen it when *I* first saw it ? When you got up on your ear and called me names, and said I had brought you eleven miles to look at a sapling, didn't I *explain* to you that all the whale-ships in the North Seas had been wooding off of it for more than twenty-seven years ? And did **you** s'pose the tree could last for-*ever*, con-*found* it ? I

don't see why you want to keep back things that way, and try
to injure a person that's never done *you* any harm."

Somehow this man's presence made me uncomfortable, and
I was glad when a native arrived at that moment to say that

ELEVEN MILES TO SEE.

Muckawow, the most companionable and luxurious among the
rude war-chiefs of the Islands, desired us to come over and help
him enjoy a missionary whom he had found trespassing on his
grounds.

I think it was about ten days afterward that, as I finished a
statement I was making for the instruction of a group of friends
and acquaintances, and which made no pretence of being extraordinary, a familiar voice chimed instantly in on the heels of
my last word, and said:

"But, my dear sir, there was *nothing* remarkable about that
horse, or the circumstance either—nothing in the world! I
mean no sort of offence when I say it, sir, but you really do
not know anything whatever about speed. Bless your heart,
if you could only have seen my mare Margaretta; *there* was a
beast!—*there* was lightning for you! Trot! Trot is no name

for it—she flew! How she *could* whirl a buggy along! I started her out once, sir—Colonel Bilgewater, *you* recollect that animal perfectly well—I started her out about thirty or thirty-five yards ahead of the awfullest storm I ever saw in my life, and it chased us upwards of eighteen miles! It did, by the everlasting hills! And I'm telling you nothing but the unvarnished truth when I say that not one single drop of rain fell on me—not a single *drop*, sir! And I swear to it! But my dog was a-swimming behind the wagon all the way!"

CHASED BY A STORM.

For a week or two I stayed mostly within doors, for I seemed to meet this person everywhere, and he had become utterly hateful to me. But one evening I dropped in on Captain Perkins and his friends, and we had a sociable time. About ten o'clock I chanced to be talking about a merchant friend of mine, and without really intending it, the remark slipped out that he was a little mean and parsimonious about paying his workmen. Instantly, through the steam of a hot whiskey punch on the opposite side of the room, a remembered voice shot—and for a moment I trembled on the imminent verge of profanity:

"Oh, my dear sir, really you expose yourself when you parade *that* as a surprising circumstance. Bless your heart and hide, you are ignorant of the very A B C of meanness! ignorant as the unborn babe! ignorant as unborn *twins!* You don't know *any thing* about it! It is pitiable to see you, sir, a well-spoken and prepossessing stranger, making such an enormous pow-wow here about a subject concerning which your ignorance is perfectly humiliating! Look me in the eye, if you please; look me in the eye. John James Godfrey was the son of poor but honest parents in the State of Mississippi—boyhood friend of mine—bosom comrade in later years. Heaven rest his noble spirit, he is gone from us now. John James Godfrey was hired by the Hayblossom Mining Company in California to do some blasting for them—the "Incorporated Company of Mean Men," the boys used to call it.

Well, one day he drilled a hole about four feet deep and put in an awful blast of powder, and was standing over it ramming it down with an iron crowbar about nine foot long, when the cussed thing struck a spark and fired the powder, and scat! away John Godfrey whizzed like a skyrocket, him and his crowbar! Well, sir, he kept on going up in the air higher and higher, till he didn't look any bigger than a boy—and he kept going on up higher and higher, till he didn't look any big-

LEAVING WORK.

ger than a doll—and he kept on going up higher and higher, till he didn't look any bigger than a little small bee—and then

he went out of sight! Presently he came in sight again, looking like a little small bee—and he came along down further
and further, till he looked as big as a doll again—and down
further and further, till he was as big as a boy again—and further and further, till he was a full-sized man once more; and
then him and his crowbar came a wh-izzing down and lit right
exactly in the same old tracks and went to r-ramming down,
and r-ramming down, and r-ramming down again, just the same
as if nothing had happened! Now do you know, that poor
cuss warn't gone only sixteen minutes, and yet that Incorporated Company of Mean Men DOCKED HIM FOR THE LOST TIME!'"

I said I had the headache, and so excused myself and went
home. And on my diary I entered "another night spoiled"
by this offensive loafer. And a fervent curse was set down
with it to keep the item company. And the very next day I
packed up, out of all patience, and left the Island.

Almost from the very beginning, I regarded that man as a
liar.

.   .   .   .

The line of points represents an interval of years. At the
end of which time the opinion hazarded in that last sentence
came to be gratifyingly and remarkably endorsed, and by
wholly disinterested persons. The man Markiss was found
one morning hanging to a beam of his own bedroom (the doors
and windows securely fastened on the inside), dead; and on
his breast was pinned a paper in his own handwriting begging
his friends to suspect no innocent person of having any thing
to do with his death, for that it was the work of his own hands
entirely. Yet the jury brought in the astounding verdict that
deceased came to his death "by the hands of some person or
persons unknown!" They explained that the perfectly undeviating consistency of Markiss's character for thirty years towered aloft as colossal and indestructible testimony, that whatever statement he chose to make was entitled to instant and
unquestioning acceptance as a *lie*. And they furthermore
stated their belief that he was not dead, and instanced the

strong circumstantial evidence of his own word that he *was* dead—and beseeched the coroner to delay the funeral as long as possible, which was done.   And so in the tropical climate of Lahaina the coffin stood open for seven days, and then even the loyal jury gave him up.   But they sat on him again, and changed their verdict to "suicide induced by mental aberration"—because, said they, with penetration, "he said he was dead, and he *was* dead; and would he have told the truth if he had been in his right mind ?   *No,* sir."

CHAPTER LXXVIII.

AFTER half a year's luxurious vagrancy in the islands, I took shipping in a sailing vessel, and regretfully returned to San Francisco—a voyage in every way delightful, but without an incident: unless lying two long weeks in a dead calm, eighteen hundred miles from the nearest land, may rank as an incident. Schools of whales grew so tame that day after day they played about the ship among the porpoises and the sharks without the least apparent fear of us, and we pelted them with empty bottles for lack of better sport. Twenty-four hours afterward these bottles would be still lying on the glassy water under our noses, showing that the ship had not moved out of her place in all that time. The calm was absolutely breathless, and the surface of the sea absolutely without a wrinkle. For a whole day and part of a night we lay so close to another ship that had drifted to our vicinity, that we carried on conversations with her passengers, introduced each other by name, and became pretty intimately acquainted with people we had never heard of before, and have never heard of since. This was the only vessel we saw during the whole lonely voyage. We had fifteen passengers, and to show how hard pressed they were at last for occupation and amusement, I will mention that the gentlemen gave a good part of their time every day, during the calm, to trying to sit on an empty champagne bottle (lying on its side), and thread a needle without touching their heels to the deck, or falling over; and the ladies sat in the shade of the mainsail, and watched the enterprise with absorbing interest. We were at sea five Sundays; and yet, but for the almanac, we never would have known but that all the other days were Sundays too.

I was home again, in San Francisco, without means and without employment. I tortured my brain for a saving scheme of some kind, and at last a public lecture occurred to me! I sat down and wrote one, in a fever of hopeful anticipation. I showed it to several friends, but they all shook their heads. They said nobody would come to hear me, and I would make a humiliating fail-

OUR AMUSEMENTS.

ure of it. They said that as I had never spoken in public, I would break down in the delivery, anyhow. I was disconsolate now. But at last an editor slapped me on the back and told me to "go ahead." He said, "Take the largest house in town, and charge a dollar a ticket." The audacity of the proposition was charming; it seemed fraught with practical worldly wisdom, however. The proprietor of the several theatres endorsed the advice, and said I might have his handsome new opera-house at half price—fifty dollars. In sheer desperation I took it—on credit, for sufficient reasons. In three days I did a hundred and fifty dollars' worth of printing and advertising, and was the most distressed and frightened creature on the Pacific coast. I could not sleep—who could, under such circumstances? For other people there was facetiousness in the last line of my posters, but to me it was plaintive with a pang when I wrote it:

"Doors open at 7½. The trouble will begin at 8."

That line has done good service since. Showmen have borrowed it frequently. I have even seen it appended to a newspaper advertisement reminding school pupils in vacation what time next term would begin. As those three days of suspense dragged by, I grew more and more unhappy. I had sold two hundred tickets among my personal friends, but I feared they might not come. My lecture, which had seemed "humorous" to me, at first, grew steadily more and more dreary, till not a vestige of fun seemed left, and I grieved that I could not bring a coffin on the stage and turn the thing into a funeral. I was so panic-stricken, at last, that I went to three old friends, giants in stature, cordial by nature, and stormy-voiced, and said:

"This thing is going to be a failure; the jokes in it are so dim that nobody will ever see them; I would like to have you sit in the parquette, and help me through."

They said they would. Then I went to the wife of a popular citizen, and said that if she was willing to do me a very great kindness, I would be glad if she and her husband would sit prominently in the left-hand stage-box, where the whole house could see them. I explained that I should need help, and would turn toward her and smile, as a signal, when I had been delivered of an obscure joke—"and then," I added, "don't wait to investigate, but *respond !*"

She promised. Down the street I met a man I never had seen before. He had been drinking, and was beaming with smiles and good nature. He said:

"My name's Sawyer. You don't know me, but that don't matter. I haven't got a cent, but if you knew how bad I wanted to laugh, you'd give me a ticket. Come, now, what do you say ?"

"Is your laugh hung on a hair-trigger ?—that is, is it critical, or can you get it off *easy ?*"

My drawling infirmity of speech so affected him that he laughed a specimen or two that struck me as being about the article I wanted, and I gave him a ticket, and appointed him to sit in the second circle, in the centre, and be responsible for that division of the house. I gave him minute instructions about how to detect indistinct jokes, and then went away, and left him chuckling placidly over the novelty of the idea.

I ate nothing on the last of the three eventful days—I only suffered. I had advertised that on this third day the box-office would be opened for the sale of reserved seats. I crept down to the theatre at four in the afternoon to see if any sales had been made. The ticket seller was gone, the box-office was locked up. I had to swallow suddenly, or my heart would have got out. " No sales," I said to myself; " I might have known it." I thought of suicide, pretended illness, flight. I thought of these things in earnest, for I was very miserable and scared. But of course I had to drive them away, and prepare to meet my fate. I could not wait for half-past seven—I wanted to face the horror, and end it—the feeling of many a man doomed to hang,

SEVERE CASE OF STAGE-FRIGHT.

no doubt. I went down back streets at six o'clock, and entered the theatre by the back door. I stumbled my way in the dark among the ranks of canvas scenery, and stood on the stage. The house was gloomy and silent, and its emptiness depressing. I went into the dark among the scenes again, and for an hour and a half gave myself up to the horrors, wholly unconscious of everything else. Then I heard a murmur; it rose higher and higher, and ended in a crash, mingled with cheers. It made my hair raise, it was so close to me, and so loud. There was a pause, and then another; presently came a third, and before I well knew what I was about, I was in the middle of the stage, staring at a sea of faces, bewildered

by the fierce glare of the lights, and quaking in every limb
with a terror that seemed like to take my life away. The
house was full, aisles and all!

The tumult in my heart and brain and legs continued a full
minute before I could gain any command over myself. Then
I recognized the charity and the friendliness in the faces before
me, and little by little my fright melted away, and I began to

MY THREE PARQUETTE ALLIES.

talk Within three or four minutes I was comfortable, and
even content. My three chief allies, with three auxiliaries,
were on hand, in the parquette, all sitting together, all armed

SAWYER IN THE CIRCLE.

with bludgeons, and all
ready to make an onslaught
upon the feeblest joke that
might show its head. And
whenever a joke did fall,
their bludgeons came down
and their faces seemed to
split from ear to ear; Sawyer, whose hearty counte-
nance was seen looming
redly in the centre of the
second circle, took it up,
and the house was carried
handsomely. Inferior jokes
never fared so royally before. Presently I delivered a bit of

serious matter with impressive unction (it was my pet), and the audience listened with an absorbed hush that gratified me more than any applause; and as I dropped the last word of the clause, I happened to turn and catch Mrs. ——'s intent and waiting eye; my conversation with her flashed upon me, and in spite of all I could do I smiled. She took it for the signal, and promptly delivered a mellow laugh that touched off the whole audience; and the explosion that followed was the triumph of the evening. I thought that that honest man Sawyer would choke himself; and as for the bludgeons, they performed like pile-drivers. But my poor little morsel of pathos was ruined. It was taken in good faith as an intentional joke, and the prize one of the entertainment, and I wisely let it go at that.

All the papers were kind in the morning; my appetite returned; I had abundance of money. All's well that ends well.

CHAPTER LXXIX.

I LAUNCHED out as a lecturer, now, with great boldness. I had the field all to myself, for public lectures were almost an unknown commodity in the Pacific market. They are not so rare, now, I suppose. I took an old personal friend along to play agent for me, and for two or three weeks we roamed through Nevada and California and had a very cheerful time of it. Two days before I lectured in Virginia City, two stage-coaches were robbed within two miles of the town. The daring act was committed just at dawn, by six masked men, who sprang up alongside the coaches, presented revolvers at the heads of the drivers and passengers, and commanded a general dismount. Everybody climbed down, and the robbers took their watches and every cent they had. Then they took gun-powder and blew up the express specie boxes and got their contents. The leader of the robbers was a small, quick-spoken man, and the fame of his vigorous manner and his intrepidity was in everybody's mouth when we arrived.

The night after instructing Virginia, I walked over the desolate "divide" and down to Gold Hill, and lectured there. The lecture done, I stopped to talk with a friend, and did not start back till eleven. The "divide" was high, unoccupied ground, between the towns, the scene of twenty midnight murders and a hundred robberies. As we climbed up and stepped out on this eminence, the Gold Hill lights dropped out of sight at our backs, and the night closed down gloomy and dismal. A sharp wind swept the place, too, and chilled our perspiring bodies through.

"I tell you I don't like this place at night," said Mike the agent.

"Well, don't speak so loud," I said. "You needn't remind anybody that we are here."

Just then a dim figure approached me from the direction of Virginia—a man, evidently. He came straight at me, and I stepped aside to let him pass; he stepped in the way and confronted me again. Then I saw that he had a mask on and was holding something in my face—I heard a click-click and recognized a revolver in dim outline. I pushed the barrel aside with my hand and said:

"Don't!"

He ejaculated sharply:

"Your watch! Your money!"

I said:

"You can have them with pleasure—but take the pistol away from my face, please. It makes me shiver."

"No remarks! Hand out your money!"

"Certainly—I—"

"Put up your hands! Don't you go for a weapon! Put 'em up! Higher!"

I held them above my head.

A pause. Then:

"Are you going to hand out your money or not?"

I dropped my hands to my pockets and said:

Certainly! I—"

"Put up your *hands*! Do you want your head blown off? Higher!"

I put them above my head again.

Another pause.

Are you going to hand out your money or *not?* Ah-ah—again? Put up your hands! By George, you want the head shot off you awful bad!"

"Well, friend, I'm trying my best to please you. You tell

me to give up my money, and when I reach for it you tell me to put up my hands. If you would only—. Oh, now—don't! All six of you at me! That other man will get away while.— Now please take some of those revolvers out of my face—*do*, if you *please!* Every time one of them clicks, my liver comes up into my throat! If you have a mother—any of you—or if any of you have ever *had* a mother—or a—grandmother—or a—"

"Cheese it! *Will* you give up your money, or have we got to—. There-there—none of that! Put up your *hands!*"

"Gentlemen—I know you are gentlemen by your—"

"Silence! If you want to be facetious, young man, there are times and places more fitting. *This* is a serious business."

"You prick the marrow of my opinion. The funerals I have attended in my time were comedies compared to it. Now *I* think—"

"Curse your palaver! Your money!—your money!— your money! Hold!—put up your hands!"

"Gentlemen, listen to reason. You *see* how I am situated —now *don't* put those pistols so close—I smell the powder. You see how I am situated. If I had four hands—so that I could hold up two and—"

"Throttle him! Gag him! Kill him!"

"Gentlemen, *don't!* Nobody's watching the other fellow. Why don't some of you—. Ouch! Take it away, please! Gentlemen, you see that I've got to hold up my hands; and so I can't take out my money—but if you'll be so kind as to take it out for me, I will do as much for you some—"

"Search him Beauregard—and stop his jaw with a bullet, quick, if he wags it again. Help Beauregard, Stonewall."

Then three of them, with the small, spry leader, adjourned to Mike and fell to searching him. I was so excited that my lawless fancy tortured me to ask my two men all manner of facetious questions about their rebel brother-generals of the South, but, considering the order they had received, it was but common prudence to keep still. When everything had been taken from me,—watch, money, and a multitude of trifles of small value,—I supposed I was free, and forthwith put my cold hands into my empty pockets and began an inoffensive

A PREDICAMENT.

jig to warm my feet and stir up some latent courage—but instantly all pistols were at my head, and the order came again:

"Be still! Put up your hands! And *keep* them up!"

They stood Mike up alongside of me, with strict orders to keep his hands above his head, too, and then the chief highwayman said:

"Beauregard, hide behind that boulder; Phil Sheridan, you hide behind that other one; Stonewall Jackson, put yourself behind that sage-bush there. Keep your pistols bearing on these fellows, and if they take down their hands within ten minutes, or move a single peg, let them have it!"

Then three disappeared in the gloom toward the several ambushes, and the other three disappeared down the road toward Virginia.

It was depressingly still, and miserably cold. Now this whole thing was a practical joke, and the robbers were personal friends of ours in disguise, and twenty more lay hidden within ten feet of us during the whole operation, listening. Mike knew all this, and was in the joke, but I suspected nothing of it. To me it was most uncomfortably genuine.

When we had stood there in the middle of the road five minutes, like a couple of idiots, with our hands aloft, freezing to death by inches, Mike's interest in the joke began to wane. He said :

" The time's up, now, aint it ? "

" No, you keep still. Do you want to take any chances with those bloody savages ? "

Presently Mike said :

" *Now* the time's up, anyway. I'm freezing."

" Well freeze. Better freeze than carry your brains home in a basket. Maybe the time *is* up, but how do *we* know?—got no watch to tell by. I mean to give them good measure. I calculate to stand here fifteen minutes or die. Don't you move."

So, without knowing it, I was making one joker very sick of his contract. When we took our arms down at last, they were aching with cold and fatigue, and when we went sneaking off, the dread I was in that the time might not yet be up and that we would feel bullets in a moment, was not sufficient to draw all my attention from the misery that racked my stiffened body.

The joke of these highwayman friends of ours was mainly a joke upon themselves ; for they had waited for me on the cold hill-top two full hours before I came, and there was very little fun in that ; they were so chilled that it took them a couple of weeks to get warm again. Moreover, I never had a thought that they would kill me to get money which it was so perfectly easy to get without any such folly, and so they did not really frighten me bad enough to make their enjoyment worth the trouble they had taken. I was only afraid that their weapons would go off accidentally. Their very numbers inspired me with confidence that no blood would be intentionally spilled. They were not smart ; they ought to have sent only *one* highwayman, with a double-barrelled shot gun, if they desired to see the author of this volume climb a tree.

However, I suppose that in the long run I got the largest share of the joke at last; and in a shape not foreseen by the highwaymen; for the chilly exposure on the "divide" while I was in a perspiration gave me a cold which developed itself into a troublesome disease and kept my hands idle some three months, besides costing me quite a sum in doctor's bills. Since

BEST PART OF THE JOKE.

then I play no practical jokes on people and generally lose my temper when one is played upon me.

When I returned to San Francisco I projected a pleasure journey to Japan and thence westward around the world; but a desire to see home again changed my mind, and I took a berth in the steamship, bade good-bye to the friendliest land and livest, heartiest community on our continent, and came by the way of the Isthmus to New York—a trip that was not much of a pic-nic excursion, for the cholera broke out among us on the passage and we buried two or three bodies at sea every day. I found home a dreary place after my long absence; for half the children I had known were now wearing whiskers or waterfalls, and few of the grown people I had been acquainted with remained at their hearthstones prosperous and happy—some of them had wandered to other scenes, some were in jail, and the rest had been hanged. These changes touched me deeply, and I went away and joined the famous Quaker City European Excursion and carried my tears to foreign lands.

Thus, after seven years of vicissitudes, ended a "pleasure trip" to the silver mines of Nevada which had originally been intended to occupy only three months. However, I usually miss my calculations further than that.

MORAL.

If the reader thinks he is done, now, and that this book has no moral to it, he is in error. The moral of it is this: If you are of any account, stay at home and make your way by faithful diligence; but if you are "no account," go away from home, and then you will *have* to work, whether you want to or not. Thus you become a blessing to your friends by ceasing to be a nuisance to them—if the people you go among suffer by the operation.

APPENDIX.

APPENDIX.

A.

BRIEF SKETCH OF MORMON HISTORY.

MORMONISM is only about forty years old, but its career has been full of stir and adventure from the beginning, and is likely to remain so to the end. Its adherents have been hunted and hounded from one end of the country to the other, and the result is that for years they have hated all "Gentiles" indiscriminately and with all their might. Joseph Smith, the finder of the Book of Mormon and founder of the religion, was driven from State to State with his mysterious copperplates and the miraculous stones he read their inscriptions with. Finally he instituted his "church" in Ohio and Brigham Young joined it. The neighbors began to persecute, and apostasy commenced. Brigham held to the faith and worked hard. He arrested desertion. He did more—he added converts in the midst of the trouble. He rose in favor and importance with the brethren. He was made one of the Twelve Apostles of the Church. He shortly fought his way to a higher post and a more powerful—President of the Twelve. The neighbors rose up and drove the Mormons out of Ohio, and they settled in Missouri. Brigham went with them. The Missourians drove them out and they retreated to Nauvoo, Illinois. They prospered there, and built a temple which made some pretensions to architectural grace and achieved some celebrity in a section of country where a brick court-house with a tin dome and a cupola on it was contemplated with reverential awe. But the Mormons were badgered and harried again by their neighbors. All the proclamations Joseph Smith could issue denouncing polygamy and repudiating it as utterly anti-Mormon were of no avail; the people of the neighborhood, on both sides of the Mississippi, claimed that polygamy was practised by the Mormons, and not only polygamy but a little of everything that was bad. Brigham returned from a mission to England, where he had established a Mormon newspaper, and he brought back with him several hundred converts to his preaching. His influence among the brethren augmented with every move he made. Finally Nauvoo was invaded by the Missouri and Illinois

Gentiles, and Joseph Smith killed. A Mormon named Rigdon assumed the Presidency of the Mormon church and government, in Smith's place, and even tried his hand at a prophecy or two. But a greater than he was at hand. Brigham seized the advantage of the hour and without other authority than superior brain and nerve and will, hurled Rigdon from his high place and occupied it himself. He did more. He launched an elaborate curse at Rigdon and his disciples; and he pronounced Rigdon's "prophecies" emanations from the devil, and ended by "handing the false prophet over to the buffetings of Satan for a thousand years"—probably the longest term ever inflicted in Illinois. The people recognized their master. They straightway elected Brigham Young President, by a prodigious majority, and have never faltered in their devotion to him from that day to this. Brigham had forecast—a quality which no other prominent Mormon has probably ever possessed. He recognized that it was better to move to the wilderness than *be* moved. By his command the people gathered together their meagre effects, turned their backs upon their homes, and their faces toward the wilderness, and on a bitter night in February filed in sorrowful procession across the frozen Mississippi, lighted on their way by the glare from their burning temple, whose sacred furniture their own hands had fired! They camped, several days afterward, on the western verge of Iowa, and poverty, want, hunger, cold, sickness, grief and persecution did their work, and many succumbed and died—martyrs, fair and true, whatever else they might have been. Two years the remnant remained there, while Brigham and a small party crossed the country and founded Great Salt Lake City, purposely choosing a land which was *outside the ownership and jurisdiction of the hated American nation.* Note that. This was in 1847. Brigham moved his people there and got them settled just in time to see disaster fall again. For the war closed and Mexico ceded Brigham's refuge to the enemy—the United States! In 1849 the Mormons organized a "free and independent" government and erected the "State of Deseret," with Brigham Young as its head. But the very next year Congress deliberately snubbed it and created the "Territory of Utah" out of the same accumulation of mountains, sage-brush, alkali and general desolation,—but made Brigham Governor of it. Then for years the enormous migration across the plains to California poured through the land of the Mormons and yet the church remained staunch and true to its lord and master. Neither hunger, thirst, poverty, grief, hatred, contempt, nor persecution could drive the Mormons from their faith or their allegiance; and even the thirst for gold, which gleaned the flower of the youth and strength of many nations was not able to entice them! That was the final test. An experiment that could survive that was an experiment with some substance to it somewhere.

Great Salt Lake City throve finely, and so did Utah. One of the last things which Brigham Young had done before leaving Iowa, was to appear in the pulpit dressed to personate the worshipped and lamented prophet Smith, and confer the prophetic succession, with all its dignities, emoluments and authorities, upon "President Brigham Young!" The people accepted the pious fraud with the maddest enthusiasm, and Brigham's power was sealed and secured for all time. Within five years afterward he openly added polygamy to the tenets of the church by authority of a "revelation" which he pretended had been received nine years before by Joseph Smith, albeit Joseph is amply on record as denouncing polygamy to the day of his death.

Now was Brigham become a second Andrew Johnson in the small beginning and steady progress of his official grandeur. He had served successively as a disciple in the ranks; home missionary; foreign missionary; editor and publisher; Apostle; President of the Board of Apostles; President of all Mormondom, civil and ecclesiastical; successor to the great Joseph by the will of heaven; "prophet," "seer," "revelator." There was but one dignity higher which he *could* aspire to, and he reached out modestly and took that—he proclaimed himself a God!

He claims that he is to have a heaven of his own hereafter, and that he will be its God, and his wives and children its goddesses, princes and princesses. Into it all faithful Mormons will be admitted, with their families, and will take rank and consequence according to the number of their wives and children. If a disciple dies before he has had time to accumulate enough wives and children to enable him to be respectable in the next world any friend can marry a few wives and raise a few children for him *after he is dead*, and they are duly credited to his account and his heavenly status advanced accordingly.

Let it be borne in mind that the majority of the Mormons have always been ignorant, simple, of an inferior order of intellect, unacquainted with the world and its ways; and let it be borne in mind that the wives of these Mormons are necessarily after the same pattern and their children likely to be fit representatives of such a conjunction; and then let it be remembered that *for forty years* these creatures have been driven, driven, driven, relentlessly! and mobbed, beaten, and shot down; cursed, despised, expatriated; banished to a remote desert, whither they journeyed gaunt with famine and disease, disturbing the ancient solitudes with their lamentations and marking the long way with graves of their dead—and all because they were simply trying to live and worship God in the way which *they* believed with all their hearts and souls to be the true one. Let all these things be borne in mind, and then it will not be hard to account for the deathless hatred which the Mormons bear our people and our government.

That hatred has "fed fat its ancient grudge" ever since Mormon Utah developed into a self-supporting realm and the church waxed rich and strong. Brigham as Territorial Governor made it plain that Mormondom was for the Mormons. The United States tried to rectify all that by appointing territorial officers from New England and other anti-Mormon localities, but Brigham prepared to make their entrance into his dominions difficult. Three thousand United States troops had to go across the plains and put these gentlemen in office. And after they were in office they were as helpless as so many stone images. They made laws which nobody minded and which could not be executed. The federal judges opened court in a land filled with crime and violence and sat as holiday spectacles for insolent crowds to gape at—for there was nothing to try, nothing to do, nothing on the dockets! And if a Gentile brought a suit, the Mormon jury would do just as it pleased about bringing in a verdict, and when the judgment of the court was rendered no Mormon cared for it and no officer could execute it. Our Presidents shipped one cargo of officials after another to Utah, but the result was always the same—they sat in a blight for awhile, they fairly feasted on scowls and insults day by day, they saw every attempt to do their official duties find its reward in darker and darker looks, and in secret threats and warnings of a more and more dismal nature—and at last they either succumbed and became despised tools and toys of the Mormons, or got scared and discomforted beyond all endurance and left the Territory. If a brave officer kept on courageously till his pluck was proven, some pliant Buchanan or Pierce would remove him and appoint a stick in his place. In 1857 General Harney came very near being appointed Governor of Utah. And so it came very near being Harney governor and Cradlebaugh judge!— two men who never had any idea of fear further than the sort of murky comprehension of it which they were enabled to gather from the dictionary. Simply (if for nothing else) for the variety they would have made in a rather monotonous history of Federal servility and helplessness, it is a pity they were not fated to hold office together in Utah.

Up to the date of our visit to Utah, such had been the Territorial record. The Territorial government established there had been a hopeless failure, and Brigham Young was the only real power in the land. He was an absolute monarch—a monarch who defied our President—a monarch who laughed at our armies when they camped about his capital—a monarch who received without emotion the news that the august Congress of the United States had enacted a solemn law against polygamy, and then went forth calmly and married twenty-five or thirty more wives.

B.

THE MOUNTAIN MEADOWS MASSACRE.

THE persecutions which the Mormons suffered so long—and which they consider they still suffer in not being allowed to govern themselves—they have endeavored and are still endeavoring to repay. The now almost forgotten "Mountain Meadows massacre" was their work. It was very famous in its day. The whole United States rang with its horrors. A few items will refresh the reader's memory. A great emigrant train from Missouri and Arkansas passed through Salt Lake City and a few disaffected Mormons joined it for the sake of the strong protection it afforded for their escape. In that matter lay sufficient cause for hot retaliation by the Mormon chiefs. Besides, these one hundred and forty-five or one hundred and fifty unsuspecting emigrants being in part from Arkansas, where a noted Mormon missionary had lately been killed, and in part from Missouri, a State remembered with execrations as a bitter persecutor of the saints when they were few and poor and friendless, here were substantial additional grounds for lack of love for these wayfarers. And finally, this train was rich, very rich in cattle, horses, mules and other property—and how could the Mormons consistently keep up their coveted resemblance to the Israelitish tribes and not seize the "spoil" of an enemy when the Lord had so manifestly "delivered it into their hand?"

Wherefore, according to Mrs. C. V. Waite's entertaining book, "The Mormon Prophet," it transpired that—

"A 'revelation' from Brigham Young, as Great Grand Archee or God, was dispatched to President J. C. Haight, Bishop Higbee and J. D. Lee (adopted son of Brigham), commanding them to raise all the forces they could muster and trust, follow those cursed Gentiles (so read the revelation), attack them disguised as Indians, and with the arrows of the Almighty make a clean sweep of them, and leave none to tell the tale ; and if they needed any assistance they were commanded to hire the Indians as their allies, promising them a share of the booty. They were to be neither slothful nor negligent in their duty, and to be punctual in sending the teams back to him before winter set in, for this was the mandate of Almighty God."

The command of the "revelation" was faithfully obeyed. A large party of Mormons, painted and tricked out as Indians, overtook the train of emigrant wagons some three hundred miles south of Salt Lake City, and made an attack. But the emigrants threw up earthworks, made fortresses of their wagons and defended themselves gallantly and successfully for five days! Your Missouri or Arkansas gentleman is not much afraid of the sort of scurvy apologies for "Indians" which the southern part of Utah affords. He would stand up and fight five hundred of them.

At the end of the five days the Mormons tried military strategy. They retired to the upper end of the "Meadows," resumed civilized apparel, washed off their paint, and then, heavily armed, drove down in wagons to the beleaguered emigrants, bearing a flag of truce! When the emigrants saw white men coming they threw down their guns and welcomed them with cheer after cheer! And, all unconscious of the poetry of it, no doubt, they lifted a little child aloft, dressed in white, in answer to the flag of truce!

The leaders of the timely white "deliverers" were President Haight and Bishop John D. Lee, of the Mormon Church. Mr. Cradlebaugh, who served a term as a Federal Judge in Utah and afterward was sent to Congress from Nevada, tells in a speech delivered in Congress how these leaders next proceeded:

"They professed to be on good terms with the Indians, and represented them as being very mad. They also proposed to intercede and settle the matter with the Indians. After several hours parley they, having (apparently) visited the Indians, gave the *ultimatum* of the savages; which was, that the emigrants should march out of their camp, leaving everything behind them, even their guns. It was promised by the Mormon bishops that they would bring a force and guard the emigrants back to the settlements. The terms were agreed to, the emigrants being desirous of saving the lives of their families. The Mormons retired, and subsequently appeared with thirty or forty armed men. The emigrants were marched out, the women and children in front and the men behind, the Mormon guard being in the rear. When they had marched in this way about a mile, at a given signal the slaughter commenced. The men were almost all shot down at the first fire from the guard. Two only escaped, who fled to the desert, and were followed one hundred and fifty miles before they were overtaken and slaughtered. The women and children ran on, two or three hundred yards further, when they were overtaken and with the aid of the Indians they were slaughtered. Seventeen individuals only, of all the emigrant party, were spared, and they were little children, the eldest of them being only seven years old. Thus, on the 10th day of September, 1857, was consummated one of the most cruel, cowardly and bloody murders known in our history."

The number of persons butchered by the Mormons on this occasion was *one hundred and twenty.*

With unheard-of temerity Judge Cradlebaugh opened his court and pro-

37†

ceeded to make Mormondom answer for the massacre. And what a spectacle it must have been to see this grim veteran, solitary and alone in his pride and his pluck, glowering down on his Mormon jury and Mormon auditory, deriding them by turns, and by turns " breathing threatenings and slaughter ! "

An editorial in the *Territorial Enterprise* of that day says of him and of the occasion :

" He spoke and acted with the fearlessness and resolution of a Jackson ; but the jury failed to indict, or even report on the charges, while threats of violence were heard in every quarter, and an attack on the U. S. troops intimated, if he persisted in his course.

" Finding that nothing could be done with the juries, they were discharged, with a scathing rebuke from the judge. And then, sitting as a committing magistrate, *he commenced his task alone.* He examined witnesses, made arrests in every quarter, and created a consternation in the camps of the saints greater than any they had ever witnessed before, since Mormondom was born. At last accounts terrified elders and bishops were decamping to save their necks ; and developments of the most startling character were being made, implicating the highest Church dignitaries in the many murders and robberies committed upon the Gentiles during the past eight years."

Had Harney been Governor, Cradlebaugh would have been supported in his work, and the absolute proofs adduced by him of Mormon guilt in this massacre and in a number of previous murders, would have conferred gratuitous coffins upon certain citizens, together with occasion to use them. But Cumming was the Federal Governor, and he, under a curious pretense of impartiality, sought to screen the Mormons from the demands of justice. On one occasion he even went so far as to publish his protest against the use of the U. S. troops in aid of Cradlebaugh's proceedings.

Mrs. C. V. Waite closes her interesting detail of the great massacre with the following remark and accompanying summary of the testimony—and the summary is concise, accurate and reliable :

" For the benefit of those who may still be disposed to doubt the guilt of Young and his Mormons in this transaction, the testimony is here collated and circumstances given which go not merely to implicate but to fasten conviction upon them by ' confirmations strong as proofs of Holy Writ : '

" 1. The evidence of Mormons themselves, engaged in the affair, as shown by the statements of Judge Cradlebaugh and Deputy U. S. Marshal Rodgers.

" 2. The failure of Brigham Young to embody any account of it in his Report as Superintendent of Indian Affairs. Also his failure to make any allusion to it whatever from the pulpit, until several years after the occurrence.

" 3. The flight to the mountains of men high in authority in the Mormon Church and State, when this affair was brought to the ordeal of a judicial investigation.

" 4. The failure of the *Deseret News*, the Church organ, and the only paper then published in the Territory, to notice the massacre until several months afterward, and then only to deny that Mormons were engaged in it.

" 5. The testimony of the children saved from the massacre.

" 6. The children and the property of the emigrants found in possession of the Mormons, and that possession traced back to the very day after the massacre.

" 7. The statements of Indians in the neighborhood of the scene of the massacre: these statements are shown, not only by Cradlebaugh and Rodgers, but by a number of military officers, and by J. Forney, who was, in 1859, Superintendent of Indian Affairs for the Territory.   To all these were such statements freely and frequently made by the Indians.

" 8. The testimony of R. P. Campbell, Capt. 2d Dragoons, who was sent in the Spring of 1859 to Santa Clara, to protect travelers on the road to California and to inquire into Indian depredations."

C.

CONCERNING A FRIGHTFUL ASSASSINATION THAT WAS NEVER CONSUMMATED.

[IF ever there was a harmless man, it is Conrad Wiegand, of Gold Hill, Nevada. If ever there was a gentle spirit that thought itself unfired gunpowder and latent ruin, it is Conrad Wiegand. If ever there was an oyster that fancied itself a whale; or a jack-o'lantern, confined to a swamp, that fancied itself a planet with a billion-mile orbit; or a summer zephyr that deemed itself a hurricane, it is Conrad Wiegand. Therefore, what wonder is it that when he says a thing, he thinks the world listens; that when he does a thing the world stands still to look; and that when he suffers, there is a convulsion of nature? When I met Conrad, he was "Superintendent of the Gold Hill Assay Office"—and he was not only its Superintendent, but its entire force. And he was a street preacher, too, with a mongrel religion of his own invention, whereby he expected to regenerate the universe. This was years ago. Here latterly he has entered journalism; and his journalism is what it might be expected to be: colossal to ear, but pigmy to the eye. It is extravagant grandiloquence confined to a newspaper about the size of a double letter sheet. He doubtless edits, sets the type, and prints his paper, all alone; but he delights to speak of the concern as if it occupies a block and employs a thousand men.

[Something less than two years ago, Conrad assailed several people mercilessly in his little "People's Tribune," and got himself into trouble. Straightway he airs the affair in the "Territorial Enterprise," in a communication over his own signature, and I propose to reproduce it here, in all its native simplicity and more than human candor. Long as it is, it is well worth reading, for it is the richest specimen of journalistic literature the history of America can furnish, perhaps:]

From the Territorial Enterprise, Jan. 20, 1870.

A SEEMING PLOT FOR ASSASSINATION MISCARRIED.

TO THE EDITOR OF THE ENTERPRISE : Months ago, when Mr. Sutro incidentally exposed mining management on the Comstock, and among others roused me to protest against its continuance, in great kindness you warned me that any attempt by publications, by public meetings and by legislative action, aimed at the correction of chronic mining evils in Storey County, must entail upon me (*a*) business ruin, (*b*) the burden of all its costs, (*c*) personal violence, and if my purpose were persisted in, then (*d*) assassination, and after all nothing would be effected.

YOUR PROPHECY FULFILLING.

In large part at least your prophecies have been fulfilled, for (*a*) assaying, which was well attended to in the Gold Hill Assay Office (of which I am superintendent), in consequence of my publications, has been taken elsewhere, so the President of one of the companies assures me. With no reason *assigned*, other work has been taken away. With but one or two important exceptions, our assay business now consists simply of the *gleanings* of the vicinity. (*b*) Though my own personal donations to the People's Tribune Association have already exceeded $1,500, outside of our own numbers we have received (in money) less than $300 as contributions and subscriptions for the journal. (*c*) On Thursday last, on the main street in Gold Hill, near noon, with neither warning nor cause assigned, by a powerful blow I was felled to the ground, and while down I was kicked by a man who it would seem had been led to *believe* that I had spoken derogatorily of him. By whom he was so induced to believe I am as yet unable to say. On Saturday last I was again assailed and beaten by a man who first informed me why he did so, and who persisted in making his assault even after the erroneous impression under which he *also* was at first laboring had been clearly and repeatedly pointed out. This same man, after failing through intimidation to elicit from me the names of our editorial contributors, against giving which he knew me to be pledged, beat himself weary upon me with a raw hide, I not resisting, and then pantingly threatened me with permanent disfiguring mayhem, if ever again I should introduce his name into print, and who but a few minutes before his attack upon me assured me that the only reason I was "permitted" to reach home alive on Wednesday evening last (at which time the PEOPLE'S TRIBUNE was issued) was, that he deems me only half-witted, and be it remembered the very next morning I *was* knocked down and kicked by a man who seemed to be *prepared* for flight.

[*He sees doom impending :*]

WHEN WILL THE CIRCLE JOIN?

How long before the whole of your prophecy will be fulfilled I cannot say, but under the shadow of so much fulfillment in so short a time, and with such threats from a man who is one of the most prominent exponents of the San Francisco mining-ring staring me and this whole community defiantly in the face and *pointing* to a completion of your augury, do you blame me for feeling that this communication is the last I shall ever write for the Press, especially when a sense alike of personal self-respect, of duty to this money-oppressed and fear-ridden community, and of American fealty to the spirit of true Liberty all command me, and each more loudly than love of life itself, to declare the name of that prominent man to be JOHN B. WINTERS, President of the Yellow Jacket Company, a political aspirant and a military General? The name of his partially duped accomplice and abettor in this last marvelous assault, is no other than PHILIP LYNCH, Editor and Proprietor of the Gold Hill *News.*

Despite the insult and wrong heaped upon me by John B. Winters, on Saturday afternoon, only a glimpse of which I shall be able to afford your readers, so much do I deplore clinching (by publicity) a serious mistake of any one, man or woman, committed under natural and not self-wrought passion, in view of his great apparent excitement at the time and in view of the almost perfect privacy of the assault, I am far from sure that I should not have given him space for repentance before exposing him, were it not that he himself has so far exposed the matter as to make it the common talk of the town that he has horsewhipped me. That fact having been made public, all the facts in connection need to be also, or silence on my part would seem *more* than singular, and with many would be proof either that I was conscious of some unworthy aim in publishing the article, or else that my " non-combatant " principles are but a convenient cloak alike of physical and moral cowardice. I therefore shall try to present a graphic but truthful picture of this whole affair, but shall forbear all comments, presuming that the editors of our own journal, if others do not, will speak freely and fittingly upon this subject in our next number, whether I shall then be dead or living, for my death will not stop, though it may suspend, the publication of the PEOPLE'S TRIBUNE.

[*The "non-combatant" sticks to principle, but takes along a friend or two of a conveniently different stripe :*]

THE TRAP SET.

On Saturday morning John B. Winters sent verbal word to the Gold Hill Assay Office that he desired to see me at the Yellow Jacket office. Though such a request struck me as decidedly cool in view of his own recent discourtesies to me there alike as a publisher and as a stockholder in the Yellow Jacket mine, and though it seemed to me more like a summons than the courteous request by one gentleman to another for a favor, hoping that some conference with Sharon looking to the betterment of mining matters in Nevada might arise from it, I felt strongly inclined to overlook what *possibly* was simply an oversight in courtesy. But as then it had only been two days since I had been bruised and beaten under a hasty and false apprehension of facts, my caution was somewhat aroused. Moreover I remembered sensitively his contemptuousness of manner to me at my last interview in his office. I therefore felt it needful, if I went at all, to go accompanied by a friend whom he would not dare to treat with incivility, and whose presence with me might secure exemption from insult. Accordingly I asked a neighbor to accompany me.

THE TRAP ALMOST DETECTED.

Although I was not then aware of this fact, it would seem that previous to my request this same neighbor had heard Dr. Zabriskie state publicly in a saloon, that Mr. Winters had told him he had decided either to kill or to horsewhip me, but had not finally decided on which. My neighbor, therefore, felt unwilling to go down with me until he had *first* called on Mr. Winters alone. He therefore paid him a visit. From that interview he assured me that he gathered the impression that he did not believe I would have any difficulty with Mr. Winters, and that he (Winters) would call on me at four o'clock in my own office.

MY OWN PRECAUTIONS.

As Sheriff Cummings was in Gold Hill that afternoon, and as I desired to converse with him about the previous assault, I invited him to my office, and he came. Although a half hour had passed beyond four o'clock, Mr. Winters had not called, and we both of us began preparing to go home. Just then, Philip Lynch, Publisher of the Gold Hill *News,* came in and said, blandly and cheerily, as if bringing good news :

" Hello, John B. Winters wants to see you."

I replied, " Indeed ! Why he sent me word that he would call on me *here* this afternoon at four o'clock ! "

" O, well, it don't do to be too ceremonious just now, he's in my office, and that will do as well—come on in, Winters wants to consult with you alone. He's got something to say to you."

Though slightly uneasy at this change of programme, yet believing that in an *editor's* house I ought to be safe, and anyhow that I would be within hail of the street, I hurriedly, and but partially whispered my dim apprehensions to Mr. Cummings, and asked him if he would not keep near enough to hear my voice in case I should call. He consented to do so while waiting for some other parties, and to come in if he heard my voice or thought I had need of protection.

On reaching the editorial part of the *News* office, which viewed from the street is dark, I did not see Mr. Winters, and again my misgivings arose. Had I paused long enough to consider the case, I should have not invited Sheriff Cummings in, but as Lynch went down stairs, he said : " *This* way, Wiegand—it's best to be private," or some such remark.

[I do not desire to strain the reader's fancy, hurtfully, and yet it would be a favor to me if he would try to fancy this lamb in battle, or the duelling ground or at the head of a vigilance committee—M. T. :]

I followed, and *without* Mr. Cummings, and without arms, which I never do or will carry, unless as a soldier in war, or unless I should yet come to feel I must fight a duel, or to join and aid in the ranks of a *necessary* Vigilance Committee. But by following I made a fatal mistake. Following was entering a trap, and whatever animal suffers itself to be *caught* should expect the common fate of a caged rat, as I fear events to come will prove.

Traps commonly are not set for *benevolence*.

[*His body-guard is shut out :*]

THE TRAP INSIDE.

I followed Lynch down stairs. At their foot a door to the left opened into a small room. From *that* room another door opened into yet *another* room, and once entered I found myself inveigled into what many will ever henceforth regard as a private subterranean Gold Hill den, admirably adapted in proper hands to the purposes of murder, raw or disguised, for from it, with both or even one door closed, when too late, I saw that I *could* not be heard by Sheriff Cummings, and from it, BY VIOLENCE AND BY FORCE, I was prevented from making a peaceable exit, when I thought I saw the studious object of this " consultation" was no other than to compass my killing, *in the presence of Philip Lynch as a witness*, as soon as by insult a proverbially excitable man should be exasperated to the point of assailing Mr. Winters, so that Mr. Lynch, by his conscience and by his well known tenderness of heart toward the rich and potent would be *compelled* to testify that he saw Gen. John B. Winters kill Conrad Wiegand in " self-defence." But I am going too fast.

OUR HOST.

Mr. Lynch was present during the most of the time (say a little short of an hour), but three times he left the room. His testimony, therefore, would be available only as to the bulk of what transpired. On entering this carpeted den I was invited to a seat near one corner of the room. Mr. Lynch took a seat near the window. J. B. Winters sat (at first) near the door, and began his remarks essentially as follows :

" I have come here to exact of you a retraction, in black and white, of those damnably false charges which you have preferred against me in that —— —— infamous lying sheet of yours, and you must declare yourself their author, that you published them knowing them to be false, and that your motives were malicious."

" Hold, Mr. Winters. Your language is insulting and your demand an enormity. I trust I was not invited here either to be insulted or coerced. I supposed myself here by invitation of Mr. Lynch, at your request."

" Nor did I come here to insult you. I have already told you that I am here for a very different purpose."

" Yet your language *has* been offensive, and even now shows strong excitement. If insult is repeated I shall either leave the room or call in Sheriff Cummings, whom I just left standing and waiting for me outside the door."

" No, you won't, sir. You may just as well understand it at once as not. *Here* you are my man, and I'll tell you why ! Months ago you put your property out of your hands, boasting that you did so to escape losing it on prosecution for libel."

"It is true that I did convert all my immovable property into personal property, such as I could trust safely to others, and chiefly to escape ruin through possible libel suits."

"Very good, sir. Having placed yourself beyond the pale of the law, *may God help your soul if you* DON'T make precisely such a retraction as I have demanded. I've got you now, and by —— before you can get out of this room you've *got* to both write and sign precisely the retraction I have demanded, and before you go, anyhow—you —— —— low-lived —— lying —— ——, I'll teach you what *personal* responsibility is *outside* of the law; and, by ——, Sheriff Cummings and all the friends you've got in the world besides, can't save you, you —— ——, etc.! *No,* sir. I'm *alone* now, and I'm *prepared* to be shot down just here and now rather than be villified by you as I have been, and suffer you to escape me after publishing those charges, not only here where I am known and universally respected, but where I am *not* personally known and may be injured."

I confess this speech, with its terrible and but too plainly *implied* threat of killing me if I did not sign the paper he demanded, terrified me, especially as I saw he was working himself up to the highest possible pitch of passion, and instinct told me that any reply other than one of seeming concession to his demands would only be fuel to a raging fire, so I replied:

"Well, if I've *got* to sign ——," and then I paused some time. Resuming, I said, "But, Mr. Winters, you are greatly excited. Besides, I see you are laboring under a total misapprehension. It is your duty not to inflame but to calm yourself. I am prepared to show you, if you will only point out the article that you allude to, that *you* regard as 'charges' what no calm and logical mind has any *right* to regard as such. *Show* me the charges, and I will try, at all events; and if it becomes plain that no charges *have* been preferred, then plainly there can be nothing to retract, and no one could rightly *urge* you to demand a retraction. You should beware of making so serious a mistake, for however *honest* a man may be, every one is liable to misapprehend. Besides you *assume* that *I* am the author of some certain article which you have not pointed out. It is *hasty* to do so."

He then pointed to some numbered paragraphs in a TRIBUNE article, headed "What's the Matter with Yellow Jacket?" saying "*That's* what I refer to."

To gain time for general reflection and resolution, I took up the paper and looked it over for awhile, he remaining silent, and as I hoped, cooling. I then resumed. saying, "As I supposed. I do not *admit* having written that article, nor nave you any right to *assume* so important a point, and then base important action upon your assumption. You might deeply regret it afterwards. In my published Address to the People, I notified the world that no information as to the authorship of any article would be given without the consent of the writer. I therefore cannot honorably tell you *who* wrote that article, nor can you exact it."

"If you are *not* the author, then I *do* demand to know who is?"

"I must decline to say."

"Then, by ——, I brand *you* as its author, and shall treat you accord-ingly."

"Passing that point, the most important misapprehension which I notice is, that you regard them as 'charges' at all, when their context, both at their beginning and end, show they are not. These words introduce them : '*Such an investigation* [just before indicated], *we think MIGHT result in showing some of the following points.*' Then follow eleven specifications, and the succeeding paragraph shows that the suggested investigation 'might EX-ONERATE those who are generally believed guilty.' You see, therefore, the context *proves* they are not preferred *as* charges, and this you seem to have overlooked."

While making those comments, Mr. Winters frequently interrupted me in such a way as to convince me that he was *resolved* not to consider candidly the thoughts contained in my words. He insisted upon it that they *were* charges, and "By ——," he would make me take them back *as* charges, and he referred the question to Philip Lynch, to whom I then appealed as a literary man, as a logician, and as an editor, calling his attention especially to the introductory paragraph just before quoted.

He replied, "If they are *not* charges, they certainly are *insinuations*," whereupon Mr. Winters renewed his demands for retraction precisely such as he had before named, except that he would allow me to state who *did* write the article if I did not myself, and this time shaking his fist in my face with more cursings and epithets.

When he threatened me with his clenched fist, instinctively I tried to rise from my chair, but Winters then forcibly thrust me down, as he did every other time (at least seven or eight), when under similar imminent danger of bruising by his fist (or for aught I could know worse than that after the first stunning blow), which he could easily and safely to himself have dealt me so long as he kept me down and stood over me.

This fact it was, which more than anything else, convinced me that by plan and plot I was purposely made powerless in Mr. Winters' hands, and that he did not mean to allow me that advantage of being afoot, which he possessed. Moreover, I then became convinced, that Philip Lynch (and for what *reason* I wondered) would do absolutely nothing to protect me in his own house. I realized then the situation thoroughly. I had found it equally vain to protest or argue, and I would make no unmanly appeal for pity, still less apologize. Yet my life had been by the plainest possible implication threatened. I was a weak man. I was unarmed. I was help-lessly down, and Winters was afoot and probably armed. Lynch was the only "witness." The statements demanded, if given and not explained, would utterly sink me in my own self-respect, in my family's eyes, and in the eyes of the community. On the other hand, should I give the author's name how could I ever expect that confidence of the People which I should no longer deserve, and how much dearer to me and to my family was *my* life than the life of the real author to *his* friends. Yet life seemed dear and each minute that remained seemed precious if not solemn. I sincerely trust that neither you nor any of your readers, and especially none with families, may ever be placed in such seeming *direct* proximity to death while obliged to decide the one question I was compelled to, viz.: What should I do—I, a man of family, and *not* as Mr. Winters is, "alone."

[*The reader is requested not to skip the following.—M. T.:*]

STRATEGY AND MESMERISM.

To gain time for further reflection, and hoping that by a *seeming* acquiescence I might regain my personal liberty, at least till I could give an alarm, or take advantage of some momentary inadvertence of Winters, and then without a *cowardly* flight escape, I resolved to write a certain kind of retraction, but previously had inwardly decided

First.—That I would studiously avoid every action which might be *construed* into the drawing of a weapon, even by a self-infuriated man, no matter what amount of insult might be heaped upon me, for it seemed to me that this great excess of compound profanity, foulness and epithet must be more than a mere indulgence, and therefore must have some object. "Surely in vain the net is spread in the sight of any bird." Therefore, as before without thought, I thereafter by intent kept my hands away from my pockets, and generally in sight and spread upon my knees.

Second.—I resolved to make no motion with my arms or hands which could possibly be construed into aggression.

Third.—I resolved completely to govern my outward manner and suppress indignation. To do this, I must govern my spirit. To do that, by force of imagination I was obliged like actors on the boards to resolve myself into an unnatural mental state and see all things through the eyes of an assumed *character.*

Fourth.—I resolved to try on Winters, silently, and unconsciously to himself a mesmeric power which I possess over certain kinds of people, and which at times I have found to work even in the dark over the lower animals.

Does any one smile at these last counts? God save you from ever being *obliged* to beat in a game of chess, whose stake is your life, you having but four poor pawns and pieces and your adversary with his full force unshorn. But if you are, provided you have any strength with breadth of will, do not despair. Though mesmeric power may not *save* you, it may help you ; *try* it at all events. In this instance I was conscious of power coming into me, and by a law of nature, I know Winters was correspondingly weakened. If I could have gained more time I am sure he would not even have struck me.

It takes time both to form such resolutions and to recite them. That time, however, I gained while thinking of my retraction, which I first wrote in pencil, altering it from time to time till I got it to suit me, my aim being to make it look like a concession to demands, while in fact it should tersely speak the truth into Mr. Winters' mind. When it was finished, I copied it in ink, and if correctly copied from my first draft it should read as follows. In copying I do not think I made any material change.

To Philip Lynch, Editor of the Gold Hill News: I learn that Gen. John B. Winters believes the following (pasted on) clipping from the PEOPLE'S TRIBUNE of January to contain distinct charges of mine against him personally, and that as such he desires me to retract them unqualifiedly.

In compliance with his request, permit me to say that, although Mr. Winters and I see this matter differently, in view of his strong feelings in the premises, I hereby declare that I do not know those " charges " (if such they are) to be true, and I hope that a critical examination would altogether disprove them. CONRAD WIEGAND.

Gold Hill, January 15, 1870.

I then read what I had written and handed it to Mr. Lynch, whereupon Mr. Winters said :

" That's not satisfactory, and it won't do ; " and then addressing himself to Mr. Lynch, he further said : " How does it strike *you?* "

" Well, I confess I don't see that it *retracts* anything."

" Nor do I," said Winters ; " in fact, I regard it as adding insult to injury. Mr. Wiegand you've got to do better than that. *You* are not the man who can pull wool over *my* eyes."

" That, sir, is the only retraction I can write."

" No it isn't, sir, and if you so much as *say* so again you do it at your peril, for I'll thrash you to within an inch of your life, and, by ——, sir, I don't pledge myself to spare you even that inch either. I want you to understand I have asked you for a very different paper, and that paper you've got to sign."

" Mr. Winters, I assure you that I *do* not wish to irritate you, but, at the same time, it is utterly *impossible* for me to write any other paper than that which I have written. If you are resolved to *compel* me to *sign* something, Philip Lynch's hand must write at your dictation, and if, when written, I *can* sign it I will do so, but such a document as you say you *must* have from me, I never can sign. I mean what I say."

" Well, sir, what's to be done must be done quickly, for I've been here long enough already. I'll put the thing in another shape (and then pointing to the paper) ; don't you know those charges to be false ? "

" I do not."

" Do you know them to be true ? "

" Of my own personal knowledge I do not."

" Why then did you print them ? "

" Because rightly considered in their connection they are *not* charges, but pertinent and useful *suggestions* in answer to the queries of a correspondent who stated facts which are inexplicable."

" Don't you know that *I* know they are false ? "

" If you *do,* the proper course is simply to deny them and court an investigation."

" And do YOU claim the right to make ME come out and deny anything you may choose to write and print ? "

To that question I think I made no reply, and he then further said : " Come, now, we've talked about the matter long enough. I want your final answer—did you write that article or not ? "

" I cannot in honor tell you *who* wrote it."

" Did you not see it before it was printed ? "

" Most certainly, sir."

" And did you deem it a fit thing to publish ? "

" Most assuredly, sir, or I would never have consented to its appearance. Of its *authorship* I can say nothing whatever, but for its *publication* I assume full, sole and personal responsibility."

" And do you then retract it or not ? "

" Mr. Winters, if my refusal to sign such a paper as you have demanded *must* entail upon me all that your language in this room fairly implies, then I ask a few minutes for prayer."

" Prayer ! —— —— you, this is not your *hour* for prayer—your time to pray was when you were writing those —— lying charges. Will you sign or not ? "

" You already have my answer."

" What ! do you still refuse ? "

" I do, sir."

" Take *that*, then," and to my amazement and inexpressible relief he drew only a rawhide instead of what I expected—a bludgeon or pistol. With it, as he spoke, he struck at my left ear downwards, as if to tear it off, and afterwards on the side of the head. As he moved away to get a better chance for a more effective shot, for the first time I gained a chance under peril to rise, and I did so pitying him from the very bottom of my soul, to think that one so naturally capable of true dignity, power and nobility could, by the temptations of this State, and by unfortunate associations and aspirations, be so deeply debased as to find in such brutality anything which he could call satisfaction—but the great hope for us all is in progress and growth, and John B. Winters, I trust, will yet be able to comprehend my feelings.

He continued to beat me with all his great force, until absolutely weary, exhausted and panting for breath. I still adhered to my purpose of non-aggressive defence, and made no other use of my arms than to defend my head and face from further disfigurement. The mere pain arising from the blows he inflicted upon my person was of course transient, and my clothing to some extent deadened its severity, as it now hides all remaining traces.

When I supposed he was through, taking the butt end of his weapon and shaking it in my face, he warned me, if I correctly understood him, of more yet to come, and furthermore said, if ever I again dared introduce his name to print, in either my own or any other public journal, he would cut off my left ear (and I do not *think* he was jesting) and send me home to my family a visibly mutilated man, to be a standing warning to all low-lived puppies who seek to blackmail gentlemen and to injure their good names. And when he *did* so operate, he informed me that his implement would not be a whip but a knife.

When he had said this, unaccompanied by Mr. Lynch, as I remember it, he left the room, for I sat down by Mr. Lynch, exclaiming: "The man is mad—he is *utterly* mad—this step is his ruin—it is a mistake—it would be ungenerous in me, despite of all the ill usage I have here received, to expose him, at least until he has had an opportunity to reflect upon the matter. I shall be in no haste."

"Winters *is* very mad just now," replied Mr. Lynch, "but when he is himself he is one of the finest men I ever met. In fact, he told me the reason he did not meet you upstairs was to spare you the humiliation of a beating in the sight of others."

I submit that that unguarded remark of Philip Lynch convicts him of having been privy in advance to Mr. Winters' intentions whatever they may have been, or at least to his meaning to make an assault upon me, but I leave to others to determine how much censure an *editor* deserves for inveigling a weak, non-combatant man, also a publisher, to a pen of his own to be horsewhipped, if no worse, for the simple printing of what is verbally in the mouth of nine out of ten men, and women too, upon the street.

While writing this account two theories have occurred to me as *possibly* true respecting this most remarkable assault :

First—The aim *may* have been simply to extort from me such admissions as in the hands of money and influence would have sent me to the Penitentiary for libel. This, however, seems unlikely, because any statements elicited by fear or force could not be evidence in law or could be so explained as to have no force. The statements wanted so badly must have been desired for some other purpose.

Second—The other theory has so dark and wilfully murderous a look that I shrink from writing it, yet as in all probability my death at the earliest practicable moment has already been decreed, I feel I should do all I can before my hour arrives, at least to show others how to break up that aristocratic rule and combination which has robbed all Nevada of true freedom, if not of manhood itself. Although I do not prefer this hypothesis as a "*charge*," I feel that as an American citizen I still have a right both to think and to speak my thoughts even in the land of Sharon and Winters, and as much so respecting the theory of a brutal assault (especially when I have been its subject) as respecting any other apparent enormity. I give the matter simply as a suggestion which may explain to the proper authorities and to the people whom they should represent, a well ascertained but notwithstanding a darkly mysterious fact. The scheme of the assault *may* have been

First—To terrify me by making me conscious of my own helplessness after making actual though not legal threats against my life.

Second—To imply that I could save my life only by writing or signing certain specific statements which if not subsequently explained would eternally have branded me as infamous and would have consigned my family to shame and want, and to the dreadful compassion and patronage of the rich.

Third—To blow my brains out *the moment I had signed,* thereby preventing me from making any subsequent explanation such as *could* remove the infamy.

Fourth—Philip Lynch to be compelled to testify that I was killed by John B. Winters in self-defence, for the conviction of Winters would bring *him* in as an accomplice. If that *was* the programme in John B. Winters' mind nothing saved my life but my persistent *refusal* to sign, when that refusal seemed clearly to me to be the choice of death.

The remarkable assertion made to me by Mr. Winters, that pity only spared my life on Wednesday evening last, almost compels me to believe that at first he *could* not have intended me to leave that room alive; and why I was allowed to, unless through mesmeric *or some other invisible influence,* I cannot divine. The more I reflect upon this matter, the more probable as true does this horrible interpretation become.

The narration of these things I might have spared both to Mr. Winters and to the public had he himself observed silence, but as he has both verbally spoken and suffered a thoroughly garbled statement of facts to appear in the Gold Hill *News* I feel it due to myself no less than to this community, and to the entire independent press of America and Great Britain, to give a true account of what even the Gold Hill *News* has pronounced a disgraceful affair, and which it deeply regrets because of some alleged telegraphic mistake in the account of it. [Who received the erroneous telegrams?]

Though he may not deem it prudent to take my life just now, the publication of this article I feel sure must compel Gen. Winters (with his peculiar views about *his* right to exemption from criticism by *me*) to resolve on my violent death, though it may take years to compass it. Notwithstanding *I* bear *him* no ill will; and if W. C. Ralston and William Sharon, and other members of the San Francisco mining and milling Ring feel that he above all other men in this State and California is the most fitting man to supervise and control Yellow Jacket matters, until I am able to vote more than half their stock I presume he will be retained to grace his present post.

Meantime, I cordially invite all who know of any sort of important villainy which only *can* be cured by exposure (and who would expose it if they felt sure they would not be betrayed under bullying threats), to communicate with the PEOPLE'S TRIBUNE; for until I *am* murdered, so long as I can raise the means to publish, I propose to continue my *efforts* at least to revive the liberties of the State, to curb oppression, and to benefit man's world and God's earth.   CONRAD WIEGAND.

[It does seem a pity that the Sheriff was shut out, since the good sense of a general of militia and of a prominent editor failed to teach them that the merited castigation of this weak, half-witted child was a thing that ought to have been done in the street, where the poor thing could have a chance to run. When a journalist maligns a citizen, or attacks his good name on hearsay evidence, he deserves to be thrashed for it, even if he *is* a "non-combatant" weakling; but a generous adversary would at least allow such a lamb the use of his legs at such a time.—M. T.]

NEW ILLUSTRATED MONTHLY.

CHEAPEST PAPER IN THE WORLD.

A large 8 page Illustrated Journal, devoted to Literature, Agriculture, Domestic Economy, Wit and Humor. One of the most interesting and popular papers of the age is sent to subscribers one year for

ONE DOLLAR. ONE DOLLAR.

To each subscriber is sent at once on receipt of subscription price ($1.00), one of the following

PREMIUMS.   PREMIUMS.   PREMIUMS.

A fine steel line engraving of

STUART'S WASHINGTON,

full length, from the original painting by Gabriel Stuart, 1797.

The finest and most renowned painting of Washington extant. Value $2.50. Or the beautiful chromo called

THE BURIAL OF THE BIRD;

Being a gem of a picture worth three times the cost of the whole.

We employ the best writers,—in fact, no other paper in the Union has such a combination of them.

MARK TWAIN
writes for it.

JOHN HAY
writes for it.

Rev. JOHN TODD
writes for it.

And scores of other talented authors.

The sheet is filled with original matter, and is one of the handsomest of its kind, as well as one of the most valuable.

If you wish to see one of the finest papers in the country, filled with the choicest reading matter, send for sample of THE PUBLISHER, which will be sent to any one enclosing us two cents to prepay postage.

Liberal club rates and good commissions given to agents.

Book premiums given. This is a rare chance for men, women, and children, invalids and others, to get popular and valuable books at the cost of a little trouble. Children can get up clubs easily, and receive beautiful books for themselves, or cash commissions.

Send for samples or agencies to

AMERICAN PUBLISHING CO.,
Hartford, Conn.

AFTERWORD

Henry B. Wonham

During the fall of 1869, as he began dredging up memories of Nevada and California for a series of "Around the World" letters in the *Buffalo Express*, Samuel Langhorne Clemens, alias Mark Twain, was on the move. Having just published the most popular travel book ever written by an American, he spent part of that fall gearing up for another grueling lecture tour that would take him from Pittsburgh on a circuitous route to Jamestown, New York. In a letter written to Frank Fuller during a rare lull on the tour, he complained that he was "dead tired of being in one place so long," and he later confided to another friend, fellow *Quaker City* passenger Emily Severance, "I am in a fidget to move. It isn't a novel sensation, though — I never was any other way."[1] Indeed, by his thirty-fourth birthday in November of 1869, Sam Clemens could look back on nearly eighteen years of perpetual motion — and with *The Innocents Abroad* achieving sensational popularity on both sides of the Atlantic, there seemed to be nothing that could bring Mark Twain's legendary peregrinations to an end.

Less than two years later, however, as he finished patching together his Western material during the early fall of 1871, the Wild Humorist of the Pacific Slope had come to rest in quiet Hartford, Connecticut. His marriage to Olivia Langdon in February of the preceding year had been the decisive event during a period of remarkable personal transformation, as Sam Clemens literally remade himself and his literary persona according to a newfound ideal of domestic stability. The once unregenerate vagabond who had complained so often of his "impatience to move — move — *Move!*" now basked in the comfort and permanence of a fully appointed Victorian household, which he described to his mother-in-law as "the daintiest, & the most exquisite & enchanting that can be found in all America — & the longer we know it the more fascinating it grows & the firmer the hold it fastens upon each fettered sense."[2] The American Vandal who had toppled false idols in Europe and the Holy Land to the delight of readers everywhere now called himself, with only a measure of irony, "Little Sammy in Fairy Land."[3] In early 1870, Little Sammy could barely contain his happiness at finding himself, after so many years of drifting, fastened and fettered to that bulwark of Victorian respectability, the home.

Roughing It, the book that came into existence during this extraordinary period of realignment in Sam Clemens' life and career, is also a record of personal transformation, albeit of a very different sort. Amazed to discover that his white kid gloves and swallowtail coat will be of little use at Pawnee receptions in the Rocky Mountains, the narrator of this uneven but irresistible volume gradually abandons the trappings of polite civilization at precisely the moment Sam Clemens seemed most interested in acquiring them. On the Western side of the Continental Divide, *Roughing It*'s credulous narrator encounters a frontier culture whose values contradict his own, a society in which constant mobility, violence, lawlessness, opportunism, and reckless materialism present a devastating affront to his genteel expectations. By gradually adopting the rough mannerisms of a seasoned old-timer, the narrator successfully remakes himself as a "vagabondizing" Westerner, much as Sam Clemens was in the process of remaking "Mark Twain" into a symbol of Victorian stability.

This peculiar symmetry between the man and his book suggests that *Roughing It* performed an important psychic function during the period of Mark Twain's radical domestication. Read against the paeans to hearth and home that Clemens was sending off to friends and family, the narrator's exuberance as he migrates westward toward an uncertain future has the look of an attempt to compensate imaginatively for something lost. "Home" may have become "a ceaseless, unsurfeiting feast for the eye & the soul, & the whole being," as Clemens wrote to Livy's mother in February of 1870,[4] but within months he was composing paeans of a different sort, in language that is unmistakably more vigorous, more descriptive, and more emotionally charged. Early in chapter 5, for example, the narrator's depiction of mornings on the overland route across the prairie reads like a hymn to motion and velocity.

> We resumed undress uniform, climbed a-top the flying coach, dangled our legs over the side, shouted occasionally at our frantic mules, merely to see them lay their ears back and scamper faster, tied our hats on to keep our hair from blowing away, and leveled an outlook over the world-wide carpet about us for things new and strange to gaze at. Even at this day it thrills me through and through to think of the life, the gladness and the wild sense of freedom that used to make the blood dance in my veins on those fine overland mornings! (48)

It is tempting to read into these lines a subtle rebuke of the life Sam Clemens had so willingly entered only months before, a life anchored in the Clemenses' new domestic routine. Anticipating the adolescent masculine sanctuary of the raft in *Huckleberry Finn*, where Huck and Jim float naked and free in defiance of a hostile civilization, the narrator of *Roughing It* is plainly euphoric in describing the overland journey as a fantasy ride into the unknown, perhaps an alternative to the fantasy of domestic bliss in which Sam Clemens had invested so much, and in which he sincerely wished to believe. From the Clemenses' dainty little mansion in Buffalo — a wedding present from Livy's parents — and later from the enormous house in Hartford, the narrator's "wild sense of freedom" had suddenly, within the space of a few months, begun to seem like a remote memory, accessible "even at this day" only through an act of imagination.

Sam Clemens' Western experiences from 1861 to 1865 were indeed no longer fresh in his mind when he announced his intention to "do up Nevada & Cal." in a July 1870 letter to his brother Orion, and the painstaking task of recollection made the composition of *Roughing It* more arduous than he had expected.[5] Yet for all the difficulty Clemens faced in recreating an image of the life he had left behind in San Francisco five years before, *Roughing It* is such an engaging book precisely because of the distance that separates the narrator from an experience he clearly values, a distance measurable not only in years but in emotional cost. In his first great success, *The Innocents Abroad*, Mark Twain had reported his contemporaneous experience with all the quirks, sarcasm, and foolishness that his wonderfully flexible journalistic persona made available. In *Roughing It* he tapped not only a new set of experiences but a new category of experience, for now the "vagabondizing" days of his past were neither immediately accessible nor entirely appropriate to his evolving persona. Memory, in other words, had come to play an important role in Sam Clemens' relationship to Mark Twain, a relationship he would continue to refine and complicate in a succession of major works after *Roughing It*, venturing deeper into the recesses of his own history for the subject matter of each new book. That process of successive forays into the past of Sam Clemens began with Mark Twain's rediscovery of the West in *Roughing It* and culminated in 1885 with the publication of his finest Mississippi Valley book, *Adventures of Huckleberry Finn* — a period of approximately fifteen years that roughly defines the major phase of his career.

Ironically, as he probed his options for the subject of his second book of travel in late 1869 and early 1870, Twain had no intention of altering the formula that had succeeded so well in *The Innocents Abroad*. It had taken him only a few months to put that book together during the spring and summer of 1868, and within a year he had begun to reap astonishing pecuniary rewards for his labor. Convinced that book writing, as opposed to lecturing and journalism, represented a lucrative and almost effortless means of marketing his work, he informed Mary Fairbanks in January 1870 that he intended to write another book "during the summer," presumably a sequel.[6] With that end in mind, the Clemenses toyed with the idea of a honeymoon in England, where Twain felt he could gather material for a "telling book" on British customs and institutions.[7] Meanwhile, Elisha Bliss — who was also reaping huge profits as the publisher of *The Innocents Abroad* — tried to convince his star author to make another tour of Europe in preparation for a follow-up volume.

By May 1870, Twain had tentatively settled on the West as the subject of his next book. He wrote to Mary Fairbanks, "Well, I guess we *shall* have to go with you to California in the Spring [of 1871], for the publishers are getting right impatient to see another book on the stocks, & I doubt if I could do better than rub up old Pacific memories & put them between covers along with some eloquent pictures."[8] This letter makes it unclear whether he intended to make a book out of his own Western experiences between 1861 and 1865, or out of contemporaneous observations of travel in California, more in the journalistic manner of *The Innocents Abroad*. To the extent that he had a plan at all, he probably intended to fill the considerable gaps in his memory of the frontier by balancing anecdotes from the past with contemporary observations, as he would eventually do in *Life on the Mississippi* (1883). Six weeks later, he had apparently decided to make do without the proposed journey, for on July 15 he contracted to write a 600-page book for Bliss's American Publishing Company, the manuscript to be delivered on January 1, 1871, only five and a half months away. Later the same day he wrote to Orion, asking for help: "as it stands, I propose to do up Nevada & Cal., beginning with the trip across the country in the stage. . . . Do you remember any of the scenes, names, incidents or adventures of the coach trip . . . for I remember next to *nothing* about the matter?"[9]

Orion had already pitched in by forwarding a file of clippings from the *Virginia City Territorial Enterprise*, which Twain intended to stitch together with Orion's and his own recollections in the form of a quasi–travel narrative and sketchbook. If that strategy failed to produce sufficient material to fill the 1,800 manuscript pages necessary for a 600-page subscription book, he felt sure there were enough miscellaneous items on his writing desk to make a book "any time you want it," as he boldly told Bliss.[10] The Western material looked promising, yet as a precaution he left the question of subject matter out of his contractual agreement with the American Publishing Company, confiding to Orion that "the subject . . . is a secret because I may possibly change it."[11] Brimming with confidence, he described his successful negotiations to his mother on July 27, noting that he planned to begin writing "about a month from now," at the end of August.[12] He was convinced the job would take no more than four months.

That projection would have been optimistic under the best of circumstances, and the Clemenses did not enjoy the best of circumstances during the fall and winter of 1870–71. On August 6 Livy's father, Jervis Langdon, died in Elmira, New York, after a long illness, bringing an abrupt end to the couple's happy period of nesting in Buffalo. Twain found time to begin work on his Western book later that month, but his father-in-law's untimely demise proved to be only the first in a series of catastrophic distractions. Early in September, a childhood friend of Livy's, Emma Nye, visited the Clemenses' Buffalo home and was promptly stricken with typhoid. "Miss Emma Nye lingered a month with typhoid fever," Twain wrote soberly to Mary Fairbanks, "& died here in our own bedroom on the 29th of Sept."[13] Livy, who was pregnant and still suffering acutely over the loss of her father when Emma Nye arrived, exhausted herself in caring for her friend and collapsed under the strain at the end of September. Not only her pregnancy but her life seemed in jeopardy as October arrived. Years later Mark Twain remembered Emma Nye's last days as "among the blackest, the gloomiest, the most wretched of my long life."[14]

Despite the ongoing turmoil, Twain may have plugged along "tolerably fairly on the book" in September and early October, as he told Bliss, but all work came to an end when Livy gave birth prematurely to a son, Langdon, on November 7, 1870.[15] Their dainty Buffalo mansion having served as a hospital for two months now, he catalogued his staggering medical expenses in a desperate letter to Orion, concluding with a terse summary of affairs: "*I am sitting still with my hands idle* — for Livy is very sick & I do not believe the baby will live five days."[16] With two months left to deliver the book to Bliss, he had written about eight chapters, perhaps 180 out of the necessary 1,800 manuscript pages, and further progress looked doubtful for the moment.

Livy's health remained tenuous through the end of the year and took a decisive turn for the worse at the end of January, when she herself was diagnosed with typhoid. Clemens' earlier crooning over household gods must have seemed like a cruel farce after one year of marriage, and as Livy slipped into the delirium that had consumed Emma Nye's life five months before, the increasing absurdity of his domestic predicament occasionally erupted in what he later described as "half insane tempests and cyclones of humor."[17] One such eruption occurred in the February installment of his regular column for the *Galaxy* magazine, which included a bitterly topical piece on the life-threatening hazards of domesticity. Sounding once again like the Mark Twain who had to "move — move — *Move*," the astonished narrator of "The Danger of Lying in Bed" inverts conventional wisdom by discovering that the greatest peril to well-being lies "NOT IN TRAVELLING, BUT IN STAYING AT HOME."[18] The home he had been so reluctant to leave six months before when he shelved proposals to visit California, England, and Europe had become anything but a refuge from the cares of the world, as he had so blithely described it to his mother-in-law. Having quietly passed over his publisher's January 1 deadline, a date Twain simply neglected to mention in correspondence after September, he had begun looking for ways to escape the obligations that tied him to his writing desk in Buffalo. One of those obligations, the book that was supposed to take four months to write, was still barely under way.

Amazingly, Twain's strategy for easing the pressures of the dreadful winter of 1870–71 was to embark on a variety of new literary projects. Perhaps as a way of distracting himself from the bleak domestic scene and of avoiding his principal literary obligation to Bliss, he whiled away much of the winter dreaming up extravagant new undertakings, like a proposed book of travel and adventure in the diamond fields of South Africa. After securing a $1,500 advance from the American Publishing Company for this misbegotten enterprise, he pushed Bliss to begin "canvassing like mad" for a collection to be called *Mark Twain's Sketches*, which he hoped to publish by spring.[19] At the same time he was casting his net elsewhere, contracting with Isaac Sheldon of the *Galaxy* to produce a new pamphlet entitled *Mark Twain's (Burlesque) Autobiography and First Romance.*

None of these impulsive projects succeeded — or, more accurately, they succeeded for a time in diverting his attention from the unwritten Western book, but failed to replace it. The forgettable burlesque autobiography received chilly reviews when it appeared in February, and Bliss managed to discourage Twain from moving forward on the sketchbook, which finally appeared in 1875 as *Sketches, New and Old*. The diamond-mine venture ended tragically when James Henry Riley, Twain's surrogate fact-finder, died in 1872, after his return from South Africa. His letters, which Twain was to have reworked into a book that would "sweep the world like a besom of destruction," languished on Twain's writing desk until the project was entirely dropped later the same year.[20] As spring arrived in 1871, both Livy and the baby appeared likely to pull through, but the fate of the Western book, now almost a year old and *still* barely under way, looked ominous.

Just as earlier in his career constant movement had seemed essential to Mark Twain's creativity, he now packed his family's belongings, put the house up for sale, sold his stake in the *Buffalo Express*, and pinned his creative hopes on a change of scenery. After the euphoric spring of 1870, Buffalo had become the scene of constant personal misfortunes and literary disappointments, and Twain seemed almost superstitious about escaping in order to start over in a new place. Hartford was their ultimate destination, but the family planned to spend the summer at the Langdon home in Elmira, where Twain intended to jump-start his stalled manuscript. Ironically, the traumatic winter in Buffalo had begun to make work on *Roughing It* look like a release from other cares. After encumbering himself for months with fruitless writing projects, he told Bliss in his last letter from Buffalo, "I want to get clear away from all hamperings, all harassments. I am going to shut myself up in a farmhouse alone, on top of an Elmira hill, & *write* — on my book."[21] The next day, March 18, 1871, he loaded his wife onto a mattress — she was still too weak to make the five-hour journey any other way — and put the family on the train for Elmira. After a catastrophic experiment in domestic living, Mark Twain was on the move again.

For the next three and a half months, Twain enjoyed one of those unexplainable bursts of creativity that visited him intermittently throughout his career, often after periods of prolonged idleness. By the end of April, after only about five weeks in Elmira, he had already doubled the output of the previous year, working his way up to approximately chapter 25. The Langdons' cottage at Quarry Farm, two and a half miles from the family home on Main Street, provided an ideal retreat where Twain found it possible to rattle off as many as 200 manuscript pages per week. In mid-April he was joined at Quarry Farm by an old friend from his days at the *Virginia City Territorial Enterprise*, Joe Goodman, who had come east in Mark Twain's wake to em-

bark on a literary career of his own. Goodman's praise for the working manuscript and his recollections of Washoe journalism helped to revive Twain's interest in the book, with the result that by May 15 he was once again brimming
with confidence, informing Bliss, "I am writing with a red-hot interest.
Nothing grieves me now — nothing troubles me, bothers me or gets my attention — I don't think of anything but the book. . . . It will be a bully book."[22]

Giddy with pleasure over his ability to write again, he scratched out an im-
promptu dedication for the book at the end of his May 15 letter to Bliss.
Though he later replaced it with a more demure tribute to his former mining
buddy Calvin Higbie, the unpublished version is worth quoting as an indica-
tion of Mark Twain's gleeful state of mind during the wonderfully productive
summer of 1871.

> To the Late Cain,
>
> This Book is Dedicated:
>
> Not on account of respect for his memory, for it merits little respect; not
> on account of sympathy with him, for his bloody deed placed him without
> the pale of sympathy, strictly speaking: but out of a mere humane commis-
> eration for him in that it was his misfortune to live in a dark age that knew
> not the beneficent Insanity Plea.[23]

The irreverence that made Mark Twain famous was once again running high,
so high in fact that by early June he was hatching plans to go back out on the
road for another lecture tour in the fall and winter. As June came to an end
and his "red-hot interest" in the Western book began to cool, he informed
Orion that he had before him fifty-six completed chapters and, by his own
reckoning, "nearly MS enough" to make a book.[24]

That estimate was based on his plan to tack a large section of previously
published material, ultimately eighteen chapters, onto the end of his Western
adventures, a strategy that would allow him, he hoped, to cut out half or most
of the overland section. In 1866 Mark Twain had sailed to the Sandwich
Islands, present-day Hawaii, as a traveling correspondent for the *Sacramento
Union*, and he now saw an opportunity to fill out the *Roughing It* manuscript
by revising his *Union* letters according to the same principle he had used in

preparing his *San Francisco Daily Alta California* letters for *The Innocents Abroad*. His calculations were off, as it turned out, and most readers consider it fortunate that the final eighteen chapters did not provide enough material to crowd out the overland episode.

Twain was busily reading proof pages between lecture stops toward the end of the year when Bliss frantically informed him that the book, including the Sandwich Islands section, was still too short, having come back from the typesetter at 570 pages instead of "between 600 and 700 Octavo pages," as the prospectus promised. This latest calamity resulted in the hurried compilation of three appendixes, pasted together from bits of discarded material and miscellaneous news items that were tacked on to the already tacked-on concluding section to ensure customer satisfaction. With the increasingly haphazard collage now rounding out to a reasonably bulky 591 pages, Bliss agreed to start printing, though he was careful to distribute a revised prospectus specifying that Mark Twain's new volume included "nearly 600 Octavo pages."

In order to discourage pirated editions, *Roughing It* was published simultaneously in England and America toward the end of February 1872, and after one year had achieved a phenomenal combined sale of 93,000 copies. George Routledge and Sons issued the English edition, which consisted of two volumes, the first entitled *Roughing It* (including chapters 1–45 of the American edition), the second entitled *The Innocents at Home* (including chapters 46–79 and a reprint of the *Burlesque Autobiography*). Initial reviews in the British press were guarded about Twain's apparent vulgarity, and condescending toward his subject matter. The London *Examiner* found it possible to forgive the author's indelicate humor on the grounds that "wild, irregular passions. . . are among the very qualities required for semi-civilized regions, such as those that form the scene of Mr. Clemens' [book]," but in offering such qualified forgiveness the reviewer found little to praise.[25] The Manchester *Guardian* was more blunt, noting that unlike Bret Harte, who "has shown the tender flower of sentiment . . . among the rude and unlovely surroundings of a digger's camp," Mark Twain "has contented himself with dwelling on the outside of things."[26]

American reviewers were more sympathetic, but surprisingly few received a crack at the book. Twain's confidence that *Roughing It* would be "bully" had understandably waned during the final stages of "composition," which involved more pasting and clipping than actual writing. By January 1872, as *Roughing It* was about to be issued, he had convinced himself that it "would be considered pretty poor stuff, & that therefore I had better not let the press get a chance at it."[27] A few negative reviews in the prominent papers and magazines would kill the advance sale of subscriptions, as he well understood, for customers who purchased a book by Mark Twain from one of the hundreds of American Publishing Company canvassers were trading on a name and on high expectations. Expectations for the sequel to *The Innocents Abroad* were very high indeed, and in early 1872 Twain was sure he had failed to meet them. To avoid disclosing the fact until sales of *Roughing It* were well established, therefore, he held back review copies from all but a few "friends of mine," like his new neighbor in Hartford, editor of the prominent *Hartford Courant*, Charles Dudley Warner.[28]

Warner's review, which appeared in the *Courant* on March 18, praised the moral underpinnings of Twain's humor and lauded his use of the authentic "*argot*" of the mining regions. Twain's future collaborator on *The Gilded Age* (1873) concluded with a favorable assessment of the book's patchwork quality, its unpredictable blend of "queer stories, funny dialogues, strange, comical and dangerous adventures," all of which combined to produce, in Warner's view, "the best picture of frontier mining life that has been written."[29] Twain must have relished this implicit assertion of his superiority over Bret Harte, whose dialect poems and sketches of mining life had made him the unparalleled leader of "the Western school" prior to *Roughing It*'s appearance. On March 20, two days after reading Warner's review, Twain wrote to Bliss that he was now "at last easy & comfortable about the new book," for he had received "sufficient testimony . . . to about satisfy me that the general verdict gives 'Roughing It' the preference over 'Innocents Abroad.' "[30]

Another key witness confirmed this testimony two months later, in Boston's starchy *Atlantic Monthly*. William Dean Howells had liked *The Innocents Abroad*, but in *Roughing It* he recognized traces of a major literary talent. Mark Twain's best work was still before him, but in *Roughing It*'s "kaleidoscopic succession" of images, personalities, and events, Howells discerned the expansive imagination of a writer he would later deem "the Lincoln of our literature." His review touched many of the same points as Warner's, but with keener appreciation.

> The grotesque exaggeration and broad irony with which the life [of the West] is described are conjecturably the truest colors that could have been used, for all existence there must have looked like an extravagant joke, the humor of which was only deepened by the nether-side of tragedy. . . . A thousand anecdotes, relevant and irrelevant, embroider the work; excursions and digressions of all kinds are the very woof of it, as it were; everything far-fetched or near at hand is interwoven, and yet the complex is a sort of "harmony of colors" which is not less than triumphant.[31]

Howells' stamp of approval carried wide cultural authority, as Twain understood when he responded gratefully in a letter that has become famous for its vivid representation of the author's troubled relationship to his book. He told Howells that the *Atlantic* review had made him feel "as uplifted & reassured . . . as a mother who has given birth to a white baby when she was awfully afraid it was going to be a mulatto."[32] When Louise Chandler Moulton of the *New York Tribune* chimed in with another favorable notice, Twain employed a slightly cooler version of the same metaphor in his letter of thanks: "I am *content*, now that the book has been praised in the Tribune — & so I thank you with all that honest glow of gratitude that comes into a mother's eyes when a stranger praises her child."[33] *Roughing It*, the problem child of Mark Twain's imagination, had indeed landed on its feet, and appeared destined to enjoy a long and successful run.

At the end of his letter to Louise Moulton, Twain complained that his new book had attracted "not the slightest mention" in the press, and he blamed Bliss for failing to send review copies to the newspapers. Clearly this was a dodge, for it had been Twain's decision to withhold the book from reviewers on the assumption that *Roughing It* would be considered "pretty poor stuff." The reviews by Howells and Moulton confirmed his growing suspicion that he had written a critical and popular hit, and as spring arrived he scrambled to get the book noticed in print, deflecting responsibility for the mishandling of review copies onto Bliss in what would become a pattern of vindictive and evasive behavior toward his publishers. A few papers fell in line by printing late reviews, and many carried excerpts from the book, but Twain's early misgivings about the quality of *Roughing It* probably cost him priceless publicity. Privately, at least, he accepted part of the blame, confessing in a letter to Bliss, "I believe I have learned, now, that if one don't secure publicity & notoriety for a book the instant it is issued, no amount of hard work & faithful advertising can accomplish it later on."[34]

This belated insight was borne out by *Roughing It*'s tumultuous sales history. In June, six months after publication, when Bliss finally caught up with the massive list of back orders, 67,395 copies had been sold, almost exactly matching the entire first year's sales total for *The Innocents Abroad*. But these phenomenal early sales figures dropped off in July, when merely 2,645 copies were bound for distribution. The trend continued through the end of 1872, leaving the American edition's total first-year sale at 75,178 — an impressive figure by any reckoning — almost all of which, however, had come during the first six months. With *The Innocents Abroad* still selling well after four years in print, *Roughing It*, true to its boom-or-bust theme, had enjoyed a magnificent but short-lived popularity.

Modern critical assessments of Mark Twain's Western book generally take sides along the Brooks/DeVoto fault line that runs throughout critical debate on the author's life and career. In his influential 1920 study, *The Ordeal of Mark Twain*, Van Wyck Brooks argued that Twain's monumental natural talent was stunted and corrupted by his participation in a materialistic frontier culture where the pursuit of immediate gratification precluded any appreciation for art. Humor thus became the perverted expression of Twain's incipient genius, a poor substitute in Brooks's view for the sort of literary greatness he might have achieved in an environment more conducive to his artistic sensibilities. For Brooks, *Roughing It* was both a chronicle of Mark Twain's disastrous embrace of frontier values and a demonstration of Brooks's larger point that as a writer Twain sold out his enormous talent in order to turn a quick profit. Parochial as this view seems, with its blatant dismissal of all things Western, Brooks articulated a powerful interpretation of Twain's career, and his argument still resonates in the work of astute critics, like Forrest G. Robinson, who share Brooks's impatience with *Roughing It*'s haphazard construction and tiresome padding.

Extending Brooks's formal and psychological line of attack into the arena of cultural studies, some of *Roughing It*'s more recent critics have focused attention on Twain's brutally condescending representation of Native Americans and Chinese immigrants, noting that the book at times plays mercilessly on xenophobic anxieties in its highly exclusive image of the frontier "community." Portions of *Roughing It* — like chapter 19, in which the narrator describes the "Goshoot Indians" as "the wretchedest type of mankind I have ever seen" (146) — undeniably reflect Twain's uncritical assimilation of racist assumptions that were pervasive in mid-nineteenth-century America. Without dismissing or apologizing for those assumptions, which make *Roughing It* Mark Twain's least politically correct book, it might be fair to point out that his exaggerated disdain for Native American cultures was more an attempt to earn a laugh at the expense of James Fenimore Cooper, Emerson Bennett, and the "Noble Savage" of popular romance than to draw a realistic picture of Native American life. As so often in Twain's career, most conspicuously in the final chapters of *Huckleberry Finn*, the exigencies of humor and the necessity to achieve stark contrast led him to deploy reductive caricatures that grate on contemporary sensibilities.

Van Wyck Brooks's disparaging account of Twain's Western experience inspired a rebuttal by Bernard DeVoto, who wrote *Mark Twain's America* in 1932 to prove that the rough-and-tumble frontier actually nourished the country's first distinctly American literary voice. Turning Brooks's argument on its head, DeVoto claimed that Mark Twain's chance-taking, high-velocity, mammon-loving existence in the West encouraged, rather than stunted, all the best tendencies in his literary development, which might have proceeded along more conventional lines and achieved more conventional results had he grown up in one of the cultural centers of Europe or New England. For DeVoto, *Roughing It* was the inspired story of Mark Twain's and America's coming of age, a brilliant representation of frontier life in all its unpredictable, chaotic splendor. Howells had articulated a similar position, noting that *Roughing It*'s lack of coherence produced a " 'harmony of colors' which is not less than triumphant," and critics who admire the book have been devising similarly ingenious means of praising its structural discontinuities ever since.

Writing thirty years after the publication of *Mark Twain's America*, Henry Nash Smith refined DeVoto's unqualified celebration of the frontier in making *Roughing It* a cornerstone of his masterful *Mark Twain: The Development of a Writer* (1962). Smith's admiration for the book echoed the opinion of other scholars, like Kenneth Lynn and Franklin Rogers, both of whom argued eloquently for *Roughing It*'s central importance to Twain's emerging technique as a writer and humorist. In the most significant recent commentary on the book, Jeffrey Steinbrink describes Twain's troubled Western narrative and the personal saga that unfolded during its year-long composition as watershed events in his literary development. According to Steinbrink's concentrated and valuable study, *Getting to Be Mark Twain* (1991), *Roughing It* marks the successful culmination of Samuel Clemens' "sorting out" of his literary persona, a decisive step in his growth as a writer.

Debate about Twain's Western book persists, yet admirers and detractors generally agree that *Roughing It* marks a crucial phase in the author's life and literary career. *The Innocents Abroad* had come into existence almost effortlessly, requiring only a few months of editorial stitching and pruning before its release to a stunned reading public in 1869. When Twain informed Mary Fairbanks of his intention to spend the summer of 1870 writing a second book, he was clearly hoping to duplicate the feat of the previous year, despite the fact that he no longer possessed a large file of richly humorous letters from which to make a new book. *Roughing It*, in other words, was the first of Twain's works that had to be "invented" from the ground up, fashioned out of a blend of memory and imagination.

In early 1870, as he celebrated his marriage to Olivia Langdon in the couple's new home, Twain was a world-famous author who had no idea how to write such a book, and very little inclination to try. With new domestic obligations quelling his perennial wanderlust, the crutch of travel no longer offered itself as an automatic way to supply and organize his humorous material, and so he was forced to cultivate other resources in himself. Dragging his heels the entire way, beset by devastating personal events, he learned that composition of a long humorous narrative requires a good deal of actual work — fifteen months' worth instead of four, as it turned out — work for which he possessed a remarkable, if halting, aptitude. It wasn't clear in 1870 what sort of sequel Twain might devise after the triumph of *The Innocents Abroad*, but all indications suggested that he would continue to excel as a writer of humorous travelogue. Instead, he surprised readers and himself by taking an enormous step in the direction of literary fiction, creating a book that continues to dazzle with the variety of its many idioms and the sheer exuberance of its depiction of frontier life.

NOTES

1. Samuel Langhorne Clemens to Frank Fuller, December 13, 1867, in *Mark Twain's Letters, Volume 2 (1867–1868)*, ed. Harriet Elinor Smith and Richard Bucci (Berkeley: U of California P, 1990) 136; SLC to Emily Severance, December 24, 1867, in *Letters, Volume 2*, 138.

2. SLC to Jane Clemens, June 1, 1867, in *Letters, Volume 2*, 49–50; SLC to Mrs. Langdon, February 20, 1870, quoted in Jeffrey Steinbrink, *Getting to Be Mark Twain* (Berkeley: U of California P, 1991) 80–81.

3. SLC to Mrs. Langdon, February 9, 1870, quoted in Steinbrink, 81.

4. SLC to Mrs. Langdon, Febraury 20, 1870, quoted in Steinbrink, 80–81.

5. SLC to Orion Clemens, July 15, 1870, in *Mark Twain's Letters*, ed. Albert Bigelow Paine, 2 vols. (New York: Harper, 1917) 1:174–75.

6. SLC to Mary Fairbanks, January 6, 1870, quoted in Steinbrink, 132.

7. SLC to Elisha Bliss, March 11, 1870, quoted in Steinbrink, 132.

8. SLC to Mary Fairbanks, May 29, 1870, in *Mark Twain to Mrs. Fairbanks*, ed. Dixon Wecter (San Marino, Calif.: Huntington Library, 1949) 131.

9. SLC to Orion Clemens, July 15, 1870, in *Mark Twain's Letters*, ed. Albert Bigelow Paine, 1:174–75.

10. SLC to Elisha Bliss, January 22, 1870, quoted in Steinbrink, 132.

11. SLC to Orion Clemens, July 15, 1870, in *Mark Twain's Letters*, ed. Albert Bigelow Paine, 1:174–75.

12. SLC to Jane Clemens, July 27, 1870, quoted in Steinbrink, 135.

13. SLC to Mary Fairbanks, October 13, 1870, in *Mark Twain to Mrs. Fairbanks*, 176.

14. Autobiographical dictation, February 15, 1906, quoted in Steinbrink, 136–37.

15. SLC to Elisha Bliss, October 13, 1870, quoted in Steinbrink, 141.

16. SLC to Orion Clemens, November 11, 1870, quoted in Steinbrink, 144.

17. Autobiographical dictation, February 15, 1906, quoted in Steinbrink, 136–37.

18. Quoted in Steinbrink, 149.

19. SLC to Elisha Bliss, January 3, 1871, quoted in Steinbrink, 147.

20. SLC to James Henry Riley, December 2, 1870, quoted in Steinbrink, 147.

21. SLC to Elisha Bliss, March 17, 1871, quoted in Steinbrink, 166.

22. SLC to Elisha Bliss, May 15, 1871, in *Mark Twain's Letters*, ed. Albert Bigelow Paine, 1:187–88.

23. SLC to Elisha Bliss, May 15, 1871, in *Mark Twain's Letters*, ed. Albert Bigelow Paine, 1:188.

24. SLC to Orion Clemens, July 2, 1871, quoted in Steinbrink, 185.

25. "Life in the Western States," London *Examiner*, April 6, 1872: 361–62, quoted in Harriet Elinor Smith, introduction to *Roughing It*, ed. Harriet Elinor Smith and Edgar Marquess Branch (Berkeley: U of California P, 1993) 885.

26. "Literature: Uncivilized America," Manchester *Guardian*, March 6, 1872: 7, quoted in Smith, 885.

27. SLC to David Gray Sr., June 10, 1880, quoted in Smith, 797.

28. SLC to Elisha Bliss, March 20, 1872, in *Mark Twain's Letters to His Publishers, 1867–1894*, ed. Hamlin Hill (Berkeley: U of California P, 1967) 70–71.

29. "'Roughing It.' Mark Twain's New Book," *Hartford Courant*, March 18, 1872: 1, quoted in Smith, 885–86.

30. SLC to Elisha Bliss, March 20, 1872, in *Mark Twain's Letters to His Publishers*, 70–71.

31. "Recent Literature," *Atlantic Monthly* 29 (June 1872): 754–55.

32. SLC to William Dean Howells, May 25–30(?), 1872, quoted in Smith, 798.

33. SLC to Louise Chandler Moulton, June 18, 1872, quoted in Smith, 888.

34. SLC to Elisha Bliss, March 4, 1873, in *Mark Twain's Letters to His Publishers*, 74.

FOR FURTHER READING

Henry B. Wonham

Mark Twain was a prolific letter writer, and his correspondence with Olivia, Elisha Bliss, Orion Clemens, Mary Fairbanks, and other friends between 1861 and 1872 is an essential resource for the study of his Western experience and its literary representation in *Roughing It*. Many of these letters are now available in the University of California's scholarly edition, *Mark Twain's Letters, Volume 1 (1853–1866)*, ed. Edgar M. Branch, Michael B. Frank, and Kenneth M. Sanderson (Berkeley: U of California P, 1988), *Volume 2 (1867–1868)*, ed. Harriet Smith, Richard Bucci, and Lin Salamo (Berkeley: U of California P, 1990), and *Volume 3 (1869)*, ed. Victor Fischer, Michael B. Frank, and Dahlia Armon (Berkeley: U of California P, 1992). Other useful collections include Dixon Wecter's two editions of correspondence, *The Love Letters of Mark Twain* (New York: Harper, 1949) and *Mark Twain to Mrs. Fairbanks* (San Marino, Calif.: Huntington Library, 1949).

Twain's early correspondence provides the theoretical framework for the most important book-length study of *Roughing It*, Franklin R. Rogers' *The Pattern for Mark Twain's "Roughing It": Letters from Nevada by Samuel and Orion Clemens, 1861–1862* (Berkeley: U of California P, 1961). In general, Twain's Western book has attracted considerably less critical attention than *The Adventures of Tom Sawyer*, *Adventures of Huckleberry Finn*, *A Connecticut Yankee in King Arthur's Court*, or *Pudd'nhead Wilson*, though *Roughing It* has a special appeal for critics who approach Twain's literary achievement in terms of his evolving technique as a humorist. From this point of view, *Roughing It* is an essential text, for it shows Mark Twain working his way through the literary pranks and burlesques of Washoe journalism toward the construction of longer fictional narratives. Kenneth Lynn mined this important vein of Twain criticism in *Mark Twain and Southwestern Humor* (Boston: Little, Brown, 1959), as did Franklin Rogers in *Mark Twain's Burlesque Patterns: As Seen in the Novels and Narratives, 1855–1885* (Dallas: Southern Methodist UP, 1960) and Henry Nash Smith in "Mark Twain as an

Interpreter of the Far West: The Structure of *Roughing It*" (in *The Frontier in Perspective*, ed. Walker D. Wyman and Clifton B. Kroeber [Madison: U of Wisconsin P, 1957]) and *Mark Twain: The Development of a Writer* (Cambridge: Harvard UP, 1962). More recently, the book has continued to find its champions among critics interested in Twain's humorous technique. See especially David E. E. Sloane's *Mark Twain as a Literary Comedian* (Baton Rouge: Louisiana State UP, 1979) and Henry B. Wonham's *Mark Twain and the Art of the Tall Tale* (New York: Oxford UP, 1993), which describes *Roughing It* as Mark Twain's "western *bildungsroman*."

For a more critical appraisal of Twain's achievement, see Forrest G. Robinson's essay "'Seeing the Elephant': Some Perspectives on Mark Twain's *Roughing It*," *American Studies* 21 (1980): 43–64. Helen L. Harris has written an important essay on the issue of Twain's representation of Native Americans, "Mark Twain's Response to the Native American," *American Literature* 46 (January 1975): 495–505, and James C. McNutt is also interesting on that subject in "Mark Twain and the American Indian: Earthly Realism and Heavenly Idealism," *American Indian Quarterly* 4 (August 1978): 223–42.

As all these critics take pains to point out, *Roughing It* is a strange hybrid, including elements of fantasy, fable, and autobiography, and thus biographical criticism of Twain's early career is another essential resource for sorting out the book's various narrative modes. In addition to the major biographies by Paine and Kaplan, more concentrated accounts by Paul Fatout (*Mark Twain in Virginia City* [Bloomington: Indiana UP, 1964]) and Effie Mona Mack (*Mark Twain in Nevada* [New York: Scribner's, 1947]) are very helpful. Harriet Elinor Smith's introduction to the University of California edition of *Roughing It*, ed. Harriet Elinor Smith and Edgar Marquess Branch (Berkeley: U of California P, 1993), is rich with biographical detail, as is Jeffrey Steinbrink's masterful account of the brief but decisive period from 1868 to 1871 in *Getting to Be Mark Twain* (Berkeley: U of California P, 1991).

ILLUSTRATORS AND ILLUSTRATIONS
IN MARK TWAIN'S FIRST AMERICAN EDITIONS

Beverly R. David & Ray Sapirstein

From the "gorgeous gold frog" stamped into the cover of *The Celebrated Jumping Frog of Calaveras County* in 1867 to the comet-riding captain on the frontispiece of *Extract from Captain Stormfield's Visit to Heaven* in 1909, illustrators and illustrations were an integral part of Mark Twain's first editions.

Twain marketed most of his major works by subscription, and illustration functioned as an important sales tool. Subscription books were packed with pictures of every type and size and were bound in brassy gold-stamped covers. The books were sold by agents who flipped through a prospectus filled with lively illustrations, selected text, and binding samples. Illustrations quickly conveyed a sense of the story, condensing the proverbial "thousand words" and outlining the scope and tone of the work, making an impression on the potential purchaser even before the full text had been printed. Book canvassers were rewarded with up to 50 percent of the selling price, which started at $3.50 and ranged as high as $7.00 for more ornate bindings. The books themselves were seldom produced until a substantial number of customers had placed orders. To justify the relatively high price and to reassure buyers that they were getting their money's worth, books published by subscription had to offer sensational volume and apparent substance. As Frank Bliss of the American Publishing Company observed, these consumers "would not pay for blank paper and wide margins. They wanted everything filled up with type or pictures." While authors of trade books generally tolerated lighter sales, gratified by attracting a "better class of readers," as Hamlin Hill put it, authors of subscription books sacrificed literary respectability for popular appeal and considerable profit.[1]

The humorist George Ade remembered Twain's books vividly, offering us a child's-eye view of the nineteenth-century subscription book market.

Just when front-room literature seemed at its lowest ebb, so far as the American boy was concerned, along came Mark Twain. His books looked at a distance, just like the other distended, diluted, and altogether tasteless volumes that had been used for several decades to balance the ends of the center table . . . so thick and heavy and emblazoned with gold that [they] could keep company with the bulky and high-priced Bible. . . . The publisher knew his public, so he gave a pound of book for every fifty cents, and crowded in plenty of wood-cuts and stamped the outside with golden bouquets and put in a steel engraving of the author, with a tissue paper veil over it, and "sicked" his multitude of broken-down clergymen, maiden ladies, grass widows, and college students on the great American public.

Can you see the boy, Sunday morning prisoner, approach the book with a dull sense of foreboding, expecting a dose of Tupper's *Proverbial Philosophy?* Can you see him a few minutes later when he finds himself linked arm-in-arm with Mulberry Sellers or Buck Fanshaw or the convulsing idiot who wanted to know if Christopher Columbus was sure-enough dead? No wonder he curled up on the hair-cloth sofa and hugged the thing to his bosom and lost all interest in Sunday school. *Innocents Abroad* was the most enthralling book ever printed until *Roughing It* appeared. Then along came *The Gilded Age*, *Life on the Mississippi*, and *Tom Sawyer*. . . . While waiting for a new one we read the old ones all over again.[2]

Publishers, editors, and Twain himself spent a good deal of time on design — choosing the most talented artists, directing their interpretations of text, selecting from the final prints, and at times removing material they deemed unfit for illustration.[3]

With the exception of *Following the Equator* (1897), books released in the twilight of Twain's career were not sold by subscription. Twain's later books, published for the trade market by Harper and Brothers, seldom contained more than a frontispiece and a dozen or so tasteful illustrations, rather than the hundreds of illustrations per volume that subscription publishing demanded. Illustration, however, remained a major component of Twain's later work in two important cases: *Extracts from Adam's Diary*, illustrated by Fred

Strothmann in 1904, and *Eve's Diary*, illustrated by Lester Ralph in 1906.

The stories behind the illustrators and illustrations of Mark Twain's first editions abound in back-room intrigue. The besotted or negligent lapses of some of the artists and the procrastinations of the engravers are legendary. The consequent production delays, mistimed releases, and copyright infringements all implied a lack of competent supervision that frequently infuriated Twain and ultimately encouraged him to launch his own publishing company.

In many cases, Twain took illustrations into account as he wrote and edited his text, using them as counterpoint and accompaniment to his words, often allowing them to inform his general narrative strategy and to influence the amount of detail he felt necessary to include in his written descriptions. In the most artful and carefully considered illustrated works, an analysis of the relationships between author and illustrator and between text and pictures illuminates key dimensions of Twain's writings and the responses they have elicited from readers. Examinations of even the most straightforward examples of decorative imagery yield insights into the publishing history of Twain's books and his attitudes toward the production process.

The original illustrations in Twain's works have often been replaced in the twentieth century by subsequent visual interpretations. But while Norman Rockwell's well-known nostalgic renderings of *Tom Sawyer* and *Huckleberry Finn* may tell us much about 1930s sensibilities, we would do well to reacquaint ourselves with the first American editions and the artwork they contained if we want to understand the books Twain wrote and the world they affected.

Illustrated books, like the illustrated weekly magazines that first appeared in the 1860s, were a significant source of visual images entering nineteenth-century homes. Because of their widespread popularity and the relative paucity of other sources of visual information, Twain's books helped to define America's perceptions of remote people, exotic scenes, and historic events. In addition to being an essential element of Mark Twain's body of work, illustrations are a documentary source in their own right, a window into Twain's world and our own.

NOTES

1. For background on subscription book publishing, see Hamlin Hill, *Mark Twain and Elisha Bliss* (Columbia: University of Missouri Press, 1964), chapter 1. See also R. Kent Rasmussen, "Subscription-book publishing" entry, *Mark Twain A to Z: The Essential Reference to His Life and Writings* (New York: Facts on File, 1995), p. 448.

2. George Ade, "Mark Twain and the Old-Time Subscription Book," *Review of Reviews* 61 (June 10, 1910): 703–4; reprinted in Frederick Anderson, ed., *Mark Twain: The Critical Heritage* (London: Routledge and Kegan Paul, 1971), pp. 337–39.

3. Beverly R. David, *Mark Twain and His Illustrators, Volume 1 (1869–1875)* (Troy, N.Y.: Whitston Publishing Company, 1986), discusses in detail Twain's involvement in the production of his early books.

READING THE ILLUSTRATIONS IN *ROUGHING IT*

Beverly R. David & Ray Sapirstein

Mark Twain's readers were in for a bumpy ride when they joined him in 1872 on a literary journey to the Nevada Territory and beyond. The cover for Twain's second subscription book illustrated one of the primitive but functional modes of Western transportation. A beared miner appears in a gold-stamped vignette, driving a buckboard wagon filled with sacks of provisions, one monogrammed "M.T." The spirited horse and driver travel along an uneven log road, the log-ends lettered to spell out the title of the book.

As he had done with *The Innocents Abroad*, Twain again relied on the marketing savvy of Elisha Bliss and the American Publishing Company. As editor and publisher, Bliss retained True Williams (1839–1897) as principal artist and Roswell Shurtleff (1838–1915) as backup. Both artists had worked on *Innocents Abroad* and were subcontracted through the illustrating firm Fay and Cox, hence the firm's trademark on the list of illustrations.[1] Williams was to be the workhorse, producing the majority of the drawings. Albert Bigelow Paine, Twain's friend and biographer, and an authority on illustration, remembered Williams as "a man of great talent" but commented that "it was necessary to lock him in a room when industry was required, with nothing more exciting than cold water as a beverage."[2] Shurtleff drew the more polished full-page prints, including "The South Pass" (100), an impressive view perched high in the Rocky Mountains, and the magnificently composed frontispiece, "The Miner's Dream," which featured Twain as the dreamer, seated asleep on a barrel. To appeal to subscription book buyers' taste for visual indulgence, Bliss added a second frontispiece to face the first, Williams' "Camping in the Snow."

When the two illustrators ran over deadline, Bliss recruited E. F. Mullen, an over-the-hill semi-reformed alcoholic, to produce images for the Mono Lake section and for the final pages of the book. Under severe pressure for a Christmas 1871 release, Bliss accelerated the time-consuming illustration process by culling plates from works his firm had already published. Thus

Roughing It contained several engravings borrowed from Albert D. Richardson's *Beyond the Mississippi* and Thomas Knox's *Overland Through Asia*. The appropriated images included "Goshoot Indians Hanging Around Stations" by James Carter Beard (147), an unconvincing "Hawaiian" boy blowing a horn, drawn by Henry Louis Stephens and signed by the engraver, Richardson (489), detail from an image of a house in Denver, "Prairie Dogs" (50), the hanging liar tailpiece by A. W. Waud (557), and scenes of a Nevada quartz mill by Asa Coolidge Warren (253–56). Bliss also borrowed five prints from J. Ross Browne's *Adventures in the Apache Country: A Tour Through Arizona and Sonora*, published in 1869 by Harper and Brothers and not an American Publishing Company product. These included a print of Mono Lake (265) and several prints of characters altered to correspond to Twain's story.[3]

Both Williams and Shurtleff were skilled caricaturists and inserted several colorful local figures. Readers encounter Calvin Higbie, to whom *Roughing It* is dedicated, in chapter 40, in which he and Twain become short-term millionaires. In several images, Jim Gillis, the veteran storyteller, joins the millionaire crew. In addition to the full-page presentation of the famous "turnip" letter (509), Horace Greeley (of "Go west, young man" fame) appears in "Greeley's Ride," which parallels Twain's satire by depicting the great promoter of the West so terrifically jolted that his head "shot clean through the roof" of Hank Monk's hell-bent stagecoach (151–52). Even True Williams makes a cameo appearance; the illustrator drew a self-portrait to depict the character "Williams," the heroic conqueror of the blustery, tale-telling "Admiral" (453). As in *Innocents Abroad*, slapstick cartoons and sublime scenery are accompanied by formal portraits of notable figures. Although there was no royalty in the West as there had been in the Europe of *The Innocents Abroad*, the artists drew likenesses of the closest American equivalents, the autocratic Mormon leaders Heber Kimball (112) and Brigham Young (113).

Noteworthy among the illustrations are the many images portraying Twain himself as the lead player in the events and scences he described. The reader is continually guided by Twain's presence in the text and illustrations; they etch his persona as well as his words into the reader's consciousness. Like a foreign correspondent delivering on-the-spot news from abroad, Twain recorded not only the story but *his* story, his own reactions and involvement in the scene. Predictably, Twain's persona often stole the show; his descriptions of exotic people, places, and customs were secondary, merely a foil for his comic presentation. Frequently, the illustrators satirically transcribed Twain's own self-deprecating tales, depicting him dancing with the "grace of a kangaroo" (420), being "unexpectedly elevated" by the Genuine Mexican Plug (180), and coming down with a "severe case of stage fright" as a lecturer (561). This last comic image was used on posters and advertising materials for the book.

The illustrations featuring Mark Twain were central to the development of his public persona, distilling his likeness to trademark physical idiosyncrasies and scattering it liberally throughout the book. In the words of Louis Budd, a prominent observer of Twain as a public personality, he was "bound to be cartooned. . . . Sometimes he was meant to be identified by his thatch of hair, mustache, and nose — generally considered his most graphic features."[4] Twain deliberately conceived his physical style for easy caricature and recognition, admitting that he had a "talent for posturing."[5] In fact, his likeness was so iconic and easily reproducible that throughout his life he spawned a host of impostors eager to bask in his fame.

The illustrations in *Roughing It*, which conjoin a "look," a recognizable personal style, with an attitude or outlook, much in the manner of today's celebrities, establish that the cult of personality surrounding Mark Twain originated with his earliest works. As he explains in chapter 78 of *Roughing It*, he ultimately capitalized on his popularity as a lecturer, answering the demand for his personal presence both in life and on the printed page.

At a time before photographs could be reproduced in printer's ink, Twain fashioned himself as a package calculated to become a popular icon. According to Budd, who has thoroughly studied Twain's penchant for self-promotion, "he thought . . . of his signature as a logo — a brand name, even — rather than a pen name. As early as 1873, at an attorney's suggestion, he started trying to establish 'Mark Twain' as a protected trademark."[6] Twain's name, wry attitude, and physical features were his trademarks. By reducing him to caricature and presenting him in outrageous and memorable scenes, Twain's illustrators were instrumental in forging his celebrity.

Roughing It continued the assault on sentimental idealism begun in *The Innocents Abroad*, exposing a tawdry and corrupt American West rather than the oft-imagined wilderness paradise of early-nineteeth-century arts and letters. Although Twain blamed the book's slow sales on the poor quality of the engravings and paper,[7] the crudely drawn and executed illustrations clearly articulated Twain's satiric purpose to readers, differentiating *Roughing It* from high-toned travel narratives and memoirs. The images accompanying Twain's text suggest the book's kinship with pulpy comic monthlies, editorial cartoons, and dime novels, which similarly used the frontier West as the stage for countless tall tales of exploits, exotica, oddities, and perverse curiosities.

As in *Innocents Abroad*, the engravings in *Roughing It* reflect Twain's divided attitude, in this case toward the idealization of the Western frontier. Two types of images vie for dominance in the book: irreverent, ludicrous scribblings and fanciful panoramas of natural splendor and majesty. The competition between these two modes reflects and underscores Twain's own dilemma. While he stripped bare the image of the West as a society morally purified by its proximity to unspoiled nature, he equally celebrated natural scenery, perpetuating the image of the West as a wilderness idyll.

The first edition of *Roughing It* contained 591 pages with 304 illustrations, which in bulk and proportion of text to pictures was typical of subscription books. Early reviews were not complimentary on this point, however, suggesting that the engravings were "crude in design . . . and coarse in execution."[8] Though a valuable and comic treatise on the nineteenth-century Pacific gold rush frontier, the finished book showed too many seams, betraying its origin as a cut-and-paste operation with inconsistent text and careless drawings. Its sales fell far short of those of Twain's first subscription book, *The Innocents Abroad*.

NOTES

1. *Innocents Abroad* was also illustrated by arrangement with Fay and Cox, "the first syndicated illustration business"; see William Murrell, *A History of American Graphic Humor, 1865–1938* (New York: Macmillan Company, for the Whitney Museum of American Art, 1938), p. 14. See also Sinclair Hamilton, *Early American Book Illustrators and Wood Engravers, 1670–1870* (Princeton: Princeton University Library, 1958), pp. 207, 223–24. Fay and Cox was also a wood engraving firm.

2. Albert Bigelow Paine, *Mark Twain: A Biography*, 3 vols. (New York: Harper and Brothers, 1912), 1:366. For more on Williams, see Nathan M. Wood, "True Williams, Pen Drew Literary Giant of Old," *Watertown [N.Y.] Daily Times*, August 30, 1938, p. 11. Until recently, very little biographical information on Williams has been available. Unearthed by Barbara Schmidt, instructional media coordinator at Tarleton State University in Stephenville, Texas, and a regular contributor to the Mark Twain Forum on the Internet, this article provides significant biographical information, including his dates and publishing history. We are indebted to Barbara Schmidt for generously sharing this reference and her pioneering research on Williams' later career, which she is working on for a forthcoming article. Biographical information on Williams is presented in greater detail in this series in "Reading the Illustrations in Tom Sawyer," in *The Adventures of Tom Sawyer*, The Oxford Mark Twain (New York: Oxford University Press, 1996).

3. For more detail regarding the sources of the appropriated prints, see Beverly R. David, *Mark Twain and His Illustrators, Volume 1 (1869–1875)* (Troy, N.Y.: Whitston Publishing Company, 1986), pp. 133–43.

4. Louis J. Budd, *Our Mark Twain: The Making of His Public Personality* (Philadelphia: University of Pennsylvania Press, 1983), p. 76.

5. Ibid., p. 24.

6. Louis J. Budd, "A 'Talent for Posturing'; The Achievement of Mark Twain's Public Personality," in Sara deSaussure Davis and Philip D. Beidler, eds., *The Mythologizing of Mark Twain* (Tuscaloosa: University of Alabama Press, 1984), p. 79.

7. Samuel L. Clemens to Elisha Bliss, March 4, 1873, in *Mark Twain's Letters to His Publishers, 1867–1894*, Hamlin Hill, ed. (Berkeley: University of California Press, 1967), p. 74.

8. Unsigned review, *Overland Monthly*, June 1872, no. 8, pp. 580–81; reprinted in Frederick Anderson, ed., *Mark Twain: The Critical Heritage* (London: Routledge and Kegan Paul, 1971), p. 51.

A NOTE ON THE TEXT

Robert H. Hirst

This text of *Roughing It* is a photographic facsimile of a copy of the first American edition dated 1872 on the title page. Although books printed from the first edition plates were manufactured until at least 1903, the earliest copies of the first edition came from the bindery on January 30, 1872. Two copies were deposited with the Copyright Office on February 19, and the first known review of the book appeared on February 23. The copy reproduced here is an example of Jacob Blanck's state B (*BAL* 3337). More precisely, it is an example of state *Ad,* as defined in the Mark Twain Project's edition of this title (*Roughing It,* ed. Harriet Elinor Smith, Edgar M. Branch, Lin Salamo, and Robert Pack Browning, The Works of Mark Twain, University of California Press, 1993, pp. 914–15). It is therefore an early impression (no earlier than the fourth), certainly among the 75,168 copies printed and bound by the end of December 1872. It has 'Eastern' instead of the original 'eastern' (330); the words 'he' and 'his' are both lost to type damage (242); a hyphen is missing from 'breast-pin' (123); only the period survives from the original exclamation point after 'death!' (123); and the error 'hearties' has been corrected to 'heartiest' (569). The original volume is in the collection of the Mark Twain House in Hartford, Connecticut (810/C625r/1872/c. 3). But because of the missing words on page 242, that page has been reproduced from a copy of an earlier impression (*Ac*) in the Mark Twain Papers, The Bancroft Library, University of California at Berkeley (PS1318/A1/1872/copy 5/MARK).

THE MARK TWAIN HOUSE

The Mark Twain House is a museum and research center dedicated to the study of Mark Twain, his works, and his times. The museum is located in the nineteen-room mansion in Hartford, Connecticut, built for and lived in by Samuel L. Clemens, his wife, and their three children, from 1874 to 1891. The Picturesque Gothic-style residence, with interior design by the firm of Louis Comfort Tiffany and Associated Artists, is one of the premier examples of domestic Victorian architecture in America. Clemens wrote *Adventures of Huckleberry Finn*, *The Adventures of Tom Sawyer*, *A Connecticut Yankee in King Arthur's Court*, *The Prince and the Pauper*, and *Life on the Mississippi* while living in Hartford.

The Mark Twain House is open year-round. In addition to tours of the house, the educational programs of the Mark Twain House include symposia, lectures, and teacher training seminars that focus on the contemporary relevance of Twain's legacy. Past programs have featured discussions of literary censorship with playwright Arthur Miller and writer William Styron; of the power of language with journalist Clarence Page, comedian Dick Gregory, and writer Gloria Naylor; and of the challenges of teaching *Adventures of Huckleberry Finn* amidst charges of racism.

CONTRIBUTORS

Beverly R. David is professor emerita of humanities and theater at Western Michigan University in Kalamazoo. She is currently working on volume 2 of *Mark Twain and His Illustrators*, and on a Mark Twain mystery entitled *Murder at the Matterhorn*. She has written a number of sections on illustration for the *Mark Twain Encyclopedia* and her *Mark Twain and His Illustrators, Volume 1 (1869–1875)* was published in 1989. Dr. David resides in Allegan, Michigan, in the summer and Green Valley, Arizona, in the winter.

Shelley Fisher Fishkin, professor of American Studies and English at the University of Texas at Austin, is the author of the award-winning books *Was Huck Black? Mark Twain and African-American Voices* (1993) and *From Fact to Fiction: Journalism and Imaginative Writing in America* (1985). Her most recent book is *Lighting Out for the Territory: Reflections on Mark Twain and American Culture* (1996). She holds a Ph.D. in American Studies from Yale University, has lectured on Mark Twain in Belgium, England, France, Israel, Italy, Mexico, the Netherlands, and Turkey, as well as throughout the United States, and is president-elect of the Mark Twain Circle of America.

Robert H. Hirst is the General Editor of the Mark Twain Project at The Bancroft Library, University of California in Berkeley. Apart from that, he has no other known eccentricities.

George Plimpton holds degrees from Harvard and Cambridge, and is a writer, editor, and television host. His works include *Rabbit's Umbrella* (1956), *Out of My League* (1961), *Paper Lion* (1966), *The Bogey Man* (1968*)*, *Shadow-Box* (1976), *Fireworks* (1984), *The X-Factor* (1990), and *The Best of Plimpton* (1990). He has edited *American Journey: The Times of Robert Kennedy* (1970, with Jean Stein), *Pierre's Book* (1971), *The Fancy* (1973), nine volumes of *Writers at Work* (1957-87), *Women Writers at Work* (1989), and *The Norton Book of Sports* (1992), among other books. For television he has hosted *Greatest Sports Legends*, *Survival Anglia*, *Writers' Workshop*, and Disney's *Mousterpiece Theater*. He has been editor in chief of the *Paris Review* since 1953, and lives in New York City.

Ray Sapirstein is a doctoral student in the American Civilization Program at the University of Texas at Austin. He curated the 1993 exhibition *Another Side of Huckleberry Finn: Mark Twain and Images of African Americans* at the Harry Ransom Humanities Research Center at the University of Texas at Austin. He is currently completing a dissertation on the photographic illustrations in several volumes of Paul Laurence Dunbar's poetry.

Henry B. Wonham, assistant professor of English at the University of Oregon, has recently published articles in *American Literature* and *Arizona Quarterly*. He is the author of *Mark Twain and the Art of the Tall Tale* (1993), and the editor of a collection of essays, *Criticism and the Color Line: Desegregating American Literary Studies* (1996). His book *The Short Fiction of Charles W. Chesnutt* is forthcoming from G. K. Hall. He lives in Eugene, Oregon.

ACKNOWLEDGMENTS

There are a number of people without whom The Oxford Mark Twain would not have happened. I am indebted to Laura Brown, senior vice president and trade publisher, Oxford University Press, for suggesting that I edit an "Oxford Mark Twain," and for being so enthusiastic when I proposed that it take the present form. Her guidance and vision have informed the entire undertaking.

Crucial as well, from the earliest to the final stages, was the help of John Boyer, executive director of the Mark Twain House, who recognized the importance of the project and gave it his wholehearted support.

My father, Milton Fisher, believed in this project from the start and helped nurture it every step of the way, as did my stepmother, Carol Plaine Fisher. Their encouragement and support made it all possible. The memory of my mother, Renée B. Fisher, sustained me throughout.

I am enormously grateful to all the contributors to The Oxford Mark Twain for the effort they put into their essays, and for having been such fine, collegial collaborators. Each came through, just as I'd hoped, with fresh insights and lively prose. It was a privilege and a pleasure to work with them, and I value the friendships that we forged in the process.

In addition to writing his fine afterword, Louis J. Budd provided invaluable advice and support, even going so far as to read each of the essays for accuracy. All of us involved in this project are greatly in his debt. Both his knowledge of Mark Twain's work and his generosity as a colleague are legendary and unsurpassed.

Elizabeth Maguire's commitment to The Oxford Mark Twain during her time as senior editor at Oxford was exemplary. When the project proved to be more ambitious and complicated than any of us had expected, Liz helped make it not only manageable, but fun. Assistant editor Elda Rotor's wonderful help in coordinating all aspects of The Oxford Mark Twain, along with literature editor T. Susan Chang's enthusiastic involvement with the project in its final stages, helped bring it all to fruition.

I am extremely grateful to Joy Johannessen for her astute and sensitive copyediting, and for having been such a pleasure to work with. And I appreciate the conscientiousness and good humor with which Kathy Kuhtz Campbell heroically supervised all aspects of the set's production. Oxford president Edward Barry, vice president and editorial director Helen McInnis, marketing director Amy Roberts, publicity director Susan Rotermund, art director David Tran, trade editorial, design and production manager Adam Bohannon, trade advertising and promotion manager Woody Gilmartin, director of manufacturing Benjamin Lee, and the entire staff at Oxford were as supportive a team as any editor could desire.

The staff of the Mark Twain House provided superb assistance as well. I would like to thank Marianne Curling, curator, Debra Petke, education director, Beverly Zell, curator of photography, Britt Gustafson, assistant director of education, Beth Ann McPherson, assistant curator, and Pam Collins, administrative assistant, for all their generous help, and for allowing us to reproduce books and photographs from the Mark Twain House collection. One could not ask for more congenial or helpful partners in publishing.

G. Thomas Tanselle, vice president of the John Simon Guggenheim Memorial Foundation, and an expert on the history of the book, offered essential advice about how to create as responsible a facsimile edition as possible. I appreciate his very knowledgeable counsel.

I am deeply indebted to Robert H. Hirst, general editor of the Mark Twain Project at The Bancroft Library in Berkeley, for bringing his outstanding knowledge of Twain editions to bear on the selection of the books photographed for the facsimiles, for giving generous assistance all along the way, and for providing his meticulous notes on the text. The set is the richer for his advice. I would also like to express my gratitude to the Mark Twain Project, not only for making texts and photographs from their collection available to us, but also for nurturing Mark Twain studies with a steady infusion of matchless, important publications.

I would like to thank Jeffrey Kaimowitz, curator of the Watkinson Library at Trinity College, Hartford (where the Mark Twain House collection is kept), along with his colleagues Peter Knapp and Alesandra M. Schmidt, for having been instrumental in Robert Hirst's search for first editions that could be safely reproduced. Victor Fischer, Harriet Elinor Smith, and especially Kenneth M. Sanderson, associate editors with the Mark Twain Project, reviewed the note on the text in each volume with cheerful vigilance. Thanks are also due to Mark Twain Project associate editor Michael Frank and administrative assistant Brenda J. Bailey for their help at various stages.

I am grateful to Helen K. Copley for granting permission to publish photographs in the Mark Twain Collection of the James S. Copley Library in La Jolla, California, and to Carol Beales and Ron Vanderhye of the Copley Library for making my research trip to their institution so productive and enjoyable.

Several contributors — David Bradley, Louis J. Budd, Beverly R. David, Robert Hirst, Fred Kaplan, James S. Leonard, Toni Morrison, Lillian S. Robinson, Jeffrey Rubin-Dorsky, Ray Sapirstein, and David L. Smith — were particularly helpful in the early stages of the project, brainstorming about the cast of writers and scholars who could make it work. Others who participated in that process were John Boyer, James Cox, Robert Crunden, Joel Dinerstein, William Goetzmann, Calvin and Maria Johnson, Jim Magnuson, Arnold Rampersad, Siva Vaidhyanathan, Steve and Louise Weinberg, and Richard Yarborough.

Kevin Bochynski, famous among Twain scholars as an "angel" who is gifted at finding methods of making their research run more smoothly, was helpful in more ways than I can count. He did an outstanding job in his official capacity as production consultant to The Oxford Mark Twain, supervising the photography of the facsimiles. I am also grateful to him for having put me in touch via e-mail with Kent Rasmussen, author of the magisterial *Mark Twain A to Z*, who was tremendously helpful as the project proceeded, sharing insights on obscure illustrators and other points, and generously being "on call" for all sorts of unforeseen contingencies.

I am indebted to Siva Vaidhyanathan of the American Studies Program of the University of Texas at Austin for having been such a superb research assistant. It would be hard to imagine The Oxford Mark Twain without the benefit of his insights and energy. A fine scholar and writer in his own right, he was crucial to making this project happen.

Georgia Barnhill, the Andrew W. Mellon Curator of Graphic Arts at the American Antiquarian Society in Worcester, Massachusetts, Tom Staley, director of the Harry Ransom Humanities Research Center at the University of Texas at Austin, and Joan Grant, director of collection services at the Elmer Holmes Bobst Library of New York University, granted us access to their collections and assisted us in the reproduction of several volumes of The Oxford Mark Twain. I would also like to thank Kenneth Craven, Sally Leach, and Richard Oram of the Harry Ransom Humanities Research Center for their help in making HRC materials available, and Jay and John Crowley, of Jay's Publishers Services in Rockland, Massachusetts, for their efforts to photograph the books carefully and attentively.

I would like to express my gratitude for the grant I was awarded by the University Research Institute of the University of Texas at Austin to defray some of the costs of researching The Oxford Mark Twain. I am also grateful to American Studies director Robert Abzug and the University of Texas for the computer that facilitated my work on this project (and to UT systems analyst Steve Alemán, who tried his best to repair the damage when it crashed). Thanks also to American Studies administrative assistant Janice Bradley and graduate coordinator Melanie Livingston for their always generous and thoughtful help.

The Oxford Mark Twain would not have happened without the unstinting, wholehearted support of my husband, Jim Fishkin, who went way beyond the proverbial call of duty more times than I'm sure he cares to remember as he shared me unselfishly with that other man in my life, Mark Twain. I am also grateful to my family — to my sons Joey and Bobby, who cheered me on all along the way, as did Fannie Fishkin, David Fishkin, Gennie Gordon, Mildred Hope Witkin, and Leonard, Gillis, and Moss

Plaine — and to honorary family member Margaret Osborne, who did the same.

My greatest debt is to the man who set all this in motion. Only a figure as rich and complicated as Mark Twain could have sustained such energy and interest on the part of so many people for so long. Never boring, never dull, Mark Twain repays our attention again and again and again. It is a privilege to be able to honor his memory with The Oxford Mark Twain.

Shelley Fisher Fishkin
Austin, Texas
April 1996